PULP FICTION: THE VILLAINS

Edited by Otto Penzler

Introduction by Harlan Ellison

PULP FICTION: THE VILLAINS

Edited by Otto Penzler
Introduction by Harlan Ellison

Quercus

First published in Great Britain in 2007 by
Quercus
21 Bloomsbury Square
London
WC1A 2NS

A CIP catalogue record for this book is available from the British Library.

ISBN (HB) 1-84724-076-3
ISBN-13 (HB) 978-1-84724-076-7
ISBN (TPB) 1-84724-077-1
ISBN-13 (TPB) 978-1-84724-077-4

Typeset by Deltatype Ltd, Birkenhead, Merseyside
Printed and bound in Great Britain by
Clays Ltd, St Ives plc.

10 9 8 7 6 5 4 3 2 1

CONTENTS

For Sheila Mitchell
and
H.R.F. Keating
My dear friends and hoteliers par excellence

FOREWORD

After World War I, the popularity of American pulpwood magazines increased rapidly, reaching their peak of success in the 1920s and 1930s, as more than 500 titles a month hit the newsstands. With their reasonable prices (mostly a dime or fifteen cents a copy), brilliantly colored covers depicting lurid and thrilling scenes, and a writing style that emphasized action and adventure above philosophizing and introspection, millions of copies of this new, uniquely American literature were sold every week.

At first, the magazines sought to publish something for all tastes, so a single issue might feature a western story, an aviation adventure, a mystery, a science fiction tale and a sports report. New titles came along and most of the old ones quickly morphed into special interest publications. The very first issues of *Black Mask*, for example, often had western scenes on the covers, but by the mid-1920s it had become devoted almost entirely to mystery fiction – the most popular and widely disseminated genre in the pulps.

One of the elements that made the detective magazines so popular was the heroic figures in the center of the action. The hard-boiled cop or, especially, private detective, was the idealization of the lone individual, representing justice and decency, pitted against virulent gangs, corrupt politicians or other agencies who violated that sense of goodness with which most readers identified. The fact that the best of these crime fighting tough guys became series characters, taking on one group of thugs after another, always emerging victorious in spite of the almost hopeless odds he (and these protagonists were almost always male) encountered.

Many of the most memorable of these protagonists became staples of *Black Mask*, *Detective Fiction Weekly*, *Dime Detective* and the other major pulp publications. Dashiell Hammett's Continental Op, Carroll John Daly's Race Williams, Frank Gruber's Oliver Quade, Ramon Decolta's (Raoul Whitfield) Jo Gar, Norbert Davis' Max Latin, George Harmon Coxe's Flash Casey. W.T. Ballard's Bill Lennox, Robert Reeves' Cellini Smith and Frederick Nebel's Cardigan are just a few of the detectives who appeared month after month to the delight of a reading public whose appetite for this sort of no-nonsense, shoot-first-and-ask-questions-later fiction remained unsated until the end of the second World War.

Other great crime fighting figures had their own magazines. Most of these super-heroes, an amalgam of hard-boiled dicks and science fiction inventions, had powers beyond that of ordinary mortals, and almost all wore costumes and masks. The first and most famous was the Shadow, who had 'the power to cloud men's minds'; over time, the biggest seller was Doc Savage, the Man of Bronze, who had 'superhuman strength and protean genius whose life is dedicated to the destruction of evildoers'; the most ferocious was the Spider, who killed bad guys without mercy and used his cigarette lighter to brand the foreheads of villains with a vermillion seal of tensed hairy legs and poison fangs as a symbol of his dedication to justice; The Phantom Detective, a master of a thousand disguises who combined the indestructible resilience of the masked crusaders with the cerebral dexterity of such old-fashioned detectives as Sherlock Holmes and Ellery Queen; and such less-than-successful heroes as the Black Bat, the Ghost, the Whisperer, the Purple Scar, the Masked Detective, the Crimson Mask and the last of the giants of justice created for the pulps, the Avenger.

Depression-era crowds eagerly snatched up each new episode of their favorite crime fighting protagonist, rooting for and identifying with the stalwart men of action and intellect. In addition to the hero, there was another essential element in each adventure – a monstrous opponent.

For a hero to be worthy of the name, it was utterly required that he do battle with a villain so despicable, so vile, so conscienceless that only a man of supreme strength of body and mind, and an incorruptible soul, could hope to emerge victorious.

Here, in *The Crimes of Richmond City*, you will see the almost overwhelming odds faced by MacBride and Kennedy as they attempt to right the wrongs they are forced to encounter. Other detectives, in other tales, had no lesser difficulties to overcome.

The pulps were also home to a different kind of crook, and readers were able to identify with them, too. These larcenous entities were, admittedly, thieves, but not your common, or garden variety, robber.

Virtually all the thieves who became successful series characters in the pulps (and, indeed, in all of crime fiction) were Robin Hood-type crooks. They did not commit violent acts, and they stole from the rich. Not just any rich person, mind you, but always someone who had come by his fortune illicitly. This was an exceptionally agreeable manner of behaving during the Depression era, when literally millions of Americans were jobless, standing in slow-moving bread lines to procure minimal sustenance for themselves and their families. The impoverished multitudes blamed the actions of Wall Street brokers, bankers, big businessmen and factory owners for their plight, so what could be more attractive than to see someone break into their posh apartments and crack their safes, or nick the diamond necklaces from the fat necks of their bloated wives? Furthermore, these crooks generally donated their swag to charity or to a worthy individual (after deducting a sufficient amount to ensure their own rather lavish lifestyle, of course).

Perhaps not strangely, but nevertheless an apparent contradiction to their chosen careers, a large percentage of these redistributionist thieves, after several successful adventures, become detectives. Often they are suspected of a murder or another crime which they did not commit, so must discover the true culprit in order to exonerate themselves. In other instances, they have friends in the police department who need their help. A long tradition of criminals behaving in this manner pre-dates the pulp era (Raffles worked as much as a solver of crime in his later exploits as he did as a cracksman). The American master criminal, Frederick Irving Anderson's creation, the Infallible Godahl (not included in this collection because he did not appear in the pulps), was so brilliant that he planned and executed capers so meticulously that he was never arrested. Eventually, the police paid him a large stipend *not* to commit crimes, since they knew they could never catch him and wanted to avoid the embarrassment of seeing headlines with yet another successful burglary.

All types of criminals appear in this substantial omnibus of crime. It is left to your own ethical proclivities to determine whether you identify with the safecrackers, con men, burglars and villains or with the police who are paid to catch them.

Otto Penzler

INTRODUCTION

I, FELON BY HARLAN ELLISON®

Not that it's any of your damned business, but the first time I went to jail was in 1945. I was eleven years old. In 1958 I wrote a story about it. The title was 'Free With This Box!' I was twenty-four. Now shuddup and leave me alone.

There are three volumes in this group of homages to the pulp writers of a dear and departed era in popular literature. One of them, I'm told, is *Pulp Fiction: The Crimefighters*, the third will be *Pulp Fiction: The Women*, and this one, dealing with the villains. As I am not a woman, it is manifest why I was not solicited by the *éminence grise* of this project, the esteemed editor Mr Otto (we calls him 'Slow Hand Poppa') Penzler, to pen the introductory exegesis for the book about the broads; and as you will understand in mere moments, selecting me to front a book extolling the virtues of cops, pseudo-cops, hemi/semi/demi cops and p.i. cops is about as apropos as a piñata at a paraplegics' picnic.

I was importuned by Penzler to write a foreword for a book of stories about *crooks*. We're talkin' here thieves, thugs, knaves, poltroons, bilkers, milkers, murderers, arsonists, liars, blackmailers, footpads, cat burglars, shakedown artists, pigeon-drop and 3-card monte swindlers, bloodthirsters and backstabbers . . . in short, criminals.

Now, you may ask, what is this delicate flower of advanced age, this pinnacle of society, this world-famous and multiple award-winning credit to his species, getting at? Is he, heaven forfend, suggesting that it is right and proper, even condign that this Penzler fellah thinks Ellison is *as one with* this fictional cadre of creeps and culprits, similar in spirit or outlook or past experience? Is that what we are to believe?

What is it witchu? Didn't I tell you to shuddup and leave me alone?

First of all, I grew up *reading* the pulps. I was born in '34 and, unlike most of the Jessica Simpson-admiring twerps of contemporary upbringing, for whom nostalgia is what they had for breakfast, I actually *remember* what a hoot it was to plonk myself into the Ouroboros root-nest of the ancient oak tree in the front yard of our little house at 89 Harmon Drive, Painesville, Ohio, with the latest issue of *Black Book Detective Magazine* or *The*

Shadow. Ah me, those wood-chip-scented, cream-colored pulp pages dropping their dandruff onto the lap of my knickers . . .

(Those were corduroy boys' pants, here in America. In England, as I later discovered to my priapic delight, the same word is used to designate female panties – ah yes, in the aphorism of G.B. Shaw: 'The United States and England are two countries divided by a common language.')

. . . and while Jack Wheeldon and his cronies yelled 'kike' as they rode their Schwinns past my eyrie, I went away from that place and that time with the adventures of masked riders, square-jawed crimefighters, mightily-thewed barbarian warriors, spacemen accompanied by gorgeous women in brass brassieres, and culprits too smooth and sagacious to be nobbled by some cigar-masticating flatfoot from the Central Office. There was something called 'escapism' in the pop lit of those days. It's too bad that word has fallen on such hard times. Escapism now, I'm told, is Not A Good Thing. Yet in its place we have 'entertainment' that deifies the idle, the infamous, the egregious and the shallow. In place of Raffles and Flambeau and Jimmy Valentine we have rapper thugs for whom human speech is not their natural tongue, a morbid fascination with those missing and presumed buried or drowned in the Bahamas, the need for a daily fix of tabloid ink infusion anent the presumed grotesqueries of child molesters, serial killers, televangelist alarmists, racists and ratfinks and raucous riffraff. We have been led down the societal garden path to a place where an honest crook who carries no firearm and would not stoop to such ignominious behavior as a carjacking or ballbatting of an ATM is no-price, and we are surfeited with 'entertainment' that cheapens us, distances us, turns us into an unworthy people who accept no responsibility for our bad actions and fills us with a sense of American Idol entitlement that has no substance in reality.

If I seem to be extolling the chimerical 'virtues' of felons and crooks, one might assume in much the same way as the naive and gullible praised Dillinger, Capone, Ma Barker and her boys, back in the day, well, I live in the real world and I do truly *really* understand that Billy the Kid and Murder, Inc. and even Bonnie & Clyde were way less than icons to hold up to one's children . . . *but* . . . nonetheless . . .

I would rather spend time reading about Boston Blackie and Fantomas and Harry Lime than have to put up with one more pelvic twitch of Christina Aguilera or pelvic piercing of Pink. What used to be a necessary and even enriching, innervating, if not ennobling retreat to the made-up worlds of high crimes and low misdemeanors in the pulps, has been relentlessly, ceaselessly, tirelessly bastardized by corporate and advertising thugs (far worse than the Bad Guys you'll find in this volume), into a pounding, remorseless assault of empty trivial crap that fills the air, saturates our perceptions of the received world, and turns us away from ourselves and our true values and our important pursuits. Distractions that make the tomfoolery and toughtalk of the pulps seem as rich and golden as the

Analects of Confucius or a paraphrasing of Lao Tzu. In the stories in this book, taken from the heart and core of that popular entertainment engine of the '20s, '30s and '40s, you will experience an escapism that steals nothing from you, reduces you not one scintilla, pleasures and distracts you the way a tall champagne flute of good, tart lemonade does on a blistering August afternoon.

The fictions may creak a bit in the joints, some of the writing may be too prolix for modern tastes (don't forget, they were writing for ½¢ to a penny-a-word in those halcyon days of post-Depression America), and we have been exposed to an electronically-linked world for so long now, that some of the attitudes and expressions in these fables may seem giggle-worthy, but this is a muscular writing that sustained us through some very tough times, and their preserved quality of sheer entertainment value is considerable. So be kind.

As for me, well, I come to this book with credentials that are not trumpeted in the 'official biographies' or in a WHO'S WHO or the *Encyclopedia of American Authors*. But mine is exactly the proper vita for a book'a'crooks.

As I said, I grew up *in situ* with the pulp detective magazines. And in my earliest days as a professional I *wrote* for the metamorphosed hardboiled pulps in digest-size (which stick-in-the-mud Penzler has trouble perceiving as equally valid cred for 'pulp' as the larger-sized magazines). I wrote for *Manhunt, Mantrap, Mayhem, Guilty, Sure-Fire Detective, Trapped, The Saint Mystery Magazine* (both U.S. and U.K editions), *Mike Shayne's, Tightrope, Crime and Justice Detective Story*, and *Terror Detective Story Magazine*, just to glaze your eyes and bore yo ass with a select few of the rags for which I toiled. So that's a *second* good reason for me being the one who stands here at the prow of the ship, urging you aboard.

But the cred that stands, the one that beats the bulldog, is that I *was* a felon. I mentioned my first incarceration at age eleven, a spree of petty theft involving comic character pinback buttons concealed in boxes of Wheaties; but that was just the first. Age thirteen, ran off and wound up in a huge free-standing cell in the old (now-razed) Kansas City slam, all alone save for a carny geek who went nuts without his bottle of gin a day, and impressed me forever with the stench of rotgut sweated out via armpits. Booted out of Ohio State University in 1954, in part, for shoplifting. Saw the inside of the Columbus jail on that one.

US Army brigs of various venues, 1957–59, mostly for insubordination. 1960: I'm in New York, living down in the Village, guy I had a beef with phones in bullshit charges of 'possession of firearms' to the cops, they bust me, toss me in The Tombs (see my book MEMOS FROM PURGATORY), and finally the Grand Jury looks at it, the D.A. knows it's bullshit so he urges them to return No True Bill, and that was that.

Civil Rights days. I was in jails in Mississippi, Georgia, Alabama with

Martin, and on and on. In Louisiana, a couple of redneck cops grabbed me on a back road in Plaquemine Parish, hauled me in, stripped me to the waist, cuffed me behind my back, lifted me up between them, hung the cuffs over a meat hook turned into the top-half of a Dutch door, and took turns walloping me across the belly with a plastic kiddie ballbat, careful to leave barely a mark on the outside. Did that till the Boss of Plaquemine, the infamous Leander Peres showed up, thumbed through my wallet full of i.d. and credit cards, discovered I was from Hollywood, knew there'd be a *geshry* (as we say in Yiddish) if I vanished, had his boys take me down, and redeposited me: in a ditch somewhere out on a dark back road, with this admonition, which I recall with telephonic accuracy more than four decades later: 'Nex' tahm you show yo ass in Plack-uh-mun, jew-boy, we gonna jus' kill you.'

Is it appropriate that Otto picked me for the introductory remarks about crooks and felons? You better believe it, dawg. Now go thee hence, inside further, and enjoy yourself.

Tell 'em Harlan sent you. And now, just shuddup and leave me alone. A tired old felon slumped and maundering about his days on the other side of the law.

Harlan Ellison

THE CAT-WOMAN

ERLE STANLEY GARDNER

Of the many pulp creations of Erle Stanley Gardner (1889–1970), one of his personal favorites was Ed Jenkins, known as the Phantom Thief, his first significant series character (after Bob Larkin, who lasted only two adventures), who appeared in 74 novellas, more than any other protagonist.

Much of Gardner's career is important and inspiring because of the sheer numbers. In the decade before the first novel about Perry Mason, *The Case of the Velvet Claws* (1933), he averaged approximately 1,200,000 published words a year – the equivalent of one 10,000-word novella every three days, for 365 days. And he had a day job as a lawyer.

He dictated cases to his secretary and, in 1932, it finally occurred to him that he could dictate fiction, too, which greatly speeded up the writing process, enabling him to produce novels for the first time. *Velvet Claws* famously took 3½ days, though Gardner mostly said it was really four days, since he needed a half day to think up the plot.

Jenkins made his debut with 'Beyond the Law' in the January 1925 issue of *Black Mask* and was one of the most popular series in the history of the magazine. When he decided to write no more about him, readers caused such an uproar that he was forced to continue producing his capers. 'The Cat-Woman' was first published in the February 1927 issue of *Black Mask*.

THE CAT-WOMAN

ERLE STANLEY GARDNER

Big Bill Ryan slid his huge bulk into the vacant chair opposite my own and began toying with the heavy watch chain which stretched across the broad expanse of his vest.

'Well,' I asked, showing only mild annoyance, for Big Ryan had the reputation of never wasting time, his own or anyone else's.

'Ed, I hear you've gone broke. I've got a job for you.'

He spoke in his habitual, thin, reedy voice. In spite of his bulk his mouth was narrow and his tone shrill. However, I fancied I could detect a quiver of excitement underlying his words, and I became cold. News travels fast in the underworld. He knew of my financial setback as soon as I did, almost. My brokers had learned my identity – that I was a crook, and they had merely appropriated my funds. They were reputable business men. I was a crook. If I made complaint the courts would laugh at me. I've had similar experiences before. No matter how honest a man may appear he'll always steal from a crook – not from any ethical reasons, but because he feels he can get away with it.

'What's on your mind?' I asked Ryan, not affirming or denying the rumor concerning my financial affairs.

His pudgy fingers seemed to be fairly alive as he twisted and untwisted the massive gold chain.

'It's just a message,' he said, at length, and handed me a folded slip of paper.

I looked it over. It was a high class of stationery, delicately perfumed, bearing a few words in feminine handwriting which was as perfect and characterless as copper plate.

> 'Two hours after you get this message meet me at Apartment 624, Reedar Arms Apartments. The door will be open.
>
> H. M. H.'

I scowled over at Ryan and shook my head. 'I've walked into all the traps I intend to, Ryan.'

His little, pig eyes blinked rapidly and his fingers jammed his watch chain into a hard knot.

'The message is on the square, Ed. I can vouch for that. What the job will be that opens up I can't tell. You'll have to take the responsibility of that; but there won't be any police trap in that apartment.'

I looked at the note again. The ink was dark. Evidently the words had been written some little time ago. The message did not purport to be to anyone in particular. Big Ryan was a notorious fence, a go-between of crooks. Apparently he had been given the note with the understanding that he was to pick out the one to whom it was to be delivered. The note would clear his skirts, yet he must be in on the game. He'd have to get in touch with the writer after he made a delivery of the note so that the time of the appointment would be known.

I reached a decision on impulse, and determined to put Ryan to the test. 'All right, I'll be there.'

I could see a look of intense relief come over his fat face. He couldn't keep back the words. 'Bully for you, Ed Jenkins!' he shrilled. 'After I heard you were broke I thought I might get you. You're the one man who could do it. Remember, two hours from now,' and, with the words, he pulled out his turnip watch and carefully checked the time. Then he heaved up from the chair and waddled toward the back of the restaurant.

I smiled to myself. He was going to telephone 'H. M. H.' and I filed that fact away for future reference.

Two hours later I stepped from the elevator on the sixth floor of the Reedar Arms Apartments, took my bearings and walked directly to the door of 624. I didn't pause to knock but threw the door open. However, I didn't walk right in, but stepped back into the hallway.

'Come in, Mr. Jenkins,' said a woman's voice.

The odor of incense swirled out into the hall, and I could see the apartment was in half-light, a pink light which came through a rose-colored shade. Ordinarily I trust the word of no man, but I was in desperate need of cash, and Big Bill Ryan had a reputation of being one who could be trusted. I took a deep breath and walked into the apartment, closing the door after me.

She was sitting back in an armchair beneath a rose-shaded reading lamp, her bare arm stretched out with the elbow resting on a dark table, the delicate, tapering fingers holding a long, ivory cigarette holder in which burned a half-consumed cigarette. Her slippered feet were placed on a stool and the light glinted from a well-proportioned stretch of silk stocking. It was an artistic job, and the effect was pleasing. I have an eye for such things, and I stood there for a moment taking in the scene, appreciating it. And then I caught the gaze of her eyes.

Cat eyes she had; eyes that seemed to dilate and contract, green eyes that were almost luminous there in the half-light.

I glanced around the apartment, those luminous, green eyes studying me as I studied the surroundings. There was nothing at all in the apartment to suggest the personality of such a woman. Everything about the place was suggestive merely of an average furnished apartment. At the end of the room, near the door of a closet, I saw a suitcase. It merely confirmed my previous suspicion. The woman had only been in that apartment for a few minutes. She rented the place merely as a meeting ground for the crook she had selected to do her bidding. When Big Bill Ryan had picked a man for her, he had telephoned her and she had packed her negligee in the suitcase and rushed to the apartment.

She gave a little start and followed my gaze, then her skin crinkled as her lips smiled. That smile told me much. The skin seemed hard as parchment. She was no spring chicken, as I had suspected from the first.

The cat-woman shrugged her shoulders, reached in a little handbag and took out a blue-steel automatic which she placed on the table. Then she hesitated, took another great drag at the cigarette and narrowed her eyes at me.

'It is no matter, Mr. Jenkins. I assure you that my desire to conceal my identity, to make it appear that this was my real address, was to protect myself only in case I did not come to terms with the man Ryan sent. We had hardly expected to be able to interest a man of your ability in the affair, and, now that you are here, I shan't let you go, so there won't be any further need of the deception. I will even tell you who I am and where I really live – in a moment.'

I said nothing, but watched the automatic. Was it possible she knew so little about me that she fancied I could be forced to do something at the point of a pistol?

As though she again read my mind, she reached into the handbag and began taking out crisp bank notes. They were of five-hundred-dollar denomination, and there were twenty of them. These she placed on the table beside the gun.

'The gun is merely to safeguard the money,' she explained with another crinkling smile. 'I wouldn't want you to take the cash without accepting my proposition.'

I nodded. As far as possible I would let her do the talking.

'Mr. Jenkins, or Ed, as I shall call you now that we're acquainted, you have the reputation of being the smoothest worker in the criminal game. You are known to the police as The Phantom Crook, and they hate, respect and fear you. Ordinarily you are a lone wolf, but because you are pressed for ready cash, I think I can interest you in something I have in mind.'

She paused and sized me up with her cat-green eyes. If she could read anything on my face she could have read the thoughts of a wooden Indian.

'There are ten thousand dollars,' she said, and there was a subtle, purring something about her voice. 'That money will be yours when you leave this room if you agree to do something for me. Because I can trust you, I will pay you in advance.'

Again she stopped, and again I sat in immobile silence.

'I want you to break into a house – my own house – and steal a very valuable necklace. Will you do it?'

She waited for a reply.

'That is all you wish?' I asked, killing time, waiting.

She wrinkled her cheeks again.

'Oh yes, now that you speak of it, there is one other thing. I want you to kidnap my niece. I would prefer that you handle the entire matter in your own way, but I will give you certain suggestions, some few instructions.'

She paused waiting for a reply, and I let my eyes wander to the cash piled on the table. Very evidently she had intended that the actual cash should be a strong point in her argument and it would disappoint her if I didn't look hungrily at it.

'How long shall I hold your niece captive?'

She watched me narrowly, her eyes suddenly grown hard.

'Ed Jenkins, once you have my niece you can do anything with her or about her that you want. You must keep her for two days. After that you may let her go or you may keep her.'

'That is all?' I asked.

'That is all,' she said, and I knew she lied, as she spoke.

I arose. 'I am not interested, but it has been a pleasure to have met you. I appreciate artistry.'

Her face darkened, and the corners of her upper lip drew back, the feline snarl of a cat about to spring. I fancied her hand drifted toward the automatic.

'Wait,' she spat, 'you don't know all.'

I turned at that, and, by an effort, she controlled herself. Once more the purring note came into her voice.

'The necklace you will steal is my own. I am the legal guardian of my niece and I will give you my permission to kidnap her. What is more, I will allow you to see her first, to get her own permission. You will not be guilty of any crime whatever.'

I came back and sat down in the chair.

'I have the necklace and it is insured for fifty thousand dollars,' she said in a burst of candor. 'I must have the money, simply must. To sell the necklace would be to cause comment of a nature I cannot explain. If I secrete the necklace I will be detected by the insurance company. If the notorious Ed Jenkins breaks into my house, steals my necklace, kidnaps my niece, the insurance company will never question but what the theft was genuine. You will, of course, not actually take the necklace. You will take a paste copy. The insurance company will pay me fifty thousand dollars, and, when occasion warrants, I can again produce the necklace.'

I nodded. 'You intend then that I shall be identified as the thief, that the police shall set up a hue and cry for me?'

She smiled brightly. 'Certainly. That's why I want you to kidnap my niece. However, that should mean nothing to you. You have a reputation of being able to slip through the fingers of the police any time you wish.'

I sighed. I had enjoyed immunity from arrest in California because of a legal technicality; but I was broke and in need of cash. All honest channels of employment were closed to me, and, after all, the woman was right. I had been able to laugh at the police.

I reached forward and took the money, folded the crisp bills and put them in my pocket.

'All right. I will accept. Remember one thing, however, if you attempt to double-cross me, to play me false in any way, I will keep the money and also get revenge. Whatever your game is you must keep all the cards on the table as far as my own connection with it is concerned. Otherwise . . . ?'

I paused significantly.

'Otherwise?' she echoed, and there was a taunt in her voice.

I shrugged my shoulders. 'Otherwise you will be sorry. Others have thought they could use Ed Jenkins for a cat's-paw, could double-cross him. They never got away with it.'

She smiled brightly. 'I would hardly give you ten thousand dollars in cash unless I trusted you, Ed. Now that we've got the preliminaries over with we may as well get to work and remove the stage setting.'

With that she arose, stretched with one of those toe stretching extensions of muscles which reminded me of a cat arising from a warm sofa, slipped out of the negligee and approached the suitcase. From the suitcase she took a tailored suit and slipped into it in the twinkling of an eye. She threw the negligee into the suitcase, took a hat from the closet, reached up and switched out the light.

'All right, Ed. We're ready to go.'

She had her own machine in a nearby garage, a long, low roadster of the type which is purchased by those who demand performance and care nothing for expense of operation. I slipped into the seat and watched her dart through the traffic. She had skill, this cat-woman, but there was a ruthlessness about her driving. Twice, pedestrians barely managed to elude the nickeled bumpers. On neither occasion did she so much as glance backward to make sure she had not given them a glancing blow in passing.

At length we slowed up before an impressive house in the exclusive residential district west of Lakeside. With a quick wriggle she slipped out from behind the steering wheel, vaulted lightly to the pavement and extended her long, tapering fingers to me. 'Come on, Ed. Here's where we get out.'

I grinned as she held the door open. Whatever her age she was in perfect condition, splendidly formed, quick as a flash of light, and she almost gave the impression of assisting me from the car.

I was shown into a drawing-room and told to wait.

While the cat-woman was gone I looked about me, got the lay of the land, and noticed the unique furnishings of the room. Everywhere were evidences of the striking personality of the woman. A tiger rug was on the floor, a leopard skin on the davenport. A huge painted picture hung over the fireplace, a picture of a cat's head, the eyes seeming to have just a touch of luminous paint in them. In the semi-darkness of the nook the cat's eyes blazed forth and dominated the entire room. It was impossible to keep the eyes away from that weird picture; those steady, staring eyes drew my gaze time after time.

At length there was the rustle of skirts and I rose.

The cat-woman stood in the doorway. On her arm was a blonde girl attired in flapper style, painted and powdered, and, seemingly, a trifle dazed.

'My niece, Jean Ellery, Ed. Jean, may I present Mr. Ed Jenkins. You folks are destined to see a good deal of each other so you'd better get acquainted.'

I bowed and advanced. The girl extended her hand, a limp, moist morsel of flesh. I took it and darted a glance at the cat-woman. She was standing tense, poised, her lips slightly parted, her eyes fixed upon the girl, watching her every move.

'Hullo, Ed. Mr. Jenkins. I understand you're goin' to kidnap me. Are you a cave-man or do you kidnap 'em gently?'

There was a singsong expression about her voice, the tone a child uses in reciting a piece of poetry the import of which has never penetrated to the brain.

'So you want to be kidnapped, do you, Jean?'

'Uh, huh.'

'Aren't you afraid you may never get back?'

'I don't care if I never come back. Life here is the bunk. I want to get out where there's somethin' doin', some place where I can see life. Action, that's what I'm lookin' for.'

With the words she turned her head and let her vacant, blue eyes wander to the cat-woman. Having spoken her little piece, she wanted to see what mark the teacher gave her. The cat-woman flashed a glance of approval, and the doll-faced blonde smiled up at me.

'All right, Jean,' she said. 'You run along. Mr. Jenkins and I have some things to discuss.'

The blonde turned and walked from the room, flashing me what was meant to be a roguish glance from over her shoulder. The cat-woman curled up in a chair, rested her head on her cupped hands, and looked at me. There in the half-light her eyes seemed as luminous as those of the cat in the painting over the fireplace.

'Tomorrow at ten will be about right, Ed. Now, here are some of the things you must know. This house really belongs to Arthur C. Holton, the big oil man, you know. I have been with him for several years as private secretary and general house manager. Tomorrow night our engagement is to be announced and he is going to present me with the famous tear-drop necklace as an engagement present. I will manage everything so that the presentation takes place at about nine-thirty. Just before ten I will place the necklace on my niece to let her wear the diamonds for a few minutes, and she will leave the room for a moment, still wearing the diamonds.

'Really, I'll slip the genuine necklace in my dress and put an imitation around my niece's neck. She will leave the room and an assistant will bind and gag her and place her in a speedy roadster which I have purchased for you and is to be waiting outside. Then you must show your face. It won't look like a kidnapping and a theft unless I have some well-known crook show himself for a moment at the door.

'You can pretend that you have been double-crossed in some business deal by Mr. Holton. You suddenly jump in the doorway and level a gun at the guests. Then you can tell them that this is merely the first move in your revenge, that you will make Mr. Holton regret the time he double-crossed you. Make a short speech and then run for the machine. I have a little cottage rented down on the seashore, and I have had Jean spend several days there already, under another name, of course, and you can go there as Jean's husband, one who has just returned from a trip East. You will be perfectly safe from detection because all the neighbors know Jean as Mrs. Compton. You will post as Mr. Compton and adopt any disguise you wish. But, remember; you must not stop and open the luggage compartment until you reach the cottage.'

She spilled all that and then suddenly contracted her eyes until the pupils seemed mere slits.

'That may sound unimportant to you, Ed, but you've got to play your part letter perfect. There is a lot that depends on your following instructions to the letter. In the meantime I will give you plenty of assurance that I will shoot square with you.'

I sat there, looking at this cat-woman curled up in the chair before the crackling fire, and had all I could do to keep from bursting out laughing right in her face. I've seen some wild, farfetched plots, but this had anything cheated I had ever heard of.

'Think how it will add to your reputation,' she went on, the singing, purring note in her soothing tone.

I yawned. 'And you can double-cross me and have me arrested ten minutes later, or tip the police off to this little cottage you have reserved for me, and I'll spend many, many years in jail while you laugh up your sleeve.'

She shook her head. 'What earthly reason would I have for wanting to have you arrested? No, Ed, I've anticipated that. Tomorrow we go to a notary public and I'll execute a written confession of my part in the affair.

This confession will be placed in safekeeping where it will be delivered to the police in the event you are caught. *That* will show you how my interests are the same as your own, how I cannot afford to have you captured. This paper will contain my signed statement that I have authorized you to steal the jewels, and my niece will also execute a document stating the kidnapping is with her consent. Think it over, Ed. You will be protected, but I must have that insurance money, and have it in such a way that no one will suspect me.'

I sat with bowed head, thinking over the plan. I had already digested everything she had told me. What I was worrying about was what she hadn't told me.

I arose and bowed.

'I'll see you tomorrow then?'

She nodded, her green eyes never leaving my face.

'Meet me at the office of Harry Atmore, the lawyer at eleven and ask for Hattie M. Hare. He will see that you are protected in every way. I guarantee that you won't have any cause for alarm about my double-crossing you.'

Apparently there was nothing more to be gained by talking with this woman and I left her.

I had ten thousand dollars in my pocket, a cold suspicion in my mind and a determination to find out just what the real game was. I didn't know just how deep Big Ryan was mixed in this affair – not yet I didn't, but I proposed to find out. In the meantime I wasn't taking any chances, and I slipped into my apartment without any brass band to announce my presence.

At first I thought everything was in proper order, and then I noticed something was missing. It was a jade handled, Chinese dagger, one that I had purchased at a curio store not more than a month ago. What was more, the Chinaman who sold it to me had known who I was. That dagger could be identified by the police as readily as my signature or my fingerprints.

I sat down by the window in my easy chair and thought over the events of the evening. I couldn't see the solution, not entirely, but I was willing to bet the cat-woman wouldn't have slept easily if she had known how much I was able to put together. Right then I could have dropped the whole thing and been ten thousand dollars ahead; but there was big money in this game that was being played. I couldn't forget how Big Bill Ryan had twisted and fumbled at his watch chain when he had delivered that note to me. He was a smooth fence, was Big Ryan, and he wouldn't have let his fat fingers get so excited over a mere thirty or forty thousand dollar job. There was a million in this thing or I missed my guess.

At last I figured I'd checked things out as far as I could with the information I had, and rolled in.

At eleven on the dot I presented myself at the office of Harry Atmore. Atmore was a shyster criminal lawyer who charged big fees, knew when and where to bribe, and got results for his clients. I gave the stenographer my name, told her that I had an appointment, and was shown into the private office of Henry Atmore, attorney-at-law.

Atmore sat at a desk, and his face was a study. He was trying to control his expression, but his face simply would twitch in spite of himself. He held forth a flabby hand, and I noticed that his palm was moist and that his hand trembled. To one side of the table sat the cat-woman and the blonde. Both of them smiled sweetly as I bowed.

Atmore got down to business at once. He passed over two documents for my inspection. One was a simple statement from Hattie M. Hare to the effect that I had been employed by her to steal the Holton, 'tear-drop' necklace, and that we were jointly guilty of an attempt to defraud the insurance company. The other was a statement signed by Jean Ellery to the effect that I had arranged with her to kidnap her, but that she gave her consent to the kidnapping, and that it was being done at her request.

I noticed that the Hare statement said nothing about the kidnapping, and the other said nothing about the necklace. I filed those facts away for future reference.

'Now here's what we'll do, Jenkins,' Atmore said, his moist hand playing with the corners of some papers which lay on his desk, 'we'll have both of these statements placed in an envelope and deposited with a trust company to be held indefinitely, not to be opened, and not to be withdrawn. That will prevent any of the parties from withdrawing them, but if you should ever be arrested the district attorney, or the grand jury could, of course, subpoena the manager of the trust company and see what is in the envelope. The idea of these statements is not to give you immunity from prosecution, but to show you that Miss Hare is as deep in the mud as you are in the mire. She can't afford to have you arrested or to even let you get caught. Of course, if you *should* get arrested on some other matter we're relying on you to play the game. You've never been a squealer, and I feel my clients can trust you.'

I nodded casually. It was plain he was merely speaking a part. His plan had already been worked out.

'I have one suggestion,' I said.

He inclined his head. 'Name it.'

'That you call in a notary public and have them acknowledge the confessions.'

The lawyer looked at his client. He was a beady-eyed, sallow-faced rat of a man. His great nose seemed to have drawn his entire face to a point, and his mouth and eyes were pinched accordingly. Also his lip had a tendency to draw back and show discolored, long teeth, protruding in front. He was like a rat, a hungry, cunning rat.

The cat-woman placed her ivory cigarette holder to her vivid lips, inhaled a great drag and then expelled two streams of white smoke from her dilated nostrils. She nodded at the lawyer, and, as she nodded, there was a hard gleam about her eyes.

'Very well,' was all she said, but the purring note had gone from her voice.

Atmore wiped the back of his hand across his perspiring forehead, called in a notary, and, on the strength of his introduction, had the two documents acknowledged. Then he slipped them in one of the envelopes, wrote 'Perpetual Escrow' on the back, signed it, daubed sealing wax all over the flap and motioned to me.

'You can come with me, Jenkins, and see that I put this in the Trust Company downstairs.'

I arose, accompanied the lawyer to the elevator and was whisked down to the office of the Trust Company. We said not a word on the trip. The lawyer walked to the desk of the vice-president, handed him the envelope, and told him what he wanted.

'Keep this envelope as a perpetual escrow. It can be opened by no living party except with an order of court. After ten years you may destroy it. Give this gentleman and myself a duplicate receipt.'

The vice-president looked dubiously at the envelope, weighed it in his hand, sighed, and placed his signature on the envelope, gave it a number with a numbering machine, dictated a duplicate receipt, which he also signed, and took the envelope to the vaults.

'That should satisfy you,' said Atmore, his beady eyes darting over me, the perspiration breaking out on his forehead. 'That is all fair and above board.'

I nodded and started toward the door. I could see the relief peeping in the rat-like eyes of the lawyer.

At the door I stopped, turned, and clutched the lawyer by the arm. 'Atmore, do you know what happens to people who try to double-cross me?'

He was seized with a fit of trembling, and he impatiently tried to break away.

'You have a reputation for being a square shooter, Jenkins, and for always getting the man who tries to double-cross you.'

I nodded.

There in the marble lobby of that trust company, with people all around us, with a special officer walking slowly back and forth, I handed it to this little shyster.

'All right. You've just tried to double-cross me. If you value your life hand me that envelope.'

He shivered again.

'W-w-w-what envelope?'

I gave him no answer, just kept my eyes boring into his, kept his trembling arm in my iron clutch, and kept my face thrust close to his.

He weakened fast. I could see his sallow skin whiten.

'Jenkins, I'm sorry. I told her we couldn't get away with it. It was her idea, not mine.'

I still said nothing, but kept my eyes on his.

He reached in his pocket and took out the other envelope. My guess had been right. I knew his type. The rat-like cunning of the idea had unquestionably been his, but he didn't have the necessary nerve to bluff it through. He had prepared two envelopes. One of them had been signed and sealed before my eyes, but in signing and sealing it he had followed the mental pattern of another envelope which had already been signed and sealed and left in his pocket, an envelope which contained nothing but blank sheets of paper. When he put the envelope with the signed confession into his coat pocket he had placed it back of the dummy envelope. The dummy envelope he had withdrawn and deposited in his 'perpetual escrow.'

I took the envelope from him, broke the seals, and examined the documents. They were intact, the signed, acknowledged confessions.

I turned back to the shyster.

'Listen, Atmore. There is a big fee in this for you, a fee from the woman, perhaps from someone else. Go back and tell them that you have blundered, that I have obtained possession of the papers and they will expose you, fire you for a blunderer, make you the laughing stock of every criminal rendezvous in the city. If you keep quiet about this no one will ever know the difference. Speak and you ruin your reputation.'

I could see a look of relief flood his face, and I knew he would lie to the cat-woman about those papers.

'Tell Miss Hare I'll be at the house at nine forty-five on the dot,' I said. 'There's no need of my seeing her again until then.'

With that I climbed into my roadster, drove to the beach and looked over the house the cat-woman had selected for me. She had given me the address as well as the key at our evening interview, just before I said good night. Of course, she expected me to look the place over.

It was a small bungalow, the garage opening on to the sidewalk beneath the first floor. I didn't go in. Inquiry at a gasoline station showed that the neighbors believed Compton was a traveling salesman, away on a trip, but due to return. The blonde had established herself in the community. So much I found out, and so much the cat-woman had expected me to find out.

Then I started on a line she hadn't anticipated.

First I rented a furnished apartment, taking the precaution first to slip on a disguise which had always worked well with me, a disguise which made me appear twenty years older.

Second, I went to the county clerk's office, looked over the register of actions, and found a dozen in which the oil magnate had been a party. There were damage suits, quiet title actions, actions on oil leases, and on options. In all of these actions he had been represented by Morton, Huntley & Morton. I got the address of the lawyers from the records, put up a good stall with their telephone girl, and found myself closeted with old H. F. Morton, senior member of the firm.

He was a shabby, grizzled, gray-eyed old campaigner and he had a habit of drumming his fingers on the desk in front of him.

'What was it you wanted, Mr. Jenkins?'

I'd removed my disguise and given him my right name. He may or may not have known my original record. He didn't mention it.

I shot it to him right between the eyes.

'If I were the lawyer representing Arthur C. Holton I wouldn't let him marry Miss Hattie Hare.'

He never batted an eyelash. His face was as calm as a baby's. His eyes didn't even narrow, but there came a change in the tempo of his drumming on the desk.

'Why?' he asked.

His tone was mild, casual, but his fingers were going rummy-tum-tum; rummy-tum-tum; rummy-tum-tummy-tum tummy-tum tum.

I shook my head. 'I can't tell you all of it, but she's in touch with a shyster lawyer planning to cause trouble of some kind.'

'Ah, yes. Mr.-er-Jenkins. You are a friend of Mr. Holton?'

I nodded. 'He doesn't know it though.'

'Ah, yes,' rummy-tum-tum; rummy-tum-tum; 'what is it I can do for you in the matter?'

'Help me prevent the marriage.'

Rummy-tum-tum; rummy-tum-tum.

'How?'

'Give me a little information as a starter. Mr. Holton has a great deal of property?'

At this his eyes did narrow. The drumming stopped.

'This is a law office. Not an information bureau.'

I shrugged my shoulders. 'Miss Hare will have her own personal attorney. If the marriage should go through and anything should happen to Mr. Holton another attorney would be in charge of the estate.'

He squirmed at that, and then recommenced his drumming.

'Nevertheless, I cannot divulge the confidential affairs of my client. This much is common knowledge. It is street talk, information available to anyone who will take the trouble to look for it. Mr. Holton is a man of great wealth. He owns much property, controls oil producing fields, business property, stocks, bonds. He was married and lost his wife when his child was born. The child was a boy and lived but a few minutes. Mr. Holton created a trust for that child, a trust which terminated with the premature death of the infant. Miss Hare has been connected with him as his secretary and general household executive for several years. Mr. Holton is a man of many enemies, strong character and few friends. He is hated by the working class, and is hated unjustly, yet he cares nothing for public opinion. He is noted as a collector of jewels and paintings. Of late he has been influenced in many respects by Miss Hare, and has grown very fond of her.

'How do you propose to prevent his marriage, and what do you know of Miss Hare?'

I shook my head.

'I won't tell you a thing unless you promise to give me all the information I want, and keep me posted.'

His face darkened. 'Such a proposition is unthinkable. It is an insult to a reputable attorney.'

I knew it, but I made the stall to keep him from finding out that I had all the information I wanted. I only wanted a general slant on Holton's affairs, and, most of all, I wanted a chance to size up his attorney, to get acquainted with him so he would know me later.

'Stick an ad in the personal columns of the morning papers if you want to see me about anything,' I said as I made for the door.

He watched me meditatively. Until I had left the long, book-lined corridor, and emerged from the expensive suite of offices, I could still hear his fingers on the desk.

Rummy-tum-tum; rummy-tum-tum; rummy-tum-tummy-tum-tummy-tum-tum.

I went to a hotel, got a room and went to sleep. I was finished with my regular apartment. That was for the police.

At nine-forty-five I sneaked into the back door of Holton's house, found one of the extra servants waiting for me, and was shown into a closet near the room where the banquet was taking place. The servant was a crook, but one I couldn't place. I filed his map away for future reference, and he filed mine.

Ten minutes passed. I heard something that might or might not have been a muffled scream, shuffling footsteps going down the hall. Silence, the ringing of a bell.

I stepped to the door of the banquet room, and flung it wide. Standing there on the threshold I took in the scene of hectic gaiety. Holton and the cat-woman sat at the head of the table. Couples in various stages of intoxication were sprinkled about. Servants stood here and there, obsequious, attentive. A man sat slightly apart, a man who had his eyes riveted on the door of an ante-room. He was the detective from the insurance company.

For a minute I stood there, undiscovered.

The room was a clatter of conversation. The detective half arose, his eyes on the door of the ante-room. Holton saw me, stopped in the middle of a sentence, and looked me over.

'Who are you, and what do you want?'

I handed it out in bunches. 'I'm Ed Jenkins, the phantom crook. I've got a part of what I want. I'll come back later for the rest.'

The detective reached for his hip, and I slammed the door and raced down the corridor. Taking the front steps in a flying leap I jumped into the seat of the powerful speedster, noticed the roomy luggage compartment, the running engine, the low, speedy lines, slammed in the gear, slipped in the clutch, and skidded out of the drive as the detective started firing from the window.

I didn't go direct to the beach house.

On a dark side-road I stopped the car, went back and opened up the luggage compartment and pulled out the bound and gagged girl. She was one I had never seen before, and she was mad. And she was the real Jean Ellery or else I was dumb.

I packed her around, parked her on the running board, took a seat beside her, left on the gag and the cords, and began to talk. Patiently, step by step, I went over the history of the whole case, telling her everything. When I had finished I cut the cords and removed the gag.

'Now either beat it, go ahead and scream, or ask questions, whichever you want,' I told her.

She gave a deep breath, licked her lips, wiped her face with a corner of her party gown, woefully inspected a runner in the expensive stockings, looked at the marks on her wrists where the ropes had bitten, smoothed out her garments and turned to me.

'I think you're a liar,' she remarked casually.

I grinned.

That's the way I like 'em. Here this jane had been grabbed, kidnapped, manhandled, jolted, forced to sit on the running board of a car and listen to her kidnapper talk a lot of stuff she naturally wouldn't believe, and then was given her freedom. Most girls would have fainted. Nearly all of 'em would have screamed and ran when they got loose. Here was a jane who was as cool as a cucumber, who looked over the damage to her clothes, and then called me a liar.

She was a thin slip of a thing, twenty or so, big, hazel eyes, chestnut hair, slender figure, rosebud mouth, bobbed hair and as unattainable as a girl on a magazine cover.

'Read this,' I said, and slipped her the confession of the cat-woman.

She read it in the light of the dash lamp, puckered her forehead a bit, and then handed it back.

'So you are Ed Jenkins— Why should auntie have wanted me kidnapped?'

I shrugged my shoulders. 'That's what I want to know. It's the one point in the case that isn't clear. Want to stick around while I find out?'

She thought things over for a minute.

'Am I free to go?'

I nodded.

'Guess I'll stick around then,' she said as she climbed back into the car, snuggling down next to the driver's seat. 'Let's go.'

I got in, started the engine, and we went.

A block from the beach house I slowed up.

'The house is ahead. Slip out as we go by this palm tree, hide in the shadows and watch what happens. I have an idea you'll see some action.'

I slowed down and turned my face toward her, prepared to argue the thing out, but there was no need for argument. She was gathering her skirts about her. As I slowed down she jumped. I drove on to the house, swung the car so it faced the door of the garage and got out.

I had to walk in front of the headlights to fit the key to the door of the garage, and I was a bit nervous. There was an angle of this thing I couldn't get, and it worried me. I thought something was due to happen. If there hadn't been so much money involved I'd have skipped out. As it was, I was playing my cards trying to find out what was in the hand of the cat-woman.

I found out.

As though the swinging of the garage door had been a signal, two men jumped out from behind a rosebush and began firing at the luggage compartment of the car.

They had shotguns, repeaters, and they were shooting chilled buckshot at deadly range through the back of that car. Five times they shot, and then they vanished, running like mad.

Windows began to gleam with lights, a woman screamed, a man stuck his head out into the night. Around the corner there came the whine of a starting motor, the purr of an automobile engine, the staccato barks of an exhaust and an automobile whined off into the night.

I backed the speedster, turned it and went back down the street. At the palm tree where I'd left the flapper I slowed down, doubtfully, hardly expecting to see her again.

There was a flutter of white, a flash of slim legs, and there she was sitting on the seat beside me, her eyes wide, lips parted. 'Did you get hurt?'

I shook my head and jerked my thumb back in the direction of the luggage compartment.

'Remember, I wasn't to stop or open that compartment until I got to the beach house,' I said.

She looked back. The metal was riddled with holes, parts of the body had even been ripped into great, jagged tears.

'Your beloved auntie didn't want you kidnapped. She wanted you murdered. Right now she figures that you're dead, that I am gazing in shocked surprise at the dead body of a girl I've kidnapped, the police on my trail, the neighborhood aroused. Naturally she thinks I'll have my hands full for a while, and that she won't be bothered with me any more, either with me or with you.'

The girl nodded.

'I didn't say so before, but I've been afraid of Aunt Hattie for a long time. It's an awful thing to say about one's own aunt, but she's absolutely selfish, selfish and unscrupulous.'

I drove along in silence for a while.

'What are you going to do?' asked the kid.

'Ditch this car, get off the street, hide out for a few days, and find out what it's all about. Your aunt tried to double-cross me on a deal where there's something or other at stake. I intend to find out what. She and I will have our accounting later.'

She nodded, her chin on her fist, thinking.

'What are *you* going to do?'

She shrugged her shoulders. 'Heaven knows. If I go back I'll probably be killed. Having gone this far, Aunt Hattie can't afford to fail. She'll have me killed if I show up. I guess I'll have to hide out, too.'

'Hotel?' I asked.

I could feel her eyes on my face, sizing me up, watching me like a hawk.

'I can't get a room in a hotel at this hour of the night in a party dress.'

I nodded.

'Ed Jenkins, are you a gentleman?'

I shook my head. 'Hell's fire, no. I'm a crook.'

She looked at me and grinned. I could feel my mouth soften a bit.

'Ed, this is no time to stand on formalities. You know as well as I do that I'm in danger. My aunt believes me dead. If I can keep under cover, leaving her under that impression, I'll stand a chance. I can't hide out by myself. Either my aunt or the police would locate me in no time. You're an experienced crook, you know all the dodges, and I think I can trust you. I'm coming with you.'

I turned the wheel of the car.

'All right,' I said. 'It's your best move, but I wanted you to suggest it. Take off those paste diamonds and leave 'em in the car. I've got to get rid of this car first, and then we'll go to my hideout.'

An hour later I showed her into the apartment. I had run the car off the end of a pier. The watchman was asleep and the car had gurgled down into deep water as neatly as a duck. The watchman had heard the splash, but that's all the good it did him.

The girl looked around the place.

'Neat and cozy,' she said. 'I'm trusting you, Ed Jenkins. Good night.'

I grinned.

'Good night,' I said.

I slept late the next morning. I was tired. It was the girl who called me.

'Breakfast's ready,' she said.

I sat up in bed and rubbed my eyes.

'Breakfast?'

She grinned.

'Yep. I slipped down to the store, bought some fruit and things, and brought you the morning papers.'

I laughed outright. Here I had kidnapped a girl and now she was cooking me breakfast. She laughed, too.

'You see, I'm about broke, and I can't go around in a party dress. I've got to touch you for enough money to buy some clothes, and it's always easier to get money out of a man when he's well-fed. Aunt Hattie told me that.'

'You've got to be careful about showing yourself, too,' I warned her. 'Some one is likely to recognize you.'

She nodded and handed me the morning paper.

All over the front page were smeared our pictures, hers and mine. Holton had offered a reward of twenty thousand dollars for my arrest. The insurance company had added another five.

Without that, I knew the police would be hot on the trail. Their reputation was at stake. They'd leave no stone unturned. Having the girl with me was my best bet. They'd be looking for me alone, or with a girl who was being held a prisoner. They'd hardly expect to find me in a downtown apartment with a girl cooking me breakfast.

I handed Jean a five-hundred-dollar bill.

'Go get yourself some clothes. Get quiet ones, but ones that are in style. I'm disguising myself as your father. You look young and chic, wear 'em short, and paint up a bit. Don't wait, but get started as soon as we eat.'

She dropped a curtsey.

'You're so good to me, Ed,' she said, but there was a wistful note in her voice, and she blinked her eyes rapidly. 'Don't think I don't appreciate it, either,' she added. 'You don't have to put up with me, and you're being a real gentleman. . . .'

That was that.

I was a little nervous until the girl got back from her shopping. I was afraid some one would spot her. She bought a suit and changed into that right at the jump, then got the rest of her things. She put in the day with needle and thread, and I did some thinking, also I coached the girl as to her part. By late afternoon we were able to buy an automobile without having anything suggest that I was other than an elderly, fond parent and the girl a helter-skelter flapper.

'Tonight you get educated as a crook,' I told her.

'Jake with me, Ed,' she replied, flashing me a smile. Whatever her thoughts may have been she seemed to have determined to be a good sport, a regular pal, and never let me see her as other than cheerful.

We slid our new car around where we could watch Big Bill Ryan's place. He ran a little cafe where crooks frequently hung out, and he couldn't take a chance on my having a spotter in the place. One thing was certain. If he was really behind the play he intended to have me caught and executed for murder. He knew me too well to think he could play button, button, who's got the button with me and get away with it.

We waited until eleven, parked in the car I'd purchased, watching the door of the cafe and Big Ryan's car. It was crude but effective. Ryan and the cat-woman both thought I had been left with the murdered body of Jean Ellery in my car, a car which had to be got rid of, a body which had to be concealed, and with all the police in the state on my track. They hardly expected I'd put in the evening watching Big Ryan with the kid leaning on my shoulder.

At eleven Ryan started out, and his face was all smiles. He tried to avoid being followed, but the car I'd purchased had all sorts of speed, and I had no trouble in the traffic. After that I turned out the lights and tailed him into West Forty-ninth Street. I got the number of the house as he stopped, flashed past once to size it up and then kept moving.

'Here's where you get a real thrill,' I told the girl as I headed the car back toward town. 'I've a hunch Harry Atmore's mixed up in this thing as a sort of cat's-paw all around, and I want to see what's in his office.'

We stopped a block away from Atmore's office building. I was a fatherly-looking old bird with mutton chop whiskers and a cane.

'Ever done any burglarizing?' I asked as I clumped my way along the sidewalk.

She shook her head.

'Here's where you begin,' I said, piloted her into the office building, avoided the elevator, and began the long, tedious climb.

Atmore's lock was simple, any door lock is, for that matter. I had expected I'd have to go take a look through the files. It wasn't necessary. From the odor of cigar smoke in the office there'd been a late conference there. I almost fancied I could smell the incense-like perfume of the cat-woman and the aroma of her cigarettes. Tobacco smoke is peculiar. I can tell just about how fresh it is when I smell a room that's strong with it. This was a fresh odor. On the desk was a proof of loss of the necklace, and a memo to call a certain number. I looked up the number in the telephone book. It was the number of the insurance company. That's how I found it, simply looked up the insurance companies in the classified list and ran down the numbers.

The insurance money would be paid in the morning.

That house on West Forty-ninth Street was mixed up in the thing somehow. It was a new lead, and I drove the kid back to the apartment and turned in. The situation wasn't ripe as yet.

Next morning I heard her stirring around, getting breakfast. Of course it simplified matters to eat in the apartment; but if the girl was going to work on the case with me she shouldn't do all the housework. I started to tell her so, rolled over, and grabbed another sleep. It was delicious lying there, stretching out in the warm bed, and hearing the cheery rattle of plates, knives and forks, cups and spoons. I had been a lone wolf so long, an outcast of society, that I thrilled with a delicious sense of intimacy at the idea of having Jean Ellery puttering around in my kitchen. Almost I felt like the father I posed as.

I got up, bathed, shaved, put on my disguise and walked out into the kitchen. The girl was gone. My breakfast was on the table, fruit, cream, toast in the toaster, coffee in the percolator, all ready to press a button and eat. The morning paper was even propped up by my plate.

I switched on the electricity; and wondered about the girl. Anxiously I listened for her step in the apartment. She was company, and I liked her.

The kid didn't say much, but she had a sense of humor, a ready dimple, a twinkle in her eyes, and was mighty easy to look at.

She came in as I was finishing my coffee.

'Hello, Ed. I'm the early bird this morning, and I've caught the worm. That house out on Forty-ninth Street is occupied by old Doctor Drake. He's an old fellow who used to be in San Francisco, had a breakdown, retired, came here, lost his money, was poor as could be until three months ago, and then he suddenly blossomed out with ready money. He's retiring, crabbed, irascible, keeps to himself, has no practice and few visitors.'

I looked her over, a little five-foot-three flapper, slim, active, graceful, but looking as though she had nothing under her chic hat except a hair bob.

'How did you know I wanted to find out about that bird; and how did you get the information?'

She ignored the first question, just passed it off with a wave of the hand.

'The information was easy. I grabbed some packages of face powder, went out in the neighborhood and posed as a demonstrator representing the factory, giving away free samples, and lecturing on the care of the complexion. I even know the neighborhood gossip, all the scandals, and the love affairs of everyone in the block. Give me some of that coffee, Ed. It smells good.'

I grinned proudly at her. The kid was there. It would have been a hard job for me to get that information. She used her noodle. A doctor, eh? Big Ryan had gone to see him when he knew he would have the insurance money. The aunt wanted the girl killed. The engagement had been announced. Then there was the matter of my jade-handled dagger. Those things all began to mill around in my mind. They didn't fit together exactly, but they all pointed in one direction, and that direction made my eyes open a bit wider and my forehead pucker. The game was drawing to the point where I would get into action and see what could be done along the line of checkmating the cat-woman.

A thought flashed through my mind. 'Say, Jean, it's going to be a bit tough on you when it comes time to go back. What'll you tell people, that you were kidnapped and held in a cave or some place? And they'll have the police checking up on your story, you know?'

She laughed a bit and then her mouth tightened. 'If you had been one of the soft-boiled kind that figured you should have married me or some such nonsense I wouldn't have stayed. It was only because you took me in on terms of equality that I remained. You take care of your problems and I'll take care of mine; and we'll both have plenty.'

'That being the case, Jean,' I told her, 'I'm going to stage a robbery and a burglary tonight. Are you coming?'

She grinned at me.

'Miss Jean Ellery announces that it gives her pleasure to accept the invitation of Ed Jenkins to a holdup and burglary. When do we start?'

I shrugged my shoulders. 'Some time after eight or nine. It depends. In the meantime we get some sleep. It's going to be a big night.'

With that I devoted my attention to the paper. After all, the kid was right. I could mind my own business and she could mind hers. She knew what she was doing. Hang it, though, it felt nice to have a little home to settle back in, one where I could read the papers while the girl cleaned off the table, humming a little song the while. All the company I'd ever had before had been a dog, and he was in the hospital recovering from the effects of our last adventure. I was getting old, getting to the point where I wanted company, someone to talk to, to be with.

I shrugged my shoulders and got interested in what I was reading. The police were being panned right. My reputation of being a phantom crook was being rubbed in. Apparently I could disappear, taking an attractive girl and a valuable necklace with me, and the police were absolutely powerless.

Along about dark I parked my car out near Forty-ninth Street. I hadn't much that was definite to go on, but I was playing a pretty good hunch. I knew Big Ryan's car, and I knew the route he took in going to the house of Dr. Drake. I figured he'd got the insurance money some time during the day. Also I doped it out that the trips to the house of Dr. Drake were made after dark. It was pretty slim evidence to work out a plan of campaign on, but, on the other hand, I had nothing to lose.

We waited there two hours before we got action, and then it came, right according to schedule. Big Bill Ryan's car came under the street light, slowed for a bad break that was in the gutter at that point, and then Big Ryan bent forward to shift gears as he pulled out of the hole. It was a bad spot in the road and Bill knew it was there. He'd driven over it just the same way the night I'd followed him.

When he straightened up from the gearshift he was looking down the business end of a wicked pistol. I don't ordinarily carry 'em, preferring to use my wits instead, but this job I wanted to look like the job of somebody else anyway, and the pistol came in handy.

Of course, I was wearing a mask.

There wasn't any need for argument. The gun was there. Big Bill Ryan's fat face was there, and there wasn't three inches between 'em. Big Bill kicked out the clutch and jammed on the brake.

There was a puzzled look on his face as he peered at me. The big fence knew every crook in the game, and he probably wondered who had the nerve to pull the job. It just occurred to me that he looked too much interested and not enough scared, when I saw what I'd walked into. Big Bill had the car stopped dead before he sprung his trap. That was so I couldn't drop off into the darkness. He wanted me.

The back of the car, which had been in shadow, seemed to move, to become alive. From beneath a robe which had been thrown over the seat and floor there appeared a couple of arms, the glint of the street light on metal arrested my eye; and it was too late to do anything, even if I could have gotten away with it.

There were two gunmen concealed in the back of that car. Big Bill Ryan ostensibly was driving alone. As a matter of fact he had a choice of bodyguard. Those two guns were the best shots in crookdom, and they obeyed orders.

Big Bill spoke pleasantly.

'I hadn't exactly expected this, Jenkins, but I was prepared for it. You see I credit you with a lot of brains. How you found out about the case, and how you learned enough to intercept me on this little trip is more than I know. However, I've always figured you were the most dangerous man in the world, and I didn't take any chances.

'You're a smart man, Jenkins; but you're running up against a stone wall. I'm glad this happened when there was a reward out for you in California. It'll be very pleasant to surrender you to the police, thereby cementing my pleasant relations and also getting a cut out of the reward money. Come, come, get in and sit down. Grab his arms, boys.'

Revolvers were thrust under my nose. Grinning faces leered at me. Grimy hands stretched forth and grabbed my shoulders. The car lurched forward and sped away into the night, headed toward the police station. In such manner had Ed Jenkins been captured by a small-time crook and a couple of guns. I could feel myself blush with shame. What was more, there didn't seem to be any way out of it. The guns were awaiting orders, holding fast to me, pulling me over the door. Ryan was speeding up. If I could break away I'd be shot before I could get off of the car, dead before my feet hit ground. If I stayed where I was I'd be in the police station in ten minutes, in a cell in eleven, and five minutes later the reporters would be interviewing me, and the papers would be grinding out extras.

It's the simple things that are hard to beat. This thing was so blamed simple, so childish almost, and yet, there I was.

We flashed past an intersection, swung to avoid the lights of another car that skidded around the corner with screeching tires, and then we seemed to be rocking back and forth, whizzing through the air. It was as pretty a piece of driving as I have ever seen. Jean Ellery had come around the paved corner at full speed, skidding, slipping, right on the tail of the other machine, had swung in sideways, hit the rear bumper and forced Ryan's car around and over, into the curb, and then she had sped on her way, uninjured. Ryan's car had crumpled a front wheel against the curb, and we were all sailing through the air.

Personally, I lit on my feet and kept going. I don't think anyone was hurt much, although Ryan seemed to make a nosedive through the windshield, and the two guns slammed forward against the back of the front seat and then pitched out. Being on the running board, I had just taken a little loop-the-loop through the atmosphere, gone into a tail spin, and pancaked to the earth.

The kid was there a million. If she had come up behind on a straight stretch there would have been lots of action. Ryan would have spotted her, and the guns would have gone into action. She'd either have been captured with me, or we'd both have been shot. By slamming into us from around a corner, however, she'd played her cards perfectly. It had been damned clever driving. What was more it had been clever headwork. She'd seen what had happened when I stuck the gun into Ryan's face, had started my car, doubled around the block, figured our speed to a nicety, and slammed down the cross street in the nick of time.

These things I thought over as I sprinted around a house, through a backyard, into an alley, and into another backyard. The kid had gone sailing off down the street, and I had a pretty strong hunch she had headed for the apartment. She'd done her stuff, and the rest was up to me.

Hang it! My disguise was in my car, and here I was, out in the night, my face covered by a mask, a gun in my pocket, and a reward out for me, with every cop in town scanning every face that passed him on the street. Oh well, it was all in a lifetime and I had work to do. I'd liked to have handled Bill Ryan; seeing I couldn't get him, I had to play the next best bet, Dr. Drake.

His house wasn't far, and I made it in quick time. I was working against time.

I took off my mask, walked boldly up the front steps and rang the doorbell.

There was the sound of shuffling feet, and then a seamed, sallow face peered out at me. The door opened a bit, and two glittering, beady eyes bored into mine.

'What d'yuh want?'

I figured him for Doctor Drake. He was pretty well along in years, and his eyes and forehead showed some indications of education. There was a glittering cupidity about the face, a cunning selfishness that seemed to be the keynote of his character.

'I'm bringing the money.'

His head thrust a trifle farther forward and his eyes bored into mine.

'What money?'

'From Bill Ryan.'

'But Mr. Ryan said he would be here himself.'

I shrugged my shoulders.

I had made my play and the more I kept silent the better it would be. I knew virtually nothing about this end of the game. He knew everything. It would be better for me to let him convince himself than to rush in and ruin it trying to talk too much of detail.

At length the door came cautiously open.

'Come in.'

He led the way into a sort of office. The furniture was apparently left over from some office or other, and it was good stuff, massive mahogany, dark with years; old-fashioned book-cases; chairs that were almost antiques; obsolete text books, all of the what-nots that were the odds and ends of an old physician's office.

Over all lay a coating of gritty dust.

'Be seated,' said the old man, shuffling across to the swivel chair before the desk. I could see that he was breaking fast, this old man. His forehead and eyes retained much of strength, indicated some vitality. His mouth was sagging, weak. Below his neck he seemed to have decayed, the loose, flabby muscles seemed incapable of functioning. His feet could hardly be lifted from the floor. His shoulders lurched forward, and his spine curved into a great hump. Dandruff sprinkled over his coat, an affair that had once been blue serge and which was now spotted with egg, grease, syrup and stains.

'Where is the money?'

I smiled wisely, reached into an inner pocket, half pulled out a wallet, then leered at him after the fashion of a cheap crook, one of the smart-aleck, cunning kind.

'Let's see the stuff first.'

He hesitated, then heaved out of his chair and approached a bookcase. Before the door he suddenly stiffened with suspicion. He turned, his feverish eyes glittering wildly in the feeble light of the small incandescent with which the room was redly illuminated.

'Spread out the money on the table.'

I laughed.

'Say, bo, the coin's here, all right; but if you want to see the long green you gotta produce.'

He hesitated a bit, and then the telephone rang, a jangling, imperative clamor. He shuffled back to the desk, picked up the receiver in a gnarled, knotty hand, swept back the unkempt hair which hung over his ear, and listened.

As he listened I could see the back straighten, the shoulders straighten. A hand came stealing up the inside of the coat.

Because I knew what to expect I wasn't surprised. He bent forward, muttered something, hung up the receiver, spun about and thrust forward an ugly pistol, straight at the chair in which I had been sitting. If ever there was desperation and murder stamped on a criminal face it was on his.

The only thing that was wrong with his plans was that I had silently shifted my position. When he swung that gun around he pointed it where I had been, but wasn't. The next minute I had his neck in a stranglehold, had the gun, and had him all laid out for trussing. Linen bandage was available, and it always makes a nice rope for tying people up with. I gagged him on general principles and then I began to go through that bookcase.

In a book on interior medicine that was written when appendicitis was classified as fatal inflammation of the intestines, I found a document, yellow with age. It was dated in 1904 but it had evidently been in the sunlight some, and had seen much had usage. The ink was slightly faded, and there were marks of old folds, dog-eared corners, little tears. Apparently the paper had batted around in a drawer for a while, had perhaps been rescued at one time or another from a wastebasket, and, on the whole, it was genuine as far as date was concerned. It couldn't have had all that hard usage in less than twenty-two years.

There was no time then to stop and look at it. I took out my wallet, dropped it in there, and then went back to the bookcase, turning the books upside down, shaking them, fluttering the leaves, wondering if there was something else.

I was working against time and knew it. Big Bill Ryan wouldn't dare notify the police. He wouldn't want to have me arrested at the home of Doctor Drake; but he would lose no time in getting the house surrounded by a bunch of gunmen of his own choosing, of capturing me as I sought to escape the house, and then taking me to police headquarters.

It was a matter of seconds. I could read that paper any time; but I could only go through that bookcase when I was there, and it looked as though I wouldn't be in that house again, not for some time. At that I didn't have time to complete the search. I hadn't covered more than half of the books when I heard running steps on the walk, and feet came pounding up the steps.

As a crook my cue was to make for the back door, to plunge out into the night, intent on escape. That would run me into the guns of a picked reception committee that was waiting in the rear. I knew Big Ryan, knew that the hurrying impatience of those steps on the front porch was merely a trap. I was in a house that was surrounded. The automobile with engine running out in front was all a part of the stall. Ryan had probably stopped his machine half a block away, let out his men, given them a chance to surround the house, and then he had driven up, stopped the car with the engine running and dashed up the steps. If Dr. Drake had me covered all right; if I had managed to overpower the old man, I would break and run for the rear.

All of these things flashed through my mind in an instant. I was in my element again. Standing there before the rifled bookcase, in imminent danger, I was as cool as a cake of ice, and I didn't waste a second.

The door of the bookcase I slammed shut. The books were in order on the shelves. As for myself, I did the unexpected. It is the only safe rule.

Instead of sneaking out the back door, I reached the front door in one jump, threw it open and plunged my fist in the bruised, bleeding countenance of Big Bill Ryan. That automobile windshield hadn't used him too kindly, and he was badly shaken. My maneuver took him by surprise. For a split fraction of a second I saw him standing like a statue. The next instant my fist had crashed home.

From the side of the house a revolver spat. There was a shout, a running of dark figures, and I was off. Leaping into the driver's seat of the empty automobile, I had slammed in the gears, shot the clutch, stepped on the throttle and was away.

I chuckled as I heard the chorus of excited shouts behind, the futile rattle of pistol shots. There would be some explaining for Big Bill Ryan to do. In the meantime I was headed for the apartment. I was going to decorate Jean Ellery with a medal, a medal for being the best assistant a crook ever had.

I left the car a couple of blocks from the apartment and walked rapidly down the street. I didn't want the police to locate the stolen car too near my apartment, and yet I didn't dare to go too far without my disguise. The walk of two blocks to my apartment was risky.

My own machine, the one in which Jean had made the rescue, was parked outside. I looked it over with a grin. She was some driver. The front bumper and license plate had been torn off, and the paint on the radiator was scratched a bit, but that was all.

I worried a bit about that license number. I'd bought that car as the old man with the flapper daughter, and I had it registered in the name I had taken, the address as the apartment where Jean and I lived. Losing that license number was something to worry about.

I made record time getting to the door of the apartment, fitting the latchkey and stepping inside. The place was dark, and I pressed the light switch, then jumped back, ready for anything. The room was empty. On the floor was a torn article of clothing. A shoe was laying on its side over near the other door. A rug was rumpled, a chair overturned. In the other room there was confusion. A waist had been ripped to ribbons and was lying by another shoe. The waist was one that Jean had been wearing. The shoes were hers.

I took a quick glance around, making sure the apartment was empty, and then I got into action. Foot by foot I covered that floor looking for something that would be a clue, some little thing that would tell me of the persons who had done the job. Big Bill had acted mighty quick if he had been the one. If it had been the police, why the struggle? If it was a trap, why didn't they spring it?

There was no clue. Whoever it was had been careful to leave nothing behind. I had only a limited amount of time, and I knew it. Once more I was working against time, beset by adverse circumstances, fighting overwhelming odds.

I made a run for the elevator, got to the ground floor, rushed across the street, into the little car Jean had driven, and, as I stepped on the starter and switched on the lights, there came the wail of a siren, the bark of an exhaust, and a police car came skidding around the corner and slid to a stop before the apartment house.

As for me, I was on my way.

Mentally I ran over the characters in the drama that had been played about me, and I picked on Harry Atmore. The little, weak, clever attorney with his cunning dodges, his rat-like mind, his cowering spirit was my meat. He was the weak point in the defense, the weak link in the chain.

I stopped at a telephone booth in a drug store. A plastered-haired sheik was at the telephone fixing up a couple of heavy dates for a wild night. I had to wait while he handed out what was meant to be a wicked line. Finally he hung up the receiver and sauntered toward his car, smirking his self-satisfaction. I grabbed the instrument and placed the warm receiver to my ear.

Atmore wasn't at home. His wife said I'd find him at the office. I didn't call the office. It would suit me better to walk in unannounced if I could get him by himself. I climbed into my machine and was on my way.

I tried the door of Atmore's office and found it was open. There was a light in the reception room. Turning, I pulled the catch on the spring lock, slammed the door and turned out the light. Then I walked into the private office.

There must have been that on my face which showed that I was on a mission which boded no good to the crooked shyster, an intentness of purpose which was apparent. He gave me one look, and then shrivelled down in his chair, cowering, his rat-like nose twitching, his yellow teeth showing.

I folded my arms and glared at him.

'Where's the girl?'

He lowered his gaze and shrugged his shoulders.

I advanced. Right then I was in no mood to put up with evasions. Something seemed to tell me that the girl was in danger, that every second counted, and I had no time to waste on polite formalities. That girl had grown to mean something to me. She had fitted in, uncomplaining, happy, willing, and she had saved me when I had walked into a trap there with Big Bill Ryan. As long as I was able to help that girl she could count on me. There had never been very much said, but we understood each other, Jean Ellery and I. She had played the game with me, and I would play it with her.

'Atmore,' I said, pausing impressively between the words, 'I want to know where that girl is, and I mean to find out.'

He ducked his hand, and I sprang, wrenched his shoulder, pulled him backward, crashed a chair to the floor, struck the gun up, kicked his wrist, smashed my fist in his face and sprawled him on the floor. He didn't get up. I was standing over him, and he crawled and cringed like a whipped cur.

'Miss Hare has her. Bill Ryan got her located through the number on a machine, and Hattie Hare went after her. She is a devil, that woman. She has the girl back at the Holton house.'

I looked at his writhing face for a moment trying to determine if he was lying. I thought not. Big Ryan had undoubtedly traced that license number. That was but the work of a few minutes on the telephone with the proper party. He couldn't have gone after the girl himself because he had been at

Dr. Drake's too soon afterward. On the other hand, he had gone to a public telephone because he had undoubtedly telephoned Dr. Drake and told him of his accident, probably warned him against me. From what the doctor had said, Ryan knew I was there, and he had dropped everything to come after me. What more natural than that he should have telephoned the cat-woman to go and get the girl.

I turned and strode toward the door.

'Listen, you rat,' I snapped. 'If you have lied to me, you'll die!'

His eyes rolled a bit, his mouth twitched, but he said nothing. I ran into the dark outer office, threw open the door, snapped the lock back on the entrance door, banged it and raced to the elevator. Then I turned and softly retraced my steps, slipped into the dark outer office, and tiptoed to the door of the private office. By opening it a crack I could see the lawyer huddled at his desk, frantically clicking the hook on the telephone.

In a minute he got central, snapped a number, waited and then gave his message in five words. 'He's on his way out,' he said, and hung up.

I only needed one guess. He was talking to the cat-woman. They had prepared a trap, had baited it with the girl, and were waiting for me to walk into it.

I went back into the hall, slipped down the elevator, went to my car and stepped on the starter. As I went I thought. Time was precious. Long years of being on my own resources had taught me to speed up my thinking processes. For years I had been a lone wolf, had earned the name of being the phantom crook, one who could slip through the fingers of the police. Then there had been a welcome vacation while I enjoyed immunity in California, but now all that was past. I was my own man, back in the thick of things. I had accomplished everything I had done previously by thinking fast, reaching quick decisions, and putting those decisions into instant execution. This night I made up my mind I would walk into the trap and steal the bait; whether I could walk out again depended upon my abilities. I would be matching my wits against those of the cat-woman, and she was no mean antagonist. Witness the manner in which she had learned that the girl had not been murdered, that I had convinced the girl of the woman's duplicity, had taken her in as a partner, the manner in which the cat-woman had known she could reach me through the girl, that I would pick on Atmore as being the weak link in the chain.

I stopped at a drug store long enough to read the paper I had taken from the book at Dr. Drake's house, and to telephone. I wanted to know all the cards I held in my hand before I called for a showdown.

The document was a strange one. It was nothing more nor less than a consent that the doctor should take an unborn baby and do with it as he wished. It was signed by the expectant mother. Apparently it was merely one of thousands of such documents which find their way into the hands of doctors. Yet I was certain it represented an important link in a strong chain.

Upon the back of the document were three signatures. One of them was the signature of Hattie M. Hare. There were addresses, too, also telephone numbers. Beneath the three signatures were the words 'nurses and witnesses.'

I consulted the directory, got the number of H. F. Morton, and got him out of bed.

'This is Mr. Holton,' I husked into the telephone. 'Come to my house at once.'

With the words I banged the receiver against the telephone a couple of times and hung up. Then I sprinted into the street, climbed into the machine and was off.

I had no time to waste, and yet I was afraid the trap would be sprung before I could get the bait. It was late and a ring at the doobell would have been a telltale sign. I parked the machine a block away, hit the backyards and approached the gloomy mass of shadows which marked the home of Arthur C. Holton, the oil magnate. I was in danger and knew it, knew also that the danger was becoming more imminent every minute.

I picked a pantry window. Some of the others looked more inviting, but I picked one which I would hardly have been expected to have chosen. There had already been a few minutes' delay. Seconds were precious. I knew the house well enough to take it almost at a run. When I have once been inside a place I can generally dope out the plan of the floors, and I always remember those plans.

In the front room there was just the flicker of a fire in the big fireplace. Above the tiles there glowed two spots of fire. I had been right in my surmise about the painting of the cat's head. The eyes had been tinted with luminous paint.

In the darkness there came a faint, dull, 'click.' It was a sound such as is made by a telephone bell when it gives merely the jump of an electrical contact, a sound which comes when a receiver has been removed from an extension line. With the sound I had out my flashlight and was searching for the telephone. If anyone was using an extension telephone in another part of the house I wanted to hear what was being said.

It took me a few seconds to locate the instrument, and then I slipped over to it and eased the receiver from the hook. It was the cat-woman who was talking:

'Yes, Arthur C. Holton's residence, and come right away. You know he threatened to return. Yes, I know it's Ed Jenkins. I tell you I saw his face. Yes, the phantom crook. Send two cars and come at once.'

There was a muttered assent from the cop at the other end of the line, and then the click of two receivers. Mine made a third.

So that was the game, was it? In some way she had known when I entered the place. I fully credited those luminous, cat-eyes of hers with being able to see in the dark. She had laid a trap for me, baited it with the girl, and now she had summoned the police. Oh well, I had been in worse difficulties before.

I took the carpeted stairway on the balls of my feet, taking the stairs two at a time. There was a long corridor above from which there opened numerous bedrooms. I saw a flutter of pink at one end of the hall, a mere flash of woman's draperies. I made for that point, and I went at top speed. If my surmise was correct I had no time to spare, not so much as the tick of a watch.

The door was closed and I flung it open, standing not upon ceremony or formalities. I was racing with death.

Within the room was a dull light, a reflected, diffused light which came from the corridor, around a corner, against the half-open door, and into the room. There was a bed and a white figure was stretched upon the bed, a figure which was struggling in the first panic of a sudden awakening. When I had flung the door open it had crashed against the wall, rebounded so that it was half closed, and then remained shivering on its hinges, catching and reflecting the light from the hall.

In that semi-darkness the cat-woman showed as a flutter of flowing silk. She moved with the darting quickness of a cat springing on its prey. She had turned her head as I crashed into the room, and her eyes, catching the light from the hall, glowed a pale, baleful green, a green of hate, of tigerish intensity of rage.

Quick as she was, I was quicker. As the light caught the flicker of cold steel I flung her to one side, slammed her against the wall. She was thin, lithe, supple, but the warm flesh of her which met my hands through the thin veil of sheer silk was as hard as wire springs. She recoiled from the wall, poised lightly on her feet, gave me a flicker of the light from those cat-eyes once more, and then fluttered from the room, her silks flapping in the breeze of her progress. Two hands shot from the bed and grasped me by the shoulders, great, hairy hands with clutching fingers.

'Jenkins! Ed Jenkins!' exclaimed a voice.

I shook him off and raced for the door. From the street below came the sound of sliding tires, the noise of feet hurrying on cement, pounding on gravel. Someone dashed up the front steps and pounded on the door, rang frantically at the bell. The police had arrived, excited police who bungled the job of surrounding the house.

There was yet time. I had been in tighter pinches. I could take the back stairs, shoot from the back door and try the alley. There would probably be the flash of firearms, the whine of lead through the night air, but there would also be the element of surprise, the stupidity of the police, the flat-footed slowness of getting into action. I had experienced it all before.

In one leap I made the back stairs and started to rush down. The front door flew open and there came the shrill note of a police whistle. I gathered my muscles for the next flying leap, and then stopped, caught almost in midair.

I had thought of the girl!

Everything that had happened had fitted in with my theory of the case, and in that split fraction of a second I knew I was right. Some flash of inner intuition, some telepathic insight converted a working hypothesis, a bare theory, into an absolute certainty. In that instant I knew the motive of the cat-woman, knew the reason she had rushed from that other room. Jean Ellery had been used by her to bait the trap for Ed Jenkins, but she had had another use, had served another purpose. She was diabolically clever, that cat-woman, and Jean Ellery was to die.

I thought of the girl, of her charm, her ready acceptance of life as the working partner of a crook, and I paused in mid flight, turned a rapid flip almost in the air and was running madly down the corridor, toward the police.

There are times when the mind speeds up and thoughts become flashes of instantaneous conceptions, when one lives ages in the space of seconds. All of the thoughts which had pieced together the real solution of the mystery, the explanation of the actions of the cat-woman had come to me while I was poised, balanced for a leap on the stairs. My decision to return had been automatic, instantaneous. I could not leave Jean Ellery in danger.

The door into which the cat-woman had plunged was slightly ajar. Through it could be seen the gleam of light, a flicker of motion. I was almost too late as I hurtled through that door, my outstretched arm sweeping the descending hand of the cat-woman to one side.

Upon the bed, bound, gagged, her helpless eyes staring into the infuriated face of the cat-woman, facing death with calm courage, watching the descent of the knife itself, was the form of Jean Ellery. My hand had caught the downthrust of the knife just in time.

The cat-woman staggered back, spitting vile oaths, lips curling, eyes flashing, her words sounding like the explosive spats of an angry cat. The knife had clattered to the floor and lay at my very feet. The green-handled dagger, the jade-hilted knife which had been taken from my apartment. At that instant a shadow blotted the light from the hallway and a voice shouted:

'Hands up, Ed Jenkins!'

The cat-woman gave an exclamation of relief.

'Thank God, officer, you came in the nick of time!'

There was the shuffling of many feet: peering faces, gleaming shields, glinting pistols, and I found myself grabbed by many hands, handcuffs snapped about my wrists, cold steel revolvers thrust against my neck. I was pushed, jostled, slammed, pulled, dragged down the stairs and into the library.

The cat-woman followed, cajoling the officers, commenting on their bravery, their efficiency, spitting epithets at me.

And then H. F. Morton walked into the open door, took in the situation with one glance of his steely eyes, deposited his hat and gloves on a chair, walked to the great table, took a seat behind it and peered over the tops of his glasses at the officers, at the cat-woman, at myself.

The policeman jostled me toward the open front door.

The lawyer held up a restraining hand.

'Just a minute,' he said, and there was that in the booming authority of the voice which held the men, stopped them in mid-action.

'What is this?' he asked, and, with the words, dropped his hands to the table and began to drum regularly, rhythmically, 'rummpy-tum-tum; rummpy-tum-tum; rummpy-tum-tumpty-tum-tumpty-tum-tum.'

'Aw g'wan,' muttered one of the officers as he pulled me forward.

'Shut up, you fool. He's the mayor's personal attorney!' whispered another, his hands dragging me back, holding me against those who would have taken me from the house.

The word ran through the group like wildfire. There were the hoarse sibilants of many whispers, and then attentive silence.

''Tis Ed Jenkins, sor,' remarked one of the policemen, one who seemed to be in charge of the squad. 'The Phantom Crook, sor, caught in this house from which he kidnapped the girl an' stole the necklace, an' 'twas murder he was after tryin' to commit this time.'

The lawyer's gray eyes rested on my face.

'If you want to talk, Jenkins, talk now.'

I nodded.

'The girl, Jean Ellery. She is the daughter of Arthur C. Holton.'

The fingers stopped their drumming and gripped the table.

'What?'

I nodded. 'It was supposed that his child was a boy, a boy who died shortly after birth. As a matter of fact, the child was a girl, a girl who lived, who is known as Jean Ellery. A crooked doctor stood for the substitution, being paid a cash fee. A nurse originated the scheme, Miss Hattie M. Hare. The boy could never be traced. His future was placed in the doctor's hands before birth and when coincidence played into the hands of this nurse she used all her unscrupulous knowledge, all her cunning. The girl was to be brought up to look upon the nurse as her aunt, her only living relative. At the proper time the whole thing was to be exposed, but the doctor was to be the one who was to take the blame. Hattie M. Hare was to have her connection with the scheme kept secret.

'But the doctor found out the scheme to make him the goat. He had in his possession a paper signed by the nurse, a paper which would have foiled the whole plan. He used this paper as a basis for regular blackmail.

'It was intended to get this paper, to bring out the girl as the real heir, to have her participate in a trust fund which had been declared for the child of Arthur C. Holton, to have her inherit all the vast fortune of the oil magnate;

– and to remember her aunt Hattie M. Hare as one of her close and dear relatives, to have her pay handsomely for the so-called detectives and lawyers who were to "unearth" the fraud, to restore her to her place, to her estate.

'And then there came another development, Arthur C. Holton became infatuated with the arch-conspirator, Hattie M. Hare. He proposed marriage, allowing himself to be prevailed upon to make a will in her favor, to make a policy of life insurance to her.

'The girl ceased to be an asset, but became a menace. She must be removed. Also Arthur C. Holton must die that Miss Hattie M. Hare might succeed in his estate without delay. But there was a stumbling block, the paper which was signed by Hattie M. Hare, the paper which might be connected with the substitution of children, which would brand her a criminal, which would be fatal if used in connection with the testimony of the doctor.

'Doctor Drake demanded money for his silence and for that paper. He demanded his money in cash, in a large sum. The woman, working with fiendish cunning, decided to use me as a cat's-paw to raise the money and to also eliminate the girl from her path as well as to apparently murder the man who stood between her and his wealth. I was to be enveigled into apparently stealing a necklace worth much money, a necklace which was to be insured, and the insurance payable to Miss Hare; I was to be tricked into kidnapping a girl who would be murdered; I was to be persuaded to make threats against Mr. Holton, and then I was to become the apparent murderer of the oil magnate. My dagger was to be found sticking in his breast. In such manner would Miss Hare bring about the death of the man who had made her the beneficiary under his will, buy the silence of the doctor who knew her for a criminal, remove the only heir of the blood, and make me stand all the blame, finally delivering me into the hands of the law.

'There is proof. I have the signed statement in my pocket. Doctor Drake will talk. Harry Atmore will confess . . . . There she goes. Stop her!'

The cat-woman had seen that her play was ended. She had realized that she was at the end of her rope, that I held the evidence in my possession, that the bound and gagged girl upstairs would testify against her. She had dashed from the room while the stupefied police had held me and stared at her with goggle eyes.

Openmouthed they watched her flight, no one making any attempt to take after her, eight or ten holding me in their clumsy hands while the cat-woman, the arch criminal of them all dashed out into the night.

H. F. Morton looked at me and smiled.

'Police efficiency, Jenkins,' he said.

Then he faced the officers. 'Turn him loose.'

The officers shifted uneasily. The man in charge drew himself up stiffly and saluted. 'He is a noted criminal with a price on his head, the very devil of a crook, sor.'

Morton drummed steadily on the desk.

'What charge have you against him?'

The officer grunted.

'Stealin' Mr. Holton's necklace, an' breakin' into his house, sor.'

'Those charges are withdrawn,' came from the rear of the room in deep, firm tones.

I turned to see Arthur C. Holton. He had dressed and joined the group. I did not even know when he had entered the room, how much he had heard. By his side, her eyes starry, stood Jean Ellery, and there were gleaming gems of moisture on her cheeks.

The policeman grunted.

'For kidnappin' the young lady an' holdin' her. If she stayed against her will 'twas abductin', an' she wouldn't have stayed with a crook of her own accord, not without communicatin' with her folks.'

That was a poser. I could hear Jean suck in her breath to speak the words that would have freed me but would have damned her in society forever; but she had not the chance.

Before I could even beat her to it, before my confession would have spared her name and sent me to the penitentiary, H. F. Morton's shrewd mind had grasped all the angles of the situation, and he beat us all to it.

'You are wrong. The girl was not kidnapped. Jenkins never saw her before.'

The policeman grinned broadly.

'Then would yez mind tellin' me where she was while all this hue an' cry was bein' raised, while everyone was searchin' for her?'

Morton smiled politely, urbanely.

'Not at all, officer. She was at my house, as the guest of my wife. Feeling that her interests were being jeopardized and that her life was in danger, I had her stay incognito in my own home.'

There was tense, thick silence.

The girl gasped. The clock ticked. There was the thick, heavy breathing of the big-bodied policemen.

'Rummy-tum-tum; rummy-tum-tum; rumiddy, tumptidy, tumpy tum-tum,' drummed the lawyer. 'Officer, turn that man loose. Take off those handcuffs. Take . . . off . . . those . . . handcuffs . . . I . . . say. You haven't a thing against him in California.'

As one in a daze, the officer fitted his key to the handcuffs, the police fell back, and I stood a free man.

'Good night,' said the lawyer pointedly, his steely eyes glittering into those of the officers.

Shamefacedly, the officers trooped from the room.

Jean threw herself into my arms.

'Ed, you came back because of me! You risked your life to save mine, to see that a wrong was righted, to see that I was restored to my father! Ed, dear, you are a man in a million.'

I patted her shoulder.

'You were a good pal, Jean and I saw you through,' I said. 'Now you must forget about it. The daughter of a prominent millionaire has no business knowing a crook.'

Arthur Holton advanced, hand outstretched.

'I was hypnotized, fooled, taken in by an adventuress and worse. I can hardly think clearly, the events of the past few minutes have been so swift, but this much I do know. I can never repay you for what you have done, Ed Jenkins. I will see that your name is cleared of every charge against you in every state, that you are a free man, that you are restored to citizenship, and that you have the right to live,' and here he glanced at Jean: 'You will stay with us as my guest?'

I shook my head. It was all right for them to feel grateful, to get a bit sloppy now that the grandstand play had been made, but they'd probably feel different about it by morning.

'I think I'll be on my way,' I said, and started for the door.

'Ed!' It was the girl's cry, a cry which was as sharp, as stabbing as a quick pain at the heart. '*Ed, you're not leaving!*'

By way of answer I stumbled forward. Hell, was it possible that the difficulty with that threshold was that there was a mist in my eyes? Was Ed Jenkins, the phantom crook, known and feared by the police of a dozen states, becoming an old woman?

Two soft arms flashed about my neck, a swift kiss planted itself on my cheek, warm lips whispered in my ear.

I shook myself free, and stumbled out into the darkness. She was nothing but a kid, the daughter of a millionaire oil magnate. I was a crook. Nothing but hurt to her could come to any further acquaintance. It had gone too far already.

I jumped to one side, doubled around the house, away from the street lights, hugging the shadow which lay near the wall. From within the room, through the half-open window there came a steady, throbbing, thrumming sound: 'Rummy-tum-tum; rummy-tum-tum; rummy-tum-tummy; tum-tummy-tum-tum.'

H. F. Morton was thinking.

THE DILEMMA OF THE DEAD LADY

CORNELL WOOLRICH

The master of noir fiction, Cornell Woolrich (1903–1968) wrote literally hundreds of stories, of which fewer than you might think have happy endings.

It was difficult to find the right story for this volume because so many of his characters are shades of gray. People with whom we empathize choose to murder someone, or are put in positions where there seems to be no choice. Policemen, the upholders of the law, are frequently fascistic thugs who enjoy torturing suspects. Pretty girls with faces of angels turn out to be liars and cheats, and often worse. Even situations concluded in a way that another author would resolve justly, a Woolrich character often still faces a future barren of love, joy, or hope.

'The Dilemma of the Dead Lady' has had a varied life. Inspired by a cruise he took with his mother in 1931, he twists the memories into one of his most horrifying suspense stories. Although it was common for Woolrich to visit great terrors on ordinary, decent people, in this tale the central character is such a lowlife that we almost feel he deserves whatever befalls him.

After its original publication in the July 4, 1936, issue of *Detective Fiction Weekly*, it was retitled 'Wardrobe Trunk' for its book publication in *The Blue Ribbon* (1946) as by William Irish. Oddly, Woolrich rewrote it as a radio play titled 'Working Is for Fools' which was never produced but did appear in the March 1964 issue of *Ellery Queen's Mystery Magazine*.

THE DILEMMA OF THE DEAD LADY

CORNELL WOOLRICH

I

It was already getting light out, but the peculiar milky-white Paris street lights were still on outside Babe Sherman's hotel window. He had the room light on, too, such as it was, and was busy packing at a mile-a-minute rate. The boat ticket was in the envelope on the bureau. All the bureau drawers were hanging out, and his big wardrobe trunk was yawning wide open in the middle of the room. He kept moving back and forth between it and the bureau with a sort of catlike tread, transferring things.

He was a good-looking devil, if you cared for his type of good looks – and women usually did. Then later on, they always found out how wrong they'd been. They were only a sideline with him, anyway; they were apt to get tangled around a guy's feet, trip him up when he least expected it. Like this little – what was her name now? He actually couldn't remember it for a minute, and didn't try to; he wouldn't be using it any more now, anyway. She'd come in handy, though – or rather her life's savings had – right after he'd been cleaned at the Longchamps track. And then holding down a good job like she did with one of the biggest jewelry firms on the Rue de la Paix had been damned convenient for his purposes. He smiled when he thought of the long, slow build-up it had taken – calling for her there twice a day, taking her out to meals, playing Sir Galahad. Boy, he'd had to work hard for his loot this time, but it was worth it! He unwrapped the little tissue-paper package in his breastpocket, held the string of pearls up to the light, and looked at them. Matched, every one of them – and with a diamond clasp. They'd bring plenty in New York! He knew just the right fence, too.

The guff he'd had to hand her, though, when she first got around to pointing out new articles in the display cases, each time one was added to the stock! 'I'd rather look at you, honey.' Not seeming to take any interest, not even glancing down. Until finally, when things were ripe enough to suit him: 'Nice pearls, those. Hold 'em up to your neck a minute, let's see how they look on you.'

'Oh, I'm not allow' to take them out! I am only suppose' to handle the briquets, gold cigarette cases—' But she would have done anything he asked her by that time. With a quick glance at the back of M'sieu Proprietor, who was right in the room with them, she was holding them at her throat for a stolen moment.

'I'll fasten the catch for you – turn around, look at the glass.'

'No, no, please—' They fell to the floor, somehow. He picked them up and handed them back to her; they were standing at the end of the long case, he on his side, she on her side. And when they went back onto the velvet tray inside the case, the switch had already been made. As easy as that!

He was all dressed, even had his hat on the back of his skull, but he'd left his shoes off, had been going around in his stocking feet, hence the catlike tread. Nor was this because he intended beating this cheesy side-street hotel out of his bill, although that wouldn't have been anything new to his experience either. He could possibly have gotten away with it at that – there was only what they called a 'concierge' on duty below until seven, and at that he was always asleep. But for once in his life he'd paid up. He wasn't taking any chances of getting stopped at the station. He wanted to get clear of this damn burg and clear of this damn country without a hitch. He had a good reason, $75,000-worth of pearls. When they said it in francs it sounded like a telephone number. Besides, he didn't like the looks of their jails here; you could smell them blocks away. One more thing: you didn't just step on the boat like in New York. It took five hours on the boat train getting to it, and a wire to Cherbourg to hold you and send you back could make it in twenty minutes. So it was better to part friends with everyone. Not that the management of a third-class joint like this would send a wire to Cherbourg, but they would go to the police, and if the switch of the pearls happened to come to light at about the same time. . . .

He sat down on the edge of the bed and picked up his right shoe. He put the pearls down for a minute, draped across his thigh, fumbled under the mattress and took out a tiny screwdriver. He went to work on the three little screws that fastened his heel. A minute later it was loose in his hand. It was hollow, had a steel rim on the end of it to keep it from wearing down. He coiled the pearls up, packed them in. There was no customs inspection at this end, and before he tackled the Feds at the other side, he'd think up something better. This would do for now.

It was just when he had the heel fitted in place again, but not screwed on, that the knock on the door came. He got white as a sheet for a minute, sat there without breathing. Then he remembered that he'd left word downstairs last night that he was making the boat train; it was probably the porter for his wardrobe trunk. He got his windpipe going again, called out in his half-baked French, 'Too soon, gimme another ten minutes!'

The knocking hadn't quit from the time it began, without getting louder it kept getting faster and faster all the time. The answer froze him when it came through the door: 'Let me in, let me in, Bébé, it's me!'

He knew who 'me' was, all right! He began to swear viciously but soundlessly. He'd already answered like a fool, she knew he was there! If he'd only kept his trap shut, she might have gone away. But if he didn't let her in now, she'd probably rouse the whole hotel! He didn't want any publicity if he could help it. She could make it tough for him, even without knowing about the pearls. After all, she had turned over her savings to him. Her knocking was a frantic machine-gun tattoo by now, and getting louder all the time. Maybe he could stall her off for an hour or two, get rid of her long enough to make the station, feed her some taffy or other. . . .

He hid the screwdriver again, stuck his feet into his shoes without lacing them, shuffled over to the door and unlocked it. Then he tried to stand in the opening so that she couldn't see past him into the room.

She seemed half-hysterical, there were tears standing in her eyes. 'Bébé, I waited for you there last night, what happen'? Why you do these to me, what I have done?'

'What d'ya mean by coming here at this hour?' he hissed viciously at her. 'Didn't I tell you never to come here!'

'Nobody see me, the concierge was asleep, I walk all the way up the stairs—' She broke off suddenly. 'You are all dress', at these hour? You, who never get up ontil late! The hat even—'

'I just got in,' he tried to bluff her, looking up and down the passageway. The motion was his undoing; in that instant she had peered inside, across his shoulder, possibly on the lookout for some other girl. She saw the trunk standing there open in the middle of the room.

He clapped his hand to her mouth in the nick of time, stifling her scream. Then pulled her roughly in after him and locked the door.

He let go of her then. 'Now, there's nothing to get excited about,' he said soothingly. 'I'm just going on a little business trip to, er—' He snapped his fingers helplessly, couldn't think of any French names. 'I'll be back day after tomorrow—'

But she wasn't listening, was at the bureau before he could stop her, pawing the boat ticket. He snatched it from her, but the damage had already been done. 'But you are going to New York! This ticket is for one! You said never a word—' Anyone but a heel like Babe Sherman would have been wrung by the misery in her voice. 'I thought that you and I, we—'

He was getting sick of this. 'What a crust!' he snarled. 'Get hep to yourself! I should marry you! Why, we don't even talk the same lingo!'

She reeled as though an invisible blow had struck her, pulled herself together again. She had changed now. Her eyes were blazing. 'My money!' she cried hoarsely. 'Every sou I had in the world I turned over to you! My *dot*, my marriage dowry, that was suppose' to be! No, no, you are not going to do these to me! You do not leave here ontil you have give it back—' She darted at the locked door. 'I tell my story to the gendarmes—'

He reared after her, stumbled over the rug but caught her in time, flung her backward away from the door. The key came out of the keyhole, dropped to the floor, he kicked it sideways out of her reach. 'No, you don't!' he panted.

Something was holding her rigid, though his hands were no longer on her. He followed the direction of her dilated eyes, down toward the floor. His loosened heel had come off just now. She was staring, not at that, but at the lustrous string of pearls that spilled out of it like a tiny snake, their diamond catch twinkling like an eye.

Again she pounced, and again he forestalled her, whipped them up out of her reach. But as he did so, they straightened out and she got a better look at them than she would have had they stayed coiled in a mass. 'It is number twenty-nine, from the store!' she gasped. 'The one I showed you! Oh, *mon Dieu*, when they find out, they will blame me! They will send me to St. Lazare—'

He had never yet killed anyone, didn't intend to even now. But death was already in the room with the two of them. She could have still saved herself, probably, by using her head, subsiding, pretending to fall in with his plans for the time being. That way she might have gotten out of there alive. But it would have been superhuman; no one in her position would have had the self-control to do it. She was only a very frightened French girl after all. They were both at a white-heat of fear and self-preservation; she lost her head completely, did the one thing that was calculated to doom her. She flung herself for the last time at the door, panic-stricken, with a hoarse cry for help. And he, equally panic-stricken, and more concerned about silencing her before she roused the house than even about keeping her in the room with him, took the shortest way of muffling her voice. The inaccurate way, the deadly way. He flung the long loop of pearls over her head from behind like a lasso, foreshortened them into a choking noose, dragged her stumbling backward. They were strung on fine platinum wire, almost unbreakable. She turned and turned, three times over, like a dislodged tenpin, whipping the thing inextricably around her throat, came up against him, coughing, clawing at herself, eyes rolling. Too late he let go, there wasn't any slack left, the pearls were like gleaming white nail heads driven into her flesh.

He clawed now, too, trying to free her as he saw her face begin to mottle. There wasn't room for a finger hold; to pluck at one loop only tightened the other two under it. Suddenly she dropped vertically, like a plummet, between his fumbling hands, twitched spasmodically for an instant at his feet, then lay there still, face black now, eyes horrible protuberances. Dead. Strangled by a thing of beauty, a thing meant to give pleasure.

2

Babe Sherman was a realist, also known as a heel. He saw from where he was that she was gone, without even bending over her. No face could turn that color and ever be alive again. No eyes could swell in their sockets like that and ever see again. He didn't even bend down over her, to feel for her heart; didn't say a word, didn't make a sound. The thought in his mind was: 'Now I've done it. Added murder to all the rest. It was about the only thing missing!'

His first move was to the door. He stood there listening. Their scuffle hadn't taken long; these old Paris dumps had thick stone walls. Her last cry at the door, before he'd corralled her, had been a hoarse, low-pitched one, not a shrill, woman's scream. There wasn't a sound outside. Then he went to the window, peered through the mangy curtains, first from one side, then the other. He was low enough – third story – and the light had been on, but the shutters were all tightly closed on the third floor of the building across the way, every last one of them. He carefully fitted his own together; in France they come inside the vertical windows.

He went back to her, and he walked all around her. This time the thought was, appropriately enough: 'How is it I've never done it before now? Lucky, I guess.' He wasn't as cool as he looked, by any means, but he wasn't as frightened as a decent man would have been, either; there'd been too many things in his life before this, the edge had been taken off long ago. He had no conscience.

He stooped over her for the first time, but only to fumble some more with the necklace. He saw that it would have to stay; opening the catch was no good, only a wire clipper could have severed it, and he had none. He spoke aloud for the first time since he'd been 'alone' in the room. 'Y' wanted 'em back,' he said gruffly, 'well, y' got 'em!' A defense mechanism, to show himself how unfrightened he was. And then, supreme irony, her given name came back to him at last, for the first time since she'd put in an appearance, 'Manon,' he added grudgingly. The final insult!

He straightened up, flew at the door like an arrow almost before the second knocking had begun, to make sure that it was still locked. This time it *was* the porter, sealing him up in there, trapping him! 'M'sieu, the baggages.'

'Wait! One little minute! Go downstairs again, then come back—'

But he wouldn't go away. 'M'sieu hasn't much time. The boat train leaves in fifteen minutes. They didn't tell me until just now. It takes nearly that long to the sta—'

'Go back, go back I tell you!'

'Then m'sieu not want to make his train—'

But he had to, it meant the guillotine if he stayed here even another twenty-four hours! He couldn't keep her in the damned place with him forever; he couldn't smuggle her out, he couldn't even blow and leave her behind! In ten minutes after he was gone they'd find her in the room, and a wire could get to Cherbourg four and a half hours before his train!

He broke for just a minute. He groaned, went around in circles in there, like a trapped beast. Then he snapped right out of it again. The answer was so obvious! His only safety lay in taking her with him, dead or not! The concierge had been asleep, hadn't seen her come in. Let her employer or her landlord turn her name over to the Missing Persons Bureau – or whatever they called it here – a week or ten days from now. She'd be at the bottom of the deep Atlantic long before that. The phony pearls in the showcase would give them their explanation. And she had no close relatives here in Paris. She'd already told him that. The trunk, of course, had been staring him in the face the whole time.

He put his ear to the keyhole, could hear the guy breathing there on the other side of the door, waiting! He went at the trunk, pitched out all the things he'd been stuffing in it when she interrupted him. Like all wardrobes, one side was entirely open, for suits to be hung in; the other was a network of small compartments and drawers, for shoes, shirts, etc. It wasn't a particularly well-made trunk; he'd bought it secondhand. He cleared the drawers out, ripped the thin lath partitions out of the way bodily. The hell with the noise, it was no crime partly to destroy your own trunk. Both sides were open now, four-square; just the metal shell remained.

He dragged her over, sat her up in the middle of it, folded her legs up against her out of the way, and pushed the two upright halves closed over her. She vanished, there was no resistance, no impediment, plenty of room. Too much, maybe. He opened it again, packed all his shirts and suits tightly around her, and the splintered partitions and the flattened-out drawers. There wasn't a thing left out, not a thing left behind, not a nail even. Strangest of biers, for a little fool that hadn't known her man well enough!

Then he closed it a second time, locked it, tilted it this way and that. You couldn't tell. He scanned his boat ticket, copied the stateroom number onto the baggage label the steamship company had given him: 42-A. And the label read: NEEDED IN STATEROOM. It couldn't go into the hold, of course. Discovery would be inevitable in a day or two at the most. He moistened it, slapped it against the side of the trunk.

He gave a last look around. There wasn't a drop of blood, nothing to give him away. The last thing he saw before he let the porter in was the hollow heel that had betrayed him to her, lying there. He picked it up and slipped it in his pocket, flat.

He opened the door and jerked his thumb. The blue-bloused porter straighted up boredly. '*Allons!*' Babe said. 'This goes right in the taxi with me, understand?'

The man tested it, spit on his hands, grabbed it. 'He'll soak you an extra half-fare.'

'I'm paying,' Babe answered. He sat down on the edge of the bed and finished lacing his shoes. The porter bounced the trunk on its edges out of the room and down the passageway.

Babe caught up with him at the end of it. He wasn't going to stay very far away from it, from now on. He was sweating a little under his hat band; otherwise he was okay. She hadn't meant anything to him anyway, and he'd done so many lousy things before now. . . .

He'd never trusted that birdcage French elevator from the beginning, and when he saw Jacques getting ready to tilt the trunk onto it, he had a bad half-minute. The stairs wouldn't be any too good for it, either; it was a case of six of one, half a dozen of the other. 'Will it hold?' he asked.

'Sure, if we don't get on with it.' It wobbled like jelly, though, under it. Babe wiped his forehead with one finger. 'Never dropped yet,' the porter added.

'It only has to once,' thought Babe. He deliberately crossed his middle and index fingers and kept them that way, slowly spiraling around the lethargic apparatus down the stair well.

Jacques closed the nutty-looking little wicket gate, reached over it to punch the bottom button, and then came after him. They'd gone half a flight before anything happened. Then there was a sort of groan, a shudder, and the thing belatedly started down after them.

It seemed to Babe as if they'd already been waiting half an hour, when it finally showed up down below. He'd been in and out and had a taxi sputtering at the door. The concierge was hanging around, and by looking at him, Babe could tell Manon had spoken the truth. He had been asleep until now, hadn't seen her go up.

The porter lurched the trunk ahead of him down the hall, out onto the Rue l'Ecluse, and then a big row started right in. One of those big French rows that had always amused Sherman until now. It wasn't funny this time.

The driver didn't mind taking it, but he wanted it tied on in back, on top, or even at the side, with ropes. The porter, speaking for Babe, insisted that it go inside the body of the cab. It couldn't go in front because it would have blocked his gears.

Sherman swore like a maniac. 'Two fares!' he hollered. 'Damn it, I'll never make the North Station—' A baker and a scissors-grinder had joined in, taking opposite sides, and a gendarme was slouching up from the corner to find out what it was about. Before they got through, they were liable to, at that. . . .

He finally got it in for two and a half fares; it just about made the side door, taking the paint off it plentifully. The gendarme changed his mind and turned back to his post at the crossing. Sherman got in with it, squeezed around it onto the seat, and banged the door. He slipped the porter a five-franc note. 'Bon voyage!' the concierge yelled after him.

'Right back at ya!' he gritted. He took a deep breath that seemed to come up from his shoes, almost. 'Hurdle number one,' he thought. 'Another at the station, another at Cherbourg – and I'm in the clear!'

The one at the Gare du Nord was worse than the one before. This time it was a case of baggage car versus the compartment he was to occupy. It wasn't that he was afraid to trust it to the baggage car, so much – five hours wouldn't be very dangerous – it was that he was afraid if he let it go now, it would go right into the hold of the ship without his being able to stop it, and that was where the risk lay. He couldn't get rid of her at sea once they put her in the hold.

The time element made his second hurdle bad, too; it had narrowed down to within a minute or two of train time. He couldn't buy the whole compartment, as he had the extra taxi fare, because there was already somebody else in it, one of the bulldog-type Yanks who believed in standing up for his rights. The driver had made the Gare as only a Paris driver can make a destination, on two wheels, and 'All aboard!' had already been shouted up and down the long platform. The station-master had one eye on his watch and one on his whistle. Once he tooted that, the thing would be off like a shot – the boat trains are the fastest things in Europe – and Sherman would be left there stranded, without further funds to get him out and with a death penalty crime and a 'hot' pearly necklace on his hands. . . .

3

He kept running back and forth between his compartment and the stalled baggage hand-truck up front, sweating like a mule, waving his arms – the conductor on one side of him, the baggage-master on the other.

'Put it in the car aisle, outside my door,' he pleaded. 'Stand it up in the vestibule for me, can't you do that?'

'Against the regulations.' And then ominously, 'Why is this trunk any different from all the others? Why does m'sieu insist on keeping it with him?'

'Because I lost one once that way,' was all Babe could think of.

The whistle piped shrilly, doors slammed, the thing started to move. The baggage-master dropped out. 'Too late! It will have to be sent after you now!' He turned and ran back to his post.

Sherman took out his wallet, almost emptied it of napkin-size banknotes – what was left of Manon's savings – about forty dollars in our money. His luck was he'd left that much unchanged yesterday, at the Express, 'Don't do this to me, Jacques! Don't make it tough for me! It'll miss my boat if I don't get it on this train with me!' His voice was hoarse, cracked by now. The wheels were slowly gathering speed, his own car was coming up toward them. They'd been up nearer the baggage car.

The conductor took a quick look up and down the platform. The money vanished. He jerked his head at the waiting truck-man; the man came up alongside the track, started to run parallel to the train, loaded truck and all. Babe caught at the next vestibule hand-rail as it came abreast, swung himself in, the conductor after him. 'Hold onto me!' the latter warned. Babe clasped him around the waist from behind. The conductor, leaning out, got a grip on the trunk from above. The truckman hoisted it from below, shoved it in on them. It went aboard as easily as a valise.

They got it up off the steps and parked it over in the farther corner of the vestibule. The conductor banged the car door shut. 'I'll lose my job if they get wise to this!'

'You don't know anything about it,' Babe assured him. 'I'll get it off myself at Cherbourg. Just remember to look the other way.'

He saw the fellow counting over the palm-oil, so he handed him the last remaining banknote left in his wallet – just kept some silver for the dockhand at Cherbourg. 'You're a good guy, Jacques,' he told him wearily, slapped him on the back, and went down the car to his compartment. Hurdle number two! Only one more to go. But all this fuss and feathers wasn't any too good, he realized somberly. It made him and trunk too conspicuous, too easily remembered later on. Well, the hell with it, as long as they couldn't prove anything!

His compartment mate looked up, not particularly friendly. Babe tried to figure him, and he tried to figure Babe. Or maybe he had already.

'Howja find it?' he said finally. Just that. Meaning he knew Babe had been working Paris in one way or another. Babe got it.

'I don't have to talk to you!' he snarled. 'Whaddya think y'are, an income tax blank?'

'Tell you what I am, a clairvoyant; read the future. First night out you'll be drumming up a friendly little game – with your own deck of cards. Nickels and dimes, just to make it interesting.' He made a noise with his lips that was the height of vulgarity. 'Lone wolf, I notice, though. Matter, Sûreté get your shill?'

Babe balled a fist, held it back by sheer will power. 'Read your own future.' He slapped himself on the shoulder with his other hand. 'Find out about the roundhouse waiting for you up in here.'

The other guy went back to his Paris *Herald* contemptuously. He must have known he'd hit it right the first time, or Babe wouldn't have taken it from him. 'You know where to find me,' he muttered. 'Now or after we're aboard. I'll be in 42-A.'

The label on that wardrobe trunk of his outside flashed before Babe's mind. He took a deep breath, that was almost a curse in itself, and closed his eyes. He shut up, didn't say another word. When he opened his eyes again a minute later, they were focused for a second down at the feet of the guy opposite him. Very flat, that pair of shoes looked, big – and very flat.

The motion of the train seemed to sicken him for a moment. But this guy was going back alone. A muffed assignment? Or just a vacation? They didn't take 3,000-mile jaunts for vacations. They didn't take vacations at all! Maybe the assignment hadn't had a human quarry – just data or evidence from one of the European police files?

The irises of the other man's eyes weren't on him at all, were boring into the paper between his fists – which probably meant he could have read the laundry mark on the inside of Babe's collar at the moment, if he'd been called on to do so. Federal or city? Babe couldn't figure. Didn't look government, though. The dick showed too plainly all over him – the gentleman with the whiskers didn't use types that gave themselves away to their quarry that easy.

'So I not only ride the waves with a corpse in my cabin with me, but with a dick in the next bunk! Oh, lovely tie-up!' He got up and went outside to take a look at his trunk. Looked back through the glass after he'd shut the door; the guy's eyes hadn't budged from his paper. There's such a thing as underdoing a thing; there's also such a thing as overdoing it, Babe told himself knowingly. The average human glances up when someone leaves the room he's in. 'You're good,' he cursed him, 'but so am I!'

The trunk was okay. He hung around it for a while, smoking a cigarette. The train rushed northwestward through France, with dead Manon and her killer not a foot away from one another, and the ashes of a cigarette were the only obsequies she was getting. They were probably missing her by now at the jewelry shop on the Rue de la Paix, phoning to her place to find out why she hadn't showed. Maybe a customer would come in today and want to be shown that pearly necklace, number twenty-nine; maybe no one would ask to see it for a week or a month.

He went back in again, cleaned his nails with a pocket-knife. Got up and went out to look, in another half-hour. Came back in again. Gee, Cherbourg was far away! At the third inspection, after another half-hour, he got a bad jolt. A fresh little flapper was sitting perched up on top of it, legs crossed, munching a sandwich! The train motion gave him a little qualm again. He slouched up to her. She gave him a smile, but he didn't give her one back. She was just a kid, harmless, but he couldn't bear the sight.

'Get off it, Susie,' he said in a muffled voice, and swept his hand at her vaguely. 'Get crumbs all over it, it ain't a counter.'

She landed on her heels. 'Oh, purrdon me!' she said freshly. 'We've got the President with us!' Then she took a second look at his face. He could tell she was going mushy on him in another minute, so he went back in again. The flatfoot – if he was one – was preferable to that, the way he felt right now.

Cherbourg showed about one, and he'd already been out there in the vestibule with it ten minutes before they started slowing up. The train ran right out onto the new double-decker pier the French had put up, broadside to the boat; all you had to do was step up the companionway.

His friend the conductor brushed by, gave him the office, accomplished the stupendous feat of not seeing the huge trunk there, and went ahead to the next vestibule. The thing stopped. Babe stuck his head out. Then he found out he wouldn't even need a French middleman, the ship's stewards were lined up in a row on the platform to take on the hand-luggage for the passengers. One of them came jumping over. 'Stand by,' Babe said. The passengers had right of way first, of course. They all cleared out – but *not* the wise guy. Maybe he'd taken the door at the other end of the coach, though.

Then the third hurdle reared – sky-high. 'In the stateroom?' the steward gasped respectfully. 'That's out of the question, sir – a thing that size! That has to go in the hold!'

About seven minutes of this, two more stewards and one of the ship's officers – and he wasn't getting anywhere. 'Tell you what,' he said finally, groggy with what he was going through, 'just lemme have it with me the first day, till I can get it emptied a little and sorted out. Then you can take it down the hold.' He was lighting one cigarette from another and throwing them away half-smoked, his eyebrows were beaded with sweat, the quay was just a blur in front of him. . . .

'We can't do that, man!' the officer snapped. 'The hold's loaded through the lower hatches. We can't transfer things from above down there, once we're out at sea!'

Behind Babe a voice said gruffly: 'Lissen, I'm in there with him and I got something to say – or haven't I? Your objection is that it'll take up too much room in there, cramp the party sharing the cabin with him, right? Well, cut out this bellyaching, the lot of you, and put it where the guy wants it to go! It's all right with me, I waive my rights—'

4

Babe didn't turn around. He knew what had just happened behind him though, knew by the way their opposition flattened out. Not another word was said. He knew as well as if he'd seen it with his own eyes: the guy had palmed his badge at them behind his back!

He would have given anything to have it go into the hold now, instead, but it was too late! He swallowed chokedly, still didn't turn, didn't say thanks. He felt like someone who has just had a rattlesnake dropped down the back of his neck while he's tied hand and foot.

He got down from the car, and they hopped in to get it. He didn't give it another look. He headed slowly toward the companionway he'd been directed to, to show his ticket, and was aware of the other man strolling along at his elbow. 'What's your game?' he said, out of the corner of his mouth, eyes straight ahead.

There was mockery in the slurring answer. 'Just big-hearted. Might even help you make out your customs' declaration on what y'got in it—'

Babe stumbled over something on the ground before him that wasn't there at all, stiff-armed himself against a post, went trudging on. He didn't have anything in his shoulder for this guy before. He had something in his heart for him now – death.

He looked up at the triple row of decks above him while an officer was checking his ticket and passport at the foot of the companionway. It was called the *American Statesman*. 'You're going to be one short when you make the Narrows seven days from now!' he told it silently. 'This copper's never going to leave you alive.'

They maneuvered the trunk down the narrow ship's corridor and into the stateroom by the skin of its teeth. It was a tight squeeze. It couldn't, of course, go under either one of the bunks. One remaining wall was taken up by the door, the other by the folding washstand, which opened like a desk. The middle of the room was the only answer, and that promptly turned the cabin into nothing more than a narrow perimeter around the massive object. That his fellow passenger, who wasn't any sylph, should put up with this was the deadest give-away ever, to Babe's way of thinking, that he was on to something. Some of these punks had a sixth sense, almost, when it came to scenting crime in the air around them. He wouldn't need more than one, though, in about a day more, if Babe didn't do something in a hurry! It was July, and there were going to be two of them in there with it.

He tried half-heartedly to have it shunted down to the hold after all – although that would have been just jumping from a very quick frying pan to a slower but just as deadly fire – but they balked. It would have to be taken out again onto the quay and then shipped aboard from there, they pointed out. There was no longer time enough. And he'd cooked up a steam of unpopularity for himself as it was that wouldn't clear away for days.

The dick didn't show right up, but a pair of his valises came in, and Sherman lamped the tags. 'E. M. Fowler, New York.' He looked out, and he saw where he'd made still another mistake. He'd bought a cabin on the A-deck, the middle of the three, just under the promenade deck; a C-cabin would have been the right one, below deck level. This one had no porthole opening directly above the water, but a window flush with the deck outside. But then he hadn't known he was going to travel with a corpse, and her money had made it easy to buy the best. Now he'd have to smuggle her outside with him, all the way along the passageway, down the stairs, and out across the lowest deck – when the time came.

He beat it out in a hurry, grinding his hands together. Should have thought of it sooner, before he'd let them haul it in there! He'd ask to be changed, that was all. Get the kind he wanted, away from that bloodhound and by himself. Sure they could switch him, they must have some last-minute cancellations! Always did.

The purser spread out a chart for him when he put it to him in his office, seemed about to do what he wanted; Sherman felt better than he had at any time since five that morning. Then suddenly he looked up at him as though he'd just remembered something. 'You Mr. Sherman, 42-A?' Babe nodded. 'Sorry, we're booked solid; you'll have to stay in there.' He put the chart away.

Arguing was no use. He knew what had happened; Fowler and his badge again. He'd forseen this move, beat him to it, blocked it! 'You weren't bragging, brother, when you called yourself a clairvoyant!' he thought bitterly. But the guy couldn't actually *know* what was in the trunk, what was making him act like this? Just a hunch? Just the fact that he'd sized Babe up as off-color, and noticed the frantic way Babe had tried to keep the trunk with him when he boarded the train? Just the way any dick baited anyone on the other side of the fence, not sure but always hoping for the worst? Well, he was asking for it and he was going to get it – and not the way he expected, either. He'd foreclosed his own life by nailing Babe down in the cabin with him!

Just the same, he felt the need of a good stiff pick-up. They were already under way when he found his way into the bar, the jurisdiction of the French Republic was slipping behind them, it was just that pot-bellied old gent now with the brass buttons, the captain. The straight brandy put him in shape; the hell with both sides of the pond! Once he got rid of her there wouldn't be any evidence left, he could beat any extradition rap they tried to slap on him. Water scotches a trail in more ways than one.

He spent the afternoon between the bar and 42, to make sure Fowler didn't try to tackle the trunk with a chisel or pick the lock while his back was turned. But the dick didn't go near the cabin, stayed out of sight the whole time. The sun, even going down, was still plenty hot; Sherman opened the window as wide as it would go and turned on the electric fan above the door. It would have to be tonight, for plenty of good reasons! One of the least was that he couldn't keep checking on the thing like this every five minutes without going bughouse.

A steward went all over the ship pounding a portable dinner gong, and Sherman went back to the cabin, more to keep his eye on Fowler than to freshen up. He wouldn't have put on one of his other suits now even if he could have gotten at it.

Fowler came in, went around on his side of the trunk, and stripped to his undershirt. Sherman heard a rustle and a click, and he'd turned off the fan and pulled down the shade. Almost instantaneously the place got stuffy.

Babe said, 'What's the idea? You ain't that chilly in July!'

Fowler gave him a long, searching look across the top of the trunk. 'You seem to want ventilation pretty badly,' he said, very low.

It hit Sherman, like everything the guy seemed to say, and he forgot what he was doing for a minute, splashed water on his hair from force of habit. When it was all ganged up in front of his eyes, he remembered his comb was in there, too, he didn't have a thing out. He tried combing with his fingers and it wouldn't work. He stalled around while the dick slicked his own, waiting for him to get out and leave it behind.

The dick did some stalling of his own. It started to turn itself an endurance, the second dinner gong went banging by outside the window. Sherman, nerves tight as elastic bands, thought: 'What the hell is he up to?' His own shirt was hanging on a hook by the door, he saw Fowler glance at it just once, but didn't get the idea in time. Fowler parked a little bottle of liquid shoe-blackening on the extreme edge of the trunk, stopper out, right opposite the shirt. Then he brushed past between the two, elbows slightly out. He had no right to come around on that side; it was Sherman's side of the place. The shirt slipped off the hook and the shoe-polish toppled and dumped itself on top of it on the floor. The shirt came up black and white, mostly black, in his hand.

'Oops, sorry!' he apologized smoothly. 'Now I've done it – have it laundered for you—'

Sherman got the idea too late, he'd maneuvered him into opening the trunk in his presence and getting a clean one out, or else giving up his evening meal; he couldn't go in there wearing that piebald thing!

He jerked the thing away from the detective, gave him a push that sent him staggering backward, and went after him arm poised to sock him. 'I saw you! Y'did that purposely!' he snarled. He realized that he was giving himself away, lowered his arm. 'Hand over one of yours,' he ordered grimly.

Fowler shook his head, couldn't keep the upward tilt from showing at the corners of his mouth though. 'One thing I never do, let anybody else wear my things.' He fished out a couple of singles. 'I'll pay you for it, or I'll have it laundered for you—' Then very smoothly, 'Matter, mean to say you haven't got another one in that young bungalow of yours?'

Sherman got a grip on himself; this wasn't the time or the place. After all, he still held the trump in his own hands – and that was whether the trunk was to be opened or to stay closed. He punched the bell for the steward and sat down on the edge of his berth, pale but leering.

'Bring me my meal in here, I can't make the dining saloon.'

Fowler shrugged on his coat and went out, not looking quite so pleased with himself as he had a minute ago. Sherman knew, just the same, that his own actions had only cinched the suspicions lurking in the other's mind about the trunk. The first round had been the detective's after all.

That thought, and having to eat with his dinner tray parked on top the trunk – there was no other place for it – squelched the little appetite he'd had to begin with. He couldn't swallow, had to beat it around the other side and stick his head out the window, breathing in fresh air, to get rid of the mental images that had begun popping into his dome.

'Going soft, am I?' he gritted. After a while he pulled his head in again. There were a few minor things he could do right now, while the dick was in the dining room, even if the main job had to wait for tonight. Tonight Fowler would be right in here on top of him, it would have to be done with lightning-like rapidity. He'd better get started now, paving the way.

5

He closed the window and fastened it, so the shade wouldn't blow in on him. He set the untouched tray of food down outside the door, then locked it. The boat was a pre-war model reconditioned, one of the indications of this was the footwide grilled vent that pierced the three inside partitions just below the ceiling line – a continuous slitted band that encircled the place except on the deck side. It was the best they could do in 1914 to get a little circulation into the air. He couldn't do anything about that, but it was well over anyone's head.

He got out his keys and turned the trunk so that it opened *away* from the door. He squatted down, took a deep breath, touched the key to the lock, swung back the bolts, and parted the trunk. He didn't look up, picked up a handkerchief, unfolded it, and spread it over her face. He got out a couple of the shirts that had been farthest away, protected by other things, and his comb, and then he took a file that was in there and went to work on the pearls.

It was hard even to force any two of them far enough apart to get at the platinum wire underneath without damaging them in the filing, but he managed to force a split in their ranks right alongside the clasp, which stood out a little because of its setting. The wire itself was no great obstacle, it was just getting the file in at it. In five minutes the place he had tackled wore out under the friction, and it shattered to invisibility. Three pearls dropped off before he could catch them and rolled some place on the floor. He let them go for a minute, poised the file to change hands with it and unwind the gnarled necklace – and heard Fowler saying quietly: 'What's the idea of the lock-out? Do I get in, or what?'

His face was peering in and down at Sherman through that damnable slotted ventilator, high up but on a line with the middle of the door, smiling – but not a smile of friendliness or good omen.

Sherman died a little then inside himself, as he would never die again, not even if a day came when he would be kneeling under the high knife at Vincennes or sitting in the electric chair at Ossining. Something inside him curled up, but because there was no blade or voltage to follow the shock, he went ahead breathing and thinking.

His eyes traveled downward from Fowler's outlined face to the top of the trunk in a straight line. Her handkerchief-masked-head was well below it on his side, her legs stayed flat up against her as he'd first folded them, from long confinement and now rigor. He thought: 'He doesn't see her from where he is. He can't or he wouldn't be smiling like that!'

But the opening ran all around, on the side of him and in back of him. He must be up on a stool out there; all he'd have to do would be jump down, shift it farther around to where he could see, and spring up on it again. If he did that in time, he could do it much quicker than Babe could get the trunk closed. 'He hasn't thought of it yet!' Babe told himself frantically. 'Oh, Joseph and Mary, keep it from occurring to him! If I can hold him up there just a split minute, keep talking to him, not give him time to think of it—'

His eyes bored into Fowler's trying to hold him by that slight ocular magnetism any two people looking at each other have. He said very slowly: 'I'll tell you why I locked the door like that; just a minute before you showed up—'

Whang! The two halves of the trunk came together between his outstretched arms. The rest of it was just reflex action, snapping the bolts home, twisting the key in the lock. He went down lower on his haunches and panted like a fish out of water.

He went over to the door and opened it, still weak on his pins. Fowler got down off the folding stool he'd dragged up. If he was disappointed, he didn't show it.

'I didn't hear you knock,' Sherman said. There was no use throwing himself at him right now, absolutely none, it would be a fatal mistake. 'I'll get him tonight – late,' he said to himself.

Fowler answered insolently. 'Why knock, when you know ahead of time the door's going to be locked? You never get to see things that way.'

'More of that mind-reading stuff.' Sherman tried to keep the thing as matter-of-fact as possible between them, for his own sake, not let it get out of bounds and go haywire before he was ready. 'I don't mind telling you you're getting on my nerves, buddy.'

He spotted one of the pearls, picked it up before Fowler saw what it was, put it in his pocket. 'First you gum up a good shirt on me. Then you pull a Peeping Tom act—' He kept walking aimlessly around, eyes to the floor. He saw the second one and pocketed that, too, with a swift snake of the arm. His voice rose to a querulous protest. 'What are you, some kind of a stool pigeon? Am I marked lousy, or what?' Trying to make it sound like no more than the natural beef of an unjustly persecuted person.

Fowler said from his side of the trunk: 'Couple little things like that shouldn't get on your nerves—' pause – 'unless you've got something else on them already.'

Sherman didn't answer that one, there didn't seem to be a satisfactory one for it. He couldn't locate the third pearl either – if there had been one. He wasn't sure any more whether two or three had rolled off her neck.

He flung himself down on his bunk, lay there on his back sending up rings of cigarette smoke at the ceiling. Fowler, hidden on his side of the trunk, belched once or twice, moved around a little, finally began rattling the pages of a magazine. The ship steamed westward, out into the open Atlantic. They both lay there, waiting, waiting. . . .

The human noises around them grew less after an hour or so; suddenly the deck lights outside the window went out without warning. It was midnight.

A minute later, Sherman heard the door open and close, and Fowler had gone out of the cabin. He sat up and looked across the trunk. He'd left his coat and vest and tie on his berth – gone to the washroom. He listened, heard his footsteps die away down the oilcloth-covered passageway outside. That was exactly what Babe Sherman was waiting for.

He swung his legs down and made a beeline across the cabin, didn't bother locking the door this time, it was quiet enough now to hear him coming back anyway. He went through that coat and vest with a series of deft scoops, one to a pocket, that showed how good he must have once been at the dip racket. The badge was almost the first thing he hit, settling his doubts on that score once and for all – if he'd still had any left. New York badge, city dick. Sherman had no gun with him, didn't work that way as a rule. He thought, 'He almost certainly has. If I could only locate it before he comes back—' He didn't intend to use it in any case – too much noise – but unless he got his hands on it ahead of time, it was going to be very risky business!

The fool had left one of his two valises open under the bunk, ready to haul out his pajamas! Sherman went all through it in no time flat, without messing it too much either. Not in it. It was either in the second one, or he carried it in a hip-holster, but probably the former was the case. Then one of those hunches that at times visit the deserving and the undeserving alike, smote him from nowhere; he tipped the upper end of the mattress back and put his hand on it! A minute later it was broken and the cartridges were spilling out into his palm. He jammed it closed, put it back, and heaved himself back onto his own bunk just as the slap-slap of Fowler's footsteps started back along the passageway. 'Now, buddy!' he thought grimly.

Fowler finished undressing and got under the covers. 'Gosh, the air's stale in here!' he muttered, more to himself than Sherman. 'Seems to get ranker by the minute!'

'Whaddya want me to do, hand yuh a bunch of violets?' Babe snarled viciously. He got up and went out, for appearance's sake, then stayed just outside the door, head bent, listening. Fowler didn't make a move, at least not to or at the trunk. Sherman took good aim out through the open window that gave onto the little cubicle between their cabin and the next, let fly with the handful of bullets. They cleared the deck beautifully, every last one of them.

He went back in again, saw that Fowler already had his eyes closed, faking it probably. He took off his coat and shoes, put out the light, lay down like he was. The motion of the boat, and the black and orange frieze of the ventilator high up near the ceiling – the corridor lights stayed on all night – were all that remained. And the breathing of two mortal enemies, the stalker and the stalked. . . .

Sherman, who had cursed the ventilator to hell and back after it had nearly betrayed him that time, now suddenly found that it was going to come in handy after all. It let in just enough light, once your eyes got used to the change, so that it wouldn't be necessary to turn on the cabin light again when the time came to get her out. He couldn't have risked that under any circumstances, even if it took him half the night to find the keyhole of the trunk with the key. This way it wouldn't.

The guy was right at that, though, it *was* getting noticeable in here.

He planned it step by step first, without moving his shoulders from the berth. Get rid of her first and then attend to the dick later was the best way. She couldn't wait, the dick could. They had six days to go yet, and the dick couldn't just drop from sight without it backfiring in some way. Down here wasn't the right spot either. They might run into heavy weather in a day or two, and if he watched his opportunity he might be able to catch the dick alone on the upper deck after the lights went out. Even raise a 'Man overboard!' after he went in, if it seemed advisable. Or if not, be the first to report his disappearance the day after.

So now for her. He knew the set-up on these boats. There was always a steward on night duty at the far end of the corridor, to answer any possible calls. He'd have to be gotten out of the way to begin with, sent all the way down to the pantry for something, if possible. Yet he mustn't rap on the door here in answer to the call and wake up the flatfoot. And he mustn't come back too quickly and catch Babe out of the cabin – although that was the lesser danger of the two and could always be explained away by the washroom. Now for it; nothing like knowing every step in advance, couldn't be caught off-base that way.

6

There is an art in being able to tell by a person's breathing if he is asleep or just pretending to be; it was one of Sherman's many little accomplishments. But there is another art, too, that goes with it – that of being able to breathe so you fool the person doing the listening. This, possibly, may have been the other man's accomplishment. His breathing deepened, got scratchier – but very slowly. It got into its stride, and little occasional burblings welled up in it, very artistically. Not snores by any means, just catches in the larynx. Sherman, up on his elbow, thought: 'He's off. He couldn't breathe that way for very long if he wasn't – be too much of a strain.'

He got up off the bunk and put on his coat, so the white of his undershirt wouldn't show. He picked up the shirt that Fowler had ruined and balled it up tightly into fist-size, or not much bigger. He got out the trunk key and put it down on the floor right in front of the trunk, between his bent legs. He spit muffedly into his free hand, soaked the hollow of it. Then he gave that a half-turn up against the lock and each of the clamps. The lock opened quietly enough, but the clamps had a snap to them that the saliva alone wouldn't take care of. He smothered them under the ganged-up shirt as he pressed each one back. He got it down to a tiny click. Then he took a long, hard look over at Fowler through the gloom. That suction was still working in his throat.

The trunk split apart fairly noiselessly, with just one or two minor squeaks, and he had to turn his head for a minute – for a different reason this time. The way it had opened, though, was all to the good, one side of it shielded him from Fowler's bunk.

He had to go carefully on the next step, couldn't just remove her. There were too many loose things in there, all the busted partitions and drawers would clack together and racket. He got them out first, piece by piece. She came last, and wasn't very heavy.

Now here was where the steward came into it. He had a choice of risks: not to bother with the steward at all, to try sneaking down the passageway in the opposite direction with her. That was out entirely. All the steward would have to do was stick his head out of the little room where the call-board was and spot him. Or, to leave her out, but in here, in the dark, and tackle the steward outside. He didn't like that one either. Fowler might open his eyes from one moment to the next and let out a yell. So he had to get her out of here, and yet keep the steward from coming near her outside. The inset between the cabins, outside the door, was the answer – but the steward must *not* turn the corner and come all the way! It was all a question of accurate timing.

He was as far as the cabin door now, but that was a problem in itself. He was holding her up against him like a ventriloquist's dummy, legs still folded up flat while she hung down straight. He got the door open without any creaking, but a sunburst of orange seemed to explode around him and his burden. It didn't reach all the way to Fowler's berth, but it could very well tickle his eyelids open if it was left on too long.

He stepped across the raised threshold with her, holding onto the door so it wouldn't swing with the ship's motion. Then without letting go of it he managed to let her down to the floor out there. He turned and went in again alone, to ring for the steward; as he did so an optical illusion nearly floored him for a second. It was that Fowler had suddenly stiffened to immobility in the midst of movement. But he was in the same position that he had been before – or seemed to be – and his lids were down and the clucking was still going on in his throat. There was no time to worry about it, either he was awake or he wasn't – and he wasn't, must have just stirred in his sleep.

The steward's bell, Sherman knew, didn't make any sound in the cabin itself, only way out at the call-board. He punched it, got back to the door before it had time to swing too far shut or open, and then eased it closed. She was right beside him on the floor out there, but he didn't look at her, listened carefully. In a minute he heard the put-put of shoeleather coming down from the other end of the passageway. Now!

He drifted negligently around the corner, started up toward the steward to head him off; the man was still two of those lateral insets away. They came together between his, Babe's and the next.

'Did you ring, sir?'

Sherman put his head on the steward's arm appealingly. 'I feel rotten,' he said in a low voice. 'Get me some black coffee, will you? Too many brandies all afternoon and evening.' He looked the part, from what he'd just gone through – if nothing else.

'Yes, sir, right away,' the steward said briskly. And then instead of turning back, he took a step to get around Sherman and continue on down the passageway, toward where the body was!

'What're you going that way for?' Sherman managed to say, gray now.

'The main pantry's closed, sir, at this hour. We have a little one for sandwiches and things in back of the smoking room, I'll heat you some up there—'

'Here I go!' was all Sherman had time to think. The whole boat went spinning around him dizzily for a minute, but his reflexes kept working for him. Without even knowing what he was doing, he got abreast of the steward – on the side where she was – and accompanied him back, partly turned toward him. The steward was a shorter man, only Sherman's outthrust shoulder kept him from seeing what lay sprawled there as the inset opened out to one side of them. He pulled the same stunt he had on Fowler when he was getting the trunk closed under his nose, kept jabbering away with his eyes glued on the steward's, holding them steady on his own face.

The steward stepped past, and the opening closed behind him again. Sherman dropped back, but still guarding it with his body. His jaws were yammering automatically: '—never could stand the coffee in Paris, like drinking mud. All right, you know where to find me—'

The steward went on and disappeared at the upper end. Sherman, in the inset, crumpled to his hands and knees for a minute, like an animal, stomach heaving in and out. This last tension had been too much for him, coming on top of everything else. 'All to keep from dying twenty years too soon!' he thought miserably, fighting his wretchedness.

He got himself in shape again in a hurry, had to, and a minute later was groping up the corridor in the opposite direction, lopsidedly, borne down by her dimensions if not her weight on one side, his other arm out to steady himself against the wall.

There was no one out at the stairlanding now that the steward was out of the way, and only a single overhead light was burning. He decided to chuck the stairs and do it right from this A-deck. One deck higher or lower couldn't make any difference if he went far enough back to the stern. And there might be other stewards on night duty on the other deck levels.

He put her down for a minute on a wicker settee out there, unhooked the double doors to the deck, and looked out. Deserted and pitch dark. A minute later she was out there with him, and the end of his long, harrowing purgatory was in sight. Babe couldn't keep his hands from trembling.

He didn't go right to the rail with her. There was still the necklace, for one thing, and then the nearer the stern the better to make a clean-cut job of it. You couldn't see your hand in front of your face beyond the rail, but the deck wall on the other side of him showed up faintly white in the gloom, broken by black squares that were the cabin windows.

Near the end of the superstructure there was a sharp indentation, an angle where it jutted farther out, and in this were stacked sheaves of deck chairs, folded up flat and held in place by a rope. There were, however, three that had been left unfolded side by side, perhaps made use of by some late strollers and that the deck steward had missed putting away, and one of them even had a steamer rug left bunched across it.

He let her down on one of them and bent over her to finish freeing the necklace. The handkerchief had remained in place all this time, for some reason. But it was one of his own and huge, touched her shoulders. He had to discard it to be able to see what he was doing. Loosened, the breeze promptly snatched it down the deck and it vanished. His hands reached for the loose end of the necklace, where he had already filed it through close to the clasp – and then stayed that way, poised, fingers pointing inward in a gesture that was like a symbol of avarice defeated.

The platinum strand was there, but invisible now in the dark, naked of pearls! Not two or three but the whole top row had dropped off, one by one, somehow, somewhere along the way! The motion of carrying her, of picking her up and setting her down so repeatedly, must have loosened them one at a time, jogged them off through that break in the wire he himself had caused. And since it obviously hadn't happened while she was still in the trunk, what it amounted to was: he had left a trail of pearls behind him, every step of the way he had come with her from the cabin out here – like that game kids play with chalk marks called Hare-and-hounds – but with death for its quarry. An overwhelming sense of futility and disaster assailed him.

They wouldn't stay in one place, they'd roll around, but they were there behind him just the same, pointing the way. It was only the top row that had been stripped clean, the other two had been tourniqueted in too tight for any to fall off. . . .

He had no more than made the discovery, with his fingertips and not his eyes, than a figure loomed toward him out of the deck gloom, slowly, very slowly, and Fowler's voice drawled suavely:

'I'll take the rest of 'em now, that go with the ones I been pickin' up on the way.'

Sherman automatically gave the blanket beside him a fillip that partly covered her, then stood up and went out toward him, knees already crouched for the spring that was to come. The gloom made Fowler seem taller than he was. Sherman could sense the gun he was holding leveled at him by the rigid foreshortening of his one arm. The thing was, was it still empty or had he reloaded it since?

7

He started circling, with Fowler for an axis, trying to maneuver him closer to the rail. That brought the chair more clearly into Fowler's line of vision, but the position of his head never changed, slowly turned in line with Sherman. Suddenly it dawned on Sherman that the dick didn't know the whole story even yet; hadn't tumbled yet to what was on that chair! Must have taken it for just a bunched-up steamer rug in the dark. Sure! Otherwise he'd be hollering blue murder by this time, but all he'd spoken about was the pearls. Hadn't seen Sherman carry her out after all, then; thought he was just on the trail of a jewel smuggler.

'But in a minute more he'll see her; he's bound to!' he told himself. 'Dark or not, his eyes'll be deflected over that way. And that's when—'

While his feet kept carrying him slowly sidewise across the deck, from the chair toward the rail, he muttered: '*You* will? Who says so?'

Fowler palmed his badge at him with his left hand. 'This says so. Now come on, why make it tough for yourself? I've got you dead to rights and you know it! They're so hot they're smoking. Fork 'em over and don't keep me waiting out here all night, or I'll—'

Sherman came up against the rail. Had he reloaded that persuader or hadn't he? 'I can only be wrong once about it,' he figured grimly. He jerked his head at the chair. 'The tin always wins. Help yourself!' His knees buckled a notch lower.

He saw the pupils of Fowler's eyes follow the direction his head had taken, start back again, then stop dead – completely off him. 'Oh, so you *are* working with a shill after all! What's she showing her teeth, grinning so about? D'ye think I'm a kid—?'

He never finished it. Sherman's stunning blow – the one he'd promised him in the train – his whole body following it, landed in an arc up from where he'd been standing. His fist caught Fowler on the side of the neck, nearly paralyzing his nerve centers for a minute, and the impact of Sherman's body coming right after it sent him down to the deck with Sherman on top of him. The gun clicked four times into the pit of Sherman's stomach before they'd even landed, and the impact with which the back of the dick's head hit the deck told why it didn't click the two remaining times. He was stunned for a minute, lay there unresisting. Less than a minute – much less – but far too long!

Sherman got up off him, pulled him up after him, bent him like a jackknife over the rail, then caught at his legs with a vicious dip. The gun, which was still in the dick's hand, fell overboard as he opened it to claw at the empty night. His legs cleared the rail at Sherman's heave like those of a pole vaulter topping a bar, but his faculties had cleared just in time for his finish. His left hand closed despairingly around a slim, vertical deck-support as the rest of his body went over. The wrench nearly pulled it out of its socket, turned him completely around in mid-air so that he was facing Sherman's way for a brief instant. His face was a piteous blur against the night that would have wrung tears from the Evil One himself.

But a human being was sending him to his death, and they can be more remorseless than the very devils of hell. 'I don't want to die!' the blurred face shrieked out. The flat of Sherman's foot, shooting out between the lower deck-rails like a battering-ram, obliterated it for a minute. The gripping hand flew off the upright support into nothingness. When Sherman's foot came back through the rails again, the face was gone. The badge was all that was left lying there on the deck.

The last thing Sherman did was pick that up and shie it out after him. 'Take that with you, Cop, you'll need it for your next pinch!'

Carrying out his original purpose, after what had just happened, was almost like an anticlimax; he was hardly aware of doing so at all, just a roundtrip to the rail and back. He leaned up against the deck wall for a minute, panting with exertion. The partly denuded necklace, freed at last from its human ballast, in the palm of his hand. 'You've cost me plenty!' he muttered to it. He dumped it into his pocket.

Suddenly the deck lights had flashed on all around him, as if lightning had struck the ship. He cringed and turned this way and that. They were standing out there, bunched by the exit through which he himself had come a little while ago, stewards and ship's officers, all staring ominously down toward him. He knew enough not to try to turn and slink away; he was in full sight of them, and a second group had showed up behind him, meanwhile, at the lower end of the deck, cutting him off in that direction. That last scream Fowler ripped out from the other side of the rail, probably; the wind must have carried it like an amplifier all over the ship at once.

'But they didn't see me do it!' he kept repeating to himself vengefully, as they came down the deck toward him from both directions, treading warily, spread out fanwise to block his escape. 'They didn't see me do it! They gave it the lights out here just a minute too late!'

The chief officer had a gun out in his hand, and a look on his face to match it. They meant business. One by one the cabin windows facing the deck lighted up; the whole ship was rousing. This wasn't just another hurdle any more; this was a dead end – the last stop, and he knew it.

Suddenly he came to a decision. The net was closing in on him and in a minute more his freedom of action would be gone forever. He didn't waste it, but used it while he still had it to cut himself free from the first crime even while the second was tangling around him tighter every enstant.

He found the rail with the backs of his elbows, leaned there negligently, waiting for them. Right as they came up, his elbows slipped off the rail again, his hands found his trouser pockets in a gesture that looked simply like cocky bravado. Then he withdrew them again, gave one a slight unnoticeable backhand-flip through the rails. The motion, screened by his body, remained unobserved; their eyes were on his face. The necklace had gone back to Manon, the job had blown up – but it couldn't be helped, he had his own skin to think of now.

The chief officer's eyes were as hard as the metal that pointed out of his fist at Sherman's middle. 'What'd you do with that man Fowler?' he clipped.

Sherman grinned savagely back around his ear. 'What'd *I* do with him? I left him pounding his ear in 42-A. We're not Siamese twins. Is there a regulation against coming out here to stretch my legs—?'

The night steward cut in with: 'I didn't like how he acted when he ordered the cawfee a while ago, sir. That's why I reported to you. When I took it in to him they were both gone, and the insides of this man's trunk were all busted up and lying around, like they had a fierce fight—'

A woman leaning out of one of the cabin windows shrilled almost hysterically: 'Officer! Officer! I heard somebody fall to the deck right outside my window here, the sound woke me up, and then somebody screamed: "I don't want to die!" And when I jumped up to look out—' Her voice broke uncontrollably for a minute.

The officer was listening intently, but without turning his head away from Sherman or deflecting the gun.

'—he was kicking at a *face* through the rails! I saw it go down—! I – I fainted away for a minute, after that!' She vanished from the window, someone's arm around her, sobbing loudly in a state of collapse.

The net was closing around him, tighter, every minute. 'We all heard the scream,' the officer said grimly, 'but that tells us what it meant—'

The bulky captain showed up, one of his shirttails hanging out under his hurriedly donned uniform-jacket. He conferred briefly with the chief officer, who retreated a pace or two without taking his gun off Sherman. The latter stood there, at bay against the rail, a husky deckhand gripping him by each shoulder now.

The gun was lowered, only to be replaced by a pair of hand-cuffs. The captain stepped forward. 'I arrest you for murder! Hold out your hands! Mr. Moulton, put those on him!'

The deckhands jerked his forearms out into position, his cuffs shot back. The red welt across his knuckles where he'd bruised them against Fowler's jawbone revealed itself to every eye there.

He flinched as the cold steel locked around him. 'I didn't do it – he fell overboard!' he tried to say. 'It's her word against mine—!' But the net was too tight around him, there was no room left to struggle, even verbally.

The captain's voice was like a roll of drums ushering in an execution – the first of the hundreds, the thousands of questions that were going to torment him like gadflies, drive him out of his mind, until the execution that was even now rushing toward him remorselessly from the far side of the ocean would seem like a relief in comparison. 'What was your motive in doing away with this man, sending him to his death?'

He didn't answer. The malevolent gods of his warped destiny did it for him, sending another of the stewards hurrying up from the deck below, the answer in both his outstretched hands, a thin flat badge, a gnarled string of pearls, half-gone.

'I found this and this, sir, on the B-deck just now! I thought I heard a scream out there a while back and I went out to look. Just as I turned to come in again this, this shield landed at my feet, came sailing in from nowhere on the wind like a boomerang. I put on the lights thinking someone had had an accident down on that deck, and a little while afterward I caught sight of this necklace down at the very end. The wind had whipped it around one of the deck-supports like a paper streamer—'

Sherman just looked at the two objects, white and still. The night had thrown back the evidence he had tried to get rid of, right into his very teeth! There were two executions waiting for him now, the tall knife at Vincennes, the electric chair at one of the Federal penitentiaries – and though he could only die once, what consolation was it that only by one death could he cheat the other?

The captain said: 'He's as good as dead already! Take him down below and keep him under double guard until we can turn him over to the Federal authorities when we reach Quarantine.'

Sherman stumbled off in the middle of all of them, unresisting. But he did crack up completely when the captain – just as they were taking him inside – folded a yellow wireless message and showed it to the chief officer. 'Funny part of it is,' he heard him say, 'this came in not fifteen minutes ago, from the New York City police authorities, asking us to hold this man Fowler for them, for blackmail, for preying on people on ships and trains, impersonating a detective abroad. The badge is phony, of course. If our friend here had kept his hands off him for just a quarter of an hour more—'

Sherman didn't hear the rest of it. There was a rush of blood to his ears that drowned it out, and the laughter of the Furies seemed to shriek around him while they prodded him with white-hot irons. All he knew was that he was going to die for a murder that could have been avoided, in order to cover up one that otherwise would quite probably never have been revealed!

THE HOUSE OF KAA

RICHARD B. SALE

A prolific writer for the pulps, Richard B. Sale (1911–1993) also wrote such successful novels as *Lazarus #7* (1942), *Passing Strange* (1942), *Not Too Narrow – Not Too Deep* (1936), which was filmed in 1940 as *Strange Cargo*, and *For the President's Eyes Only* (1971). He devoted most of his writing energy to writing and directing movies, including *Mr. Belvedere Goes to College* (1949), the Frank Sinatra vehicle *Suddenly* (1954), and *Gentlemen Marry Brunettes* (1955).

Among his pulp fiction, he is most remembered for the reporter/detective series about Daffy Dil, written for *Detective Fiction Weekly*, and his adventure-packed tales written for *Ten Detective Aces* about The Cobra, one of the early examples of what is generally known among pulp aficionados as a 'Weird Menace' or 'Avenger' story. Such characters as The Shadow, The Avenger, The Spider, Operator 5, and The Phantom Detective were among the most popular figures in the pulps. They mainly dressed in costumes, usually with masks, sometimes with capes, as they wreaked justice without bothering about the police, judges or juries.

In 'The House of Kaa,' first published in the February 1934 issue of *Ten Detective Aces*, villains abound and The Cobra kills them with impunity. No masked avenger is worth his salt unless confronted by larger-than-life crooks, and those in the following story meet the standard.

THE HOUSE OF KAA

RICHARD B. SALE

Jack Kirk, whose profession had never been anything but sordid murder, paused before the dreary brownstone house on Rokor Street. He glanced all about him in a wary and frightened sort of way.

He could have sworn that some one was following him. If not some one – *something!* A black, misshapen, baroque giant. A flitting spectre.

Kirk had seen a shadow – only for an instant.

Then the shadow had disintegrated like the whispering dissipation of a gliding ghost.

Kirk shook his shoulders and blamed it on his imagination. He went slowly up the short flight of stairs in the front of the house and glanced at the sign over the door. It read:

GORGAN & WILKINS – REPTILE
IMPORTERS

Quickly, Kirk pulled a key from his pocket, inserted it in the lock, and opened the door. He entered with alacrity, slamming it after him.

The main hall was dark as pitch. But Kirk knew where he was going. He ascended the long, creaking staircase to the second floor of the dreary place. A solitary light on the second floor led him to a door marked 'Office.'

He rapped sharply four times and entered.

Three men were in the room. He recognized them as Maxie Gorgan, John Wilkins, and the man from India, Wentworth Lane. They had been talking but now they looked up at him.

'Sit down, Jack,' Gorgan smirked. 'Lane here is reporting on our – ah – Indian importations.' He grinned knowingly.

Kirk smiled and sat down. Lane bit his lip angrily.

'You can be as sarcastic as you like, Maxie,' he snapped, 'but I tell you it's so. I don't know about this end, but I do know that the police are close to catching us in Bombay. There was an American operative on my trail for several days before I left for London. You know, the one we checked on.'

'What do they suspect you of?' Gorgan leered. 'Maybe they think you're maltreating snakes!' He laughed harshly. 'Listen, Lane, you're an agent for a company. You're an importer of reptiles from India.'

'But the trouble is – the only reptiles I ever import to you are regal pythons. It's damned suspicious.'

'If you're afraid—' Gorgan began coldly.

Lane leaped to his feet, his eyes blazing.

'You want me to deny I am. Well, I'm not lying for any one. And you can't make me! I *am* afraid! And I'm going to get out!'

Gorgan eyed Wilkins surreptitiously and nodded. Kirk, watching the proceedings, was mildly amused. He failed to see what had gotten Lane's wind up so. Lane had been a good reliable man on the Bombay end.

'Just a second, Lane,' Wilkins purred softly. 'Maybe you're right. Maybe we've misjudged you. We don't want you to quit.'

'No,' Gorgan added with a trace of acerbity, 'you can't quit.'

'Well, I'm going to nevertheless,' Lane declared stridently. His voice lowered as he leaned forward. 'Did you ever hear of the Cobra?' he whispered.

Gorgan and Wilkins looked dumb. They shook their heads.

'Did you, Kirk?'

Jack Kirk smiled amusedly.

'Yeah,' he replied. 'Sure, I've heard of him. Some sort of a guy who thinks he's a public avenger. Goes around alone.'

Lane nodded. 'That's he – the Cobra.'

'But he's supposed to be in India.' Kirk was enjoying this baiting Lane. 'You know how those yarns get around the underworld. The last thing they had on that guy was when he put down the Persian uprising in Bombay. Last month, I think.'

Lane said, 'Yes, last month. And we started this business last month. It was all right when we got away with those emeralds and that Mahar diamond. I thought the whole layout was foolproof. But I haven't felt right since I shipped the Kubij opal to you. That's a damned unlucky stone. It belonged to Sarankh, a rajah of the Hindustan country. I hired three dacoits to steal it, paid them well, and sent the stone through the customs with our regular snake freight.

'Right after that, this American detective came around and asked a lot of queer questions. But we have a good front with this reptile-importing set-up and I got around him.

'Then the Cobra stepped in – and I was so upset over the affair that I took the first and fastest boat here to see you. I tell you, a child could guess the answer from the fact that the only snakes we ship are pythons!'

Wilkins laughed. 'Don't be an ass!'

Jack Kirk leaned forward. 'What's this about the Cobra, Lane?' he asked frowning. 'What happened?'

'The three dacoits I hired,' Lane explained soberly, 'were found dead the day before I left for London – *dead from cobra venom!* And there were tiny darts in their throats!'

'Darts?' Kirk echoed, feeling his own throat in dread.

Lane smiled mirthlessly. 'Yes, darts. The mark of the Cobra. A dart in the throat covered with noxious cobra venom. That's how the devil gets his name.'

'Listen,' Gorgan snarled, 'don't let him hypnotize you, Jack. This Cobra stuff is crazy! I've had enough of this cock-and-bull yarn, Lane. You're welching and you're taking the easiest way out. There's nothing wrong. The Kubij opal will arrive tomorrow with our python shipment.'

'I tell you, I'm afraid!' Lane cried. 'I'm quitting, Maxie. I'm getting out. I don't want any money from the jewels. I want my life. You can split my share among the three of you.'

Maxie Gorgan rose steadily to his feet. His voice was icy and sinister. His hand stole stealthily inside of his coat.

'You can't quit this game, Lane,' he warned.

Lane looked at him coolly, evenly.

'You heard me, Maxie,' he replied fearlessly. 'When the Cobra steps in – I step out. And that's final.'

The three shots from Gorgan's pistol sounded like one. Three hot slugs buried themselves in Lane's chest like lightning. Lane stared at Gorgan's tense face in stupefaction. His lips moved soundlessly. He struggled bravely to speak. Blood poured from his mouth. His legs sagged and he fell forward on his face, crashing to the floor with an ominous thump. He did not move after he hit.

Kirk wet his lips and put out the cigarette he had been smoking.

'God, Max!' Wilkins exclaimed in horror. 'You shouldn't have done it!'

Gorgan shrugged and put his gun back.

'It's his own funeral. I told him. We can't afford to have a welcher, Wilky. There's too much money involved. Besides, there's only a split of three now, and dead men tell no tales. Kirk – get rid of this stiff. Use the car outside. Dump him out at Yorkshire.'

Kirk sighed.

'Okay, chief,' he said.

Jack Kirk did not notice the black sedan which followed him and his macabre burden through Surrey. Kirk was intent upon the operation of his vehicle, since even the slightest accident would incur the intervention of police. And with a dead man to be explained, Kirk was taking no chances.

The black car tailed him tenaciously out past Surrey into the suburbs of London.

Nor could Kirk see the figure at the wheel of the mystery car – a dark incongruous figure, covered by a black cloak, its face concealed by the dark shadows of the turbid night.

To a prowling cat, whose green eyes might have pierced the darkness, the hawklike featres of Deen Bradley would have been discernible. Deen was an operative of the Bombay Department of Justice. High-foreheaded, dark-skinned, he had black eyes which glittered coldly like ebony diamonds, hard, unemotional. He had no mustache. His face was thin and sharp. His lips, narrow and straight-lined.

He handled the car with natural dexterity, never shifting his cobra eyes from the red tail-light of the cadaver-car before him.

At Yorkshire, Kirk left the main highway and swerved to the right. Deen followed quickly, stepping down on the gas.

The American suddenly saw the brake-light of the other machine flare into being. Kirk slowed momentarily and, as he did so, a limp bundle tumbled lifelessly from the rolling car.

Then, Kirk sped away with amazing alacrity, his engine roaring sonorously into the night.

The fog drifting across the open countryside swallowed the lights of his car.

Deen slammed his brakes to the floor of the sedan, and the automobile skidded perilously to a halt. Beside it, in a ditch, lay the bundle which had been thrown from Kirk's car.

Deen leaped from the sedan and ran forward. He found a man, bleeding profusely and unconscious. He bent down and lifted up the fellow on his right arm.

The face of Wentworth Lane stared at him, eyes sightless and horrible.

'Zah!' Deen muttered in repugnance. 'So it is murder, too!'

He grasped the wrist of the unconscious Lane and felt for a possible flicker of life.

Instantly he jumped to his feet and dashed for the sedan, carrying Lane in his arms. His strength was astonishing. He carried Lane, who was heavy-set, as though the latter was a child. Carefully he laid the wounded man on the cushions. Then he hopped agilely into the front seat and pressed the accelerator to the floor.

Twenty minutes later, Lane was on a white-enameled operating table in the Yorkshire hospital while two doctors bent over him, working furiously to save his life. Deen stood by, anxiously waiting.

Presently one of the doctors looked up and shook his head.

'He's dying.'

Deen frowned. He asked, 'There is no chance?'

'None. I don't see how he keeps alive. Two bullets through his right lung. A third against his spine. It's miraculous!'

The dying man gasped paroxysmally.

'Can he be made to talk?' asked Deen.

The doctor shrugged dubiously. He turned to a nurse.

'Adrenalin,' he snapped.

He leaned over the naked chest of Lane and drove a hypodermic syringe into the flesh directly over the heart. Then he emptied the contents.

Momentarily, there was no visible result.

Then Lane's staring eyes gained the power of sight and recognition. They glanced around furtively. Finally they rested on Deen's dark face.

'You—'

'Yes. It is I. From India. I followed you. Quick, you must speak. You are dying.'

Lane coughed rackingly.

'Gorgan,' he muttered whisperingly. 'Pythons – code word is – House of Kaa—'

His lips had hardly stopped moving when he sighed. His body relaxed.

The doctors made preparations to transfer the corpse into the mortuary for identification and signing of the death certificate. With the American to establish identity—

But when they glanced around for him, Deen was gone.

That night, the police found the cadaver of Jack Kirk in Rokor Street, London. Kirk was sprawled crazily in the gutter – dead. Protruding from his throat was a small dart, about a half an inch long.

The chief medical examiner found that Kirk had died as the result of the violent neurotoxic destruction of cobra venom.

And throughout the underworld of London, a dire, foreboding wail echoed – a wail that spelled the nemesis of criminals.

The Cobra had come to England!

'Well, what are we going to do?' Commissioner Marshall asked sharply.

Inspector Ryder shrugged. The two men were sitting in the commissioner's office at the C. I. D. headquarters in Scotland Yard. In Marshall's hand was the coroner's report on the Jack Kirk murder the night preceding.

'I'd suggest nothing,' the inspector said with a flip of his hand. 'The department has been after Kirk for two years. He was a killer. One of the few English bandits who carried and used a gun. He was working for that Gorgan-Wilkins reptile firm over on Rokor Street. There's something damned queer going on over there, too. As far as I'm concerned, chief, I'd let it go.'

'You mean – drop the case entirely?'

'Yes, sir.' Ryder leaned forward. 'We've had excellent reports about this Cobra from Bombay headquarters. It was he who brought those Persian renegades to justice after they murdered Kilgore, one of the C. I. D.'s best men.'

'I remember that,' Marshall nodded.

Ryder grimaced. 'We owe him a good turn. Commissioner – I don't know who or what the Cobra is. But I *do* know that he gets results because he goes outside of the law. He saved me a lot of trouble getting Kirk. And there must be a reason. I wager that important business has brought the Cobra to London.'

'Very well,' the commissioner sighed. 'Drop investigation.'

At that moment, there was a knock on the door. An attendant looked in. 'Mr. Bradley to see you, sir.'

'Send him in.'

The door opened, and the dark-skinned, hawk-faced Deen Bradley walked in.

'Happy to know you, Bradley,' Marshall exclaimed, rising and shaking hands with sincere enthusiasm. 'Meet Inspector Ryder. Bradley is one of the best in Bombay, Ryder.'

'I know,' the inspector said. 'Thanks for helping us out on that Kilgore case down there.'

'I did very little,' Deen replied softly. 'In reality, you should thank him who calls himself the Cobra.'

'That's a coincidence!' Marshall cried. 'Your Bombayan avenger happens to be in London. Did you read it? The Kirk affair.'

'The commissioner's called off an investigation,' Ryder remarked, eyeing the American keenly.

Deen nodded without a trace of emotion, said: 'Very wise.'

'But what brings you here?' Marshall queried. 'Bombay cabled me to watch for you and give you any aid you asked.'

Deen sat down and pulled a peculiar greenish cigarette holder from his pocket. Slowly, he inserted a cigarette in it and lighted it.

'For the last month,' he began, 'there have been strange robberies in India along the eastern coast. Emeralds and diamonds of priceless value have been purloined by hired dacoits. Most notorious was the recent theft of the Kubij opal of the Rajah Sarankh.'

'We heard of that,' put in Ryder.

'All these jewels are being exported from India,' Deen continued. 'Somehow they are being smuggled out – past the customs officials. More paradoxical – they are being smuggled *into* England past the watchful scrutiny of your revenue officers here.

'I resolved to investigate. It was no general sneak-thief job, I knew. It appeared to be an international imbroglio, carefully planned and executed. A jewel ring. I tracked a Wentworth Lane to London to lead me to the lost jewels. Last night, he too was murdered – by his own cohorts.'

'But how can these jewels get into England past the customs?' the inspector demanded. 'They are very rigid, you know.'

'True, they are rigid,' Deen murmured. 'But do the customs men cut open the bellies of regal pythons to look for stolen jewels?'

Ryder stared at the American, dumbfounded.

'Good Gad!' he cried sharply. 'Smuggling by snakes! You mean, then, that Gorgan-Wilkins reptile outfit is the center of the ring! They import nothing but pythons. And they hardly ever sell any of the snakes. The reptiles just disappear. I checked that when I first became suspicious of that company.'

'You see,' Deen explained, 'it is very simple. The jewels are stolen in India by hired dacoits. Then, securely wrapped, they are placed in food which is swallowed by the pythons immediately prior to shipment. Since a big snake takes ten to eighteen days to assimilate and digest its food before throwing off waste, the seven-day sea trip to London is completed within that time. When the snakes arrive, they are killed and the jewels recovered from the stomach!'

'Amazing!' breathed the commissioner. 'We'll arrest them at once!'

'No.' Deen's voice was clear and firm. 'You must not arrest them yet. You must help me. We will need evidence – the Kubij opal, perhaps. And I have a simple plan.'

Maxie Gorgan eyed John Wilkins thoughtfully as the latter paced the floor of the House of Kaa in Rokor Street. Wilkins was highly excited and nervous. He had been smoking incessantly.

'You're acting like a kid,' Gorgan muttered.

'I can't help it, Maxie,' Wilkins said. 'This thing's getting my goat. First you knock off Lane—'

'Keep your mouth shut!'

'Aw, no one can hear us. Anyway, Lane dies first. Then Kirk, after dumping him, is found dead right outside with one of those damned poisoned darts in his throat. I wouldn't give a hang, Maxie, if it weren't for that Cobra story that Lane told us before you rubbed him out.'

'You're getting scared over nothing,' Gorgan said. 'Suppose this guy who calls himself the Cobra *is* on to us. What of it? He's outside the law, isn't he? And he's a lone wolf, isn't he? And above all, remember, he's a man – a single man. And he'll have to come to us. He can't go to the police. One man. I can handle him, Wilky.'

Wilkins shook his head.

'I'm leery. Suppose they're on to the shipment we got today. The pythons. They're here, aren't they?'

'Yeah,' Gorgan growled. 'And when you lose those jitters, we'll go down and get the Kubij opal.'

'I don't like it, Maxie,' Wilkins protested. 'The whole organization is shot. With Kirk gone, who's going to fence the jewels after we melt them down? With Lane gone – who's going to take over the Bombay end of the business?'

The doorbell at the front of the house jingled stridently.

A deep pall of silence covered the office. Gorgan's hand crept inside his coat and brought out an ugly automatic. He waved Wilkins away and went to the window.

A solitary man was standing before them. A tall, gaunt man with piercing black eyes. No one else was in sight.

'Let him in,' Gorgan said curtly. 'Keep him covered all the time. Lock the door after you. Hurry!'

Wilkins complied nervously and went downstairs.

He presently reappeared behind Deen Bradley who entered the office smoking a cigarette, that same peculiar green holder held tightly between his teeth. He bowed to Gorgan

'Sit down,' Maxie said, nodding to a chair.

Deen seated himself and smiled mirthlessly. 'You may remove that finger from the trigger of your gun,' he purred. 'I am unarmed.'

Gorgan flushed guiltily and his eyes narrowed. He lifted the pistol from his pocket and laid it on the desk in front of him, his right hand still curled around it.

'Frisk him, Wilky,' he said.

'I did before,' Wilkins replied. 'No gun, Maxie.'

Gorgan nodded. He said, 'Okay, then. What do you want?'

Deen shifted the cigarette holder to the corner of his mouth. 'I know you killed Lane,' he said quietly.

Instantly Maxie Gorgan hurled himself to his feet and glowered at the American, the heavy Luger held tensely in his hand and aimed point-blank at Deen's skull.

'No need to fire,' Deen said jocosely. 'I could never prove it.'

Gorgan hesitated, eyeing Deen warily. He sat down and fingered the trigger of the gun longingly.

'Who in hell are you?' he spat, 'and what do you want? You'd better get down to business, mister. You're due for a slug.'

'My name is Sam Trent,' Deen replied. 'I want to cut in.'

'*Cut in?*'

'I know that Lane and Kirk were cogs in your jewel-smuggling organization,' Deen said. 'Since they are defunct, the necessity of engaging a capable man to assume charge of the Bombay headquarters is imminent. I learned all this from Lane. I saw, in India, that his courage was dissipating, that he would attempt to withdraw, so I followed him to London. Zah! There you have it. You need a man. I am he.'

'You know a helluva lot for a stranger,' Gorgan exclaimed belligerently, both disturbed and interested. 'Maybe – since you're so smart – you also know the code word?'

Gorgan expected to catch Deen there. He paused triumphantly and his gun rose to a level with Deen's chest.

'But, of course,' Deen said mildly. '*House of Kaa.*'

Wilkins leaped to his feet like a shot. He cried, '*Kaa!* He knows it, Maxie. He must be straight. Lane would never have trusted him. How else could he have gotten hold of that? Kirk didn't even know. It was between Lane and you and me. For telegraphic correspondence to assure identification.'

'So Lane told you, eh?' Gorgan mused.

'Yes.'

'You know about the – business, too?'

'You refer to the shipping of the jewels in the pythons—'

'Okay.' Maxie held up his hand. 'You know all right.' He turned to Wilkins. 'This may be a cross. I don't see how, but it may be. Better check him.'

Deen smiled. 'And how do you "check" me?'

Gorgan regarded him coldly. 'Lane told us more than once about a Yankee dick at the Bombay office who was always asking questions. We anticipated the guy might try something. His name is Deen Bradley. Maybe you're on the level. Maybe you're not. Wilkins – check those fingerprints he just left on the chair.'

Deen frowned as Wilkins hurried forward and sprinkled a quantity of grayish powder on the spot where his hand had rested.

'You see,' Gorgan said, grinning evilly, 'Lane sent me a copy of that Yank dick's prints from India. We were taking no chances.'

Deen's lips were a thin, bloodless line. The green cigarette holder stiffened between his teeth. Wilkins opened a file drawer and brought out two photographs. Carefully he compared them with the marks on the arm of the chair.

'The same, Maxie!'

Gorgan sighed, relieved. 'I thought so. I thought if I prattled on a little, he'd leave his prints somewhere. So you're Deen Bradley, the famous Bombay operative, eh?' His voice snapped into a vicious snarl. 'Well, you're on your last case! You're through. What do you think we are – pulling a raw stunt like this?'

Wilkins was trembling with excitement.

'What are we going to do, Maxie?' he demanded.

Gorgan smiled without humor.

'We'll take him down into the snake room. We'll put him in the pit and let him make friends with the big boy. The thirty-foot constrictor. The one we haven't fed for three weeks. Let's see how a rat can fight a python. And then we'll get the Kubij opal from the new shipment and take it on the lam. This business is all washed up, Wilky. We've made enough out of it.'

Gorgan rose, his pistol ominously steady in his hand. 'Okay, Deen,' he growled. 'Keep ahead of me. If you make any funny moves, this lead bites you instead of the snake.'

Deen rose silently, his immobile face void of expression. He left the office, Gorgan's automatic prodding painfully into his back. They descended the stairs.

The descent took them into the cellar of the house, which Deen noted, was not damp at all, the floors being amazingly desiccated. Before a huge metal door, the two men stopped him. Wilkins accepted the proffered pistol while Maxie unlocked the door. It swung open. Gorgan snapped on the lights. They entered, leaving the metal door unlocked behind them.

Deen stared in astonishment at the room. It was enormous, the entire breadth of the house above. In the center of the room was a pit, about twenty feet deep. It was lined with opaque glass and was empty. An iron railing surrounded it. Near the railing, on the far side, was a large packing case.

'A pretty showroom, isn't it?' Gorgan leered. 'Watch!'

Deen gazed into the bottom of the pit, fascinated. Gorgan went to the wall and pulled down a short lever. The glass partition on one side began to rise. Instantly there was a sickening slithery scrape. The macabre head of a huge serpent slid out of the compartment in the wall to wind a path across the bottom of the pit, shaking the kinks and curls out of its great length. It was orange-brown and repugnantly thick. It raised its terrible snout, hungrily searching.

'He wants living food,' Gorgan growled alarmingly.

He moved threateningly on Deen while Wilkins still held the pistol in Deen's back.

With a lightning blow, Deen twisted around and cracked Wilkins on the side of the jaw with fearful strength. The punch clipped the man cleanly, eliciting a resounding crack. Wilkins fell like an ox. The pistol dropped from his nerveless hand as a red welt flamed on his chin.

Deen dived for the gun, conscious of Gorgan behind him.

He felt a ringing blow on his head, as Gorgan slashed down his clenched fists like a lunatic. It stunned him momentarily. He fell dazedly on his side and struggled courageously for the pistol.

Maxie Gorgan reached it first. He lifted it and fired.

The slug ripped through Deen's coat and buried itself in the opaque glass of the snake pit behind the detective.

Painfully, Deen strove to raise himself, hanging precariously to the iron railing at his back.

Gorgan raised the gun quickly for a second shot.

'Wait!' Deen called breathlessly.

Gorgan hesitated, then relaxed his trigger finger still holding the heavy automatic at Deen's head. 'What do you want? Talk fast!'

Deen nodded dejectedly.

'I admit defeat,' he said in a low voice. 'I have failed and therefore deserve to die. But before you kill me, I have one last request to make.'

'What is it?' Gorgan snapped.

'I would like to smoke a last cigarette,' Deen replied. 'Surely you can not deny a doomed man that courtesy?'

A crafty look narrowed Gorgan's eyes as he threw a surreptitious glance at the glass pit and the huge python. He lowered the gun and nodded.

'Okay,' he said. 'Go ahead.'

Deen rapidly felt in his pockets for his odd greenish cigarette holder. He found it and placed it between his teeth. Then he found a cigarette and started to make a pretense of lighting it.

Simultaneously, Gorgan sprang forward when Deen's head was slightly turned, and with almost preternatural strength, shoved the detective through the railing, hurling him cruelly into the glass pit.

Deen turned a complete somersault and landed thuddingly on his feet at the bottom. He turned. The regal serpent was not three feet away from him, its elliptical eyes regarding him with sinister austerity.

Meanwhile, Gorgan, certain that the detective was safely in the python pit, turned savagely to John Wilkins who had recovered from Deen's furious blow and was struggling to regain his feet.

'Your ace is in!' Gorgan snarled at him. 'You're through, Wilky. This is just the chance I've wanted. Lane dead. Kirk dead. The dick with the python. And now – *you!* There'll be no split on the jewels. They're all mine, mine!'

Crackling like a madman, he aimed the deadly Luger.

Wilkins gaped at him in horror and shrilly screamed.

Crack! Crack!

Jagged blue holes appeared in Wilkins' forehead as red blood poured copiously down his neck where the two bullets ripped his skull to pieces on the way out.

His legs collapsed suddenly, even while his eyes rolled sightlessly at Gorgan's smoking gun. He fell – right into the glass pit and on top of the python's back!

The great reptile reared up in pain and shock. Its terrible head slashed around in a razorlike strike and knocked Wilkins' dead body clear across the bottom of the pit from the force of the blow. The curved rows of fangs bit into Wilkins' clothes. They were not venomous but chewed into the cadaver viciously.

The two crushing loops of the serpentine phantasmagoria fell over the dead man, encircled him, and began to contract, the muscles rippling comberlike beneath the scaly skin.

It was a horrid spectacle – a python crushing a dead man.

Deen stood by, unhurt, watching the gruesome scene in lethargic fascination.

Suddenly, above him, he heard a harsh, bitter cry. Gorgan had watched his plans go awry. Wilkins' corpse had diverted the snake from the detective. The snake would try and swallow the cadaver but would get no further than the head, since it is impossible for any living constrictor to gulp down a man because of the width of the shoulders. He would have to kill Deen himself.

Bestially, Gorgan flung up the pistol.

Deen was taken almost unawares. He saw the ugly black nozzle of the automatic draw a bead on his eyes. With the alacrity of a bullet, he hurled himself to the floor of the pit. Simultaneously, the gun spat flame and death.

The slug tore Deen's coat and crashed against the glass of the pit, crumbling the glass and leaving irregular footing against the side of the wall.

Deen had lifted himself on his hands, half-kneeling. The peculiar green cigarette holder was between his teeth again. It was held taut, stiff against his gleaming white teeth.

Gorgan was pulling the trigger of the pistol frantically but the lead was going wild, breaking down the glass of the pit.

There was a piercing, whistling *hiss* like that of an angry, hooded hamadryad.

Gorgan was suddenly transfixed. His eyes bulged maniacally. A purplish cyanotic color pervaded his flesh. His lips moved jabberingly but uttered no sound. A thin trickle of blood course slowly down from his throat, from a minute hole directly above his jugular vein. A tiny black hole – a dart-hole.

Gruesomely, Maxie Gorgan fought against the powerful nerve-destroying cobra venom which was seeping through his blood stream and tearing the vortex of his vasomotor system and lungs to shreds. His breath came in agonizing, sobbing gulps and each one was filled with inhuman pain. His face slowly grew black as the toxin destruction grew greater.

For a second, his voice gained audibility.

'You—' he rasped, a death rattle sounding in his throat – 'the Cobra. . . .'

He fell forward into the pit, smashing down on his face and rolling over on his back, dead.

Deen climbed out of the pit where the python had swallowed the head of Wilkins and was fighting to engulf the man's shoulders, an impossibility. He stepped on the scant indentations of broken glass which the bullets had created.

The sound of axes tearing wood floated down to the cellar. He glanced at his watch. True to the hour, the police – as he had outlined in his plan with Ryder and Marshall – were raiding the gloomy House of Kaa.

Inspector Ryder burst into the pit-room, almost at the same instant, service revolver in hand. He surveyed the wreckage of the pit and whistled in horror. Quickly he put a hot bullet through the skull of the regal python. He gazed down and saw the noxious dart imbedded in the upturned throat of Maxie Gorgan.

'The Cobra!' Ryder exclaimed.

'Yes,' Deen said. 'The Cobra saved my life. Quick, may I have your revolver?'

Ryder regarded Deen keenly. The green cigarette holder in Deen's hand caught his eye. For the time being, he said nothing. He handed his gun over.

Deen went around the pit to the packing case which stood next to the railing. He found a hammer and ripped the top unceremoniously off the base. There were three more pythons within, all small specimens, from six to ten feet in length.

One had a small white piece of adhesive tape on the back of its head.

Fearlessly, Deen reached in and yanked the snake out with both his hands. Holding one hand behind the neck, he laid the snake on the floor, placed the gun against its brain and pulled the trigger. The snake thrashed slightly and was still.

Then, opening a knife, the detective slit open the belly, cut away the fatty tissues and lacerated the stomach.

When Deen stood up, a gleaming, dazzling flash of red fire struck Inspector Ryder in the eyes.

'The Kubij Opal!' he cried.

'Exactly,' Deen murmured. 'The case is over.'

Ryder eyed the green cigarette holder in the detective's other hand.

'But what of the Cobra?' he asked.

Deen hastily pocketed the holder. His eyes twinkled.

'The Cobra disappeared just before you came in.'

THE INVISIBLE MILLIONAIRE

LESLIE CHARTERIS

It is almost impossible to measure the success of Leslie Charteris' famous creation, Simon Templar, better known as the Saint.

The Saint is anything but. He is an adventurer, a romantic hero who works outside the law and has grand fun doing it. Like so many crooks in literature, he is imbued with the spirit of Robin Hood, which suggests that it is perfectly all right to steal, so long as it is from someone with wealth. Most of the more than forty books about the Saint are collections of short stories or novellas, and in the majority of tales he also functions as a detective. Unconstricted by being an official policeman, he steps outside the law to retrieve money or treasure that may not have been procured in an honorable fashion, either to restore it to its proper owner or to enrich himself.

'Maybe I am a crook,' Templar once says, 'but in between times I'm something more. In my simple way I am a kind of justice.'

In addition to the many books about the Saint, there were ten films about him, mainly starring George Sanders or Louis Hayward, a comic strip, a radio series that ran for much of the 1940s and a television series starring Roger Moore, an international success with 118 episodes.

Leslie Charteris (1907–1993), born in Singapore, became an American citizen in 1946.

'The Invisible Millionaire' was first published in the June 1938 issue of *Black Mask*.

THE INVISIBLE MILLIONAIRE

LESLIE CHARTERIS

I

The girl's eyes caught Simon Templar as he entered the room, ducking his head instinctively to pass under the low lintel of the door; and they followed him steadily across to the bar. They were blue eyes with long lashes, and the face to which they belonged was pretty without any distinctive feature, crowned with curly yellow hair. And besides anything else, the eyes held an indefinable hint of strain.

Simon knew all this without looking directly at her. But he had singled her out at once from the double handful of riverside week-enders who crowded the small barroom as the most probable writer of the letter which he still carried in his pocket – the letter which had brought him out to the Bell that Sunday evening on what anyone with a less incorrigibly optimistic flair for adventure would have branded from the start as a fool's errand. She was the only girl in the place who seemed to be unattached: there was no positive reason why the writer of that letter should have been unattached, but it seemed likely that she would be. Also she was the best looker in a by no means repulsive crowd; and that was simply no clue at all except to Simon Templar's own unshakable faith in his guardian angel, who had never thrown any other kind of damsel in distress into his buccaneering path.

But she was still looking at him. And even though he couldn't help knowing that women often looked at him with more than ordinary interest, it was not usually done quite so fixedly. His hopes rose a notch, tentatively; but it was her turn to make the next move. He had done all that had been asked of him when he walked in there punctually on the stroke of eight.

He leaned on the counter, with his wide shoulders seeming to take up half the length of the bar, and ordered a pint of beer for himself and a bottle of Vat 69 for Hoppy Uniatz, who trailed up thirstily at his heels. With the tankard in his hands, he waited for one of those inevitable moments when all the customers had paused for breath at the same time.

'Anyone leave a message for me?' he asked.

His voice was quiet and casual, but just clear enough for everyone in the room to hear. Whoever had sent for him, unless it was merely some pointless practical joker, should need no more confirmation than that. He hoped it would be the girl with the blue troubled eyes. He had a weakness for girls with eyes of that shade, the same colour as his own.

The barman shook his head.

'No sir. I haven't had any messages.'

Simon went on gazing at him reflectively, and the barman misinterpreted his expression. His mouth broadened and said: 'That's all right, sir. I'd know if there was anything for you.'

Simon's fine brows lifted a little puzzledly.

'I haven't seen you before,' he said.

'I've seen your picture often enough, sir. I suppose you could call me one of your fans. You're the Saint, aren't you?'

The Saint smiled slowly.

'You don't look frightened.'

'I never had the chance to be a rich racketeer, like the people you're always getting after. Gosh, though, I've had a kick out of some of the things you've done to 'em! And the way you're always putting it over on the police – I'll bet they'd give anything for an excuse to lock you up. . . .'

Simon was aware that the general buzz of conversation, after starting to pick up again, had died a second time and was staying dead. His spine itched with the feel of stares fastening on his back. And at the same time the barman became feverishly conscious of the audience which had been captured by his runaway enthusiasm. He began to stammer, turned red and plunged confusedly away to obliterate himself in some unnecessary fussing over the shelves of bottles behind him.

The Saint grinned with his eyes only, and turned tranquilly round to lean his back against the bar and face the room.

The collected stares hastily unpinned themselves and the voices got going again; but Simon was as oblivious of those events as he would have been if the rubber-necking had continued. At that moment his mind was capable of absorbing only one fearful and calamitous realisation. He had turned to see whether the girl with the fair curly hair and the blue eyes had also been listening, and whether she needed any more encouragement to announce herself. And the girl was gone.

She must have got up and gone out even in the short time that the barman had been talking. The Saint's glance swept on to identify the other faces in the room – faces that he had noted and automatically catalogued as he came in. They were all the same, but her face was not one of them. There was an empty glass beside her chair, and the chair itself was already being taken by a dark slender girl who had just entered.

Interest lighted the Saint's eyes again as he saw her, awakened instantly as he appreciated the subtle perfection of the sculptured cascade of her brown hair, crystallised as he approved the contours of her slim yet mature figure revealed by a simple flowered cotton dress. Then he saw her face for the first time, and held his tankard a shade tighter. Here, indeed, was something to call beautiful, something on which the word could be used without hesitation even under his most dispassionate scrutiny. She was like – 'Peaches in autumn,' he said to himself, seeing the fresh bloom of her cheeks against the russet shades of her hair. She raised her head with a smile, and his blood sang carillons. Perhaps after all. . . .

And then he saw that she was smiling and speaking to an ordinarily good-looking young man in a striped blazer who stood possessively over her; and inward laughter overtook him before he could feel the sourness of disappointment.

He loosened one elbow from the bar to run a hand through his dark hair, and his eyes twinkled at Mr. Uniatz.

'Oh well, Hoppy,' he said. 'It looks as if we can still be taken for a ride, even at our age.'

Mr. Uniatz blinked at him. Even in isolation, the face that nature had planted on top of Mr. Uniatz' bull neck could never have been mistaken for that of a matinee idol with an inclination toward intellectual pursuits and the cultivation of the soul; but when viewed in exaggerating contrast with the tanned piratical chiselling of the Saint's features it had a grotesqueness that was sometimes completely shattering to those who beheld it for the first time. To compare it with the face of a gorilla which had been in violent contact with a variety of blunt instruments during its formative years would be risking the justifiable resentment of any gorilla which had been in violent contact with a variety of blunt instruments during its formative years. The best that can be said of it is that it contained in mauled and primitive form all the usual organs of sight, smell, hearing and ingestion, and prayerfully let it go at that. And yet it must also be said that Simon Templar had come to regard it with a fondness which even its mother could scarcely have shared. He watched it with good-humoured patience, waiting for it to answer.

'I dunno, boss,' said Mr. Uniatz.

He had not thought over the point very deeply. Simon knew this, because when Mr. Uniatz was thinking his face screwed itself into even more frightful contortions than were stamped on it in repose. Thinking of any kind was an activity which caused Mr. Uniatz excruciating pain. On this occasion he had clearly escaped much suffering because his mind – if such a word can be used without blasphemy in connection with any of Mr. Uniatz' cerebral processes – had been elsewhere.

'Something is bothering you, Hoppy,' said the Saint. 'Don't keep it to yourself, or your head will start aching.'

'Boss,' said Mr. Uniatz gratefully, 'do I have to drink dis wit' de paper on?'

He held up the parcel he was nursing.

Simon looked at him blankly for a moment, and then felt weak in the middle.

'Of course not,' he said. 'They only wrapped it up because they thought we were going to take it home. They haven't got to know you yet, that's all.'

An expression of sublime relief spread over Mr. Uniatz' homely countenance as he pawed off the wrapping paper from the bottle of Vat 69. He pulled out the cork, placed the neck of the bottle in his mouth and tilted his head back. The soothing fluid flowed in a cooling stream down his asbestos gullet. All his anxieties were at rest.

For the Saint, consolation was not quite so easy. He finished his tankard and pushed it across the bar for a refill. While he was waiting for it to come back, he pulled out of his pocket and read over again the note that had brought him there. It was on a plain sheet of good note paper, with no address.

DEAR SAINT,

I'm not going to write a long letter, because if you aren't going to believe me it won't make any difference how many pages I write.

I'm only writing to you at all because I'm utterly desperate. How can I put it in the baldest possible way? I'm being forced into making myself an accomplice in one of the most gigantic frauds that can ever have been attempted, and I can't go to the police for the same reason that I'm being forced to help.

There you are. It's no use writing any more. If you can be at the Bell at Hurley at eight o'clock on Sunday evening I'll see you and tell you everything. If I can only talk to you for half an hour, I know I can make you believe me.

Please, for God's sake, at least let me talk to you.

My name is

NORA PRESCOTT

Nothing there to encourage too many hopes in the imagination of anyone whose mail was as regularly cluttered with crank letters as the Saint's; and yet the handwriting looked neat and sensible, and the brief blunt phrasing had somehow carried more conviction than a ream of protestations. All the rest had been hunch – that supernatural affinity for the dark trails of ungodliness which had pitchforked him into the middle of more brews of mischief than any four other freebooters of his day.

And for once the hunch had been wrong. If only it hadn't been for that humdrumly handsome excrescence in the striped blazer. . . .

Simon looked up again for another tantalizing eyeful of the dark slender girl.

He was just in time to get a parting glimpse of her back as she made her way to the door, with the striped blazer hovering over her like a motherly hen. Then she was gone; and everyone else in the bar suddenly looked nondescript and obnoxious.

The Saint sighed.

He took a deep draught of his beer and turned back to Hoppy Uniatz. The neck of the bottle was still firmly clamped in Hoppy's mouth, and there was no evidence to show that it had ever been detached therefrom since it was first inserted. His Adam's apple throbbed up and down with the regularity of a slow pulse. The angle of the bottle indicated that at least a pint of its contents had already reached his interior.

Simon gazed at him with reverence.

'You know, Hoppy,' he remarked, 'when you die we shan't even have to embalm you. We'll just put you straight into a glass case, and you'll keep for years.'

The other customers had finally returned to their own business, except for a few who were innocently watching for Mr. Uniatz to stiffen and fall backwards; and the talkative young barman edged up again with a show of wiping off the bar.

'Nothing much here to interest you tonight, sir, is there?' he began chattily.

'There was,' said the Saint ruefully, 'but she went home.'

'You mean the dark young lady, sir?'

'Who else?'

The man nodded knowingly.

'You ought to come here more often, sir. I've often seen her in here alone. Miss Rosemary Chase, that is. Her father's Mr. Marvin Chase, the millionaire. He just took the New Manor for the season. Had a nasty motor accident only a week ago. . . .'

Simon let him go on talking, without paying much attention. The dark girl's name wasn't Nora Prescott, anyhow. That seemed to be the only important item of information – and with it went the last of his hopes. The clock over the bar crept on to twenty minutes past eight. If the girl who had written to him had been as desperate as she said, she wouldn't come as late as that – she'd have been waiting there when he arrived. The girl with the strained blue eyes had probably been suffering from nothing worse than biliousness or thwarted love. Rosemary Chase had happened merely by accident. The real writer of the letter was almost certainly some fat and frowsy female among those he had passed over without a second thought, who was doubtless still gloating over him from some obscure corner, gorging herself with the spectacle of her inhibition's hero in the flesh.

A hand grasped his elbow, turning him round, and a lightly accented voice said: 'Why, Mr. Templar, what are you looking so sad about?'

The Saint's smile kindled as he turned.

'Giulio,' he said, 'if I could be sure that keeping a pub would make anyone as cheerful as you, I'd go right out and buy a pub.'

Giulio Trapani beamed at him teasingly.

'Why should you need anything to make you cheerful? You are young, strong, handsome, rich – and famous. Or perhaps you are only waiting for a new romance?'

'Giulio,' said the Saint, 'that's a very sore point, at the moment.'

'Ah! Perhaps you are waiting for a love letter which has not arrived?'

The Saint straightened up with a jerk. All at once he laughed. Half-incredulous sunshine smashed through his despondency, lighted up his face. He extended his palm.

'You old son of a gun! Give!'

The landlord brought his left hand from behind his back, holding an envelope. Simon grabbed it and ripped it open. He recognized the handwriting at a glance. The note was on a sheet of hotel paper.

Thank God you came. But I daren't be seen speaking to you after the barman recognised you.

Go down to the lock and walk up the towpath. Not very far along on the left there's a boathouse with green doors. I'll wait for you there. Hurry.

The Saint raised his eyes, and sapphires danced in them.

'Who gave you this, Giulio?'

'Nobody. It was lying on the floor outside when I came through. You saw the envelope – "Deliver at once to Mr. Templar in the bar." So that's what I do. Is it what you were waiting for?'

Simon stuffed the note into his pocket, and nodded. He drained his tankard.

'This is the romance you were talking about – maybe,' he said. 'I'll tell you about it later. Save some dinner for me. I'll be back.' He clapped Trapani on the shoulder and swung round, newly awakened, joyously alive again. Perhaps, in spite of everything, there was still adventure to come. . . . 'Let's go, Hoppy!'

He took hold of Mr. Uniatz' bottle and pulled it down. Hoppy came upright after it with a plaintive gasp.

'Chees, boss—'

'Have you no soul?' demanded the Saint sternly as he herded him out of the door. 'We have a date with a damsel in distress. The moon will be mirrored in her beautiful eyes, and she will pant out a story while we fan the gnats away from her snowy brow. Sinister eggs are being hatched behind the scenes. There will be villains and mayhem and perhaps even moider. . . .'

He went on talking lyrical nonsense as he set a brisk pace down the lane toward the river; but when they reached the towpath even he had dried up. Mr. Uniatz was an unresponsive audience, and Simon found that some of the things he was saying in jest were oddly close to the truth that he believed. After all, such fantastic things had happened to him before.

He didn't fully understand the change in himself as he turned off along the riverbank beside the dark shimmering sleekness of the water. The ingrained flippancy was still with him – he could feel it like a translucent film over his mind – but underneath it he was all open and expectant, a receptive void in which anything might take shape. And something was beginning to take shape there – something still so nebulous and formless that it eluded any conscious survey, and yet something as inescapably real as a promise of thunder in the air. It was as if the hunch that had brought him out to the Bell in the first place had leapt up from a whisper to a great shout; and yet everything was silent. Far away, to his sensitive ears, there was the ghostly hum of cars on the Maidenhead road; close by, the sibilant lap of the river, the lisp of leaves, the stertorous breathing and elephantine footfalls of Mr. Uniatz; but those things were only phases of the stillness that was everywhere. Everything in the world was quiet, even his own nerves, and they were almost too quiet. And ahead of him, presently, loomed the shape of a building like a boathouse. His pencil flashlight stabbed out for a second and caught the front of it. It had green doors.

Quietly he said: 'Nora.'

There was no answer, no hint of movement anywhere. And he didn't know why, but in the same quiet way his right hand slid up to his shoulder rig and loosened the automatic in the spring clip under his arm.

He covered the last two yards in absolute silence, put his hand to the handle of the door and drew it back quickly as his fingers slid on a sticky dampness. It was queer, he thought even then, even as his left hand angled the flashlight down, that it should have happened just like that, when everything in him was tuned and waiting for it, without knowing what it was waiting for. Blood – on the door.

II

Simon stood for a moment, and his nerves seemed to grow even calmer and colder under an edge of sharp bitterness.

Then he grasped the door handle again, turned it and went in. The inside of the building was pitch dark. His torch needled the blackness with a thin jet of light that splashed dim reflections from the glossy varnish on a couple of punts and an electric canoe. Somehow he was quite sure what he would find, so sure that the certainty chilled off any rise of emotion. He knew what it must be; the only question was, who? Perhaps even that was not such a question. He was never quite sure about that. A hunch that had almost missed its mark had become stark reality with a suddenness that disjointed the normal co-ordinates of time and space: it was as if, instead of discovering things, he was trying to remember things he had known before and had forgotten. But he saw her at last, almost tucked under the shadow of the electric canoe, lying on her side as if she were asleep.

He stepped over and bent his light steadily on her face, and knew then that he had been right. It was the girl with the troubled blue eyes. Her eyes were open now, only they were not troubled any more. The Saint stood and looked down at her. He had been almost sure when he saw the curly yellow hair. But she had been wearing a white blouse when he saw her last, and now there was a splotchy crimson pattern on the front of it. The pattern glistened as he looked at it.

Beside him, there was a noise like an asthmatic foghorn loosening up for a burst of song.

'Boss,' began Mr. Uniatz.

'Shut up.'

The Saint's voice was hardly more than a whisper, but it cut like a razor blade. It cut Hoppy's introduction cleanly off from whatever he had been going to say; and at the same moment as he spoke Simon switched off his torch, so that it was as if the same tenuous whisper had sliced off even the ray of light, leaving nothing around them but blackness and silence.

Motionless in the dark, the Saint quested for any betraying breath or sound. To his tautened eardrums, sensitive as a wild animal's, the hushed murmurs of the night outside were still an audible background against which the slightest stealthy movement even at a considerable distance would have stood out like a bugle call. But he heard nothing then, though he waited for several seconds in uncanny stillness.

He switched on the torch again.

'Okay, Hoppy,' he said. 'Sorry to interrupt you, but that blood was so fresh that I wondered if someone mightn't still be around.'

'Boss,' said Mr. Uniatz aggrievedly, 'I was doin' fine when ya stopped me.'

'Never mind,' said the Saint consolingly. 'You can go ahead now. Take a deep breath and start again.'

He was still partly listening for something else, wondering if even then the murderer might still be within range.

'It ain't no use now,' said Mr. Uniatz dolefully.

'Are you going to get temperamental on me?' Simon demanded sufferingly. 'Because if so—'

Mr. Uniatz shook his head.

'It ain't dat, boss. But you gotta start wit' a full bottle.'

Simon focused him through a kind of fog. In an obscure and apparently irrelevant sort of way, he became aware that Hoppy was still clinging to the bottle of Vat 69 with which he had been irrigating his tonsils at the Bell, and that he was holding it up against the beam of the flashlight as though brooding over the level of the liquid left in it. The Saint clutched at the buttresses of his mind.

'What in the name of Adam's grandfather,' he said, 'are you talking about?'

'Well, boss, dis is an idea I get out of a book. De guys walks in a saloon, he buys a bottle of scotch, he pulls de cork, an' he drinks de whole bottle straight down wit'out stopping. So I was tryin' de same t'ing back in de pub, an' was doin' fine when ya stopped me. Lookit, I ain't left more 'n two-t'ree swallows. But it ain't no use goin' on now,' explained Mr. Uniatz, working back to the core of his grievance. 'You gotta start wit' a full bottle.'

Nothing but years of training and self-discipline gave Simon Templar the strength to recover his sanity.

'Next time you'd better take the bottle away somewhere and lock yourself up with it,' he said with terrific moderation. 'Just for the moment, since we haven't got another bottle, is there any danger of your noticing that someone has been murdered around here?'

'Yeah,' said Mr. Uniatz brightly. 'De wren.'

Having contributed his share of illumination, he relapsed into benevolent silence. This, his expectant self-effacement appeared to suggest, was not his affair. It appeared to be something which required thinking about; and Thinking was a job for which the Saint possessed an obviously supernatural aptitude which Mr. Uniatz had come to lean upon with a childlike faith that was very much akin to worship.

The Saint was thinking. He was thinking with a level and passionless detachment that surprised even himself. The girl was dead. He had seen plenty of men killed before, sometimes horribly; but only one other woman. Yet that must not make any difference. Nora Prescott had never meant anything to him: he would never even have recognized her voice. Other women of whom he knew just as little were dying everywhere, in one way or another, every time he breathed; and he could think about it without the slightest feeling. Nora Prescott was just another name in the world's long roll of undistinguished dead.

But she was someone who had asked him for help, who had perhaps died because of what she had wanted to tell him. She hadn't been just another twittering fluffhead going into hysterics over a mouse. She really had known something – something that was dangerous enough for someone else to commit murder rather than have it revealed.

'. . . one of the most gigantic frauds that can ever have been attempted.'

The only phrase out of her letter which gave any information at all came into his head again, not as a merely provocative combination of words, but with some of the clean-cut clarity of a sober statement of fact. And yet the more he considered it, the closer it came to clarifying precisely nothing.

And he was still half listening for a noise that it seemed as if he ought to have heard. The expectation was a subtle nagging at the back of his mind, the fidget for attention of a thought that still hadn't found conscious shape.

His torch panned once more round the interior of the building. It was a plain wooden structure, hardly more than three walls and a pair of double doors which formed the fourth, just comfortably roomy for the three boats which it contained. There was a small window on each side, so neglected as to be almost opaque. Overhead, his light went straight up to the bare rafters which supported the shingle roof. There was no place in it for anybody to hide except under one of the boats; and his light probed along the floor and eliminated that possibility.

The knife lay on the floor near the girl's knees – an ordinary cheap kitchen knife, but pointed and sharp enough for what it had had to do. There was a smear of blood on the handle; and some of it must have gone on the killer's hand, or more probably on his glove, and in that way been left on the doorknob. From the stains and rents on the front of the girl's dress, the murderer must have struck two or three times; but if he was strong he could have held her throat while he did it, and there need have been no noise.

'Efficient enough,' the Saint summed it up aloud, 'for a rush job.'

He was thinking: 'It must have been a rush job, because he couldn't have known she was going to meet me here until after she'd written that note at the Bell. Probably she didn't even know it herself until then. Did he see the note? Doesn't seem possible. He could have followed her. Then he must have had the knife on him already. Not an ordinary sort of knife to carry about with you. Then he must have known he was going to use it before he started out. Unless it was here in the boathouse and he just grabbed it up. No reason why a knife like that should be lying about in a place like this. Bit too convenient. Well, so he knew she'd got in touch with me, and he'd made up his mind to kill her. Then why not kill her before she even got to the Bell? She might have talked to me there, and he couldn't have stopped her – could he? Was he betting that she wouldn't risk talking to me in public? He could have been. Good psychology, but the hell of a nerve to bet on it. Did he find out she'd written to me? Then I'd probably still have the letter. If I found her murdered, he'd expect me to go to the police with it. Dangerous. And he knew I'd find her. Then why—'

The Saint felt something like an inward explosion as he realised what his thoughts were leading to. He knew then why half of his brain had never ceased to listen – searching for what intuition had scented faster than reason.

Goose pimples crawled up his spine onto the back of his neck.

And at that same moment he heard the sound.

It was nothing that any other man might have heard at all. Only the gritting of a few tiny specks of gravel between a stealthy shoe sole and the board stage outside. But it was what every nerve in his body had unwittingly been keyed for ever since he had seen the dead girl at his feet. It was what he inevitably had to hear, after everything else that had happened. It spun him round like a jerk on the string wound round a top.

He was in the act of turning when the gun spoke.

Its bark was curt and flat and left an impression of having been curiously thin, though his ears rang with it afterwards. The bullet zipped past his ear like a hungry mosquito; and from the hard fierce note that it hummed he knew that if he had not been starting to turn at the very instant when it was fired it would have struck him squarely in the head. Pieces of shattered glass rattled on the floor.

Lights smashed into his eyes as he whirled at the door, and a clear clipped voice snapped at him: 'Drop that gun! You haven't got a chance!'

The light beat on him with blinding intensity from the lens of a pocket searchlight that completely swallowed up the slim ray of his own torch. He knew that he hadn't a chance. He could have thrown bullets by guesswork; but to the man behind the glare he was a target on which patterns could be punched out.

Slowly his fingers opened off the big Luger, and it plonked on the boards at his feet.

His hand swept across and bent down the barrel of the automatic which Mr. Uniatz had whipped out like lightning when the first shot crashed between them.

'You too, Hoppy,' he said resignedly. 'All that scotch will run away if they make a hole in you now.'

'Back away,' came the next order.

Simon obeyed.

The voice said: 'Go on, Rosemary – pick up the guns. I'll keep 'em covered.'

A girl came forward into the light. It was the dark slender girl whose quiet loveliness had unsteadied Simon's breath at the Bell.

III

She bent over and collected the two guns by the butts, holding them aimed at Simon and Hoppy, not timidly, but with a certain stiffness which told the Saint's expert eye that the feel of them was unfamiliar. She moved backwards and disappeared again behind the light.

'Do you mind,' asked the Saint ceremoniously, 'if I smoke?'

'I don't care.' The clipped voice, he realised now, could only have belonged to the young man in the striped blazer. 'But don't try to start anything, or I'll let you have it. Go on back in there.'

The Saint didn't move at once. He took out his cigarette case first, opened it and selected a cigarette. The case came from his breast pocket, but he put it back in the pocket at his hip, slowly and deliberately and holding it lightly, so that his hand was never completely out of sight and a nervous man would have no cause to be alarmed at the movement. He had another gun in that pocket, a light but beautifully balanced Walther; but for the time being he left it there, sliding the cigarette case in behind it and bringing his hand back empty to get out his lighter.

'I'm afraid we weren't expecting to be held up in a place like this,' he remarked apologetically. 'So we left the family jools at home. If you'd only let us know—'

'Don't be funny. If you don't want to be turned over to the police, you'd better let *me* know what you're doing here.'

The Saint's brows shifted a fraction of an inch.

'I don't see what difference it makes to you, brother,' he said slowly. 'But if you're really interested, we were just taking a stroll in the moonlight to work up an appetite for dinner, and we happened to see the door of this place open—'

'So that's why you both had to pull out guns when you heard us.'

'My dear bloke,' Simon argued reasonably, 'what do you expect anyone to do when you creep up behind them and start sending bullets whistling round their heads?'

There was a moment's silence.

The girl gasped.

The man spluttered: 'Good God, you've got a nerve! After you blazed away at us like that – why, you might have killed one of us!'

The Saint's eyes strained uselessly to pierce beyond the light. There was an odd hollow feeling inside him, making his frown unnaturally rigid. Something was going wrong. Something was going as immortally cockeyed as it was possible to go. It was taking him a perceptible space of time to grope for a bearing in the reeling void. Somewhere the scenario had gone as paralysingly off the rails as if a Wagnerian soprano had bounced into a hotcha dance routine in the middle of *Tristan*.

'Look,' he said. 'Let's be quite clear about this. Is your story going to be that you thought I took a shot at you?'

'I don't have to think,' retorted the other. 'I heard the bullet whizz past my head. Go on – get back in that boathouse.'

Simon dawdled back.

His brain felt as if it was steaming. The voice behind the light, now that he was analysing its undertones, had a tense unsophistication that didn't belong in the script at all. And the answers it gave were all wrong. Simon had had it all figured out one ghostly instant before it began to happen. The murderer hadn't just killed Nora Prescott and faded away, of course. He had killed her and waited outside, knowing that Simon Templar must find her in a few minutes, knowing that that would be his best chance to kill the Saint as well and silence whatever the Saint knew already and recover the letter. That much was so obvious that he must have been asleep not to have seen it from the moment when his eyes fell on the dead girl. Well, he had seen it now. And yet it wasn't clicking. The dialogue was all there, and yet every syllable was striking a false note.

And he was back inside the boathouse, as far as he could go, with the square bow of a punt against his calves and Hoppy beside him.

The man's voice said: 'Turn a light on, Rosemary.'

The girl came round and found a switch. Light broke out from a naked bulb that hung by a length of flex from one of the rafters, and the young man in the striped blazer flicked off his torch.

'Now,' he started to say, 'we'll—'

'Jim!'

The girl didn't quite scream, but her voice tightened and rose to within a semitone of it. She backed against the wall, one hand to her mouth, with her face white and her eyes dilated with horror. The man began to turn toward her, and then followed her wide and frozen stare. The muzzle of the gun he was holding swung slack from its aim on the Saint's chest as he did so – it was an error that in some situations would have cost him his life, but Simon let him live. The Saint's head was whirling with too many questions, just then, to have any interest in the opportunity. He was looking at the gun which the girl was still holding, and recognizing it as the property of Mr. Uniatz.

'It's Nora,' she gasped. 'She's—'

He saw her gather herself with an effort, force herself to go forward and kneel beside the body. Then he stopped watching her. His eyes went to the gun that was still wavering in the young man's hand.

'Jim,' said the girl brokenly, 'she's dead!'

The man took a half step toward the Saint.

'You swine!' he grunted. 'You killed her—'

'Go on,' said the Saint gently. 'And then I took a pot at you. So you fired back in self-defence, and just happened to kill us. It'll make a swell story even if it isn't a very new one, and you'll find yourself quite a hero. But why all the play acting for our benefit? We know the gag.'

There was complete blankness behind the anger in the other's eyes. And all at once the Saint's somersaulting cosmos stabilized itself with a jolt – upside down, but solid.

He was looking at the gun which was pointing at his chest, and realising that it was his own Luger.

And the girl had got Hoppy's gun. And there was no other artillery in sight.

The arithmetic of it smacked him between the eyes and made him dizzy. Of course there was an excuse for him, in the shape of the first shot and the bullet that had gone snarling past his ear. But even with all that, for him out of all people in the world, at his time of life . . .

'Run up to the house and call the police, Rosemary,' said the striped blazer in a brittle bark.

'Wait a minute,' said the Saint.

His brain was not fogged any longer. It was turning over as swiftly and smoothly as a hair-balanced flywheel, registering every item with the mechanical infallibility of an adding machine. His nerves were tingling.

His glance whipped from side to side. He was standing again approximately where he had been when the shot cracked out, but facing the opposite way. On his right quarter was the window that had been broken, with the shards of glass scattered on the floor below it – he ought to have understood everything when he heard them hit the floor. Turning the other way, he saw that the line from the window to himself continued on through the open door.

He look a long drag on his cigarette.

'It kind of spoils the scene,' he said quietly, 'but I'm afraid we've both been making the same mistake. You thought I fired at you—'

'I don't have—'

'All right, you don't have to think. You heard the bullet whizz past your head. You said that before. You're certain I shot at you. Okay. Well, I was just as certain that you shot at me. But I know now I was wrong. You never had a gun until you got mine. It was that shot that let you bluff me. I'd heard the bullet go past *my* head, and so it never even occurred to me that you were bluffing. But we were both wrong. The shot came through that window – it just missed me, went on out through the door and just missed you. And somebody else fired it!'

The other's face was stupid with stubborn incredulity.

'Who fired it?'

'The murderer.'

'That means you,' retorted the young man flatly. 'Hell, I don't want to listen to you. You see if you can make the police believe you. Go on and call them, Rosemary. I can take care of these two.'

The girl hesitated.

'But, Jim—'

'Don't worry about me, darling. I'll be all right. If either of these two washouts tries to get funny, I'll give him plenty to think about.'

The Saint's eyes were narrowing.

'You lace-pantie'd bladder of hot air,' he said in a cold even voice that seared like vitriol. 'It isn't your fault if God didn't give you a brain, but he did give you eyes. Why don't you use them? I say the shot was fired from outside, and you can see for yourself where the broken windowpane fell. Look at it. It's all on the floor in here. If you can tell me how I could shoot at you in the doorway and break a window behind me, and make the broken glass fall inwards, I'll pay for your next marcel wave. Look at it, nitwit.'

The young man looked.

He had been working closer to the Saint, with his free fist clenched and his face flushed with wrath, since the Saint's first sizzling insult smoked under his skin. But he looked. Somehow, he had to do that. He was less than five feet away when his eyes shifted. And it was then that Simon jumped him.

The Saint's lean body seemed to lengthen and swoop across the intervening space. His left hand grabbed the Luger, bent the wrist behind it agonisingly inwards, while the heel of his open right hand settled under the other's chin. The gun came free; and the Saint's right arm straightened jarringly and sent the young man staggering back.

Simon reversed the automatic with a deft flip and held it on him. Even while he was making his spring, out of the corner of his eye he had seen Hoppy Uniatz flash away from him with an electrifying acceleration that would have stunned anyone who had misguidedly judged Mr. Uniatz on the speed of his intellectual reactions; now he glanced briefly aside and saw that Hoppy was holding his gun again and keeping the girl pinioned with one arm.

'Okay, Hoppy,' he said. 'Keep your Betsy and let her go. She's going to call the police for us.'

Hoppy released her, but the girl did not move. She stood against the wall, rubbing slim wrists that had been bruised by Mr. Uniatz' untempered energy, looking from Simon to the striped blazer with scared, desperate eyes.

'Go ahead,' said the Saint impatiently. 'I won't damage little Jimmy unless he makes trouble. If this was one of my murdering evenings, you don't think I'd bump him and let you get away, do you? Go on and fetch your policeman – and we'll see whether the boy friend can make them believe *his* story!'

IV

They had to wait for some time. . . .

After a minute Simon turned the prisoner over to Hoppy and put his Luger away under his coat. He reached for his cigarette case again and thoughtfully helped himself to a smoke. With the cigarette curling blue drifts past his eyes, he traced again the course of the bullet that had so nearly stamped the finale on all his adventures. There was no question that it had been fired from outside the window – and that also explained the peculiarly flat sound of the shot which had faintly puzzled him. The cleavage lines on the few scraps of glass remaining in the frame supplied the last detail of incontrovertible proof. He devoutly hoped that the shining lights of the local constabulary would have enough scientific knowledge to appreciate it.

Mr. Uniatz, having brilliantly performed his share of physical activity, appeared to have been snared again in the unfathomable quagmires of the Mind. The tortured grimace that had cramped itself into his countenance indicated that some frightful eruption was taking place in the small core of grey matter which formed a sort of glutinous marrow inside his skull. He cleared his throat, producing a noise like a piece of sheet iron getting between the blades of a lawn mower, and gave the fruit of his travail to the world.

'Boss,' he said, 'I dunno how dese mugs t'ink dey can get away wit' it.'

'How which mugs think they can get away with what?' asked the Saint somewhat vacantly.

'Dese mugs,' said Mr. Uniatz, 'who are tryin' to take us for a ride, like ya tell me in de pub.'

Simon had to stretch his memory backwards almost to breaking point to hook up again with Mr. Uniatz' train of thought; and when he had finally done so he decided that it was wisest not to start any argument.

'Others have made the same mistake,' he said casually and hoped that would be the end of it.

Mr. Uniatz nodded sagely.

'Well, dey all get what's comin' to dem,' he said with philosophic complacency. 'When do I give dis punk de woiks?'

'When do you— What?'

'Dis punk,' said Mr. Uniatz, waving his Betsy at the prisoner. 'De mug who takes a shot at us.'

'You don't,' said the Saint shortly.

The equivalent of what on anybody else's face would have been a slight frown carved its fearsome corrugations into Hoppy's brow.

'Ya don't mean he gets away wit' it after all?'

'We'll see about that.'

'Dijja hear what he calls us?'

'What was that?'

'He calls us washouts.'

'That's too bad.'

'Yeah, dat's too bad.' Mr. Uniatz glowered disparagingly at the captive. 'Maybe I better go over him wit' a paddle foist. Just to make sure he don't go to sleep.'

'Leave him alone,' said the Saint soothingly. 'He's young, but he'll grow up.'

He was watching the striped blazer with more attention than a chance onlooker would have realised. The young man stood glaring at them defiantly – not without fear, but that was easy to explain if one wanted to. His knuckles tensed up involuntarily from time to time; but a perfectly understandable anger would account for that. Once or twice he glanced at the strangely unreal shape of the dead girl half hidden in the shadows, and it was at those moments that Simon was studying him most intently. He saw the almost conventionalised horror of death that takes the place of practical thinking with those who have seen little of it, and a bitter disgust that might have had an equally conventional basis. Beyond that, the sullen scowl which disfigured the other's face steadily refused him the betraying evidence that might have made everything so much simpler. Simon blew placid and meditative smoke rings to pass the time; but there was an irking bafflement behind the cool patience of his eyes.

It took fifteen minutes by his watch for the police to come, which was less than he had expected.

They arrived in the persons of a man with a waxed moustache in plain clothes, and two constables in uniform. After them, breathless when she saw the striped blazer still inhabited by an apparently undamaged owner, came Rosemary Chase. In the background hovered a man who even without his costume could never have been mistaken for anything but a butler.

Simon turned with a smile.

'Glad to see you, Inspector,' he said easily.

'Just "Sergeant,"' answered the plain-clothes man in a voice that sounded as if it should have been 'sergeant major.'

He saw the automatic that Mr. Uniatz was still holding, and stepped forward with a rather hollow but courageous belligerence.

'Give me that gun!' he said loudly.

Hoppy ignored him and looked inquiringly at the only man whom he took orders from; but Simon nodded. He politely offered his own Luger as well. The sergeant took the two guns, squinted at them sapiently and stuffed them into his side pockets. He looked relieved, and rather clever.

'I suppose you've got licences for these firearms,' he said temptingly.

'Of course,' said the Saint in a voice of saccharine virtue.

He produced certificate and permit to carry from his pocket. Hoppy did the same. The sergeant pored over the documents with surly suspicion for some time before he handed them to one of the constables to note down the particulars. He looked so much less clever that Simon had difficulty in keeping a straight face. It was as if the Official Mind, jumping firmly to a foregone conclusion, had spent the journey there developing an elegantly graduated approach to the obvious climax, and therefore found the entire structure staggering when the first step caved in under its feet.

A certain awkwardness crowded itself into the scene.

With a businesslike briskness that was only a trifle too elaborate, the sergeant went over to the body and brooded over it with portentous solemnity. He went down on his hands and knees to peer at the knife, without touching it. He borrowed a flashlight from one of the constables to examine the floor around it. He roamed about the boathouse and frowned into dark corners. At intervals he cogitated. When he could think of nothing else to do, he came back and faced his audience with dogged valour.

'Well,' he said less aggressively, 'while we're waiting for the doctor I'd better take your statements.' He turned. 'You're Mr. Forrest, sir?'

The young man in the striped blazer nodded.

'Yes.'

'I've already heard the young lady's story, but I'd like to hear your version.'

Forrest glanced quickly at the girl and almost hesitated. He said: 'I was taking Miss Chase home, and we saw a light moving in here. We crept up to find out what it was, and one of these men fired a shot at us. I turned my torch on them and pretended I had a gun too, and they surrendered. We took their guns away; and then this man started arguing and trying to make out that somebody else had fired the shot, and he managed to distract my attention and get his gun back.'

'Did you hear any noise as you were walking along? The sort of noise this – er – deceased might have made as she was being attacked?'

'No.'

'I – did – not – hear – the – noise – of – the – deceased – being – attacked,' repeated one of the constables with a notebook and pencil, laboriously writing it down.

The sergeant waited for him to finish and turned to the Saint.

'Now, Mr. Templar,' he said ominously. 'Do you wish to make a statement? It is my duty to warn you—'

'Why?' asked the Saint blandly.

The sergeant did not seem to know the answer to that.

He said gruffly: 'What statement do you wish to make?'

'Just what I told Comrade Forrest when we were arguing. Mr. Uniatz and I were ambling around to work up a thirst, and we saw this door open. Being rather inquisitive and not having anything better to do, we just nosed in, and we saw the body. We were just taking it in when somebody fired at us; and then Comrade Forrest turned on the spotlight and yelled "Hands up!" or words to that effect, so to be on the safe side we handed up, thinking he'd fired the first shot. Still, he looked kind of nervous when he had hold of my gun, so I took it away from him in case it went off. Then I told Miss Chase to go ahead and fetch you. Incidentally, as I tried to tell Comrade Forrest, I've discovered that we were both wrong about that shooting. Somebody else did it from outside the window. You can see for yourself if you take a look at the glass.'

The Saint's voice and manner were masterpieces of matter-of-fact veracity. It is often easy to tell the plain truth, and be disbelieved; but Simon's pleasant imperturbability left the sergeant visibly nonplused. He went and inspected the broken glass at some length, and then he came back and scratched his head.

'Well,' he admitted grudgingly, 'there doesn't seem to be much doubt about that.'

'If you want any more proof,' said the Saint nonchalantly, 'you can take our guns apart. Comrade Forrest will tell you that we haven't done anything to them. You'll find the magazines full and the barrels clean.'

The sergeant adopted the suggestion with morbid eagerness, but he shrugged resignedly over the result.

'That seems to be right,' he said with stoic finality. 'It looks as if both you gentlemen were mistaken.' He went on scrutinising the Saint grimly. 'But it still doesn't explain why you were in here with the deceased.'

'Because I found her,' answered the Saint reasonably. 'Somebody had to.'

The sergeant took another glum look around. He did not audibly acknowledge that all his castles in the air had settled soggily back to earth, but the morose admission was implicit in the majestic stolidity with which he tried to keep anything that might have been interpreted as a confession out of his face. He took refuge in an air of busy inscrutability, as if he had just a little more up his sleeve than he was prepared to share with anyone else for the time being; but there was at least one member of his audience who was not deceived, and who breathed a sigh of relief at the lifting of what might have been a dangerous suspicion.

'Better take down some more details,' he said gruffly to the constable with the notebook, and turned to Rosemary Chase. 'The deceased's name is Nora Prescott – is that right, miss?'

'Yes.'

'You knew her quite well?'

'Of course. She was one of my father's personal secretaries,' said the dark girl; and the Saint suddenly felt as if the last knot in the tangle had been untied.

V

He listened with tingling detachment while Rosemary Chase talked and answered questions. The dead girl's father was a man who had known and helped Marvin Chase when they were both young, but who had long ago been left far behind by Marvin Chase's sensational rise in the financial world. When Prescott's own business was failing, Chase had willingly lent him large sums of money, but the failure had still not been averted. Illness had finally brought Prescott's misfortunes to the point where he was not even able to meet the interest on the loan, and when he refused further charity Chase had sent him to Switzerland to act as an entirely superfluous 'representative' in Zurich and had given Nora Prescott a job himself. She had lived more as one of the family than as an employee. No, she had given no hint of having any private troubles or being afraid of anyone. Only she had not seemed to be quite herself since Marvin Chase's motor accident. . . .

The bare supplementary facts clicked into place in the framework that was already there as if into accurately fitted sockets, filling in sections of the outline without making much of it more recognizable. They filed themselves away in the Saint's memory with mechanical precision; and yet the closeness which he felt to the mystery that hid behind them was more intuitive than methodical, a weird sensitivity that sent electric shivers coursing up his spine.

A grey-haired ruddy-cheeked doctor arrived and made his matter-of-fact examination and report.

'Three stab wounds in the chest – I'll be able to tell you more about them after I've made the post-mortem, but I should think any one of them might have been fatal. Slight contusions on the throat. She hasn't been dead much more than an hour.'

He stood glancing curiously over the other faces.

'Where's the ambulance?' said the sergeant grumpily.

'They've probably gone to the house,' said the girl. 'I'll send them down if I see them – you don't want us getting in your way any more, do you?'

'No, miss. This isn't very pleasant for you, I suppose. If I want any more information I'll come up and see you in the morning. Will Mr. Forrest be there if we want to see him?'

Forrest took a half step forward.

'Wait a minute,' he blurted. 'You haven't—'

'They aren't suspicious of you, Jim,' said the girl with a quiet firmness. 'They might just want to ask some more questions.'

'But you haven't said anything about Templar's—'

'Of course.' The girl's interruption was even firmer. Her voice was still quiet and natural, but the undercurrent of determined warning in it was as plain as a siren to the Saint's ears. 'I know we owe Mr. Templar an apology, but we don't have to waste Sergeant Jesser's time with it. Perhaps he'd like to come up to the house with us and have a drink – that is, if you don't need him any more, Sergeant.'

Her glance only released the young man's eye after it had pinned him to perplexed and scowling silence. And once again Simon felt that premonitory crisping of his nerves.

'All this excitement certainly does dry out the tonsils,' he remarked easily. 'But if Sergeant Jesser wants me to stay. . . .'

'No sir.' The reply was calm and ponderous. 'I've made a note of your address, and I don't think you could run away. Are you going home tonight?'

'You might try the Bell first, in case we decide to stop over.'

Simon buttoned his coat and strolled toward the door with the others; but as they reached it he stopped and turned back.

'By the way,' he said blandly, 'do you mind if we take our lawful artillery?'

The sergeant gazed at him and dug the guns slowly out of his pocket. Simon handed one of them to Mr. Uniatz and leisurely fitted his own automatic back into the spring holster under his arm. His smile was very slight.

'Since there still seems to be a murderer at large in the neighborhood,' he said, 'I'd like to be ready for him.'

As he followed Rosemary Chase and Jim Forrest up a narrow footpath away from the river, with Hoppy Uniatz beside him and the butler bringing up the rear, he grinned inwardly over that delicately pointed line and wondered whether it had gone home where he intended it to go. Since his back had been turned to the real audience, he had been unable to observe their reaction; and now their backs were turned to him in an equally uninformative reversal. Neither of them said a word on the way, and Simon placidly left the silence to get tired of itself. But his thoughts were very busy as he sauntered after them along the winding path and saw the lighted windows of a house looming up through the thinning trees that had hidden it from the riverbank. This, he realised with a jolt, must be the New Manor, and therefore the boathouse where Nora Prescott had been murdered was presumably a part of Marvin Chase's property. It made no difference to the facts, but the web of riddles seemed to draw tighter around him. . . .

They crossed a lawn and mounted some steps to a flagged terrace. Rosemary Chase led them through open french windows into an inoffensively furnished drawing room, and the butler closed the windows behind him as he followed. Forrest threw himself sulkily into an armchair, but the girl had regained a composure that was just a fraction too detailed to be natural.

'What kind of drinks would you like?' she asked.

'Beer for me,' said the Saint with the same studied urbanity. 'Scotch for Hoppy. I'm afraid I should have warned you about him – he likes to have his own bottle. We're trying to wean him, but it isn't going very well.'

The butler bowed and oozed out.

The girl took a cigarette from an antique lacquer box, and Simon stepped forward politely with his lighter. He had an absurd feeling of unreality about this new atmosphere that made it a little difficult to hide his sense of humour, but all his senses were vigilant. She was even lovelier than he had thought at first sight, he admitted to himself as he watched her face over the flame – it was hard to believe that she might be an accomplice to wilful and messy and apparently mercenary murder. But she and Forrest had certainly chosen a very dramatic moment to arrive. . . .

'It's nice of you to have us here,' he murmured, 'after the way we've behaved.'

'My father told me to bring you up,' she said. 'He seems to be quite an admirer of yours, and he was sure you couldn't have had anything to do with – with the murder.'

'I noticed – down in the boathouse – you knew my name,' said the Saint thoughtfully.

'Yes – the sergeant used it.'

Simon looked at the ceiling.

'Bright lads, these policemen, aren't they? I wonder how *he* knew?'

'From – your gun licence, I suppose.'

Simon nodded.

'Oh yes. But before that. I mean, I suppose he must have told your father who I was. Nobody else could have done it, could they?'

The girl reddened and lost her voice; but Forrest found his. He jerked himself angrily out of his chair.

'What's the use of all this beating about the bush, Rosemary?' he demanded impatiently. 'Why don't you tell him we know all about that letter that Nora wrote him?'

The door opened, and the butler came back with a tray of bottles and glasses and toured the room with them. There was a strained silence until he had gone again. Hoppy Uniatz stared at the newly opened bottle of whiskey which had been put down in front of him, with a rapt and menacing expression which indicated that his grey matter was in the throes of another paroxysm of Thought.

Simon raised his glass and gazed appreciatively at the sparkling brown clearness within it.

'All right,' he said. 'If you want it that way. So you knew Nora Prescott had written to me. You came to the Bell to see what happened. Probably you watched through the windows first; then when she went out, you came in to watch me. You followed one of us to the boathouse—'

'And we ought to have told the police—'

'Of course.' The Saint's voice was mild and friendly. 'You ought to have told them about the letter. I'm sure you could have quoted what was in it. Something about how she was being forced to help in putting over a gigantic fraud, and how she wanted me to help her. Sergeant Jesser would have been wild with excitement about that. Naturally he'd've seen at once that that provided an obvious motive for me to murder her, and none at all for the guy whose fraud was going to be given away. It really was pretty noble of you both to take so much trouble to keep me out of suspicion, and I appreciate it a lot. And now that we're all pals together, and there aren't any policemen in the audience, why don't you save me a lot of headaches and tell me what the swindle is?'

The girl stared at him.

'Do you know what you're saying?'

'I usually have a rough idea,' said the Saint coolly and deliberately. 'I'll make it even plainer, if that's too subtle for you. Your father's a millionaire, they tell me. And when there are any gigantic frauds in the wind, I never expect to find the Big Shot sitting in a garret toasting kippers over a candle.'

Forrest started toward him.

'Look here, Templar, we've stood about enough from you—'

'And I've stood plenty from you,' said the Saint without moving. 'Let's call it quits. We were both misunderstanding each other at the beginning, but we don't have to go on doing it. I can't do anything for you if you don't put your cards on the table. Let's straighten it out now. Which of you two cooled off Nora Prescott?'

He didn't seem to change his voice, but the question came with a sharp stinging clarity like the flick of a whip. Rosemary Chase and the young man gaped at him frozenly, and he waited for an answer without a shift of his lazily negligent eyes. But he didn't get it.

The rattle of the door handle made everyone turn, almost in relief at the interruption. A tall cadaverous man, severely dressed in a dark suit and high old-fashioned collar, his chin bordered with a rim of black beard, pince-nez on a loop of black ribbon in his hand, came into the room and paused hesitantly.

Rosemary Chase came slowly out of her trance.

'Oh, Doctor Quintus,' she said in a quiet forced voice. 'This is Mr. Templar and . . . er. . . .'

'Hoppy Uniatz,' Simon supplied.

Dr. Quintus bowed; and his black sunken eyes clung for a moment to the Saint's face.

'Delighted,' he said in a deep burring bass; and turned back to the girl. 'Miss Chase, I'm afraid the shock has upset your father a little. Nothing at all serious, I assure you, but I think it would be unwise for him to have any more excitement just yet. However, he asked me to invite Mr. Templar to stay for dinner. Perhaps later . . .'

Simon took another sip at his beer, and his glance swung idly over to the girl with the first glint of a frosty sparkle in its depths.

'We'd be delighted,' he said deprecatingly. 'If Miss Chase doesn't object. . . .'

'Why, of course not.' Her voice was only the minutest shred of a decibel out of key. 'We'd love to have you stay.'

The Saint smiled his courteous acceptance, ignoring the wrathful half movement that made Forrest's attitude rudely obvious. He would have stayed anyway, whoever had objected. It was just dawning on him that out of the whole fishy setup, Marvin Chase was the one man he had still to meet.

VI

'Boss,' said Mr. Uniatz, rising to his feet with an air of firm decision, 'should I go to de terlet?'

It was not possible for Simon to pretend that he didn't know him; nor could he take refuge in temporary deafness. Mr. Uniatz' penetrating accents were too peremptory for that to have been convincing. Simon swallowed, and took hold of himself with the strength of despair.

'I don't know, Hoppy,' he said bravely. 'How do you feel?'

'I feel fine, boss. I just t'ought it might be a good place.'

'It might be,' Simon conceded feverishly.

'Dat was a swell idea of yours, boss,' said Mr. Uniatz, hitching up his bottle.

Simon took hold of the back of a chair for support.

'Oh, not at all,' he said faintly. 'It's nothing to do with me.'

Hoppy looked puzzled.

'Sure, you t'ought of it foist, boss,' he insisted generously. 'Ya said to me, de nex time I should take de bottle away someplace an' lock myself up wit' it. So I t'ought I might take dis one in de terlet. I just t'ought it might be a good place,' said Mr. Uniatz, rounding off the résumé of his train of thought.

'Sit down!' said the Saint with paralysing ferocity.

Mr. Uniatz lowered himself back onto his hams with an expression of pained mystification, and Simon turned to the others.

'Excuse us, won't you?' he said brightly. 'Hoppy's made a sort of bet with himself about something, and he has a rather one-track mind.'

Forrest glared at him coldly. Rosemary half put on a gracious smile, and took it off again. Dr. Quintus almost bowed, with his mouth open. There was a lot of silence, in which Simon could feel the air prickling with pardonable speculations on his sanity. Every other reaction that he had been deliberately building up to provoke had had time to disperse itself under cover of the two consecutive interruptions. The spell was shattered, and he was back again where he began. He knew it, and resignedly slid into small talk that might yet lead to another opening.

'I heard that your father had a nasty motor accident, Miss Chase,' he said.

'Yes.'

The brief monosyllable offered nothing but the baldest affirmation; but her eyes were fixed on him with an expression that he tried unavailingly to read.

'I hope he wasn't badly hurt.'

'Quite badly burned,' rumbled the doctor. 'The car caught fire, you know. But fortunately his life isn't in danger. In fact, he would probably have escaped with nothing worse than a few bruises if he hadn't made such heroic efforts to save his secretary, who was trapped in the wreckage.'

'I read something about it,' lied the Saint. 'He was burned to death, wasn't he? What was his name, now?'

'Bertrand Tamblin.'

'Oh yes. Of course.'

Simon took a cigarette from his case and lighted it. He looked at the girl. His brain was still working at fighting pitch; but his manner was quite casual and disarming now – the unruffled conversational manner of an accepted friend discussing a minor matter of mutual interest.

'I just remembered something you said to the sergeant a little while ago, Miss Chase – about your having noticed that Nora Prescott seemed to be rather under a strain since Tamblin was killed.'

She looked back at him steadily, neither denying it nor encouraging him.

He said in the same sensible and persuasive way: 'I was wondering whether you'd noticed them being particularly friendly before the accident – as if there was any kind of attachment between them.'

He saw that the eyes of both Forrest and Dr. Quintus turned toward the girl, as if they both had an unexpectedly intense interest in her answer. But she looked at neither of them.

'I can't be sure,' she answered, as though choosing her words carefully. 'Their work brought them together all the time, of course. Mr. Tamblin was really Father's private secretary and almost his other self, and when Nora came to us she worked for Mr. Tamblin nearly as much as Father. I thought sometimes that Mr. Tamblin was – well, quite keen on her – but I don't know whether she responded. Of course I didn't ask her.'

'You don't happen to have a picture of Tamblin, do you?'

'I think there's a snapshot somewhere. . . .'

She stood up and went over to an inlaid writing table and rummaged in the drawer. It might have seemed fantastic that she should do that, obeying the Saint's suggestion as if he had hypnotized her; but Simon knew just how deftly he had gathered up the threads of his broken dominance and woven them into a new pattern. If the scene had to be played in that key, it suited him as well as any other. And with that key established, such an ordinary and natural request as he had made could not be refused. But he noticed that Dr. Quintus followed her with his hollow black eyes all the way across the room.

'Here.'

She gave Simon a commonplace Kodak print that showed two men standing on the steps of a house. One of them was apparently of medium height, a little flabby, grey-haired in the small areas of his head where he was not bald. The other was a trifle shorter and leaner, with thick smooth black hair and metal-rimmed glasses.

The Saint touched his forefinger on the picture of the older man.

'Your father?'

'Yes.'

It was a face without any outstanding features, creased in a tolerant if somewhat calculating smile. But Simon knew how deceptive a face could be, particularly in that kind of reproduction.

And the first thought that was thrusting itself forward in his mind was that there were two people dead, not only one – two people who had held similar and closely associated jobs, who from the very nature of their employment must have shared a good deal of Marvin Chase's confidence and known practically everything about his affairs, two people who must have known more about the intricate details of his business life than anyone else around him. One question clanged in the Saint's head like a deep jarring bell: Was Nora Prescott's killing the first murder to which that unknown swindle had led, or the second?

All through dinner his brain echoed the complex repercussions of that explosive idea, under the screen of superficial conversation which lasted through the meal. It gave that part of the evening a macabre spookiness. Hoppy Uniatz, hurt and frustrated, toyed halfheartedly with his food, which is to say that he did not ask for more than two helpings of any one dish. From time to time he washed down a mouthful with a gulp from the bottle which he had brought in with him, and put it down again to leer at it malevolently, as if it had personally welshed on him; Simon watched him anxiously when he seemed to lean perilously close to the candles which lighted the table, thinking that it would not take much to cause his breath to ignite and burn with a blue flame. Forrest had given up his efforts to protest at the whole procedure. He ate most of the time in sulky silence, and when he spoke at all he made a point of turning as much of his back to the Saint as his place at the table allowed: plainly he had made up his mind that Simon Templar was a cad on whom good manners would be wasted. Rosemary Chase talked very little, but she spoke to the Saint when she spoke at all, and she was watching him all the time with enigmatic intentness. Dr. Quintus was the only one who helped to shoulder the burden of maintaining an exchange of urbane trivialities. His reverberant basso bumbled obligingly into every conversational opening, and said nothing that was worth remembering. His eyes were like pools of basalt at the bottom of dry caverns, never altering their expression, and yet always moving, slowly, in a way that seemed to keep everyone under ceaseless surveillance.

Simon chatted genially and emptily, with faintly mocking calm. He had shown his claws once, and now it was up to the other side to take up the challenge in their own way. The one thing they could not possibly do was ignore it, and he was ready to wait with timeless patience for their lead. Under his pose of idle carelessness he was like an arrow on a drawn bow with ghostly fingers balancing the string.

Forrest excused himself as they left the dining room. Quintus came as far as the drawing room but didn't sit down. He pulled out a large gold watch and consulted it with impressive deliberation.

'I'd better have another look at the patient,' he said. 'He may have settled down again by now.'

The door closed behind him.

Simon leaned himself against the mantelpiece. Except for the presence of Mr. Uniatz, who in those circumstances was no more obtrusive than a piece of primitive furniture, he was alone with Rosemary Chase for the first time since so many things had begun to happen. And he knew that she was also aware of it.

She kept her face averted from his tranquil gaze, taking out a cigarette and lighting it for herself with impersonal unapproachability, while he waited. And then suddenly she turned on him as if her own restraint had defeated itself.

'Well?' she said with self-consciously harsh defiance. 'What are you thinking, after all this time?'

The Saint looked her in the eyes. His own voice was contrastingly even and unaggressive.

'Thinking,' he said, 'that you're either a very dangerous crook or just a plain damn fool. But hoping you're just the plain damn fool. And hoping that if that's the answer, it won't be much longer before your brain starts working again.'

'You hate crooks, don't you?'

'Yes.'

'I've heard about you,' she said. 'You don't care what you do to anyone you think is a crook. You've even – killed them.'

'I've killed rats,' he said. 'And I'll probably do it again. It's the only treatment that's any good for what they've got.'

'Always?'

Simon shrugged.

'Listen,' he said, not unkindly. 'If you want to talk theories we can have a lot of fun, but we shan't get very far. If you want me to admit that there are exceptions to my idea of justice, you can take it as admitted; but we can't go on from there without getting down to cases. I can tell you this, though. I've heard that there's something crooked being put over here, and from what's happened since it seems to be true. I'm going to find out what the swindle is and break it up if it takes fifty years. Only it won't take me nearly as long as that. Now if you know something that you're afraid to tell me because of what it might make me do to you or somebody else who matters to you, all I can say is that it'll probably be a lot worse if I have to dig it out for myself. Is that any use?'

She moved closer toward him, her brown eyes searching his face.

'I wish—'

It was all she had time to say. The rush of sounds that cut her off hit both of them at the same time, muffled by distance and the closed door of the room, and yet horribly distinct, stiffening them both together as though they had been clutched by invisible clammy tentacles. A shrill incoherent yell, hysterical with terror but unmistakably masculine. A heavy thud. A wild shout of *'Help!'* in the doctor's deep thundery voice. And then a ghastly inhuman wailing gurgle that choked off into deathly silence.

VII

Balanced on a knife edge of uncanny self-control, the Saint stood motionless, watching the girl's expression for a full long second before she turned away with a gasp and rushed at the door. Hoppy Uniatz flung himself after her like a wild bull awakened from slumber: he could have remained comatose through eons of verbal fencing, but this was a call to action, clear and unsullied, and such simple clarions had never found him unresponsive. Simon started the thin edge of an instant later than either of them; but it was his hand that reached the doorknob first.

He threw the door wide and stepped out with a smooth combination of movements that brought him through the opening with a gun in his hand and his eyes streaking over the entire scene outside in one whirling survey. But the hall was empty. At the left and across from him, the front door was closed; at the opposite end a door which obviously communicated with the service wing of the house was thrown open to disclose the portly emerging figure of the butler with the white frightened faces of other servants peering from behind him.

The Saint's glance swept on upwards. The noises that had brought him out had come from upstairs, he was certain: that was also the most likely place for them to have come from, and it was only habitual caution that had made him pause to scan the hall as he reached it. He caught the girl's arm as she came by him.

'Let me go up first,' he said. He blocked Hoppy's path on his other side, and shot a question across at the butler without raising his voice. 'Are there any other stairs, Jeeves?'

'Y-yes sir—'

'All right. You stay here with Miss Chase. Hoppy, you find these back stairs and cover them.'

He raced on up the main stairway.

As he took the treads three at a time, on his toes, he was trying to find a niche for one fact of remarkable interest. Unless Rosemary Chase was the greatest natural actress that a generation of talent scouts had overlooked, or unless his own judgment had gone completely cockeyed, the interruption had hit her with the same chilling shock as it had given him. It was to learn that that he had stayed to study her face before he moved: he was sure that he would have caught any shadow of deception, and yet if there had really been no shadow there to catch it meant that something had happened for which she was totally unprepared. And that in its turn might mean that all his suspicions of her were without foundation. It gave a jolt to the theories he had begun to put together that threw them into new and fascinating outlines, and he reached the top of the stairs with a glint of purely speculative delight shifting from the grim alertness of his eyes.

From the head of the staircase the landing opened off in the shape of a squat long-armed T. All the doors that he saw at first were closed; he strode lightly to the junction of the two arms, and heard a faint movement down the left-hand corridor. Simon took a breath and jumped out on a quick slant that would have been highly disconcerting to any marksman who might have been waiting for him round the corner. But there was no marksman.

The figures of two men were piled together on the floor, in the middle of a sickening mess; and only one of them moved.

The one who moved was Dr. Quintus, who was groggily trying to scramble up to his feet as the Saint reached him. The one who lay still was Jim Forrest; and Simon did not need to look at him twice to see that his stillness was permanent. The mess was blood – pools and gouts and splashes of blood, in hideous quantity, puddling on the floor, dripping down the walls, soddening the striped blazer and mottling the doctor's clothes. The gaping slash that split Forrest's throat from ear to ear had almost decapitated him.

The Saint's stomach turned over once. Then he was grasping the doctor's arm and helping him up. There was so much blood on him that Simon couldn't tell what his injuries might be.

'Where are you hurt?' he snapped.

The other shook his head muzzily. His weight was leaden on Simon's supporting grip.

'Not me,' he mumbled hoarsely. 'All right. Only hit me – on the head. Forrest—'

'Who did it?'

'Dunno. Probably same as – Nora. Heard Forrest . . . yell. . . .'

'Where did he go?'

Quintus seemed to be in a daze through which outside promptings only reached him in the same form as outside noises reach the brain of a sleepwalker. He seemed to be making a tremendous effort to retain some sort of consciousness, but his eyes were half closed and his words were thick and rambling, as if he were dead drunk.

'Suppose Forrest was – going to his room – for something. . . . Caught murderer – sneaking about. . . . Murderer – stabbed him. . . . I heard him yell. . . . Rushed out. . . . Got hit with – something. . . . Be all right – soon. Catch him—'

'Well, where did he go?'

Simon shook him, roughly slapped up the sagging head. The doctor's chest heaved as though it were taking part in his terrific struggle to achieve coherence. He got his eyes wide open.

'Don't worry about me,' he whispered with painful clarity. 'Look after – Mr. Chase.'

His eyelids fluttered again.

Simon let him go against the wall, and he slid down almost to a sitting position, clasping his head in his hands.

The Saint balanced his Luger in his hand, and his eyes were narrowed to chips of sapphire hardness. He glanced up and down the corridor. From where he stood he could see the length of both passages which formed the arms of the T-plan of the landing. The arm on his right finished with a glimpse of the banisters of a staircase leading down – obviously the back stairs whose existence the butler had admitted, at the foot of which Hoppy Uniatz must already have taken up his post. But there had been no sound of disturbance from that direction. Nor had there been any sound from the front hall where he had left Rosemary Chase with the butler. And there was no other normal way out for anyone who was upstairs. The left-hand corridor, where he stood, ended in a blank wall; and only one door along it was open.

Simon stepped past the doctor and over Forrest's body, and went silently to the open door.

He came to it without any of the precautions that he had taken before exposing himself a few moments before. He had a presentiment amounting to conviction that they were unnecessary now. He remembered with curious distinctness that the drawing-room curtains had not been drawn since he entered the house. Therefore anyone who wanted to could have shot at him from outside long ago. No one had shot at him. Therefore. . . .

He was looking into a large white-painted airy bedroom. The big double bed was empty, but the covers were thrown open and rumpled. The table beside it was loaded with medicine bottles. He opened the doors in the two side walls. One belonged to a spacious built-in cupboard filled with clothing; the other was a bathroom. The wall opposite the entrance door was broken by long casement windows, most of them wide open. He crossed over to one of them and looked out. Directly beneath him was the flat roof of a porch.

The Saint put his gun back in its holster and felt an unearthly cold dry calm sinking through him. Then he climbed out over the sill onto the porch roof below, which almost formed a kind of blind balcony under the window. He stood there recklessly, knowing that he was silhouetted against the light behind, and lighted a cigarette with leisured, tremorless hands. He sent a cloud of blue vapor drifting toward the stars; and then with the same leisured passivity he sauntered to the edge of the balustrade, sat on it and swung his legs over. From there it was an easy drop onto the parapet which bordered the terrace along the front of the house, and an even easier drop from the top of the parapet to the ground. To an active man the return journey would not present much more difficulty.

He paused long enough to draw another lungful of night air and tobacco smoke, and then strolled on along the terrace. It was an eerie experience, to know that he was an easy target every time he passed a lighted window, to remember that the killer might be watching him from a few yards away, and still to hold his steps down to the same steady pace; but the Saint's nerves were hardened to an icy quietness, and all his senses were working together in taut-strung vigilance.

He walked three quarters of the way round the building and arrived at the back door. It was unlocked when he tried it; and he pushed it open and looked down the barrel of Mr. Uniatz' Betsy.

'I bet you'll shoot somebody one of these days, Hoppy,' he remarked; and Mr. Uniatz lowered the gun with a faint tinge of disappointment.

'What ya find, boss?'

'Quite a few jolly and interesting things.' The Saint was only smiling with his lips. 'Hold the fort a bit longer, and I'll tell you.'

He found his way through the kitchen, where the other servants were clustered together in dumb and terrified silence, back to the front hall where Rosemary Chase and the butler were standing together at the foot of the stairs. They jumped as if a gun had been fired when they heard his footsteps; and then the girl ran toward him and caught him by the lapels of his coat.

'What is it?' she pleaded frantically. 'What happened?'

'I'm sorry,' he said as gently as he could.

She stared at him. He meant her to read his face for everything except the fact that he was still watching her like a spectator on the dark side of the footlights.

'Where's Jim?'

He didn't answer.

She caught her breath suddenly with a kind of sob, and turned toward the stairs. He grabbed her elbows and turned her back and held her.

'I wouldn't go up,' he said evenly. 'It wouldn't do any good.'

'Tell me, then. For God's sake, tell me! Is he' – she choked on the word – 'dead?'

'Jim, yes.'

Her face was whiter than chalk, but she kept her feet. Her eyes dragged at his knowledge through a brightness of unheeded tears.

'Why do you say it like that? What else is there?'

'Your father seems to have disappeared,' he said, and held her as she went limp in his arms.

VIII

Simon carried her into the drawing room and laid her down on a sofa. He stood gazing at her introspectively for a moment; then he bent over her again quickly and stabbed her in the solar plexus with a stiff forefinger. She didn't stir a muscle.

The monotonous *cheep-cheep* of a telephone bell ringing somewhere outside reached his ears, and he saw the butler starting to move mechanically toward the door. Simon passed him and saw the instrument half hidden by a curtain on the other side of the hall. He took the receiver off the hook and said: 'Hullo.'

'May I speak to Mr. Templar, please?'

The Saint put a hand on the wall to save himself from falling over.

'Who wants him?'

'Mr. Trapani.'

'Giulio!' Simon exclaimed. The voice was familiar now, but its complete unexpectedness had prevented him from recognizing it before. 'It seems to be about sixteen years since I saw you – and I never came back for dinner.'

'That's quite all right, Mr. Templar. I didn't expect you, when I knew what had happened. I only called up now because it's getting late and I didn't know if you would want a room for tonight.'

The Saint's brows drew together.

'What the hell is this?' he demanded slowly. 'Have you taken up crystal gazing or something?'

Giulio Trapani chuckled.

'No, I am not any good at that. The police sergeant stopped here on his way back, and he told me. He said you had got mixed up with a murder, and

Miss Chase had taken you home with her. So of course I knew you would be very busy. Has she asked you to stay?'

'Let me call you back in a few minutes, Giulio,' said the Saint. 'Things have been happening, and I've got to get hold of the police again.' He paused, and a thought struck him. 'Look, is Sergeant Jesser still there, by any chance?'

There was no answer.

Simon barked: 'Hullo.'

Silence. He jiggled the hook. The movements produced no corresponding clicks in his ear. He waited a moment longer, while he realized that the stillness of the receiver was not the stillness of a broken connection, but a complete inanimate muteness that stood for something less easily remedied than that.

He hung the receiver up and traced the course of the wiring with his eyes. It ran along the edge of the wainscoting to the frame of the front door and disappeared into a hole bored at the edge of the wood. Simon turned right round with another abrupt realization. He was alone in the hall – the butler was no longer in sight.

He slipped his pencil flashlight out of his breast pocket with his left hand and let himself out of the front door. The telephone wires ran up outside along the margin of the door frame and continued up over the exterior wall. The beam of his torch followed them up, past a lighted window over the porch from which he had climbed down a few minutes ago, to where they were attached to a pair of porcelain insulators under the eaves. Where the wires leading on from the insulators might once have gone was difficult to decide: they dangled slackly downwards now, straddling the balcony and trailing away into the darkness of the drive.

The Saint switched off his light and stood motionless. Then he flitted across the terrace, crossed the drive and merged himself into the shadow of a big clump of laurels on the edge of the lawn. Again he froze into breathless immobility. The blackness ahead of him was stygian, impenetrable, even to his noctambulant eyes, but hearing would serve his temporary purpose almost as well as sight. The night had fallen so still that he could even hear the rustle of the distant river; and he waited for minutes that seemed like hours to him, and must have seemed like weeks to a guilty prowler who could not have travelled very far after the wires were broken. And while he waited, he was trying to decide at exactly what point in his last speech the break had occurred. It could easily have happened at a place where Trapani would think he had finished and rung off. . . . But he heard nothing while he stood there – not a snap of a twig or the rustle of a leaf.

He went back to the drawing room and found the butler standing there, wringing his hands in a helpless sort of way.

'Where have you been?' he inquired coldly.

The man's loose bloodhound jowls wobbled.

'I went to fetch my wife, sir.' He indicated the stout red-faced woman who was kneeling beside the couch, chafing the girl's nerveless wrists. 'To see if she could help Miss Chase.'

Simon's glance flickered over the room like a rapier blade and settled pricklingly on an open french window.

'Did you have to fetch her in from the garden?' he asked sympathetically.

'I – I don't understand, sir.'

'Don't you? Neither do I. But that window was closed when I saw it last.'

'I opened it just now, sir, to give Miss Chase some fresh air.'

The Saint held his eyes ruthlessly, but the butler did not try to look away.

'All right,' he said at length. 'We'll check up on that presently. Just for the moment, you can both go back to the kitchen.'

The stout woman got to her feet with the laboured motions of a rheumatic camel.

''Oo do you think you are,' she demanded indignantly, 'to be bossing everybody about in his 'ouse?'

'I am the Grand Gugnune of Waziristan,' answered the Saint pleasantly. 'And I said – get back to the kitchen.'

He followed them back himself and went on through to find Hoppy Uniatz. The other door of the kitchen conveniently opened into the small rear hall into which the back stairs came down and from which the back door also opened. Simon locked and bolted the back door and drew Hoppy into the kitchen doorway and propped him up against the jamb.

'If you stand here,' he said, 'you'll be able to cover the back stairs and this gang in the kitchen at the same time. And that's what I want you to do. None of them is to move out of your sight – not even to get somebody else some fresh air.'

'Okay, boss,' said Mr. Uniatz dimly. 'If I only had a drink—'

'Tell Jeeves to buy you one.'

The Saint was on his way out again when the butler stopped him.

'Please, sir, I'm sure I could be of some use—'

'You are being useful,' said the Saint and closed the door on him.

Rosemary Chase was sitting up when he returned to the drawing room.

'I'm sorry,' she said weakly. 'I'm afraid I fainted.'

'I'm afraid you did,' said the Saint. 'I poked you in the tummy to make sure it was real, and it was. It looks as if I've been wrong about you all the evening. I've got a lot of apologies to make, and you'll have to imagine most of them. Would you like a drink?'

She nodded; and he turned to the table and operated with a bottle and siphon. While he was doing it, he said with matter-of-fact naturalness: 'How many servants do you keep here?'

'The butler and his wife, a housemaid and a parlourmaid.'

'Then they're all rounded up and accounted for. How long have you known them?'

'Only about three weeks – since we've been here.'

'So that means nothing. I should have had them corralled before, but I didn't think fast enough.' He brought the drink over and gave it to her. 'Anyway, they're corralled now, under Hoppy's thirsty eye, so if anything else happens we'll know they didn't have anything to do with it. If that's any help. . . . Which leaves only us – and Quintus.'

'What happened to him?'

'He said he got whacked on the head by our roving bogeyman.'

'Hadn't you better look after him?'

'Sure. In a minute.'

Simon crossed the room and closed the open window and drew the curtains. He came back and stood by the table to light a cigarette. There had been so much essential activity during the past few minutes that he had had no time to do any constructive thinking; but now he had to get every possible blank filled in before the next move was made. He put his lighter away and studied her with cool and friendly encouragement, as if they had a couple of years to spare in which to straighten out misunderstandings.

She sipped her drink and looked up at him with dark stricken eyes from which, he knew, all pretence and concealment had now been wiped away. They were eyes that he would have liked to see without the grief in them; and the pallor of her face made him remember its loveliness as he had first seen it. Her red lips formed bitter words without flinching.

'I'm the one who ought to have been killed. If I hadn't been such a fool this might never have happened. I ought to be thrown in the river with a weight round my neck. Why don't you say so?'

'That wouldn't be any use now,' he said. 'I'd rather you made up for it. Give me the story.'

She brushed the hair off her forehead with a weary gesture.

'The trouble is – I can't. There isn't any story that's worth telling. Just that I was – trying to be clever. It all began when I read a letter that I hadn't any right to read. It was in this room. I'd been out. I came in through the french windows, and I sat down at the desk because I'd just remembered something I had to make a note of. The letter was on the blotter in front of me – the letter you got. Nora must have just finished it, and then left the room for a moment, just before I came in, not thinking anyone else would be around. I saw your name on it. I'd heard of you, of course. It startled me so much that I was reading on before I knew what I was doing. And then I couldn't stop. I read it all. Then I heard Nora coming back. I lost my head and slipped out through the window again without her seeing me.'

'And you never spoke to her about it?'

'I couldn't – later. After all that, I couldn't sort of come out and confess that I'd read it. Oh, I know I was a damn fool. But I was scared. It seemed as if she must know something dreadful that my father was involved in. I didn't know anything about his affairs. But I loved him. If he was doing something crooked, whatever it was, I'd have been hurt to death; but still I wanted to try and protect him. I couldn't talk about it to anybody but Jim. We decided the only thing was to find out what it was all about. That's why we followed Nora to the Bell, and then followed you to the boathouse.'

'Why didn't you tell me this before?'

She shrugged hopelessly.

'Because I was afraid to. You remember I asked you about how much you hated crooks? I was afraid that if my father was mixed up in – anything wrong – you'd be even more merciless than the police. I wanted to save him. But I didn't think – all this would happen. It was hard enough not to say anything when we found Nora dead. Now that Jim's been killed, I can't go on with it any more.'

The Saint was silent for a moment, weighing her with his eyes; and then he said: 'What do you know about this guy Quintus?'

IX

'Hardly anything,' she said. 'He happened to be living close to where the accident happened, and Father was taken to his house. Father took such a fancy to him that when they brought him home he insisted on bringing Doctor Quintus along to look after him – at least, that's what I was told. I know what you're thinking.' She looked at him steadily. 'You think there's something funny about him.'

'"Phony" is the way I pronounce it,' answered the Saint bluntly.

She nodded.

'I wondered about him too – after I read that letter. But how could I say anything?'

'Can you think of anything that might have given him a hold over your father?'

She moved her hands desperately.

'How could I know? Father never talked business at home. I never heard anything – discreditable about him. But how could I know?'

'You've seen your father since he was brought home?'

'Of course. Lots of times.'

'Did he seem to have anything on his mind?'

'I can't tell—'

'Did he seem to be worried or frightened?'

'It's so *hard*,' she said. 'I don't know what I really saw and what I'm making myself imagine. He was badly hurt, you know, and he was still trying to keep some of his business affairs going, so that took a lot out of him, and Doctor Quintus never let me stay with him very long at a time. And then he didn't feel like talking much. Of course he seemed shaky, and not a bit like himself; but after an accident like that you wouldn't expect anything else. . . .

I don't know what to think about anything. I thought he always liked Jim, and now— Oh, God, what a mess I've made!'

The Saint smoothed the end of his cigarette in an ash tray, and there was an odd kind of final contentment in his eyes. All the threads were in his hands now, all the questions answered – except for the one answer that would cover all the others. Being as he was, he could understand Rosemary Chase's story, forgetting the way it had ended. Others might have found it harder to forgive; but to him it was just the old tale of amateur adventuring leading to tragic disaster. And even though his own amateur adventures had never led there, they were still close enough for him to realise the hairbreadth margin by which they had escaped it. . . . And the story she told him gathered up many loose ends.

He sat down beside her and put his hand on her arm.

'Don't blame yourself too much about Jim,' he said steadyingly. 'He made some of the mess himself. If he hadn't thrown me off the track by the way he behaved, things might have been a lot different. Why the hell did he have to do that?'

'He'd made up his mind that you'd only come into this for what you could get out of it – that if you found out what Nora knew, you'd use it to blackmail Father, or something like that. He wasn't terribly clever. I suppose he thought you'd killed her to keep the information to yourself—'

The Saint shrugged wryly.

'And I thought one of you had killed her to keep her mouth shut. None of us has been very clever – yet.'

'What are we going to do?' she said.

Simon thought. And he may have been about to answer when his ears caught a sound that stopped him. His fingers tightened on the girl's wrist for an instant, while his eyes rested on her like bright steel; and then he got up.

'Give me another chance,' he said in a soft voice that could not even have been heard across the room.

And then he was walking across to greet the doctor as the footsteps that had stopped him arrived at the door and Quintus came in.

'Doctor Quintus!' The Saint's air was sympathetic, his face full of concern. He took the doctor's arm. 'You shouldn't have come down alone. I was just coming back for you, but there've been so many other things—'

'I know. And they were probably more valuable than anything you could have done for me.'

The blurry resonance of the other's voice was nearly normal again. He moved firmly over to the table on which the tray of drinks stood.

'I'm going to prescribe myself a whiskey and soda,' he said.

Simon fixed it for him. Quintus took the glass and sat down gratefully on the edge of a chair. He rubbed a hand over his dishevelled head as though trying to clear away the lingering remnants of fog. He had washed his face and hands, but the darkening patches of red stain on his clothing were still gruesome reminders of the man who had not come down.

'I'm sorry I was so useless, Mr. Templar,' he said heavily. 'Did you find anything?'

'Not a thing.' The Saint's straightforwardness sounded completely ingenuous. 'Mr. Chase must have been taken out of the window – I climbed down from there myself, and it was quite easy. I walked most of the way round the house, and nothing happened. I didn't hear a sound, and it was too dark to see anything.'

Quintus looked across at the girl.

'There isn't anything I can say, Miss Chase. I can only tell you that I would have given my own right hand to prevent this.'

'But *why?*' she said brokenly. 'Why are all these things happening? What is it all about? First Nora, and then – Jim. . . . And now my father. What's happened to him? What have they done with him?'

The doctor's lips tightened.

'Kidnapped, I suppose,' he said wretchedly. 'I suppose everything has been leading up to that. You father's a rich man. They'd expect him to be worth a large ransom – large enough to run any risks for. Jim's death was – well, just a tragic accident. He happened to run into one of them in the corridor, so he was murdered. If that hadn't confused them, they'd probably have murdered me.'

'They?' interposed the Saint quickly. 'You saw them, then.'

'Only one man, the one who hit me. He was rather small, and he had a handkerchief tied over his face. I didn't have a chance to notice much. I'm saying "they" because I don't see how one man alone could have organized and done all this. . . . It must be kidnapping. Possibly they were trying to force or bribe Nora to help them from the inside, and she was murdered because she threatened to give them away.'

'And they tried to kill me in case she had told me about the plot.'

'Exactly.'

Simon put down the stub of his cigarette and searched for a fresh one.

'Why do you think they should think she might have told me anything?' he inquired.

Quintus hesitated expressionlessly. He drank slowly from his glass and brought his cavernous black eyes back to the Saint's face.

'With your reputation – if you will forgive me – finding you on the scene . . . I'm only theorising, of course—'

Simon nodded good-humouredly.

'Don't apologize,' he murmured. 'My reputation is a great asset. It's made plenty of clever crooks lose their heads before this.'

'It *must* be kidnapping,' Quintus repeated, turning to the girl. 'If they'd wanted to harm your father, they could easily have done it in his bedroom when they had him at their mercy. They wouldn't have needed to take him away. You must be brave and think about that. The very fact that they took him away proves that they must want him alive.'

The Saint finished chain-lighting the fresh cigarette and strolled over to the fireplace to flick away the butt of the old one. He stood there for a moment, and then turned thoughtfully back to the room.

'Talking of this taking away,' he said, 'I did notice something screwy about it. I didn't waste much time getting upstairs after I heard the commotion. And starting from the same commotion, our kidnapping guy or guys had to dash into the bedroom, grab Mr. Chase, shove him out of the window and lower him to the ground. All of which must have taken a certain amount of time.' He looked at the doctor. 'Well, I wasted a certain amount of time myself in the corridor, finding out whether you were hurt, and so forth. So those times begin to cancel out. Then, when I got in the bedroom, I saw at once that the bed was empty. I looked in the cupboard and the bathroom, just making sure the old boy was really gone; but that can't have taken more than a few seconds. Then I went straight to the window. And then, almost immediately, I climbed out of it and climbed down to the ground to see if I could see anything, because I knew Marvin Chase could only have gone out that way. Now you remember what I told you? *I didn't hear a sound.* Not so much as the dropping of a pin.'

'What do you mean?' asked the girl.

'I mean this,' said the Saint. 'Figure out our timetable for yourselves – the kidnappers' and mine. They can't have been more than a few seconds ahead of me. And from below the window they had to get your father to a car, shove him in and take him away – *if they took him away*. But I told you! I walked all round the house, slowly, listening, and I didn't hear anything. When did they start making those completely noiseless cars?'

Quintus half rose from his chair.

'You mean – they might still be in the grounds? Then we're sure to catch them! As soon as the police get here – you've sent for them, of course?'

Simon shook his head.

'Not yet. And that's something else that makes me think I'm right. I haven't called the police yet because I can't. I can't call them because the telephone wires have been cut. And they were cut *after* all this had happened – after I'd walked round the house and come back in and told Rosemary what had happened!'

The girl's lips were parted, her wide eyes fastened on him with a mixture of fear and eagerness. She began to say: 'But they might—'

The crash stopped her.

Her eyes switched to the left, and Simon saw blank horror leap into her face as he whirled toward the sound. It had come from one of the windows, and it sounded like smashing glass. . . . It was the glass. He saw the stir of the curtains and the gloved hand that came between them under a shining gun barrel, and flung himself fiercely backwards.

X

He catapulted himself at the main electric-light switches beside the door – without conscious decision, but knowing that his instinct must be right. More slowly, while he was moving, his mind reasoned it out: the unknown man who had broken the window had already beaten him to the draw, and in an open gun battle with the lights on the unknown had a three-to-one edge in choice of targets. . . . Then the Saint's shoulder hit the wall, and his hand sliced up over the switches just as the invader's revolver spoke once, deafeningly.

Blam!

Simon heard the spang of the bullet some distance from him, and more glass shattered. Quintus gasped deeply. The Saint's ears sang with the concussion, but through the buzzing he was trying to determine whether the gunman had come in.

He moved sideways, noiselessly, crouching, his Luger out in his hand. Nothing else seemed to move. His brain was working again in a cold fever of precision. Unless the pot-shot artist had hoped to settle everything with the first bullet, he would expect the Saint to rush the window. Therefore the Saint would not rush the window. . . . The utter silence in the room was battering his brain with warnings.

His fingers touched the knob of the door, closed on it and turned it without a rattle until the latch disengaged. Gathering his muscles, he whipped it suddenly open, leapt through it out into the hall and slammed it behind him. In the one red-hot instant when he was clearly outlined against the lights of the hall, a second shot blasted out of the dark behind him and splintered the woodwork close to his shoulder; but his exposure was too swift and unexpected for the sniper's marksmanship. Without even looking back, Simon dived across the hall and let himself out the front door.

He raced around the side of the house and dropped to a crouch again as he reached the corner that would bring him in sight of the terrace outside the drawing-room windows. He slid an eye round the corner, prepared to yank it back on an instant's notice, and then left it there with the brow over it lowering in a frown.

It was dark on the terrace, but not too dark for him to see that there was no one standing there.

He scanned the darkness on his right, away from the house; but he could find nothing in it that resembled a lurking human shadow. And over the whole garden brooded the same eerie stillness, the same incredible absence of any hint of movement, that had sent feathery fingers creeping up his spine when he was out there before. . . .

The Saint eased himself along the terrace, flat against the wall of the house, his forefinger tight on the trigger and his eyes probing the blackness of the grounds. No more shots came at him. He reached the french windows with the broken pane, and stretched out a hand to test the handle. They wouldn't open. They were still fastened on the inside – as he had fastened them.

He spoke close to the broken pane.

'All clear, souls. Don't put the lights on yet, but let me in.'

Presently the window swung back. There were shutters outside, and he folded them across the opening and bolted them as he stepped in. Their hinges were stiff from long disuse. He did the same at the other window before he groped his way back to the door and relit the lights.

'We'll have this place looking like a fortress before we're through,' he remarked cheerfully; and then the girl ran to him and caught his sleeve.

'Didn't you see anyone?'

He shook his head.

'Not a soul. The guy didn't even open the window – just stuck his gun through the broken glass and sighted from outside. I have an idea he was expecting me to charge through the window after him, and then he'd 've had me cold. But I fooled him. I guess he heard me coming round the house, and took his feet off the ground.' He smiled at her reassuringly. 'Excuse me a minute while I peep at Hoppy – he might be worried.'

He should have known better than to succumb to that delusion. In the kitchen a trio of white-faced women and one man who was not much more sanguine jumped round with panicky squeals and goggling eyes as he entered; but Mr. Uniatz removed the bottle which he was holding to his lips with dawdling reluctance.

'Hi, boss,' said Mr. Uniatz with as much phlegmatic cordiality as could be expected of a man who had been interrupted in the middle of some important business; and the Saint regarded him with new respect.

'Doesn't anything ever worry you, Hoppy?' he inquired mildly.

Mr. Uniatz waved his bottle with liberal nonchalance.

'Sure, boss, I hear de firewoiks,' he said. 'But I figure if anyone is getting' hoit it's some udder guy. How are t'ings?'

'T'ings will be swell, so long as I know you're on the job,' said the Saint reverently, and withdrew again.

He went back to the drawing room with his hands in his pockets, not hurrying; and in spite of what had happened he felt more composed than he had been all the evening. It was as if he sensed that the crescendo was coming to a climax beyond which it could go no further, while all the time his own unravellings were simplifying the tangled undercurrents toward one final resolving chord that would bind them all together. And the two must coincide and blend. All he wanted was a few more minutes, a few more answers. . . . His smile was almost indecently carefree when he faced the girl again.

'All is well,' he reported, 'and I'm afraid Hoppy is ruining your cellar.'

She came up to him, her eyes searching him anxiously.

'That shot when you ran out,' she said. 'You aren't hurt?'

'Not a bit. But it's depressing to feel so unpopular.'

'What makes you think you're the only one who's unpopular?' asked the doctor dryly.

He was still sitting in the chair where Simon had left him, and Simon followed his glance as he screwed his neck round indicatively. Just over his left shoulder a picture on the wall had a dark-edged hole drilled in it, and the few scraps of glass that still clung to the frame formed a jagged circle around it.

The Saint gazed at the bullet scar, and for a number of seconds he said nothing. He had heard the impact, of course, and heard the tinkle of glass; but since the shot had missed him he hadn't given it another thought. Now that its direction was pointed out to him, the whole sequence of riddles seemed to fall into focus.

The chain of alibis was complete.

Anyone might have murdered Nora Prescott – even Rosemary Chase and Forrest. Rosemary Chase herself could have fired the shot at the boathouse, an instant before Forrest switched on his torch, and then rejoined him. But Forrest wasn't likely to have cut his own throat; and even if he had done that, he couldn't have abducted Marvin Chase afterwards. And when Forrest was killed, the Saint himself was Rosemary Chase's alibi. The butler might have done all these things; but after that he had been shut in the kitchen with Hoppy Uniatz to watch over him, so that the Saint's own precaution acquitted him of having fired those last two shots a few minutes ago. Dr. Quintus might have done everything else, might never have been hit on the head upstairs at all; but he certainly couldn't have fired those two shots either – and one of them had actually been aimed at him. Simon went back to his original position by the fireplace to make sure of it. The result didn't permit the faintest shadow of doubt. Even allowing for his dash to the doorway, if the first shot had been aimed at the Saint and had just missed Quintus instead, it must have been fired by someone who couldn't get within ten feet of the bull's-eye at ten yards range – an explanation that wasn't even worth considering.

And that left only one person who had never had an alibi – who had never been asked for one because he had never seemed to need one. The man around whom all the commotion was centred – and yet the one member of the cast, so far as the Saint was concerned, who had never yet appeared on the scene. Someone who, for all obvious purposes, might just as well have been nonexistent.

But if Marvin Chase himself had done all the wild things that had been done that night, it would mean that the story of his injuries must be entirely fictitious. And it was hardly plausible that any man would fabricate and elaborate such a story at a time when there was no conceivable advantage to be gained from it.

Simon thought about that, and everything in him seemed to be standing still.

The girl was saying: 'These people wouldn't be doing all this if they just wanted to kidnap my father. Unless they were maniacs. They can't get any ransom if they kill off everyone who's ever had anything to do with him, and that's what they seem to be trying to do—'

'Except you,' said the Saint, almost inattentively. 'You haven't been hurt yet.'

He was thinking: 'The accident happened a week ago – days before Nora Prescott wrote to me, before there was ever any reason to expect me on the scene. But all these things that a criminal might want an alibi for have happened *since* I came into the picture, and probably on my account. Marvin Chase might have been a swindler, and he might have rubbed out his secretary in a phony motor accident because he knew too much; but for all he could have known that would have been the end of it. He didn't need to pretend to be injured himself, and take the extra risk of ringing in a phony doctor to build up the atmosphere. Therefore he didn't invent his injuries. Therefore his alibi is as good as anyone else's. Therefore we're right back where we started.'

Or did it mean that he was at the very end of the hunt? In a kind of trance he walked over to the broken window and examined the edges of the smashed pane. On the point of one of the jags of glass clung a couple of kinky white threads – such as might have been ripped out of a gauze bandage. Coming into the train of thought that his mind was following, the realization of what they meant gave him hardly any sense of shock. He already knew that he was never going to meet Marvin Chase.

Dr. Quintus was getting to his feet.

'I'm feeling better now,' he said. 'I'll go for the police.'

'Just a minute,' said the Saint quietly. 'I think I can have someone ready for them to arrest when they get here.'

XI

He turned to the girl and took her shoulders in his hands.

'I'm sorry, Rosemary,' he said. 'You're going to be hurt now.'

Then, without stopping to face the bewildered fear that came into her eyes, he went to the door and raised his voice.

'Send the butler along, Hoppy. See that the curtains are drawn where you are, and keep an eye on the windows. If anyone tries to rush you from any direction, give 'em the heat first and ask questions afterwards.'

'Okay, boss,' replied Mr. Uniatz obediently.

The butler came down the hall as if he were walking on eggs. His impressively fleshy face was pallid and apprehensive, but he stood before the Saint with a certain ineradicable dignity.

'Yes sir?'

Simon beckoned him to the front door; and this time the Saint was very careful. He turned out all the hall lights before he opened the door, and then drew the butler quickly outside without fully closing it behind them. They stood where the shadow of the porch covered them in solid blackness.

'Jeeves,' he said, and in contrast with all that circumspection his voice was extraordinarily clear and carrying, 'I want you to go to the nearest house and use their phone to call the police station. Ask for Sergeant Jesser. I want you to give him a special message.'

'Me, sir?'

Simon couldn't see the other's face, but he could imagine the expression on it from the tremulous tone of the reply. He smiled to himself, but his eyes were busy on the dark void of the garden.

'Yes, you. Are you scared?'

'N-no sir. But—'

'I know what you mean. It's creepy, isn't it? I'd feel the same way myself. But don't let it get you down. Have you ever handled a gun?'

'I had a little experience during the war, sir.'

'Swell. Then here's a present for you.' Simon felt for the butler's flabby hand and pressed his own Luger into it. 'It's all loaded and ready to talk. If anything tries to happen, use it. And this is something else. I'll be with you. You won't hear me and you won't see me, but I'll be close by. If anyone tries to stop you or do anything to you, he'll get a nasty surprise. So don't worry. You're going to get through.'

He could hear the butler swallow.

'Very good, sir. What was the message you wished me to take?'

'It's for Sergeant Jesser,' Simon repeated with the same careful clarity. 'Tell him about the murder of Mr. Forrest and the other things that have happened. Tell him I sent you. And tell him I've solved the mystery, so he needn't bother to bring back his gang of coroners and photographers and fingerprint experts and what not. Tell him I'm getting a confession now, and I'll have it all written out and signed for him by the time he gets here. Can you remember that?'

'Yes sir.'

'Okay, Jeeves. On your way.'

He slipped his other automatic out of his hip pocket and stood there while the butler crossed the drive and melted into the inky shadows beyond. He could hear the man's softened footsteps even when he was out of sight, but they kept regularly on until they faded in the distance, and there was no disturbance. When he felt as sure as he could hope to be that the butler was beyond the danger zone, he put the Walther away again and stepped soundlessly back into the darkened hall.

Rosemary Chase and the doctor stared blankly at him as he re-entered the drawing room; and he smiled blandly at their mystification.

'I know,' he said. 'You heard me tell Jeeves that I was going to follow him.'

Quintus said: 'But why—'

'For the benefit of the guy outside,' answered the Saint calmly. 'If there is a guy outside. The guy who's been giving us so much trouble. If he's hung around as long as this, he's still around. He hasn't finished his job yet. He missed the balloon pretty badly on the last try, and he daren't pull out and leave it missed. He's staying right on the spot, wondering like hell what kind of a fast play he can work to save his bacon. So he heard what I told the butler. I meant him to. And I think it worked. I scared him away from trying to head off Jeeves with another carving-knife performance. Instead of that, he decided to stay here and try to clean up before the police arrive. And that's also what I meant him to do.'

The doctor's deep-set eyes blinked slowly

'Then the message you sent was only another bluff?'

'Partly. I may have exaggerated a little. But I meant to tickle our friend's curiosity. I wanted to make sure that he'd be frantic to find out more about it. So he had to know what's going on in this room. I'll bet money that he's listening to every word I'm saying now.'

The girl glanced at the broken window, beyond which the venetian shutters hid them from outside but would not silence their voices, and then glanced at the door; and she shivered. She said: 'But then he knows you didn't go with the butler—'

'But he knows it's too late to catch him up. Besides, this is much more interesting now. He wants to find out how much I've really got up my sleeve. And I want to tell him.'

'But you said you were only bluffing,' she protested huskily. 'You don't really know anything.'

The Saint shook his head.

'I only said I was exaggerating a little. I haven't got a confession yet, but I'm hoping to get one. The rest of it is true. I know everything that's behind tonight's fun and games. I know why everything has been done, and who did it.'

They didn't try to prompt him, but their wide-open eyes clung to him almost as if they had been hypnotized. It was as if an unreasoned fear of what he might be going to say made them shrink from pressing him, while at the same time they were spellbound by a fascination beyond their power to break.

The Saint made the most of his moment. He made them wait while he sauntered to a chair, and settled himself there, and lighted a cigarette, as if they were only enjoying an ordinary casual conversation. The theatrical pause was deliberate, aimed at the nerves of the one person whom he had to drive into self-betrayal.

'It's all so easy, really, when you sort it out,' he said at length. 'Our criminal is a clever guy, and he'd figured out a swindle that was so simple and audacious that it was practically foolproof – barring accidents. And to make up for the thousandth fraction of risk, it was bound to put millions into his hands. Only the accident happened; and one accident led to another.'

He took smoke from his cigarette and returned it through musingly half-smiling lips.

'The accident was when Nora Prescott wrote to me. She had to be in on the swindle, of course; but he thought he could keep her quiet with the threat that if she exposed him her father would lose the sinecure that was practically keeping him alive. It wasn't a very good threat, if she'd been a little more sensible, but it scared her enough to keep her away from the police. It didn't scare her out of thinking that a guy like me might be able to wreck the scheme somehow and still save something out of it for her. So she wrote to me. Our villain found out about that but wasn't able to stop the letter. So he followed her to the Bell tonight, planning to kill me as well, because he figured that once I'd received that letter I'd keep on prying until I found something. When Nora led off to the boathouse, it looked to be in the bag. He followed her, killed her and waited to add me to the collection. Only on account of another accident that happened then, he lost his nerve and quit.'

Again the Saint paused.

'Still our villain knew he had to hang on to me until I could be disposed of,' he went on with the same leisured confidence. 'He arranged to bring me up here to be got rid of as soon as he knew how. He stalled along until after dinner, when he'd got a plan worked out. He'd just finished talking it over with his accomplice—'

'Accomplice?' repeated the doctor.

'Yes,' said the Saint flatly. 'And just to make sure we understand each other, I'm referring to a phony medico who goes under the name of Quintus.'

The doctor's face went white, and his hands whitened on the arms of his chair; but the Saint didn't stir.

'I wouldn't try it,' he said. 'I wouldn't try anything, brother, if I were you. Because if you do, I shall smash you into soup meat.'

Rosemary Chase stared from one to the other.

'But – you don't mean—'

'I mean that that motor accident of your father's was a lie from beginning to end.' Simon's voice was gentle. 'He needed a phony doctor to back up the story of those injuries. He couldn't have kept it up with an honest one, and that would have wrecked everything. It took me a long time to see it, but that's because we're all ready to take too much for granted. You told me you'd seen your father since it happened, so I didn't ask any more questions. Naturally you didn't feel you had to tell me that when you saw him he was smothered in bandages like a mummy, and his voice was only a hoarse croak; but he needed Quintus to keep him that way.'

'You must be out of your mind!' Quintus roared hollowly.

The Saint smiled.

'No. But you're out of a job. And it was an easy one. I said we all take too much for granted. You're introduced as a doctor, and so everybody believes it. Now you're going to have another easy job – signing the confession I promised Sergeant Jesser. You'll do it to save your own skin. You'll tell how Forrest wasn't quite such a fool as he seemed; how he listened outside Marvin Chase's room and heard you and your pal cooking up a scheme to have your pal bust this window here and take a shot at you, just for effect, and then kill me and Hoppy when we came dashing into the fight; how Forrest got caught there, and how he was murdered so he couldn't spill the beans—'

'And what else?' said a new voice.

Simon turned his eyes toward the doorway and the man who stood there – a man incongruously clad in dark wine-coloured silk pajamas and bedroom slippers, whose head was swathed in bandages so that only his eyes were visible, whose gloved right hand held a revolver aimed at the Saint's chest. The Saint heard Rosemary come to her feet with a stifled cry, and answered to her rather than to anyone else.

'I told you you were going to be hurt, Rosemary,' he said. 'Your father was killed a week ago. But you'll remember his secretary. This is Mr. Bertrand Tamblin.'

XII

'You're clever, aren't you?' Tamblin said viciously.

'Not very,' said the Saint regretfully. 'I ought to have tumbled to it long ago. But as I was saying, we all take too much for granted. Everyone spoke of you as Marvin Chase, and so I assumed that was who you were. I got thrown off the scent a bit further when Rosemary and Forrest crashed into the boathouse at an awkward moment, when you got up the wind and scrammed. I didn't get anywhere near the mark until I began to think of you as the invisible millionaire – the guy that all the fuss was about and yet who couldn't be seen. Then it all straightened out. You killed Marvin Chase, burnt his body in a fake auto crash and had yourself brought home by Quintus in his place. Nobody argued about it; you had Quintus to keep you covered; you knew enough about his affairs to keep your end up in any conversation – you could even fool his daughter on short interviews, with your face bandaged and talking in the sort of faint unrecognizable voice that a guy who'd been badly injured might talk in. And you were all set to get your hands on as much of Marvin Chase's dough as you could squeeze out of banks and bonds before anyone got suspicious.'

'Yes?'

'Oh yes. . . . It was a grand idea until the accidents began to happen. Forrest was another accident. You got some of his blood on you – it's on you now – and you were afraid to jump back into bed when you heard me coming up the stairs. You lost your head again and plunged into a phony kidnapping. I don't believe that you skipped out of your window at all just then – you simply hopped into another room and hid there till the coast was clear. I wondered about that when I didn't hear any car driving off, and nobody took a shot at me when I walked round the house.'

'Go on.'

'Then you realized that someone would send for the police, and you had to delay that until you'd carried out your original plan of strengthening Quintus' alibi and killing Hoppy and me. You cut the phone wires. That was another error: an outside gang would have done that first and taken no chances, not run the risk of hanging around to do it after the job was pulled. Again you didn't shoot at me when I went out of doors the second time, because you wanted to make it look as if Quintus was also being shot at first. Then when you chose your moment, I was lucky enough to be too fast for you. When you heard me chasing round the outside of the house, you pushed off into the night for another think. I'd 've had the hell of a time catching you out there in the dark, so I let you hear me talking to the butler because I knew it would fetch you in.'

Tamblin nodded.

'You only made two mistakes,' he said. 'Forrest would have been killed anyway, only I should have chosen a better time for it. I heard Rosemary talking to him one night outside the front door, directly under my window, when he was leaving – that is how I found out that Nora had written to you and where she was going to meet you.'

'And the other mistake?' Simon asked coolly.

'Was when you let your own cleverness run away with you. When you arranged your clever scheme to get me to walk in here to provide the climax for your dramatic revelations, and even left the front door ajar to make it easy for me. You conceited fool! You've got your confession; but did you think I'd let it do you any good? Your bluff only bothered me for a moment when I was afraid Quintus had ratted. As soon as I found he hadn't, I was laughing at you. The only difference you've made is that now I shall have to kill Rosemary as well. Quintus had ideas about her, and we could have used her to build up the story—'

'Bertrand,' said the Saint gravely, 'I'm afraid you are beginning to drivel.'

The revolver that was aimed on him did not waver.

'Tell me why,' Tamblin said interestedly.

Simon trickled smoke languidly through his nostrils. He was still leaning back in his chair, imperturbably relaxed, in the attitude in which he had stayed even when Tamblin entered the room.

'Because it's your turn to be taking too much for granted. You thought my cleverness had run away with me, and so you stopped thinking. It doesn't seem to have occurred to you that since I expected you to come in, I may have expected just how sociable your ideas would be when you got here. You heard me give Jeeves a gun, and so you've jumped to the conclusion that I'm unarmed. Now will you take a look at my left hand? You notice that it's in my coat pocket. I've got you covered with another gun, Bertrand, and I'm ready to bet I can shoot faster than you. If you don't believe me, just start squeezing that trigger.'

Tamblin stood gazing motionlessly at him for a moment; and then his head tilted back and a cackle of hideous laughter came through the slit in the bandages over his mouth.

'Oh no, Mr. Templar,' he crowed. 'You're the one who took too much for granted. You decided that Quintus was a phony doctor, and so you didn't stop to think that he might be a genuine pickpocket. When he was holding on to you in the corridor upstairs – you remember? – he took the magazines out of both your guns. You've got one shot in the chamber of the gun you've got left, and Quintus has got you covered as well now. You can't get both of us with one bullet. You've been too clever for the last time.'

It was no bluff. Simon knew it with a gambler's instinct, and knew that Tamblin had the last laugh.

'Take your hand out of your pocket,' Tamblin snarled. 'Quintus is going to aim at Rosemary. If you use that gun, you're killing her as surely as if—'

The Saint saw Tamblin's forefinger twitch on the trigger, and waited for the sharp bite of death.

The crisp thunder of cordite splintered the unearthly stillness; but the Saint felt no shock, no pain. Staring incredulously, he saw Tamblin stagger as if a battering-ram had hit him in the back; saw him sway weakly, his right arm drooping until the revolver slipped through his fingers; saw his knees fold and his body pivot slantingly over them like a falling tree. . . . And saw the cubist figure and pithecanthropoid visage of Hoppy Uniatz coming through the door with a smoking Betsy in its hairy hand.

He heard another thud on his right, and looked round. The thud was caused by Quintus' gun hitting the carpet. Quintus' hands waved wildly in the air as Hoppy turned toward him.

'Don't shoot!' he screamed. 'I'll give you a confession. I haven't killed anyone. Tamblin did it all. Don't shoot me—'

'He doesn't want to be shot, Hoppy,' said the Saint. 'I think we'll let the police have him – just for a change. It may help to convince them of our virtue.'

'Boss,' said Mr. Uniatz, lowering his gun, 'I done it.'

The Saint nodded. He got up out of his chair. It felt rather strange to be alive and untouched.

'I know,' he said. 'Another half a second, and he'd 've been the most famous gunman on earth.'

Mr. Uniatz glanced cloudily at the body on the floor.

'Oh, him,' he said vaguely. 'Yeah. . . . But listen, boss – I done it!'

'You don't have to worry about it,' said the Saint. 'You've done it before. And Comrade Quintus' squeal will let you out.'

Rosemary Chase was coming toward him, pale but steady. It seemed to Simon Templar that a long time had been wasted in which he had been too busy to remember how beautiful she was and how warm and red her lips were. She put out a hand to him; and because he was still the Saint and always would be, his arm went round her.

'I know it's tough,' he said. 'But we can't change it.'

'It doesn't seem so bad now, somehow,' she said. 'To know that at least my father wasn't doing all this. . . . I wish I knew how to thank you.'

'Hoppy's the guy to thank,' said the Saint, and looked at him. 'I never suspected you of being a thought reader, Hoppy, but I'd give a lot to know what made you come out of the kitchen in the nick of time.'

Mr. Uniatz blinked at him.

'Dat's what I mean, boss, when I say I done it,' he explained, his brow furrowed with the effort of amplifying a statement which seemed to him to be already obvious enough. 'When you call out de butler, he is just opening me anudder bottle of scotch. An' dis time I make de grade. I drink it down to de last drop wit'out stopping. So I come right out to tell ya.' A broad beam of ineffable pride opened up a gold mine in the centre of Mr. Uniatz' face. 'I done it, boss! Ain't dat sump'n?'

FAITH

DASHIELL HAMMETT

Not only is Dashiell Hammett regarded as one of the greatest of all pulp writers, he is often recognized as one of the most important and influential, as well as popular, American writers of the twentieth century. His work has never been out of print, being reprinted again and again in many parts of the world. His stories have been anthologized more frequently than such Nobel laureates as Theodore Dreiser, Thomas Mann, Pearl S. Buck and John Galsworthy.

How rare it is, then, to be able to offer a story that you cannot have read before. 'Faith' appears in print here for the very first time anywhere.

The copy of the typescript from which the story was set has Hammett's address, 1309 Hyde Street, San Francisco, on it. It provides an unusual opportunity to see a story in the form in which it was originally mailed out – before e-mail and before agents worked as middlemen. It is clean, with a few minor corrections made in his hand, a few words crossed out.

Candidly, it is not his greatest story, a bit thin when compared with 'The House on Turk Street' or 'Dead Yellow Women.' Still, it's more than just a literary scrap, providing a searing look at hobo life in the Great Depression. These men lived on the roughest fringes of society, stealing when they had to, drinking when there was money, brawling with each other and with railroad security guards and other elements of the law enforcement community.

Were they criminal? Was the protagonist of 'Faith'? You decide.

FAITH

DASHIELL HAMMETT

Sprawled in a loose evening group on the river bank, the fifty-odd occupants of the slapboard barrack that was the American bunk-house listened to Morphy damn the canning-factory, its superintendent, its equipment, and its pay. They were migratory workingmen, these listeners, simple men, and they listened with that especial gravity which the simple man – North American Indian, Zulu, or hobo – affects.

But when Morphy had finished one of them chuckled.

Without conventions any sort of group life is impossible, and no division of society is without its canons. The laws of the jungles are not the laws of the drawing-room, but they are as certainly existent, and as important to their subjects. If you are a migratory workingman you may pick your teeth wherever and with whatever tool you like, but you may not either by word or act publicly express satisfaction with your present employment; nor may you disagree with any who denounce the conditions of that employment. Like most conventions, this is not altogether without foundation in reason.

So now the fifty-odd men on the bank looked at him who had chuckled, turned upon him the stare that is the social lawbreaker's lot everywhere: their faces held antagonism suspended in expectancy of worse to come; physically a matter of raised brows over blank eyes, and teeth a little apart behind closed lips.

'What's eatin' you?' Morphy – a big bodied dark man who said 'the proletariat' as one would say 'the seraphim' – demanded. 'You think this is a good dump?'

The chuckler wriggled, scratching his back voluptuously against a prong of uptorn stump that was his bolster, and withheld his answer until it seemed he had none. He was a newcomer to the Bush River cannery, one of the men hurried up from Baltimore that day: the tomatoes, after an unaccountable delay in ripening, had threatened to overwhelm the normal packing force.

'I've saw worse,' the newcomer said at last, with the true barbarian's lack of discomfiture in the face of social disapproval. 'And I expect to see worse.'

'Meanin' what?'

'Oh, I ain't saying!' The words were light-flung, airy. 'But I know a few things. Stick around and you'll see.'

No one could make anything of that. Simple men are not ready questioners. Someone spoke of something else.

The man who had chuckled went to work in the process-room, where half a dozen Americans and as many Pollocks cooked the fresh-canned tomatoes in big iron kettles. He was a small man, compactly plump, with round maroon eyes above round cheeks whose original ruddiness had been tinted by sunburn to a definite orange. His nose was small and merrily pointed, and a snuff-user's pouch in his lower lip, exaggerating the lift of his mouth at the corners, gave him a perpetual grin. He held himself erect, his chest arched out, and bobbed when he walked, rising on the ball of the propelling foot midway each step. A man of forty-five or so, who answered to the name Feach and hummed through his nose while he guided the steel-slatted baskets from truck, to kettle, to truck.

After he had gone, the men remembered that from the first there had been a queerness about Feach, but not even Morphy tried to define that queerness. 'A nut,' Morphy said, but that was indefinite.

What Feach had was a secret. Evidence of it was not in his words only: they were neither many nor especially noteworthy, and his silence held as much ambiguity as his speech. There was in his whole air – in the cock of his round, boy's head, in the sparkle of his red-brown eyes, in the nasal timbre of his voice, in his trick of puffing out his cheeks when he smiled – a sardonic knowingness that seemed to mock whatever business was at hand. He had for his work and for the men's interests the absent-minded, bantering sort of false-seriousness that a busy parent has for its child's affairs. His every word, gesture, attention, seemed thinly to mask preoccupation with some altogether different thing that would presently appear: a man waiting for a practical joke to blossom.

He and Morphy worked side by side. Between them the first night had put a hostility which neither tried to remove. Three days later they increased it.

It was early evening. The men, as usual, were idling between their quarters and the river, waiting for bed-time. Feach had gone indoors to get a can of snuff from his bedding. When he came out Morphy was speaking.

'Of course not,' he was saying. 'You don't think a God big enough to make all this would be crazy enough to do it, do you? What for? What would it get Him?'

A freckled ex-sailor, known to his fellows as Sandwich, was frowning with vast ponderance over the cigarette he was making, and when he spoke the deliberation in his voice was vast.

'Well, you can't always say for certain. Sometimes a thing looks one way, and when you come to find out, is another. It don't *look* like there's no God. I'll say *that*. But—'

Feach, tamping snuff into the considerable space between his lower teeth and lip, grinned around his fingers, and managed to get derision into the snapping of the round tin lid down on the snuff-can.

'So you're one of *them* guys?' he challenged Morphy.

'Uh-huh.' The big man's voice was that of one who, confident of his position's impregnability, uses temperateness to provoke an assault. 'If somebody'd *show* me there was a God, it'd be different. But I never been showed.'

'I've saw wise guys like you before!' The jovial ambiguity was suddenly gone from Feach; he was earnest, and indignant. 'You want what you call proof before you'll believe anything. Well, you wait – you'll get your proof *this* time, and plenty of it.'

'That's what I'd like to have. You ain't got none of this proof *on* you, have you?'

Feach sputtered.

Morphy rolled over on his back and began to roar out a song to the Maryland sky, a mocking song that Wobblies sing to the tune of 'When the bugle calls up yonder I'll be there.'

'You will eat, by and by,
In that glorious land they call the sky—
'Way up high!
Work and pray,
Live on hay.
You'll get pie in the sky when you die.'

Feach snorted and turned away, walking down the river bank. The singer's booming notes followed him until he had reached the pines beyond the two rows of frame huts that were the Pollocks' quarters.

By morning the little man had recovered his poise. For two weeks he held it – going jauntily around with his cargo of doubleness and his bobbing walk, smiling with puffed cheeks when Morphy called him 'Parson' – and then it began to slip away from him. For a while he still smiled, and still said one thing while patently thinking of another; but his eyes were no longer jovially occupied with those other things: they were worried.

He took on the look of one who is kept waiting at a rendezvous, and tries to convince himself that he will not be disappointed. His nights became restless; the least creaking of the clapboard barrack or the stirring of a sleeping man would bring him erect in bed.

One afternoon the boiler of a small hoisting engine exploded. A hole was blown in the store-house wall, but no one was hurt. Feach raced the others to the spot and stood grinning across the wreckage at Morphy. Carey, the superintendent, came up.

'Every season it's got to be something!' he complained. 'But thank God this ain't as bad as the rest – like last year when the roof fell in and smashed everything to hell and gone.'

Feach stopped grinning and went back to work.

Two nights later a thunderstorm blew down over the canning-factory. The first distant rumble awakened Feach. He pulled on trousers, shoes, and shirt, and left the bunk-house. In the north, approaching clouds were darker than the other things of night. He walked toward them, breathing with increasing depth, until, when the clouds were a black smear overhead, his chest was rising and falling to the beat of some strong rhythm.

When the storm broke he stood still, on a little hummock that was screened all around by bush and tree. He stood very straight, with upstretched arms and upturned face. Rain – fat thunder-drops that tapped rather than pattered – drove into his round face. Jagged streaks of metal fire struck down at ground and tree, house and man. Thunder that could have been born of nothing less than the impact of an enormous something upon the earth itself, crashed, crashed, crashed, reverberations lost in succeeding crashes as they strove to keep pace with the jagged metal streaks.

Feach stood up on his hummock, a short man compactly plump, hidden from every view by tree and undergrowth; a little man with a pointed nose tilted at the center of the storm, and eyes that held fright when they were not blinking and squinting under fat rain-drops. He talked aloud, though the thunder made nothing of his words. He talked into the storm, cursing God for half an hour without pause, with words that were vilely blasphemous, in a voice that was suppliant.

The storm passed down the river. Feach went back to his bunk, to lie awake all night, shivering in his wet underwear and waiting. Nothing happened.

He began to mumble to himself as he worked. Carey, reprimanding him for over-cooking a basket of tomatoes, had to speak three times before the little man heard him. He slept little. In his bunk, he either tossed from side to side or lay tense, straining his eyes through the darkness for minute after minute. Frequently he would leave the sleeping-house to prowl among the buildings, peering expectantly into each shadow that house or shed spread in his path.

Another thunderstorm came. He went out into it and cursed God again. Nothing happened. He slept none after that, and stopped eating. While the others were at table he would pace up and down beside the river, muttering to himself. All night he wandered around in distorted circles, through the pines, between the buildings, down to the river, chewing the ends of his fingers and talking to himself. His jauntiness was gone: a shrunken man who slouched when he walked, and shivered, doing his daily work only because it required neither especial skill nor energy. His eyes were more red than brown, and dull except when they burned with sudden fevers. His finger-nails ended in red arcs where the quick was exposed.

On his last night at the cannery, Feach came abruptly into the center of the group that awaited the completion of night between house and river. He shook his finger violently at Morphy.

'That's crazy!' he screeched. 'Of course there's a God! There's got to be! That's crazy!'

His red-edged eyes peered through the twilight at the men's faces: consciously stolid faces once they had mastered their first surprise at this picking up of fortnight-old threads: the faces of men to whom exhibitions of astonishment were childish. Feach's eyes held fear and a plea.

'Got your proof with you tonight?' Morphy turned on his side, his head propped on one arm, to face his opponent. 'Maybe you can *show* me why there's *got* to be a God?'

'Ever' reason!' Moisture polished the little man's face, and muscles writhed in it. 'There's the moon, and the sun, and the stars, and flowers, and rain, and—'

'Pull in your neck!' The big man spit for emphasis. 'What do you know about them things? Edison could've made 'em for all you know. Talk sense. Why has there got to be a God?'

'Why? I'll tell you why!' Feach's voice was a thin scream; he stood tiptoe, and his arms jerked in wild gestures. 'I'll tell you why! I've stood up to Him, and had His hand against me. I've been cursed by Him, and cursed back. That's how I know! Listen: I had a wife and kid once, back in Ohio on a farm she got from her old man. I come home from town one night and the lightning had came down and burnt the house flat – with them in it. I got a job in a mine near Harrisburg, and the third day I'm there a cave-in gets fourteen men. I'm down with 'em, and get out without a scratch. I work in a box-factory in Pittsburgh that burns down in less'n a week. I'm sleeping in a house in Galveston when a hurricane wrecks it, killing ever'body but me and a fella that's only crippled. I shipped out of Charleston in the *Sophie*, that went down off Cape Flattery, and I'm the only one that gets ashore. That's when I began to know for sure that it was God after me. I had sort of suspected it once or twice before – just from queer things I'd noticed – but I hadn't been certain. But now I knew what was what, and I wasn't wrong either! For five years I ain't been anywhere that something didn't happen. Why was I hunting a job before I came up here? Because a boiler busts in the Deal's Island packing-house where I worked before and wiped out the place. That's why!'

Doubt was gone from the little man; in the quarter-light he seemed to have grown larger, taller, and his voice rang.

Morphy, perhaps alone of the audience not for the moment caught in the little man's eloquence, laughed briefly.

'An' what started all this hullabaloo?' he asked.

'I done a thing,' Feach said, and stopped. He cleared his throat sharply and tried again. 'I done a thi—' The muscles of throat and mouth went on speaking, but no sound came out. 'What difference does that make?' He no longer bulked large in the dimness, and his voice was a whine. 'Ain't it enough that I've had Him hounding me year after year? Ain't it enough that everywhere I go He—'

Morphy laughed again.

'A hell of a Jonah you are!'

'All right!' Feach gave back. 'You wait and see before you get off any of your cheap jokes. You can laugh, but it ain't ever' man that's stood up to God and wouldn't give in. It ain't ever' man that's had Him for a enemy.'

Morphy turned to the others and laughed, and they laughed with him. The laughter lacked honesty at first, but soon became natural; and though there were some who did not laugh, they were too few to rob the laughter of apparent unanimity.

Feach shut both eyes and hurled himself down on Morphy. The big man shook him off, tried to push him away, could not, and struck him with an open hand. Sandwich picked Feach up and led him in to his bed. Feach was sobbing – dry, old-man sobs.

'They won't listen to me, Sandwich, but I know what I'm talking about. Something's coming here – you wait and see. God wouldn't forget me after all these years He's been riding me.'

'Course not,' the freckled ex-sailor soothed him. 'Everything'll come out all right. You're right.'

After Sandwich had left him Feach lay still on his bunk, chewing his fingers and staring at the rough board ceiling with eyes that were perplexed in a blank, hurt way. As he bit his fingers he muttered to himself. 'It's something to have stood up to Him and not give in. . . . He wouldn't forget . . . chances are it's something new. . . . He wouldn't!'

Presently fear pushed the perplexity out of his eyes, and then fear was displaced by a look of unutterable anguish. He stopped muttering and sat up, fingers twisting his mouth into a clown's grimace, breath hissing through his nostrils. Through the open door came the noise of stirring men: they were coming in to bed.

Feach got to his feet, darted through the door, past the men who were converging upon it, and ran up along the river – a shambling, jerky running. He ran until one foot slipped into a hole and threw him headlong. He scrambled up immediately and went on. But he walked now, frequently stumbling.

To his right the river lay dark and oily under the few stars. Three times he stopped to yell at the river.

'No! No! They're wrong! There's got to be a God! There's got to!'

Half an hour was between the first time he yelled and the second, and a longer interval between the second and third; but each time there was a ritualistic sameness to word and tone. After the third time the anguish began to leave his eyes.

He stopped walking and sat on the butt of a fallen pine. The air was heavy with the night-odor of damp earth and mold, and still where he sat, though a breeze shuffled the tops of the trees. Something that might have been a rabbit padded across the pine-needle matting behind him; a suggestion of frogs' croaking was too far away to be a definite sound. Lightning-bugs moved sluggishly among the trees: yellow lights shining through moth-holes in an irregularly swaying curtain.

Feach sat on the fallen pine for a long while, only moving to slap at an occasional pinging mosquito. When he stood up and turned back toward the canning-factory he moved swiftly and without stumbling.

He passed the dark American bunk-house, went through the unused husking-shed, and came to the hole that the hoisting engine had made in the store-house wall. The boards that had been nailed over the gap were loosely nailed. He pulled two of them off, went through the opening, and came out carrying a large gasoline can.

Walking downstream, he kept within a step of the water's edge until to his right a row of small structures showed against the sky like evenly spaced black teeth in a dark mouth. He carried his can up the slope toward them, panting a little, wood-debris crackling under his feet, the gasoline sloshing softly in its can.

He set the can down at the edge of the pines that ringed the Polacks' huts, and stuffed his lower lip with snuff. No light came from the double row of buildings, and there was no sound except the rustling of tree and bush in the growing breeze from southward.

Feach left the pines for the rear of the southernmost hut. He tilted the can against the wall, and moved to the next hut. Wherever he paused the can gurgled and grew lighter. At the sixth building he emptied the can. He put it down, scratched his head, shrugged, and went back to the first hut.

He took a long match from his vest pocket and scraped it down the back of his leg. There was no flame. He felt his trousers; they were damp with dew. He threw the match away, took out another, and ignited it on the inside of his vest. Squatting, he held the match against the frayed end of a wall-board that was black with gasoline. The splintered wood took fire. He stepped back and looked at it with approval. The match in his hand was consumed to half its length; he used the rest of it starting a tiny flame on a corner of the tar-paper roofing just above his head.

He ran to the next hut, struck another match, and dropped it on a little pile of sticks and paper that leaned against the rear wall. The pile became a flame that bent in to the wall.

The first hut has become a blazing thing, flames twisting above as if it were spinning under them. The seething of the fire was silenced by a scream that became the whole audible world. When that scream died there were others. The street between the two rows of buildings filled with red-lighted figures: naked figures, underclothed figures – men, women and children – who achieved clamor. A throaty male voice sounded above the others. It was inarticulate, but there was purpose in it.

Feach turned and ran toward the pines. Pursuing bare feet made no sound. Feach turned his head to see if he were being hunted, and stumbled. A dark athlete in red flannel drawers pulled the little man to his feet and accused him in words that had no meaning to Feach. He snarled at his captor, and was knocked down by a fist used club-wise against the top of his head.

Men from the American bunk-house appeared as Feach was being jerked to his feet again. Morphy was one of them.

'Hey, what are you doing?' he asked the athlete in red drawers.

'These one, 'e sit fire to 'ouses. I see 'im!'

Morphy gaped at Feach.

'You did that?'

The little man looked past Morphy to where two rows of huts were a monster candelabra among the pines, and as he looked his chest arched out and the old sparkling ambiguity came back to his eyes.

'Maybe I done it,' he said complacently, 'and maybe Something used me to do it. Anyways, if it hadn't been that it'd maybe been something worse.'

PASTORALE

JAMES M. CAIN

It would be only a slight exaggeration to say that James M. Cain (1892–1977) wrote stories and novels so hard-boiled that he made the other pulp writers of his era seem like sissies. No one wrote prose that was as lean as his. No word was wasted – a style that influenced many outstanding authors who followed him, notably Albert Camus and Elmore Leonard, whose works have been as generous with words as Scrooge was with shillings.

While other tough-guy writers recognized that not all women were warm and fuzzy, Cain elevated their malevolence to heights seldom matched, then or now. Perhaps the fact that he was married four times contributed to his feelings toward the female of the species.

In such memorable masterpieces as *Double Indemnity* and *The Postman Always Rings Twice*, Cain's women are so desirable that men will, literally, kill for them. He once said that he wrote about the most terrifying thing he knew: the wish that comes true. The men in these novels and other stories are not entirely rational in their longings and it is their grave misfortune that they are successful in their quests for the wrong women.

It is cheating a little to use 'Pastorale' in an omnibus of pulp fiction because it was originally published in the March 1938 issue of *The American Mercury* which, as one of the leading intellectual journals of its time, was anything but pulpy. However, when the great tough writers of the 1930s are listed, the big three are Hammett, Chandler and Cain, so here it is.

PASTORALE

JAMES M. CAIN

I

Well, it looks like Burbie is going to get hung. And if he does; what he can lay it on is, he always figured he was so damn smart.

You see, Burbie, he left town when he was about sixteen year old. He run away with one of them travelling shows, 'East Lynne' I think it was, and he stayed away about ten years. And when he come back he thought he knowed a lot. Burbie, he's got them watery blue eyes what kind of stick out from his face, and how he killed the time was to sit around and listen to the boys talk down at the poolroom or over at the barber shop or a couple other places where he hung out, and then wink at you like they was all making a fool of theirself or something and nobody didn't know it but him.

But when you come right down to what Burbie had in his head, why it wasn't much. 'Course, he generally always had a job, painting around or maybe helping out on a new house, like of that, but what he used to do was to play baseball with the high school team. And they had a big fight over it, 'cause Burbie was so old nobody wouldn't believe he went to the school, and them other teams was all the time putting up a squawk. So then he couldn't play no more. And another thing he liked to do was sing at the entertainments. I reckon he liked that most of all, 'cause he claimed that a whole lot of the time he was away he was on the stage, and I reckon maybe he was at that, 'cause he was pretty good, 'specially when he dressed hisself up like a old-time Rube and come out and spoke a piece what he knowed.

Well, when he come back to town he seen Lida and it was a natural. 'Cause Lida, she was just about the same kind of a thing for a woman as Burbie was for a man. She used to work in the store, selling dry goods to the men, and kind of making hats on the side. 'Cepting only she didn't stay on the dry goods side no more'n she had to. She was generally over where the boys was drinking Coca-Cola, and all the time carrying on about did they like it with ammonia or lemon, and could she have a swallow outen their glass. And what she had her mind on was the clothes she had on, and was she dated up for Sunday night. Them clothes was pretty snappy, and she made them herself. And I heard some of them say she wasn't hard to date up, and after you done kept your date why maybe you wasn't going to be disappointed. And why Lida married the old man I don't know, lessen she got tired working at the store and tooken a look at the big farm where he lived at, about two mile from town.

By the time Burbie got back she'd been married about a year and she was about due. So her and him commence meeting each other, out in the orchard back of the old man's house. The old man would go to bed right after supper and then she'd sneak out and meet Burbie. And nobody wasn't supposed to know nothing about it. Only everybody did, 'cause Burbie, after he'd get back to town about eleven o'clock at night, he'd kind of slide into the poolroom and set down easy like. And then somebody'd say, 'Yay, Burbie, where you been?' And Burbie, he'd kind of look around, and then he'd pick out somebody and wink at him, and that was how Burbie give it some good advertising.

So the way Burbie tells it, and he tells it plenty since he done got religion down to the jailhouse, it wasn't long before him and Lida thought it would be a good idea to kill the old man. They figured he didn't have long to live nohow, so he might as well go now as wait a couple of years. And another thing, the old man had kind of got hep that something was going on, and they figured if he throwed Lida out it wouldn't be no easy job to get his money even if he died regular. And another thing, by that time the Klux was kind of talking around, so Burbie figured it would be better if him and Lida was to get married, else maybe he'd have to leave town again.

So that was how come he got Hutch in it. You see, he was afeared to kill the old man hisself and he wanted some help. And then he figured it would be pretty good if Lida wasn't nowheres around and it would look like robbery. If it would of been me, I would of left Hutch out of it. 'Cause Hutch, he was mean. He'd been away for a while too, but him going away, that wasn't the same as Burbie going away. Hutch was sent. He was sent for ripping a mail sack while he was driving the mail wagon up from the station, and before he come back he done two years down to Atlanta.

But what I mean, he wasn't only crooked, he was mean. He had a ugly look to him, like when he'd order hisself a couple of fried eggs over to the restaurant, and then set and eat them with his head humped down low and his arm curled around his plate like he thought somebody was going to steal it off him, and handle his knife with his thumb down near the tip, kind of like a nigger does a razor. Nobody didn't have much to say to Hutch, and I reckon that's why he ain't heard nothing about Burbie and Lida, and et it all up what Burbie told him about the old man having a pot of money hid in the fireplace in the back room.

So one night early in March, Burbie and Hutch went out and done the job. Burbie he'd already got Lida out of the way. She'd let on she had to go to the city to buy some things, and she went away on No. 6, so everybody knowed she was gone. Hutch, he seen her go, and come running to Burbie saying now was a good time, which was just what Burbie wanted. 'Cause her and Burbie had already put the money in the pot, so Hutch wouldn't think it was no put-up job. Well, anyway, they put $23 in the pot, all changed into pennies and nickels and dimes so it would look like a big pile, and that was all the money Burbie had. It was kind of like you might say the savings of a lifetime.

And then Burbie and Hutch got in the horse and wagon what Hutch had, 'cause Hutch was in the hauling business again, and they went out to the old man's place. Only they went around the back way, and tied the horse back of the house so nobody couldn't see it from the road, and knocked on the back door and made out like they was just coming through the place on their way back to town and had stopped by to get warmed up, 'cause it was cold as hell. So the old man let them in and give them a drink of some hard cider what he had, and they got canned up a little more. They was already pretty canned, 'cause they both of them had a pint of corn on their hip for to give them some nerve.

And then Hutch he got back of the old man and crowned him with a wrench what he had hid in his coat.

2

Well, next off Hutch gets sore as hell at Burbie 'cause there ain't no more'n $23 in the pot. He didn't do nothing. He just set there, first looking at the money, what he had piled up on a table, and then looking at Burbie.

And then Burbie commences soft-soaping him. He says hope my die he thought there was a thousand dollars anyway in the pot, on account the old man being like he was. And he says hope my die it sure was a big surprise to him how little there was there. And he says hope my die it sure does make him feel bad, on account he's the one had the idea first. And he says hope my die it's all his fault and he's going to let Hutch keep all the money, damn if he ain't. He ain't going to take none of it for hisself at all, on account of how bad he feels. And Hutch, he don't say nothing at all, only look at Burbie and look at the money.

And right in the middle of while Burbie was talking, they heard a whole lot of hollering out in front of the house and somebody blowing a automobile horn. And Hutch jumps up and scoops the money and the wrench off the table in his pockets, and hides the pot back in the fireplace. And then he grabs the old man and him and Burbie carries him out the back door, hists him in the wagon, and drives off. And how they was to drive off without them people seeing them was because they come in the back way and that was the way they went. And them people in the automobile, they was a bunch of old folks from the Methodist church what knowed Lida was away and didn't think so much of Lida nohow and come out to say hello. And when they come in and didn't see nothing, they figured the old man had went in to town and so they went back.

Well, Hutch and Burbie was in a hell of a fix all right. 'Cause there they was, driving along somewheres with the old man in the wagon and they didn't have no more idea than a bald-headed coot where they was going or what they was going to do with him. So Burbie, he commence to whimper. But Hutch kept a-setting there, driving the horse, and he don't say nothing.

So pretty soon they come to a place where they was building a piece of county road, and it was all tore up and a whole lot of toolboxes laying out on the side. So Hutch gets out and twists the lock off one of them with the wrench, and takes out a pick and a shovel and throws them in the wagon. And then he got in again and drove on for a while till he come to the Whooping Nannie woods, what some of them says has got a ghost in it on dark nights, and it's about three miles from the old man's farm. And Hutch turns in there and pretty soon he come to a kind of a clear place and he stopped. And then, first thing he's said to Burbie, he says,

'Dig that grave!'

So Burbie dug the grave. He dug for two hours, until he got so damn tired he couldn't hardly stand up. But he ain't hardly made no hole at all. 'Cause the ground is froze and even with the pick he couldn't hardly make a dent in it scarcely. But anyhow Hutch stopped him and they throwed the old man in and covered him up. But after they got him covered up his head was sticking out. So Hutch beat the head down good as he could and piled the dirt up around it and they got in and drove off.

After they'd went a little ways, Hutch commence to cuss Burbie. Then he said Burbie'd been lying to him. But Burbie, he swears he ain't been lying. And then Hutch says he *was* lying and with that he hit Burbie. And after he knocked Burbie down in the bottom of the wagon he kicked him and then pretty soon Burbie up and told him about Lida. And when Burbie got done telling him about Lida, Hutch turned the horse around. Burbie asked then what they was going back for and Hutch says they're going back for to git a present for Lida. So they come back for to git a present for Lida. So they come back to the grave and Hutch made Burbie cut off the old man's head with the shovel. It made Burbie sick, but Hutch made him stick at it, and after a while Burbie had it off. So Hutch throwed it in the wagon and they get in and start back to town once more.

Well, they wasn't no more'n out of the woods before Hutch takes hisself a slug of corn and commence to holler. He kind of raved to hisself, all about how he was going to make Burbie put the head in a box and tie it up with a string and take it out to Lida for a present, so she'd get a nice surprise when she opened it. Soon as Lida comes back he says Burbie has got to do it, and then he's going to kill Burbie. 'I'll kill you!' he says. 'I'll kill you, damn you! I'll kill you!' And he says it kind of singsongy, over and over again.

And then he takes hisself another slug of corn and stands up and whoops.

Then he beat on the horse with the whip and the horse commence to run. What I mean, he commence to gallop. And then Hutch hit him some more. And then he commence to screech as loud as he could. 'Ride him, cowboy!' he hollers. 'Going East! Here come old broadcuff down the road! Whe-e-e-e-e!' And sure enough, here they come down the road, the horse a-running hell to split, and Hutch a-hollering, and Burbie a-shivering, and the head a-rolling around in the bottom of the wagon, and bouncing up in the air when they hit a bump, and Burbie damn near dying every time it hit his feet.

3

After a while the horse got tired so it wouldn't run no more, and they had to let him walk and Hutch set down and commence to grunt. So Burbie, he tries to figure out what the hell he's going to do with the head. And pretty soon he remembers a creek what they got to cross, what they ain't crossed on the way out 'cause they come the back way. So he figures he'll throw the head overboard when Hutch ain't looking. So he done it. They come to the creek, and on the way down to the bridge there's a little hill, and when the wagon tilted going down the hill the head rolled up between Burbie's feet, and he held it there, and when they got in the middle of the bridge he reached down and heaved it overboard.

Next off, Hutch give a yell and drop down in the bottom of the wagon. 'Cause what it sounded like was a pistol shot. You see, Burbie done forgot that it was a cold night and the creek done froze over. Not much, just a thin skim about a inch thick, but enough that when that head hit it it cracked pretty loud in different directions. And that was what scared Hutch. So when he got up and seen the head setting out there on the ice in the moonlight, and got it straight what Burbie done, he let on he was going to kill Burbie right there. And he reached for the pick. And Burbie jumped out and run, and he didn't never stop till he got home at the place where he lived at, and locked the door, and climbed in bed and pulled the covers over his head.

Well, the next morning a fellow come running into town and says there's hell to pay down at the bridge. So we all went down there and first thing we seen was that head laying out there on the ice, kind of rolled over on one ear. And next thing we seen was Hutch's horse and wagon tied to the bridge rail, and the horse damn near froze to death. And the next thing we seen was the hole in the ice where Hutch fell through. And the next thing we seen down on the bottom next to one of the bridge pilings, was Hutch.

So the first thing we went to work and done was to get the head. And believe me a head laying out on thin ice is a pretty damn hard thing to get, and what we had to do was to lasso it. And the next thing we done was to get Hutch. And after we fished him out he had the wrench and the $23 in his pockets and the pint of corn on his hip and he was stiff as a board. And near as I can figure out, what happened to him was that after Burbie run away he climbed down on the bridge piling and tried to reach the head and fell in.

But we didn't know nothing about it then, and after we done got the head and the old man was gone and a couple of boys that afternoon found the body and not the head on it, and the pot was found, and them old people from the Methodist church done told their story and one thing and another, we figured out that Hutch done it, 'specially on account he must have been drunk and he done time in the pen and all like of that, and nobody ain't thought nothing about Burbie at all. They had the funeral and Lida cried like hell and everybody tried to figure out what Hutch wanted with the head and things went along thataway for three weeks.

Then one night down to the poolroom they was having it some more about the head, and one says one thing and one says another, and Benny Heath, what's a kind of a constable around town, he started a long bum argument about how Hutch must of figured if they couldn't find the head to the body they couldn't prove no murder. So right in the middle of it Burbie kind of looked around like he always done and then he winked. And Benny Heath, he kept on a-talking, and after he got done Burbie kind of leaned over and commence to talk to him. And in a couple of minutes you couldn't of heard a man catch his breath in that place, accounten they was all listening at Burbie.

I already told you Burbie was pretty good when it comes to giving a spiel at a entertainment. Well, this here was a kind of spiel too. Burbie act like he had it all learned by heart. His voice trimmled and ever couple of minutes he'd kind of cry and wipe his eyes and make out like he can't say no more, and then he'd go on.

And the big idea was what a whole lot of hell he done raised in his life. Burbie said it was drink and women what done ruined him. He told about all the women what he knowed, and all the saloons he's been in, and some of it was a lie 'cause if all the saloons was as swell as he said they was they'd of throwed him out. And then he told about how sorry he was about the life he done led, and how hope my die he come home to his old home town just to get out the devilment and settle down. And he told about Lida, and how she wouldn't let him cut it out. And then he told how she done led him on till he got the idea to kill the old man. And then he told about how him and Hutch done it, and all about the money and the head and all the rest of it.

And what it sounded like was a piece what he knowed called 'The Face on the Floor,' what was about a bum what drawed a picture on the barroom floor of the woman what done ruined him. Only the funny part was that Burbie wasn't ashamed of hisself like he made out he was. You could see he was proud of hisself. He was proud of all them women and all the liquor he'd drunk and he was proud about Lida and he was proud about the old man and the head and being slick enough not to fall in the creek with Hutch. And after he got done he give a yelp and flopped down on the floor and I reckon maybe he thought he was going to die on the spot like the bum what drawed the face on the barroom floor, only he didn't. He kind of lain there a couple of minutes till Benny got him up and put him in the car and tooken him off to jail.

So that's where he's at now, and he's went to work and got religion down there, and all the people what comes to see him, why he sings hymns to them and then he speaks them his piece. And I hear tell he knows it pretty good by now and has got the crying down pat. And Lida, they got her down there too, only she won't say nothing 'cepting she done it same as Hutch and Burbie. So Burbie, he's going to get hung, sure as hell. And if he hadn't felt so smart, he would of been a free man yet.

Only I reckon he done been holding it all so long he just had to spill it.

THE SAD SERBIAN

FRANK GRUBER

Few pulp writers were as prolific as Frank Gruber (1904–1969) who, at the peak of his career, produced three or four full-length novels a year, many about series characters Johnny Fletcher and his sidekick, Sam Cragg, numerous short stories, many featuring Oliver Quade, 'the Human Encyclopedia,' and screenplays, including such near-classics as *The Mask of Dimitrios*, *Terror By Night* and, with Steve Fisher, *Johnny Angel*. He also wrote two dozen western novels.

In addition to a relentless work ethic and a fertile imagination, he developed an eleven-point formula for his novels which certainly helped speed the writing process. In his autobiography, *The Pulp Jungle*, which is also an informal history of pulp magazines and the era in which they flourished, he outlined the formula for his mystery stories.

The successful adventure, he believed, needed a colorful hero, a theme with information the reader is unlikely to know, a villain more powerful than the hero, a vivid background for the action, an unusual murder method or unexpected circumstances surrounding the crime, unusual variations on the common motives of greed and hate, a well-hidden clue, a trick or twist that will snatch victory from the jaws of defeat, constantly moving action, a protagonist who has a personal involvement, and a smashing climax. These key points, of course, may well describe all of pulp fiction – and a lot of later adventure and crime stories as well.

'The Sad Serbian' first appeared in the March 1939 issue of *Black Mask*.

THE SAD SERBIAN

FRANK GRUBER

To look at me reading the death notices while I'm having my breakfast in Thompson's, you'd think I was an undertaker. I'm not, but my job is just as cheerful. Take this business today. I've got a bunch of cards with names, and I'm comparing them with the names in the death notices. I do this every morning and about twice a year I find a name I'm looking for. I strike pay-dirt this morning with the name Druhar.

I finish my breakfast and go out and hunt for my jaloppy, which I've got parked a couple of blocks down the street. I climb in and head for the North Side; 598 Blackhawk Street.

These foreigners certainly bury them early in the morning. Although it's only nine-thirty, they've already taken the crepe down from the door. There are a couple of kids hanging around and I ask them: 'At what church are they having the mass for Mrs. Druhar?'

'Saint John's on Cleveland Avenue,' one of the kids replies.

I miss them at the church, so the only thing I can do is go out to the cemetery, which, according to the paper, is St Sebastian's, seven miles outside the city limits. It takes me about an hour to get out there, so when I get to the cemetery, they're breaking up; going back to the cars that have brought them out. I grab an old envelope out of my pocket and wave it around as if it's a telegram, or something.

'Mr. Tony Druhar!' I yell.

A big fellow, who is just about to climb into a green sedan, says: 'Here I am.'

I run over and see that the license number on the sedan checks with the number on one of my cards. So I pull out the old repossess warrant and stick it into Mr. Druhar's hand. 'Sorry, Mr. Druhar,' I say. 'I'm taking your car, on account of you haven't done right by the Mid-West Finance Company.'

This Druhar looks stupidly at the piece of paper in his hand for a minute. Then he lets out a roar you could have heard over on Grant Avenue. 'Why, you lousy, grave-robbing—! Is this a time to pull something like this, when I have just buried my poor grandmother?'

'That's how I found you,' I tell him. 'It says in the paper: "Mourned by her sons, so-and-so, and grandsons, Tony Druhar, and so-and-so."'

Some people certainly get mad. This Druhar fellow jumps up and down and takes off his hat and throws it on the ground and jumps on it. Then three fellows just as big as Druhar climb out of his sedan and surround me.

'So you're a skip-tracer!' one of them says, and lets a handful of knuckles fly in my direction.

I'm lucky enough to duck them, but I can see that this isn't the safest place in the world right now for Sam Cragg. I get a lucky break, though. A motorcycle cop who's escorted the funeral out here is just a little way off, and when Druhar starts all his yelling, he comes over.

'What's the trouble?' he asks.

Druhar starts swearing again, but I grab hold of the cop's arm. 'I've got a repossess warrant for this car. This Druhar has missed six payments, and the Mid-West Finance Company wants $188 or the car.'

The cop gives me a funny look and takes the warrant from Tony Druhar. He looks at it and then he looks at me. 'I'll bet you hate yourself, mister, when you look at your face in the mirror every morning.'

'Maybe I do,' I tell the cop, 'but if I didn't have this job somebody else would, and I haven't got a pull, so I can't get on the WPA, and I have to eat.'

'Why?' asks the cop.

I can see he's all on the other side, so I give him some law. 'Officer, this is a regular warrant, good anywhere in this country. As an officer of the law, I'm calling on you to see that it's properly served. I want this car or $188.'

There's some hullabaloo, but after a while Druhar and his pals get together and make me a proposition, which I am sap enough to accept. I'm a softie, and you oughtn't to be a skip-tracer if you are a softie. They've pooled up $32 and they say that Druhar will have the rest of the money for me tomorrow. I'm just cagy enough, though, to make them all give me their names and addresses and prove them by letters and stuff they've got with them.

That's where I made my big mistake and how I got mixed up with the phoney prince.

Next morning I drive up to 736 Gardner Street. Gardner Street is a little one-block chopped up street that has been dumped in between Stanton Park and Ogden Avenue. There are only about thirty houses on the street, and everyone of them should have been condemned twenty years ago. Druhar is supposed to live on the first floor of one of these dumps.

I can't ring the doorbell because there isn't a doorbell, so I bang the door with my fist. Nothing happens so I bang it again. Then I figure I have been given the runaround and I get sore, and push on the door. It goes open and I walk into the place. Druhar is at home. He's lying on the floor.

He's dead.

For a minute I look down at him and all sorts of cold shivers run up and down my back. This Druhar is a big fellow, but somebody has twisted his neck so that his face is looking over his shoulder.

There's a slip of paper sticking out of Druhar's pants pocket. I don't like corpses any better than the next fellow, but I reach down and pull out this piece of paper. And then my eyes pop out. The paper reads:

> 'For value received, I promise to pay to Tony Druhar, Five Thousand Dollars.' W. C. Roberts.

A promissory note, good in any man's court, if this W. C. Roberts has got $5000.

I look at the thing and finally stick it in my pocket. After all, Tony Druhar, dead or alive, owes the Mid-West Finance Company about $156.00.

I back out of the house and I'm on the porch when I see the taxicab that is pulled up behind my jaloppy. The prince is coming across the sidewalk.

Of course I don't know that he's a prince then. I find that out later. But he certainly dresses the part. He's wearing a black, single-breasted coat, which is open, showing a fawn-colored waistcoat. Under it is a pair of striped trousers and below that, believe it or not, white spats. On his head he's got a pearl-gray Homburg. He's carrying a pair of yellow pigskin gloves and a cane. So help me, he's coming up to Druhar's house.

'Good morning, sir,' he says to me in a voice that drips with some foreign accent. His face is long and very sad and aristocratic. 'I'm looking for Mr. Druhar.'

What I want to do is jump into my jaloppy and get the hell out of there, but I know how cops are, and it's just my luck that either the prince or the taxicab driver will remember the license number of my car, so I figure I may as well face the thing out.

'Mr. Druhar,' I say, 'is inside the house. He's dead.'

The prince's mouth falls open, but only for a second. Then he reaches into his waistcoat and brings out a monocle and sticks it in his eye. He looks at me and says, 'I do not understand.'

'Maybe he doesn't either, but he's dead just the same.'

He lets out a sigh. 'That is too bad. I am Prince Peter Strogovich. This Druhar had applied to me for a position, and I was just about to employ him. It is sad.'

The prince takes the monocle out of his eye and polishes it with his gloves. 'You say he is inside? The police do not yet know?'

They know soon enough. Some of the neighbors have been attracted by the triple event – my jaloppy, the taxicab and the prince in his fancy outfit. They have gathered and they've heard some of our talk, so there's a lot of chattering and running around.

In about five minutes, a squad car rolls up. In a few minutes more, there are ten or twelve cops around, an ambulance, and the emergency squad from the Fire Department.

There's a lot of excitement and when it all sifts down, the prince and myself are down at Headquarters, and Captain Riordan is swearing and asking a lot of questions.

Most of the swearing is at me. 'I don't like your story at all,' he tells me. 'You were pretty sore at this Druhar. According to the neighbors, and his friends, you cut a pretty scene yesterday at the funeral of his grandmother. My idea is that you went there this morning to collect the money and you got into a fight with him.'

'Wait a minute, Captain,' I cut in. 'Call up Oscar Berger, who's the Argus Adjustment Agency. Ask him if I've killed any of my skips before.'

'There's always a time to start, you know.'

The captain grunts and picks up the telephone. He calls the office and says, 'Hello, Mr. Berger? This is Police Headquarters. I've got a man here by the name of Sam Cragg who says he works for you. . . . What's the charge? Why, he said he was after a fellow who owed some money and it seems that the fellow got his neck twisted. What?' He listens for a minute, then he turns to me. 'He wants to know if you collected the money.'

I give the captain my opinion of Oscar Berger, which the captain translates into 'No.' He listens a minute more and then says, 'O.K.,' and hangs up.

'Berger says he fired you a couple of days ago.'

I really get sore then. That was about the kind of loyalty you can expect from a man who'd run that kind of a collection agency.

Prince Peter comes to my assistance.

'Captain, I do not think this man killed Mr. Druhar. I do not think he is strong enough to do it. Besides, there are no marks on him, and Mr. Druhar would not have submitted without fighting.'

'I could figure that out myself,' snaps the captain. 'He could have come on Druhar from the back and caught him by surprise.'

The prince shrugs. 'At any rate, you are not going to hold me? I have important matters. . . .'

'You can go,' says the captain. He scowls at me. 'I still don't like your story, but I'm going to give you the benefit of the doubt. If I find out anything more, I can pick you up easily enough.'

That's enough for me. I get out of Headquarters as quickly as I can. Outside, Prince Peter is just climbing into a taxicab.

I get a street car and ride back to Gardner Street where the jaloppy is still parked. It's there all right, only it hasn't got any tires or headlights now. The damn crooks in the neighborhood have stripped them off.

When I start swearing even the kids on the street duck into the houses. I've got a good mind just to leave the rest of the junk right there, but when I get to Division Street I go into a saloon and telephone a garage.

By the time I get down to the rattle-trap building on Wells Street where AAA has its lousy offices, I'm in a swell mood – for murder.

I slam into the office and Betty Marshall, who practically runs the business from the inside, gives me the ha-ha. 'So you finally landed in jail!'

'And it's no thanks to our boss that I'm not still there. Is he inside?'

He's trying to lock his office door, when I push it open and knock him halfway across the room. 'Listen, Berger,' I says to him, 'what kind of a double-crosser are you?'

He ducks behind the desk. 'Now take it easy, Cragg. I was just going to call Goldfarb, my lawyer, and have him spring you.'

'I'll bet you were! Every day of the week I do things for you that keep me awake nights, and that's the kind of loyalty you give me.'

'Now, now, Sam,' he soft-soaps me. 'I got a nice bunch of easy skips for you. To make it up, I'll pay you the regular five buck rate on them, although these are so easy you oughtn't to get more than three on them. It's the new account I landed, the O. W. Sugar Jewelry Company.'

'You call those easy skips? Hell, three-fourths of the people that buy jewelry on the installment plan pawn it before they finish paying for it!'

'Yeah, but they're all working people in the lower brackets. You've just got to find out where they work and threaten to garnishee their wages and they'll kick in.'

I take the cards he gives me. Like I said before, I hadn't any pull and couldn't get on the WPA.

These Sugar Jewelry skips are no better or worse than others I've handled. I find the first one, a middle-age Italian woman, cracking pecans in a little dump near Oak and Milton – the Death Corner. She gets eight cents a pound for shelling the pecans and if she works hard she can shell two pounds an hour. Why a woman like that ever bought a wrist watch I don't know, but she did – and I make her promise to pay a dollar a week on the watch.

I am working on the second skip on Sedgwick near Division, when I get the surprise of my life. Prince Pete Strogovich, cane and white spats and all, comes out of a little confectionery store. I step into a doorway and watch him saunter across the street and go into a saloon. Then I walk into the confectionery store. It's a dump; dirty showcases, stationery, candy boxes and empty soft drink bottles standing all around. There's a magazine rack on one side.

Next to it sits the biggest woman I've ever seen in my life. She's six feet one or two inches tall and big all around. She weighs two-ninety or three hundred and none of it is flabby fat.

'What can I do for you?' she asks, her voice a hoarse bass.

I pretend not to hear her and started pawing over the magazines.

'Can I help you?' she goes on. 'What magazines are you looking for?'

I make up the name of a dick mag.

'I don't carry that one, but there's plenty of detective magazines, just as good.'

'They're not just as good,' I retort. 'That's the trouble with you storekeepers. You're always trying to sell something just as good.'

She starts panting like she has the asthma and I give her a look. Her eyes are slits in her fat cheeks, but they're glittering slits. She's good and sore.

'Get the hell out of here!' she snaps at me. She starts getting up from the big reinforced chair and I beat it to the door.

When I get outside Prince Peter's coming out of the saloon, dabbing a handkerchief to his aristocratic mouth. I walk across the street and meet him on the corner.

'Hi, Pete!' I say to him.

He knows me all right. But he isn't overjoyed to meet me. 'What are you doing here?' he asks.

'Nothin' much, Pete, just trying to locate a skip.'

'Skip?' he asks. 'What is a skip?'

'Well, suppose you buy a suit of clothes on the installment plan, or a diamond ring or a car. You try to beat the firm out of the money and move without leaving a forwarding address. A skip tracer runs you down and hands you a summons. That's me.'

'Then you are a detective, no?'

'Well, I do detective work, all right, but I'm not exactly a detective.'

'So!' The prince gets out his monocle and begins polishing it on his gloves. He's sizing me up. After a minute, he decides I'm O.K. 'My friend, would you do a job for me? For two weeks I have been looking for a man and I can not find him. He – he owes me some money, just like your skips. You think, perhaps, you can find him?'

'Probably, but you see, I work for a collection agency and I only look for people they want.'

'But I would pay you well. Here!' He whips out a leather wallet and pulls out a couple of bills. Fifties. I take them from his hand and rub them. 'You're paying me a hundred dollars to find this man for you?'

'One hundred dollars now. When you find him I give you four hundred dollars more. You work for me, huh?'

I fold the bills four ways and put them into my pocket. Argus Adjustment Agency pays me five dollars for finding a skip. Sometimes I find two in one day. Sometimes I don't find two in a week.

'What's this fellow's name?'

'Roberts,' the prince says, 'W. C. Roberts.'

I don't tumble right away, not until the prince says: 'He owes me five thousand dollars. He has give me the note and promise to pay. . . .'

And then I know. W. C. Roberts is the name on Tony Druhar's note, the one I'd slipped out of his pocket and had in my own right now. I say: 'What was the last address you had of this Roberts, and what does he look like?'

'I do not know what he looks like,' the prince says. 'But his last address is – was,' he pulls a tiny notebook from his pocket, '518 Rookery Building.'

I write the address down on a card.

'He isn't there, any more, I take it.'

'No, he have moved and not give the new address. But you find him?'

'For five hundred bucks I'd find John Wilkes Booth,' I tell him.

'Booth? I do not know him.'

'Never mind. And where'll I find you?'

He thinks that over before giving me the answer. 'At the Gregorian Towers on Michigan Boulevard.'

I write that down, too, then I ask him the question that's been bothering me for a long time. 'Say, Prince, would you mind telling me what nationality you are?'

He likes that. He pulls himself up straight and sticks the monocle in his eye. 'I am Serbian,' he says proudly. 'My cousin was the king of Serbia. King Peter Karageorgovich.'

Me, I don't even know where Serbia is. The name's vaguely familiar, but that's about all. I make up my mind to look it up sometime.

I leave the prince and get on a south-bound Sedgwick Street car, but at Chicago Avenue it moves too slow and I get off and grab a cab. I have a hundred bucks and I want to see what it's like to spend money.

The Rookery Building is one of those old office buildings that was built right after the war – the Civil War. One of these days they're going to tear it down and use the ground as a parking lot.

I go straight to the superintendent's office. 'I'm looking for a Mr. W. C. Roberts, who used to have an office in this building,' I say to him.

'Is that so?' The supe comes back at me. 'Some other people are looking for him, too – including the cops.'

'Ha, the cops! And why're they looking for him?'

'You ain't never heard of W. C. Roberts, mister?'

'What'd he do, kill someone?'

'Uh-uh.' He gives me a funny look, then reaches into his pocket and brings out a slip of paper. He hands it to me and I look at it. It has some writing on it:

> 'For value received I promise to pay to William Kilduff, five thousand dollars.
>
> W. C. Roberts.'

I pull out my own note – the one made out to Tony Druhar. I show it to the superintendent. 'Hello, sucker,' says the superintendent. 'How much you pay for yours?'

I stall. 'The usual amount, I guess.'

'Five bucks?'

'Ten.'

'You *are* a sucker. Us Irish only paid five. I heard some Polacks and Serbians paid as high as twenty bucks.'

'Oh,' I say, not knowing what this was all about, 'so it depends on the nationality how big a sucker you are?'

'Yeah, sure. Most of us Irish know now we got gypped. But those hunkies – I hear they're still going for it. They refuse to believe that Roberts is a crook. That phoney prince keeps them bulled.'

'Prince? You mean Prince Peter Strogovich?'

'Yeah, the guy with the fancy duds,' he says.

'He claims to be a Serbian prince.' I laugh. 'I'll bet he gives his fellow countrymen a good line. Like to hear him some time.'

'Why don't you go to one of their meetings, then? I think tonight is the Serbians' night. They hold their meeting at some hall on Halsted Street, near North Avenue.'

'Say, what's this Roberts' guy look like?' I ask.

'That's the funny part of it. No one knows. He never came to his office here. A dame ran it for him. When the cops came in one day, she just went out and never came back.'

'Cagy, huh? Well, so long, sucker!'

'So long, sucker!'

When I get out of the Rookery Building I walk over to Adams Street and go into a saloon and have two good hookers of rye. I need them. This set-up is the screwiest I've ever run across in all my life.

Promissory notes, five bucks apiece. . . . Serbians.

I have another snort, then go back to the office of AAA, on Wells near Randolph. Betty has just come from getting her hair done. I give it the once-over. 'Like it?' she asked.

It's set in the new up-and-at-'em style. 'You dames get screwier every day,' I tell her.

'Is that so?' she says, coldly. 'Well, it's a good thing I didn't get my hair done for *you*.'

It's an idea I haven't thought about before, but I make a mental note of it. Inside his private office, Oscar Berger rubs his hands together. He can do it better than a Maxwell Street clothing merchant.

'Well, how many did you find?'

'One, but I got some good leads on two more.'

'Only one, and such good prospects!'

'Nuts, Berger,' I say to him, 'They're as tough as any others and you know it. Look, tell me something, ever hear of a crook by the name of W. C. Roberts?'

'Yeah, sure. Haven't you? But maybe that case broke when you were on your vacation.'

'It must have. What'd Roberts do?'

'Nothing much. Except swindle about five thousand hunkies in this man's town. He's an inventor, see, or claims to be one. He gets a bunch of these hunkies together and tells them he invented four-wheel brakes for automobiles, but Henry Ford or General Motors swiped the patent from him. He invented wireless, but Marconi gypped him out of the patent. So what? So he wants to sue Henry Ford and General Motors. But lawsuits cost money and that's what he hasn't got much of. So he gets the hunkies to finance the lawsuits. Mr. Roberts gives them notes. They lend him ten bucks now, they get five thousand when he collects from the big shots.'

'How much does he collect?'

Berger screws up his mouth. 'Ten or fifteen billion. Boxcar numbers.'

'And the chumps fall for it?'

'They like it! According to the papers, ten or fifteen thousand hunkies kicked in from five to a hundred bucks per each.'

'And Roberts skipped?'

'Wouldn't you?'

'That depends. If the suckers were milked dry, maybe. But I understand there's a lot of Bulgarians and Serbians and such still believe in Roberts.'

'Oh, sure, that's the sweet part of it. Roberts warned them even before the law jumped on him, that he was expecting something like that. On account of Mr. Ford, Westinghouse and Edison owning the cops and sicking them on him. Slick guy, this Roberts.'

'Yeah? What'd he look like?'

'That's the funny part of it. No one knows. He doesn't show himself. When the cops tried to get him, they discovered that no one would even admit ever having seen him.'

'Not bad,' I say, 'not bad at all.'

Oscar Berger gives me the once-over. 'What's your interest in this? Roberts didn't put the bite into you, did he?'

'No. When someone offers me over four per cent interest I know he's crooked. Not that I'd ever get enough to invest at four per cent.'

When I come out of Berger's office, Betty is putting lipstick on her mouth. 'All right, sister,' I say to her, 'I'm going to give you a break tonight. Where do you live?'

'At 4898 Winthrop, but if you come up you're traveling just for the exercise.'

'I like exercise,' I tell her. 'I'll be there at seven.'

'I won't be home. . . . What'll I wear?'

Nice, girl, Betty. 'Nothing fancy. We'll go to some quiet spot.'

I still have the best part of my hundred bucks the Serbian prince had given me. I get a haircut and a shave and have a bite at Harding's Grill on Madison. Then I take a taxi to 4898 Winthrop Avenue, which is a block north of Lawrence and one east of Broadway.

The place is a second-rate apartment hotel. They won't let me upstairs without being announced and when I get Betty on the phone she says she'll be right down.

She's down in five minutes. I almost don't recognize her. She's wearing a silver evening dress that must have cost her at least a month's pay. Her hair's brushed soft and shiny.

She certainly doesn't look like the type of girl who'd work for a sleezy outfit like AAA. I say to her: 'You look very interesting.'

'You never noticed it before,' she says.

'How could I? All the time I'm working for Triple A I've got a grouch. Skip tracing is a lousy business.'

'I'm figuring on quitting myself,' Betty says. 'One of your chumps came into the office last week. He was a big fellow, but he bawled like a baby. You were going to garnishee his wages unless he paid ten dollars a month on a cheap piano he bought for his daughter who wanted to be a musician, but changed her mind and eloped with a greaseball.'

'Nix,' I say. 'Let me forget skip tracing for one night. I dream about it.'

'All right. Where we going?'

'A little place I discovered,' I tell her. 'You've never seen one like it.'

I flag a taxi. Betty looks at me suspiciously when I give the driver the address, but she doesn't make any comment until we climb out on Halsted Street, down near North Avenue.

She looks around while I pay the driver. 'What is this, one of your jokes?'

We're in front of a dump that has a sign on the window. 'Plennert's Café. Lodge Hall for Rent.'

'No. A fellow told me this place would be interesting.'

The café is a cheap saloon. You have to go through the saloon to get into the lodge hall, in the rear.

Betty's game, I've got to say that for her. We go through the saloon into the lodge hall. There are rows of folding chairs set up in the hall and most of them are filled with men, women and kids. You can cut the smoke.

Almost all the men in the place are dark complected. Some of them have to shave twice a day. The women are swarthy, too, although here and there you can see a blonde, just by way of contrast.

Betty comes in for a lot of gawking. She's glad when I pull her down in a seat near the rear.

'What is this?' she whispers to me. Her face is red and I know she doesn't like it any too well.

I say, 'This is a patriotic meeting of the Sons and Daughters of Serbia. Look, up there on the platform, there's something you'll never see again – a Serbian prince.'

Yeah, Prince Peter. He's pouring out a glass of water on a speaker's stand and the way some of the Serbs on the platform stand around, you can tell that they think a lot of Prince Pete.

There are about eight men on the platform and one woman. The woman is as big as three of the men. Yeah, she's the amazon who keeps the confectionery store on Sedgwick Street. She's sitting on a stout wooden bench near the side of the stage, where she can watch Prince Pete. She's pretty interested in him.

The prince drinks his water and holds up his hands. The room becomes as still as a cemetery at midnight.

'My country people,' the prince says in English. And then he starts jabbering in the damnedest language. He sounds off for ten minutes and I don't understand a word of it – until everyone in the place begins clapping hands and cheering and one or two of the younger fellows yell in English:

'The hell with Henry Ford! The hell with General Motors! We'll stick with Mr. Roberts!'

'Fun, isn't it?' I say to Betty, next to me.

'Is it? I suppose this is your idea of a joke.'

'Not at all. You see in this room about two hundred of the choicest suckers in the city of Chicago. And do they like it? Listen, to them.'

About twenty or thirty of the Serbians climb up onto the platform. Prince Pete gives them some aristocratic condescension and they like it. Every one of them.

'You want to see the prince's monocle?' I ask Betty. 'Wait here a minute.'

I push through the crowd and climb up on the platform.

'Hello, Prince,' I say to his royal highness.

Sure enough, the monocle comes out. He gets it out of his fancy vest and sticks it into his eye. Then he says: 'Ah, Mister Cragg! How *do* you do?'

'Fine. And you – you're doing all right yourself, I see.'

He drops his voice. 'You have information for me, yes?'

'I have information, no. But I've got a clue. Another day or two—'

'Good! You let me know damn quick, yes? This,' he shrugs deprecatingly, 'it is part of the game. You understand?'

'Yeah, sure, I understand.'

I go back to Betty. 'Well, you got enough?'

'Oh, no,' she replies sweetly. 'I'd like to attend another patriotic meeting. How about the Bulgarians, haven't they got one tonight?'

'No, theirs is Thursday. But there's a beer stube over on North Avenue—'

She gets up quick. In the saloon, the amazon gets up from a chair and grabs my arm. 'You're the man was in my store this afternoon,' she says.

I try to take my arm out of her grip and can't. 'That's right, I wanted to buy a detective magazine. Uh, you got it for me?'

'Don't try to kid me, young man,' she snaps at me. 'I'm not as dumb as I look. I saw you talking to the Prince. That's why I came out here. What's he up to?'

I take hold of her wrist and this time she lets me take it off my arm. 'Sorry, madam,' I tell her. 'The affair between the prince and myself is confidential.'

Her eyes leave me for a second and she sizes up Betty. 'This your girl?'

'Uh-huh. Why?'

'You're a cop,' she says. 'I can always smell one. You're a private dick. And you're working for the Prince. Well, I want you to do a little job for me. And I'll pay you twice what he paid you.'

'He's paying me a grand.'

'That's a lie! Pete hasn't got that kind of money. I'll give you six hundred.' She's wearing a tweed suit that would have made a fine tent for Mr. Ringling's biggest elephant. She digs a fist into a pocket and brings out a roll of bills. She counts out six hundred dollars, in fifties.

'Here, now tell me what the Prince hired you for?'

I struck the word ethics out of my dictionary when I became a skip tracer. But Betty is breathing down my neck. I say to the fat woman. 'That's against the rules. A dick never betrays a confidence.'

Her piggish eyes glint like they had that afternoon when she'd got sore at me. She says, 'All right, you don't have to tell me that. I think I can guess. But I want you to work for me just the same. I think Pete's two-timing me.'

'Two-timing *you?*'

She shows her teeth. They are as big as a horse's. 'He's got a woman somewhere. I want you to shadow him.'

'And then? After I see him with the dame?'

'You give me her name and address, that's all. I'll do the rest.'

She would, too. She'd probably snatch the woman bald-headed. But that isn't my worry. Not yet. I say to the amazon: 'Oke, I'll work for you.'

'Start tonight. Shadow the Prince. I – I can't do it myself.' She scowls. 'I'm too conspicuous . . . my size.'

Betty pokes me in the back with her fist, but I pretend not to notice. 'All right, Miss—'

'Kelly, Mamie Kelly. You know my address. When you get results, give me a buzz on the phone.'

She waddles out of the saloon and about two second later, the prince comes in. He catches up with Betty and me at the door says, 'Ah, Mr. Cragg!' and looks at Betty like she was modeling lingerie. But he doesn't stop.

When we get outside, he's waving his yellow cane at a taxicab. By luck there's another parked across the street. Even though it is facing the wrong way, I want it and want it bad.

I grab hold of Betty's wrist. 'Come on!'

She jerks away. 'What're you going to do? You louse, you can't double-cross your – your client, like that.'

'Double-cross, hell!' I snort. 'That's the only game the prince understands. We're following him!'

I drag her across the street and heave her into the cab. 'Follow that yellow taxi!' I tell the driver. 'Five bucks if you keep on his tail.'

'For ten bucks, I'll run him down!' says the cabby.

He makes a beautiful U turn, just missing a street car. Then we are off, up Halsted Street.

'Some fun,' Betty says to me. But she doesn't mean it.

I grin at her. 'Now, kid, you got to take the good with the bad. I work like a dog all week for Oscar Berger. I do things that make me ashamed to look in a mirror and what do I get? Twenty, maybe thirty measly bucks a week. And now comes a chance to make some real dough – and you squawk!'

'It's dirty money,' she says.

I reach into my pocket and pull out Tony Druhar's five thousand dollar promissory note. 'Look, Betty, I almost got thrown in the can this morning, because a guy was killed. I found this on his body.'

She looks at the piece of paper. 'Why, it's an I.O.U. for five thousand dollars!'

'Uh-huh, and every one of these Serbians tonight has at least one chunk of paper like this. Prince Pete's one of the higher-ups in as lousy a racket I ever heard of. That's why I'm working on all these angles. I'd do it even if I wasn't getting a cent.'

Well, maybe I would at that. But I know it is a lot more fun doing with a flock of fifties in my pocket, and the promise of some more.

It goes over. Betty hands the note back to me and her eyes are shining. 'I didn't understand, Sam. I think – I think you're swell!'

'So're you, kid!' I say. I throw my arm about her. And then the cab stops all of a sudden and the driver yells. 'Here, buddy!'

'What? Where is he?'

'He just went into The Red Mill.'

I look around and see that we are on Lawrence near Broadway. I climb out of the cab and help Betty, then hand the cabby a five dollar bill.

I say to Betty, 'Maybe, we'll get a chance to do some of that dancing you wanted.'

We go inside and the headwaiter looks at Betty's silver evening dress and gives me a big smile. 'Good evening, sir. A table near the front?'

'Umm,' I say, looking around as if night clubs were regular stuff with me. 'Something not too public, if you know what I mean?'

'Yes, sir!'

He starts off down the side along the booths. At the fourth booth I stop. 'Well, well, Prince!'

He's in the booth with as dizzy a blonde as I ever saw. He looks up at me and the monocle almost falls from his eye. 'You!' he says.

'Yeah, me. Ain't it a coincidence?'

Then he sees Betty and catches hold of himself. He comes to his feet and bows. I say: 'Betty, allow me to introduce his royal highness, Prince Peter Strogovich . . . or something.'

So help me, he takes her hand and kisses it. Then he says, 'But won't you join us? Ah, Mitzi, this is my old friend, Mr. Cragg. And Miss—'

'Betty Marshall.'

The headwaiter is disappointed. He's losing a tip. I wave him away. 'We're joining our friends.'

Mitzi is giving Betty the once-over. She says, bluntly: 'I saw him first.'

'My eyes aren't very good,' Betty gives her back.

It's over the Prince's head. He gives Betty an eye-massage, his face still sad, but lecherous. 'That is a beautiful dress you are wearing, Miss Marshall.'

I say, 'Ain't it? Look, Betty, your nose is shiny. Why don't you and Mitzi go spruce up?'

'I was just going to do that,' Betty says. 'Coming along, Mitzi?'

Mitzi gives me a dirty look, but she gets up. When the girls are gone, the prince says to me, 'She is charming, no?'

'She's only my secretary. Her steady is a prize fighter, who's very jealous. And now that we've got that cleared away, let's talk business. You've been holding out on me, Prince. You want me to find W. C. Roberts and all the time you're working for him.'

'Of course I am working for him. But I do not know Mr. Roberts. I have never seen him. Always, he sends me just letters.'

'What about the dough you collect from these hunkies, these countrymen of yours.'

'I send it to him, all! Then he mail me the commission, ten per cent.'

'A very likely story. You collect from these people and mail it to Roberts. He trusts you?'

The prince scowls sadly. 'That is the trouble. He does not trust me. One time, just for a joke, you know, I send him not as much money as I collect. Next week I get the letter from him. He know how much I have hold out.'

'Ah, he's got a spotter. Someone who goes to the meetings and checks up on you. Right?'

The prince shrugs wearily. 'That is what I think. But I do not know who it is. I have try to find out and I cannot.'

I make a guess. 'Maybe the spotter's name was Tony Druhar!'

The prince gets sore about that. 'What you mean by that, Mr. Cragg?'

'Nothing. I was just joking.'

'It is not a good joke. I go to see Mr. Druhar, yesterday, because he wants sell me note for ten dollars.'

'You said you were seeing him because he'd applied to you for a job of some kind.'

'When I say that I do not know you. It was because of note. I buy note sometimes at bargain.'

He's lying like hell. Maybe a Serbian's note is a bargain at five dollars, but it isn't to an Irishman.

I say, 'You send this money to Mr. Roberts; to what address?'

'I send the letter to General Delivery. In two-three days I get back letter, with my commission.'

'Where's the letter mailed, Chicago?'

'Yes, that is why I know Mr. Roberts still live here.'

'Well, it's a nice racket for you, Prince. As long as you get your dough, what're you kicking about? Why do you want to see Roberts?'

He doesn't like that. He gives me a once-over through his monocle. 'Mr. Cragg, I pay you five hundred dollars to find Mr. Roberts. You wish to continue working for me?'

'Why, certainly, Prince!' I tell him. 'I was just trying to get a line on Mr. Roberts. . . . Ah, here're the girls.'

They look like they'd chewed up the olive branch in the ladies' room. I get up and say to Betty: 'Gosh, I just remembered we're supposed to be at Bill's party.'

'I was about to remind you,' Betty says smartly.

I say, 'So long, Prince. Be seeing you in a day or two.'

He grabs hold of Betty's hand and tries to kiss it. She jerks it away. 'I just washed it,' she tells him.

'But your telephone number? And your address? I like to send you the flowers.'

'I've got hay fever,' Betty says. 'I can't stand flowers. And I haven't got a telephone. I never learned how to work one. So long, Prince.'

'Good-by!' snaps Mitzi. 'It was nice meeting you.'

We exit.

Outside, Betty says, 'Nice boy, that Prince. Some woman's husband is going to shoot him one of these days.'

'You forget Mamie Kelly. She's got something on him.'

'You going to snitch on him?'

'Not yet. Still a few things to settle with him.'

'You get anything out of him?'

'Uh-huh, the reason he wants me to find this Roberts. He tried holding out one week and discovered Roberts has a checker on him. My hunch is the Prince prefers a hundred per cent to ten.'

The Red Mill is only a couple of blocks from Betty's apartment hotel. I walk east on Lawrence Avenue with her. I turn her into Winthrop and we are almost to Ainslee before she's aware of it. Then she says, 'You're taking me home? What a large evening!'

'Be a large one next time. Maybe tomorrow?'

'You'll probably take me to the Bulgarian or Siberian meeting.'

I leave her outside her apartment hotel. She's sore when she goes inside. I can't help it. I'll see her in the morning. There's a couple of little things I still have to do and I have to get up early in the morning.

I go to a stationery store on Broadway that is still open and buy a large children's book, one with stiff covers. I have the clerk wrap it in the reddest paper he has in the store, some glossy Christmas wrapping paper.

Then I get an address label from him and a bunch of postage stamps.

It's a long ride downtown so I take the elevated. I get off at Quincy and walk over to the post office and mail the red package at the mailing window. Then I go to my cheap hotel on Jackson Street and go to bed.

Seven-thirty I get up and have breakfast at Thompson's – without the Death Notices, this time. After which I hoof over to the post office to see if my little trick works.

There are a couple of thousand lock boxes in the General Delivery room at the main Chicago post office. To watch them all, during the rush hours would take eighteen pairs of eyes. That's why I mailed the book to Mr. Roberts. The postal clerk would put a card in his box, saying there was a package for him. He'd have to call at one of the windows for it.

So I fool around at a writing stand near the windows. I fill out eighteen or twenty post-office money orders for fancy amounts and tear them up or stick them in my pocket. I make one out every time someone comes from a box and goes to one of the windows to get a package.

It's nine forty-five when the red package is handed out. I'm almost caught sleeping, because I'd been expecting a man and this is a girl, a young girl probably just out of high school.

I'm right behind her when she goes out of the post office. She doesn't even suspect she's followed. She walks north up Clark Street to Monroe, then turns east and goes into a building. I ride up in the same elevator with her to the tenth floor.

When she goes in a door I walk over and look at the inscription on it. It reads: 'Harker Service Company.'

I wait about five minutes, then go inside. The girl I'd followed from the post office is at a typewriter, but another, a big horsy-faced dame is behind a desk just inside the door. Beside her, against the wall is a big cabinet with narrow pigeon-holes. There are letters in most of the pigeon-holes and another stack on the desk in front of the girl. The red package is there, too.

I say, 'I understand you run a business mail service here.'

'That's right,' the girl replies. 'We also take telephone calls, forward mail and provide you with a business address. No room number is necessary. The charge is only $2.00 per month.'

'That's fine,' I say. 'Now, tell me, does a man named Brown get his mail here?'

She freezes up, right away. 'Our service is absolutely confidential!'

'But I got a letter from Brown; he gave this address. I want to see him.'

'In that case, you'd have to leave a message for him. Although,' her face twists, 'there's no Mr. Brown in our service.'

'I must have got the address wrong then,' I say.

I go out. There's a cigar stand in the lobby on the first floor, with a marble game next to it. I buy a package of cigarettes and shove a nickel in the slot of the marble game. There was a sticker on the glass: 'For Amusement Only. No Prizes or Awards.'

It's a bumper game; the steel marbles make electric contact with springs and light up lights and register a score. I waste three nickels, then get some change from the cigar stand. 'You're playing that just for fun, you know,' the cigar stand man warns me.

'Sure, I'm killing time, that's all.'

I spend a dollar on the game, then loaf around for a half hour and spend another dollar. It's about eleven-thirty by then and the man at the cigar stand's getting nervous about me.

I buy a candy bar and get the change in nickels and shove them into the marble game. 'That's costing you money,' the fellow at the stand says.

'So's the dame I'm s'posed to meet here!' I snap at him.

He chuckles. 'Boy, how you can take it. Two hours!'

I pump two of the steel marbles into the slot and slam them both out with the plunger. Lights go up, a bell rings.

'Jackpot!' the cigar stand man yelps.

'No prizes, huh?' I glare at him. There's a little knob in the front of the machine. I pushed it and a small door pops open exposing a box almost filled with nickels. There are about five pounds of nickels. I stow them in my coat pocket while the cigar stand chap looks on, sick. He's still afraid that I'm a cop.

I quit then. It's just twelve when I go into the Gregorian Towers on North Michigan and ride up to Prince Peter's apartment.

He's just having his breakfast. He's wearing a purple dressing gown on which is embroidered a big red monogram.

'You have found him, Mr. Cragg?' he asks eagerly.

'Practically,' I say. 'But the expenses on this job are very heavy. If you could let me have another hundred. . . .'

He doesn't like that. 'What do you mean, you have found him – practically?'

'Well, I got past the post office, anyway. A girl gets his mail at General Delivery and takes it to an address on Monroe Street.'

'How do you know it is Mr. Roberts' mail?' he cuts in. 'Hah! Four days I have waited at General Delivery and cannot spot this girl, his messenger.'

'I can understand that. There're about five thousand boxes there. I knew I couldn't watch them all, so last night after I left you I bought a big flat book, that I knew was too big to put into a post-office box. I had it wrapped in red paper and mailed it Mr. Roberts. When the girl got this red package, I followed her.'

'To what number on Monroe Street?'

'The Davis Building. Room 1023. It's a mail address outfit.'

'Mail address? What is that?'

There was a loud knock on the prince's door. He says: 'The waiter for these dishes. . . . Come in!'

The door opens and Mamie Kelly, all three hundred pounds of her, comes in. The prince jumps to his feet and turns about four shades whiter.

'Madame!' he exclaims.

She comes all the way into the room. She has something under her arm, a flat red package. The string's broken on the package and the paper disarranged. I can see the cover of a children's book.

I say: 'Well, Prince, I must be going.'

Mamie Kelly blocks the way to the door. She says, 'Stick around, young fellow. Something I want to ask you.'

'Yeah, sure,' I say. 'I'll run over to your store after a while. I've got to report at my office.'

She shakes her big head. 'No.' She takes the book from under her arm and says, 'Look, Pete!' and slams it over the prince's head. He goes down to the floor and stays there.

'Get up, you dirty rat!' Mamie Kelly yells.

The prince begins to whine. He sounds like a dog that has been whipped. Big Mamie reaches down and twists one of her meat hooks in the back of his purple dressing gown. She picks him up and tosses him into an easy chair. Man Mountain Dean couldn't have done it easier.

All of a sudden I think of something. Tony Druhar, the Serbian I'd found dead – with his face turned around to his spine. . . .

Maybe you think I don't feel funny. A three-hundred-pound woman, all muscle and bone. My skin gets hot and cold and begins to crawl. What the hell, a man – you could belt him in the jaw, butt him in the stomach or kick him where it'll do the most good. But a woman – can you do those things to a woman?

The prince is as big as me, if not bigger. Yet Mamie Kelly handles him as if he was a baby. She turns to me and says, 'So you think you're smart, sending me this book?'

'Me?' I say.

'None of that, now! Della Harker's a cousin of mine. I never got a package before. When you came in there, with your phoney stuff she got me on the telephone. I saw you from across the street fooling around with that damn pin game.'

'Mamie!' yelps the Prince, suddenly. '*You* – you are W. C. Roberts?'

'Of course I am. How the hell you suppose I got all the money to set you up in this swell hotel? You think I made it in that lousy store I run on Sedgwick for a blind?'

The prince is about ready to faint. I'm not far from it, myself. I'm concentrating on the door, wondering if I can get to it and out, before she can head me off.

Mamie Kelly says, 'I give you all that dough, buy you the fancy clothes and what do you do in return? You spend the money on blond floozies, and try to muscle in on my racket. You think I don't know about Druhar?'

'Druhar?' the prince gasps.

'Yes, Druhar, the punk. He was starving, and I gave him a job at the store. He had to nose around, and then try to sell me out to you. Well, he got what he deserved.'

'*You* killed him?'

'Like that!' she makes a motion with her two hands like wringing out a wet dishrag.

I take a deep breath and make a dash for the door.

I don't get to it. Mamie takes a quick step to one side and falls against me. She knocks me spinning and before I can get up, she swoops down on me and grabs my left arm. She twists it behind my back in a hammerlock.

I yell and heave up, trying to turn a forward somersault. A bunch of nickels fall on the floor. And then—

I yelled to high heaven. She breaks my arm. The big, fat murderess! The bones grate in my elbow and I yell bloody murder.

I guess that saves my life. After all, it's a hotel and she doesn't want a flock of cops busting in. She lets go my arm to grab my neck. I have just enough strength left to roll away.

She comes after me again, her big face twisted in a snarl. I can't see her eyes at all, they're buried in the fat of her cheeks. I'm so scared of her that I go a little crazy. I kick a chair in her way and she knocks it aside with one punch of her fist.

I try for the door again. She heads me off. I back away and step on some of the nickels that've spilled from my pocket.

And then I know what to do. It's my only chance. Two minutes more in this room with the amazon – and I'd wind up like Tony Druhar. Only more broken bones.

My left arm is hanging limp at my side and I'm dizzy with the pain of it. But there's nothing wrong with my right arm. I rip open my coat with my right hand, shrug out of the right side of it and reach over to slide it down my left shoulder.

Mamie makes a noise like a female gorilla and starts for me. I jump back and find myself against the wall. But I've got the coat in my hand now, the coat with about five pounds of nickels in the pockets. A half-pound of them in the toe of a sock would have made a dandy black-jack.

She comes at me and I swing the coat with all that's left in me. The noise she makes when she hits the floor reminds me of the time I got drunk at a dance and fell into the bass drum.

Prince Pete thinks this is a good time to make his getaway, but I beat him to the door and swing the weighted coat in his face.

'Wait a minute, pal,' I say to him. 'You made a bargain with me – four hundred bucks more if I found W. C. Roberts for you. There's Roberts. Now kick in. I need the dough, on account of I figure on quitting my skip tracing job and maybe getting married!'

He pays. Then I pick up the telephone and call police headquarters.

YOU'LL ALWAYS REMEMBER ME

STEVE FISHER

It was the goal, the dream, of the penny-a-word writers for the pulps to break out, to get into the higher-paying slick magazines, to have books published, or to get a break in Hollywood. Of the handful who made it, few enjoyed more success than Steve Fisher (1912–1980), the extraordinarily prolific pulp writer (almost 200 stories between 1935 and 1938) who became a sought-after screenwriter.

Of the twenty novels written under his own name and as Stephen Gould and Grant Lane, the most famous is *I Wake Up Screaming*, the basis for the classic film noir starring Victor Mature.

Among the many notable motion pictures on which he received screen credit are such war films as *To the Shores of Tripoli*, *Destination Tokyo* and *Berlin Correspondent*. Crime films include *Lady in the Lake* and *Song of the Thin Man*. He also wrote more than 200 television scripts for such popular shows as *Starsky & Hutch*, *McMillan & Wife* and *Barnaby Jones*.

'You'll Always Remember Me' is not a subtle story, as expected of a tale written for a pulp magazine, but its theme still resonates more than a half-century after it was written. What should society do with juvenile killers who cannot be tried as adults? William March explored this successfully in his play *The Bad Seed*, which later became a controversial movie.

This story, with its chilling last paragraph, was originally published in the March 1938 issue of *Black Mask*.

YOU'LL ALWAYS REMEMBER ME

STEVE FISHER

I could tell it was Pushton blowing the bugle and I got out of bed tearing half of the bed clothes with me. I ran to the door and yelled, 'Drown it! Drown it! Drown it!' and then I slammed the door and went along the row of beds and pulled the covers off the rest of the guys and said:

'Come on, get up. Get up! Don't you hear Pushton out there blowing his stinky lungs out?'

I hate bugles anyway, but the way this guy Pushton all but murders reveille kills me. I hadn't slept very well, thinking of the news I was going to hear this morning, one way or the other, and then to be jarred out of what sleep I could get by Pushton climaxed everything.

I went back to my bed and grabbed my shoes and puttees and slammed them on the floor in front of me, then I began unbuttoning my pajamas. I knew it wouldn't do any good to ask the guys in this wing. They wouldn't know anything. When they did see a paper all they read was the funnies. That's the trouble with Clark's. I know it's one of the best military academies in the West and that it costs my old man plenty of dough to keep me here, but they sure have some dopy ideas on how to handle kids. Like dividing the dormitories according to ages. Anybody with any sense knows that it should be according to grades because just take for instance this wing. I swear there isn't a fourteen-year-old-punk in it that I could talk to without wanting to push in his face. And I have to live with the little pukes.

So I kept my mouth shut and got dressed, then I beat it out into the company street before the battalion got lined up for the flag raising. That's a silly thing, isn't it? Making us stand around with empty stomachs, shivering goose pimples while they pull up the flag and Pushton blows the bugle again. But at that I guess I'd have been in a worse place than Clark's Military Academy if my pop hadn't had a lot of influence and plenty of dollars. I'd be in a big school where they knock you around and don't ask you whether you like it or not. I know. I was there a month. So I guess the best thing for me to do was to let the academy have their Simple Simon flag-waving fun and not kick about it.

I was running around among the older guys now, collaring each one and asking the same question: 'Were you on home-going yesterday? Did you see a paper last night? What about Tommy Smith?' That was what I wanted to know. What about Tommy Smith.

'He didn't get it,' a senior told me.

'You mean the governor turned him down?'

'Yeah. He hangs Friday.'

That hit me like a sledge on the back of my head and I felt words rushing to the tip of my tongue and then sliding back down my throat. I felt weak, like my stomach was all tied up in a knot. I'd thought sure Tommy Smith would have had his sentence changed to life. I didn't think they really had enough evidence to swing him. Not that I cared, particularly, only he had lived across the street and when they took him in for putting a knife through his old man's back – that was what they charged him with – it had left his two sisters minus both father and brother and feeling pretty badly.

Where I come in is that I got a crush on Marie, the youngest sister. She's fifteen. A year older than me. But as I explained, I'm not any little dumb dope still in grammar school. I'm what you'd call bright.

So that was it; they were going to swing Tommy after all, and Marie would be bawling on my shoulder for six months. Maybe I'd drop the little dame. I certainly wasn't going to go over and take that for the rest of my life.

I got lined up in the twelve-year-old company, at the right end because I was line sergeant. We did squads right and started marching toward the flag pole. I felt like hell. We swung to a company front and halted.

Pushton started in on the bugle. I watched him with my eyes burning. Gee, I hate buglers, and Pushton is easy to hate anyway. He's fat and wears horn-rimmed glasses. He's got a body like a bowling ball and a head like a pimple. His face looks like yesterday's oatmeal. And does he think being bugler is an important job! The little runt struts around like he was Gabriel, and he walks with his buttocks sticking out one way and his chest the other.

I watched him now, but I was thinking more about Tommy Smith. Earlier that night of the murder I had been there seeing Marie and I had heard part of Tommy's argument with his old man. Some silly thing. A girl Tommy wanted to marry and the old man couldn't see it that way. I will say he deserved killing, the old grouch. He used to chase me with his cane. Marie says he used to get up at night and wander around stomping that cane as he walked.

Tommy's defense was that the old boy lifted the cane to bean him. At least that was the defense the lawyer wanted to present. He wanted to present that, with Tommy pleading guilty, and hope for an acquittal. But Tommy stuck to straight denials on everything. Said he hadn't killed his father. The way everything shaped up the State proved he was a drunken liar and the jury saw it that way.

Tommy was a nice enough sort. He played football at his university, was a big guy with blond hair and a ruddy face, and blue eyes. He had a nice smile, white and clean like he scrubbed his teeth a lot. I guess his old man had been right about that girl, though, because when all this trouble started she dropped right out of the picture, went to New York or somewhere with her folks.

I was thinking about this when we began marching again; and I was still thinking about it when we came in for breakfast about forty minutes later, after having had our arms thrown out of joint in some more silly stuff called setting-up exercises. What they won't think of! As though we didn't get enough exercise running around all day!

Then we all trooped in to eat.

I sat at the breakfast table cracking my egg and watching the guy across from me hog six of them. I wanted to laugh. People think big private schools are the ritz and that their sons, when they go there, mix with the cream of young America. Bushwa! There are a few kids whose last names you might see across the front of a department store like Harker Bros., and there are some movie stars' sons, but most of us are a tough, outcast bunch that couldn't get along in public school and weren't wanted at home. Tutors wouldn't handle most of us for love or money. So they put us here.

Clark's will handle any kid and you can leave the love out of it so long as you lay the money on the line. Then the brat is taken care of so far as his parents are concerned, and he has the prestige of a fancy Clark uniform.

There wasn't another school in the State that would have taken me, public or private, after looking at my record. But when old man Clark had dough-ray-me clutched in his right fist he was blind to records like that. Well, that's the kind of a bunch we were.

Well, as I say, I was watching this glutton stuff eggs down his gullet which he thought was a smart thing to do even though he got a bellyache afterward, when the guy on my right said:

'I see Tommy Smith is going to hang.'

'Yeah,' I said, 'that's rotten, ain't it?'

'Rotten?' he replied. 'It's wonderful. It's what that rat has coming to him.'

'Listen,' said I, 'one more crack like that and I'll smack your stinking little face in.'

'You and how many others?' he said.

'Just me,' I said, 'and if you want to come outside I'll do it right now.'

The kid who was table captain yelled: 'Hey, you two pipe down. What's the argument anyway?'

'They're going to hang Tommy Smith,' I said, 'and I think it's a dirty rotten shame. He's as innocent as a babe in the woods.'

'Ha-ha,' said the table captain, 'you're just bothered about Marie Smith.'

'Skirt crazy! Skirt crazy!' mumbled the guy stuffing down the eggs.

I threw my water in his face, then I got up, facing the table captain, and the guy on my right. 'Listen,' I said, 'Tommy Smith is innocent. I was there an hour before the murder happened, wasn't I? What do you loud-mouthed half-wits think you know about it? All you morons know is what you read in the papers. Tommy didn't do it. I should know, shouldn't I? I was right there in the house before it happened. I've been around there plenty since. I've talked to the detectives.'

I sat down, plenty mad. I sat down because I had seen a faculty officer coming into the dining-room. We all kept still until he walked on through. Then the table captain sneered and said:

'Tommy Smith is a dirty stinker. He's the one that killed his father all right. He stuck a knife right through his back!'

'A lie! A lie!' I screamed.

'How do you know it's a lie?'

'Well, I – I know, that's all,' I said.

'Yeah, you know! Listen to him! You know! That's hot. I think I'll laugh!'

'Damn it,' I said. 'I *do* know!'

'How? How? Tell us that!'

'Well, maybe *I* did it. What do you think about that?'

'You!' shouted the table captain. 'A little fourteen-year-old wart like you killing anybody! Ha!'

'Aw, go to hell,' I said, 'that's what you can do. Go straight to hell!'

'A little wart like you killing anybody,' the table captain kept saying, and he was holding his sides and laughing.

All that Monday I felt pretty bad thinking about Tommy, what a really swell guy he had been, always laughing, always having a pat on the back for you. I knew he must be in a cell up in San Quentin now, waiting, counting the hours, maybe hearing them build his scaffold.

I imagine a guy doesn't feel so hot waiting for a thing like that, pacing in a cell, smoking up cigarettes, wondering what it's like when you're dead. I've read some about it. I read about Two Gun Crowley, I think it was, who went to the chair with his head thrown back and his chest out like he was proud of it. But there must have been something underneath, and Crowley, at least, knew that *he* had it coming to him. The real thing must be different than what you read in the papers. It must be pretty awful.

But in spite of all this I had sense enough to stay away from Marie all day. I could easily have gone to her house which was across the street from the campus, but I knew that she and her sister, Ruth, and that Duff Ryan, the young detective who had made the arrest – because, as he said, he thought it was his duty – had counted on the commutation of sentence. They figured they'd have plenty of time to clear up some angles of the case which had been plenty shaky even in court. No, sir. Sweet Marie would be in no mood for my consolation and besides I was sick of saying the same things over and over and watching her burst into tears every time I mentioned Tommy's name.

I sat in the study hall Monday evening thinking about the whole thing. Outside the window I could see the stars crystal clear; and though it was warm in the classroom I could feel the cold of the air in the smoky blue of the night, so that I shivered. When they marched us into the dormitory at eight-thirty Simmons, the mess captain, started razzing me about Tommy being innocent again, and I said:

'Listen, putrid, you wanta get hurt?'

'No,' he said, then he added: 'Sore head.'

'You'll have one sore face,' I said, 'if you don't shut that big yap of yours.'

There was no more said and when I went to bed and the lights went off I lay there squirming while that fat-cheeked Pushton staggered through taps with his bugle. I was glad that Myers had bugle duty tomorrow and I wouldn't have to listen to Pushton.

But long after taps I still couldn't sleep for thinking of Tommy. What a damn thing that was – robbing me of my sleep! But I tell you, I did some real fretting, and honestly, if it hadn't been for the fact that God and I parted company so long ago, I might have even been sap enough to pray for him. But I didn't. I finally went to sleep. It must have been ten o'clock.

I didn't show around Marie's Tuesday afternoon either, figuring it was best to keep away. But after chow, that is, supper, an orderly came beating it out to the study hall for me and told me I was wanted on the telephone. I chased up to the main building and got right on the wire. It was Duff Ryan, that young detective I told you about.

'You've left me with quite a load, young man,' he said.

'Explain,' I said. 'I've no time for nonsense.' I guess I must have been nervous to say a thing like that to the law, but there was something about Duff Ryan's cool gray eyes that upset me and I imagined I could see those eyes right through the telephone.

'I mean about Ruth,' he said softly, 'she feels pretty badly. Now I can take care of her all right, but little Marie is crying her eyes out and I can't do anything with her.'

'So what?' I said.

'She's your girl, isn't she, Martin?' he asked.

'Listen,' I said, 'in this school guys get called by their last name. Martin sounds sissy. My name is Thorpe.'

'I'm sorry I bothered you, Martin,' Duff said in that same soft voice. 'If you don't want to cooperate—'

'Oh, I'll cooperate,' I said. 'I'll get right over. That is, provided I can get permission.'

'I've already arranged that,' Duff told me. 'You just come on across the street and don't bother mentioning anything about it to anyone.'

'O.K.,' I said, and hung up. I sat there for a minute. This sounded fishy to me. Of course, Duff *might* be on the level, but I doubted it. You can never tell what a guy working for the law is going to do.

I trotted out to the campus and on across to the Smith house. Their mother had died a long while ago, so with the father murdered, and Tommy in the death house, there were only the two girls left.

Duff answered the door himself. I looked up at the big bruiser and then I sucked in my breath. I wouldn't have known him! His face was almost gray. Under his eyes were the biggest black rings I had ever seen. I don't mean the kind you get fighting. I mean the other kind, the serious kind you get from worry. He had short clipped hair that was sort of reddish, and shoulders that squared off his figure, tapering it down to a nice V.

Of course, he was plenty old, around twenty-six, but at this his being a detective surprised you because ordinarily he looked so much like a college kid. He always spoke in a modulated voice and never got excited over anything. And he had a way of looking at you that I hated. A quiet sort of way that asked and answered all of its own questions.

Personally, as a detective, I thought he was a big flop. The kind of detectives that I prefer seeing are those giant fighters that blaze their way through a gangster barricade. Duff Ryan was none of this. I suppose he was tough but he never showed it. Worst of all, I'd never even seen his gun!

'Glad you came over, Martin,' he said.

'The name is Thorpe,' I said.

He didn't answer, just stepped aside so I could come in. I didn't see Ruth, but I spotted Marie right away. She was sitting on the divan with her legs pulled up under her, and her face hidden. She had a hankerchief pressed in her hand. She was a slim kid, but well developed for fifteen, so well developed in fact that for a while I had been razzed about this at school.

Like Tommy, she had blond hair, only hers was fluffy and came part way to her shoulders. She turned now and her face was all red from crying, but I still thought she was pretty. I'm a sucker that way. I've been a sucker for women ever since I was nine.

She had wide spaced green eyes, and soft, rosy skin, and a generous mouth. Her only trouble, if any, was that she was a prude. Wouldn't speak to anybody on the Clark campus except me. Maybe you think I didn't like that! I'd met her at Sunday school or rather coming out, since I had been hiding around waiting for it to let out, and I walked home with her four Sundays straight before she would speak to me. That is, I walked along beside her holding a one-way conversation. Finally I skipped a Sunday, then the next one she asked me where I had been, and that started the ball rolling.

'Thorpe,' she said – that was another thing, *she* always called me by my last name because that was the one I had given her to start with – 'Thorpe, I'm so glad you're here. Come over here and sit down beside me.'

I went over and sat down and she straightened up, like she was ashamed that she had been crying, and put on a pretty good imitation of a smile. 'How's everything been?' she said.

'Oh, pretty good,' I said. 'The freshmen are bellyaching about Latin this week, and just like algebra, I'm already so far ahead of them it's a crying shame.'

'You're so smart, Thorpe,' she told me.

'Too bad about Tommy,' I said. 'There's always the chance for a reprieve though.'

'No,' she said, and her eyes began to get dim again, 'no, there isn't. This – this decision that went through Sunday night – that's the— Unless, of course, something comes up that we – the lawyer can—' and she began crying.

I put my arm round her which was a thing she hadn't let me do much, and I said, 'Come on, kid. Straighten up. Tommy wouldn't want you to cry.'

About five minutes later she did straighten up. Duff Ryan was sitting over in the corner looking out the window but it was just like we were alone.

'I'll play the piano,' she said.

'Do you know anything hot yet?'

'Hot?' she said.

'Something popular, Marie,' I explained. Blood was coming up into my face.

'Why, no,' she replied. 'I thought I would—'

'Play hymns!' I half screamed. 'No! I don't want to hear any of those damned hymns!'

'Why, Thorpe!'

'I can't help it,' I said. 'I've told you about that enough times. Those kind of songs just drone along in the same pitch and never get anywhere. If you can't play something decent stay away from the piano.'

My fists were tight now and my fingers were going in and out. She knew better than to bring up that subject. It was the only thing we had ever argued about. Playing hymns. I wanted to go nuts every time I heard '*Lead Kindly Light*' or one of those other goofy things. I'd get so mad I couldn't see straight. Just an obsession with me, I guess.

'All right,' she said, 'but I wish you wouldn't swear in this house.'

I said, 'All right, I won't swear in this house.'

'Or anywhere else,' she said.

I was feeling good now. 'O.K., honey, if you say so.'

She seemed pleased and at least the argument had gotten her to quit thinking about Tommy for a minute. But it was then that her sister came downstairs.

Ruth was built on a smaller scale than Marie so that even though she was nineteen she wasn't any taller. She had darker hair too, and an oval face, very white now, making her brown eyes seem brighter. Brighter though more hollow. I will say she was beautiful.

She wore only a rich blue lounging robe which was figure-fitting though it came down past her heels and was clasped in a high collar around her pale throat.

'I think it's time for you to come to bed, Marie,' she said. 'Hello, Thorpe.'

'Hello,' I said.

Marie got up wordlessly and pressed my hand, and smiled again, that faint imitation, and went off. Ruth stood there in the doorway from the dining-room and as though it was a signal – which I suspect it was – Duff Ryan got up.

'I guess it's time for us to go, Martin,' he said.

'You don't say,' I said.

He looked at me fishily. 'Yeah. I do say. We've got a job to do. Do you know what it is, Martin? We've got to kill a kitten. A poor little kitten.'

I started to answer but didn't. The way he was saying that, and looking at me, put a chill up my back that made me suddenly ice cold. I began to tremble all over. He opened the door and motioned for me to go out.

That cat thing was a gag of some kind, I thought, and I was wide awake for any funny stuff from detectives, but Duff Ryan actually had a little kitten hidden in a box under the front steps of the house. He picked it up now and petted it.

'Got hit by a car,' he said. 'It's in terrible pain and there isn't a chance for recovery. I gave it a shot of stuff that eased the pain for a while but it must be coming back. We'll have to kill the cat.'

I wanted to ask him why he hadn't killed it in the first place, whenever he had picked it up from under the car, but I kept my mouth shut and we walked along, back across the street to the Clark campus. There were no lights at all here and we walked in darkness, our feet scuffing on the dirt of the football gridiron.

'About that night of the murder, Martin,' Duff said. 'You won't mind a few more questions, will you? We want to do something to save Tommy. I made the arrest but I've been convinced since that he's innocent. I want desperately to save him before it's too late. It's apparent that we missed on something because – well, the way things are.'

I said, 'Are you sure of Tommy's innocence, or are you stuck on Ruth?'

'Sure of his innocence,' he said in that soft voice. 'You want to help, don't you, Martin? You don't want to see Tommy die?'

'Quit talking to me like a kid,' I said. 'Sure I want to help.'

'All right. What were you doing over there that night?'

'I've answered that a dozen times. Once in court. I was seeing Marie.'

'Mr. Smith – that is, her father – chased you out of the house though, didn't he?'

'He asked me to leave,' I said.

'No, he didn't, Martin. He ordered you out and told you not to come back again.'

I stopped and whirled toward him. 'Who told you that?'

'Marie,' he said. 'She was the only one who heard him. She didn't want to say it before because she was afraid Ruth would keep her from seeing you. That little kid has a crush on you and she didn't think that had any bearing on the case.

'Well, it hasn't has it?'

'Maybe not,' snapped Duff Ryan, 'but he did chase you out, didn't he? He threatened to use his cane on you?'

'I won't answer,' I said.

'You don't have to,' he told me. 'But I wish you'd told the truth about it in the first place.'

'Why?' We started walking again. 'You don't think *I* killed him, do you?' I shot a quick glance in his direction and held my breath.

'No,' he said, 'nothing like that, only—'

'Only what?'

'Well, Martin, haven't you been kicked out of about every school in the State?'

'I wouldn't go so far as to say *every* school.'

Duff said, 'Quite a few though, eh?'

'Enough,' I said.

'That's what I thought,' he went on quietly, 'I went over and had a look at your record, Martin. I wish I had thought of doing that sooner.'

'Listen—'

'Oh, don't get excited,' he said, 'this may give us new leads, that's all. We've nothing against you. But when you were going to school at Hadden, you took the goat, which was a class mascot, upstairs with you one night and then pushed him down the stairs so that he broke all his legs. You did that, didn't you?'

'The goat slipped,' I said.

'Maybe,' whispered Duff. He lit a cigarette, holding onto the crippled cat with one hand. 'But you stood at the top of the stairs and watched the goat suffer until somebody came along.'

'I was so scared I couldn't move.'

'Another time,' Duff continued, 'at another school, you pushed a kid into an oil hole that he couldn't get out of and you were ducking him – maybe trying to kill him – when someone came along and stopped you.'

'He was a sissy. I was just having some fun!'

'At another school you were expelled for roping a newly born calf and pulling it up on top of a barn where you stabbed it and watched it bleed to death.'

'I didn't stab it! It got caught on a piece of tin from the drain while I was pulling it up. You haven't told any of this to Marie, have you?'

'No,' Duff said.

'All those things are just natural things,' I said. 'Any kid is liable to do them. You're just nuts because you can't pin the guilt on anybody but the guy who is going to die Friday and you're trying to make me look bad!'

'Maybe,' Duff answered quietly, and we came into the chapel now and stopped. He dropped his cigarette, stepped on it, then patted the cat. Moonlight shone jaggedly through the rotting pillars. I could see the cat's eyes shining. 'Maybe,' Duff breathed again, 'but didn't you land in a reform school once?'

'Twice,' I said.

'And once in an institution where you were observed by a staff of doctors? It was a State institution, I think. Sort of a rest home.'

'I was there a month,' I said. 'Some crab sent me there, or had me sent. But my dad got me out.'

'Yes,' Duff replied, 'the crab had you sent there because you poisoned two of his Great Dane dogs. Your dad had to bribe somebody to get you out, and right now he pays double tuition for you here at Clark's.'

I knew all this but it wasn't anything sweet to hear coming from a detective. 'What of it?' I said. 'You had plenty of chance to find that out.'

'But we weren't allowed to see your records before,' Duff answered. 'As a matter of fact I paid an orderly to steal them for me, and then return them.'

'Why, you dirty crook!'

I could see the funny twist of his smile there in the moonlight. His face looked pale and somehow far away. He looked at the cat and petted it some more. I was still shaking. Scared, I guess.

He said, 'Too bad we have to kill you, kitten, but it's better than that pain.'

Then, all at once I thought he had gone mad. He swung the cat around and began batting its head against the pillar in the chapel. I could see the whole thing clearly in the moonlight, his arm swinging back and forth, the cat's head being battered off, the bright crimson blood spurting all over.

He kept on doing it and my temples began to pound. My heart went like wild fire. I wanted to reach over and help him. I wanted to take that little cat and squeeze the living guts out of it. I wanted to help him smash its brains all over the chapel. I felt dizzy. Everything was going around. I felt myself reaching for the cat.

But I'm smart. I'm no dummy. I'm at the head of my class. I'm in high school. I knew what he was doing. He was testing me. *He wanted me to help him.* The son of a— wasn't going to trick *me* like that. Not Martin Thorpe. I put my arms behind me and grabbed my wrists and with all my might I held my arms there and looked the other way.

I heard the cat drop with a thud to the cement, then I looked up, gasping to catch my breath. Duff Ryan looked at me with cool gray eyes, then he walked off. I stood there, still trying to get my breath and watching his shadow blend with the shadows of the dark study hall. I was having one hell of a time getting my breath.

But I slept good all night. I was mad and I didn't care about Tommy any more. Let him hang. I slept good but I woke up ten minutes before reveille remembering that it was Pushton's turn at the bugle again. He and Myers traded off duty every other day.

I felt pretty cocky and got up putting on only my slippers and went down to the eleven-year-old wing. Pushton was sitting on the edge of the bed working his arms back and forth and yawning. The fat little punk looked like an old man. He took himself that seriously. You would have thought maybe he was a general.

'What you want, Thorpe?' he said.

'I want your bugle. I'm going to break the damn thing.'

'You leave my bugle alone,' he said. 'My folks aren't as rich as yours and I had to save all my spending money to buy it.' This was true. They furnished bugles at school but they were awful and Pushton took his music so seriously that he had saved up and bought his own instrument.

'I know it,' I said, 'so the school won't be on my neck if I break it.' I looked around. 'Where is it?'

'I won't tell you!'

I looked under the bed, under his pillow, then I grabbed him by the nose. 'Come on, Heinie. Where is it?'

'Leave me alone!' he wailed. 'Keep your hands off me.' He was talking so loud now that half the wing was waking up.

'All right, punk,' I said. 'Go ahead and blow that thing, and I hope you blow your tonsils out.'

I went back to my bed and held my ears. Pushton blew the bugle all right, I never did find out where he had the thing hidden.

I dressed thinking well, only two more days and Tommy gets it. I'd be glad when it was over. Maybe all this tension would ease up then and Marie wouldn't cry so much because once he was dead there wouldn't be anything she could do about it. Time would go by and eventually she would forget him. One person more or less isn't so important in the world anyway, no matter how good a guy he is.

Everything went swell Wednesday right through breakfast and until after we were marching out of the chapel and into the schoolroom. Then I ran into Pushton who was trotting around with his bugle tucked under his arm. I stopped and looked him up and down.

His little black eyes didn't flicker. He just said, 'Next time you bother me, Thorpe, I'm going to report you.'

'Go ahead, punk,' I said, 'and see what happens to you.'

I went on into school then, burning up at his guts, talking to *me* that way.

I was still burned up and sore at the guy when a lucky break came, for me, that is, not Pushton. It was during the afternoon right after we had been dismissed from the class room for the two-hour recreation period.

I went into the main building, which was prohibited in the day time so that I had to sneak in, to get a book I wanted to read. It was under my pillow.

I slipped up the stairs, crept into my wing, got the book and started out. It was then that I heard a pounding noise.

I looked around, then saw it was coming from the eleven-year-old wing.

I walked in and there it was! You wouldn't have believed anything so beautiful could have been if you hadn't seen it with your own eyes. At least that was the way I felt about it. For, who was it, but Pushton.

The bugler on duty has the run of the main building and it was natural enough that he was here but I hadn't thought about it. There was a new radio set, a small portable, beside his bed. I saw that the wires and ear phone – which you have to use in the dormitory – were connected with the adjoining bed as well and guessed that it belonged to another cadet. But Pushton was hooking it up. He was leaning half-way out the window trying, pounding with a hammer, to make some kind of a connection on the aerial wire.

Nothing could have been better. The window was six stories from the ground with cement down below. No one knew I was in the building. I felt blood surge into my temples. My face got red, hot red, and I could feel fever throbbing in my throat. I moved forward slowly, on cat feet, my hands straight at my sides. I didn't want him to hear me. But I was getting that dizzy feeling now. My fingers were itching.

Then suddenly I lunged over, I shoved against him. He looked back once, and that was what I wanted. He looked back for an instant, his fat face green with the most unholy fear I have ever seen. Then I gave him another shove and he was gone. Before he could call out, before he could say a word, he was gone, falling through the air!

I risked jumping up on the bed so I could see him hit, and I did see him hit. Then I got down and straightened the bed and beat it out.

I ran down the stairs as fast as I could. I didn't see anybody. More important, no one saw me. But when I was on the second floor I ran down the hall to the end and lifted the window. I jumped out here, landing squarely on my feet.

I waited for a minute, then I circled the building from an opposite direction. My heart was pounding inside me. It was difficult for me to breathe. I managed to get back to the play field through an indirect route.

Funny thing, Pushton wasn't seen right away. No one but myself had seen him fall. I was on the play field at least ten minutes, plenty long enough to establish myself as being there, before the cry went up. The kids went wild. We ran in packs to the scene.

I stood there with the rest of them looking at what was left of Pushton. He wouldn't blow any more bugles. His flesh was like a sack of water that had fallen and burst full of holes. The blood was splattered out in jagged streaks all around him.

We stood around about five minutes, the rest of the kids and I, nobody saying anything. Then a faculty officer chased us away, and that was the last I saw of Pushton.

Supper was served as usual but there wasn't much talk. What there was of it seemed to establish the fact that Pushton had been a thick-witted sort and had undoubtedly leaned out too far trying to fix the aerial wire and had fallen.

I thought that that could have easily been the case, all right, and since I had hated the little punk I had no conscience about it. It didn't bother me nearly so much as the fact that Tommy Smith was going to die. I had liked Tommy. And I was nuts about his sister, wasn't I?

That night study hall was converted into a little inquest meeting. We were all herded into one big room and Major Clark talked to us as though we were a bunch of Boy Scouts. After ascertaining that no one knew any more about Pushton's death than what they had seen on the cement, he assured us that the whole thing had been unavoidable and even went so far as to suggest that we might spare our parents the worry of telling them of so unfortunate an incident. All the bloated donkey was worrying about was losing a few tuitions.

Toward the end of the session Duff Ryan came in and nodded at me, and then sat down. He looked around at the kids, watched Major Clark a while, and then glanced back at me. He kept doing that until we were dismissed. He made me nervous.

Friday morning I woke up and listened for reveille but it didn't come. I lay there, feeling comfortable in the bed clothes, and half lazy, but feeling every minute that reveille would blast me out of my place. Then I suddenly realized why the bugle hadn't blown. I heard the splash of rain across the window and knew that we wouldn't have to raise the flag nor take our exercises this morning. On rainy days we got to sleep an extra half-hour.

I felt pretty good about this and put my hands behind my head there on the pillow and began thinking. They were pleasant, what you might call mellow thoughts. A little thing like an extra half-hour in bed will do that.

Things were working out fine and after tonight I wouldn't have anything to worry about. For Duff Ryan to prove Tommy was innocent *after* the hanging would only make him out a damn fool. I was glad it was raining. It would make it easier for me to lay low, to stay away from Marie until the final word came. . . .

That was what I thought in the morning, lying there in bed. But no. Seven-thirty that night Duff came over to the school in a slicker. He came into the study hall and got me. His eyes were wild. His face was strained.

'Ruth and I are going to see the lawyer again,' he said, 'you've got to stay with Marie.'

'Nuts,' I said.

He jerked me out of the seat, then he took his hands off me as though he were ashamed. 'Come on,' he said. 'This is no time for smart talk.'

So I went.

Ruth had on a slicker too and was waiting there on the front porch. I could see her pretty face. It was pinched, sort of terrible. Her eyes were wild too. She patted my hand, half crying, and said, 'You be good to Marie, honey. She likes you, and you're the only one in the world now that can console her.'

'What time does Tommy go?' I asked.

'Ten-thirty,' said Duff.

I nodded. 'O.K.' I stood there as they crossed the sidewalk and got into Duff Ryan's car and drove away. Then I went in to see Marie. The kid looked scared, white as a ghost.

'Oh, Thorpe,' she said, 'they're going to kill him tonight!'

'Well, I guess there's nothing we can do,' I said.

She put her arms around me and cried on my shoulder. I could feel her against me, and believe me, she was nice. She had figure, all right. I put my arms around her waist and then I kissed her neck and her ears. She looked at me, tears on her cheeks, and shook her head. 'Don't.'

She said that because I had never kissed her before, but now I saw her lips and I kissed her. She didn't do anything about it, but kept crying.

Finally I said, 'Well, let's make fudge. Let's play a game. Let's play the radio. Let's do *something*. This thing's beginning to get me.'

We went to the kitchen and made fudge for a while.

But I was restless. The rain had increased. There was thunder and lightning in the sky now. Again I had that strange feeling of being cold, although the room was warm. I looked at the clock and it said ten minutes after eight. Only ten minutes after eight! And Tommy wasn't going to hang until ten-thirty!

'You'll always stay with me, won't you, Thorpe?' said Marie.

'Sure,' I told her, but right then I felt like I wanted to push her face in. I had never felt that way before. I couldn't understand what was the matter with me. Everything that had been me was gone. My wit and good humor.

I kept watching the clock, watching every minute that ticked by, and thinking of Tommy up there in San Quentin in the death cell pacing back and forth. I guess maybe he was watching the minutes too. I wondered if it was raining up there and if rain made any difference in a hanging.

We wandered back into the living-room and sat down at opposite ends of the divan. Marie looking at nothing, her eyes glassy, and me watching and hating the rain, and hearing the clock.

Then suddenly Marie got up and went to the piano. She didn't ask me if she could or anything about it. She just went to the piano and sat down. I stared after her, even opened my mouth to speak. But I didn't say anything.

After all, it was *her* brother who was going to die, wasn't it? I guess for one night at least she could do anything she wanted to do.

But then she began playing. First, right off, '*Lead Kindly Light*,' and then '*Onward Christian Soldiers*,' and then '*Little Church in the Wildwood*.' I sat there wringing my hands with that agony beating in my ears. Then I leapt to my feet and began to shout at her.

'Stop that! Stop it! Do you want to drive me crazy?'

But her face was frozen now. It was as though she was in a trance. I ran to her and shook her shoulder, but she pulled away from me and played on.

I backed away from her and my face felt as though it was contorted. I backed away and stared at her, her slim, arched back. I began biting my fingernails, and then my fingers. That music was killing me. Those hymns . . . those silly, inane hymns. Why didn't she stop it? The piano and the rain were seeping into my blood stream.

I walked up and down the room. I walked up and down the room faster and faster. I stopped and picked up a flower vase and dropped it, yelling: '*Stop it! For the love of heaven, stop!*'

But she kept right on. Again I began staring at her, at her back, and her throat, and the profile of her face. I felt blood surging in me. I felt those hammers in my temples. . . .

I tried to fight it off this time. I tried to go toward her to pull her away from that damn piano but I didn't have the strength to move in her direction. I stood there feeling the breath go out of me, feeling my skin tingle. And I didn't want to be like that. I looked at my hands and one minutes they were tight fists and the next my fingers were working in and out like mad.

I looked toward the kitchen, and then I moved quietly into it. She was still slamming at the piano when I opened the drawer and pulled out the knife I had used to kill her father.

At least it was a knife like it. I put it behind me and tiptoed back into the room. She wasn't aware that I had moved. I crept up on her, waited.

Her hands were flying over the piano keys. Once more I shouted, and my voice was getting hoarse: 'Stop it!'

But of course she didn't. She didn't and I swore. I swore at her. She didn't hear this either. But I'd show the little slut a thing or two.

I was breathing hard, looking around the room to make sure no one was here. Then I lifted the knife and plunged down with it.

I swear I never knew where Duff Ryan came from. It must have been from behind the divan. A simple place like that and I hadn't seen him, merely because I had been convinced that he went away in the car. But he'd been in the room all the time waiting for me to do what I almost did.

It had been a trick, of course, and this time I'd been sap enough to fall into his trap. He had heard me denounce hymns, he knew I'd be nervous tonight, highly excitable, so he had set the stage and remained hidden and Marie had done the rest.

He had told Marie then, after all.

Duff Ryan grabbed my wrist just at the right moment, as he had planned on doing, and of course being fourteen I didn't have much chance against him. He wrested away the knife, then he grabbed me and shouted:

'Why did you murder Marie's father?'

'Because the old boy hated me! Because he thought Marie was too young to know boys! Because he kicked me out and hit me with his cane!' I said all this, trying to jerk away from him, but I couldn't so I went on:

'That's why I did it. Because I had a lot of fun doing it! So what? What are you going to do about it? I'm a kid, you can't hang *me!* There's a law against hanging kids. I murdered Pushton too. I shoved him out the window! How do you like that? All you can do is put me in reform school!'

As my voice faded, and it faded because I had begun to choke, I heard Ruth at the telephone. She had come back in too. She was calling long distance. San Quentin.

Marie was sitting on the divan, her face in her hands. You would have thought she was sorry for me. When I got my breath I went on:

'I came back afterward, while Tommy was in the other room. I got in the kitchen door. The old man was standing there and I just picked up the knife and let him have it. I ran before I could see much. But Pushton. Let me tell you about Pushton—'

Duff Ryan shoved me back against the piano. 'Shut up,' he said. 'You didn't kill Pushton. You're just bragging now. But you did kill the old man and that's what we wanted to know!'

Bragging? I was enraged. But Duff Ryan clipped me and I went out cold.

So I'm in reform school now and – will you believe it? – I can't convince anyone that I murdered Pushton. Is it that grown-ups are so unbelieving because I'm pretty young? Are they so stupid that they still look upon fourteen-year-old boys as little innocents who have no minds of their own? That is the bitterness of youth. And I am sure that I won't change or see things any differently. I told the dopes that too, but everyone assures me I will.

But the only thing I'm really worried about is that no one will believe about Pushton, not even the kids here at the reform school, and that hurts. It does something to my pride.

I'm not in the least worried about anything else. Things here aren't so bad, nor so different from Clark's. Doctors come and see me now and then but they don't think anything is wrong with my mind.

They think I knifed Old Man Smith because I was in a blind rage when I did it, and looking at it that way, it would only be second-degree murder even if I were older. I'm not considered serious. There are lots worse cases here than mine. Legally, a kid isn't responsible for what he does, so I'll be out when I'm twenty-one. Maybe before, because my old man's got money. . . .

You'll always remember me, won't you? Because I'll be out when I'm older and you might be the one I'll be seeing.

FINGER MAN

RAYMOND CHANDLER

Arguably the greatest mystery writer of the 20th century, Raymond Chandler (1888–1959) brought a literary sensibility to that least likely of places – pulp magazines. Pulps were very clearly and specifically designed to be fast, cheap, action-filled entertainment for the masses. No literary aspirations or pretensions were welcomed by the hard-working editors of even the best of them, notably *Black Mask* and *Dime Detective*. Still, Dashiell Hammett brought important realism to his pulp stories, and Chandler elevated the form even further.

Philip Marlowe, the hero of all seven of Chandler's novels, appears in this printing of 'Finger Man,' a novella filled with bad guys and corruption. When the story was first published in the October 1934 issue of *Black Mask*, the first-person narrator was unnamed. For its first book appearance, the anonymous shamus in 'Finger Man' was given the Marlowe name, as Chandler had become the 'hottest' mystery writer in America because of his Marlowe novels. The majority of Chandler's short fiction was collected in three paperback originals published by Avon in its 'Murder Mystery Monthly' series, *5 Murderers* (1944), *Five Sinister Characters* (1945) and *Finger Man* (1946) and his detectives, whether named Carmody, Dalmas, Malvern, Mallory or unnamed, were transformed into Marlowe. As the detectives evolved from the earliest experiments to the more complex and nuanced hero he envisioned and later compared to a modern-day knight, the adventures became classics of the American crime story.

FINGER MAN

RAYMOND CHANDLER

ONE

I got away from the Grand Jury a little after four, and then sneaked up the backstairs to Fenweather's office. Fenweather, the D.A., was a man with severe, chiseled features and the gray temples women love. He played with a pen on his desk and said: 'I think they believed you. They might even indict Manny Tinnen for the Shannon kill this afternoon. If they do, then is the time you begin to watch your step.'

I rolled a cigarette around in my fingers and finally put it in my mouth. 'Don't put any men on me, Mr. Fenweather. I know the alleys in this town pretty well, and your men couldn't stay close enough to do me any good.'

He looked towards one of the windows. 'How well do you know Frank Dorr?' he asked, with his eyes away from me.

'I know he's a big politico, a fixer you have to see if you want to open a gambling hell or a bawdy house – or if you want to sell honest merchandise to the city.'

'Right.' Fenweather spoke sharply, and brought his head around towards me. Then he lowered his voice. 'Having the goods on Tinnen was a surprise to a lot of people. If Frank Dorr had an interest in getting rid of Shannon who was the head of the Board where Dorr's supposed to get his contracts, it's close enough to make him take chances. And I'm told he and Manny Tinnen had dealings. I'd sort of keep an eye on him, if I were you.'

I grinned. 'I'm just one guy,' I said. 'Frank Dorr covers a lot of territory. But I'll do what I can.'

Fenweather stood up and held his hand across the desk. He said: 'I'll be out of town for a couple of days, I'm leaving tonight, if this indictment comes through. Be careful – and if anything should happen to go wrong, see Bernie Ohls, my chief investigator.'

I said: 'Sure.'

We shook hands and I went out past a tired-looking girl who gave me a tired smile and wound one of her lax curls up on the back of her neck as she looked at me. I got back to my office soon after four-thirty. I stopped outside the door of the little reception room for a moment, looking at it. Then I opened it and went in, and of course there wasn't anybody there.

There was nothing there but an old red davenport, two odd chairs, a bit of carpet, and a library table with a few old magazines on it. The reception room was left open for visitors to come in and sit down and wait – if I had any visitors and they felt like waiting.

I went across and unlocked the door into my private office, lettered '*Philip Marlowe . . . Investigations.*'

Lou Harger was sitting on a wooden chair on the side of the desk away from the window. He had bright yellow gloves clamped on the crook of a cane, a green snap-brim hat set too far back on his head. Very smooth black hair showed under the hat and grew too low on the nape of his neck.

'Hello. I've been waiting,' he said, and smiled languidly.

''Lo, Lou. How did you get in here?'

'The door must have been unlocked. Or maybe I had a key that fitted. Do you mind?'

I went around the desk and sat down in the swivel chair. I put my hat down on the desk, picked up a bulldog pipe out of an ash tray and began to fill it up.

'It's all right as long as it's you,' I said. 'I just thought I had a better lock.'

He smiled with his full red lips. He was a very good-looking boy. He said: 'Are you still doing business, or will you spend the next month in a hotel room drinking liquor with a couple of Headquarters boys?'

'I'm still doing business – if there's any business for me to do.'

I lit a pipe, leaned back and stared at his clear olive skin, straight, dark eyebrows.

He put his cane on top of the desk and clasped his yellow gloves on the glass. He moved his lips in and out.

'I have a little something for you. Not a hell of a lot. But there's carfare in it.'

I waited.

'I'm making a little play at Las Olindas tonight,' he said. 'At Canales' place.'

'The white smoke?'

'Uh-huh. I think I'm going to be lucky – and I'd like to have a guy with a rod.'

I took a fresh pack of cigarettes out of a top drawer and slid them across the desk. Lou picked them up and began to break the pack open.

I said: 'What kind of play?'

He got a cigarette halfway out and stared down at it. There was a little something in his manner I didn't like.

'I've been closed up for a month now. I wasn't makin' the kind of money it takes to stay open in this town. The Headquarters boys have been putting the pressure on since repeal. They have bad dreams when they see themselves trying to live on their pay.'

I said: 'It doesn't cost any more to operate here than anywhere else. And here you pay it all to one organization. That's something.'

Lou Harger jabbed the cigarette in his mouth. 'Yeah – Frank Dorr,' he snarled. 'That fat, bloodsuckin' sonofabitch!'

I didn't say anything. I was way past the age when it's fun to swear at people you can't hurt. I watched Lou light his cigarette with my desk lighter. He went on, through a puff of smoke: 'It's a laugh, in a way. Canales bought a new wheel – from some grafters in the sheriff's office. I know Pina, Canales' head croupier, pretty well. The wheel is one they took away from me. It's got bugs – and I know the bugs.'

'And Canales don't . . . That sounds just like Canales,' I said.

Lou didn't look at me. 'He gets a nice crowd down there,' he said. 'He has a small dance floor and a five-piece Mexican band to help the customers relax. They dance a bit and then go back for another trimming, instead of going away disgusted.'

I said: 'What do *you* do?'

'I guess you might call it a system,' he said softly, and looked at me under his long lashes.

I looked away from him, looked around the room. It had a rust-red carpet, five green filing cases in a row under an advertising calendar, an old costumer in the corner, a few walnut chairs, net curtains over the windows. The fringe of the curtains was dirty from blowing about in the draft. There was a bar of late sunlight across my desk and it showed up the dust.

'I get it like this,' I said. 'You think you have that roulette wheel tamed and you expect to win enough money so that Canales will be mad at you. You'd like to have some protection along – me. I think it's screwy.'

'It's not screwy at all,' Lou said. 'Any roulette wheel has a tendency to work in a certain rhythm. If you know the wheel very well indeed—'

I smiled and shrugged. 'Okey, I wouldn't know about that. I don't know enough roulette. It sounds to me like you're being a sucker for your own racket, but I could be wrong. And that's not the point anyway.'

'What is?' Lou asked thinly.

'I'm not much stuck on bodyguarding – but maybe that's not the point either. I take it I'm supposed to think this play is on the level. Suppose I don't, and walk out on you, and you get in a box? Or suppose I think everything is aces, but Canales don't agree with me and gets nasty.'

'That's why I need a guy with a rod,' Lou said, without moving a muscle except to speak.

I said evenly: 'If I'm tough enough for the job – and I didn't know I was – that still isn't what worries me.'

'Forget it,' Lou said. 'It breaks me up enough to know you're worried.'

I smiled a little more and watched his yellow gloves moving around on top of the desk, moving too much. I said slowly: 'You're the last guy in the world to be getting expense money that way just now. I'm the last guy to be standing behind you while you do it. That's all.'

Lou said: 'Yeah.' He knocked some ash off his cigarette down on the glass top, bent his head to blow it off. He went on, as if it was a new subject: 'Miss Glenn is going with me. She's a tall redhead, a swell looker. She used to model. She's nice to people in any kind of a spot and she'll keep Canales from breathing on my neck. So we'll make out. I just thought I'd tell you.'

I was silent for a minute, then I said: 'You know damn well I just got through telling the Grand Jury it was Manny Tinnen I saw lean out of that car and cut the ropes on Art Shannon's wrists after they pushed him on the roadway, filled with lead.'

Lou smiled faintly at me. 'That'll make it easier for the grafters on the big time; the fellows who take the contracts and don't appear in the business. They say Shannon was square and kept the Board in line. It was a nasty bump-off.'

I shook my head. I didn't want to talk about that. I said: 'Canales has a noseful of junk a lot of the time. And maybe he doesn't go for redheads.'

Lou stood up slowly and lifted his cane off the desk. He stared at the tip of one yellow finger. He had an almost sleepy expression. Then he moved towards the door, swinging his cane.

'Well, I'll be seein' you some time,' he drawled.

I let him get his hand on the knob before I said: 'Don't go away sore, Lou. I'll drop down to Las Olindas, if you have to have me. But I don't want any money for it, and for Pete's sake don't pay any more attention to me than you have to.'

He licked his lips softly and didn't quite look at me. 'Thanks, keed. I'll be careful as hell.'

He went out then and his yellow glove disappeared around the edge of the door.

I sat still for about five minutes and then my pipe got too hot. I put it down, looked at my strap watch, and got up to switch on a small radio in the corner beyond the end of the desk. When the A.C. hum died down the last tinkle of a chime came out of the horn, then a voice was saying: 'KLI now brings you its regular early evening broadcast of local news releases. An event of importance this afternoon was the indictment returned late today against Maynard J. Tinnen by the Grand Jury. Tinnen is a well-known City Hall lobbyist and man about town. The indictment, a shock to his many friends, was based almost entirely on the testimony—'

My telephone rang sharply and a girl's cool voice said in my ear: 'One moment, please. Mr. Fenweather is calling you.'

He came on at once. 'Indictment returned. Take care of the boy.'

I said I was just getting it over the radio. We talked a short moment and then he hung up, after saying he had to leave at once to catch a plane.

I leaned back in my chair again and listened to the radio without exactly hearing it. I was thinking what a damn fool Lou Harger was and that there wasn't anything I could do to change that.

TWO

It was a good crowd for a Tuesday but nobody was dancing. Around ten o'clock the little five-piece band got tired of messing around with a rhumba that nobody was paying any attention to. The marimba player dropped his sticks and reached under his chair for a glass. The rest of the boys lit cigarettes and sat there looking bored.

I leaned sidewise against the bar, which was on the same side of the room as the orchestra stand. I was turning a small glass of tequila around on the top of the bar. All the business was at the center one of the three roulette tables.

The bartender leaned beside me, on his side of the bar.

'The flame-top gal must be pickin' them,' he said.

I nodded without looking at him. 'She's playing with fistfuls now,' I said. 'Not even counting it.'

The red-haired girl was tall. I could see the burnished copper of her hair between the heads of the people behind her. I could see Lou Harger's sleek head beside hers. Everybody seemed to be playing standing up.

'You don't play?' the bartender asked me.

'Not on Tuesdays. I had some trouble on a Tuesday once.'

'Yeah? Do you like that stuff straight, or could I smooth it out for you?'

'Smooth it out with what?' I said. 'You got a wood rasp handy?'

He grinned. I drank a little more of the tequila and made a face.

'Did anybody invent this stuff on purpose?'

'I wouldn't know, mister.'

'What's the limit over there?'

'I wouldn't know that either. How the boss feels, I guess.'

The roulette tables were in a row near the far wall. A low railing of gilt metal joined their ends and the players were outside the railing.

Some kind of a confused wrangle started at the center table. Half a dozen people at the two end tables grabbed their chips up and moved across.

Then a clear, very polite voice, with a slightly foreign accent, spoke out: 'If you will just be patient, madame . . . Mr. Canales will be here in a minute.'

I went across, squeezed near the railing. Two croupiers stood near me with their heads together and their eyes looking sidewise. One moved a rake slowly back and forth beside the idle wheel. They were staring at the red-haired girl.

She wore a high-cut black evening gown. She had fine white shoulders, was something less than beautiful and more than pretty. She was leaning on the edge of the table, in front of the wheel. Her long eyelashes were twitching. There was a big pile of money and chips in front of her.

She spoke monotonously, as if she had said the same thing several times already.

'Get busy and spin that wheel! You take it away fast enough, but you don't like to dish it out.'

The croupier in charge smiled a cold, even smile. He was tall, dark, disinterested: 'The table can't cover your bet,' he said with calm precision. 'Mr. Canales, perhaps—' He shrugged neat shoulders.

The girl said: 'It's your money, highpockets. Don't you want it back?'

Lou Harger licked his lips beside her, put a hand on her arm, stared at the pile of money with hot eyes. He said gently: 'Wait for Canales. . . .'

'To hell with Canales! I'm hot – and I want to stay that way.'

A door opened at the end of the tables and a very slight, very pale man came into the room. He had straight, lusterless black hair, a high bony forehead, flat, impenetrable eyes. He had a thin mustache that was trimmed in two sharp lines almost at right angles to each other. They came down below the corners of his mouth a full inch. The effect was Oriental. His skin had a thick, glistening pallor.

He slid behind the croupiers, stopped at a corner of the center table, glanced at the red-haired girl and touched the ends of his mustache with two fingers, the nails of which had a purplish tint.

He smiled suddenly, and the instant after it was as though he had never smiled in his life. He spoke in a dull, ironic voice.

'Good evening, Miss Glenn. You must let me send somebody with you when you go home. I'd hate to see any of that money get in the wrong pockets.'

The red-haired girl looked at him, not very pleasantly.

'I'm not leaving – unless you're throwing me out.'

Canales said: 'No? What would you like to do?'

'Bet the wad – dark meat!'

The crowd noise became a deathly silence. There wasn't a whisper of any kind of sound. Harger's face slowly got ivory-white.

Canales' face was without expression. He lifted a hand, delicately, gravely, slipped a large wallet from his dinner jacket and tossed it in front of the tall croupier.

'Ten grand,' he said in a voice that was a dull rustle of sound. 'That's my limit – always.'

The tall croupier picked the wallet up, spread it, drew out two flat packets of crisp bills, riffled them, refolded the wallet and passed it along the edge of the table to Canales.

Canales did not take it. Nobody moved, except the croupier.

The girl said: 'Put it on the red.'

The croupier leaned across the table and very carefully stacked her money and chips. He placed her bet for her on the red diamond. He placed his hand along the curve of the wheel.

'If no one objects,' Canales said, without looking at anyone, 'this is just the two of us.'

Heads moved. Nobody spoke. The croupier spun the wheel and send the ball skimming in the groove with a light flirt of his left wrist. Then he drew his hands back and placed them in full view on the edge of the table, on top of it.

The red-haired girl's eyes shone and her lips slowly parted.

The ball drifted along the groove, dipped past one of the bright metal diamonds, slid down the flank of the wheel and chattered along the tines beside the numbers. Movement went out of it suddenly, with a dry click. It fell next the double-zero, in red twenty-seven. The wheel was motionless.

The croupier took up his rake and slowly pushed the two packets of bills across, added them to the stake, pushed the whole thing off the field of play.

Canales put his wallet back in his breast pocket, turned and walked slowly back to the door, went through it.

I took my cramped fingers off the top of the railing, and a lot of people broke for the bar.

THREE

When Lou came up I was sitting at a little tile-top table in a corner, fooling with some more of the tequila. The little orchestra was playing a thin, brittle tango and one couple was maneuvering self-consciously on the dance floor.

Lou had a cream-colored overcoat on, with the collar turned up around a lot of white silk scarf. He had a fine-drawn glistening expression. He had white pigskin gloves this time and he put one of them down on the table and leaned at me.

'Over twenty-two thousand,' he said softly. 'Boy, what a take!'

I said: 'Very nice money, Lou. What kind of car are you driving?'

'See anything wrong with it?'

'The play?' I shrugged, fiddled with my glass. 'I'm not wised up on roulette, Lou . . . I saw plenty wrong with your broad's manners.'

'She's not a broad,' Lou said. His voice got a little worried.

'Okey. She made Canales look like a million. What kind of car?'

'Buick sedan. Nile green, with two spotlights and those little fender lights on rods.' His voice was still worried.

I said: 'Take it kind of slow through town. Give me a chance to get in the parade.'

He moved his glove and went away. The red-haired girl was not in sight anywhere. I looked down at the watch on my wrist. When I looked up again

Canales was standing across the table. His eyes looked at me lifelessly above his trick mustache.

'You don't like my place,' he said.

'On the contrary.'

'You don't come here to play.' He was telling me, not asking me.

'Is it compulsory?' I asked dryly.

A very faint smile drifted across his face. He leaned a little down and said: 'I think you are a dick. A smart dick.'

'Just a shamus,' I said. 'And not so smart. Don't let my long upper lip fool you. It runs in the family.'

Canales wrapped his fingers around the top of a chair, squeezed on it. 'Don't come here again – for anything.' He spoke very softly, almost dreamily. 'I don't like pigeons.'

I took the cigarette out of my mouth and looked it over before I looked at him. I said: 'I heard you insulted a while back. You took it nicely . . . So we won't count this one.'

He had a queer expression for a moment. Then he turned and slid away with a little sway of the shoulders. He put his feet down flat and turned them out a good deal as he walked. His walk, like his face, was a little negroid.

I got up and went out through the big white double doors into a dim lobby, got my hat and coat and put them on. I went out through another pair of double doors onto a wide veranda with scrollwork along the edge of its roof. There was sea fog in the air and the windblown Monterey cypresses in front of the house dripped with it. The grounds sloped gently into the dark for a long distance. Fog hid the ocean.

I had parked the car out on the street, on the other side of the house. I drew my hat down and walked soundlessly on the damp moss that covered the driveway, rounded a corner of the porch, and stopped rigidly.

A man just in front of me was holding a gun – but he didn't see me. He was holding the gun down at his side, pressed against the material of his overcoat, and his big hand made it look quite small. The dim light that reflected from the barrel seemed to come out of the fog, to be part of the fog. He was a big man, and he stood very still, poised on the balls of his feet.

I lifted my right hand very slowly and opened the top two buttons of my coat, reached inside and drew out a long .38 with a six-inch barrel. I eased it into my overcoat pocket.

The man in front of me moved, reached his left hand up to his face. He drew on a cigarette cupped inside his hand and the glow put brief light on a heavy chin, wide, dark nostrils, and a square, aggressive nose, the nose of a fighting man.

Then he dropped and cigarette and stepped on it and a quick, light step made faint noise behind me. I was far too late turning.

Something swished and I went out like a light.

FOUR

When I came to I was cold and wet and had a headache a yard wide. There was a soft bruise behind my right ear that wasn't bleeding. I had been put down with a sap.

I got up off my back and saw that I was a few yards from the driveway, between two trees that were wet with fog. There was some mud on the backs of my shoes. I had been dragged off the path, but not very far.

I went through my pockets. My gun was gone, of course, but that was all – that and the idea that this excursion was all fun.

I nosed around through the fog, didn't find anything or see anyone, gave up bothering about that, and went along the blank side of the house to a curving line of palm trees and an old type arc light that hissed and flickered over the entrance to a sort of lane where I had stuck the 1925 Marmon touring car I still used for transportation. I got into it after wiping the seat off with a towel, teased the motor alive, and choked it along to a big empty street with disused car tracks in the middle.

I went from there to De Cazens Boulevard, which was the main drag of Las Olindas and was called after the man who built Canales' place long ago. After a while there was town, buildings, dead-looking stores, a service station with a night-bell, and at last a drugstore which was still open.

A dolled-up sedan was parked in front of the drugstore and I parked behind that, got out, and saw that a hatless man was sitting at the counter, talking to a clerk in a blue smock. They seemed to have the world to themselves. I started to go in, then I stopped and took another look at the dolled-up sedan.

It was a Buick and of a color that could have been Nile-green in daylight. It had two spotlights and two little egg-shaped amber lights stuck up on thin nickel rods clamped to the front fenders. The window by the driver's seat was down. I went back to the Marmon and got a flash, reached in and twisted the license holder of the Buick around, put the light on it quickly, then off again.

It was registered to Louis N. Harger.

I got rid of the flash and went into the drugstore. There was a liquor display at one side, and the clerk in the blue smock sold me a pint of Canadian Club, which I took over to the counter and opened. There were ten seats at the counter, but I sat down on the one next to the hatless man. He began to look me over, in the mirror, very carefully.

I got a cup of black coffee two-thirds full and added plenty of the rye. I drank it down and waited for a minute, to let it warm me up. Then I looked the hatless man over.

He was about twenty-eight, a little thin on top, had a healthy red face, fairly honest eyes, dirty hands and looked as if he wasn't making much money. He wore a gray whipcord jacket with metal buttons on it, pants that didn't match.

I said carelessly, in a low voice: 'Your bus outside?'

He sat very still. His mouth got small and tight and he had trouble pulling his eyes away from mine, in the mirror.

'My brother's,' he said, after a moment.

I said: 'Care for a drink? . . . Your brother is an old friend of mine.'

He nodded slowly, gulped, moved his hand slowly, but finally got the bottle and curdled his coffee with it. He drank the whole thing down. Then I watched him dig up a crumpled pack of cigarettes, spear his mouth with one, strike a match on the counter, after missing twice on his thumbnail, and inhale with a lot of very poor nonchalance that he knew wasn't going over.

I leaned close to him and said evenly: 'This doesn't *have* to be trouble.'

He said: 'Yeah . . . Wh-what's the beef?'

The clerk sidled towards us. I asked for more coffee. When I got it I stared at the clerk until he went and stood in front of the display window with his back to me. I laced my second cup of coffee and drank some of it. I looked at the clerk's back and said: 'The guy the car belongs to doesn't have a brother.'

He held himself tightly, but turned towards me. 'You think it's a hot car?'

'No.'

'You don't think it's a hot car?'

I said: 'No. I just want the story.'

'You a dick?'

'Uh-huh – but it isn't a shakedown, if that's what worries you.'

He drew hard on his cigarette and moved his spoon around in his empty cup.

'I can lose my job over this,' he said slowly. 'But I needed a hundred bucks. I'm a hack driver.'

'I guessed that,' I said.

He looked surprised, turned his head and stared at me. 'Have another drink and let's get on with it,' I said. 'Car thieves don't park them on the main drag and then sit around in drugstores.'

The clerk came back from the window and hovered near us, busying himself with rubbing a rag on the coffee urn. A heavy silence fell. The clerk put the rag down, went along to the back of the store, behind the partition, and began to whistle aggressively.

The man beside me took some more of the whiskey and drank it, nodding his head wisely at me. 'Listen – I brought a fare out and was supposed to wait for him. A guy and a jane come up alongside me in the Buick and the guy offers me a hundred bucks to let him wear my cap and drive my hack into town. I'm to hang around here an hour, then take his heap to the Hotel Carillon on Towne Boulevard. My cab will be there for me. He gives me the hundred bucks.'

'What was his story?' I asked.

'He said they'd been to a gambling joint and had some luck for a change. They're afraid of holdups on the way in. They figure there's always spotters watchin' the play.'

I took one of his cigarettes and straightened it out in my fingers. 'It's a story I can't hurt much,' I said. 'Could I see your cards?'

He gave them to me. His name was Tom Sneyd and he was a driver for the Green Top Cab Company. I corked my pint, slipped it into my side pocket, and danced a half-dollar on the counter.

The clerk came along and made change. He was almost shaking with curiosity.

'Come on, Tom,' I said in front of him. 'Let's go get that cab. I don't think you should wait around here any longer.'

We went out, and I let the Buick lead me away from the straggling lights of Las Olindas, through a series of small beach towns with little houses built on sandlots close to the ocean, and bigger ones built on the slopes of the hills behind. A window was lit here and there. The tires sang on the moist concrete and the little amber lights on the Buick's fenders peeped back at me from the curves.

At West Cimarron we turned inland, chugged on through Canal City, and met the San Angelo Cut. It took us almost an hour to get to 5640 Towne Boulevard, which is the number of the Hotel Carillon. It is a big, rambling slate-roofed building with a basement garage and a forecourt fountain on which they play a pale green light in the evening.

Green Top Cab No. 469 was parked across the street, on the dark side. I couldn't see where anybody had been shooting into it. Tom Sneyd found his cap in the driver's compartment, climbed eagerly under the wheel.

'Does that fix me up? Can I go now?' His voice was strident with relief.

I told him it was all right with me, and gave him my card. It was twelve minutes past one as he took the corner. I climbed into the Buick and tooled it down the ramp to the garage and left it with a colored boy who was dusting cars in slow motion. I went around to the lobby.

The clerk was an ascetic-looking young man who was reading a volume of *California Appellate Decisions* under the switchboard light. He said Lou was not in and had not been in since eleven, when he came on duty. After a short argument about the lateness of the hour and the importance of my visit, he rang Lou's apartment, but there wasn't any answer.

I went out and sat in my Marmon for a few minutes, smoked a cigarette, imbibed a little from my pint of Canadian Club. Then I went back into the Carillon and shut myself in a pay booth. I dialed the *Telegram*, asked for the City Desk, got a man named Von Ballin.

He yelped at me when I told him who I was. 'You still walking around? That ought to be a story. I thought Manny Tinnen's friends would have had you laid away in old lavender by this time.'

I said: 'Can that and listen to this. Do you know a man named Lou

Harger? He's a gambler. Had a place that was raided and closed up a month ago.'

Von Ballin said he didn't know Lou personally, but he knew who he was.

'Who around your rag would know him real well?'

He thought a moment. 'There's a lad named Jerry Cross here,' he said, 'that's supposed to be an expert on night life. What did you want to know?'

'Where would he go to celebrate,' I said. Then I told him some of the story, not too much. I left out the part where I got sapped and the part about the taxi. 'He hasn't shown at his hotel,' I ended. 'I ought to get a line on him.'

'Well, if you're a friend of his—'

'Of his – not of his crowd,' I said sharply.

Von Ballin stopped to yell at somebody to take a call, then said to me softly, close to the phone: 'Come through, boy. Come through.'

'All right. But I'm talking to you, not to your sheet. I got sapped and lost my gun outside Canales' joint. Lou and his girl switched his car for a taxi they picked up. Then they dropped out of sight. I don't like it too well. Lou wasn't drunk enough to chase around town with that much dough in his pockets. And if he was, the girl wouldn't let him. She had the practical eye.'

'I'll see what I can do,' Von Ballin said. 'But it don't sound promising. I'll give you a buzz.'

I told him I lived at the Merritt Plaza, in case he had forgotten, went out and got into the Marmon again. I drove home and put hot towels on my head for fifteen minutes, then sat around in my pajamas and drank hot whiskey and lemon and called the Carillon every once in a while. At two-thirty Von Ballin called me and said no luck. Lou hadn't been pinched, he wasn't in any of the Receiving Hospitals, and he hadn't shown at any of the clubs Jerry Cross could think of.

At three I called the Carillon for the last time. Then I put my light out and went to sleep.

In the morning it was the same way. I tried to trace the red-haired girl a little. There were twenty-eight people named Glenn in the phone book, and three women among them. One didn't answer, the other two assured me they didn't have red hair. One offered to show me.

I shaved, showered, had breakfast, walked three blocks down the hill to the Condor Building.

Miss Glenn was sitting in my little reception room.

FIVE

I unlocked the other door and she went in and sat in the chair where Lou had sat the afternoon before. I opened some windows, locked the outer door of the reception room, and struck a match for the unlighted cigarette she held in her ungloved and ringless left hand.

She was dressed in a blouse and plaid skirt with a loose coat over them, and a close-fitting hat that was far enough out of style to suggest a run of bad luck. But it hid almost all of her hair. Her skin was without make-up and she looked about thirty and had the set face of exhaustion.

She held her cigarette with a hand that was almost too steady, a hand on guard. I sat down and waited for her to talk.

She stared at the wall over my head and didn't say anything. After a little while I packed my pipe and smoked for a minute. Then I got up and went across to the door that opened into the hallway and picked up a couple of letters that had been pushed through the slot.

I sat down at the desk again, looked them over, read one of them twice, as if I had been alone. While I was doing this I didn't look at her directly or speak to her, but I kept an eye on her all the same. She looked like a lady who was getting nerved for something.

Finally she moved. She opened up a big black patent-leather bag and took out a fat manila envelope, pulled a rubber band off it and sat holding the envelope between the palms of her hands, with her head tilted way back and the cigarette dribbling gray smoke from the corners of her mouth.

She said slowly: 'Lou said if I ever got caught in the rain, you were the boy to see. It's raining hard where I am.'

I stared at the manila envelope. 'Lou is a pretty good friend of mine,' I said. 'I'd do anything in reason for him. Some things not in reason – like last night. That doesn't mean Lou and I always play the same games.'

She dropped her cigarette into the glass bowl of the ash tray and left it to smoke. A dark flame burned suddenly in her eyes, then went out.

'Lou is dead.' Her voice was quite toneless.

I reached over with a pencil and stabbed at the hot end of the cigarette until it stopped smoking.

She went on: 'A couple of Canales' boys got him in my apartment – with one shot from a small gun that looked like my gun. Mine was gone when I looked for it afterwards. I spent the night there with him dead . . . I had to.'

She broke quite suddenly. Her eyes turned up in her head and her head came down and hit the desk. She lay still, with the manila envelope in front of her lax hands.

I jerked a drawer open and brought up a bottle and a glass, poured a stiff one and stepped around it, heaved her up in her chair. I pushed the edge of the glass hard against her mouth – hard enough to hurt. She struggled and swallowed. Some of it ran down her chin, but life came back into her eyes.

I left the whiskey in front of her and sat down again. The flap of the envelope had come open enough for me to see currency inside, bales of currency.

She began to talk to me in a dreamy sort of voice.

'We got all big bills from the cashier, but makes quite a package at that.

There's twenty-two thousand even in the envelope. I kept out a few odd hundreds.

'Lou was worried. He figured it would be pretty easy for Canales to catch up with us. You might be right behind and not be able to do very much about it.'

I said: 'Canales lost the money in full view of everybody there. It was good advertising – even if it hurt.'

She went on exactly as though I had not spoken. 'Going through the town we spotted a cab driver sitting in his parked cab and Lou had a brain wave. He offered the boy a C note to let him drive the cab into San Angelo and bring the Buick to the hotel after a while. The boy took us up and we went over on another street and made the switch. We were sorry about ditching you, but Lou said you wouldn't mind. And we might get a chance to flag you.

'Lou didn't go into his hotel. We took another cab over to my place. I live at the Hobart Arms, eight hundred block on South Minter. It's a place where you don't have to answer questions at the desk. We went up to my apartment and put the lights on and two guys with masks came around the half-wall between the living room and the dinette. One was small and thin and the other one was a big slob with a chin that stuck out under his mask like a shelf. Lou made a wrong motion and the big one shot him just the once. The gun just made a flat crack, not very loud, and Lou fell down on the floor and never moved.'

I said: 'It might be the ones that made a sucker out of me. I haven't told you about that yet.'

She didn't seem to hear that either. Her face was white and composed, but as expressionless as plaster. 'Maybe I'd better have another finger of the hooch,' she said.

I poured us a couple of drinks, and we drank them. She went on: 'They went through us, but we didn't have the money. We had stopped at an all-night drugstore and had it weighed and mailed it at a branch post office. They went through the apartment, but of course we had just come in and hadn't had time to hide anything. The big one slammed me down with his fist, and when I woke up again they were gone and I was alone with Lou dead on the floor.'

She pointed to a mark on the angle of her jaw. There was something there, but it didn't show much. I moved around in my chair a little and said: 'They passed you on the way in. Smart boys would have looked a taxi over on that road. How did they know where to go?'

'I thought that out during the night,' Miss Glenn said. 'Canales knows where I live. He followed me home once and tried to get me to ask him up.'

'Yeah,' I said, 'but why did they go to your place and how did they get in?'

'That's not hard. There's a ledge just below the windows and a man could edge along it to the fire escape. They probably had other boys covering Lou's hotel. We thought of that chance but we didn't think about my place being known to them.'

'Tell me the rest of it,' I said.

'The money was mailed to me,' Miss Glenn explained. 'Lou was a swell boy, but a girl has to protect herself. That's why I had to stay there last night with Lou dead on the floor. Until the mail came. Then I came over here.'

I got up and looked out of the window. A fat girl was pounding a typewriter across the court. I could hear the clack of it. I sat down, stared at my thumb.

'Did they plant the gun?' I asked.

'Not unless it's under him. I didn't look there.'

'They let you off too easy. Maybe it wasn't Canales at all. Did Lou open his heart to you much?'

She shook her head quietly. Her eyes were slate-blue now, and thoughtful, without the blank stare.

'All right,' I said. 'Just what did you think of having me do about it all?'

She narrowed her eyes a little, then put a hand out and pushed the bulging envelope slowly across the desk.

'I'm no baby and I'm in a jam. But I'm not going to the cleaners just the same. Half of this money is mine, and I want it with a clean getaway. One-half net. If I'd called the law last night, there'd have been a way to chisel me out of it . . . I think Lou would like you to have his half, if you want to play with me.'

I said: 'It's big money to flash at a private dick, Miss Glenn,' and smiled wearily. 'You're a little worse off for not calling cops last night. But there's an answer to anything they might say. I think I'd better go over there and see what's broken, if anything.'

She leaned forward quickly and said: 'Will you take care of the money? . . . Dare you?'

'Sure. I'll pop downstairs and put it in a safe-deposit box. You can hold one of the keys – and we'll talk split later on. I think it would be a swell idea if Canales knew he had to see me, and still sweller if you hid out in a little hotel where I have a friend – at least until I nose around a bit.'

She nodded. I put my hat on and put the envelope inside my belt. I went out, telling her there was a gun in the top left-hand drawer, if she felt nervous.

When I got back she didn't seem to have moved. But she said she had phoned Canales' place and left a message for him she thought he would understand.

We went by rather devious ways to the Lorraine, at Brant and Avenue C. Nobody shot at us going over, and as far as I could see we were not trailed.

I shook hands with Jim Dolan, the day clerk at the Lorraine, with a twenty folded in my hand. He put his hand in his pocket and said he would be glad to see that 'Miss Thompson' was not bothered.

I left. There was nothing in the noon paper about Lou Harger of the Hobart Arms.

SIX

The Hobart Arms was just another apartment house, in a block lined with them. It was six stories high and had a buff front. A lot of cars were parked at both curbs all along the block. I drove through slowly and looked things over. The neighborhood didn't have the look of having been excited about anything in the immediate past. It was peaceful and sunny, and the parked cars had a settled look, as if they were right at home.

I circled into an alley with a high board fence on each side and a lot of flimsy garages cutting it. I parked beside one that had a For Rent sign and went between two garbage cans into the concrete yard of the Hobart Arms, along the side to the street. A man was putting golf clubs into the back of a coupe. In the lobby a Filipino was dragging a vacuum cleaner over the rug and a dark Jewess was writing at the switchboard.

I used the automatic elevator and prowled along an upper corridor to the last door on the left. I knocked, waited, knocked again, went in with Miss Glenn's key.

Nobody was dead on the floor.

I looked at myself in the mirror that was the back of a pull-down bed, went across and looked out of a window. There was a ledge below that had once been a coping. It ran along to the fire escape. A blind man could have walked in. I didn't notice anything like footmarks in the dust on it.

There was nothing in the dinette or kitchen except what belonged there. The bedroom had a cheerful carpet and painted gray walls. There was a lot of junk in the corner, around a wastebasket, and a broken comb on the dresser held a few strands of red hair. The closets were empty except for some gin bottles.

I went back to the living room, looked behind the wall bed, stood around for a minute, left the apartment.

The Filipino in the lobby had made about three yards with the vacuum cleaner. I leaned on the counter beside the switchboard.

'Miss Glenn?'

The dark Jewess said: 'Five-two-four,' and made a check mark on the laundry list.

'She's not in. Has she been in lately?'

She glanced up at me. 'I haven't noticed. What is it – a bill?'

I said I was just a friend, thanked her and went away. That established the fact that there had been no excitement in Miss Glenn's apartment. I went back to the alley and the Marmon.

I hadn't believed it quite the way Miss Glenn told it anyhow.

I crossed Cordova, drove a block and stopped beside a forgotten drugstore that slept behind two giant pepper trees and a dusty, cluttered window. It had a single pay booth in the corner. An old man shuffled towards me wistfully, then went away when he saw what I wanted, lowered a pair of steel spectacles on the end of his nose and sat down again with his newspaper.

I dropped my nickel, dialed, and a girl's voice said: 'Telegrayam!' with a tinny drawl. I asked for Von Ballin.

When I got him and he knew who it was, I could hear him clearing his throat. Then his voice came close to the phone and said very distinctly: 'I've got something for you, but it's bad. I'm sorry as all hell. Your friend Harger is in the morgue. We got a flash about ten minutes ago.'

I leaned against the wall of the booth and felt my eyes getting haggard. I said: 'What else did you get?'

'Couple of radio cops picked him up in somebody's front yard or something, in West Cimarron. He was shot through the heart. It happened last night, but for some reason they only just put out the identification.'

I said: 'West Cimarron, huh? . . . Well, that takes care of that. I'll be in to see you.'

I thanked him and hung up, stood for a moment looking out through the glass at a middle-aged gray-haired man who had come into the store and was pawing over the magazine rack.

Then I dropped another nickel and dialed the Lorraine, asked for the clerk.

I said: 'Get your girl to put me on to the redhead, will you, Jim?'

I got a cigarette out and lit it, puffed smoke at the glass of the door. The smoke flattened out against the glass and swirled about in the close air. Then the line clicked and the operator's voice said: 'Sorry, your party does not answer.'

'Give me Jim again,' I said. Then, when he answered, 'Can you take time to run up and find out why she doesn't answer the phone? Maybe she's just being cagey.'

Jim said: 'You bet. I'll shoot right up with a key.'

Sweat was coming out all over me. I put the receiver down on a little shelf and jerked the booth door open. The gray-haired man looked up quickly from the magazines, then scowled and looked at his watch. Smoke poured out of the booth. After a moment I kicked the door shut and picked up the receiver again.

Jim's voice seemed to come to me from a long way off. 'She's not here. Maybe she went for a walk.'

I said: 'Yeah – or maybe it was a ride.'

I pronged the receiver and pushed on out of the booth. The gray-haired stranger slammed a magazine down so hard that it fell to the floor. He stooped to pick it up as I went past him. Then he straightened up just behind me and said quietly, but very firmly: 'Keep the hands down, and quiet. Walk on out to your heap. This is business.'

Out of the corner of my eye I could see the old man peeking short-sightedly at us. But there wasn't anything for him to see, even if he could see that far. Something prodded my back. It might have been a finger, but I didn't think it was.

We went out of the store very peacefully.

A long gray car had stopped close behind the Marmon. Its rear door was open and a man with a square face and a crooked mouth was standing with one foot on the running board. His right hand was behind him, inside the car.

My man's voice said: 'Get in your car and drive west. Take this first corner and go about twenty-five, not more.'

The narrow street was sunny and quiet and the pepper trees whispered. Traffic threshed by on Cordova a short block away. I shrugged, opened the door of my car and got under the wheel. The gray-haired man got in very quickly beside me, watching my hands. He swung his right hand around, with a snub-nosed gun in it.

'Careful getting your keys out, buddy.'

I was careful. As I stepped on the starter a car door slammed behind, there were rapid steps, and someone got into the back seat of the Marmon. I let in the clutch and drove around the corner. In the mirror I could see the gray car making the turn behind. Then it dropped back a little.

I drove west on a street that paralleled Cordova and when we had gone a block and a half a hand came down over my shoulder from behind and took my gun away from me. The gray-haired man rested his short revolver on his leg and felt me over carefully with his free hand. He leaned back satisfied.

'Okey. Drop over to the main drag and snap it up,' he said. 'But that don't mean trying to sideswipe a prowl car, if you lamp one . . . Or if you think it does, try it and see.'

I made the two turns, speeded up to thirty-five and held it there. We went through some nice residential districts, and then the landscape began to thin out. When it was quite thin the gray car behind dropped back, turned towards town and disappeared.

'What's the snatch for?' I asked.

The gray-haired man laughed and rubbed his broad red chin. 'Just business. The big boy wants to talk to you.'

'Canales?'

'Canales – hell! I said the *big boy*.'

I watched traffic, what there was of it that far out, and didn't speak for a few minutes. Then I said: 'Why didn't you pull it in the apartment, or in the alley?'

'Wanted to make sure you wasn't covered.'

'Who's this big boy?'

'Skip that – till we get you there. Anything else?'

'Yes. Can I smoke?'

He held the wheel while I lit up. The man in the back seat hadn't said a word at any time. After a while the gray-haired man made me pull up and move over, and he drove.

'I used to own one of these, six years ago, when I was poor,' he said jovially.

I couldn't think of a really good answer to that, so I just let smoke seep down into my lungs and wondered why, if Lou had been killed in West Cimarron, the killers didn't get the money. And if he really had been killed at Miss Glenn's apartment, why somebody had taken the trouble to carry him back to West Cimarron.

SEVEN

In twenty minutes we were in the foothills. We went over a hogback, drifted down a long white concrete ribbon, crossed a bridge, went halfway up the next slope and turned off on a gravel road that disappeared around a shoulder of scrub oak and manzanita. Plumes of pampas grass flared on the side of the hill, like jets of water. The wheels crunched on the gravel and skidded on the curves.

We came to a mountain cabin with a wide porch and cemented boulder foundations. The windmill of a generator turned slowly on the crest of a spur a hundred feet behind the cabin. A mountain blue jay flashed across the road, zoomed, banked sharply, and fell out of sight like a stone.

The gray-haired man tooled the car up to the porch, beside a tan-colored Lincoln coupe, switched off the ignition and set the Marmon's long parking brake. He took the keys out, folded them carefully in their leather case, put the case away in his pocket.

The man in the back seat got out and held the door beside me open. He had a gun in his hand. I got out. The gray-haired man got out. We all went into the house.

There was a big room with walls of knotted pine, beautifully polished. We went across it walking on Indian rugs and the gray-haired man knocked carefully on a door.

A voice shouted: 'What is it?'

The gray-haired man put his face against the door and said: 'Beasley – and the guy you wanted to talk to.'

The voice inside said to come on in. Beasley opened the door, pushed me through it and shut it behind me.

It was another big room with knotted pine walls and Indian rugs on the floor. A driftwood fire hissed and puffed on a stone hearth.

The man who sat behind a flat desk was Frank Dorr, the politico.

He was the kind of man who liked to have a desk in front of him, and shove his fat stomach against it, and fiddle with things on it, and look very wise. He had a fat, muddy face, a thin fringe of white hair that stuck up a little, small sharp eyes, small and very delicate hands.

What I could see of him was dressed in a slovenly gray suit, and there was a large black Persian cat on the desk in front of him. He was scratching the cat's head with one of his little neat hands and the cat was leaning against his hand. Its busy tail flowed over the edge of the desk and fell straight down.

He said: 'Sit down,' without looking away from the cat.

I sat down in a leather chair with a very low seat. Dorr said: 'How do you like it up here? Kind of nice, ain't it? This is Toby, my girl friend. Only girl friend I got. Ain't you, Toby?'

I said: 'I like it up here – but I don't like the way I got here.'

Dorr raised his head a few inches and looked at me with his mouth slightly open. He had beautiful teeth, but they hadn't grown in his mouth. He said: 'I'm a busy man, brother. It was simpler than arguing. Have a drink?'

'Sure I'll have a drink,' I said.

He squeezed the cat's head gently between his two palms, then pushed it away from him and put both hands down on the arms of his chair. He shoved hard and his face got a little red and he finally got up on his feet. He waddled across to a built-in cabinet and took out a squat decanter of whiskey and two gold-veined glasses.

'No ice today,' he said, waddling back to the desk. 'Have to drink it straight.'

He poured two drinks, gestured, and I went over and got mine. He sat down again. I sat down with my drink. Dorr lit a long brown cigar, pushed the box two inches in my direction, leaned back and stared at me with complete relaxation.

'You're the guy that fingered Manny Tinnen,' he said. 'It won't do.'

I sipped my whiskey. It was good enough to sip.

'Life gets complicated at times,' Dorr went on, in the same even, relaxed voice. 'Politics – even when it's a lot of fun – is tough on the nerves. You know me. I'm tough and I get what I want. There ain't a hell of a lot I want any more, but what I want – I want bad. And ain't so damn particular how I get it.'

'You have that reputation,' I said politely.

Dorr's eyes twinkled. He looked around for the cat, dragged it towards him by the tail, pushed it down on its side and began to rub its stomach. The cat seemed to like it.

Dorr looked at me and said very softly: 'You bumped Lou Harger.'

'What makes you think so?' I asked, without any particular emphasis.

'You bumped Lou Harger. Maybe he needed the bump – but you gave it to him. He was shot once through the heart, with a thirty-eight. You wear a thirty-eight and you're known to be a fancy shot with it. You were with Harger at Las Olindas last night and saw him win a lot of money. You were supposed to be acting as bodyguard for him, but you got a better idea. You caught up with him and that girl in West Cimarron, slipped Harger the dose and got the money.'

I finished my whiskey, got up and poured myself some more of it.

'You made a deal with the girl,' Dorr said, 'but the deal didn't stick. She got a cute idea. But that don't matter, because the police got your gun along with Harger. And you got the dough.'

I said: 'Is there a tag out for me?'

'Not till I give the word . . . And the gun hasn't been turned in . . . I got a lot of friends, you know.'

I said slowly: 'I got sapped outside Canales' place. It served me right. My gun was take from me. I never caught up with Harger, never saw him again. The girl came to me this morning with the money in an envelope and a story that Harger had been killed in her apartment. That's how I have the money – for safekeeping. I wasn't sure about the girl's story, but her bringing the money carried a lot of weight. And Harger was a friend of mine. I started out to investigate.'

'You should have let the cops do that,' Dorr said with a grin.

'There was a chance the girl was being framed. Besides there was a possibility I might make a few dollars – legitimately. It has been done, even in San Angelo.'

Dorr stuck a finger towards the cat's face and the cat bit it, with an absent expression. Then it pulled away from him, sat down on a corner of the desk and began to lick one toe.

'Twenty-two grand, and the jane passed it over to you to keep,' Dorr said. 'Ain't that just like a jane?

'You got the dough,' Dorr said. 'Harger was killed with your gun. The girl's gone – but I could bring her back. I think she'd make a good witness, if we needed one.'

'Was the play at Las Olindas crooked?' I asked.

Dorr finished his drink and curled his lips around his cigar again. 'Sure,' he said carelessly. 'The croupier – a guy named Pina – was in on it. The wheel was wired for the double-zero. The old crap. Copper button on the floor, copper button on Pina's shoe sole, wires up his leg, batteries in his hip pockets. The old crap.'

I said: 'Canales didn't act as if he knew about it.'

Dorr chuckled. 'He knew the wheel was wired. He didn't know his head croupier was playin' on the other team.'

'I'd hate to be Pina,' I said.

Dorr made a negligent motion with his cigar. 'He's taken care of . . . The play was careful and quiet. They didn't make any fancy long shots, just even money bets, and they didn't win all the time. They couldn't. No wired wheel is that good.'

I shrugged, moved about in my chair. 'You know a hell of a lot about it,' I said. 'Was all this just to get me set for a squeeze?'

He grinned softly: 'Hell, no! Some of it just happened – the way the best plans do.' He waved his cigar again, and a pale gray tendril of smoke curled past his cunning little eyes. There was a muffled sound of talk in the outside room. 'I got connections I got to please – even if I don't like all their capers,' he added simply.

'Like Manny Tinnen?' I said. 'He was around City Hall a lot, knew too much. Okey, Mister Dorr. Just what do you figure on having me do for you? Commit suicide?'

He laughed. His fat shoulders shook carefully. He put one of his small hands out with the palm towards me. 'I wouldn't think of that,' he said dryly, 'and the other way's better business. The way public opinion is about the Shannon kill. I ain't sure that louse of a D.A. wouldn't convict Tinnen without you – if he could sell the folks the idea you'd been knocked off to button your mouth.'

I got up out of my chair, went over and leaned on the desk, leaned across it towards Dorr.

He said: 'No funny business!' a little sharply and breathlessly. His hand went to a drawer and got it half open. His movements with his hands were very quick in contrast with the movements of his body.

I smiled down at the hand and he took it away from the drawer. I saw a gun just inside the drawer.

I said: 'I've already talked to the Grand Jury.'

Dorr leaned back and smiled at me. 'Guys make mistakes,' he said. 'Even smart private dicks . . . You could have a change of heart – and put it in writing.'

I said very softly. 'No. I'd be under a perjury rap – which I couldn't beat. I'd rather be under a murder rap – which I can beat. Especially as Fenweather will *want* me to beat it. He won't want to spoil me as a witness. The Tinnen case is too important to him.'

Dorr said evenly: 'Then you'll have to try and beat it, brother. And after you get through beating it there'll still be enough mud on your neck so no jury'll convict Manny on your say-so alone.'

I put my hand out slowly and scratched the cat's ear. 'What about the twenty-two grand?'

'It *could* be all yours, if you want to play. After all, it ain't my money . . . If Manny gets clear, I might add a little something that *is* my money.'

I tickled the cat under its chin. It began to purr. I picked it up and held it gently in my arms.

'Who did kill Lou Harger, Dorr?' I asked, not looking at him.

He shook his head. I looked at him, smiling. 'Swell cat you have,' I said.

Dorr licked his lips. 'I think the little bastard likes you,' he grinned. He looked pleased at the idea.

I nodded – and threw the cat in his face.

He yelped, but his hands came up to catch the cat. The cat twisted neatly in the air and landed with both front paws working. One of them split Dorr's cheek like a banana peel. He yelled very loudly.

I had the gun out of the drawer and the muzzle of it into the back of Dorr's neck when Beasley and the square-faced man dodged in.

For an instant there was a sort of tableau. Then the cat tore itself loose from Dorr's arms, shot to the floor and went under the desk. Beasley raised his snub-nosed gun, but he didn't look as if he was certain what he meant to do with it.

I shoved the muzzle of mine hard into Dorr's neck and said: 'Frankie gets it first, boys . . . And that's not a gag.'

Dorr grunted in front of me. 'Take it easy,' he growled to his hoods. He took a handkerchief from his breast pocket and began to dab at his split and bleeding cheek with it. The man with the crooked mouth began to sidle along the wall.

I said: 'Don't get the idea I'm enjoying this, but I'm not fooling either. You heels stay put.'

The man with the crooked mouth stopped sidling and gave me a nasty leer. He kept his hands low.

Dorr half turned his head and tried to talk over his shoulder to me. I couldn't see enough of his face to get any expression, but he didn't seem scared. He said: 'This won't get you anything. I could have you knocked off easy enough, if that was what I wanted. Now where are you? You can't shoot anybody without getting in a worse jam than if you did what I asked you to. It looks like a stalemate to me.'

I thought that over for a moment while Beasley looked at me quite pleasantly, as though it was all just routine to him. There was nothing pleasant about the other man. I listened hard, but the rest of the house seemed to be quite silent.

Dorr edged forward from the gun and said: 'Well?'

I said: 'I'm going out. I have a gun and it looks like a gun that I could hit somebody with, if I have to. I don't want to very much, and if you'll have Beasley throw my keys over and the other one turn back the gun he took from me, I'll forget about the snatch.'

Dorr moved his arms in the lazy beginning of a shrug. 'Then what?'

'Figure out your deal a little closer,' I said. 'If you get enough protection behind me, I might throw in with you . . . And if you're as tough as you think you are, a few hours won't cut any ice one way or the other.'

'It's an idea,' Dorr said and chuckled. Then to Beasley: 'Keep your rod to yourself and give him his keys. Also his gun – the one you got today.'

Beasley sighed and very carefully inserted a hand into his pants. He tossed my leather keycase across the room near the end of the desk. The man with the twisted mouth put his hand up, edged it inside his side pocket and I eased down behind Dorr's back, while he did it. He came out with my gun, let it fall to the floor and kicked it away from him.

I came out from behind Dorr's back, got my keys and the gun up from the floor, moved sidewise towards the door of the room. Dorr watched with an empty stare that meant nothing. Beasley followed me around with his body and stepped away from the door as I neared it. The other man had trouble holding himself quiet.

I got to the door and reversed a key that was in it. Dorr said dreamily: 'You're just like one of those rubber balls on the end of an elastic. The farther you get away, the suddener you'll bounce back.'

I said: 'The elastic might be a little rotten,' and went through the door, turned the key in it and braced myself for shots that didn't come. As a bluff, mine was thinner than the gold on a week-end wedding ring. It worked because Dorr let it, and that was all.

I got out of the house, got the Marmon started and wrangled it around and sent it skidding past the shoulder of the hill and so on down to the highway. There was no sound of anything coming after me.

When I reached the concrete highway bridge it was a little past two o'clock, and I drove with one hand for a while and wiped the sweat off the back of my neck.

EIGHT

The morgue was at the end of a long and bright and silent corridor that branched off from behind the main lobby of the County Building. The corridor ended in two doors and a blank wall faced with marble. One door had 'Inquest Room' lettered on the glass panel behind which there was no light. The other opened into a small, cheerful office.

A man with gander-blue eyes and rust-colored hair parted in the exact center of his head was pawing over some printed forms at a table. He looked up, looked me over, and then suddenly smiled.

I said: 'Hello, Landon . . . Remember the Shelby case?'

The bright blue eyes twinkled. He got up and came around the table with his hand out. 'Sure. What can we do—' He broke off suddenly and snapped his fingers. 'Hell! You're the guy that put the bee on that hot rod.'

I tossed a butt through the open door into the corridor. 'That's not why I'm here,' I said. 'Anyhow not this time. There's a fellow named Louis Harger . . . picked up shot last night or this morning, in West Cimarron, as I get it. Could I take a look-see?'

'They can't stop you,' Landon said.

He led the way through the door on the far side of his office into a place that was all white paint and white enamel and glass and bright light. Against one wall was a double tier of large bins with glass windows in them. Through the peepholes showed bundles in white sheeting, and, further back, frosted pipes.

A body covered with a sheet lay on a table that was high at the head and sloped down to the foot. Landon pulled the sheet down casually from a man's dead, placid, yellowish face. Long black hair lay loosely on a small pillow, with the dankness of water still in it. The eyes were half open and stared incuriously at the ceiling.

I stepped close, looked at the face, Landon pulled the sheet on down and rapped his knuckles on a chest that rang hollowly, like a board. There was a bullet hole over the heart.

'Nice clean shot,' he said.

I turned away quickly, got a cigarette out and rolled it around in my fingers. I stared at the floor.

'Who identified him?'

'Stuff in his pockets,' Landon said. 'We're checking his prints, of course. You know him?'

I said: 'Yes.'

Landon scratched the base of his chin softly with his thumbnail. We walked back into the office and Landon went behind his table and sat down.

He thumbed over some papers, separated one from the pile and studied it for a moment.

He said: 'A sheriff's radio car found him at twelve thirty-five A.M., on the side of the old road out of West Cimarron, a quarter of a mile from where the cutoff starts. That isn't traveled much, but the prowl car takes a slant down it now and then looking for petting parties.'

I said: 'Can you say how long he had been dead?'

'Not very long. He was still warm, and the nights are cool along there.'

I put my unlighted cigarette in my mouth and moved it up and down with my lips. 'And I bet you took a long thirty-eight out of him,' I said.

'How did you know that?' Landon asked quickly.

'I just guess. It's that sort of hole.'

He stared at me with bright, interested eyes. I thanked him, said I'd be seeing him, went through the door and lit my cigarette in the corridor. I walked back to the elevators and got into one, rode to the seventh floor, then went along another corridor exactly like the one below except that it didn't lead to the morgue. It led to some small, bare offices that were used by the District Attorney's investigators. Halfway along I opened a door and went into one of them.

Bernie Ohls was sitting humped loosely at a desk placed against the wall. He was the chief investigator Fenweather had told me to see, if I got into any kind of a jam. He was a medium-sized bland man with white eyebrows and an out-thrust, very deeply cleft chin. There was another desk against the other wall, a couple of hard chairs, a brass spittoon on a rubber mat and very little else.

Ohls nodded casually at me, got out of his chair and fixed the door latch. Then he got a flat tin of little cigars out of his desk, lit one of them, pushed the tin along the desk and stared at me along his nose. I sat down in one of the straight chairs and tilted it back.

Ohls said: 'Well?'

'It's Lou Harger,' I said. 'I thought maybe it wasn't.'

'The hell you did. I could have told you it was Harger.'

Somebody tried the handle of the door, then knocked. Ohls paid no attention. Whoever it was went away.

I said slowly: 'He was killed between eleven-thirty and twelve thirty-five. There was just time for the job to be done where he was found. There wasn't time for it to be done the way the girl said. There wasn't time for me to do it.'

Ohls said: 'Yeah. Maybe you could prove that. And then maybe you could prove a friend of yours didn't do it with your gun.'

I said: 'A friend of mine wouldn't be likely to do it with my gun – if he was a friend of mine.'

Ohls grunted, smiled sourly at me sidewise. He said: 'Most anyone would think that. That's why he might have done it.'

I let the legs of my chair settle to the floor. I stared at him.

'Would I come and tell you about the money and the gun – everything that ties me to it?'

Ohls said expressionlessly: 'You would – if you knew damn well somebody else had already told it for you.'

I said: 'Dorr wouldn't lose much time.'

I pinched my cigarette out and flipped it towards the brass cuspidor. Then I stood up.

'Okey. There's no tag out for me yet – so I'll go over and tell my story.'

Ohls said: 'Sit down a minute.'

I sat down. He took his little cigar out of his mouth and flung it away from him with a savage gesture. It rolled along the brown linoleum and smoked in the corner. He put his arms down on the desk and drummed with the fingers of both hands. His lower lip came forward and pressed his upper lip back against his teeth.

'Dorr probably knows you're here now,' he said. 'The only reason you ain't in the tank upstairs is they're not sure but it would be better to knock you off and take a chance. If Fenweather loses the election, I'll be all washed up – if I mess around with you.'

I said: 'If he convicts Manny Tinnen, he won't lose the election.'

Ohls took another of the little cigars out of the box and lit it. He picked his hat off the desk, fingered it a moment, put it on.

'Why'd the redhead give you that song and dance about the bump in her apartment, the stiff on the floor – all that hot comedy?'

'They wanted me to go over there. They figured I'd go to see if a gun was planted – maybe just to check up on her. That got me away from the busy part of town. They could tell better if the D.A. had any boys watching my blind side.'

'That's just a guess,' Ohls said sourly.

I said: 'Sure.'

Ohls swung his thick legs around, planted his feet hard and leaned his hands on his knees. The little cigar twitched in the corner of his mouth.

'I'd like to get to know some of these guys that let loose of twenty-two grand just to color up a fairy tale,' he said nastily.

I stood up again and went past him towards the door.

Ohls said: 'What's the hurry?'

I turned around and shrugged, looked at him blankly. 'You don't act very interested,' I said.

He climbed to his feet, said wearily: 'The hack driver's most likely a dirty little crook. But it might just be Dorr's lads don't know he rates in this. Let's go get him while his memory's fresh.'

NINE

The Green Top Garage was on Deviveras, three blocks east of Main. I pulled the Marmon up in front of a fireplug and got out. Ohls slumped in the seat and growled: 'I'll stay here. Maybe I can spot a tail.'

I went into a huge echoing garage, in the inner gloom of which a few brand new paint jobs were splashes of sudden color. There was a small, dirty, glass-walled office in the corner and a short man sat there with a derby hat on the back of his head and a red tie under his stubbled chin. He was whittling tobacco in the palm of his hand.

I said: 'You the dispatcher?'

'Yeah.'

'I'm looking for one of your drivers,' I said. 'Name of Tom Sneyd.'

He put down the knife and the plug and began to grind the cut tobacco between his two palms. 'What's the beef?' he asked cautiously.

'No beef. I'm a friend of his.'

'More friends, huh? . . . He works nights, mister . . . So he's gone I guess. Seventeen twenty-three Renfrew. That's over by Gray Lake.'

I said: 'Thanks. Phone?'

'No phone.'

I pulled a folded city map from an inside pocket and unfolded part of it on the table in front of his nose. He looked annoyed.

'There's a big one on the wall,' he growled, and began to pack a short pipe with his tobacco.

'I'm used to this one,' I said. I bent over the spread map, looking for Renfrew Street. Then I stopped and looked suddenly at the face of the man in the derby. 'You remembered that address damn quick,' I said.

He put his pipe in his mouth, bit hard on it, and pushed two quick fingers into the pocket of his open vest.

'Couple other mugs was askin' for it a while back.'

I folded the map very quickly and shoved it back into my pocket as I went through the door. I jumped across the sidewalk, slid under the wheel and plunged at the starter.

'We're headed,' I told Bernie Ohls. 'Two guys got the kid's address there a while back. It might be—'

Ohls grabbed the side of the car and swore as we took the corner on squealing tires. I bent forward over the wheel and drove hard. There was a red light at Central. I swerved into a corner service station, went through the pumps, popped out on Central and jostled through some traffic to make a right turn east again.

A colored traffic cop blew a whistle at me and then stared hard as if trying to read the license number. I kept on going.

Warehouses, a produce market, a big gas tank, more warehouses, railroad tracks, and two bridges dropped behind us. I beat three traffic signals by a hair and went right through a fourth. Six blocks on I got the siren from a motorcycle cop. Ohls passed me a bronze star and I flashed it out of the car, twisting it so the sun caught it. The siren stopped. The motorcycle kept right behind us for another dozen blocks, then sheered off.

Gray Lake is an artificial reservoir in a cut between two groups of hills, on the east fringe of San Angelo. Narrow but expensively paved streets wind around in the hills, describing elaborate curves along their flanks for the benefit of a few cheap and scattered bungalows.

We plunged up into the hills, reading street signs on the run. The gray silk of the lake dropped away from us and the exhaust of the old Marmon roared between crumbling banks that shed dirt down on the unused sidewalks. Mongrel dogs quartered in the wild grass among the gopher holes.

Renfrew was almost at the top. Where it began there was a small neat bungalow in front of which a child in a diaper and nothing else fumbled around in a wire pen on a patch of lawn. Then there was a stretch without houses. Then there were two houses, then the road dropped, slipped in and out of sharp turns, went between banks high enough to put the whole street in shadow.

Then a gun roared around a bend ahead of us.

Ohls sat up sharply, said: 'Oh-oh! That's no rabbit gun,' slipped his service pistol out and unlatched the door on his side.

We came out of the turn and saw two more houses on the down side of the hill, with a couple of steep lots between them. A long gray car was slewed across the street in the space between the two houses. Its left front tire was flat and both its front doors were wide open, like the spread ears of an elephant.

A small, dark-faced man was kneeling on both knees in the street beside the open right-hand door. His right arm hung loose from his shoulder and there was blood on the hand that belonged to it. With his other hand he was trying to pick up an automatic from the concrete in front of him.

I skidded the Marmon to a fast stop and Ohls stumbled out.

'Drop that, you!' he yelled.

The man with the limp arm snarled, relaxed, fell back against the running boat, and a shot came from behind the car and snapped in the air not very far from my ear. I was out on the road by that time. The gray car was angled enough towards the houses so that I couldn't see any part of its left side except the open door. The shot seemed to come from about there. Ohls put two slugs into the door. I dropped, looked under the car and saw a pair of feet. I shot at them and missed.

About that time there was a thin but very sharp crack from the corner of the nearest house. Glass broke in the gray car. The gun behind it roared and plaster jumped out of the corner of the house wall, above the bushes. Then I saw the upper part of a man's body in the bushes. He was lying downhill on his stomach and he had a light rifle to his shoulder.

He was Ton Sneyd, the taxi driver.

Ohls grunted and charged the gray car. He fired twice more into the door, then dodged down behind the hood. More explosions occurred behind the car. I kicked the wounded man's gun out of his way, slid past him and sneaked a look over the gas tank. But the man behind had had too many angles to figure.

He was a big man in a brown suit and he made a clatter running hard for the lip of the hill between the two bungalows. Ohls' gun roared. The man whirled and snapped a shot without stopping. Ohls was in the open now. I saw his hat jerk off his head. I saw him stand squarely on well-spread feet, steady his pistol as if he was on the police range.

But the big man was already sagging. My bullet had drilled through his neck. Ohls fired at him very carefully and he fell and the sixth and last slug from his gun caught the man in the chest and twisted him around. The side of his head slapped the curb with a sickening crunch.

We walked towards him from opposite ends of the car. Ohls leaned down, heaved the man over on his back. His face in death had a loose, amiable expression, in spite of the blood all over his neck. Ohls began to go through his pockets.

I looked back to see what the other one was doing. He wasn't doing anything but sitting on the running board holding his right arm against his side and grimacing with pain.

Tom Sneyd scrambled up the bank and came towards us.

Ohls said: 'It's a guy named Poke Andrews. I've seen him around the poolrooms.' He stood up and brushed off his knee. He had some odds and ends in his left hand. 'Yeah, Poke Andrews. Gun work by the day, hour or week. I guess there was a livin' in it – for a while.'

'It's not the guy that sapped me,' I said. 'But it's the guy I was looking at when I got sapped. And if the redhead was giving out any truth at all this morning, it's likely the guy that shot Lou Harger.'

Ohls nodded, went over and got his hat. There was a hole in the brim. 'I wouldn't be surprised at all,' he said, putting his hat on calmly.

Tom Sneyd stood in front of us with his little rifle held rigidly across his chest. He was hatless and coatless, and had sneakers on his feet. His eyes were bright and mad, and he was beginning to shake.

'I knew I'd get them babies!' he crowed. 'I knew I'd fix them lousy bastards!' Then he stopped talking and his face began to change color. It got green. He leaned down slowly, dropped his rifle, put both his hands on his bent knees.

Ohls said: 'You better go lay down somewhere, buddy. If I'm any judge of color, you're goin' to shoot your cookies.'

TEN

Tom Sneyd was lying on his back on a day bed in the front room of his little bungalow. There was a wet towel across his forehead. A little girl with honey-colored hair was sitting beside him, holding his hand. A young woman with hair a couple of shades darker than the little girl's sat in the corner and looked at Tom Sneyd with tired ecstasy.

It was very hot when we came in. All the windows were shut and all the blinds down. Ohls opened a couple of front windows and sat down beside them, looked out towards the gray car. The dark Mexican was anchored to its steering wheel by his good wrist.

'It was what they said about my little girl,' Tom Sneyd said from under the towel. 'That's what sent me screwy. They said they'd come back and get her, if I didn't play with them.'

Ohls said: 'Okey, Tom. Let's have it from the start.' He put one of his little cigars in his mouth, looked at Tom Sneyd doubtfully, and didn't light it.

I sat in a very hard Windsor chair and looked down at the cheap, new carpet.

'I was readin' a mag, waiting for time to eat and go to work,' Tom Sneyd said carefully. 'The little girl opened the door. They come in with guns on us, got us all in here and shut the windows. They pulled down all the blinds but one and the Mex sat by that and kept looking out. He never said a word. The big guy sat on the bed here and made me tell him all about last night – twice. Then he said I was to forget I'd met anybody or come into town with anybody. The rest was okey.'

Ohls nodded and said: 'What time did you first see this man here?'

'I didn't notice,' Tom Sneyd said. 'Say eleven-thirty, quarter of twelve. I checked in to the office at one-fifteen, right after I got my hack at the

Carillon. It took us a good hour to make town from the beach. We was in the drugstore talkin' say fifteen minutes, maybe longer.'

'That figures back to around midnight when you met him,' Ohls said.

Tom Sneyd shook his head and the towel fell down over his face. He pushed it back up again.

'Well, no,' Tom Sneyd said. 'The guy in the drugstore told me he closed up at twelve. He wasn't closing up when we left.'

Ohls turned his head and looked at me without expression. He looked back at Tom Sneyd. 'Tell us the rest about the two gunnies,' he said.

'The big guy said most likely I wouldn't have to talk to anybody about it. If I did and talked right, they'd be back with some dough. If I talked wrong, they'd be back for my little girl.'

'Go on,' Ohls said. 'They're full of crap.'

'They went away. When I saw them go on up the street I got screwy. Renfrew is just a pocket – one of them graft jobs. It goes on around the hill half a mile, then stops. There's no way to get off it. So they had to come back this way . . . I got my twenty-two, which is all the gun I have, and hid in the bushes. I got the tire with the second shot. I guess they thought it was a blowout. I missed with the next and that put 'em wise. They got guns loose. I got the Mex then, and the big guy ducked behind the car . . . That's all there was to it. Then you come along.'

Ohls flexed his thick, hard fingers and smiled grimly at the girl in the corner. 'Who lives in the next house, Tom?'

'A man named Grandy, a motorman on the interurban. He lives all alone. He's at work now.'

'I didn't guess he was home,' Ohls grinned. He got up and went over and patted the little girl on the head. 'You'll have to come down and make a statement, Tom.'

'Sure.' Tom Sneyd's voice was tired, listless. 'I guess I lose my job, too, for rentin' out the hack last night.'

'I ain't so sure about that,' Ohls said softly. 'Not if your boss likes guys with a few guts to run his hacks.'

He patted the little girl on the head again, went towards the door and opened it. I nodded at Tom Sneyd and followed Ohls out of the house. Ohls said quietly: 'He don't know about the kill yet. No need to spring it in front of the kid.'

We went over to the gray car. We had got some sacks out of the basement and spread them over the late Andrews, weighted them down with stones. Ohls glanced that way and said absently: 'I got to get to where there's a phone pretty quick.'

He leaned on the door of the car and looked in at the Mexican. The Mexican sat with his head back and his eyes half-closed and a drawn expression on his brown face. His left wrist was shackled to the spider of the wheel.

'What's your name?' Ohls snapped at him.

'Luis Cadena,' the Mexican said it in a soft voice without opening his eyes any wider.

'Which one of you heels scratched the guy at West Cimarron last night?'

'No understand, señor,' the Mexican said purringly.

'Don't go dumb on me, spig,' Ohls said dispassionately. 'It gets me sore.' He leaned on the window and rolled his little cigar around in his mouth.

The Mexican looked faintly amused and at the same time very tired. The blood on his right hand had dried black.

Ohls said: 'Andrews scratched the guy in a taxi at West Cimarron. There was a girl along. We got the girl. You have a lousy chance to prove you weren't in on it.'

Light flickered and died behind the Mexican's half-open eyes. He smiled with a glint of small white teeth.

Ohls said: 'What did he do with the gun?'

'No understand, señor.'

Ohls said: 'He's tough. When they get tough it scares me.'

He walked away from the car and scuffed some loose dirt from the sidewalk beside the sacks that draped the dead man. His toe gradually uncovered the contractor's stencil in the cement. He read it out loud: 'Dorr Paving and Construction Company, San Angelo. It's a wonder the fat louse wouldn't stay in his own racket.'

I stood beside Ohls and looked down the hill between the two houses. Sudden flashes of light darted from the windshields of cars going along the boulevard that fringed Gray Lake, far below.

Ohls said: 'Well?'

I said: 'The killers knew about the taxi – maybe – and the girl friend reached town with the swag. So it wasn't Canales' job. Canales isn't the boy to let anybody play around with twenty-two grand of his money. The redhead was in on the kill, and it was done for a reason.'

Ohls grinned. 'Sure. It was done so you could be framed for it.'

I said: 'It's a shame how little account some folks take of human life – or twenty-two grand. Harger was knocked off so I could be framed and the dough was passed to me to make the frame tighter.'

'Maybe they thought you'd highball,' Ohls grunted. 'That would sew you up right.'

I rolled a cigarette around in my fingers. 'That would have been a little too dumb, even for me. What do we do now? Wait till the moon comes up so we can sing – or go down the hill and tell some more little white lies?'

Ohls spat on one of Poke Andrews' sacks. He said gruffly: 'This is county land here. I could take all this mess over to the sub-station at Solano and keep it hush-hush for a while. The hack driver would be tickled to death to keep it under the hat. And I've gone far enough so I'd like to get the Mex in the goldfish room with me personal.'

'I'd like it that way too,' I said. 'I guess you can't hold it down there for long, but you might hold it down long enough for me to see a fat boy about a cat.'

ELEVEN

It was late afternoon when I got back to the hotel. The clerk handed me a slip which read: 'Please phone F. D. as soon as possible.'

I went upstairs and drank some liquor that was in the bottom of a bottle. Then I phoned down for another pint, scraped my chin, changed clothes and looked up Frank Dorr's number in the book. He lived in a beautiful old house on Greenview Park Crescent.

I made myself a tall smooth one with a tinkle and sat down in an easy chair with the phone at my elbow. I got a maid first. Then I got a man who spoke Mister Dorr's name as though he thought it might blow up in his mouth. After him I got a voice with a lot of silk in it. Then I got a long silence and at the end of the silence I got Frank Dorr himself. He sounded glad to hear from me.

He said: 'I've been thinking about our talk this morning, and I have a better idea. Drop out and see me . . . And you might bring that money along. You just have time to get it out of the bank.'

I said: 'Yeah. The safe-deposit closes at six. But it's not your money.'

I heard him chuckle. 'Don't be foolish. It's all marked, and I wouldn't want to have to accuse you of stealing it.'

I thought that over, and didn't believe it – about the currency being marked. I took a drink out of my glass and said: 'I *might* be willing to turn it over to the party I got it from – in your presence.'

He said: 'Well – I told you that party left town. But I'll see what I can do. No tricks, please.'

I said of course no tricks, and hung up. I finished my drink, called Von Ballin of the *Telegram*. He said the sheriff's people didn't seem to have any ideas about Lou Harger – or give a damn. He was a little sore that I still wouldn't let him use my story. I could tell from the way he talked that he hadn't got the doings over near Gray Lake.

I called Ohls, couldn't reach him.

I mixed myself another drink, swallowed half of it and began to feel it too much. I put my hat on, changed my mind about the other half of my drink, went down to my car. The early evening traffic was thick with householders riding home to dinner. I wasn't sure whether two cars tailed me or just one. At any rate nobody tried to catch up and throw a pineapple in my lap.

The house was a square two-storied place of old red brick, with beautiful grounds and a red brick wall with a white stone coping around them. A shiny black limousine was parked under the porte-cochère at the side. I followed a red-flagged walk up over two terraces, and a pale wisp of a man in a cutaway coat let me into a wide, silent hall with dark old furniture and a glimpse of garden at the end. He led me along that and along another hall at right angles and ushered me softly into a paneled study that was dimly lit against the gathering dusk. He went away, leaving me alone.

The end of the room was mostly open french windows, through which a brass-colored sky showed behind a line of quiet trees. In front of the trees a sprinkler swung slowly on a patch of velvety lawn that was already dark. There were large dim oils on the walls, a huge black desk with books across one end, a lot of deep lounging chairs, a heavy soft rug that went from wall to wall. There was a faint smell of good cigars and beyond that somewhere a smell of garden flowers and moist earth. The door opened and a youngish man in nose-glasses came in, gave me a slight formal nod, looked around vaguely, and said that Mr. Dorr would be there in a moment. He went out again, and I lit a cigarette.

In a little while the door opened again and Beasley came in, walked past me with a grin and sat down just inside the windows. Then Dorr came in and behind him Miss Glenn.

Dorr had his black cat in his arms and two lovely red scratches, shiny with collodion, down his right cheek. Miss Glenn had on the same clothes I had seen on her in the morning. She looked dark and drawn and spiritless, and she went past me as though she had never seen me before.

Dorr squeezed himself into the high-backed chair behind the desk and put the cat down in front of him. The cat strolled over to one corner of the desk and began to lick its chest with a long, sweeping, businesslike motion.

Dorr said: 'Well, well. Here we are,' and chuckled pleasantly.

The man in the cutaway came in with a tray of cocktails, passed them around, put the tray with the shaker down on a low table beside Miss Glenn. He went out again, closing the door as if he was afraid he might crack it.

We all drank and looked very solemn.

I said: 'We're all here but two. I guess we have a quorum.'

Dorr said: 'What's that?' sharply and put his head to one side.

I said: 'Lou Harger's in the morgue and Canales is dodging cops. Otherwise we're all here. All the interested parties.'

Miss Glenn made an abrupt movement, then relaxed suddenly and picked at the arm of her chair.

Dorr took two swallows of his cocktail, put the glass aside and folded his small neat hands on the desk. His face looked a little sinister.

'The money,' he said coldly. 'I'll take charge of it now.'

I said: 'Not now or any other time. I didn't bring it.'

Dorr stared at me and his face got a little red. I looked at Beasley. Beasley had a cigarette in his mouth and his hands in his pockets and the back of his head against the back of his chair. He looked half asleep.

Dorr said softly, meditatively: 'Holding out, huh?'

'Yes,' I said grimly. 'While I have it I'm fairly safe. You overplayed your hand when you let me get my paws on it. I'd be a fool not to hold what advantage it gives me.'

Dorr said: 'Safe?' with a gentle sinister intonation.

I laughed. 'Not safe from a frame,' I said. 'But the last one didn't click so well . . . Not safe from being gun-walked again. But that's going to be harder next time too . . . But fairly safe from being shot in the back and having you sue my estate for the dough.'

Dorr stroked the cat and looked at me under his eyebrows.

'Let's get a couple of more important things straightened out,' I said. 'Who takes the rap for Lou Harger?'

'What makes you so sure *you* don't?' Dorr asked nastily.

'My alibi's been polished up. I didn't know how good it was until I knew how close Lou's death could be timed. I'm clear now . . . regardless of who turns in what gun with what fairy tale . . . And the lads that were sent to scotch my alibi ran into some trouble.'

Dorr said: 'That so?' without any apparent emotion.

'A thug named Andrews and a Mexican calling himself Luis Cadena. I daresay you've heard of them.'

'I don't know such people,' Dorr said sharply.

'Then it won't upset you to hear Andrews got very dead, and the law has Cadena.'

'Certainly not,' Dorr said. 'They were from Canales. Canales had Harger killed.'

I said: 'So that's your new idea. I think it's lousy.'

I leaned over and slipped my empty glass under my chair. Miss Glenn turned her head towards me and spoke very gravely, as if it was very important to the future of the race for me to believe what she said: 'Of course – *of course* Canales had Lou killed . . . At least, the men he sent after us killed Lou.'

I nodded politely. 'What for? A packet of money they didn't get? They wouldn't have killed him. They'd have brought him in, brought both of you in. You arranged for that kill, and the taxi stunt was to sidetrack me, not to fool Canales' boys.'

She put her hand out quickly. Her eyes were shimmering. I went ahead.

'I wasn't very bright, but I didn't figure on anything so flossy. Who the hell would? Canales had no motive to gun Lou, unless it got back the money he had been gypped out of. Supposing he could know that quick he *had* been gypped.'

Dorr was licking his lips and quivering his chins and looking from one of us to the other with his small tight eyes. Miss Glenn said drearily: 'Lou knew all about the play. He planned it with the croupier, Pina. Pina wanted some getaway money, wanted to move on to Havana. Of course Canales would have got wise, but not too soon, if I hadn't got noisy and tough. I got Lou killed – but not the way you mean.'

I dropped an inch of ash off a cigarette I had forgotten all about. 'All right,' I said grimly. 'Canales takes the rap . . . And I suppose you two chiselers think that's all I care about . . . Where was Lou going to be when Canales was *supposed* to find out he'd been gypped?'

'He was going to be gone,' Miss Glenn said tonelessly. 'A damn long way off. And I was going to be gone with him.'

I said: 'Nerts! You seem to forget *I* know *why* Lou was killed.'

Beasley sat up in his chair and moved his right hand rather delicately towards his left shoulder. 'This wise guy bother you, chief?'

Dorr said: 'Not yet. Let him rant.'

I moved so that I faced a little more towards Beasley. The sky had gone dark outside and the sprinkler had been turned off. A damp feeling came slowly into the room. Dorr opened a cedarwood box and put a long brown cigar in his mouth, bit the end off with a dry snap of his false teeth. There was the harsh noise of a match striking, then the slow, rather labored puffing of his breath in the cigar.

He said slowly, through a cloud of smoke: 'Let's forget all this and make a deal about that money . . . Manny Tinnen hung himself in his cell this afternoon.'

Miss Glenn stood up suddenly, pushing her arms straight down at her sides. Then she sank slowly down into the chair again, sat motionless. I said: 'Did he have any help?' Then I made a sudden, sharp movement – and stopped.

Beasley jerked a swift glance at me, but I wasn't looking at Beasley. There was a shadow outside one of the windows – a lighter shadow than the dark lawn and darker trees. There was a hollow, bitter, coughing plop; a thin spray of whitish smoke in the window.

Beasley jerked, rose halfway to his feet, then fell on his face with one arm doubled under him.

Canales stepped through the windows, past Beasley's body, came three steps further, and stood silent, with a long, black, small-calibered gun in his hand, the larger tube of a silencer flaring from the end of it.

'Be very still,' he said. 'I am a fair shot – even with this elephant gun.'

His face was so white that it was almost luminous. His dark eyes were all smoke-gray iris, without pupils.

'Sound carries well at night, out of open windows,' he said tonelessly.

Dorr put both his hands down on the desk and began to pat it. The black cat put its body very low, drifted down over the end of the desk and went under a chair. Miss Glenn turned her head towards Canales very slowly, as if some kind of mechanism moved it.

Canales said: 'Perhaps you have a buzzer on that desk. If the door of the room opens, I shoot. It will give me a lot of pleasure to see blood come out of your fat neck.'

I moved the fingers of my right hand two inches on the arm of my chair.

The silenced gun swayed towards me and I stopped moving my fingers. Canales smiled very briefly under his angular mustache.

'You are a smart dick,' he said. 'I thought I had you right. But there are things about you I like.'

I didn't say anything. Canales looked back at Dorr. He said very precisely: 'I have been bled by your organization for a long time. But this is something else again. Last night I was cheated out of some money. But this is trivial too. I am wanted for the murder of this Harger. A man named Cadena has been made to confess that I hired him . . . That is just a little too much fix.'

Dorr swayed gently over his desk, put his elbows down hard on it, held his face in his small hands and began to shake. His cigar was smoking on the floor.

Canales said: 'I would like to get my money back, and I would like to get clear of this rap – but most of all I would like you to say something – so I can shoot you with your mouth open and see blood come out of it.'

Beasley's body stirred on the carpet. His hands groped a little. Dorr's eyes were agony trying not to look at him. Canales was rapt and blind in his act by this time. I moved my fingers a little more on the arm of my chair. But I had a long way to go.

Canales said: 'Pina has talked to me. I saw to that. You killed Harger. Because he was a secret witness against Manny Tinnen. The D.A. kept the secret, and the dick here kept it. But Harger could not keep it himself. He told his broad – and the broad told you . . . So the killing was arranged, in a way to throw suspicion with a motive on me. First on this dick, and if that wouldn't hold, on me.'

There was silence. I wanted to say something, but I couldn't get anything out. I didn't think anybody but Canales would ever again say anything.

Canales said: 'You fixed Pina to let Harger and his girl win my money. It was not hard – because I don't play my wheels crooked.'

Dorr had stopped shaking. His face lifted, stone-white, and turned towards Canales, slowly, like the face of a man about to have an epileptic fit. Beasley was up on one elbow. His eyes were almost shut but a gun was labouring upwards in his hand.

Canales leaned forward and began to smile. His trigger finger whitened at the exact moment Beasley's gun began to pulse and roar.

Canales arched his back until his body was a rigid curve. He fell stiffly forward, hit the edge of the desk and slid along it to the floor, without lifting his hands.

Beasley dropped his gun and fell down on his face again. His body got soft and his fingers moved fitfully, then were still.

I got motion into my legs, stood up and went to kick Canales' gun under the desk – senselessly. Doing this I saw that Canales had fired at least once, because Frank Dorr had no right eye.

He sat still and quiet with his chin on his chest and a nice touch of melancholy on the good side of his face.

The door of the room came open and the secretary with the nose-glasses slid in pop-eyed. He staggered back against the door, closing it again. I could hear his rapid breathing across the room.

He gasped: 'Is – is anything wrong?'

I thought that very funny, even then. Then I realized that he might be short-sighted and from where he stood Frank Dorr looked natural enough. The rest of it could have been just routine to Dorr's help.

I said: 'Yes – but we'll take care of it. Stay out of here.'

He said: 'Yes, sir,' and went out again. That surprised me so much that my mouth fell open. I went down the room and bent over the gray-haired Beasley. He was unconscious, but had a fair pulse. He was bleeding from the side, slowly.

Miss Glenn was standing up and looked almost as dopy as Canales had looked. She was talking to me quickly, in a brittle, very distinct voice: 'I didn't know Lou was to be killed, but I couldn't have done anything about it anyway. They burned me with a branding iron – just for a sample of what I'd get. Look!'

I looked. She tore her dress down in front and there was a hideous burn on her chest almost between her two breasts.

I said: 'Okey, sister. That's nasty medicine. But we've got to have some law here now and an ambulance for Beasley.'

I pushed past her towards the telephone, shook her hand off my arm when she grabbed at me. She went on talking to my back in a thin, desperate voice.

'I thought they'd just hold Lou out of the way until after the trial. But they dragged him out of the cab and shot him without a word. Then the little one drove the taxi into town and the big one brought me up into the hills to a shack. Dorr was there. He told me how you had to be framed. He promised me the money, if I went through with it, and torture till I died, if I let them down.'

It occurred to me that I was turning my back too much to people. I swung around, got the telephone in my hands, still on the hook, and put my gun down on the desk.

'Listen! Give me a break,' she said wildly. 'Dorr framed it all with Pina, the croupier. Pina was one of the gang that got Shannon where they could fix him. I didn't—'

I said: 'Sure – that's all right. Take it easy.'

The room, the whole house seemed very still, as if a lot of people were hunched outside the door, listening.

'It wasn't a bad idea,' I said, as if I had all the time in the world. 'Lou was just a white chip to Frank Dorr. The play he figured put us both out as witnesses. But it was too elaborate, took in too many people. That sort always blows up in your face.'

'Lou was getting out of the state,' she said, clutching at her dress. 'He was scared. He thought the roulette trick was some kind of a pay-off to him.'

I said: 'Yeah,' lifted the phone and asked for police headquarters.

The room door came open again then and the secretary barged in with a gun. A uniformed chauffeur was behind him with another gun.

I said very loudly into the phone: 'This is Frank Dorr's house. There's been a killing . . .'

The secretary and the chauffeur dodged out again. I heard running in the hall. I clicked the phone, called the *Telegram* office and got Von Ballin. When I got through giving him the flash Miss Glenn was gone out of the window into the dark garden.

I didn't go after her. I didn't mind very much if she got away.

I tried to get Ohls, but they said he was still down at Solano. And by that time the night was full of sirens.

I had a little trouble but not too much. Fenweather pulled too much weight. Not all of the story came out, but enough so that the City Hall boys in the two-hundred-dollar suits had their left elbows in front of their faces for some time.

Pina was picked up in Salt Lake City. He broke and implicated four others of Manny Tinnen's gang. Two of them were killed resisting arrest, the other two got life without parole.

Miss Glenn made a clean getaway and was never heard of again. I think that's about all, except that I had to turn the twenty-two grand over to the Public Administrator. He allowed me two hundred dollars fee and nine dollars and twenty cents mileage. Sometimes I wonder what he did with the rest of it.

YOU'LL DIE LAUGHING

NORBERT DAVIS

There are happy stories about the lives of the hard-working, hard-drinking writers for the pulps, those wildly creative typing machines who produced a hundred thousand words a year and up. Walter B. Gibson, who wrote most of The Shadow novels, famously produced more than a million words a year for more than twenty straight years. Some went into other kinds of writing: for Hollywood, slick magazines, books, radio and, later, television.

And there are unhappy stories. One of the bright young talents who sold his first story to *Black Mask* while still a law student at Stanford, Norbert Davis (1909–1949), had so much writing success so quickly that he didn't bother to take the bar exam. As quickly as he could produce a new story, it sold – first to the pulps, then to the higher-paying slicks like *The Saturday Evening Post*. Combining the excitement of a fast-moving mystery with humor, there seemed to be no limit to his potential.

Several marriages went bad, his agent died unexpectedly and the slicks started to reject some of his work. Having turned his back on the pulps where he got his start, he felt it would condemn him as a failure to return to those pages. At the age of forty, he closed his garage door, started his car engine, and died of carbon monoxide poisoning.

'You'll Die Laughing' was first published in the November 1940 issue of *Black Mask*. This is its first book appearance.

YOU'LL DIE LAUGHING

NORBERT DAVIS

CHAPTER ONE

Blood from Turnips

He was a short pudgy man, and he looked faintly benign even now with his eyes almost closed and his lips twisted awry with the effort of his breathing. He had silver-white hair that curled in smooth exact waves. It was almost dawn and it was bitter cold.

The outer door of the apartment lobby was open, and the wind made a sharp hurrying sound in the dark empty canyon of the street outside.

The pudgy man was sitting on the tiled floor of the lobby with his back against the wall, resting there, his stubby legs outspread in front of him. After a long time he began to move again, pushing his body away from the wall, turning very slowly and laboriously. His breath sounded short and sharp with the effort, but he made it and rested at last on his hands and knees.

He began to crawl toward the door and there was something inexorable about his slow stubborn progress. He opened the door wider, fumbling blindly ahead of him, and crawled out into the street.

The wind whooped down and slapped the folds of his long blue overcoat tight around his legs, pushed with impatient hands as if to hurry him. But he crawled down the steps very slowly, one by one, and reached the sidewalk and turned and made his inching patient way down the hill toward the wan glow of the street light on the corner.

Behind him, the apartment lobby was empty and cold, with the wind pushing at the half-open door and making the hinges complain in fitful little squeaks. On the wall at the spot where the pudgy man had leaned his back there was an irregular smear of blood, bright red and glistening with a sinister light all of its own.

Dave Bly had hurried as much as he could, but it was after six o'clock in the evening when he came in from the street and trotted up the long dingy flight of stairs to the second story of the office building.

Janet was still waiting for him and he could hear the *tap-tap-tap* of her typewriter. He whistled once and heard the typewriter stop with a faint *ping*, saw her slim shadow through the frosted glass as she got up from her desk and started to put on her hat.

Bly ran on up a second flight of stairs to the third floor, hurrying now, with the thought of the interview ahead making something shrink inside him. He went down the third-floor corridor toward the lighted door at the end. The letters on its glass panel were squat and fat and dignified, and they made the legend—

J. S. CROZIER
Personal Loans

Bly opened the door and went into the narrow outer office. The door into the private office was open and J. S. Crozier's harsh voice came through it.

'Bly, is that you?'

'Yes, sir.'

A swivel chair squeaked and then J. S. Crozier came to the door and said: 'Well, you're late enough.'

'I had to do quite a lot of running around.'

'Let's see what you got.'

Bly handed him a neat sheaf of checks and bills and the typewritten list of delinquent debtors. J. S. Crozier thumbed through the bills and checks, and the light overhead made dark shadowed trenches of the lines in his face. He had a thick solid body that he carried stiffly erect. He wore rimless glasses that magnified his eyes into colorless blobs and a toupee that was a bulging mat of black hair so artificial it was grotesque.

'Forty-three dollars!' he said, throwing the sheaf of bills on Bly's desk. 'And half these checks will bounce. That's not much to show for a day's work, Bly.'

'No, sir.'

J. S. Crozier flicked his finger at the typewritten list. 'And what's the matter with this Mrs. Tremaine? She's been delinquent for six weeks. Did you see her?'

'She's had a serious operation. She's in the hospital.'

'Well, why didn't you try there?'

'I did,' said Bly. He hadn't, but he knew better than to try to explain why. 'They wouldn't let me see her.'

'Oh, they wouldn't! When will they?'

'Next week.'

'Huh! Well, you get in there to see her as soon as you can, and you tell her that if she doesn't pay up her loan – plus the back compound interest and the delinquent collection fee – she might just as well stay in the hospital because she won't have any furniture to come home to.'

'All right.'

J. S. Crozier grinned at him. 'Haven't got your heart in this, have you, Bly? A little on the squeamish side, eh?'

Bly didn't say anything. J. S. Crozier kept grinning at him and he let his colorless eyes move slowly from Bly's shoes, which were beginning to crack through the polish across the toes, up along the shabby topcoat to Bly's face, pale and a little drawn with pinched lines of strain around his mouth.

'I can't afford to be squeamish, Bly. Maybe you can.'

Bly didn't answer, and J. S. Crozier said reflectively: 'I'm disappointed in your work, Bly. Perhaps you aren't suited to such a menial task. Are you contemplating a change soon?'

'No,' said Bly.

'Perhaps you'd better think about it. Although I understand jobs are very hard to find these days . . . Very hard, Bly.'

Bly was quivering with a feeling of sick hopeless anger. He tried to hide it, tried so hard that the muscles of his face seemed wooden, but he knew he wasn't succeeding. J. S. Crozier chuckled knowingly. He kept Bly standing there for a full minute, and then he said with the undertone of the chuckle still in his voice: 'That's all, Bly. Good-night.'

'Good-night,' Bly said thickly.

J. S. Crozier let him get almost to the door. 'Oh, Bly.'

Bly turned. 'Yes?'

'This janitor at your place. This Gus Findley. He's been delinquent for three weeks now. Get something out of him tonight.'

'I'll try.'

'No,' J. S. Crozier said gently. 'Don't try, Bly. Do it. I feel that you have a responsibility there. He mentioned your name when he applied for the loan, so naturally I had confidence in his ability to pay. Get some money from him tonight.

Bly went out and closed the door. Janet was waiting there, a slim small girl with her face white and anxious for him under the dark brim of her hat. She took his arm, and Bly leaned heavily against her, his throat so thick with the choking anger that gripped him that he couldn't breathe. He pulled himself upright in a second and started walking because he knew J. S. Crozier would be listening for his footsteps and grinning. Janet walked close beside him. They went down the steps, and Bly's anger loosened and became a sick despair.

'He knew you were there waiting, Janet. That's why he talked so loud. So you could hear him bawl me out.'

'I know, dear. Never mind.'

'Every day he does something like that. He knows I wouldn't do his dirty work for half a minute if I could find something else. I wouldn't anyway – I'd starve first – if it weren't for you and Bill and – and hoping. . . .'

They were in the street now and she was standing small and straight beside him, looking up into his face. 'We'll go on hoping, Dave.'

'For how long?' Bly demanded bitterly. 'How long?'

'Forever, if we have to,' said Janet quietly.

Bly stared down at her. 'Thank you,' he said in a whisper. 'Thank you for you, my dear.' He grinned wryly. 'Well, I'm through crying in my beer for the moment. Shall we go squander our money on Dirty Dan's thirty-five cent de luxe dinner?'

CHAPTER TWO

The Blonde in 107

It was after ten when Bly got to the apartment building where he lived, and he had to use his key to open the entrance door. The air was thick and sluggish inside the small lobby, full of a wrangling jangle of sound made by a radio being played overly loud in one of the apartments upstairs.

Bly went on a diagonal across the lobby, rapped lightly on a door beside the staircase. He could hear limping steps inside coming across a bare floor, and then Gus Findley opened the door and peered nearsightedly at him.

'Hello, Mr. Bly. You come in?'

Bly shook his head. 'No thanks, Gus. I hate to ask you, but how about the money you owe on that loan you got from Crozier?'

Gus Findley had a tired resigned smile. 'No, Mr. Bly. I'm sorry. I ain't got it.'

Bly nodded slowly. 'All right, Gus.'

'I honest ain't got it.'

'I know. Gus, why did you borrow money from him?'

'I thought you worked for him, Mr. Bly. I thought he's all right if you work for him.'

Bly said: 'He's a shark, Gus. That contract you signed carries over a hundred percent interest. It doesn't show on the contract as interest, but there it is.'

'It don't make no difference, Mr. Bly. You shouldn't feel bad. I couldn't read very well anyway, that fine print, with my eyes not so good. I had to have the money for the hospital. My sister's boy got an operation.'

'Why didn't he go to the clinic – on charity?'

'No,' Gus said gently. 'No. I couldn't have him do that. Not my sister's boy. You know how it is.'

'Sure,' said Bly.

Gus moved his thin, stooped shoulders. 'Now he's got to have cod liver's oil and special milk and tonics. It costs so much I ain't got none left for Mr. Crozier. I ain't tryin' to cheat him, Mr. Bly. I'll pay as soon as I can.'

'Sure, Gus,' said Bly wearily, knowing that as soon as Gus could wouldn't be soon enough for J. S. Crozier. It would be the same bitter story again – garnishment of the major part of Gus's meager salary, attachment of what few sticks of furniture he owned. And more humiliation for Bly. J. S. Crozier would never miss the chance of making Bly serve the papers on Gus.

The lobby seemed colder and darker. The muffled wrangle of the radio went on unceasingly and a woman's laughter sounded through it, thin and hysterical.

'Someone having a party?' Bly asked.

Gus nodded gloomily. 'Yeah. That one below you – that Patricia Fitzgerald. She is no good. Six or eight complaints about the noise I got already. I called her up a couple of times and it don't do no good. I got the misery in my back and I don't like to climb them stairs. Would you maybe stop and ask her to keep quiet, Mr. Bly?'

'Sure,' said Bly. 'Sorry about your back, Gus.'

Gus shrugged fatalistically. 'Sometimes it's worse than others. How is your brother, Mr. Bly? The one that's in college.'

Bly grinned suddenly. 'Bill? Just swell. He's a smart kid. Going to graduate this year, and already they've offered him a job teaching in the college.'

'Good,' said Gus, pleased. 'That's good. Then maybe, when you don't have to send him money, you can marry that nice little lady I seen you with.'

'I hope so,' Bly said. 'But first I've got to get Bill through college. That's why I'm hanging onto this lousy job with Crozier so hard. I can't lose it now, just when Bill's all set to graduate. After he does, then I can take a chance on looking for another – something decent.'

'Sure, sure,' said Gus. 'And you'll find it, too.'

'If there is one, I will,' Bly said grimly. 'Well, I'll run up and see if I can tune that party down. So long, Gus.'

He went up the grimy shadowed stairs and down the long hall above. The noise of the radio was much louder here, packing itself deafeningly in between the narrow walls until it was one continued formless blare. Bly stopped before the door through which it was coming and hammered emphatically on the panels.

The woman's shrill thin laughter came faintly to him. Bly waited for a while and then began to kick the bottom of the door in a regular thumping cadence. He kept it up for almost two minutes before the door opened.

Patricia Fitzgerald, if that was her real name, was a tall thin blonde. She must have been pretty once, but she looked haggard now and wearily defiant, and there was a reckless twist to her full-lipped mouth. She was drunk enough to be slightly unsteady on her feet. Her bright hair was mussed untidily and she was wearing what looked like a black fur mitten on her right hand.

'Well?' she said over the blast of the radio.

Bly said: 'Do you have to play it that loud?'

She kept the door almost closed. 'And who do you think you are, sonny boy?'

'I'm just the poor dope that lives above you. Will you turn that radio down a little, please?'

She considered it, swaying slightly, watching Bly with eyes that were owlishly serious. 'If I turn it down will you do a favor for me, huh?'

'What?' Bly asked.

'You wait.' She closed the door.

The sound of the radio suddenly went down to a thin sweet trickle of music and the hall seemed empty without its unbearable noise.

Patricia Fitzgerald opened the door again. She no longer wore the black mitten. She was jingling some change in her right hand.

'You know where Doc's Hamburger Shack is – over two blocks on Third?'

Bly nodded. 'Yes.'

'You be a nice guy and run over there and get me a couple of hamburgers. If you do I won't make any more noise.'

'O.K.,' Bly agreed.

She gave him the change. 'You tell Doc these hamburgers are for me. He knows me and he knows how I like 'em. You tell him my name and tell him they're for me. Will you?'

'All right.'

'Be sure and tell him they're for me.'

'Sure, sure,' said Bly. 'Just keep the radio turned down like it is and everything will be dandy.'

'Hurry up, fella,' said Patricia Fitzgerald, and neither her eyes nor her voice were blurred now.

Bly nodded patiently. He went back down the hall, down the stairs and across the lobby. The last thing he heard as he opened the front door was Patricia Fitzgerald's laughter, sounding high and hysterical without the radio to muffle it.

Doc's Hamburger Shack was a white squat building on the corner of a weed-grown lot. Its moisture-steamed windows beamed out cheerily at the night, and when Bly opened the door the odor of frying meat and coffee swirled about his head tantalizingly.

Doc was leaning against the cash register. He was gaunt and tall and he had a bald perspiring head and a limply bedraggled mustache.

There was only one other customer. He was sitting at the far end of the counter. He was a short pudgy man and he looked pleasantly benign, sitting there relaxed with a cup of coffee on the counter in front of him. He had silver-white hair that curled in smooth exact waves. He watched Bly, sitting perfectly still, not moving anything but his round blandly innocent eyes.

'Hello, Doc,' Bly said, sitting down at the counter and reaching for the crumpled evening paper on it. 'I want a couple of hamburgers to go. They're not for me. They're for a blonde by the name of Patricia Fitzgerald who lives over in my apartment house. She said you'd know just how she wanted them fixed.'

Doc put his hand up and tugged at one draggled end of his mustache. 'Patricia Fitzgerald? Lives at the Marton Arms? Apartment 107?'

Bly nodded, engrossed in the sports page. 'Yeah.'

'She send you over?'

'Sure,' said Bly.

'She tell you to give her name?'

Bly looked up. 'Well, certainly.'

'O.K.,' said Doc. 'O.K.' He plopped two pats of meat on the grill and then sauntered casually down the counter and leaned across it in front of the pudgy man.

Bly went on reading his favorite sports column. The hamburger sizzled busily. Doc came sauntering back to the grill and began to prepare a couple of buns.

Bly had finished his sports column and was hunting through the paper for the comics when a siren began to growl somewhere near. After a while it died down and then another started up from a different direction.

'Must be a fire around here,' Bly observed.

'Naw,' said Doc. 'Them's police sirens. Fire sirens have a higher tone.' He put a paper sack on the counter. 'Here's your 'burgers, all wrapped up. Be careful of 'em. She don't like 'em mussed up at all.'

'O.K.,' Bly said. He paid Doc with the change Patricia Fitzgerald had given him and went to the door.

The pudgy man was sipping at his coffee, but he was watching Bly calculatingly over the rim of his cup.

There were several cars parked in front of the apartment building and one of them was a blue sedan with a long glittering radio antenna strung across its sloping top. Bly no more than half noticed it, and its identity didn't register on him until he unlocked the front door of the apartment house and very nearly bumped into a policeman who was standing just inside the entryway.

'What—' Bly said, startled.

'You live here?' the policeman asked. He was standing, spread-legged, as immovable as a rock, his thumbs hooked into his broad leather gun belt.

'Yes,' Bly answered blankly.

'You been in here before this evening?'

'Yes. I went out to get these hamburgers for the girl who lives below me in 107.'

The policeman's expression was so elaborately disinterested that it was a dead give-away. 'Dame by the name of Fitzgerald?'

'Yes. She asked me—'

The policeman came one smooth sliding step closer, suddenly caught Bly's right arm by wrist and elbow.

Bly struggled unavailingly. 'Here! What – what—'

'March,' said the policeman. 'Right up those stairs. Get tough and I'll slap you down.'

He steered Bly across the lobby and up the stairs. He went down the hall with Bly stumbling along beside him willy-nilly like a clumsy partner in some weird dance.

The door of Patricia Fitzgerald's apartment was partially open and the policeman thrust Bly roughly through it and followed him inside.

'This is the bird,' he said importantly. 'I nabbed him downstairs in the lobby.'

Bly heard the words through a thick haze that seemed to enclose his brain. He was staring unbelievably at Patricia Fitzgerald. She was lying half twisted on her back at the end of the couch. There was a bright thin line across the strained white of her throat and blood had bubbled out of it and soaked into the carpet in a pool that was still spreading sluggishly. Her eyes were wide open, and the light above her glinted in the brightness of her hair.

There were two men in the room. One was sitting on the couch. He was thick and enormously wide across the shoulders. He sat with his hands on his knees, patient and unmoving, as though he were waiting for something he didn't expect to happen very soon. His eyes were blankly empty and he wheezed a little when he breathed.

The other man was standing in the center of the room with his hands folded behind him. He was small and shabby-looking, but he had an air of queer dusty brightness about him, and his eyes were like black slick beads. He had a limp brown-paper cigarette pasted in one corner of his lower lip.

'Name?' he asked, and then more loudly, 'You! What's your name?'

'Dave Bly,' Bly said. 'Is – is she—'

'Claims he lives upstairs,' said the policeman. 'Says he went out to get some hamburgers for the dame, here. I figure they was havin' a party and he gave her the business and then run and got them hamburgers and came back all innocent, tryin' to fake himself an alibi so—'

'Outside,' said the shabby little man.

The policeman stared. 'Huh?'

'Scram.'

'Well sure, Lieutenant,' the policeman said in an injured tone. He went out and shut the door.

'I'm Vargas,' the shabby man said. 'Lieutenant of detectives. This is my partner, Farnham. What do you know about this business here?'

Bly fought to speak coherently. 'Nothing. Nothing at all. She was playing her radio too loud and I asked her to stop, and she said she would if I'd go get her a couple of hamburgers. . . .'

The big man, Farnham, got off the couch slowly and ominously. He came close to Bly, caught him by the front of the coat. Effortlessly he pulled Bly forward and then slammed him back hard against the wall. His voice was thick and sluggishly indifferent.

'You lie. She was drunk and you got in a beef with her and slapped her with a knife.'

Bly felt a sinking sense of nightmare panic. 'No! I didn't even know her! I wasn't here—'

'You lie,' Farnham droned, slamming Bly against the wall again. 'You're a dirty woman-killer. She got sassy with you and you picked up that knife and stuck it in her throat.'

Bly's voice cracked. 'I did not! Let go—'

The policeman who had brought Bly in was having some trouble in the hall, and they could hear him say indignantly: 'Here now, lady! You can't go in there! Get away from that door! Lieutenant Vargas don't want nobody— Lady! Quit it, now! There's a corpse in there – all blood . . .'

A thin querulous voice answered snappily: 'A corpse! Phooey! My dear departed husband was an undertaker, young man, and I've seen a lot more corpses than you ever will, and they don't scare me a bit. You want me to jab you right in the eye with this knitting needle?'

Evidently the policeman didn't, because the door opened and a little old lady in a rusty black dressing-gown pushed her way into the room. She had a wad of gray hair perched up on top of her head like some modernistic hat, and she wore rimless spectacles on the end of a long and inquisitive nose.

'Hah!' she said. 'I thought so. Bullying people, eh? My husband – dear Mr. Tibbet, the mortician – knew a lot of policemen when he was alive, and he always said they were extremely low-class people – rude and stupid and uncouth.'

Farnham sighed. He let go of Bly and went back and sat down on the couch again. The springs creaked under his weight, and he relaxed into his position of patient ominous waiting.

'Who're you?' Vargas asked.

'Tibbet. Mrs. Jonathan Q. Tibbet – Q. for Quinlan – and you'd better listen when I talk, young man.'

'I'm listening,' said Vargas.

'Hah!' said Mrs. Tibbet. 'Insolent, eh? And your clothes aren't pressed, either, and what's more, I'll bet you drink. Go ahead and bully me! Go ahead! I dare you! My dear dead husband was a personal friend of the mayor, and I'll call up and have you put in your place if you so much as lay a finger on me or this nice young man.'

'Lady,' said Vargas in a resigned tone, 'I wouldn't touch you for ten dollars cash, but this lad is a suspect in a murder case and—'

'Suspect!' Mrs. Tibbet repeated contemptuously. 'Bah! Did you hear me? I said *bah!*'

'I heard you,' said Vargas.

Mrs. Tibbet jabbed a steel knitting needle in his direction like a rapier. 'And why isn't he a suspect? Because he has an alibi, that's why! And I'm it. I was listening to this hussy carrying on in here. I saw this young man come and request her very courteously to stop playing her radio so loudly. I was watching right through my keyhole across the hall. He didn't even go inside the room. And when he left I heard her laughing in here. There was another man in here all the time, and if you and your low-class companion on the couch weren't so stupid and lazy you'd start finding out who it was.'

'Did you see this other gent?' Vergas asked patiently.

'Oh! So you're insinuating I'd snoop and spy on my neighbors, are you? I'll speak to the mayor about this. Mr. Tibbet laid out his first two wives, and they were very friendly all Mr. Tibbet's life, and if I tell him that his drunken policemen are insulting and bullying me, he'll—'

'Yes, yes,' said Vargas. 'Sure. Absolutely. Did you see the other guy that was in here?'

'I did not.'

'Did you hear his voice?'

'Yes. It was a very low-class voice – like yours.'

'Yeah,' said Vargas. He raised his voice. 'O'Shay!'

The policeman peered in the door. 'What, Lieutenant?'

'Escort Mrs. Tibbet back to her room.'

The policeman looked doubtful. 'Take it easy with that needle, lady. Come on, now. The lieutenant is very busy.'

Mrs. Tibbet allowed herself to be guided gingerly to the door, and then turned to fire a parting shot. 'And let me tell you that I won't hear of you bullying this nice young man any more. He's a very courteous and quiet and honest and hard-working and respectful young man, and he could no more commit a murder than I could, and if you had any sense you'd know it, but if you had any sense you wouldn't be a policeman, so I'm telling you.'

'That's right,' said Vargas, 'you are. Good-bye.'

Mrs. Tibbet went out with her escort and slammed the door violently and triumphantly. Farnham, sitting stolidly on the couch, wheezed once and then said: 'Back door.'

Vargas glanced at him with his beadily cruel eyes, then stared at Bly. 'Maybe. Yeah, maybe. What about it, sonny?'

'About what?' Bly demanded, bewildered.

Vargas said: 'Farnham thinks maybe you went around and came in the back after you left the front door.'

'I didn't!' Bly denied angrily. 'You can check up at the stand where I got these hamburgers.'

'Yeah. You said you didn't know the dame. Then why did you get her those humburgers?'

Bly's face was flushed with anger. 'I could have told you in the first place if you'd given me a chance!'

'You got a chance now. Do it.'

'Gus, the janitor, asked me to stop here on the way up and ask her to be more quiet. She was tight and she said she would if I'd run over and get some hamburgers for her. I didn't want to argue with her and I didn't have anything in particular to do, so I went. She gave me the money for them.'

'What hamburger stand?'

'Doc's place – over on Third. He'll remember.' Bly had a sudden thought. 'I was in there when I heard your sirens. I was waiting then. Do – do you know when she was killed?'

'And how,' said Vargas. 'She let out a screech like a steam engine when she got it. We got three calls from three different tenants. Did you see the guy that was in here with her?'

'No,' said Bly. 'I thought there was someone, but I didn't see him. She didn't open the door wide.'

Vargas nodded. 'O.K. Beat it. Stick around inside the building. I'll maybe want to talk to you again.'

Bly stood his ground. 'Well, you listen here. You have no right to grab me and push me around and accuse me—'

'Sure, sure,' Vargas agreed lazily. 'Your constitutional rights have been violated. Write a letter to the governor, but don't do it here. We're going to be busy. Scram, now.'

CHAPTER THREE

Fall-Guy

Bly went out into the hall. He was so blindly indignant at the manhandling he had received that it wasn't until he had reached his own room that the reaction began to take effect. When he fumbled for his key, he found that he was still carrying the paper sack with the two hamburgers inside.

The odor of them and the feel of their warmness seeping through the wrappings against his palm suddenly sickened him. He went very quickly through his apartment and dropped them, still wrapped, into the garbage pail on the enclosed back porch. He sat down then in the living-room and drew several deep steadying breaths. He noticed that his forehead was wet with nervous perspiration.

Bly had never before run into violent and criminal death, and coming as it had without the slightest warning made it seem like a hazily horrible nightmare. Even now he could see Patricia Fitzgerald as plainly as if she were in the same room with him – lying so queerly crumpled on the floor, with the bright red thread across her throat and the light glinting in the metallic yellow of her hair.

Back of him the door into the kitchen swung shut with a sudden creaking swish. Bly's breath caught in his throat. He came up out of the chair and swung around, every muscle in his body achingly tense.

There was no other sound that he could hear, no other movement. He approached the door in long stealthy strides, pushed it back open again.

The kitchen was as empty as it had been when he had gone through it just the moment before, but now, standing in the doorway, he could feel a distinct draft blowing against the back of his neck.

Puzzled, he turned around. The door into his bedroom was open. There was no other place from which the draft could be coming. Bly went across the living-room and turned on the light in the bedroom.

One of the two windows on the other side of his bed was open. Bly started at it, frowning. He remembered very distinctly that he had closed and locked both of the windows before he had left for work in the morning because it had looked like it might rain.

He stepped closer, and then he saw that the glass in the upper pane of the window had been broken at a spot which, had the window been closed, would have been just above the lock. Fragments of glass glinted on the floor below the window, and there was a long gouge in the white paint of the sill.

Bly turned and walked quickly out of the apartment and down the stairs to the first-floor hall. The policeman was still on guard in front of Patricia Fitzgerald's apartment, and he surveyed Bly with evident displeasure.

'So it's you again. What do you want now?'

Bly said: 'I want to see Vargas.'

'It's Lieutenant Vargas to you,' said the policeman. 'And what do you want to see him about?'

'I'll tell that to him.'

'O.K. smarty. He'll throw you right out of there on your can, I hope.' The policeman opened the apartment door and announced: 'Here's that dope from upstairs again.'

Vargas and Farnham had changed places now. Vargas was sitting on the couch. He had his hat pulled down over his eyes and he looked like he was dozing. Farnham was standing in the center of the room staring gloomily at the rumpled contents of an ornamental desk he had hauled out into the middle of the floor.

'There ain't nothing like that in here,' he said to Vargas.

'Look out in the kitchen,' Vargas ordered. 'Sometimes dames stick stuff away in the coffee cups or the sugar bowl. Don't paw around too much until the fingerprint guy gets here.' He pushed his hat-brim back and stared at Bly. 'Well?'

Bly said: 'There's something upstairs – in my apartment – I think you ought to look at.'

'There's plenty of things I ought to look at around here, if I could find them,' Vargas said. 'O.K. Come on.'

The policeman said: 'You want I should go along with you, Lieutenant? This guy is a suspect and—'

'If I wanted you to go along, I'd say so,' Vargas informed him. 'You get out in that hall and keep your big feet and your big mouth out of this apartment.'

'Yes, sir,' said the policeman glumly.

Vargas jerked his head at Bly. 'Come along.'

They went back upstairs to Bly's apartment, and Bly took Vargas into the bedroom and showed him the broken window.

'So what?' Vargas asked.

'I locked both those windows when I left this morning,' Bly told him. 'This apartment is directly above Patricia Fitzgerald's, and the fire-escape goes past her windows and mine. I think the man who killed her came up the fire-escape from her bedroom, broke in this window, and then went through my apartment and out into the hall.'

'You're quite a thinker,' Vargas said sourly. 'Just why should he clown around like that when he could just as well go out the back door of Fitzgerald's apartment?'

'Because of the lay-out of the apartment building,' Bly explained. 'If he went out her rear door, he couldn't get away without going past the front of the building because there is a blind alley on this side that doesn't go through the block. But if he came through here, he could go along the second-floor hall, down the back steps, and out through the garage underneath and at the rear of the building. He probably didn't want to come out the front door of Patricia Fitzgerald's apartment because someone might be watching it after she screamed.'

Vargas grunted. Hands in his pockets, he strolled closer to the window and examined it and the glass on the floor carefully. 'Look and see if you're missing anything,' he said over his shoulder.

Bly looked in his closet and the drawers of his bureau. 'No. Nothing. There's nothing around here anyone could take except a few old clothes.'

Farnham came quietly in the bedroom and nodded at Vargas. 'I couldn't find it, but I found out why I couldn't.'

'Why?' Vargas asked.

'She didn't pay none.'

Vargas swung around. 'What? You mean to say they let a tramp like her in here without payin' any rent in advance?'

'Yeah,' Farnham said. 'They had a reason for it. It seems another tenant – a party who's lived here for over a year and paid his rent on the dot every month – recommended her and said that she was a good risk.'

Vargas' eyes looked beadily bright. 'And who was this accommodating party?'

Farnham nodded at Bly.

'So?' said Vargas very softly.

He and Farnham stood there motionless, both of them watching Bly with the coldly detached interest of scientific observers, and Bly had the same sense of helpless bewilderment he had had when they were questioning him in the apartment below.

'What *is* this?' he demanded nervously. 'What are you two talking about?'

'Sonny,' said Vargas, 'it seems like every time we turn around in this case, we fall over you. We're beginning to get tired of it. When you interrupted us downstairs, we were looking for Fitzgerald's rent receipt, just because we didn't have anything better to look for. We didn't find it, because she didn't have one, because she hadn't paid any rent yet. The reason she hadn't paid any is because *you* told the guys who own this building that she was O.K. and a good risk.'

Bly swallowed hard. 'You said that – that I recommended—'

'Yeah,' said Vargas. 'You. It seems mighty funny. You don't know this Patricia Fitzgerald at all, as you say, but you run errands for her and you recommend her as a good credit risk. You'd better come up with some answers about now.'

'I never recommended her for anything to anyone!' Bly denied indignantly.

Farnham took a long step closer. 'Don't pull that stuff. I called up the bank that owns the place, and I talked to Bingham, the vice-president in charge of all their rental property. He looked it up, and said you did.'

'But I didn't!' Bly said. 'I don't know—'

Farnham took another step. 'Maybe you lost your memory. Maybe if you fell downstairs, you'd find it again.'

'I heard you,' said Mrs. Tibbet. She was standing in the doorway of the bedroom, nodding her head up and down meaningly. 'Oh, I heard you, all right. I'm a witness. Falling downstairs, eh? I know what that means. Third degree. Dear Mr. Tibbet told me all about it. I'm going to report you to the mayor.'

The policeman's anxious face appeared over her shoulder. 'Lieutenant, I couldn't help it. She sneaked up the stairs when she seen Farnham come up—'

'Scram,' said Vargas curtly. 'You too, lady. I got no time for fooling now. I'm busy. Get out of here.'

Mrs. Tibbet still had her knitting needle, and she held it up now and sighted down its thin shining length. 'Make me. Go ahead. I dare you. You're not going to beat up this poor boy, and I'm going to stay right here and see that you don't. You can't bully me. I'm not afraid of you. Not one bit. Dear Mr. Tibbet always said that policemen were bums and that he could prove it by figures.'

Vargas took a deep breath. 'Look, lady. We just found out now that this guy Bly, here, is the bird that recommended the Fitzgerald dame when she came in here.'

'That's a lie,' said Mrs. Tibbet.

Farnham wheezed indignantly. 'It ain't neither! I telephoned to Bingham, the vice-president—'

'I know him,' said Mrs. Tibbet. 'Horace Bingham. He's fat. Not as fat as you are, nor quite as sloppy, but almost. And he's even dumber than you are – if that's possible. If either one of you had asked me I could have told you who was responsible for the Fitzgerald creature's presence here, but no, you wouldn't think of a simple thing like that. You're too busy going around shouting and threatening innocent people. Mr. Tibbet always said that no detective could count above five without using his fingers and what's more—'

'That's enough for this time,' Vargas told her. 'You said you knew who was responsible for the Fitzgerald girl being here. Who is it?'

'If you had any sense you'd know by this time and wouldn't have to go around asking. It is Gus Findley, of course. The janitor.'

'Are you sure about that?' Vargas asked.

'I'll have you know,' said Mrs. Tibbet, 'that I don't go around lying to people, not even to policemen, although that would hardly count because they aren't really people. Mr. Tibbet always said that all you needed to do was furnish a policeman with a tail and he'd be at home in any tree. Gus Findley was in and out of that Fitzgerald hussy's apartment on the average of ten times a day, and in my opinion it's a scandalous affair and has been from the very first.'

Vargas jerked his head at the policeman, who was still waiting nervously in the doorway. 'Get Findley.'

Farnham said doubtfully: 'Seems like this Findley is a pretty old boy to go in for—'

'Hah!' said Mrs. Tibbet. 'Men! I could tell you a thing or two—'

'Don't bother,' Vargas advised wearily.

They waited and in five minutes the policeman came back and thrust Gus Findley roughly into the bedroom. 'Here he is, Lieutenant.'

Gus Findley blinked at them fearfully. He looked old and sick and shaken, and in the strong light his face had a leaden pallor. 'What – what is it, please?'

Vargas strolled over to him. 'Now look here, you. We know that you're responsible for Patricia Fitzgerald coming to this joint, and we know you've been hanging around in her apartment all the time. We want some facts, and we want 'em right now. Start talking.'

Gus Findley's face twisted painfully. 'She – she was my niece, sir.' He turned to Bly. 'Mr. Bly, I'm so sorry. Please don't be mad with me. She come here, and she didn't have no money, and I didn't have none I could give her on account of my sister's boy having the operation. So I – I said she could live here, and I – I told Mr. Bingham that you had recommended—'

'That's all right, Gus,' Bly said uncomfortably. 'If you had asked me, I probably would have recommended her anyway. Don't worry about it. It's O.K.'

'It's not O.K. with me,' said Vargas. 'Just tell us a little more about this matter.'

'She was no good,' Gus said miserably. 'She was never no good. Her name ain't Patricia Fitzgerald. It's Paula Findley. Her folks died, and I tried to raise her up right, but she wouldn't never do nothing I said, and then she run away with some fella and – and he didn't even marry her I don't think.'

'What fella?' Vargas asked sharply.

Gus shook his head wearily. 'I dunno. I never seen him. She said, when she come back, that he'd left her a long time ago. She said she was lookin' for the fella and that when she found him she was gonna get even with him and make herself a lotta money doin' it.'

'What was his name?' Vargas inquired.

'I dunno, sir. Seems like he had a lot of names, from what she said. Seems like he wasn't no good, either.'

'That's the boy we want,' said Farnham.

Vargas nodded absently. 'Yeah. Now listen, Findley—'

'*You* listen,' Mrs. Tibbet invited. 'Mr. Findley is an old man, and he's sick, and he's had a great shock. You're not going to ask him any more questions now. Not one more question, do you understand that? I'm going to take him right down to my apartment and give him a nice hot cup of tea, and I don't want to see any drunken, dirty, foul-mouthed detectives blundering round there while I'm doing it. You hear me, you two?'

'Oh yes, indeed,' said Vargas.

CHAPTER FOUR

Garbage Collection

Bly was ten minutes late to work the next morning, and J. S. Crozier was waiting for him, standing in the open door of his private office with his sallow face set in gleefully vindictive lines.

'Well, Bly, I'm glad to know that you feel you are so necessary here that you can afford to disregard the rules I've been at some pains to impress on your mind.'

'I'm sorry,' Bly said tightly. 'I was delayed. . . .'

The bulging mat of black hair that made up J. S. Crozier's toupee had slipped askew over one ear, and he poked at it impatiently. 'Yes, yes. I noticed, however, that you entered the building some fifteen minutes ago. I suppose your delay, as you so nicely term it, had something to do with the little lady who works as a typist in the office downstairs.'

'I spoke to her on my way up,' Bly admitted.

'No doubt, no doubt. I notice that you spend quite a little time speaking to her lately. Are you contemplating matrimony, Bly?'

'I think that's my affair – and hers,' said Bly.

J. S. Crozier raised his eyebrows elaborately. 'And mine, Bly, if you are talking to her when you are presumably working for me. Or *are* you?'

'Yes,' said Bly.

'Thank you for telling me. I was wondering. If I may presume to advise you, Bly, I would say that it would be best for you to secure a position of a little more permanence before you take any rash steps. I'm not at all satisfied with your work, Bly. You're inclined to dawdle and find any excuse to keep from working. Aren't you, Bly?'

'I try to do my best,' Bly answered.

'Yes,' said J. S. Crozier. 'Try. A good word. It is misfits and idlers like you who fill our relief rolls and burden the taxpayers. You haven't got any get-up-and-go about you, Bly. You'll never amount to anything. I feel sorry for your pretty friend downstairs if she marries you. I suppose you were so engrossed in her last night that you forgot all about the slight matter of the money Gus Findley owes me?'

Bly had to swallow and then swallow again before he could steady his voice. 'I didn't really have a chance to talk to him about it. There was a murder at my apartment house last night and—'

'A murder!' said J. S. Crozier. 'Now what kind of a fantastic fairy tale is this? I suppose you're going to try to tell me that someone murdered Gus Findley!'

'I didn't say so,' Bly said, keeping a tight grip on his temper. 'But the police were questioning him about the murdered girl and the other tenants—'

'I see,' said J. S. Crozier. 'Very interesting. Do you suppose you might possibly, by the exercise of some great ingenuity, get to see him tonight? I'm growing impatient with you and your excuses, Bly.'

'I'll see him tonight.'

'You'd better,' said J. S. Crozier grimly. 'Now I have a call for you to make, Bly. The party's name is Perkins. He lives in the Marigold Apartments on Halley. Judging from that hovel that you live in, you wouldn't know, but the Marigold is an expensive residence. This party called and wants to borrow five hundred dollars with his furniture as security. The furniture should be worth three or four times that. You go over and check up on it. Tell Perkins, if you find things satisfactory, that he can take a taxi and come back here with you, and I'll have the money for him.'

'All right,' said Bly.

J. S. Crozier pointed a blunt forefinger. 'Don't make any mistake about the value of that furniture, Bly. And check up on the title. Do you understand? Have I made it perfectly clear to your limited intelligence, or do you want me to write it down?'

'I understand,' said Bly thickly.

'All right. And don't you take a taxi, getting there. You take a street-car. I've noticed these delusions of grandeur in you. You seem to think you're too fine and sensitive a person to hold such a menial position as this, but just remember that if you had any brains you'd have a better one. Get out, Bly. And don't stall around with your lady friend on the second floor as you go, either.'

The Marigold Apartments was an immense terraced gray-stone building that filled a whole block. Even without J. S. Crozier's word for it, Bly would have been immediately aware that it was an expensive residence. The doorman, after one look at Bly, was superciliously insolent and the glittering chrome-and-black-marble expanse of the lobby made Bly painfully aware of his own shabby clothes and cracked shoes.

Mr. Perkins, it seemed, lived on the fifth floor in a triplex de luxe apartment. The desk clerk – as supercilious as the doorman, but even more expertly insolent – made very sure Bly was expected before he would allow him to go up.

The elevator boy acted as though Bly's appearance was a personal affront to him. He deliberately stopped the elevator a foot below the floor and let Bly step up, and he stayed there ostentatiously watching until he made sure Bly was going to the apartment where he was expected.

The doorbell of Mr. Perkins' apartment was a black marble knob. Bly tried pushing it without effect, finally pulled it and heard chimes ring inside on a soft rising scale. The door opened instantly and a voice said: 'Won't you come in, please, Mr. Bly?'

Bly stepped into a long low room with a far wall that was one solid expanse of windows, facing out on a private flagged terrace that looked bright and clean in the sunlight.

'Shut the door, if you please, Mr. Bly.'

Bly pushed the door shut behind him, trying to place the man who was speaking to him. He was a short, pudgy man with an air that was benignly pleasant. He had silver-white hair that curled in smooth exact waves. Suddenly Bly realized he was the same man he had seen in Doc's Hamburger Shack the night before when he had gone in to order the hamburgers for Patricia Fitzgerald. He realized that and, in the same second, without quite knowing why, he felt a little cold tingle along the back of his neck.

The pudgy man had small pink hands. He put the right one in his coat pocket now and brought it out holding a flat automatic. He was still smiling.

'Sit down in that chair. The one beside the telephone, if you please.'

Bly went sideways one cautious step after another, sank numbly in the chair beside the stand that held a chrome-and-gold telephone set.

'If this is a hold-up,' he said huskily, 'you – you're wasting your time. I didn't bring the money you wanted to borrow with me. There's no way you can get it without appearing at the office yourself.'

'No hold-up,' said the pudgy man in his softly amiable voice. 'My name is not Perkins. It is Johanssen – two s's, if you please. You have heard it, perhaps?'

'No,' said Bly numbly.

'You recognize me, though?'

Bly nodded stiffly. 'Yes. You were in Doc's Hamburger Shack last night when I came in.'

'Just so.' Johanssen stood staring at him for a second, his bland eyes speculatively wide. 'You do not look like a thief, but then one can never tell in these matters. I would like to tell you a story, Mr. Bly. You do not mind? I will not bore you?'

'No,' said Bly.

Johanssen smiled. 'Good. Since you do not know my name I will tell you I am a pawnbroker. But not the ordinary kind. You believe me, Mr. Bly? Not ordinary.'

'Yes,' said Bly.

'Good,' Johanssen repeated. 'My business is under my hat. I have no office. I go to my customers. They are all rich people, Mr. Bly. But sometimes they need cash – lots of cash – very quickly and very badly. They do not want people to know this. So they call Johanssen. I come to them with the cash. You see?'

'Yes,' Bly admitted.

'One year ago, Mr. Bly, a person called me and gave me the name of a very prominent person with whom I had done business many many times. This person wanted ten thousand dollars at once. He is good for much more, so I say I will bring it to him. But, he says, he is not at home. He is at the apartment of a friend. Will I bring it to him there?

'So I bring the money where he says. But it is not my customer that has called me. It is a thief. You are listening carefully, Mr. Bly?'

'Yes,' said Bly.

'Good. This thief, he is waiting for me on the darkness of the stairs of the apartment house. He gives me no chance, Mr. Bly. He stabs me in the back with a knife and takes my money and runs away. He thinks I am dead. But no. I crawl down the stairs and through the lobby and to the street. I crawl two blocks away before someone sees me and calls an ambulance. It was very hard, that crawling. I remember that, Mr. Bly.'

Bly swallowed. 'Why – why didn't you wake someone in the apartment house?'

'No,' said Johanssen gently. 'That would bring the police. This is not a business for police. This is Johanssen's business. You see?'

'Oh,' said Bly blankly.

'You do not understand,' Johanssen said. 'It is known everywhere that Johanssen carries large sums of money with him. It must be known, also, that it is not safe to rob Johanssen. Not because the police will come after you, but because Johanssen will come after you – and find you. Now do you understand?'

Bly had the same sense of nightmare panic he had felt the night before when he had been accused of murdering Patricia Fitzgerald.

'You're not saying – saying that I—'

'No, no. May I go on with my story? I found out who stabbed me. It took much money and time and then I did not find the man. Only some of the names he had used. I found out that he had done many crimes – not bad ones like this, only cheating and swindling. This time he is very afraid. He runs and hides, and hides so well that I cannot locate him. But I do locate his woman. He leaves her when he runs with my money. You can guess who his woman was, Mr. Bly?'

'Patricia Fitzgerald,' Bly said automatically.

'Yes. She is very angry because he left her. When I offer her five thousand dollars to point this man out to me she says she will do it if she can find him. She did. Last night he was in her apartment. He murdered her. Do you know who that man was, Mr. Bly?'

'No!' Bly exclaimed.

'I am willing to pay *you* five thousand dollars if you will tell me who it was.'

'But I don't know!' Bly said. 'I didn't see him.'

'Then,' said Johanssen gently, 'then you will give me back my five thousand dollars, please.'

'You – your what?'

'My five thousand dollars.'

'But I haven't got – I never saw—'

'Yes. It was in an envelope in the paper sack that contained the hamburgers.'

Bly's mouth opened slackly. 'Envelope – hamburgers. . . .'

'Yes. You see, this Patricia Fitzgerald did not trust me. First, before she points out the man who stabs me, she must see the money. We arrange it. I will wait in the hamburger stand. She will send someone who will mention her name. I will put the money with the hamburgers. Then she will lead this man to this apartment. I will be waiting for them. The five thousand dollars is a reward I have offered, Mr. Bly. I have even put it in the papers that I will pay that much to anyone who shows me the man who stabbed me. But you have not done so. Give me the five thousand dollars back, please, at once.'

Bly shook his head dizzily. 'But I didn't know—'

Johanssen moved the automatic slightly. 'I am not joking, Mr. Bly. Give me my five thousand dollars.'

'Listen,' Bly said desperately. 'I didn't even open the sack. I threw the whole business, just as Doc gave it to me, in the garbage.'

'Garbage?' Johanssen repeated gently. 'This is not the time to be funny, Mr. Bly. You had better realize that.'

Bly leaned forward. 'But it's true. I did just that. Wait! Gus Findley! The janitor at my apartment house! He's got a lame back and I hardly ever cook in my apartment. . . .'

'Yes?' Johanssen said very softly.

'Maybe he hasn't emptied the garbage! Let me call him up. It's a chance—'

'A chance that you are taking,' Johanssen said. There was an icy little flicker deep back in his eyes. 'You may call him up. I will listen. Be very careful what you say.'

Fumblingly, with cold and stiff fingers, Bly dialed the number of the apartment house. He could hear the buzz of the telephone ringing, going on and on interminably while the icy little flame in Johanssen's eyes grew steadier and brighter.

And then the line clicked suddenly and Gus Findley's voice said irritably: 'Yes? What you want, please?'

Bly drew in a gulping breath of relief. 'Gus! This is Dave Bly.'

'Ah! Hello, Mr. Bly. How are you? I ain't got that money to pay Mr. Crozier yet, Mr. Bly. I'm sorry, but—'

'Never mind that. Listen to me, Gus. Have you emptied the garbage in my apartment this morning?'

'No, I ain't. I'm sorry, Mr. Bly, but my back has been sore like anything and them damned police has been botherin'—'

'Gus!' said Bly. 'I want you to do a favor for me. Go up to my apartment. Go on the back porch and look in the garbage pail. There's a small paper sack right on top. It's closed. Bring the sack down with you. I'll hold the line.'

'Well, sure. . . .'

'Hurry, Gus! It's very important!'

'You ain't sick, are you, Mr. Bly? You sound—'

'Gus!' Bly exploded. 'Hurry up!'

'O.K. Sure. Hold the wire.'

Bly heard the receiver bump as Gus put it down, and then there was nothing but the empty hum of the open circuit. He waited, feeling the sweat gather in cold beads on his forehead. Johanssen had come quietly closer, and Bly could catch the black slick glint of the automatic, leveled a foot from his head.

After centuries of time the receiver bumped again and Gus said cheerfully: 'Sure, I got it. What you want I should do with it?'

Bly leaned back in his chair, sighing, and nodded once at Johanssen. 'All right. What now?'

Johanssen's eyes had lost their frosty glint. 'This Gus – he is an honest man?'

Bly nodded weakly. 'Yes.'

'Tell him to open the sack and the envelope.'

'Gus,' Bly said into the telephone, 'inside the sack you'll find an envelope. Take it out and open it.'

'Sure, Mr. Bly. Wait.' Paper crackled distantly and then Gus's voice suddenly yammered frantically. 'Mr. Bly! It's money! It's thousands – millions! Mr. Bly! Mr. Bly!'

'Take it easy, Gus,' Bly said. 'It was put in there by mistake. I'm going to let you talk to the man who owns the money. He'll tell you what to do.'

'I don't want so much money here! I'm gonna call a cop! I'm afraid—'

'Here's Mr. Johanssen. Talk to him.'

Johanssen took the telephone. Gus was still shouting at the other end of the line, and Johanssen nodded several times, beginning to smile a little more broadly, finally managed to get a word in.

'Yes, Gus. Yes, yes. It is my money. No. Don't call a policeman. Just keep it for me.' The receiver fairly crackled at that last and Johanssen held it away fro his ear, wincing. 'No, no. No one will rob you. All right. Lock yourself in. Yes, I will knock three times and then twice. Yes, I will bring a writing from Mr. Bly. All right. Yes. Just be calm.'

He hung up the receiver and nodded at Bly. 'That is a good man.' The flat automatic had disappeared.

Bly wiped his forehead with his handkerchief. 'Yes. Gus is a swell old gent. He has a tough time.'

'And you have had a tough time,' said Johanssen. 'Yes. I am very sorry, Mr. Bly. I beg your pardon. Can I do something for you to show I am sorry, please?'

'No,' Bly said. 'No. It's all right.'

Johanssen watched him. 'Mr. Bly, I am very anxious to find the man who was in that apartment. You may still have the reward if you will tell me anything that will lead me to him.'

Bly shook his head wearily. 'I don't know anything.'

'Think,' Johanssen urged. 'Something small, perhaps. Some little thing you may have noticed. Some impression.'

'No,' said Bly woodenly.

Johanssen shrugged. 'So it will be, then. But please let me do something to show I am sorry for this today.'

'No,' said Bly in an absent tone. 'If you want to do something for somebody, give Gus a couple of hundred out of the five thousand so he can get free of that shark I work for.'

'I will do that. Surely.'

'I've got to go,' Bly said. 'I'm – in a hurry.'

'Surely,' said Johanssen, opening the door. 'I am so sorry, Mr. Bly. Please forgive me.'

CHAPTER FIVE

The Black Mitten

Bly took a taxi back to the office. All the way there he leaned forward on the seat, pushing forward unconsciously trying to hurry the taxi's progress. When it stopped at the curb in front of the office building he was out of it before the driver had time to open the door. He flung a crumpled bill over his shoulder and raced up the steep stairs, past the second floor and Janet's office, up to the third floor and down the corridor.

The hammer of his feet must have warned J. S. Crozier, because he was just coming out of his private office when Bly burst through the front door. Bly closed the door behind him and leaned against it, panting.

'Well,' said J. S. Crozier, 'you're back in a hurry, Bly. And I don't see any customer. Have you some more excuses to offer this time?'

Bly was smiling. He could feel the smile tugging at the corners of his lips, but it was like a separate thing, no part of him or what he was thinking.

J. S. Crozier noticed the smile. 'Bly, what on earth is the matter with you? You've got the queerest expression—'

'I feel fine,' Bly said. 'Oh, very fine. Because I've been waiting for this for a long time.'

'Bly! What do you mean? What are you talking—'

Bly stepped away from the door. 'You've had a lot of fun with me, haven't you? You've bullied and insulted and humiliated me every chance you got. You knew I had to take it. You knew I had a brother in college who was dependent on me and my job. You knew I wanted to get ahead, but that I couldn't unless I had more training. You knew when I came here that I was taking courses in a night school, and you deliberately gave me work that kept me late so I couldn't finish those courses.'

'Bly,' said J. S. Crozier, 'are you mad? You can't—'

'Oh, yes I can. I can tell you now. You've had your fun, and now you're going to pay for it. You're going to pay pretty heavily and you're going to know I'm the one who made you pay.'

'You're being insulting,' J. S. Crozier snapped. 'You're fired, Bly. If you don't leave at once I'll call the police.'

'Oh, no,' said Bly. 'You won't call the police, because that's what I'm going to do. How does it feel to be a murderer, Mr. Crozier?'

'Eh?' said J. S. Crozier. The color washed out of his cheeks and left the lines on them looking like faint indelible pencil marks. 'Wh-what did you say?'

'Murderer.'

'You – you're crazy! Raving—'

'Murderer,' said Bly. 'You murdered Patricia Fitzgerald.'

'Bly! You're a maniac! You're drunk! I won't have you—'

'You murdered Patricia Fitzgerald and I'm the one who knows you did it. I'm the one who will get up on the stand and swear you did it. I'm the one – Bly, the poor devil it was so much fun for you to bully because you knew I couldn't strike back at you. Was the fun worth it, Mr. Crozier?'

J. S. Crozier's mouth opened, fish-like, and closed again before he could find words. 'Bly! Bly! Now you can't make mad accusations like that. You're insane, Bly! You – you're sick.'

'No. I happened to remember a couple of small things. When I came to Patricia Fitzgerald's door last night and she opened it, she was wearing what I thought was a black fur mitten. It wasn't. It was that wig of yours – your toupee. She had it wrapped around her right hand. She had been laughing at how you looked without it, or perhaps she had been trying it on herself.'

'You lie!' J. S. Crozier shouted, putting his hand up over the bulging toupee protectively. 'You lie!'

'No. I saw it. I'll swear I saw it. And another thing. Just a little while ago, when you were speaking about the Marigold Apartments and how luxurious they were, you said, "Judging from that hovel you live in. . . ." You knew where I lived, but you'd never been in my apartment – until last night. You were then. You broke in the window after you murdered Patricia Fitzgerald.'

Under the toupee the veins on J. S. Crozier's forehead stood out like purple cords. 'You're a liar and a fool!' He laughed chokingly. 'You think that evidence is enough to base a charge of murder on? Bah! Get out! Go to the police! They'll laugh at you! I'm laughing at you!' His whole body shook with insane raging mirth.

The door opened quietly and Johanssen stepped inside the office. 'May I laugh, too, please?' he asked softly.

J. S. Crozier's breath hissed through his teeth. He seemed to shrink inside his clothes. The toupee had slipped down over his forehead and it fell now and lay on the floor like an immense hairy spider. J. S. Crozier's own hair was a blond, close-clipped stubble.

Johanssen smiled and nodded at Bly. 'You should never play poker, Mr. Bly. Your face gives you away. I knew you had remembered something, so I followed you here. It is nice to meet you again, Mr. – ah – Crozier.'

'Bly,' J. S. Crozier said in a shaky whisper. 'Run for help. Quick. He'll kill me.'

'Mr. Bly will not move,' said Johanssen gently. 'No.'

Bly literally couldn't have moved if he had wanted to. He was staring, fascinated, from Johanssen to J. S. Crozier. Johanssen had his right hand in his coat pocket, but he apparently wasn't at all excited or in any hurry.

'I have been looking for you for a long time,' he said. 'It is so very, very nice to see you at last.'

J. S. Crozier began to shake. His whole body shuddered. 'Johanssen,' he begged hoarsely. 'Wait. Wait, now. Don't shoot me. Listen to me. It was an accident. I didn't mean – Johanssen! You can't just shoot me in cold blood! I'll pay back the money I stole from you! I – I've made a lot! I'll give it all to you! Johanssen, please—'

The door opened in back of Johanssen, pushing him forward. He stepped aside quickly and alertly, and Vargas came into the office. His eyes were bright and beadily malicious.

'Police,' he said casually to Crozier. 'Hello, Bly. I've been following you around today. Checking up.'

J. S. Crozier caught his breath. 'Officer!' he shouted hoarsely. 'Arrest this man! He's going to kill me!'

'Which man?' Vargas asked. 'You mean Johanssen? Why, he's a respectable businessman. Are you thinking of killing anyone, Johanssen?'

'No, Mr. Vargas,' said Johanssen.

'See?' said Vargas to Crozier. 'You must be mistaken. 'Well, I've got to run along. Behave yourself, Bly.'

'No!' J. S. Crozier pleaded. 'No, no! You can't! Take me with you!'

'What for?' Vargas inquired reasonably. 'I couldn't take you with me unless I arrested you for something. And what would I arrest you for – unless it was maybe for murdering Patricia Fitzgerald last night?'

J. S. Crozier swayed. 'That – that's absurd!'

Vargas nodded. 'Sure. That's what I thought. Well, so long.'

J. S. Crozier held on to a desk to keep upright. 'No! You can't go and leave me to this – this . . . Wait! Johanssen thinks I stabbed him and robbed him! You've got to arrest me for that! You've got to lock me up!'

Vargas looked at Johanssen in surprise. 'Did he stab you, Johanssen?'

'I have not said so.'

'So long,' said Vargas.

J. S. Crozier's face was horribly contorted. 'No, no! You can't leave me alone with – with—'

Vargas stood in the doorway. 'Well? Well, Crozier?'

'Yes,' Crozier whispered hoarsely. 'I did it. I killed her. I knew – the way she looked and acted after Bly went for the sandwiches. I twisted her arm and – and she told me . . .' His voice rose to a scream. 'Take me out of here! Get me away from Johanssen!'

Vargas' voice was quick and sharp now. 'You heard it, both of you. You're witnesses. Farnham, come on in.'

*

Farnham came stolidly into the office. 'Come on baby,' he said in his heavy indifferent voice. J. S. Crozier's legs wouldn't hold his weight, and Farnham had to half carry him out the door.

'Could have nailed him anyway on that toupee business,' Vargas said casual again. 'But this way made it more certain. Johanssen, you stick around where I can find you.'

'I will be very glad to testify. I will also wish to witness the execution, if you please.'

'I'll arrange it,' Vargas promised. 'Kid, that was clever work – that business about the toupee.'

'It just – came to me,' Bly said shakily. 'It seemed all clear at once – after Mr. Johanssen told me about the arrangement for him to wait in the hamburger stand. I knew then that Patricia Fitzgerald was playing her radio loud on purpose. She thought Gus, the janitor, would come up and then she would have sent him for the sandwiches. And then I remembered the black mitten. . . .'

High heels made a quick *tap-tap-tap* along the corridor and Janet ran into the office. 'Dave! Are you all right? I saw Mr. Crozier going downstairs with another man. He – he was crying. . . .'

Bly said: 'It's all right now, dear. Mr. Crozier was the man who murdered that girl in my apartment house. I'll tell you about it later.'

'I'll be going,' said Vargas. 'Bly you stick around where I can find you.'

'That will be easy,' Bly said bitterly. 'Just look on the handiest park bench. I was so clever I thought myself right out of a job.'

'I will go also,' said Johanssen, 'but first there is this.' He took a black thick wallet from his pocket. Carefully he counted out five one-thousand-dollar bills.

'The reward, which I have offered legally and which I have advertised in the papers. Mr. Vargas is a witness that you earned it and that I paid it.'

'It's yours,' Vargas said. 'He made a public offer of it. If he didn't pay you, you could sue him.'

'Yes,' said Johanssen. 'And then there is this.' He took a folded sheet of blue legal paper from his pocket. 'This is a lease for my apartment at the Marigold, paid a year in advance. It is too big for me. For two people it would be good. You will take it, please, Mr. Bly.'

'No!' Bly said. 'I couldn't. . . .'

'Bly,' said Vargas conversationally, 'I've been standing around here wondering when you were going to kiss this girl of yours. Don't you think it's about time you did?'

ABOUT KID DETH

RAOUL WHITFIELD

The pulp community was not a huge one. The editors knew each other, and they knew the writers. The writers, too, knew each other, and their common meeting place was often a bar. While the two greatest writers for the pulps, Raymond Chandler and Dashiell Hammett, are believed to have met only once, Hammett became very close to one of the other giants of the era, Raoul Whitfield. There seems to be a good deal of evidence that Hammett became even closer to Whitfield's wife, Prudence, but that's another story.

Whitfield was prolific and quickly became one of *Black Mask*'s best and most popular writers, both under his own name and as Ramon Decolta, as whom he wrote numerous stories about the Filipino detective Jo Gar. His career was cut short when he became ill in 1935; he never fully recovered and died ten years later at the age of forty-seven.

Joey (Kid) Deth was an unusual protagonist for the pulps, whose readers didn't mind criminals as central characters just so long as they stole only from the rich. Few aristocrats read pulp magazines, so editors encouraged Robin Hood stories without fear of offending their readers. While Deth admits he's a crook, he salvages himself to some degree by swearing (and, apparently, truly) that he never shot anyone. That is left to the thugs who are chasing him.

'About Kid Deth' was first published in the February 1931 issue of *Black Mask*. This is the first time it has been published in book form.

ABOUT KID DETH

RAOUL WHITFIELD

The Kid passed the coupé twice, on the far side of the street, before he crossed back of it, got close to the figure slumped forward over the wheel. The driver's arms were crossed loosely over the rim of black; his hat was half off his head. His face was turned sideways – there was red color staining the lips. The eyes were opened and staring in the faint light from the instrument board. The engine of the car made faint vibration.

The street was fairly deserted – the snow had turned to slush and it was raining a little. A few squares to the northward there was a power house, along the East River. Greenish lights gleamed from high windows. The Kid turned away from the dead man and walked towards the river. He was smiling twistedly. He was small in size with round, dead-gray eyes. He wore a tight-fitting coat that was short, and a dark hat pulled low over his forehead. He smoked a cigarette and coughed sharply at intervals.

He didn't see Rands until the detective came down the few steps of the lunch-wagon that was located about fifty yards from the wooden dock used by the dump carts. When he did see him Rands was lightning a cigar and watching him approach, his eyes leveled above the flare of the match in his cupped hands.

Kid Deth changed his smile to a grin and stopped a few feet from the detective. Rands was a big man with broad shoulders that were slightly rounded. His face was red and squarish. He shook the match, tossed it into the slush. He said in a cheerful voice:

'Hello, Deth – back in town, eh?'

The Kid pulled on what was left of his cigarette and widened his dead-gray eyes.

'Haven't been away, Lou,' he said in a voice that sounded strangely heavy for one of his slight build.

Rands whistled a few notes of a popular theme song and looked with faint amusement towards the tail-light of the coupé.

'No?' he said finally. 'Been sick?'

Joey Deth shook his head. 'Feelin' swell,' he replied. 'How you been, Lou?'

The detective grinned. 'Nice,' he replied. 'I've been looking for you, Kid.'

Joey Deth nodded. 'Sure,' he said. 'A guy got dead out in Frisco, maybe?'

Rands grinned. It was a hard grin. He looked serious.

'Maybe,' he agreed. 'But I don't figure *you* got *that* far away from New York, Kid.'

Joey Deth narrowed his eyes and shrugged. The big detective kept looking towards the tail-light of the coupé, but he didn't seem to be thinking about the car. There was something about that that struck Deth as being funny. But he didn't show it.

'My mother's sick,' he said slowly. 'I been sticking close to the flat.'

Lou Rands nodded his head and looked sad. 'The weather's been bad,' he said. 'She got the flu?'

The Kid nodded. A river boat whistle reached the two of them from some water spot in the distance. There was just a fine mist of rain falling. Inside the lunch-wagon old Andy was clattering dishes around. Rands said slowly:

'Guess you'd better come down to Headquarters with me, Kid. I've been looking for you.'

Joey Deth frowned. 'I've got a date at one,' he said. 'How about tomorrow?'

The detective grinned. 'Stick your hands up a little,' he said quietly.

The Kid swore. He raised his hands and Rands stepped close to him. He patted the pockets of the tight-fitting coat, unbuttoned it, patted other pockets. Then he stepped away from the Kid and nodded his head.

'Sorry,' he said.

Joey Deth lowered his hands and swore. 'Sorry – you didn't find a rod,' he breathed. 'Sure.'

The detective shrugged his shoulders. He looked towards the rear end of the coupé again, and stopped smiling.

'Before we grab the subway to Center Street – we'll have a look at that car,' he said. 'Not much parking done over this way.'

Kid Deth yawned, but his body shivered a little. Rands' blue eyes were on him, smiling.

'Better be careful – wandering around at night,' he said. '*You* might get the flu, too.'

Joey Deth shrugged. 'I'm thinkin' about moving close to Headquarters,' he said with sarcasm. 'Make things easier for you.'

Lou Rands looked towards the coupé and nodded. He didn't smile.

'One of these days you'll walk in – and you *won't* walk out, Kid,' he said quietly. 'You get too close to dead people. You always have.'

Kid Deth swore. 'It's just happened that way,' he said. 'You oughta know that – by this time. You oughta be sick of ridin' me downtown.'

The detective chuckled. 'I'm sick of a lot of things,' he said. 'But I keep on doing them. All right – let's move over near that car.'

Joey Deth looked inside the lunch-wagon. His lips twisted a little. Lou Rands wasn't watching him, and he didn't see the hate that flared in the

Kid's eyes – flared and died into a smile. They moved westward on Thirty-ninth Street, away from the East River, towards the coupé. Joey Deth tried to keep his voice steady.

'What's the pull for – *this* time?' he asked sarcastically. 'I never pack a rod, you know that. You've had me downtown a half dozen times – you never kept me there.'

The tone of Rands' voice got suddenly hard. He got his right hand buried in the right pocket of his brown coat.

'I'm going to keep you there – *this* time, Joey,' he said.

The Kid jerked his head towards the detective. He'd never heard Rands talk like this before. The big dick was usually easy going, almost jocular. But now his voice was hard – and his eyes were hard. And his right-hand fingers were gripping a rod, Joey knew that.

He asked shakily: 'What for?'

They were near the coupé now. Rands smiled with his lips, turned his big head towards the Kid's.

'You've been mixed up with killings since you were able to shove over pedlers' carts, down in Rivington Street,' he said slowly. 'They put an *a* in that name of yours – and you rate it, Kid. I've been on your tail a long time. And I've got you right.'

The Kid widened his dead-gray eyes. He said very softly:

'Like hell you have!'

Rands nodded. He stopped smiling, stopped walking. He looked towards the wheel seat of the coupé. He backed up a step, moved around to the left of Kid Deth. His right coat pocket bulked a little.

'Jeeze,' he said softly – 'that guy back of the wheel looks sick, Kid!'

Joey Deth didn't look at the figure of Barney Nasser. He'd seen Barney too many times when he'd been alive. He hated Barney, dead or alive. And he was fighting down fear now. He suddenly realized that Rands was mocking him, that Rands knew Barney Nasser was slumped across the wheel of the coupé – and that the detective knew Nasser was dead.

Instinct drove words from between his lips. They were uncertain words.

'He's drunk – maybe,' he said.

The detective narrowed his eyes on Kid Deth's. They held a grimly amused expression.

'Yeah?' Rands said. 'You think so, Kid?'

Joey Deth forced a smile. He felt cold. It was difficult for him to keep his eyes away from the right-hand pocket of the big detective's coat. He nodded.

'He looks that way,' he said thickly.

Lou Rands nodded his big head slowly. The bulk in his right coat pocket moved a little.

'Dead men look that way, too,' the detective said slowly. 'Move over near him, Kid.'

Kid Deth moved over near the coupé. He kept his eyes on the arms of

Barney Nasser. They were half closed, and he tried to make them expressionless. He was thinking of the night that Nasser had turned Charlie Gay up, almost five years ago. And he was remembering that Charlie had come down the river from the Big House, three days ago. He was thinking of four or five other humans that had hated the man slumped over the wheel.

His eyes went to the eyes of Rands. The detective was smiling down at the dead man; he reached out a hand suddenly, jerked the head up from the arms. The arms of the dead man slipped off the wheel. Lou Rands sucked in his breath sharply, let the dead man's head fall forward again. He swore.

'It's Barney Nasser,' he breathed grimly. 'He's – dead!'

Kid Deth stood motionless. He didn't speak. He was thinking that the big detective was a pretty good actor. He was afraid, and fighting fear. He said, after a little silence:

'Dead?'

Lou Rands reached into the coupé with his left hand, lifted an automatic from the seat beside Nasser. He swung towards Kid Deth, held out the gun.

'That got him,' he said softly.

The Kid stared at the automatic. Rands took his right hand away from the pocket, caught Deth's left wrist. He was strong, and his movements were swift. Instinctively the Kid tried to twist loose. He spread his fingers – the grip of the gun struck against his palm. For a second the muzzle pointed towards the detective.

The Kid closed his fingers, felt for the trigger. Even as he squeezed he realized that the detective was framing him. He hated Rands – he had hated him for years. He had never killed – and Rands had always been trying to frame him. He squeezed hard. The trigger clicked.

Rands made a chuckling sound. He said fiercely as he pulled the Kid towards his big body.

'Got you – this time, Kid – with the goods – the gun—'

He struck out with his right hand. Joey Deth jerked his head to one side – the blow caught him high on the left temple. He went backward, releasing his grip on the gun. He stumbled, sprawled to the broken pavement. Rocking on his knees he saw Lou Rands through a blur before his eyes.

The detective had something white in his hands – a handkerchief. He was wrapping the gun in it. And the gun had the imprint of his fingers on it. And Barney Nasser was dead in the coupé

Kid Deth said bitterly:

'You're – framin' me – you dirty, yellow—'

Rands cut in, sharply staring down at the swaying figure before him.

'You tried to squeeze me out, Kid. If the rod had been loaded—'

The big detective broke off. His body half turned away from the kneeling Kid. Two figures were in sight, just beyond the coupé. They had crossed the street under cover of the coupé – and the detective's back had been turned to them. Rands swore hoarsely – said something Joey Deth failed to catch.

The Kid got to his feet. He saw Rands' right hand move towards the right pocket of his coat. Then the bullets whined from two guns. They made sharp, echoed sound in the quiet street. Rands' body jerked; he wheeled away from the two men. He turned jerkily towards Kid Deth, his face white and twisted. His lips were bared in pain. He said hoarsely:

'You dirty – mob hiding – rat—'

The material of his right pocket jumped – the bullet ricocheted from the pavement close to the Kid's feet. Then Lou Rands' head fell forward – he dropped. He went down heavily, and Joey Deth knew he was dead, even before his body rolled over and was motionless.

Blocks away, towards Forty-second Street, a police whistle made a shrilling sound. There was the patter of feet, near First Avenue. They died away. The Kid lifted his right hand and touched the bruised spot over his left temple. He said softly, with fear in his voice:

'Jeeze – Jeeze – they got him!'

Then he came out of it. The police whistle shrilled again. A truck rolled along First Avenue, making back-fire racket. But it was a different sound than that of the guns that had crashed. And the police in the distance knew it.

Joey Deth got a soiled handkerchief from his pocket, put it over the fingers of his left hand. He twisted Rands' gun from his grip. He took the gun wrapped in the handkerchief, from the detective's pocket. He was breathing heavily – there wasn't much time. His brain was clear – the dead detective had been right about one thing – Kid Deth had been close to dead humans many times.

He moved close to the coupé, wiping the grip of the automatic carefully with the handkerchief. He wiped the barrel, too. Lou Rands had tried to frame him with this gun – that meant that a bullet or bullets from it had killed Barney Nasser. Perhaps Rands had murdered Nasser, perhaps not. But he had known that the gangster was dead – and he had tried to frame the Kid.

Joey dropped the weapon from the handkerchief to the coupé seat, beside Nasser's right hand. The handkerchief he slipped in his pocket. He turned away from the car, glanced at the body of the detective. Then he crossed the street, went down an alley that ran through to Fortieth Street. He was half-way through the alley when he looked back and saw the lights of a car shining on the slush near the spot where the coupé rested. The siren wail died to a low whine.

The Kid smiled twistedly, patted the dead dick's gun. On Fortieth Street he went towards the river, reached a small, wooden dock and tossed the gun into the water. He kept away from the few lights, found a stone and wrapped Rands' handkerchief around it. There was a splash as East River water swallowed the fabric. The Kid moved along the river's edge to Forty-second Street. He walked westward and picked up a cab at First Avenue. The driver looked sleepy and dumb – and that suited Joey Deth. He gave an address in Harlem, on the edge of the Black Belt.

The cab had traveled three blocks before the Kid remembered something. It pulled him up straight in the seat. He swore shakily. Then he sat back and swore softly and more steadily. Until this moment he had forgotten the lunch-wagon and Old Andy. Andy might have seen him with Lou Rands, might have heard them talking. Probably he had. And the police would see the lunch-wagon – they would question Andy. And Andy would talk.

Kid Deth sat on the seat of the cab and swayed with the motion of it. There were several things he didn't know – and each thing had to do with death. But there was one thing he *did* know – he was in a tough spot. That had to do with death, too. A hot spot on the electric chair. If Old Andy had seen, heard – and talked—

He sat up straight and lighted a cigarette. His left temple ached, throbbed. He looked through the rear window of the cab and saw only the lights of a big truck, far behind. He closed his little fingers tightly and showed white, even teeth in a smile.

'Like hell – they'll get me!' he breathed.

2

At one o'clock the Kid kept the date he had spoken about to Lou Rands. He sat at a small table near the piano, in the cellar speakeasy just beyond the Black Belt – and the girl came to him. She was a blonde of around twenty-five, with blue eyes and a face that had once been babyish. Kid Deth reached under the table with his right foot and kicked out a chair for her. She sat down, got her chin resting on cupped palms and leaned towards him.

'Well—' she said in a voice that wasn't too pleasant – 'there's hell to pay, Kid.'

Joey Deth widened his dead-gray eyes and tried to look puzzled.

'Yeah?' he replied. 'What about?'

She made a clicking sound with tongue and lips. Her blue eyes narrowed; she took one hand away from her chin and tapped pointed nails against the wood of the table. She said:

'Someone got that Rands dick. I'm thirsty – how about a beer?'

Joey ordered a beer and watched a dark-skinned man at a table across the room talk to himself as he drank. He sipped his own whiskey and frowned.

'Rands, eh?' he said softly. 'Well – he had it comin'.'

The girl nodded. There was an expression in her eyes that Joey didn't like; he hadn't been sure of her for weeks now. Since Barney Nasser had stated that he was out to get Joey – the girl had changed. She was more cautious. She was playing safe.

The waiter brought her beer. Kid Deth smiled a little.

'Who got him, Bess?' he asked quietly.

The waiter went away and the girl drank half her beer in one try. Her fingers were shaking a little when she set the glass down on the table.

'You did, Kid,' she said very slowly.

Joey Deth slitted his eyes on hers. He breathed through his nose, was silent for a short time. Then he shook his head.

'Like hell I did,' he said almost pleasantly. 'Who says so, Bess?'

She kept her blue eyes steady on his. She downed half of the remaining half glass of beer.

'Barney Nasser's brother,' she said quietly. 'I ran into him at Alma's flat. He's sore as hell.'

The Kid drew a deep breath. Barney Nasser's brother – Gil Nasser. A killer who had been tried three times for murder without a conviction. A gun who hated only a week or so, and then stopped hating because there wasn't any percentage in hating a dead human.

Joey Deth said slowly: 'Gil's hopped up – he's talkin' wild.'

The girl shook her head. 'He doesn't use the bad stuff, and you know it,' she said. 'He says Barney Nasser picked you up over near Times Square – you had some talk to get finished. He drove you over between First and the East River, and you didn't like what he said. You gave him the works. The Rands dick went over on a chance – to talk with a lunch-wagon owner named Andy Polson. Old Andy, he's called. He spotted you and took you to the car. He had the goods on you, and you gunned him out. Then you slipped the gun beside Barney's body and made a duck. That's the way Gil figures.'

Kid Deth shook his head, smiling with his narrow lips.

'It's no good, Bess,' he said. 'I never killed in my life, you know that. I don't pack a gun.'

She smiled grimly. 'Barney Nasser did,' she said. 'A .38 automatic. Gil thinks there were those kind of bullets in his lungs – and a flock of them in the dick's body. He thinks you got Barney – and when Rands grabbed you – you got him.'

Kid Deth stopped smiling. He ordered another whiskey and a beer. When the waiter went away he said:

'They're framing me, Bess – maybe we'd better try Chi for a look around.'

The girl shook her head. 'I'm putting you wise – and I'm quitting, Kid,' she said. 'You told Barney you'd lay out of New York – but Brooklyn's a part of the big town. Maybe you forgot that. From now on – where you are it won't be too healthy. I'm quitting.'

Kid Deth shrugged. 'It's quiet across the bridges,' he said. 'But Barney didn't want it that way. I went in there first—'

He broke off. The waiter brought the drinks. Joey said:

'Mac – let me know who comes in – before they start the walk, will you?'

The waiter nodded. 'Sure, Kid,' he said. 'An' we ain't seen you tonight.'

Joey Deth nodded. 'That's it, I ain't been around,' he replied.

The girl chuckled mirthlessly. 'You never did have luck with the slot machines, Kid,' she said. 'Even at Coney—'

Kid Deth leaned across the table and bared his lips. Bess Grote's eyes got big and frightened. She didn't like to see Joey looking at her this way.

'You know too much,' he said in a hard voice. 'And you're pretty anxious to quit. Maybe you know that Charlie Gay has been out of stir for three days – and that it was Barney Nasser who turned him up for the stretch.'

He watched the girl's lips tremble. She lifted her beer glass and drank.

'Charlie didn't do for Barney,' she said, as she set the glass down again. 'Charlie went – out West – right away.'

Kid Deth shook his head. 'Better be careful, Bess,' he said in a hard tone. 'I saw Charlie tonight – while I was—'

He checked himself. But the girl had a quick mind. That was one of the things he had liked about her. She was shrewd.

'While you was ridin' – with Barney,' she finished.

The Kid looked at her for several seconds. He did some thinking and reached a decision. He leaned across the wet table surface.

'I'll be right with you, Bess,' he said slowly and very softly. 'You'd better be that way with me. Things are getting tight. I never used a rod in my life. I've been around killings – and dead guys. But I never knocked a guy out. You know that.'

She wasn't afraid of him; he could see that in her eyes. And it worried him. Weeks ago she *had* been afraid of him. But she figured another way now.

'You never did for a guy – until tonight, maybe,' she said slowly.

He kicked back his chair suddenly, stood up. Her eyes stayed on his; they got hard. She made a quick movement with her right hand half out of sight, and he heard the lock snap in the gray bag she always carried. He stared down at her. She said slowly:

'Sit down, Kid – and keep your hands in sight.'

He pulled his chair up, sat down. He smiled at her. After a few seconds he spoke slowly.

'So you're playing for Gil Nasser?'

She shook her head. 'Don't get rough, that's all. I'm not playing for anyone. But I'm quitting you. And I wouldn't start for Chi with you. You wouldn't reach the station, Kid.'

Joey Deth tried not to shiver. The tone of her voice was so certain. He said very quietly:

'Barney Nasser sent word he wanted to see me. I didn't want to see him. I've been working the racket across the river – and I put the slot machines in. I didn't cut in on Barney. He was on this side – and in Jersey. But he got sore because I was takin' coin out of Brooklyn. He wanted to buy me off. He wanted to talk.'

She just smiled. Kid Deth said, with his eyes on her tired blue ones:

'He picked me up in the coupé – and we drove over near the river. We talked on the way, but we didn't say much. I got the idea he was going to boost the price he was offering. Maybe I'd have taken it and cleared, Bess.'

She said: 'Maybe,' in a doubtful tone, and lighted a cigarette. She smiled at him.

He narrowed his dead-gray eyes on hers. He said in a toneless voice:

'I needed cigarettes. We don't smoke the same brand, and there was talking to be done. I remembered a speak two squares up First Avenue. We figured it would be better not to drive. I got the cigarettes, and when I came back – Barney was dead across the wheel. I hadn't heard a shot, but there are always trucks along First Avenue, and I'm used to back-fire racket.'

Bess Grote's eyes closed momentarily. When she opened them she had stopped smiling.

'You're lying, Kid,' she said softly. 'You're lying – and you're in – for the works!'

He stiffened a little, and her right hand went to the bag. He shrugged.

'I saw the lunch-wagon, went down to question Old Andy. Rands came out and grabbed me. He took me back to the car, tried to frame me. He knocked me down.'

Kid Deth touched the bruised spot on his left temple. The girl watched him closely.

'Two guns came around the far side of the car – and opened on him. I didn't see their faces – they didn't come in close. They were medium sized, Bess. That's – what happened.'

The girl finished her beer and nodded her head. She said slowly:

'That's what *you* say, Kid. But I'm quittin' you, just the same. The others may not think the same way.'

Joey Deth looked beyond the girl. A bell jangled outside. The waiter nodded to the Kid and went towards the speak-easy street door. The one who had been talking to himself was sleeping, his head pillowed in his arms. Kid Deth muttered to himself as he looked at the man – he reminded him of Barney Nasser.

'You always did – like Charlie Gay,' he said softly.

The girl's mouth tightened. She shoved back her chair a little. There was rage in her blue eyes. It told the Kid a lot.

'You always did hate – Barney Nasser!' she snapped. 'Only you never had the guts—'

She broke off as the waiter came into the back room. He reached Joey's side.

'It's that – tall, skinny dick!' he said. 'I seen him through the peephole. The one that's tied up with that Rands dick – his partner!'

The girl shoved back her chair and got to her feet. Her movements were quick, jerky. Kid Deth looked at her and chuckled without amusement in his tone.

'Going to – tip off Charlie?' he mocked.

The girl's face was white. She swore at him. She said shakily:

'Listen – Kid – you'd better go out back – keep your rod handy—'

He shook his head. 'I don't use a rod – and you know it,' he cut in steadily.

Her eyes went to the waiter's. He spoke in a thick tone.

'We're all right – an' I got to let this guy inside. I got to—'

Kid Deth narrowed his eyes on the blue, wide ones of Bess Grote.

'Sure,' he said. 'Let him in. It's Sarlow, Rands' partner. They worked together most of the time. Let him in, Mac.'

The girl looked at Kid Deth. 'You damn' fool,' she said. 'He'll take you downtown. They'll beat hell out of you.'

Joey smiled. 'That'll suit Charlie Gay fine, Bess,' he said. 'But maybe not so well as if I went out the back way, alone.'

She turned towards him – took a step in his direction. The Kid shook his head.

'Don't,' he warned. 'I know what I'm up against. You wanted to quit a month ago – now's the right time. If you want to give me a break, just because we went places and did—'

He stopped. She faced the waiter. Her voice was hard and certain now.

'Talk to the quiet clothes bull a little – before you let him in,' she said. 'I'll ease out the back way – and maybe the Kid'll go with me.'

The waiter nodded. 'He's not dumb,' he said. 'He'll go.'

He went towards the speakeasy door. Bess Grote bent forward across the table. She said in a low voice:

'Gil's sure you did for Barney. I don't know what the bulls think about Rands' kill. But what Gil got from Old Andy – the police can get. A crook and a copper are dead – and you're sitting in between them, Kid.'

Kid Deth nodded. 'And you lied to me about Gay,' he said quietly. 'He didn't go West – and he did hate Barney Nasser. And his mob—'

Her eyes held anger again. She spoke in a low, bitter tone.

'You can't pull Charlie in this, Kid. I was with him until an hour ago. We went to a show. He never even—'

The voice of Sarlow reached them. It was a slow voice, almost a drawl. It was asking questions. The Kid spoke in a whisper.

'Better call – as you go out back, Bess. There might be a mistake—'

She turned away from him abruptly. But near the door she stopped. She half turned towards the wet-surfaced table.

'If you get a break – get clear, Kid,' she said in a whisper. 'You've been lucky – too long—'

He lifted his right hand a little, made a small gesture. Then she was out of sight – she was moving towards the alley in back. Her footfalls died.

The Kid lighted a cigarette and smiled bitterly. He touched the bruised spot on his temple, finished his drink. He moved his chair back from the table. He remembered that this partner of the dead detective had shot down Eddie Birch, less than a year ago. Sarlow was a veteran. He was hard, cold. And his partner had been killed, murdered.

Joey said slowly, half aloud: 'Another guy – looking for a chance – to frame me—'

There were footfalls in the hallway beyond the room. The outside door slammed. The waiter was whistling loudly. The Kid raised his eyes and looked into the dark eyes of Sarlow. There was a half smile on the dick's face; his right hand was buried in the pocket of his coat – his left arm swung a little at his side. He leaned carelessly against a wall, ten feet from the Kid.

'Hello, Deth,' he said in a casual tone. 'Just drinking alone?'

Joey Deth nodded. 'Just drinking alone,' he replied slowly. 'How're things, Sarlow?'

There was a flicker of light in the black color of the detective's eyes. But he kept smiling.

'Not so good, Kid,' he said softly. 'They – got Lou.'

Joey Deth parted his lips and widened his eyes. He swore softly and said in a surprised tone:

'You mean – Lou Rands – your sidekick?'

Sarlow's lean body twitched. His eyes looked hurt. He lifted his left hand and took off his hat. He had gray hair; it was rumpled. A few locks were sticking damply to his forehead. His thin face was white.

'Yeah,' he said slowly. 'Lou Rands.'

Kid Deth said: 'Hell – I'm sorry. Jeeze – that's tough, Sarlow.'

Sarlow half closed his eyes. 'Think so?' he said in a strange tone.

Joey Deth nodded a little. 'I guess Rands was all right,' he said slowly. 'He tagged me a lot, but I guess—'

Sarlow looked at the Kid's hands – they rested on the surface of the table. He took his right hand from the pocket, held his gun low.

'Get up, Kid,' he said slowly. 'I got a cab outside.'

Kid Deth shrugged his shoulders. He said very softly:

'I didn't get him, Sarlow. I'm givin' it to you straight.'

Sarlow straightened his lean body. 'You've been giving things straight – for a long time, Kid,' he said in a hard voice. 'And squirming loose.'

Joey Deth got up. He shook his head. 'Two guns got him, Sarlow,' he said. 'I know how you feel – he was your side-kick. I know how you think. But it's wrong. And he tried—'

He checked himself, thinking of the gun in Sarlow's grip. No use telling the dick that his partner had tried to frame him.

'You've been lucky – for a long time, Kid.' Sarlow's voice was almost toneless. 'We gave you rope. Lou figured you'd get the dose from the inside. But you were getting coin, across the river. Barney Nasser didn't like that. He got careless – and you gave him the works. Then Lou grabbed you—'

Kid Deth kept his eyes on the dark ones of Sarlow. He shook his head.

'I didn't get Barney,' he said. 'I'm giving it to you straight—'

His words died; Sarlow's body jerked as the first shot sounded. It came from somewhere out back. There was a second's pause – then the scream reached them. It was a woman's scream – short and high pitched. Then the gun clattered. It beat a staccato song, died abruptly. There were no more screams.

Sarlow, his body tense, kept his eyes on the Kid. When the waiter came into the room he got his back to the wall and moved his gun a little.

'Get over there – by Deth!' he ordered.

McLean walked over and stood beside the Kid. His eyes were wide and he rubbed the material of his trousers with the fingers of his right hand. The man across the room muttered to himself and rolled his head. Sarlow said:

'Who – got clear, when I came in?'

The Kid got his left hand fingers on the back of the chair from which he had risen. His face was very white. There was no color in his thin lips.

Sarlow smiled. 'Whoever it was – they got the long dose,' he said. 'Tommy gun. Sounded like a frail, Kid. Was she yours?'

Kid Deth closed his eyes and tried not to rock from side to side. One thought was beating into his brain – Bess had screamed after the first shot. And *then* the Tommy had been turned loose. It had been no mistake.

Sarlow made a chuckling sound. 'Cheer up, Kid,' he said. 'Maybe it was a miss – maybe she got clear.'

Joey drew in his breath sharply. At his side the waiter muttered to himself.

'We oughta – get out there – we oughta—'

Kid Deth tried to smile. 'Like hell we oughta!' he breathed. 'It's a frame—'

Sarlow stopped smiling and moved his gun hand a little.

'That yelp sounded as if someone was hurt,' he said grimly. 'Want to go out – and look around, Kid?'

Joey shook his head. He took his left hand away from the back of the chair. He didn't speak. Sarlow listened for several seconds. He looked at the waiter.

'A blackjack hurts,' he said slowly. 'Who went out of here – when I came in?'

McLean wet his lips with the tip of his tongue. He shook his head.

'The Kid – was alone,' he breathed.

Sarlow swore. His eyes flickered to Joey Deth's; they held hate. He looked at the waiter again.

'You tried to stall for time,' he said. 'And the Kid waited for me to come in. Who went out back – and got that dose?'

The Kid said softly: 'Mac ain't in this, Sarlow. He's – all right.'

The lean detective swore at him. 'Getting big hearted, eh?' he mocked. 'But you look sick, Kid.'

A door slammed beyond the room, out back. The three men who were standing stood motionless. The Kid and the waiter stared towards the darkness beyond the room. A narrow corridor ran to the rear door. Sound came from it now – the sound of a body falling, not too heavily.

Joey said fiercely: 'Listen – let Mac go out there, Sarlow! He'll be all right—'

The waiter took a step forward, but the lean-faced detective moved his gun arm swiftly.

'You – stick where you are – both of you!' he gritted.

Joey Deth turned his twisted face away from Sarlow. The detective changed his position slightly – he was listening to a faint sound that reached the room. It might have been the sound of a human trying to drag along the wooden floor. It stopped. A half-sobbing voice came faintly into the room

'Joey—'

Kid Deth swayed a little, in front of the partner of Lou Rands. His lips were twitching. Bess Grote called again. Her voice was very weak.

'Kid – Deth—'

The Kid said fiercely: 'Let me – go out there, Sarlow – they got her—'

Sarlow shook his head. 'And *you* got Lou,' he said grimly. 'And you lied – like you've always lied—'

There was no more sound from the dark corridor. McLean said in a husky voice:

'You're killing – that woman, Sarlow. You can't keep us in here—'

The detective looked at the Kid. 'What did you send her out back for?' he said softly. 'Maybe you – *wanted* her – to get that dose, Deth!'

Kid Deth smiled at the detective. It was a peculiar, tight-lipped smile. He nodded his head.

'Sure,' he replied, and his voice was strangely calm. 'Sure – anything you say, Sarlow. But I'm going out there, see? And if you squeeze lead—'

He broke off, walked towards the door. His movements were swift, steady. He read indecision in Sarlow's eyes. The gun muzzle came up a little. Then he saw the veins of the detective's right wrist stand out – he was squeezing the trigger—

The Kid sprang at Sarlow – swinging sideways and downward with his left arm. The gun crashed – the bullet seared Deth's right thigh. Sarlow went back under his weight, went off balance. McLean was on him now – the two of them battered him to the floor. The Kid twisted the gun from his grip.

'Outside, Mac—' he breathed heavily, getting to his feet. 'Bring her – in here—'

Sarlow pulled himself to his knees and swore at Joey.

'And I held – back on you!' he muttered thickly. 'I should have—'

Kid Deth backed against the wall. He heard the foot-falls of McLean, heard the breathing of the waiter as he moved towards the room from the corridor. The man breathed heavily, as though there was a weight in his arms.

Kid Deth watched the detective as he got to his feet. He didn't look at the body of the girl, when McLean carried her into the room. He said slowly:

'Any chance – Mac?'

There was a little silence. Then the waiter's voice reached him.

'She's finished, Kid—'

Joey Deth nodded. His eyes were expressionless. He kept them fixed on the dark ones of Sarlow.

'I'm taking the lead out of your rod,' he said after a few seconds. 'You go out the front way – and keep moving. When you get outside I'll toss the rod out. Be at Headquarters tomorrow at four. I'll walk in.'

Sarlow wiped his lips with the back of his right hand. There was a thin streaking of red across his chin.

'Yeah,' he said heavily. 'Sure you will.'

Kid Deth smiled. It was a bitter, twisted smile.

'I didn't get Barney Nasser. I didn't get your partner. I'm givin' it to you straight. I never squeezed a rod on a bull—'

He stopped, thinking of Lou Rands trying to frame him, jamming the gun in his hand. He had squeezed the rod then. And it had been empty.

'Tomorrow – at Headquarters. Four o'clock. I've got – something to do—'

He jerked his right hand towards the door. Sarlow said slowly:

'That's a lot of time – for a getaway.'

The Kid shook his head. 'I'll be in – at four,' he said. 'I've got something – to do.'

Sarlow glanced towards the body of the girl. But the Kid didn't look in that direction. He half closed his dead-gray eyes.

'Get out, dick!' he gritted. 'I need – all the time – that's left!'

3

Kid Deth stopped the taxi at Forty-second Street, near Sixth Avenue, slipped from behind the wheel. His face was pale and his gray eyes were streaked with red. He was tired and something inside of him was hurt. He hadn't thought any dead woman could hurt him so much.

He went into the coffee house and sat at the counter. He drank two cups of coffee, black – and tried to eat a doughnut. The waiter stood back of the counter and read an early edition of a tabloid. It was after four, and there was a light rain falling.

After a while he finished the coffee, tossed a quarter on the counter and went outside.

He slid back of the wheel, got the cab going. He drove down Sixth Avenue, swearing softly. He didn't think he'd been recognized, but he couldn't take a chance. The papers were carrying his pictures – he knew it would be worth a lot to any copper to bring him in. And the quiet clothes boys were out, too.

The cab was Bennie Golin's – and Bennie was all right. They were about the same size – he had borrowed clothes from Bennie. It was to Bennie's flat that he had taken the battered body of Bess Grote. He'd set the man up in business – and Bennie was paying him back a little. But Golin had been afraid; the Kid had seen the expression in his eyes when he had told him what he wanted.

'If they wise up – it's my finish, Kid,' Bennie had said.

And Kid Deth had smiled grimly. 'If who wise up?' he had asked. 'The bulls?'

Golin had shaken his head. 'To hell with *them*,' he had said. 'You ain't worryin' about them.'

Joey turned the cab eastward on Thirty-fourth Street. He drove slowly, carefully. Golin had been right. The Kid wasn't so worried about the police. But there was something he wanted to do. Something important. He wanted to rub out the murderer of Bess Grote. He wanted to do that job, and do it right. Then he wanted to walk into the Center Street building and hand himself over. He could beat the rap. Berman was a smart mouthpiece. He would come high but he would see that he wasn't framed. And he would give himself up.

He cruised northward, hunching low back of the wheel. He had spent an hour in the cab, driving past spots where he might have seen something that would have helped. But he hadn't seen anything. It was still a toss-up. Gil Nasser – or Charlie Gay. One of the two had done for Bess Grote. One of the two had bossed the kill of Lou Rands. One of the two had finished Barney Nasser, perhaps. He wasn't so sure of *that*. Rands might have got Barney, working for a frame. It wasn't likely that Gil had drummed out his own brother.

At Thirty-ninth Street he took a chance and looked towards the river. The street was deserted, but there was a light shining from Old Andy's lunch-wagon.

He sped the cab down the street. Near the wagon he turned it around, headed it towards First Avenue. The street was a cul de sac – there was only one exit for machines.

He slipped from the wheel, leaving the engine running. For a few seconds he looked towards First Avenue. Rain made pattering sounds on the street surface. There was no clattering of dishes from the lunch-wagon.

He moved towards the few steps – opened the door. Fingers of his left hand gripped the gun in his pocket. His eyes searched the narrow aisle before the counter, as he looked in through the misted glass of the door. He saw no customer.

He opened the door, stepped inside. He was breathing quickly, and the one thought running through his head was that he was a fool to have come. But he *had* come.

There was sound at one end of the counter – Old Andy got to his feet. He was a big, round-shouldered man. His eyes blinked as he looked at Joey Deth. He had sandy colored hair and big features.

Joey said: 'Yeah, Andy – it's me. How're things?'

He smiled a little. Andy's eyes went to his left pocket. The lunch-wagon owner shook his head from side to side.

'I didn't – want to tell 'em, Kid,' he said. 'I didn't want—'

Joey Deth kept on smiling. 'That's all right,' he said. 'Who got Barney Nasser, Andy?'

The lunch-wagon proprietor stared at him blankly. Kid Deth stopped smiling. He spoke in a low, hard voice.

'Give me a break, Andy – the bulls are after me. Lou Rands tried to frame me – he's been trying for a long time. But not this hard. Something was up – and something went wrong. Give me a break, Andy.'

The lunch-wagon owner shook his head. 'You ain't usin' your head – comin' here, Kid,' he breathed. 'The police – they come every few hours – and ask me something they forgot—'

Kid Deth turned and looked out towards the cab. There were no lights beyond it, near First Avenue. He faced Old Andy again.

'Listen, Andy—' he said slowly – 'someone got Bess Grote tonight. Got her rotten-like. I'm being framed, Andy – and the job's being done tough. I may not be able to beat it. I got to know things. What did Lou Rands say to you, just before he grabbed me?'

Old Andy shook his head. Kid Deth took the automatic from his pocket. He watched the lunch-wagon owner's eyes get wide, watched fear creep into them.

'You had a good memory – when Gil Nasser got to you,' he said slowly. 'And you talked to the bulls. Now – you'd better talk – to me.'

Old Andy nodded his head. His eyes were on the gun. He said shakily: 'You never – used to pack a rod, Kid—'

Joey Deth smiled grimly. 'And I never used – to be framed,' he replied. 'What happened – after I left Barney Nasser in his coupé, Andy? Better talk!'

The man back of the counter shook his head again. He tapped his right ear with a big finger. Joey Deth said softly:

'You've been working that line for years, Andy. But I know it's the bunk. You ain't deaf – not unless you want to be. You'll even hear this gun crack – before you drop. What did Rands say – to you?'

He raised the gun a little. Old Andy's lips were twitching. He stepped close to the counter.

'He'd found a man dead – Barney Nasser,' he said. 'He asked – about you, Kid.'

Kid Deth said: 'What did you tell him?'

Old Andy shook his head. 'Told him I hadn't seen you – for a week or so. Said you used to come in, after theatre time. Rands was wised up – he figured some of the boys talked things over – around here.'

Kid Deth said: 'Yeah?'

There was a little silence. The rain made a soft patter on the glass windows of the lunch-wagon. Kid Deth looked towards the cab again. He got his face close to the door glass, looked towards the Avenue. The street was empty of everything except the cab. Joey faced the lunch-wagon owner again. He spoke in a very low voice. It was toneless.

'You're lying, Andy – and I'm sick of lies. You squealed on me – and you framed me. I've never killed a guy – not until now. You know that, Andy. But you're lying. Lou Rands shot out Barney Nasser – and you know it. And you know why. But you're still workin' with Lou – still trying to frame me. Maybe you've done enough – maybe not. Anyway – you're through. To hell with you – Andy – straight to hell—'

The finger next to his left thumb started to pull back on the trigger. Old Andy's face was ghastly – his eyes were wide with fear.

'For God's sake – wait – Kid!' he breathed hoarsely.

Joey Deth said: 'Wait – for what? For more lies?'

Andy Polson shook his head. 'No – I swear I'll give it to you, Kid! I didn't know—'

He broke off. The Kid eased off pressure on the trigger. He said in a hard voice:

'You didn't know – I'd pack a gun, eh? You thought I'd never hurt – right to the finish. Well – you got it wrong, Andy. I'm walking down to Headquarters at four in the afternoon, see – and before I walk in—'

He checked himself. Old Andy stood leaning against the wall, back of the counter. There was a color in his face now – red streaked the white of his skin, his eyes were protruding, he was breathing heavily.

'Barney – an' Rands – they was together, Kid,' he muttered. 'They was workin' the slot machines together. Then Rands – he got scared. When you went across the river Barney wanted Rands to – get you, Kid. But the dick – he was afraid. He was getting' worried – about bein' so thick with Barney. And he was—'

Kid Deth said in a hard voice: 'Wait – how do *you* figure to know so much?'

The lunch-wagon owner said in a whisper: 'I passed the coin – from Barney—'

Kid Deth stood tensely, his eyes narrowed on the staring ones of Andy Polson. He cut in sharply:

'And Rands – gave Barney the dose? Because he was afraid of a break.'

Old Andy shook his head. His eyes were on the gun that the Kid was holding a little lower now.

'Barney tried – to get Rands,' he said thickly. 'I seen you go along First

Avenue. Rands came close to the car – passed it. Barney got out and followed him. The lights were out in here – something went wrong with the power. Maybe Barney didn't think I was inside. I was watchin' 'em come up.'

Kid Deth said: 'Don't lie, Andy – this counts big.'

The lunch-wagon owner stared at the gun. He moved his head from side to side.

'I ain't lyin', Kid,' he said. 'I'm an old man and—'

'What happened – with Barney Nasser back of Rands?' the Kid cut in.

'He opened up,' Polson muttered. 'But Rands was swingin' around – maybe he heard him. He got Barney right away. I seen him pick him up. He carried him to the coupé then he come back here. The lights went on while he was comin' back, and he was sore as hell. He swore he'd kill me if I crossed him up. He said it was a chance – to get you. Barney had wised him that you was ridin' with him. He'd been hidin' out – an' he'd seen you get clear of the car.'

Kid Deth said slowly: 'I didn't figure that Barney tried for *him* first,' he muttered. 'But I figured he got Nasser – and wanted to frame me—'

Old Andy nodded. 'I swear I give it to you straight, Kid—'

Joey Deth lowered the pistol. 'Who gunned out Rands?' he said slowly.

The lunch-wagon owner shook his head. 'That's all I know, Kid,' he said. 'If I can square you—'

The Kid swore softly. 'You can't – not that way,' he said in a hard tone. 'They'd figure it was a deal – in court.'

There was silence except for the patter of rain against the lunch-wagon windows.

Old Andy said slowly, breathing with an effort:

'Maybe they was – tryin' for you, Kid – and got Rands.'

Kid Deth grunted. 'Like hell they were!' he breathed. 'They were guns – and they didn't miss. They wanted Rands – and they got him. And they wanted—'

He smiled grimly. He knew something now – something important. Barney Nasser and Lou Rands had been working together. Nasser had tried to finish the detective – but the dick had got him. He'd tried to frame the Kid, but he'd been gunned out. Why?

The Kid thought: I'm getting closer. Either Gil Nasser or Charlie Gay got Rands. The mob of one of them, anyway. Or maybe Gil wasn't in on it, and Barney had his men close by, in case something went wrong in *our* talk. They saw Rands carry Barney to the coupé – and they got him. There was a chance of getting me framed, so they didn't turn loose on me. If Charlie Gay pulled the shoot – it was straight hate. He was wise that Rands had been working with Barney.

Old Andy said in a monotone: 'Barney Nasser tried to get Rands in the back. Rands got him. And there are a lot of guys – that hate the dick. You better get clear, Kid – you better jump town. I've put you wise—'

The Kid shook his head. 'Someone got Bess Grote,' he said slowly. 'It wasn't a mistake, Andy. They tricked her. Maybe she was supposed to send me out back. She didn't do it. When she went out – they got her. That's what I've got to do, Andy – get the one—'

He stopped. Old Andy half closed his eyes. He touched his sandy hair with shaking fingers.

'You never used a rod, Kid—' he started. His voice died abruptly.

The Kid heard the sound, too. He swung around, half opened the door of the lunch-wagon. But the car was coming down the center of the street. It had bright lights – and it skidded to one side as the driver worked the brakes. Figures spilled to the wet street pavement – they moved swiftly and without sound.

Kid Deth stepped back and shut the door. He snapped the bolt.

'Bulls!' he breathed fiercely. 'Out the back of the wagon—'

He turned. Old Andy was close to the counter. His right arm was lifted. The fingers held a gun leveled low, above the wood. The gun was shaking a little. The trigger finger was moving. Kid Deth let his body slump forward and downward, dived towards the counter. The gun crashed as his hands and knees hit the floor – wood spurted from the counter.

The second shot sent a bullet through the glass of the lunch-wagon door. The Kid crawled towards the end of the counter on the left, pulled himself up from his knees. He muttered huskily:

'You – crazy Swede—'

From outside of the lunch-wagon two shots sounded. Something clattered, behind the counter. Old Andy made a heavy, grunting sound. He swore weakly. Two more shots sounded from outside.

There was a low cough from Old Andy. Then his body struck the floor back of the counter. Kid Deth crawled around behind – saw the outstretched hands, the half-opened eyes. There was red on Old Andy's lips. Coffee hissed downward from the percolator.

The Kid crawled around past the body of the man who had tried to kill him. Polson was dead; crouching low, the Kid went through the door that led to the small room back of the space where Old Andy lay. There was a narrow door on his right – he opened it, stared out into the rain. No one was in sight.

There were no steps. He dropped to the street, kept the lunch-wagon between himself and the men on the far side. He crouched low, and held the automatic in his left hand. At the end of the street there was a dock; the Kid worked his way northward of it, along the river bank. He found a narrow alley that led back from the river, traveled along it. There was no sound of voices.

He could guess what had happened. The men who had come up in the car were detectives. Either they had blundered into him, or Old Andy had been expecting them. Joey could see no way that he had tipped them off. There was no phone in the lunch-wagon; even if the proprietor had seen him before he got inside there would not have been time for him to have called.

Old Andy had tried to get him – to kill the story he had just told – and his second shot had crashed through the door of the lunch-wagon. Perhaps the bullet had hit one of the men outside. In any case, they had opened up – and Andy had dropped.

He lowered his head, moved rapidly westward across the avenue. When he had reached the far side he did not look back. He guessed that the detectives were getting inside the lunch-wagon, but doing it cautiously. He was halfway to Second Avenue when he heard the shrill of a police whistle. Almost immediately it was followed by the wail of the car siren.

4

Joey Deth kept close to the fronts of tenements, reached Second Avenue. He went northward, and heard the siren wail again as he climbed the Elevated Station.

When the train reached One Hundred and Twenty-fifth Street the Kid got off, descended from the station. He walked westward, got a cab, gave the address of a flat less than four squares from the speakeasy in back of which Bess Grote had been gunned out.

McLean's flat was a half square from the address he gave. The cab driver was sleepy; he came close to hitting a milk wagon at an intersection, and the Kid swore at him beneath his breath.

He gave the driver a half dollar, walked past McLean's place once, then turned back and went inside. The waiter lived alone on the top floor – the Kid pressed the button four times, and the last time it was a short buzz. The lock made a ticking sound almost immediately, and the Kid went inside.

He climbed the stairs slowly – they were dimly lighted and there were many odors drifting through the hallways. A baby was crying fretfully as he started up the last flight. When he made the turn at the head of the stairs, to go along the hallway, he saw that McLean's door was opened on a narrow crack.

Instinctively he hesitated; his left hand reached towards his left coat pocket. Then the door was opened a little more – he saw the waiter's face. He moved up close, said softly:

'You – alone?'

McLean nodded his head. He opened the door most of the way, stepped to one side. The Kid walked inside the flat.

He went over to the uncomfortable divan and dropped down on it. He said grimly:

'The dicks – almost got me, Mac.'

McLean stood with his back to the door and narrowed his eyes on Kid Deth.

'Where – at Bennie Golin's?'

Joey shook his head. 'At Old Andy's,' he replied in a low tone. 'Maybe they were tipped – maybe they just drove in. I had a cab – stopped in to get Andy to wise me to what Rands had been spilling, before that dick grabbed me. Andy came through.'

McLean said: 'Yes?' His voice was low and husky. His eyes kept shifting around. Kid Deth looked at him and remembered that he didn't know the man well, that six months ago he hadn't known him at all. He wondered if Bennie Golin wouldn't be better for the job. Then he remembered that Bennie had a wife and a kid.

The Kid lighted a cigarette, tossed the pack towards the other man. McLean shook his head, tossed the pack back.

Joey Deth said: 'I got to be sure, Mac. You sittin' in with me, or just playing safe?'

McLean smiled. It was a hard smile. 'Didn't I go out – and bring Bess into the room, Kid? Ain't I taking a chance in having you in here?'

Joey nodded. 'Sure,' he agreed. 'But that don't answer the question. I'm in the way, Mac – and a lot of guys want to get me. But they're being careful – and that means something.'

McLean grunted. 'What?' he asked.

Kid Deth pulled on his cigarette. He shrugged. His eyes were on the waiter.

'What you sticking so close to that door for?' he asked, his voice very soft.

McLean looked surprised. He stepped away from the door, halted suddenly. He turned his body a little, so that he half faced the door. The Kid listened too. And while he listened he got his automatic out of his pocket.

He said: 'Yeah – someone's coming up, Mac.'

McLean's body jerked. He faced the Kid – his breath made a sucking sound as his eyes spotted the weapon. Joey smiled.

'*Who's* coming up, Mac?' he asked coldly.

The waiter stared at him. 'What are you – getting at, Kid?' he muttered. 'I'm a little shaky – that's all. With you – in here—'

Kid Deth nodded. 'I know,' he said. 'Who's comin' to see you, Mac? It's a funny hour – for a call.'

The steps on the stairs were not heavy – the creaking sound ceased now. The Kid had made a guess, and he knew now that it was a good one. He could read the answer in McLean's eyes.

'You, too,' he said softly. 'Jeeze – but the quitting came fast when it got started. You're all crowdin' for the kill – crowding or squealing – or quitting.'

McLean said: 'I don't get you, Kid. I told you to get clear—'

Joey Deth smiled. 'But you didn't tell me *how*,' he cut in. 'Now shut up – and when you hear the tap—'

The sound of footfalls was very faint. It died away abruptly. There was a short silence – then knuckles rapped against the wood of the flat door. They knocked four times.

Kid Deth looked at McLean's white face and smiled. He slumped on the divan, held the automatic low between his knees. He got a handkerchief from his pocket and placed it over the gun. Then he nodded at McLean, made a sign with his right hand.

McLean whispered: 'For God's sake, Kid – you never packed a rod before—'

Joey Deth smiled with half-closed eyes. He motioned again for the waiter to open the door. The handkerchief moved a little. McLean opened the door and stepped to one side. A voice said:

'It's Charlie, Mac—'

McLean's face was twisted. He said in a husky voice:

'Yeah, Charlie – all right.'

Charlie Gay stepped inside the flat. For a second he didn't see the slumped figure of the Kid. When he did see it he muttered an exclamation, dropped his right hand towards his left coat pocket.

Kid Deth said: 'Don't, Charlie!'

Gay stopped. He stood with his head shoved forward a little; his eyes on the handkerchief that was over the automatic. His breath came in short, hissing sounds. The Kid said:

'Close that door, Mac – snap the lock. Expecting anyone else?'

McLean closed the door, shook his head. He said in an uncertain tone:

'Watch what you do, Kid.'

Charlie Gay said nothing. He was medium in size with a pallid face and eyes that were set back of bushy brows. His fingers moved nervously as his hands strayed at his sides.

Joey Deth chuckled a little. '*You* do the watching, Mac,' he said.

He looked at Gay. He spoke in a low, easy tone.

'You got brains, Charlie – even if you did let Barney Nasser do a squeal on you. What did you mob out Lou Rands for?'

Charlie Gay shook his head. 'Take that rod off me, Kid,' he said. 'I wasn't in on the deal, an' you know it.'

His voice was thin, rasping. When he talked he showed no fear. He kept his eyes on the white handkerchief. McLean stood close to him – both men faced the Kid.

Joey Deth said: 'You got brains, Charlie – use 'em now. Talk straight to me. There isn't too much time, for what I've got to do.'

Charlie Gay narrowed his eyes until they were narrow slits under his brows.

'I don't get you, Kid,' he said. 'I've been away a long time—'

Joey Deth nodded. 'It'll be a longer trip, this time,' he said. 'And there won't be picture shows on Saturdays, Charlie.'

McLean said: 'Listen, Kid—'

Joey moved the gun slightly, and the material of the handkerchief wavered. McLean kept quiet. Joey looked at Charlie Gay.

'You got yourself a sweet alibi, Charlie – and then you got afraid—'

His voice shook a little. He stopped. Charlie Gay's eyes flickered on the dead-gray ones of the Kid, beneath the bushy brows.

'Take the rod off me, Kid,' he said again.

Joey Deth smiled. 'Why should I?' he asked. 'You didn't take the Tommy gun off Bess Grote – even when she screamed, Charlie.'

Gay's body twitched. 'You don't think – I ran that job, Kid?' he muttered.

Joey said: 'You know about it, Charlie.'

Gay's eyes flickered towards McLean. He said harshly:

'If you sucked me into this, Mac – it'll go tough with you! The Kid's all hopped—'

Joey Deth interrupted. 'Mac's all right, Charlie,' he said quietly. 'He's just like the rest – tryin' to play in between. He didn't suck you in. Old Andy – he did the talking.'

Charlie Gay widened his eyes. 'Old Andy—' he started, and checked himself. 'Listen, Kid—' he muttered. 'Bess – she said she was – off you. I always did – like her—'

The Kid sucked in his breath. 'Yeah?' he said sharply. 'And you gunned her out just the same.'

Charlie Gay swung on McLean. 'You squealed – you dirty—'

Joey Deth said: 'Shut up, Charlie! You'll wake the neighbors.'

McLean showed fear in his eyes. 'He got it – from Old Andy,' he said shakily. 'I'm tellin' you, Charlie – I didn't squeal.'

Kid Deth sat up a little on the divan. He leaned forward and took the handkerchief away from the automatic. He pressed it to his lips with his right hand fingers.

'It's no good, Charlie,' he said quietly. 'You wanted Barney Nasser out – and you wanted to frame me. Your mob didn't get Barney, but they got Lou Rands. They got him because I was close to him – and it was a deal to finish me. Maybe it did – I'm giving myself up at four.'

'They'll give you – the hot spot, if you go down there,' Gay said softly.

The Kid shook his head. 'I've got things they'd like to know,' he said. 'I've got coin, Charlie. I can get Berman.'

He was mocking Charlie Gay, and he could see the rage in the other man's eyes. McLean said slowly:

'It was just – that you were there, Kid – there with Barney.'

Joey Deth nodded. 'I never framed a guy for the chair,' he said. 'I never even cut in on the other guy's territory. I've worked the rackets – but I worked them right.'

There was a little silence. Charlie Gay moved the fingers of his left hand.

'How much do you want, Kid?' he asked.

Joey shook his head. 'You haven't got enough to stop me, Charlie,' he said.

'I'm giving you the dose right in here – and maybe Mac can squirm out of it. Maybe not.'

The waiter stared at him, fear widening his eyes. His voice was hoarse.

'Jeeze, Kid – you wouldn't fix it like that!'

He looked at the gun. Charlie Gay stared at it, too. His hands were restless at his side.

Joey Deth nodded. 'Why not?' he said softly. 'Gay and the Nassers – they tried to frame me. I never hurt them. And when they started to jump me – all of you started to quit or squeal. You were tipping Charlie off, Mac – you knew he was coming here. Old Andy – he got yellow when I made him talk. Even the dicks – Sarlow is after me. You all want to see me burn – because a burned guy don't talk. But Charlie here – he's not too anxious for me to get inside Headquarters.'

Charlie Gay said slowly: 'Listen, Kid – I ain't lying. I sent the guns down to get Barney. He turned me up – and Lou Rands was the dirty dick that took me in. The boys knew that – and they got him, after he'd finished Barney. That's straight.'

Kid Deth was silent for several seconds. He kept his dead-gray eyes on the flickering ones of Gay.

'How about – Bess?' he asked finally.

Charlie Gay shook his head. 'It wasn't my deal,' he breathed. 'I swear to that, Kid. I used her for an alibi. I had to have someone—'

Kid Deth said with contempt in his voice:

'Maybe if I had a gun on me – like this one's on you, *I'd* lie for my life, too.'

Charlie Gay said: 'I ain't lying, Kid. I heard about her getting the dose a half hour ago. I called Mac and told him I wanted to see him and was coming over. I wanted to know how she got it.'

Kid Deth leaned forward, sat on the edge of the divan.

'All right, Charlie,' he said. 'That just means one thing – Gil Nasser got her. *One* of you did the job. I'm giving you a choice.'

Gay stared at him. There was faint eagerness in his voice, but it was the eagerness of trickery.

'What do I do, Kid?' he asked.

Joey Deth sighed. 'We go and find Gil,' he said slowly. 'It'll be light pretty quick – and that'll make it harder. We've got the coppers to beat. Know where Gil is, Charlie?'

Charlie Gay's eyes were slits beneath his bushy brows.

'He might be – at that black boy's place – drinkin'.'

The Kid smiled with his eyes half closed. He looked beyond McLean, at the cuffs of steel on the table in a corner. He nodded.

'Sure,' he said. 'He might be there. Mac – you know where it is?'

McLean hesitated, then shook his head. The Kid chuckled. He stood up and held the automatic in front of his left thigh.

'Listen, Charlie—' he said slowly – 'we don't want to make any mistakes. Get those cuffs and put Mac's arms around something. The end of that iron bed, Charlie. You still usin' it, Mac?'

McLean nodded. He was frowning. 'You don't have to fix me like that, Kid,' he said.

Joey Deth moved his right arm towards the steel cuffs.

'Fix him – like that, Charlie,' he said slowly. His voice got hard. 'It's a lot easier than being fixed – like some other guys I know.'

5

Hank Sarlow sat in a corner of the speakeasy that 'Blackie' Wade ran for Gil Nasser. There were a half dozen men in the room; two of them were standing at the bar. It was almost dawn, and Sarlow sat with his rain-soaked hat pulled low over his forehead. He was drinking beer and muttering to himself. At intervals his head rocked from side to side, across his narrow shoulders. It was the first time he had been inside the place – he had come in pretending to be drunk. A card that he had taken from the clothes of the dead Rands had been offered to Blackie – and he had been admitted.

Sarlow knew none of the men present. He had been in the place almost an hour, and he was there because he remembered that Rands had once told him the Negro ran the place for Nasser. And because of the fact that Barney Nasser had been murdered – and Bess Grote had been shot out. Sarlow had been to several places; now he was waiting, swaying in the chair, and watching out of the corners of his eyes.

Hank Sarlow swore softly. A woman laughed shrilly, from one of the rooms above. A tall man with broad shoulders and reddish hair stepped around the corner of the bar. Sarlow had not noticed him before – he guessed that there was an entrance back of the bar. The man's eyes went around the room and Sarlow kept his head low and swaying a little. He saw the man beckon to the negro he had heard called Blackie, saw his lips move swiftly. Blackie left the room, and Sarlow could hear him faintly, climbing stairs.

There was another peal of laughter, and then sudden silence. The one with the reddish hair turned so that light struck his sharp features clearly.

Sarlow said in a whisper: 'Gil – Nasser.'

A voice called from below. 'Oh, Blackie—'

There were footfalls on the stairs that led to the third floor – Blackie was descending. The speakeasy was on the second floor – a straight, narrow flight had to be climbed to reach the bar-room. The voice below called again: 'Hey – Blackie!'

The Negro came into the room and nodded towards the red-haired one. Then he went on down the stairs. There was a sudden burst of laughter from the group about the slot machine – one man wheeled away from it.

'Drinks are on me!' he announced loudly. 'The big shot – turned up!'

The men moved towards the bar. Sarlow kept his eyes on the red-haired one. A short man with a growth of beard went over to him and touched him on the shoulder. He said something, and the red-haired one shook his head, made a gesture with his right hand. Then he turned away and went to a table behind the slot machine. He sat with his body half facing the entrance from the stairs.

Sarlow breathed: 'Gil Nasser, all right. Feelin' pretty bad—'

He raised a dirty hand and pulled his wet hat brim lower over his face. There were footfalls on the stairs again – more than one person was coming up.

Sarlow kept his head low, but his eyes were narrowed on the entrance from the hallway. His body stiffened as the first man came into the room, moved towards the bar. It was Charlie Gay.

The detective felt his heart pound as he saw Kid Deth, close beside Charlie. The left pocket of the Kid's coat was pressing against Gay's right side – the two men walked to the bar almost as one human. Gay's face was white; there was a strained expression in his eyes.

The Kid was smiling a little. He didn't see Sarlow, but he did see Gil Nasser. The detective knew that, and he knew that Gil Nasser recognized the Kid – and the man his brother had turned up.

At the bar Charlie Gay turned his white face towards the Kid, who had the ex-convict between him and the seated brother of the dead crook. He tried a smile that looked bad. He said something that Sarlow didn't catch. The Kid spoke to the bartender, who was staring at him.

'Two – whiskey straight,' he ordered.

He kept his body close to the bar, but he looked around the room. Gil Nasser was sitting low in his chair – his big shoulders hunched forward. Sarlow lowered his head and slitted his eyes.

'It's going to be – a killing!' he breathed to himself. 'The Kid has guts – he's got a rod on Charlie Gay – he went after him—'

Out of the corner of his eyes he saw that Gil Nasser was watching the Kid. Suddenly he saw the brother of the dead crook rise. He moved slowly towards the door. He was within ten feet of it when Kid Deth saw him in the mirror, swung around. The Kid got his back against the wood of the bar – his left hand shoved the material of his coat pocket out.

'All right, Nasser!' he said in a hard voice. 'That's far – enough!'

Gil Nasser swung around. He smiled with his lips bared.

'Jeeze!' he muttered. 'If it ain't – Kid Deth!'

There had been the sound of voices, the clinking of glasses in the room. Now all sound died. Men stood or sat motionless, watching the Kid or Gil Nasser.

Joey Deth said: 'Yeah, Nasser – it's Kid Deth. How're things?'

Beside the Kid, his body crouched a little, was Charlie Gay. The muscles around his lips were twitching – his eyes were on Gil Nasser's right hand. The hand was only half in sight – the fingers were buried beneath the material of his left coat lapel.

Gil Nasser said in a voice that was very hard:

'Lousy, Kid.'

Joey Deth kept a smile in his dead-gray eyes. He nodded his head.

'Sure,' he agreed. 'Lousy is right.'

Nasser's right elbow came up a little, but his hand didn't go deeper behind his coat lapel. Kid Deth said in a voice that barely filled the room.

'Charlie here – he says you gunned out Bess. You figured the bulls would grab me, so I was fixed for the hot spot or a life stretch. And Bess knew too much – so you made her quiet.'

Nasser said: 'Yeah? Did Charlie say that?'

Charlie Gay was breathing heavily. His nerve broke – he cried out.

'That's a – dam' lie, Nasser – he's got a gun on me. I never said that—'

His voice broke. The Kid looked at Gil and kept on smiling.

'He's going yellow, Nasser. The Rands job got him. His mob did for the dick, trying to frame me.'

Gil Nasser stood motionless. He said in a grim tone:

'Yeah? Did he do that job?'

Sarlow sat up a little straighter, stared at Kid Deth. But the Kid was looking at only one human in the room – and that human was watching him in the same manner.

The Kid nodded. 'After your brother tried to get Rands – and missed,' he said.

Gil Nasser's eyes widened a little. He closed his lips and moved the hand inside the coat just a little. Kid Deth said:

'Don't swing that rod, Nasser. I don't have to swing mine – just a squeeze—'

Gil Nasser bared his teeth in a smile that wasn't pretty.

'You – dam' fool!' he breathed. 'You'd never get out of here.'

Joey Deth nodded. 'I'd get out – just like you would,' he said. 'In the coroner's basket. And that's better – than being framed.'

Gil Nasser narrowed his eyes again. He took his right hand away from his coat lapel, let it fall at his side. He shrugged.

'You got me wrong, Kid,' he said. 'When did you start packin' a rod?'

There was a half smile on his face. Joey Deth didn't smile.

'When you started rubbing out women!' he said steadily.

Nasser took his eyes away from Deth's and looked at the white face of Charlie Gay. He said with a hard smile:

'Tryin' to put that deal off on me, eh? Dirty rat!'

Charlie Gay said in a voice that held a half sob of fear:

'I never said – you done it. I swear to God I never said—'

His voice died away. A woman's voice, from somewhere up above called:

'Blackie – come up here—'

Kid Deth smiled almost gently. His eyes were on Gil Nasser's.

'Blackie's quiet – from a butt rap,' he said. 'Tell her to shut up – we're talkin''.

Gil Nasser said: 'Sure, Kid – anything to keep you—'

He turned his back to the Kid, took a step towards the door that led to the hallway. But Joey saw his right arm crook – the hand flash upward. As Nasser's words died he swung around. The first bullet from his gun got Charlie Gay in the stomach – the second got the wood of the bar.

Charlie Gay staggered out – and Kid Deth stepped behind him. The third bullet caught Gay in the left arm – it battered him off balance. He screamed.

'You – lyin'—'

Sarlow stood up and aimed his gun low at Nasser, squeezed the trigger steadily. The crash of his first shot and Gil Nasser's fourth sounded simultaneously. The Kid's body jerked; he swore through clenched teeth. Gil Nasser sagged downward.

Sarlow shoved his hat back and faced the men in the room from his corner.

'The riot squad's outside,' he said hoarsely. 'Now – you just keep still – all of you.'

Charlie Gay turned towards the bar, tried to grip it with his hands, failed. He went to his knees, swayed before the Kid for a second, pitched forward. He lay on the wooden floor, less than five feet from the motionless body of Gil Nasser.

The Kid leaned against the bar and took his left hand from his coat pocket. He said to Sarlow:

'Why in hell – didn't you let him – keep shooting?'

Sarlow said: 'Keep your mouth shut, you!'

The Kid grinned. He said softly: 'Jeeze – lead hurts when it scrapes your ribs.'

He put his right hand down to his left side and pressed the ripped portion of his coat. Sarlow said in a steadier tone:

'One of you look at those two on the floor.'

A short, round-shouldered man kneeled beside Charlie Gay. He lifted a wrist, felt it. He said thickly:

'He's – out.'

Kid Deth said: 'I won't miss him – a dam' bit.' His voice was grim.

Sarlow spoke more quietly. 'Kick that gun away from Nasser,' he ordered. 'Call an ambulance – one of you.'

Gil Nasser groaned and tried to sit up. Sarlow said to Joey Deth, keeping his back against the wall in his corner:

'Slide your rod – across to me, Kid.'

Kid Deth smiled. 'You're lettin' me hold it,' he said grimly.

Sarlow nodded. 'I gave you a break,' he said. 'I got Nasser. Slide it over—'

The Kid leaned down, felt pain from his left side, and slid the automatic across the floor. It stopped near the detective's feet.

Gil Nasser sat up and held his stomach. He turned dull eyes towards Sarlow, who held his gun low. He said thickly:

'A dick – got me—'

Kid Deth looked at Nasser and smiled with his dead-gray eyes.

'When you get where Barney is – tell him you heard Bess scream – and kept working the Tommy,' he said in a low, hard voice. 'He might have guts enough left – to hate you – for that.'

Nasser stared at Joey. He wiped his lips with the back of his right hand. He swayed a little.

'She didn't send – you out—' he breathed weakly, 'She put you wise—'

Kid Deth said softly, 'Jeeze – you *did* get her. You did—'

Gil Nasser spoke in a whisper. 'That rat – Lou Rands – takin' the slot graft from Barney – waitin' for the chance to turn him up—'

Sarlow swore softly. His eyes were on the Kid's. Joey nodded his head.

'That's one – truth,' he said simply.

Gil Nasser went down on the floor and lay on his stomach. The bartender was calling a number in a high-pitched voice. The Kid shivered a little. After a few seconds Nasser's body relaxed.

Sarlow said: 'We won't need that ambulance – but let it come—'

Kid Deth touched his left side. 'There's me – and the black man, downstairs,' he said.

The detective stepped out from the corner, with his eyes narrowed and the gun held low.

'The rest of you – stay quiet,' he warned. 'Come on, Kid.'

Kid Deth walked out from the bar. They went downstairs and to the street. Blackie was leaning against an iron rail holding his head. Sarlow patted him for a rod, didn't find one. Blocks away there was the clang of an ambulance bell. Sarlow said:

'Was Lou workin' with Barney Nasser, Kid?'

Kid Deth shrugged. 'Maybe,' he replied. 'I don't know. But I didn't get him, Sarlow. I've never done a job—'

Sarlow swore softly. 'It's a lousy racket, Kid,' he said. 'You comin' down – at four?'

The Kid's eyes widened a little. 'You turning me loose?' he asked.

The lean-faced detective listened to the louder clang of the ambulance gong, stared towards the entrance of the speakeasy. It was quiet inside.

'You come down – tomorrow, at four, Kid.'

His voice was tired. He was thinking of a man he'd thought was white – and who hadn't been white. He was thinking of crooks who had used guns, and one who hadn't. He was thinking of the Kid's woman.

'Get going, Kid,' he said softly.

*

When the Kid climbed out of the taxi it was clear and cold. The photographers crowded up, and the chubby-faced Berman grinned at them.

'What's all the shooting for?' he asked. 'The Kid's just down for a chat.'

They went inside and the Kid saw Lieutenant of Detectives Cardigan and Hank Sarlow standing side by side. Berman kept a smile on his face.

When they got inside Cardigan's office the lieutenant of detectives said slowly:

'We got a slot machine racket charge against you, Kid. The D.A. wants to push it. He thinks we've got you nice.'

Berman passed the cigars. 'Yeah,' he said. 'The D.A. always thinks that. It's what costs the taxpayers coin.'

The Kid said softly: 'I'm quitting the racket, Cardigan. It's lousy.'

Cardigan looked at Sarlow. The lean-faced detective said:

'Straight, Kid?'

Joey Deth nodded. 'Jeeze – yes,' he said bitterly. 'I'm through.'

Sarlow said: 'Some rotten ones got hurt. And some others that were just pulled in. Maybe Lou Rands was one of those—'

He checked himself. Cardigan swore. Berman pulled on his cigar and frowned.

The Kid said: 'I'm through. Make a fix and I'll clear out – somewhere West—'

Sarlow and Berman looked at Cardigan. The lieutenant of detectives nodded a little.

'We might not get you on the other charges, Kid,' he said. 'And some tough ones are done, out of the game. You gave us a break – and you showed up—'

The Kid was thinking of Bess Grote. Things might have been different, he was thinking. And he knew that Sarlow was thinking of Lou Rands.

'It's a lousy racket – and I'm through,' he said again, slowly. 'That's straight.'

Cardigan said: 'How about Detective Williams? A bullet from that lunch-wagon where Old Andy was found dead has got him in the hospital. He'll live, but—'

Joey Deth cut in. His voice was emotionless.

'Old Andy was trying to get me. I didn't work a rod, Cardigan. I guess you know that. Two mobs hated me a lot – and they got tipped to my talk with Barney Nasser. Maybe Barney wasn't sure about Lou Rands – maybe he thought he was framing him. He tried to get him – and lost out. Rands wanted me, so he tried to frame me. Charlie Gay closed in and mobbed Rands out. I got loose. Bess was playing safe – trying to give me a chance to get in the clear. That's the way I figure it. Charlie used her for his alibi, but she was trying to make things smooth with Gil. She told me she'd seen him. She didn't send me out back – and Gil gave her the dose. That was what I wanted to know – and I figured to shove her killer out. But I guess—'

He stopped. There was a little silence. Berman said:

'The Kid's through, Cardigan. I know when they're through – you can feel it.'

Joey Deth said for the third time: 'It's a lousy racket.'

Cardigan half closed his eyes. He sighed, nodded his head. He picked up the French phone and said in a tired voice:

'Get me the D.A.'s office, will you? Yeah – it's important. It's about – Kid Deth.'

THE SINISTER SPHERE

FREDERICK C. DAVIS

Many writers for the pulps were extremely prolific, as they needed to be with pay rates that commonly were no more than one penny a word, but none more than Frederick C. Davis (1902–1977). He wrote about numerous characters, both under his own name, as Stephen Ransome, and, most famously, the Operator 5 thrillers as Curtis Steele.

In addition to nearly full-length novels, Davis wrote more than a thousand short stories, producing more than a million words a year, but none were more popular than his series about The Moon Man – Stephen Thatcher, the policeman by day and a notorious robber by night.

The son of the police chief, Sergeant Thatcher was utterly dedicated to helping those unable to handle the trials of America's Great Depression, even if it meant breaking the law. In the tradition of Robin Hood, he stole from the wealthy to give to the poor.

To keep his true identity a secret, Thatcher donned the most peculiar disguise in all of pulp fiction – not a mask, but a dome made of highly fragile one-way glass, fitted with a breathing apparatus that filtered air. The glass, known as Argus glass, was manufactured in France and was, at the time, unknown in the United States. As the perpetrator of innumerable crimes, he was the most-hunted criminal in the city, saving lives in equally impressive numbers along the way.

There were thirty-nine adventures about The Moon Man, all published in *Ten Detective Aces* between June 1933 to November 1939. 'The Sinister Sphere' is the first adventure of the character seen by Depression-era readers as a common man who became a hero.

THE SINISTER SPHERE

FREDERICK C. DAVIS

CHAPTER I

THE MOON MAN

It was robbery.

The French door inched open. A figure crept through, into the dark room. It paused.

It turned from side to side, as if looking around, a head that had no eyes, no nose, no mouth! From side to side it turned its head, a head that was a perfect sphere of silver! Mottled black markings covered the shining surface of the ball, reproducing the shaded areas of the full moon whose light streamed in through the windows.

If the silent figure had any face at all, it was the face of the man in the moon!

The silver, spherical head sat low on a pair of broad shoulders from which a long, black cape hung. A pair of black-gloved hands stole through slits in the sides of the cape.

The dark room was not silent. From below came the soft strains of dance music, mingled with laughter and the rhythmic moving of feet on polished floor. It was midnight; the party was at its height. The man whose head was a globe of silver nodded as though pleased.

He glided through the darkness across the room. At an inner door he drifted to a stop. He opened it carefully. The music became louder in the ears of him who had no ears. The hallway outside was empty. The cloaked figure closed the door and turned to the wall.

He removed from its nail a mirror which hung between two doors, and disclosed the circular front of a safe. His black hand twirled the combination dial. He turned his moon head, listening alertly. He heard faint clicks. When he drew up, he turned the handle of the safe door and opened it.

Locks meant little to him.

Into the safe he thrust a black-gloved hand, and brought out a sheaf of banknotes. He drew them inside his cape. He closed the safe and twirled the combination.

Suddenly a loud snap! . . . A flood of light drenched the room.

The figure whirled.

In the doorway stood a woman, her eyes widened with fright. She was forty and fat. She was wearing a spangled gown. Her one bejewelled hand dropped limply from the light-switch. She stood transfixed, staring at the figure with the silver head, and gasped:

'Martin!'

She had no need to call. Her husband was at her back. He stared over her shoulder, as startled as she.

'The Moon Man!' he exclaimed.

The man in the silver mask whirled toward the open French door.

Martin Richmond, clubman, broker, man of position, was wiry and athletic. He leaped past his wife with one bound. He sprang toward the French windows with the intention of blocking the way of the grotesque thief. The Moon Man reached it at the same instant.

Richmond flung up his arms to grapple with the intruder. He groped through empty air. An ebony hand, clenched into a fist, cracked against the point of Richmond's chin.

Richmond staggered, making a desperate attempt to clasp the man with the spherical head. His hand clutched a black one. Another thrust tumbled him backward. Something soft remained in his fingers as he sprawled. The Moon Man darted through the door slamming it shut behind him.

The door opened on a balcony. Beneath it was twenty feet of empty space. The Moon Man leaped over the railing of the balcony, throwing himself into the void.

Martin Richmond scrambled up. From below came a quick, smooth purr. He rushed onto the balcony and looked down. He saw nothing. The Moon Man was gone.

'Call the police!' Richmond gasped as he sprang back into the room.

He jerked to a stop and looked at the thing he had in his hand. It was a black silk glove.

'We've been robbed!'

The words came ringing over the wire into the ear of Detective Lieutenant Gil McEwen. He was perched at his desk, in his tiny office in headquarters. He clamped the receiver tightly to his ear.

'Who's talking?'

'Martin Richmond, Morning Drive. The Moon Man robbed me. He got away!'

'Coming right out!' snapped McEwen.

He slammed the receiver on its hook and whirled in his chair to face a young man who was standing by the window. McEwen's face was hard and wrinkled as old leather; the young man's was smooth-skinned and clean-cut. McEwen's eyes were gray and glittering; the young man's were blue and warm. McEwen was fifty, hardened, by twenty years on the force; the young man was half his age, and had just been made a detective sergeant.

He was Stephen Thatcher, son of Peter Thatcher, the chief of police.

'Steve, it's the Moon Man again!' the veteran detective snapped. 'Come on!'

'I'll be damned!' said Steve Thatcher. 'Can't we do anything to stop his robberies?'

'I'll stop him!' McEwen vowed as he grabbed for the knob. 'I'll stop him if it's the last thing I ever do!'

He went out the office on a run. Steve Thatcher ran after him with long legs flexing lithely. They thumped down the wooden steps. They rushed into the adjoining garage. A moment later they swerved a police-car into the street and dashed away with the speedometer flickering around sixty.

Martin Richmond's residence on Morning Drive was five miles away. Gill McEwen made it in less than five minutes. With Steve Thatcher at his side he hurried to the front door and knocked very urgently. Martin Richmond himself opened it.

The party was still going on. Couples were still dancing in the large room at the right. McEwen saw them through closed French doors, and followed Richmond into the library opposite. Richmond wasted no time.

'My wife found the Moon Man in our room. He'd just finished robbing our safe. It was almost an hour ago.'

'An hour ago? Why didn't you call me sooner?' McEwen snapped. 'By this time he's crawled into a hole somewhere.'

'I found that our phone wires were cut. I stopped to see how much had been stolen. Then I had to find a phone. It took some time to get my neighbors to get up and let me in. I called you as soon as I could.'

'Let me see the bedroom,' McEwen ordered.

He trod up the stairs with Steve Thatcher at his heels. Thatcher could well understand the veteran detective's anger. The Moon Man had done this sort of thing repeatedly. He had committed robberies without number in his characteristic daring, grotesque way.

The papers had been filled with his exploits. The police department had been absolutely unable to find a single clue pointing to his identity. He appeared like magic, robbed, and vanished.

The papers and the police commissioners were howling for an arrest. The public was demanding protection against the mysterious thief. And the police were helpless. Steve Thatcher could well understand why Gill McEwen was in no amiable mood.

McEwen paced about the bedroom. He examined the safe. He looked out the balcony. He ran downstairs and inspected the ground below. He came back red-faced and puffing.

'He used a car. Driveway right below. Stopped the car under the balcony, climbed on the top of it, then swung himself up. Beat it the same way. Not a tire-mark or a footprint! Not one damn' thing to tell who—'

'Look at this!' said Martin Richmond quickly.

He thrust the black silk glove toward McEwen. McEwen took it slowly, narrowed his eyes at it, and passed it to Steve Thatcher.

'I pulled it off his hand as he was rushing out the door,' Richmond explained. 'He—'

'It's a right glove,' McEwen interrupted. 'The chances are he's right-handed. Then he had to use his bare hand to open the door and make a getaway. The means he's probably left a fingerprint on the knob!'

He examined the knob. He could see nothing. Raising, he turned sharply on Steve Thatcher.

'Beat it to a phone and get Kenton up. Tell him we've got to dust this knob right away – can't wait. Get him up here quick!'

Hours later Gil McEwen hunched over his desk in Headquarters peering at a photograph. It was a photograph of a door knob. On the knob was a clearly defined impression of a thumb. It was not the thumb-print of Martin Richmond, nor of Mrs. Richmond, nor of any one else in the burglarized house. McEwen had made sure of that.

It was the thumb-print of the Moon Man!

McEwen settled back in his chair exhaustedly, and peered into the face of Kenton, the fingerprint expert.

'You're absolutely sure that this print doesn't match any in the files?'

'Absolutely sure,' Kenton answered. 'The thumb that made that print has never been recorded by any police department in the United States.'

'Hell!' grunted McEwen. 'Then it can't tell us who the Moon Man is – yet. But when I find a guy whose thumb-print matches up with this one, I'll collar him hard!'

Kenton went out. Steve Thatcher settled into a chair.

'We know, anyway, that the Moon Man is somebody who has no criminal record.'

'Yeah, but he'll soon have! The time's coming when that guy's going to make a slip. When I grab him, he's going up the river on so many counts of robbery that he'll never live to come out of prison. And I'll grab him, all right – I'll do it!'

They looked toward an older man seated beside the desk. He was portly, with a kindly face and curly white hair. He was Chief Peter Thatcher. His were the keen eyes of a born law officer. His was the straight, stern mouth of a strict disciplinarian. He was a good chief, and at present he was a very worried one.

'We've *got* to get the Moon Man, Gil,' he declared. 'We've got to stop at nothing to get him.'

'Listen!' McEwen said sharply. 'I've been on the force twenty years. I've got a reputation. No crook has ever succeeded in getting away from me once I set out on his trail. I went to Brazil to get Doak, didn't I – and I got him. I went to India to get Stephano, and I got him. I'm not going to let any smart aleck Moon Man make a fool out of me. I've sworn to get him, and I will!'

Chief Thatcher nodded slowly. 'The Police Board is clamoring for that bird's hide. So are all the papers. We've got to grab the Moon Man somehow, Gil – and quick.'

'Chief, you've got my promise. I'm not going to stop trying till I've grabbed him. Nothing's going to keep me from it. And when I make a promise, I live up to my word.'

'I know you do,' the chief said soberly. 'I'm depending on you, Gil. It's your case. It's entirely in your hands.'

Steve Thatcher looked solemn.

'I haven't been a detective long enough to be of much help,' he said quietly. 'I wish to gosh I could do more. But you know you can count on me, Gil, for—'

The door opened. A girl came in. She was twenty-two, pretty, animated. Her face resembled Gil McEwen's strongly; she was his daughter. She greeted her father cheerfully, nodded to Chief Thatcher, and went quickly to Steve. She kissed him.

On Sue McEwen's third left finger glittered a solitaire. Steve had put it there. The wedding was not far off.

'Baffled!' she exclaimed, surveying the disgruntled expressions of the three. 'Aren't the papers awful? You'd think the Moon Man was the greatest criminal of the age, the way—'

'He is, as far as I'm concerned!' her father snapped. 'Sue, we're trying to get at the bottom of this thing. We'll see you later.'

'Why chase me out?' Sue asked with a smile. 'Maybe I can help. Perhaps the thing you need is a little womanly intuition.'

'Huh!' said her father. 'You're too eager to mix yourself up in police matters, Sue. I don't think you can be of any help.'

'Don't be so sure,' Sue insisted. 'I would say, for instance, that the Moon Man must be someone far above the level of an ordinary crook. He has more intelligence. He plans his moves cleverly. So far, he has always succeeded in getting what he wants, and making a clean getaway. Going through the Rogue's Gallery would be only a waste of time. The man you want is well-bred, with a fine mind, good manners, and a broad social background.'

'Trying to make a hero of him – a thief?' her father asked skeptically.

'Not at all. After all, he is a thief, and stealing, besides being illegal, is revolting to anyone of sound character. The man deserves all the punishment you want to give him, Dad. I'm only suggesting the kind of a man he is – one whose character has been despoiled by the dishonorable business of robbery. There – have I helped?'

'Not much. Now—'

'How much did he steal this time?'

'Six hundred and fifty dollars.'

'Only six hundred and fifty?' Sue McEwen repeated in surprise. 'Why, that pushes him even lower in the scale of thieves. He's nothing but a petty pilferer!'

The parsonage of the Congregational Church of Great City was located not far from the business district. The Reverend Edward Parker lived there alone. At nine o'clock on the night following the Moon Man's latest exploit he heard a knock at his door. He opened it.

A short, squatty man stood on the step. He had a twisted nose that evidently had once been broken in a fist-fight. He had a cauliflower ear. He had scarcely any neck. He nodded, and handed through the door a sealed envelope.

'From a friend, for the needy of the parish,' he said.

Immediately the Rev. Mr. Parker accepted the envelope, the pugilistic gentleman turned and walked away. The darkness swallowed him up. Dr Parker opened the envelope. Inside it he found a bundle of banknotes. They were bound by a single band of silver paper, and they amounted to $250.

Maude Betts was a widow with no work and three children. She lived in a tenement in the warehouse district of Great City. The stove in the kitchen was cold. There was no food in or on it. Her cupboard was bare. She was about to be evicted by a landlord who declared that the four months' rent, past due, must be paid him at once. She was facing the county poor farm.

A knock sounded at her door. She dried her eyes, opened the door, and found a tough-looking young chap handing her an envelope. She took it as he said: 'From a friend.'

He went away. Mrs. Betts opened the envelope and gasped with joy. From it she removed a pack of banknotes held together by a band of silver paper. They totalled just $200.

Ethel Knapp, twenty and not bad to look at, stood in her furnished room and peered at the gas jet. For ten minutes she had been peering at it, trying to summon the courage necessary to turn it on – without a lighted match above it. She had no money. She had come to Great City from her home in Ohio to work. She had no work. She had no way of returning to her mother and father. But she did have a way of saving herself from further hunger and humiliation. The gas jet.

She raised her hand toward it. Startled, she paused. A faint rustling sound came into the room. Looking down, she saw an envelope creeping under the door. She took it up, bewildered and opened it. Inside lay money – currency held together by a band of silver paper – banknotes totalling $200!

She jerked open the door. The hall was empty. She ran down the steps. She saw a few persons on the street, and paused bewildered. She had no way of knowing that the money had been left her by the squatty, combative-looking young man who was just vanishing around the corner. But that money meant life and happiness to Ethel Knapp. . . .

For the Rev. Edward Parker, $250.
For Maude Betts, $200.
For Ethel Knapp, $200.
Just $650 in all! . . .

CHAPTER II

The Moon Man Speaks

In their delight, neither Dr Parker, nor Mrs. Betts, nor Miss Knapp noticed the oddity of the silver band which encircled the money that had so mysteriously come to them. None of them thought to associate it with the Moon Man.

Had they suspected, they might have thought the stocky chap to be the Moon Man. They would have been wrong.

Ned Dargan, ex-lightweight – he of the broken nose and cauliflower ear – walked along a dark street in a shabby section of the city. He glanced neither right nor left; he walked steadily; he knew where he was going. When he reached the black doorway of an abandoned tenement building – a structure condemned by the city but not yet demolished – he paused.

Making sure he was not observed, he entered the lightless hallway. He closed the door carefully and tightly behind him and trod up a flight of broken, uncarpeted stairs. Plaster littered them. Dust lay everywhere. The air was musty and close. Dargan walked along the upper hall to another door.

As he reached for the knob a voice called:

'Come in, Angel.'

Dargan went in, smiling. The room beyond was dark. A moment passed before his eyes became accustomed to the gloom. Gradually he was able to see a form standing behind a table, a figure that blended out of the blackness like a materializing ghost. The figure was swathed in a black cape. Its head was a smooth globe of silver.

'Evenin', boss,' said Dargan.

A chuckle came from the silver-headed man. 'You've distributed the money, Angel?'

'Yeah. Got it out right away. And it certainly was badly needed, boss.'

'I know. . . . You realize why I selected Martin Richmond as a victim, Angel?'

'I've got an idea he ain't all he seems to be.'

'Not quite that,' answered the voice that came from the silver head. 'He's quite respectable, you know. Social position, wealth, all that. But there's one thing I don't like about him, Angel. He's made millions by playing the market short, forcing prices down.'

'Nothin' wrong in that, is there?' Dargan asked.

'Not according to our standards, Angel; but the fact remains that short-selling had contributed to the suffering of those we are trying to help. I've taken little enough from Richmond's kind, Angel. I must have more – later.'

Dargan peered. 'I don't quite get you, Boss. You're takin' an awful chance – and you don't keep any of the money for yourself.'

A chuckle came from the silver globe. 'I don't want the money for myself. I want it for those who are perishing for want of the barest necessities of life. What would you do if you saw a child about to be crushed under a truck? You'd snatch her away, even at the risk of your own life.

'I can't bear to see suffering, Angel. I can no more help trying to alleviate it than I can help breathing. If there were any other way of taking money from those who hoard it, and giving it to those who desperately need it – if there were any other way than stealing, I'd take that way. But there isn't.'

'Don't think I'm questioning you, boss.' Dargan hastened to explain. 'I'm with you all the way, and you know it.'

'Yes, Angel,' said the Moon Man gently, 'I know it. You're the only man in the world I trust. You know what it is to suffer; that's why you're with me. Well, you've been scouting today. What's the result?'

Dargan wagged his head. 'Things are pretty bad, boss. The regular charities ain't reaching all the folks they should, and they're pretty slow. I don't know what some of these folks would do without your help.

'There's a steamfitter out of a job named Ernest Miller. He's got a daughter, Agnes, who's sick with consumption. The kid's goin' to die if she ain't sent to Arizona. Miller can't send her – he hasn't got any money, boss.'

The Moon Man nodded his silver head. 'Miller shall have money, Angel – all he needs.'

'Then there's the guy named Frank Lauder, I told you about.'

'Lauder will be compensated, Angel.'

'Then there're two kids – Bill and Betty Anderson – a couple of sweet kids they are. Their mother just died. They ain't got nowhere to go but to their aunt and uncle, named Anderson. The Andersons are barely gettin' along as it is, and can't take the kids in. So they'll have to go to an orphanage if somethin' ain't done for 'em.'

'They won't go to the orphanage, Angel. You've done your work well. I'll have money for all of them tomorrow.'

'Tomorrow?' Dargan peered again at the small moon which was the head of the man in the black cape. 'Boss, ain't you takin' an awful chance, followin' up so close? Last night – and now tonight! Ain't it gettin' dangerous?'

There was a pause. 'Yes, Angel, it is getting dangerous. The police now have my thumb-print.'

'Your thumb-print! Holy cripes! Now if they ever catch you they'll be able to prove you—'

'I don't think it will occur to Gil McEwen to look in the right place for me, Angel!' the Moon Man interrupted with a soft laugh. 'Still, as you suggest, I've got to be very careful. At any time McEwen might accidentally find a print which matches the one he found on the Richmond bedroom door-knob last night – and when he does—'

'Cripes, boss!' gasped Dargan.

The Moon Man straightened. 'Don't worry, Angel. Keep an eye on yourself. Report back to me tomorrow night, half an hour after midnight, here. All clear?'

'Sure, boss.'

Ned Dargan turned from the room. He closed the door tightly on the Moon Man. He peered at the panel, as though trying to penetrate it with his gaze and read the secret of the man in the room – a secret even he did not know. He walked down the stairs slowly, and eased out the front door.

'I can't figure out *who* that guy is!' he told himself wonderingly. 'But, cripes! I know he's the swellest guy that ever lived!'

Ned Dargan had a solid reason for feeling as he did about the man whose face he had never seen – the Moon Man. He'd gone bad in the ring. A weakened arm made further fighting impossible. He found it just as impossible to find work. He'd drifted downward and outward; he'd become a bum, sleeping in alleys, begging food. Until, mysteriously a message had come to him from the Moon Man.

Some day Ned Dargan was going to fight again. Some day he was going to get into the ring, knock some palooka for a row, and become champ. And if he ever did, he'd have the Moon Man to thank for it. . . .

The Moon Man stood in the center of the dismal room. He watched Dargan close the door. He listened, and in a moment heard a creak, then another. He knew those sounds the stairs made. The first was pitched at A Flat and the second at B in the musical scale. When B sounded before A Flat, someone was coming up. The Moon Man heard B follow A Flat and knew that Dargan was gone.

He turned away, opened a connecting door, and stepped into an adjoining room. He turned a key in the lock. The air was pitch black. The Moon Man made motions which divested himself of his cape. He pulled off his black gloves – luckily he had provided himself with more than one pair. He removed from his head that silver sphere, and he put all his secret regalia in a closet. The closet door he also locked.

Turning again, he silently opened a window, and eased out onto a rusted fire-escape. Rung by rung he let himself down into the alleyway behind. He paused, listening and looking around. Then he stepped forth. . . .

The street-light's glow fell into the face of Stephen Thatcher!

Steve Thatcher thought of things as he walked away from the house he had made the Moon Man's rendezvous. In his mind's ear he heard Gil McEwen saying: 'I've sworn to get the Moon Man, and I will!' McEwen, the toughest detective on the force, who never failed to bag his man!

And he heard the voice of the girl he loved: 'He's nothing but a petty pilferer!'

Steve Thatcher lowered his head as though stubbornly to butt an obstacle. A wild scheme – his! He knew it. But, also, he knew the world – cruel and relentless – and he could not stand by and do nothing to save those who were suffering. The mere thought of letting others perish, while nothing was done to save them, was unendurable.

He was a cop's son – revolt against injustice was in his blood – and not even the law could keep him from trying to right the wrongs he knew existed. Beyond the written law was a higher one to which Steve Thatcher had dedicated himself – the law of humanity.

And if he were caught? Would he find leniency at the hands of Gil McEwen and Chief Thatcher? No. He was certain of that. Even if McEwen and the chief might wish to deal kindly with him, they would be unable to. The Moon Man now was a public enemy – his fate was in the hands of the multitude. Steve Thatcher would be dealt with like any common crook – if he were caught.

He remembered Ernest Miller's daughter, who must go to Arizona or die; he remembered Frank Lauder, who must be cared for; he remembered Bill and Betty Anderson, who must have help.

'It's got to be done!' he said through closed teeth. 'Damn, it's *got* to be done!'

He walked swiftly through the night.

CHAPTER III

Another Victim!

Detective Lieutenant Gil McEwen's phone clattered. He took it up. He glared at a photograph he was holding – a photograph of the Moon Man's fingerprint – and grunted: 'Hello!'

'Detective McEwen? Listen carefully. I'm calling—'

'Speak louder!' McEwen snapped. 'I can't hear you.'

'My name is Kent Atwell, Mr. McEwen,' the voice came more plainly. 'I'm phoning you from a pay-station downtown because I don't dare phone you from my home. I've been threatened – by the Moon Man.'

'What!' barked McEwen. He knew the name of Kent Atwell. Atwell was one of Great City's most prominent citizens. His home was one of the finest. His influence went far. And here he was, huddling in a booth downtown like a rabbit in a hole, using a public phone because a threat of the Moon Man had filled him with fright! 'The devil!' McEwen said.

'I've got to see you, Mr. McEwen – immediately. The Moon Man has threatened to rob me tonight. I don't dare let you come to my home, or my office. Can I meet you somewhere?'

'Where are you?'

'In a drug store at State and Main streets.'

'You're close to the Palace Theatre,' McEwen said briskly. 'Buy a ticket and go in. Go down into the men's room – be there in ten minutes. I'm coming right along, and I'll meet you there.'

'Certainly. Thank you!'

McEwen pushed the phone back and scowled. He tramped out of his office into Chief Thatcher's. He found the chief absent, but Steve Thatcher was sitting in his father's old padded chair. The young man looked up.

'You come with me, Steve!' McEwen snapped. 'This thing is getting worse and worse! The Moon Man's going to stage another robbery – and this time he's saying so ahead of time!'

'I'll be damned!' said Steve Thatcher. 'Listen, Gil. I've just found out—'

'Never mind! Come with me!'

McEwen went out the door. Steve Thatcher frowned; but he followed. He loped down the steps, crowded into a police-car beside McEwen, and said nothing until the car was whizzing down the street.

'Of all the damned gall!' the veteran detective blurted. 'Sending a warning ahead of time! He must think he's living a charmed life – that we can never touch him. I'll show him where he's wrong – then, by damn, he'll wish he was on the moon!'

Steve Thatcher sighed. 'I was about to tell you, Gil, that I think I've found out about this mask the Moon Man wears. You've wondered how he could see his way about, with a silver globe on his head. Well, evidently he can, because the thing isn't silver at all, but glass.'

'Glass?' McEwen repeated. 'How do you know?'

'It must be. That mask of the Moon Man's has made us all curious, and I began trying to figure out how he could manage to move about with his head completely enclosed in a metal ball. Well, he can't, of course. I browsed around the library today, and found the answer – Argus glass.'

'What's Argus glass?'

Steve Thatcher smiled. 'If you were a frequenter of speakeasies in New York, you'd know. Argus glass is named for the son of the mythological god, Zeus. Argus had a countless number of eyes, and some of them were always open and watching, so the legend goes. Argus glass is a mirror when you look at it from one side, and a perfectly clear piece of glass when you see it from the other.'

'Didn't know there was any such thing!' McEwen snapped, sending the car swerving around a corner.

'Nor I, until I read about it. A big French jeweller's store has in it several pillars of the glass. They look like mirrors to the customers, but they're not. They're hollow, and inside them sit detectives on revolving chairs. They can see everything that goes on in the store, but no one can see them. It wasn't so long ago that speakeasy proprietors found out about the glass. They use it in their doors now instead of peep-holes. Nobody can see in, but they can see out.'

'Say! Maybe we can learn who the Moon Man is by tracing that glass globe!' McEwen exclaimed. 'Who makes the glass?'

'The Saint Gobain Company of France. Argus glass is the answer, Gil. The Moon Man can see as clearly as though he wasn't masked at all, but nobody can see his face. His mask must be split down the middle so he can get his head into it, and he's evidently painted the mirror surface to look like a moon.'

'By damn!' McEwen declared. 'Just let me get within reach of that guy and I'll take a whack at that glass mask. It'll turn into splinters and then we'll see who the Moon Man is!'

Stephen Thatcher smiled. He had not thought of that likelihood. A sharp blow would shatter the globe that masked the face of the Moon Man! . . . His smile faded. He was almost sorry now that he had divulged the secret. He had told McEwen this only because he was supposed to be working on the case and, to safeguard himself from suspicion, had decided that he had better make some discovery about himself.

'No kidding, Gil,' he said quietly. 'Aren't you keeping something back? Haven't you some idea who the Moon Man is?'

'Not a damn' notion!' McEwen declared. 'How about you, Steve? Who do you think he is?'

'I,' said Steve Thatcher with a sigh, 'couldn't say.'

McEwen parked the police car a block from the Palace Theatre. He strode to the ticket-booth with Steve Thatcher; they bought tickets and went in. Immediately they turned toward the downstairs men's room. They entered it to find Kent Atwell waiting.

Atwell was thin, dapper; his eyes were dark and deep-set. And at the moment he was visibly agitated. When McEwen identified himself, he immediately launched into a frightened, indignant explanation of the Moon Man's threat.

'Here!' he exclaimed, pushing a sheet of crumpled paper toward McEwen. 'Read that! The incredible presumption of it!'

The bit of paper was torn irregularly at the bottom. It was typewritten – done, McEwen could not dream, on a machine in police headquarters! Its message was terse:

DEAR MR ATWELL:

Withdraw from your bank today the sum of five thousand dollars. Place it in a safe in your home. I intend to call for it tonight. Let me warn you that if you notify the police of my intentions, you will suffer worse punishment than death. That is my promise to you.

McEwen looked blank. 'How do you know this is from the Moon Man?' he asked sharply. 'Where's the rest of it – the part that is torn off?'

Atwell turned pale. 'It's of no importance – just the typewritten signature. I accidentally tore it off and lost the piece, so—'

McEwen gestured impatiently. 'Mr. Atwell, I beg your pardon, but it is my business to know when men are telling the truth. You are not being frank with me. There was more of this message – and if I'm to help you, I've got to have it.'

'Really, there—'

'Unless you produce it right now, Mr. Atwell, you can count on no help from me,' McEwen snapped.

Atwell sighed. He fumbled in his pocket. McEwen quickly took the bit of paper he produced – the lower half of the sheet he had already read. And he scanned a second paragraph:

What do I mean by a 'worse punishment than death?' I mean disgrace and humiliation, the loss of your friends and position, becoming a pariah. I know that, while you were handling the drive for money under the United Charities, you as the treasurer of the organization helped yourself to five thousand dollars of the funds. I can and will produce proof of my statement if circumstances demand it. It is that stolen five thousand I want. You will leave it for me in your safe, as I direct, and make no move to interfere with my taking it – or I will give the facts to the newspapers.

MM

McEwen peered at Kent Atwell. 'Is this true?' he demanded sharply.

'Certainly not! There is not a particle of fact in what is written there. I preferred not to let you see that paragraph, because it is all so preposterous. I refuse to be mulcted out of money that is rightfully mine, and I'm asking you to do something to protect me from this maniac who calls himself the Moon Man.'

'I can't do a damned thing until he shows up and tries to rob you,' McEwen answered. 'He says he'll come tonight. Is there some way of my getting into your house without being seen?'

'Yes. I can tell you how. But am I to deliberately wait for him to come and—'

'If I may suggest it, Mr. Atwell,' Steve Thatcher spoke up quietly, 'you had better follow the Moon Man's directions to the letter. Get the money from the bank and put it in your safe as he directs. If he suspects that you're laying a trap for him, he may not show up; but if you appear to be acting in good faith, we may stand a chance of grabbing him.'

'Exactly. He seems to know everything and be everywhere,' McEwen agreed. 'If he learns, somehow, that you haven't been at your bank today to withdraw that sum, he may stay in hiding. Our only chance of getting him is to have that money in the house – as bait.'

Steve Thatcher smiled.

'But what,' said Kent Atwell, 'but what if your precautions fail, and the money is stolen regardless and—'

'You'll have to take that chance. This is an opportunity to grab the Moon Man tonight. If we don't make the most of it, he'll get you in some other way, and you'll be helpless.' Gil McEwen fixed the gentleman with a stern eye. 'If you have no faith in what I'm suggesting, you shouldn't have come to the police, Mr. Atwell.'

'Yes, yes – I agree!' Atwell answered. 'I will go to the bank immediately. I'll take the money home and put it in the safe. And you—'

'We'll come to your house tonight, after dark. I'll have enough men with me so that there'll be no chance of the Moon Man's escaping if he comes after that money. I'll phone you beforehand, to make arrangements.'

'I'll follow your instructions to the letter.'

Kent Atwell fumbled with his gloves and left. McEwen and Steve Thatcher waited a few minutes, then hurried from the theatre. McEwen's face was twisted into a grimace of distaste.

'I half believe that what the Moon Man wrote about Atwell is the truth,' he said. 'Damn – who is that crook, anyway? How can he know so much?' He started along the street at a stiff pace. 'Tonight, Steve – tonight, unless something goes very wrong – I'll grab him!'

'Where're you heading, Gil?' Steve Thatcher asked quickly.

'I'm going to send a cable to the Saint Gobain factory in France. I'm going to find out who they made that glass mask for!'

Steve Thatcher's eyes twinkled. Again – unseen by the veteran detective – he smiled.

Outside the windows of Police Chief Thatcher's office hung veils of darkness. Inside, lights burned brilliantly. Detective Lieutenant Gil McEwen stood in the center of the room, facing a group of six men who had just entered in answer to his call. Each of the six was a plainclothes man.

'I've just made arrangements with Atwell,' McEwen was saying, crisply. 'We're going to slip into his house so we won't be seen, in case someone is watching. We're going to be damned careful about that. You're to follow my orders strictly, and be ready to leave here as soon as I say the word.'

McEwen had chosen his men well. Each of the six was an old-timer on the force. Each had demonstrated, in the headquarters target gallery, that he was a dead shot. Each possessed a record of courage and daring.

As McEwen talked to them, the door of the chief's office opened quietly. Sue McEwen sidled in, stood aside, and listened with intense interest. His eyes strayed to those of Steve Thatcher, who was standing beside his father's desk; they exchanged a smile.

'This is our chance,' McEwen declared to his men. 'We've got to make it good. If the Moon Man gets away from us tonight, God only knows if we'll ever grab him. Wait downstairs.'

The six men turned and filed from the office. McEwen paced across the rug. Steve Thatcher looked thoughtful. The chief of police sighed and wagged his head.

'You're all set, Gil?' Chief Thatcher asked.

'Yeah. You wait right by that phone, chief, in case of an emergency. And I hope when I phone you it will be to say we've got our man.'

Sue McEwen stepped toward her father eagerly. 'How soon are you leaving, dad? I wouldn't miss this for anything.'

McEwen stared at her. 'You're not getting in on this, young lady!'

'Why not?' Sue asked. 'If I go to the house with you it won't do any harm, and I may be able to help. As long as I'm a detective's daughter, I want to make the most of it.'

'How many times have I got to tell you, Sue,' her father sighed, 'that this sort of thing is not for you? We've argued about it a thousand times. I won't let you mix yourself up in police matters.'

'You forget,' Sue answered, smiling, 'that I gave you the tip that helped send John Hirch, the forger, to prison. And didn't I figure out where Mike Opple was hiding after he killed his woman? I don't think I'm so bad at this. If you'll give me a chance tonight—'

'Nothing doing!' Gil McEwen snapped. 'You go home and go to bed!'

'Dad,' said Sue indignantly, 'I'm not a child. I'm perfectly able to take care of myself. This Moon Man fascinates me, and I'm going to—'

'I think your dad's right, Sue,' Steve Thatcher interrupted gently. 'You'd better leave this to us. There's no telling what will happen.'

Sue raised her chin defiantly. 'It's going to take more than an argument to stop me this time. I—'

The telephone jangled. Gil McEwen snatched the instrument off the chief's desk. A voice twanged into his ear:

'This is Preston, downstairs, McEwen. You told me to let you know if a message came for you. There's one coming in now!'

'Be right down!' McEwen answered quickly. He dropped the telephone and hurried to the door. 'Answer to my cable coming in over the teletype!' he exclaimed as he hurried out.

*

Steve Thatcher's eyes brightened. He hastened out the door after McEwen. They jumped down the stairs side by side, paced along the brick corridor, and squeezed into a little room. Inside it was a sergeant, a battery of telephones, a short-wave radio receiving set, and a teletype machine. The teletype was clicking and spinning out its yellow ribbon.

McEwen leaned over it and read the words as they formed:

Police Headquarters Great City – Argus Glass Sphere Shipped to Gilbert McEwen General Delivery Great City – St Gobain.

'By damn!' gasped McEwen.

He tore the strip out of the machine. He glared at it. He said unprintable things.

'By damn! He ordered that mask under *my name!*'

Steve Thatcher's eyes were twinkling. He had known what this cable would say. He had planned for this exigency. And he was enjoying the veteran detective's discomfiture.

'Looks suspicious, Gil,' he remarked. '*You're* not the Moon Man, are you?'

'Yah!' snarled McEwen. 'He's smart, isn't he? He's clever! Pulling a stunt like that – getting his damn' glass mask made under my name! Wait'll I get my hands on that guy!'

Steve Thatcher chuckled in spite of himself.

McEwen squeezed out of the teletype room. He hurried down the corridor to a door which opened into a larger room. His six detectives were there, perched on and around a table usually devoted to pinochle.

'Come on!' he snapped. 'We're going!'

The six men began trooping after McEwen. Steve Thatcher followed the veteran detective a few steps.

'You've got all your car will carry, Gil. I'd better follow you in mine. I'll be along in a minute.'

McEwen nodded his agreement and pushed through a big door into the adjoining garage, with the six following him. Steve Thatcher looked up and saw Sue McEwen coming down the stairs. He turned to her.

'I want to come with you, Steve,' she said.

'Darling, I'm sorry. I'll phone you as soon as there's news.'

'But, Steve—'

He did not wait to listen. He did not like this insistence of Sue's. It emphasized in his mind the painful disaster that would surely follow if it were ever learned that he, Steve Thatcher, son of the chief of police, was the Moon Man. He hurried out the entrance, turned sharply, and went into a drug store on the corner.

He slipped into a phone-booth and called a number which was unlisted in the directory, unobtainable by anyone, known to none save him and one other.

Two miles away, in the maze of the city, a phone rang. A stocky, broken-nosed young man picked it up. He heard a voice say over the wire:

'Hello, Angel.'

'Hello, boss.'

'Listen carefully. I want you to leave the car in front of the home of Kent Atwell at exactly five minutes before midnight tonight.'

'Sure, boss.'

'Don't wait. Take a taxi back. Leave the car right in front of the house, and make sure nobody sees you do it. I'll meet you at the usual place thirty-five minutes later.'

'Right, Boss.'

'Wish me luck, Angel.'

Then the line went dead.

CHAPTER IV

The Trap Is Set

Nine o'clock. A sedan buzzed past the front of the home of Kent Atwell. It rolled on smoothly and turned at the next corner. Halfway down the block it turned again, swinging into the driveway of a dark house. It paused in front of the garage; and out of it climbed Gil McEwen and his six detectives.

Standing silent in the darkness, they waited. A moment later another car turned from the street and crept into the driveway. It braked behind the sedan. Steve Thatcher climbed out of it and walked to Gil McEwen's side.

No one spoke. Leading the way, McEwen strode past the garage and pushed his way through a high hedge. Steve Thatcher followed, and the six men. They walked silently across the rear of an adjoining estate, and paused at a gate in the hedge. They listened a moment, then eased through.

They drifted like shadows to the rear of the home of Kent Atwell. McEwen knocked softly at the door. It opened; no light came out. McEwen, Thatcher and the six men entered. Kent Atwell closed the door, turned, and led them into a spacious library.

'Okay,' said McEwen without formality. 'You alone, Atwell?'

'Yes,' said the gentleman. 'My wife is away, and I've given the servants the night off.'

'Place all locked up?'

'Every door except the front, and every window. All the blinds are drawn.'

'Money in the safe?'

'Yes.'

Atwell crossed the room to a stack of bookshelves. From one the height of his head he removed a unit of four thick volumes. In the wall behind shone the front of a circular safe.

'Locked?' McEwen asked.

'No,' Kent answered as he replaced the books.

'Good. Now.' The detective turned. 'We're all going to keep out of sight and wait. First thing, I want to make sure there's only one way for the Moon Man to get in – the front door. Steve, take a quick look around, will you – upstairs and down.'

Steve Thatcher circled the library, and made sure every window was locked. Stepping into the rear hallway, he determined that the bolt was in place. In the other rear rooms he repeated his examination; then he climbed the steps to the second floor and entered, in turn, each of the bedrooms. McEwen, listening, heard him moving about. In a moment Steve returned.

'All set,' he announced.

'Good. Where in this room can I keep out of sight, Atwell?'

Again Atwell crossed the room. He opened a door and disclosed a closet space behind it. It offered a large, comfortable hiding-place to McEwen. The detective nodded.

'Mr. Atwell, I want you to go upstairs and prepare for bed. Pretend that you are alone. I'm going to put a man in every room upstairs and down. Every window will be watched, and every door, in case the Moon Man tries something tricky. I'm going to stay here in the library and watch the safe. Understand?'

They understood.

McEwen signalled two of his men. He conducted them across the vestibule and into the two rooms on the opposite side of the house. Stationing one man in each, he closed the doors and went up the stairs with the others following. He waited until Kent Atwell went into the master bedroom, then assigned one man to each of the remaining rooms on the second floor.

Five doors opened. Five doors closed. Behind each of them a detective began to wait. Behind one of them Steve Thatcher listened.

He heard Gil McEwen go downstairs.

McEwen stepped into the library. He closed its doors. He strode to the safe, opened it, reached inside, and removed a thick pack of banknotes. He counted them – five thousand dollars. He put them back and closed the safe.

From his pocket he removed his service automatic. He examined it very intently. Crossing the room, he opened the closet door, moved a chair inside. Stepping in, he swung the door until it was within an inch of being closed. He sat, with his automatic in his hand, and waited.

The house was utterly silent.

The vigil had begun.

An hour passed.

Another.

Silently an automobile turned the corner of the street on which the Atwell mansion sat. Its lights were dimmed. It drew to the curb near the corner and its light went out. A hand reached for the ignition switch and clicked it off. The hand was that lovely one of Miss Sue McEwen.

The young lady settled down in the cushions and looked reprovingly at the Atwell residence. Its windows were dark, save for a few chinks of light shining through the draperies on one side of the lower floor. Inside, Sue McEwen knew were her father and her fiancé and six detectives and an intended victim of the Moon Man. Inside, she knew, interesting things were almost sure to happen. She said to herself in a whisper:

'I *won't* be left out!'

She opened her handbag. From it she removed a tiny automatic. It was a fancy little thing, with handle of mother-of-pearl; but it was deadly. In the hand of an expert shot it could spout death. Sue McEwen, by dint of long and arduous practice in her own back yard, under the guidance of her father, was by way of being an expert shot.

The minutes crept past.

A quarter of twelve.

The determined young lady looked and listened and waited.

Five minutes of twelve.

A soft whirr came from behind Sue McEwen's parked roadster. She did not stir, but through the corners of her eyes she saw a coupé swing into the street. Its lights were out. It rolled along without a sound. And that, thought Miss McEwen, was strange.

The lightless car eased to a stop directly in front of the Kent Atwell home. One of its doors opened. A black figure stepped out of it and began to walk toward the farther corner. When it was halfway there another sound came from behind Sue McEwen. A second car – this time with its headlamps on and making no attempt to be quiet – purred past her. It was a taxi. It spurted toward the far corner and stopped.

The squatty young man climbed into it. The cab started up again. It swung around the corner and disappeared.

'I,' said Sue McEwen to herself suddenly, 'am going to see what that's all about!'

She started her engine. She spurted away from the curb – her tiny automatic lying in her lap – and eased past the dark car parked in front of the Atwell home. Should she get out and look it over? No; that would take time, and she wanted to follow that taxi; it might get away from her if she stopped now. She stepped on the gas.

At the next corner she swung left. And there, two blocks ahead, she saw the red tail-light of the taxi gleaming.

She followed it. It drove straight on. It was going toward the central business district of Great City. Just this side of the main thoroughfare it turned. When she reached that corner Sue McEwen also turned. For a moment the taxi was out of sight, but she picked it up again immediately. She was keeping well behind it. She was taking no chances.

'Something,' she thought, 'is up.'

The taxi went on. Sue McEwen went on. The two cars, separated by two blocks, turned into a route that took them around the nocturnally popular section of the city. Presently the taxi was rolling into a region that gave Sue McEwen some uneasiness. It was dark, lonely, dangerous; and, after all, she was alone.

But she kept following that taxi. And suddenly she saw it stop.

It paused just past an intersection. The young chunky fare got out and paid the driver. Sue McEwen could not see his face. A moment later the taxi spurted off and, at the next corner, swung out of sight. The young man walked along the black street, turned and entered a 'dog cart' in the middle of the block.

From the tower of the City Hall came the reverberations of a striking gong. The town clock was striking. It tolled twelve.

What, Sue McEwen wondered, was happening back in the Kent Atwell house? She could not guess. She wanted to keep an eye on that strange young man.

She drew to the curb, cut the ignition, and blinked off her dimmers. She waited. For twenty minutes she waited. And at the end of that time her quarry came out of the lunch cart and began walking away.

She started after him, cautiously. She saw him turn the corner. As she rounded the corner, she saw the young man make a quick move and disappear.

She saw that he had gone into the black doorway of an empty tenement.

She stopped. She got out of the car and, keeping in the deep darkness which flanked the buildings, slowly worked her way toward that doorway. It was empty now. The young man had gone inside. She listened and heard nothing. With the utmost care she eased the door open an inch and peered through. She saw nothing.

Then, taking a tight grip on her little automatic, she crept in.

The house was a black tomb – silent. She stood still until her eyes became accustomed to the darkness. Gradually she saw the details of a staircase leading to the second floor. She moved toward it. She went up the steps, one after another. And suddenly she stopped.

A board creaked under her foot.

Ned Dargan stood stock still in the darkness of the room which was the rendezvous of the Moon Man. He had heard that creak. A second later he heard another. His hand slipped into his coat pocket and came out grasping a gun. He turned slowly.

Stealing toward the closed door which communicated with the hallway, he listened. He heard no sound now. He wondered if the creaks had been caused by the loose boards warping back into place after being strained by his own weight. He decided he had better make sure. He opened the door stealthily, and stepped into the hallway.

Every nerve alert, he walked to the head of the stairs. He went down them slowly. The boards creaked again as he crossed them. He went on.

Again those sounds served as a signal. Sue McEwen heard them. She was hidden behind the door of a room directly across from that which Ned Dargan had just left. Realizing that the creaking of the board under her feet might have been heard, she had hastened along the hallway and slipped into the front room just as Dargan had opened the rear one. Now, seeing the way clear, she crept back into the hall.

She crossed it. She opened the door of the room which Dargan had left – the hidden headquarters of the Moon Man. She slipped inside and looked around. It was bare. It was musty. It looked unpromising; but Sue McEwen was tantalized by the mystery of what was happening.

She gasped. From the hallway again came creaks. The man she had seen enter the house was returning to the upper hallway. Even as she turned, Sue McEwen heard his step toward the door she had just entered.

She turned quickly away from that door. She hurried across to another, which apparently communicated with a room beyond; but it balked her. It was locked. She whirled again. In a corner she saw a closet. She jerked open its door. It was empty. She sidled inside and closed the door upon herself.

At that instant she heard a step in the room. The man had come back. He was standing within a few yards of her now – unaware of her presence. She stood straight, her tiny automatic leveled. She was determined to wait – and listen – and learn.

Now she was going to see what connection all this had with the Moon Man. Now, perhaps, she might even learn who the Moon Man was.

CHAPTER V

In Dead of Night

Faintly the sound of a tolling gong came into the library of Kent Atwell. Twelve slow strikes – midnight.

Gil McEwen, hidden in the closet, heard the trembling beats. Steve Thatcher, in a room directly above, listened to them and smiled.

He silently opened the door of the bedroom which had been assigned to him. He stepped into the hallway and closed the door behind him. Along each wall of the hall was a row of such doors, all closed. Behind one of them was Kent Atwell himself. Behind the others were detectives.

Steve Thatcher crept to the nearest door. Beneath its knob the handle of a key protruded – outward. Very slowly he turned it – without a sound. And he smiled. While making the rounds of the house he had carefully removed the keys from the inside of the bedroom doors and placed them on the outside. He passed up and down the hallway silently as a ghost. At each door he turned a key.

Now one millionaire and four detectives were securely locked in their rooms – and did not know it!

Steve Thatcher crept down the front stairs into the vestibule. Again he locked a door and imprisoned another detective. He crept to the rear hallway and made a captive of another sleuth. So far he had contrived to imprison every man save Gil McEwen.

Steve Thatcher drew the bolt of the rear entrance, slipped outside, and hurried toward the street. At the car left by Gargan, he stopped. He unlocked the rumble compartment and from it removed a black bundle. Then, quickly, he returned to the rear door of the house.

Pausing, he drew on his long, black cloak and pulled on his black silk gloves. He placed on his head the glass mask modeled as a moon. It was padded inside so that it sat firmly on his head. A deflecting plate, which came into position over his nose and mouth, sent his breath downward and out, so that it would not fog the glass and blind him. He was ready.

He stealthily opened the rear door and let himself in. Through the glass he could see as clearly as though there was nothing on his head. He trod up the rear stairs, along the hallway, then down the front flight into the vestibule. Outside the unlocked door of the library he paused.

Gil McEwen, he knew, was inside – waiting.

The Moon Man laid his black hand on the knob of the library door. He twisted it. He eased the door open and peered through the narrow crack. Within six feet of him, though unseen, sat Gil McEwen.

McEwen's closet door was partly open, but he could see only the wall opposite, the wall in which the safe was set. He could not see the door opening slowly under pressure of the Moon Man's hand. He heard not the slightest sound. The Moon Man drifted into the room.

The black-cloaked figure flattened itself against the wall. It moved toward the closet door with one arm outstretched. The other arm also moved – toward a light chair. The Moon Man picked it up. His body tensed.

Suddenly he sprang. He struck the closet door and slammed it shut. Instantly he braced the chair under the knob. A startled cry came from behind the door. The knob rattled. From inside McEwen pushed – hard. The door would not open. The tilted chair wedged it firmly in place.

'By damn!' rang through the panels.

The Moon Man turned away quickly as the door shook. McEwen was throwing himself against it. From the black space within came another muffled cry:

'Get him! Carter! Landon! Winninger! Carpen! Go after him!'

The sound of McEwen's furious voice carried through the walls. Quick movements sounded upstairs. Knobs rattled. Across the lower hallway two more knobs rattled. Upstairs and down six imprisoned detectives and one imprisoned millionaire cursed.

And the Moon Man chuckled.

Suddenly the report of a gun blasted with a hollow sound. Splinters flew from a panel of McEwen's closet. A bullet hissed across the room and shattered a window pane on the opposite side. The shattered glass fell very close to the position of the wall-safe.

'No use, McEwen!' the man in the silver mask exclaimed. 'I've already got it!'

McEwen snarled; and he did not fire again. He flung himself against the door. It literally bulged under the impact of his body. The Moon Man heard the wood of the chair crack. He hurried to the wall-safe.

He grasped the four books and flung them away. He snapped open the door of the safe. He snatched out the sheaf of banknotes. They disappeared through a slit in the side of his cape.

The closet door thumped again. This time it gave a little more. Upstairs men were pounding and cursing. Bedlam filled the house. And once more McEwen crashed against the inside of the closet door.

The Moon Man hurried into the vestibule. He jerked open the front door and sped along the walk to the street. He ducked behind the car and with quick movements divested himself of his costume. Cloak, gloves and glass mask went into the rumble compartment. The next instant Steve Thatcher's hands went to the wheel.

A shot rang sharply near the house. A bullet whizzed through the air. Steve Thatcher jerked a glance backward to see one of the lower windows opening, and a plain-clothes man leaping through – after him. Steve's motor roared. He slammed into gear and spurted away.

Another shot. Another. Then Steve Thatcher sent the coupé swerving around the corner – and he was out of range.

In the library a splintering crash sounded. A panel of the closet door cracked out under the terrible impact of Gil McEwen's hard shoulder. He reached through the opening, snatched the chair away, slammed out.

He heard the shots outside the house. He went out the front door at almost a single leap. The plainclothes man with the smoking gun saw him and shouted:

'He's getting away in that car!'

McEwen whirled like a top. He sped toward the edge of the Atwell grounds and crashed through the hedge with a flying leap. As fast as his legs could swing he ran toward the driveway in which the police cars had been left. There he stopped short and cursed.

The sedan was farthest back in the driveway. Steve Thatcher's roadster was behind it, blocking the way out! McEwen hurried to it – and saw that the ignition was locked! He spun back furiously, slipped behind the wheel of the sedan, and started the motor. With an utter disregard for law and garden, he spurted off around the opposite side of the house, jounced off the curb, twisted the wheel madly, and pressed the gas pedal against the floorboards.

The tires whined as he wrenched the car around the corner. Far away he saw a gleam of red – the tail-light of another car traveling at high speed. McEwen's eyes narrowed shrewdly. At the next corner he turned again; at the next, again. Running then along a street parallel with the fleeing coupé, he let the motor out.

He did not slow for intersections. He slowed for nothing. With the car traveling at its fastest, he plunged along the street. McEwen knew the fleeing coupé could not long keep up its break-neck speed. It must surely slow down to pass through the streets near the business center, or suffer the shots of a traffic policeman. Moreover, the city narrowed like a bottle's neck toward the river. If the fugitive coupé went on, it must soon reach the bridge.

McEwen had the advantage. No traffic officer would try to stop or shoot at his police car. Deliberately he sent the sedan catapulting through the very center of Great City, its horn blaring. Lights flashed past. Other cars scurried for the curb. Pedestrians fled to the sidewalks. In a matter of seconds McEwen had put the congested district behind him and was racing toward the bridge.

Within a block of it, where two streets intersected in a V, he turned back. He knew that he was ahead of the coupé now. He shot to the next intersection and looked up and down the cross street. The same at the next, and the next. There was no place the coupé could escape him now if it stayed in the open. Sooner or later he was sure to see it.

Soon he did!

Glancing along a dark street lined by warehouses and shabby tenements, he saw a pair of headlights blink out. Instantly McEwen shut off his own, and stopped. He saw a coupé, two blocks ahead. He saw a dark figure climb out of it, turn, and hurry back along the street. He watched with eyes as keen as an eagle's – and saw the dark figure slip into an alleyway.

McEwen got out of his car. He gripped his automatic tightly and began running through the shadows toward the alleyway. When he reached it he paused.

One second before Gil McEwen glanced down the dark alleyway, Steve Thatcher lowered the rear window on the second floor of the abandoned tenement. A quick climb up the rusty fire escape had brought him to it. In the darkness of the bare room he turned, lowering a dark bundle to the floor.

A moment later Steve Thatcher had vanished; the Moon Man had appeared.

He stepped to the closet and opened it. By the glow of a flashlight he worked quickly. He separated the sheaf of banknotes into three parcels. Each he fastened together with a band of silver paper. He snapped off the flash and turned to the connecting door.

He unlocked it. Slowly he went into the room. Ned Dargan turned at his approach. The Moon Man moved toward the table. From his one black-gloved hand dropped the four packets of currency.

'There you are, Angel.'

Dargan silently took up the money. He blinked; he thrust it into his pocket.

'Boss,' he said, 'I'm worried.'

'Why?'

'Just after I came into this place a little while ago, somebody followed me.'

'Who?'

'I don't know. I heard the stairs creak. I went down to look around, but I didn't find anybody. Cripes, boss, I don't like it!'

'Nor I, Angel. I've an idea that in future we must be more careful. You had better stop delivering the money personally – send it by messenger. And we'd better change our headquarters. I'll phone you, Angel – about a new place.'

The muffled voice broke off. The silver-masked head came up. Ned Dargan's breath went sibilantly into his lungs.

From the hallway came a creak!

Then another!

'Somebody's comin' up!' gasped Dargan.

The Moon Man moved. He rounded the table, crossed to the door. With a quick motion he shot a bolt in place.

'Out the rear window, Angel – quick!'

Ned Dargan hesitated. 'Say, listen! I ain't goin' to skip and leave you to face the music alone! I'm in this as much as you are, Boss!'

'Angel, yours is a true heart. But get out that window right now! I'll take care of myself.'

The Moon Man's voice rang commandingly. Dargan did not hesitate again. He hurried into the adjoining room. He slid up the window and ducked through.

'Make it snappy, Angel! Take the car. And if you don't hear from me again – bless you.'

'Boss—'

'Snappy, I said!'

Dargan moved. He disappeared downward in the blackness.

The closet door opened silently. Sue McEwen slipped into the room without a sound. She hesitated, peering through the open communicating door. In there, beyond the threshold, was a vague black figure.

It was turning – turning to close the connecting door.

Sue McEwen raised her tiny automatic.

'Please,' she said sharply, 'throw up your hands!'

*

The Moon Man stood frozen. Through the glass that masked his face he could see the girl, standing in the glow of the moonlight that was shafting through a window. He could see the glittering gun in her hand – aimed squarely at him.

If she learned—

'Take off your mask!' she commanded.

The Moon Man could not move.

Then a sound – the rattle of a door knob. The door connecting with the hallway opened. The girl glanced toward it, catching her breath. Then, in a sob – a sob of relief – she exclaimed:

'Dad!'

Gil McEwen came through the door. He stared at his daughter. He turned and stared into the adjoining room, at the black-cloaked figure standing there – the thing with the silver head.

'By damn!' he said.

He sprang toward the Moon Man.

Instantly Steve Thatcher leaped forward. With one movement he slammed the door shut and twisted the key. He leaped back as a gun roared, as a bullet crashed through the wood. He whirled toward the window. He ducked out – cloak and mask and all – and began dropping down the fire escape.

Gil McEwen raised his gun to fire again through the door. But he did not fire. He spun on his heel, sprang into the hallway, leaped down the stairs. He burst out the front door, and whirled into the alley.

He peered at the window above. It was open. He peered at the fire escape. It was empty. He peered down the black alley. The Moon Man was not in sight.

McEwen sped through the shadows behind the buildings, but soon he paused. Useless to hunt here! As he came back his eyes turned to a row of wooden boxes, each fitted with wooden lids, which sat at the base of the tenement rear wall. They were coal-bins; each of them was large enough to hold a man. With gun leveled he moved toward them.

McEwen paused, grumbling with disappointment. On each bin-cover was a rusty hasp, and on each hasp was a closed padlock, corroded and useless, untouched for perhaps years. He turned away.

McEwen hurried toward the police-car with his daughter following close. A moment later the quiet of that dismal district was broken by the snarling of a motor and the whining of tires as the car spurted away.

After that, for a long time, the alley behind the deserted tenement was silent.

Then, at last, a faint movement. The cover of one of the coal-bins shifted. One edge of it raised – not the front edge, which was fastened by the padlock, but the rear edge, from which the hinges had been removed. Like a Jack-in-the-box, a man came out of it.

'I'll get him! Don't worry – the day's comin' when I'm going to grab that crook!'

So said Gil McEwen as he paced back and forth across the office of Chief of Police Thatcher while bright sunlight streamed into the room – the sunlight of the morning after.

Chief Thatcher sighed and looked worried. His son looked at Gil McEwen solemnly.

'He's got us all buffaloed, that's all. A swell detective I am! The way I climbed out of Atwell's bedroom window, then went chasing an innocent man for blocks, thinking he might be the Moon Man!' In this way Steve Thatcher had explained his absence from the Atwell home immediately following the Moon Man's escape. 'Gil, I guess if he's ever caught, you'll have to do it.'

'I will do it,' said McEwen. 'That's my promise. I'm never going to stop until I grab that guy!'

And McEwen, Steve Thatcher knew, meant exactly that.

The chief's son looked at his watch. Inside its cover was a photograph. It was a portrait of Sue McEwen.

'If you only knew what you almost did!' he addressed the picture in silent thought. 'If you only knew!'

PIGEON BLOOD

PAUL CAIN

There were a lot of very bad writers who worked for the pulps. For a penny, or sometimes a half-penny, what could you expect? But there were some good ones, too, and even a few great ones. It is possible that Paul Cain (1902–1966) was one of the latter. Sadly, his output was too modest to make a positive judgment.

He wrote about a dozen short stories, seven of which were collected in *Seven Slayers* (1946), and one novel, *Fast One* (1933), which Raymond Chandler lavishly praised. The novel was really a collection of five closely connected novellas which ran in *Black Mask* magazine in 1932, then revised for its hardcover edition. Doubleday must have had meager enthusiasm for it, since it must have had a small print run because it is today one of the rarest and most valuable first editions in the collectors' market. Perhaps his publisher was right, as it was almost universally blasted by critics as too tough, too violent. Still, sophisticated readers loved it and it remains one of the high spots of the hard-boiled crime genre.

He was just a kid of sixteen when he showed up in Hollywood to write screenplays, at which he had fairly early success as Peter Ruric, a nom de plume for George Sims. When the movies failed to provide enough work (and income), he turned to the pulps and used the name Paul Cain. Nothing new was published during the last thirty years of his life. 'Pigeon Blood' was first published in the November 1933 issue of *Black Mask*; it was collected in *Seven Slayers*.

PIGEON BLOOD

PAUL CAIN

The woman was bent far forward over the steering-wheel of the open roadster. Her eyes, narrowed to long black-fringed slits, moved regularly down and up, from the glistening road ahead, to the small rear-view mirror above the windshield. The two circles of white light in the mirror grew steadily larger. She pressed the throttle slowly, steadily downward; there was no sound but the roar of the wind and the deep purr of the powerful engine.

There was a sudden sharp crack; a little frosted circle appeared on the windshield. The woman pressed the throttle to the floor. She was pale; her eyes were suddenly large and dark and afraid, her lips were pressed tightly together. The tires screeched on the wet pavement as the car roared around a long, shallow curve. The headlights of the pursuing car grew larger.

The second and third shots were wild, or buried themselves harmlessly in the body of the car; the fourth struck the left rear tire and the car swerved crazily, skidded halfway across the road. Very suddenly there was bright yellow light right ahead, at the side of the road. The woman jammed on the brakes, jerked the wheel hard over; the tires slid, screamed raggedly over the gravel in front of the gas station, the car stopped. The other car went by at seventy-five miles an hour. One last shot thudded into the back of the seat beside the woman and then the other car had disappeared into the darkness.

Two men ran out of the gas station. Another man stood in the doorway. The woman was leaning back straight in the seat and her eyes were very wide; she was breathing hard, unevenly.

One of the men put his hand on her shoulder, asked: 'Are you all right, lady?'

She nodded.

The other man asked: 'Hold-ups?' He was a short, middle-aged man and his eyes were bright, interested.

The woman opened her bag and took out a cigarette. She said shakily: 'I guess so.' She pulled out the dashboard lighter, waited until it glowed red and held it to her cigarette.

The younger man was inspecting the back of the car. He said: 'They punctured the tank. It's a good thing you stopped – you couldn't have gone much father.'

'Yes – I guess it's a very good thing I stopped,' she said, mechanically. She took a deep drag of her cigarette.

The other man said: 'That's the third hold-up out here this week.'

The woman spoke to the younger man. 'Can you get me a cab?'

He said: 'Sure.' Then he knelt beside the blown-out tire, said: 'Look, Ed – they almost cut it in two.'

The man in the doorway called to her: 'You want a cab, lady?'

She smiled, nodded, and the man disappeared into the gas station; he came back to the doorway in a minute, over to the car. 'There'll be a cab here in a little while, lady,' he said.

She thanked him.

'This is one of the worst stretches of road on Long Island – for highwaymen.' He leaned on the door of the car. 'Did they try to nudge you off the road – or did they just start shooting?'

'They just started shooting.'

He said: 'We got a repair service here – do you want us to fix up your car?'

She nodded. 'How long will it take?'

'Couple days. We'll have to get a new windshield from the branch factory in Queens – an' take off that tank. . . .'

She took a card out of her bag and gave it to him, said: 'Call me up when it's finished.'

After a little while, a cab came out of the darkness of a side street, turned into the station. The woman got out of the car and went over to the cab, spoke to the driver: 'Do you know any short-cuts into Manhattan? Somebody tried to hold me up on the main road a little while ago, and maybe they're still laying for me. I don't want any more of it – I want to go home.' She was very emphatic.

The driver was a big red-faced Irishman. He grinned, said: 'Lady – I know a million of 'em. You'll be as safe with me as you'd be in your own home.'

She raised her hand in a gesture of farewell to the three men around her car and got into the cab. After the cab had disappeared around the street, the man to whom she had given the card took it out of his pocket and squinted at it, read aloud: 'Mrs. Dale Hanan – Five-eighty Park Avenue.'

The short, middle-aged man bobbed his head knowingly. 'Sure,' he said – 'I knew she was class. She's Hanan's wife – the millionaire. Made his dough in oil – Oklahoma. His chauffeur told me how he got his start – didn't have a shoestring or a place to put it, so he shot off his big toe and collected ten grand on an accident policy – grubstake on his first well. Bright boy. He's got a big estate down at Roslyn.'

The man with the card nodded. He said: 'That's swell. We can soak him plenty.' He put the card back into his pocket.

When the cab stopped near the corner of Sixty-third and Park Avenue the woman got out, paid the driver and hurried into the apartment house. In her apartment, she put in a long-distance call to Roslyn, Long Island; when the connection had been made, she said: 'Dale – it's in the open, now. I was followed, driving back to town – shot at – the car was nearly wrecked. . . . I don't know what to do. Even if I call Crandall, now, and tell him I won't go through with it – won't go to the police – he'll probably have me killed, just to make sure. . . . Yes, I'm going to stay in – I'm scared. . . . All right, dear. 'Bye.'

She hung up, went to a wide center table and poured whiskey into a tall glass, sat down and stared vacantly at the glass – her hand was shaking a little. She smiled suddenly, crookedly, lifted the glass to her mouth and drained it. Then she put the glass on the floor and leaned back and glanced at the tiny watch at her wrist. It was ten minutes after nine.

At a few minutes after ten a black Packard town-car stopped in front of a narrow building of gray stone on East Fifty-fourth Street; a tall man got out, crossed the sidewalk and rang the bell. The car went on. When the door swung open, the tall man went into a long, brightly lighted hallway, gave his hat and stick to the checkroom attendant, went swiftly up two flights of narrow stairs to the third floor. He glanced around the big, crowded room, then crossed to one corner near a window on the Fifty-fourth Street side and sat down at a small table, smiled wanly at the man across from him, said: 'Mister Druse, I believe.'

The other man was about fifty, well set up, well-groomed in the way of good living. His thick gray hair was combed sharply, evenly back. He lowered his folded newspaper to the table, stared thoughtfully at the tall man.

He said: 'Mister Hanan,' and his voice was very deep, metallic.

The tall man nodded shortly, leaned back and folded his arms across his narrow chest. He was ageless, perhaps thirty-five, forty-five; his thin, colorless hair was close-clipped, his long, bony face deeply tanned, a sharp and angular setting for large seal-brown eyes. His mouth was curved, mobile.

He asked: 'Do you know Jeffrey Crandall?'

Druse regarded him evenly, expressionlessly for a moment, raised his head and beckoned a waiter. Hanan ordered a whiskey sour.

Druse said: 'I know Mister Crandall casually. Why?'

'A little more than an hour ago Crandall, or Crandall's men, tried to murder Mrs. Hanan, as she was driving back from my place at Roslyn.' Hanan leaned forward: his eyes were wide, worried.

The waiter served Hanan's whiskey sour, set a small bottle of Perrier and a small glass on the table in front of Druse.

Druse poured the water into the glass slowly. 'So what?'

Hanan tasted his drink. He said: 'This is not a matter for the police,

Mister Druse. I understand that you interest yourself in things of this nature, so I took the liberty of calling you and making this appointment. Is that right?' He was nervous, obviously ill at ease.

Druse shrugged. '*What* nature? I don't know what you're talking about.'

'I'm sorry – I guess I'm a little upset.' Hanan smiled. 'What I mean is that I can rely on your discretion?'

Druse frowned. 'I think so,' he said slowly. He drank half of the Perrier, squinted down at the glass as if it had tasted very badly.

Hanan smiled vacantly. 'You do not know Mrs. Hanan?'

Druse shook his head slowly, turned his glass around and around on the table.

'We have been living apart for several years,' Hanan went on. 'We are still very fond of one another, we are very good friends, but we do not get along – together. Do you understand?'

Druse nodded.

Hanan sipped his drink, went on swiftly: 'Catherine has – has always had – a decided weakness for gambling. She went through most of her own inheritance – a considerable inheritance – before we were married. Since our separation she has lost somewhere in the neighborhood of a hundred and fifteen thousand dollars. I have, of course, taken care of her debts.' Hanan coughed slightly. 'Early this evening she called me at Roslyn, said she had to see me immediately – that it was very important. I offered to come into town but she said she'd rather come out. She came out about seven.'

Hanan paused, closed his eyes and rubbed two fingers of one hand slowly up and down his forehead. 'She's in a very bad jam with Crandall.' He opened his eyes and put his hand down on the table.

Druse finished his Perrier, put down the glass and regarded Hanan attentively.

'About three weeks ago,' Hanan went on, 'Catherine's debt to Crandall amounted to sixty-eight thousand dollars – she had been playing very heavily under the usual gambler's delusion of getting even. She was afraid to come to me – she knew I'd taken several bad beatings on the market – she kept putting it off and trying to make good her losses, until Crandall demanded the money. She told him she couldn't pay – together, they hatched out a scheme to get it. Catherine had a set of rubies – pigeon blood – been in her family five or six generations. They're worth, perhaps, a hundred and seventy-five thousand – her father insured them for a hundred and thirty-five, forty years ago and the insurance premiums have always been paid. . . . ' Hanan finished his whiskey sour, leaned back in his chair.

Druse said: 'I assume the idea was that the rubies disappear; that Mrs. Hanan claim the insurance, pay off Crandall, have sixty-seven thousand left and live happily forever after.'

Hanan coughed; his face was faintly flushed. 'Exactly.'

'I assume further,' Druse went on, 'that the insurance company did not question the integrity of the claim; that they paid, and that Mrs. Hanan, in turn, paid Crandall.'

Hanan nodded. He took a tortoise-shell case out of his pocket, offered Druse a cigarette.

Druse shook his head, asked: 'Are the insurance company detectives warm – are they making Crandall or whoever he had to do the actual job, uncomfortable?'

'No. The theft was well engineered. I don't think Crandall is worrying about that.' Hanan lighted a cigarette. 'But Catherine wanted her rubies back – as had, of course, been agreed upon.' He leaned forward, put his elbows on the table. 'Crandall returned paste imitations to her – she only discovered they weren't genuine a few days ago.'

Druse smiled, said slowly: 'In that case, I should think it was Crandall who was in a jam with Mrs. Hanan, instead of Mrs. Hanan who was in a jam with Crandall.'

Hanan wagged his long chin back and forth. 'This is New York. Men like Crandall do as they please. Catherine went to him and he laughed at her; said the rubies he had returned were the rubies that had been stolen. She had no recourse, other than to admit her complicity in defrauding the insurance company. That's the trouble – she threatened to do exactly that.'

Druse widened his eyes, stared at Hanan.

'Catherine is a very impulsive woman,' Hanan went on. 'She was so angry at losing the rubies and being made so completely a fool, that she threatened Crandall. She told him that if the rubies were not returned within three days she would tell what he had done; that he had stolen the rubies – take her chances on her part in it coming out. Of course she wouldn't do it, but she was desperate and she thought that was her only chance of scaring Crandall into returning the rubies – and she made him believe it. Since she talked to him, Wednesday, she has been followed. Tomorrow is Saturday, the third day. Tonight, driving back to town, she was followed, shot at – almost killed.'

'Has she tried to get in touch with Crandall again?'

Hanan shook his head. 'She's been stubbornly waiting for him to give the rubies back – until this business tonight. Now she's frightened – says it wouldn't do any good for her to talk to Crandall now because he wouldn't believe her – and it's too easy for him to put her out of the way.'

Druse beckoned the waiter, asked him to bring the check. 'Where is she now?'

'At her apartment – Sixty-third and Park.'

'What do you intend doing about it?'

Hanan shrugged. 'That's what I came to you for. I don't know what to do. I've heard of you and your work from friends. . . . '

Druse hesitated, said slowly: 'I must make my position clear.'

Hanan nodded, lighted a fresh cigarette.

'I am one of the few people left,' Druse went on, 'who actually believes that honesty is the best policy. Honesty is my business – I am primarily a business man – I've made it pay.'

Hanan smiled broadly.

Druse leaned forward. 'I am not a fixer,' he said. 'My acquaintance is wide and varied – I am fortunate in being able to wield certain influences. But above all I seek to further justice – I mean real justice as opposed to *book* justice – I was on the Bench for many years and I realize the distinction keenly.' His big face wrinkled to an expansive grin. 'And I get paid for it – *well* paid.'

Hanan said: 'Does my case interest you?'

'It does.'

'Will five thousand dollars be satisfactory – as a retaining fee?'

Druse moved his broad shoulders in something like a shrug. 'You value the rubies at a hundred and seventy-five thousand,' he said. 'I am undertaking to get the rubies back, and protect Mrs. Hanan's life.' He stared at Hanan intently. 'What value do you put on Mrs. Hanan's life?'

Hanan frowned self-consciously, twisted his mouth down at the corners. 'That is, of course, impossible to—'

'Say another hundred and seventy-five.' Druse smiled easily. 'That makes three hundred and fifty thousand. I work on a ten per cent basis – thirty-five thousand – one-third in advance.' He leaned back, still smiling easily. 'Ten thousand will be sufficient as a retainer.'

Hanan was still frowning self-consciously. He said: 'Done,' took a checkbook and fountain pen out of his pocket.

Druse went on: 'If I fail in either purpose, I shall, of course, return your check.'

Hanan bobbed his head, made out the check in a minute, illegible scrawl and handed it across the table. Druse paid for the drinks, jotted down Hanan's telephone number and the address of Mrs. Hanan's apartment. They got up and went downstairs and out of the place; Druse told Hanan he would call him within an hour, got into a cab. Hanan watched the cab disappear in east-bound traffic, lighted a cigarette nervously and walked toward Madison Avenue.

Druse said: 'Tell her I've come from Mister Hanan.'

The telephone operator spoke into the transmitter, turned to Druse. 'You may go up – Apartment Three D.'

When, in answer to a drawled, 'Come in,' he pushed open the door and went into the apartment, Catherine Hanan was standing near the center table, with one hand on the table to steady herself, the other in the pocket of her long blue robe. She was beautiful in the mature way that women who have lived too hard, too swiftly, are sometimes beautiful. She was very dark;

her eyes were large, liquid, black and dominated her rather small, sharply sculptured face. Her mouth was large, deeply red, not particularly strong.

Druse bowed slightly, said: 'How do you do?'

She smiled, and her eyes were heavy, nearly closed. 'Swell – and you?'

He came slowly into the room, put his hat on the table, asked: 'May we sit down?'

'Sure.' She jerked her head towards a chair, stayed where she was.

Druse said: 'You're drunk.'

'Right.'

He smiled, sighed gently. 'A commendable condition. I regret exceedingly that my stomach does not permit it.' He glanced casually about the room. In the comparative darkness of a corner, near a heavily draped window, there was a man lying on his back on the floor. His arms were stretched out and back, and his legs were bent under him in a curious way, and there was blood on his face.

Druse raised his thick white eyebrows, spoke without looking at Mrs. Hanan: 'Is *he* drunk, too?'

She laughed shortly. 'Uh-huh – in a different way.' She nodded towards a golf-stick on the floor near the man. 'He had a little too much niblick.'

'Friend of yours?'

She said: 'I rather doubt it. He came in from the fire-escape with a gun in his hand. I happened to see him before he saw me.'

'Where's the gun?'

'I've got it.' She drew a small black automatic half out of the pocket of her robe.

Druse went over and knelt beside the man, picked up one of his hands. He said slowly: 'This man is decidedly dead.'

Mrs. Hanan stood, staring silently at the man on the floor for perhaps thirty seconds. Her face was white, blank. Then she walked unsteadily to a desk against one wall and picked up a whiskey bottle, poured a stiff drink. She said: 'I know it.' Her voice was choked, almost a whisper. She drank the whiskey, turned and leaned against the desk, stared at Druse with wide unseeing eyes. 'So what?'

'So pull yourself together, and forget about it – we've got more important things to think about for a little while.' Druse stood up. 'How long ago? . . .'

She shuddered. 'About a half-hour – I didn't know what to do. . . .'

'Have you tried to reach Crandall? I mean before this happened – right after you came in tonight?'

'Yes – I couldn't get him.'

Druse went to a chair and sat down. He said: 'Mister Hanan has turned this case over to me. Won't you sit down, and answer a few questions? . . .'

She sank into a low chair near the desk. 'Are you a detective?' Her voice was still very low, strained.

Druse smiled. 'I'm an attorney – a sort of extra-legal attorney.' He regarded her thoughtfully. 'If we can get your rubies back and assure your safety, and' – he coughed slightly – 'induce Mister Hanan to reimburse the insurance company, you will be entirely satisfied, will you not?'

She nodded, started to speak.

Druse interrupted her: 'Are the rubies themselves – I mean intrinsically, as stones – awfully important to you? Or was this grandstand play of yours – this business of threatening Crandall – motivated by rather less tangible factors – such as self-respect, things like that?'

She smiled faintly, nodded. 'God knows how I happen to have any self-respect left – I've been an awful ass – but I have. It was the idea of being made such a fool – after I've lost over a hundred thousand dollars to Crandall – that made me do it.'

Druse smiled. 'The rubies themselves,' he said – 'I mean the rubies as stones – entirely apart from any extraneous consideration such as self-respect – would more seriously concern Mister Hanan, would they not?'

She said: 'Sure. He's always been crazy about stones.'

Druse scratched the tip of his long nose pensively. His eyes were wide and vacant, his thick lips compressed to a long downward curved line. 'You are sure you were followed when you left Crandall's Wednesday?'

'As sure as one can be without actually knowing – it was more of a followed feeling than anything else. After the idea was planted I could have sworn I saw a dozen men, of course.'

He said: 'Have you ever had that feeling before – I mean before you threatened Crandall?'

'No.'

'It may have been simply imagination, because you expected to be followed – there was reason for you to be followed?'

She nodded. 'But it's a cinch it wasn't imagination this evening.'

Druse was leaning forward, his elbows on his knees. He looked intently at her, said very seriously: 'I'm going to get your rubies back, and I can assure you of your safety – and I think I can promise that the matter of reimbursement to the insurance company will be taken care of. I didn't speak to Mister Hanan about that, but I'm sure he'll see the justice of it.'

She smiled faintly.

Druse went on: 'I promise you these things – and in return I want you to do exactly as I tell you until tomorrow morning.'

Her smile melted to a quick, rather drunken, laugh. 'Do I have to poison any babies?' She stood up, poured a drink.

Druse said: '*That's* one of the things I *don't* want you to do.'

She picked up the glass, frowned at him with mock seriousness. 'You're a moralist,' she said. 'That's one of the things I *will* do.'

He shrugged slightly. 'I shall have some very important, very delicate work for you a little later in the evening. I thought it might be best.'

She looked at him, half smiling, a little while, and then she laughed and put down the glass and went into the bedroom. He leaned back comfortably in the chair and stared at the ceiling; his hands were on the arms of the chair and he ran imaginary scales with his big blunt fingers.

She came back into the room in a little while, dressed, drawing on gloves. She gestured with her head towards the man on the floor, and for a moment her more or less alcoholic poise forsook her – she shuddered again – her face was white, twisted.

Druse stood up, said: 'He'll have to stay where he is for a little while.' He went to the heavily draped window, to the fire-escape, moved the drape aside and locked the window. 'How many doors are there to the apartment?'

'Two.' She was standing near the table. She took the black automatic from a pocket of her suit, took up a gray suede bag from the table and put the automatic into it.

He watched her without expression. 'How many keys?'

'Two.' She smiled, took two keys out of the bag and held them up. 'The only other key is the pass-key – the manager's.'

He said: 'That's fine,' went to the table and picked up his hat and put it on. They went out into the hall and closed and locked the door. 'Is there a side entrance to the building?'

She nodded.

'Let's go out that way.'

She led the way down the corridor, down three flights of stairs to a door leading to Sixty-third Street. They went out and walked over Sixty-third to Lexington and got into a cab; he told the driver to take them to the corner of Fortieth and Madison, leaned back and looked out the window. 'How long have you and Mister Hanan been divorced?'

She was quick to answer. 'Did he say we were divorced?'

'No.' Druse turned to her slowly, smiled slowly.

'Then what makes you think we are?'

'I don't. I just wanted to be sure.'

'We are *not*.' She was very emphatic.

He waited, without speaking.

She glanced at him sidewise and saw that he expected her to go on. She laughed softly. 'He wants a divorce. He asked me to divorce him several months ago.' She sighed, moved her hands nervously on her lap. 'That's another of the things I'm not very proud of – I wouldn't do it. I don't know why – we were never in love – we haven't been married, really, for a long time – but I've waited, hoping we might be able to make something out of it. . . .'

Druse said quietly: 'I think I understand – I'm sorry I had to ask you about that.'

She did not answer.

In a little while the cab stopped; they got out and Druse paid the driver and they cut diagonally across the street, entered an office building halfway down the block. Druse spoke familiarly to the Negro elevator boy; they got off at the forty-fifth floor and went up two flights of narrow stairs, through a heavy steel fire-door to a narrow bridge and across it to a rambling two-story penthouse that covered all one side of the roof. Druse rang the bell and a thin-faced Filipino boy let them in.

Druse led the way into a very big high-ceilinged room that ran the length and almost the width of the house. It was beautifully and brightly furnished, opened on one side onto a wide terrace. They went through to the terrace; there were steamer-chairs there and canvas swings and low round tables, a great many potted plants and small trees. The tiled floor was partially covered with strips of coco-matting. There was a very wide, vividly striped awning stretched across all one side. At the far side, where the light from the living room faded into darkness, the floor came to an abrupt end – there was no railing or parapet – the nearest building of the same height was several blocks away.

Mrs. Hanan sat down and stared at the twinkling distant lights of Upper Manhattan. The roar of the city came up to them faintly, like surf very far away. She said: 'It is very beautiful.'

'I am glad you find it so.' Druse went to the edge, glanced down. 'I have never put a railing here,' he said, 'because I am interested in Death. Whenever I'm depressed I look at my jumping-off place, only a few feet away, and am reminded that life is very sweet.' He stared at the edge, stroked the side of his jaw with his fingers. 'Nothing to climb over, no windows to raise – just walk.'

She smiled wryly. 'A moralist – and morbid. Did you bring me here to suggest a suicide pact?'

'I brought you here to sit still and be decorative.'

'And you?'

'I'm going hunting.' Druse went over and stood frowning down at her. 'I'll try not to be long. The boy will bring you anything you want – even *good* whiskey, if you can't get along without it. The view will grow on you – you'll find one of the finest collections of books on satanism, demonology, witchcraft, in the world inside.' He gestured with his head and eyes. 'Don't telephone anyone – and, above all, *stay* here, even if I'm late.'

She nodded vaguely.

He went to the wide doors that led into the living room, turned, said: 'One thing more – who are Mister Hanan's attorneys?'

She looked at him curiously. 'Mahlon and Stiles.'

He raised one hand in salute. 'So long.'

She smiled, said: 'So long – good hunting.'

He went into the living room and talked to the Filipino boy a minute, went out.

In the drug store across the street from the entrance to the building, he went into a telephone booth, called the number Hanan had given him. When

Hanan answered, he said: 'I have very bad news. We were too late. When I reached Mrs. Hanan's apartment, she did not answer the phone – I bribed my way in and found her – found her dead. . . . I'm terribly sorry, old man – you've got to take it standing up. . . . Yes – strangled.'

Druse smiled grimly to himself. 'No, I haven't informed the police – I want things left as they are for the present – I'm going to see Crandall and I have a way of working it so he won't have a single out. I'm going to pin it on him so that it will stay pinned – and I'm going to get the rubies back too. . . . I know they don't mean much to you now, but the least I can do is get them back – and see that Crandall is stuck so he can't wriggle out of it.' He said the last very emphatically, was silent a little while, except for an occasionally interjected 'Yes' or 'No.'

Finally he asked: 'Can you be in around three-thirty or four? . . . I'll want to get in touch with you then. . . . Right. Good-bye.' He hung up and went out into Fortieth Street.

Jeffrey Crandall was a medium-sized man with a close-cropped mustache, wide-set greenish gray eyes. He was conservatively dressed, looked very much like a prosperous real-estate man, or broker.

He said: 'Long time no see.'

Druse nodded abstractedly. He was sitting in a deep red leather chair in Crandall's very modern office, adjoining the large room in a midtown apartment building that was Crandall's 'Place' for the moment. He raised his head and looked attentively at the pictures on the walls, one after the other.

'Anything special?' Crandall lighted a short stub of green cigar.

Druse said: 'Very special,' over his shoulder. He came to the last picture, a very ordinary Degas pastel, shook his head slightly, disapprovingly, and turned back to Crandall. He took a short-barreled derringer out of his inside coat-pocket, held it on the arm of his chair, the muzzle focused steadily on Crandall's chest.

Crandall's eyes widened slowly; his mouth hung a little open. He put one hand up very slowly and took the stub of cigar out of his mouth.

Druse repeated: 'Very special.' His full lips were curved to a thin, cold smile.

Crandall stared at the gun. He spoke as if making a tremendous effort to frame his words casually, calmly: 'What's it all about?'

'It's all about Mrs. Hanan.' Druse tipped his hat to the back of his head. 'It's all about you gypping her out of her rubies – and her threatening to take it to the police – and you having her murdered at about a quarter after ten tonight, because you were afraid she'd go through with it.'

Crandall's tense face relaxed slowly; he tried very hard to smile. He said: 'You're crazy,' and there was fear in his eyes, fear in the harsh, hollow sound of his voice.

Druse did not speak. He waited, his cold eyes boring into Crandall's.

Crandall cleared his throat, moved a little forward in his chair and put his elbows on the wide desk.

'Don't ring.' Druse glanced at the little row of ivory push-buttons on the desk, shook his head.

Crandall laughed soundlessly as if the thought of ringing had never entered his mind. 'In the first place,' he said, 'I gave her back the stones that were stolen. In the second place, I never believed her gag about telling about it.' He leaned back slowly, spoke very slowly and distinctly as confidence came back to him. 'In the third place, I wouldn't be chump enough to bump her off with that kind of a case against me.'

Druse said: 'Your third place is the one that interests me. The switched rubies, her threat to tell the story – it all makes a pip of a case against you, doesn't it?'

Crandall nodded slowly.

'That's the reason,' Druse went on, 'that if I shoot you through the heart right now, I'll get a vote of thanks for avenging the lady you made a sucker of, and finally murdered because you thought she was going to squawk.'

All the fear came back into Crandall's face suddenly. He started to speak.

Druse interrupted him, went on: 'I'm going to let you have it when you reach for your gun, of course – that'll take care of any technicalities about taking the law into my own hands – anything like that.'

Crandall's face was white, drained. He said: 'How come I'm elected? What the hell have you got against me?'

Druse shrugged. 'You shouldn't jockey ladies into trying to nick insurance companies. . . . '

'It was her idea.'

'Then you should have been on the level about the rubies.'

Crandall said: 'So help me God! I gave her back the stuff I took!' He said it very vehemently, very earnestly.

'How do you know? How do you know the man you had do the actual job didn't make the switch?'

Crandall leaned forward. 'Because *I* took them. She gave me her key and I went in the side way, while she was out, and took them myself. They were never out of my hands.' He took up a lighter from the desk and relighted the stump of cigar with shaking hands. 'That's the reason I didn't take her threat seriously. I thought it was some kind of extortion gag she'd doped out to get some of her dough back. She got back the stones I took – and if they weren't genuine they were switched before I took them, or after I gave them back.'

Druse stared at him silently for perhaps a minute, finally smiled, said: 'Before.'

Crandall sucked noisily at his cigar. 'Then, if you believe me' – he glanced at the derringer – 'What's the point?'

'The point is that if I didn't believe you, you'd be in an awfully bad spot.'

Crandall nodded, grinned weakly.

'The point,' Druse went on, 'is that you're still in an awfully bad spot because no one else will believe you.'

Crandall nodded again. He leaned back and took a handkerchief out of his breast pocket and dabbed at his face.

'I know a way out of it.' Druse moved his hand, let the derringer hang by the trigger-guard from his forefinger. 'Not because I like you particularly, nor because I think you particularly deserve it – but because it's right. I can turn up the man who really murdered her – if we can get back the rubies – the real rubies. And I think I know where they are.'

Crandall was leaning far forward, his face very alive and interested.

'I want you to locate the best peterman we can get.' Druse spoke in a very low voice, watched Crandall intently. 'We've got to open a safe – I think it'll be a safe – out on Long Island. Nothing very difficult – there'll probably be servants to handle but nothing more serious than that.'

Crandall said: 'Why can't I do it?' He smiled a little. 'I used to be in the box business, you know – before I straightened up and got myself a joint. That's the reason I took the fake rubies myself – not to let anyone else in on it.'

Druse said: 'That'll be fine.'

'When?' Crandall stood up.

Druse put the derringer back in his pocket. 'Right now – where's your car?'

Crandall jerked his head towards the street. They went out through the crowded gambling room, downstairs, got into Crandall's car. Crossing Queensborough Bridge Druse glanced at his watch. It was twenty minutes past twelve.

At three thirty-five Druse pushed the bell of the penthouse, after searching, vainly as usual, for his key. The Filipino boy opened the door, said: 'It's a very hot night, sir.'

Druse threw his hat on a chair, smiled sadly at Mrs. Hanan, who had come into the little entrance-hall. 'I've been trying to teach him English for three months,' he said, 'and all he can say is "Yes, sir," and "No, sir," and tell me about the heat.' He turned to the broadly grinning boy. 'Yes, Tony, it is a very hot night.'

They went through the living room, out onto the terrace. It was cool there, and dim; a little light came out through the wide doors, from the living room.

Mrs. Hanan said: 'I'd about given you up.'

Druse sat down, sighed wearily. 'I've had a very strenuous evening – sorry I'm so late.' He looked up at her. 'Hungry?'

'Starved.'

'Why didn't you have Tony fix you something?'

'I wanted to wait.' She had taken off her suit-coat, hat; in her smartly cut tweed skirt, white mannish shirt, she looked very beautiful.

Druse said: 'Supper, or breakfast, or something will be ready in a few minutes – I ordered it for four.' He stood up. 'Which reminds me – we're having a guest. I must telephone.'

He went through the living room, up four broad, shallow steps to the little corner room that he used as an office. He sat down at the broad desk, drew the telephone towards him, dialed a number.

Hanan answered the phone. Druse said: 'I want you to come to my place, on top of the Pell Building, at once. It is very important. Ring the bell downstairs – I've told the elevator boy I'm expecting you. . . . I can't tell you over the phone – please come alone, and right away.' He hung up and sat staring vacantly at his hands a little while, and then got up and went back to the terrace, sat down.

'What did you do with yourself?'

Mrs. Hanan was lying in one of the low chairs. She laughed nervously. 'The radio – tried to improve my Spanish and Tony's English – chewed my fingernails – almost frightened myself to death with one of your damned demon books.' She lighted a cigarette. 'And you?'

He smiled in the darkness. 'I earned thirty-five thousand dollars.'

She sat up, said eagerly: 'Did you get the rubies?'

He nodded.

'Did Crandall raise much hell?'

'Enough.'

She laughed exultantly. 'Where are they?'

Druse tapped his pocket, watched her face in the pale orange glow of her cigarette.

She got up, held out her hand. 'May I see them?'

Druse said: 'Certainly.' He took a long flat jewel-case of black velvet out of his inside coat-pocket and handed it to her.

She opened the case and went to the door to the living room, looked at its contents by the light there, said: 'They are awfully beautiful, aren't they?'

'They are.'

She snapped the case closed, came back and sat down.

Druse said: 'I think I'd better take care of them a little while longer.'

She leaned forward and put the case on his lap; he took it up and put it back in his pocket. They sat silently, watching the lights in buildings over towards the East River. After awhile the Filipino boy came out and said that they were served.

'Out guest is late.' Druse stood up. 'I make a rule of never waiting breakfast – anything but breakfast.'

They went together through the living room, into the simply furnished dining room. There were three places set at the glittering white and silver table. They sat down and the Filipino boy brought in tall and spindly cocktail glasses of iced fruit; they were just beginning when the doorbell rang. The Filipino boy glanced at Druse, Druse nodded, said: 'Ask the gentleman to come in here.' The Filipino boy went out and there were voices in the entrance-hall, and then Hanan came into the doorway.

Druse stood up. He said: 'You must forgive us for beginning – you are a little late.' He raised one hand and gestured towards the empty chair.

Hanan was standing in the doorway with his feet wide apart, his arms stiff at his sides, as if he had been suddenly frozen in that position. He stared at Mrs. Hanan and his eyes were wide, blank – his thin mouth was compressed to a hard, straight line. Very suddenly his right hand went towards his left armpit.

Druse said sharply: 'Please sit down.' Though he seemed scarcely to have moved, the blunt derringer glittered in his hand.

Mrs. Hanan half rose. She was very pale; her hands were clenched convulsively on the white tablecloth.

Hanan dropped his hand very slowly. He stared at the derringer and twisted his mouth into a terribly forced smile, came slowly forward to the empty chair and sat down.

Druse raised his eyes to the Filipino boy who had followed Hanan into the doorway, said: 'Take the gentleman's gun, Tony – and serve his cocktail.' He sat down, held the derringer rigidly on the table in front of him.

The Filipino boy went to Hanan, felt gingerly under his coat, drew out a small black automatic and took it to Druse. Then he went out through the swinging-door to the kitchen. Druse put the automatic in his pocket. He turned his eyes to Mrs. Hanan, said: 'I'm going to tell you a story. After I've finished, you can both talk all you like – but please don't interrupt.'

He smiled with his mouth – the rest of his face remained stonily impassive. His eyes were fixed and expressionless, on Hanan. He said: 'Your husband has wanted a divorce for some time. His principal reason is a lady – her name doesn't matter – who wants to marry him – and whom he wants to marry. He hasn't told you about her because he has felt, perhaps justifiably, that you knowing about her would retard, rather than hasten, an agreement. . . .'

The Filipino boy came in from the kitchen with a cocktail, set it before Hanan. Hanan did not move, or look up. He stared intently at the flowers in the center of the table. The Filipino boy smiled self-consciously at Druse and Mrs. Hanan, disappeared into the kitchen.

Druse relaxed a little, leaned back; the derringer was still focused unwaveringly on Hanan.

'In the hope of uncovering some adequate grounds for bringing suit,' Druse went on, 'he has had you followed for a month or more – unsuccessfully, need I add? After you threatened Crandall, you discovered suddenly that you were being followed and, of course, ascribed it to Crandall.'

He paused. It was entirely silent for a moment, except for the faint, faraway buzz of the city and the sharp, measured sound of Hanan's breathing.

Druse turned his head towards Mrs. Hanan. 'After you left Mister Hanan at Roslyn, last night, it suddenly occurred to him that this was his golden opportunity to dispose of you, without any danger to himself. You wouldn't give him a divorce – and it didn't look as if he'd be able to force it by discovering some dereliction on your part. And now, you had threatened Crandall – Crandall would be logically suspected if anything happened to you. Mister Hanan sent his men – the men who had been following you – after you when you left the place at Roslyn. They weren't very lucky.'

Druse was smiling slightly. Mrs. Hanan had put her elbows on the table, her chin in her hands; she regarded Hanan steadily.

'He couldn't go to the police,' Druse went on – 'they would arrest Crandall, or watch him, and that would ruin the whole plan. And the business about the rubies would come out. That was the last thing he wanted' – Druse widened his smile – 'because he switched the rubies himself – some time ago.'

Mrs. Hanan turned to look at Druse; very slowly she matched his smile.

'You never discovered that your rubies were fake,' he said, 'because that possibility didn't occur to you. It was only after they'd been given back by Crandall that you became suspicious and found out they weren't genuine.' He glanced at Hanan and the smile went from his face, leaving it hard and expressionless again. 'Mister Hanan is *indeed* "crazy about stones."'

Hanan's thin mouth twitched slightly; he stared steadily at the flowers.

Druse sighed. 'And so – we find Mister Hanan, last night, with several reasons for wishing your – shall we say, disappearance? We find him with the circumstance of being able to direct suspicion at Crandall, ready to his hand. His own serious problem lay in finding a third, responsible, party before whom to lay the whole thing – or enough of it to serve his purpose.'

Mrs. Hanan had turned to face Hanan. Her eyes were half closed and her smile was very hard, very strange.

Druse stood up slowly, went on: 'He had the happy thought of calling me – or perhaps the suggestion. I was an ideal instrument, functioning as I do, midway between the law and the underworld. He made an appointment, and arranged for one of his men to call on you by way of the fire-escape, while we were discussing the matter. The logical implication was that I would come to you when I left him, find you murdered, and act immediately on the information he had given me about Crandall. My influence and testimony would have speedily convicted Crandall. Mister Hanan would have better than a divorce. He'd have the rubies, without any danger of his having switched them ever being discovered – and he'd have' – Druse grinned sourly – 'the check he had given me as an advance. Failing in the two things I had contracted to do, I would of course return it to him.'

Hanan laughed suddenly; a terribly forced, high-pitched laugh.

'It is very funny,' Druse said. 'It would all have worked very beautifully if you' – he moved his eyes to Mrs. Hanan – 'hadn't happened to see the man who came up the fire-escape to call on you, before he saw you. The man whose return Mister Hanan has been impatiently waiting. The man' – he dropped one eyelid in a swift wink – 'who confessed to the whole thing a little less than an hour ago.'

Druse put his hand into his inside pocket and took out the black velvet jewel-case, snapped it open and put it on the table. 'I found them in the safe at your place at Roslyn,' he said. 'Your servants there objected very strenuously – so strenuously that I was forced to tie them up and lock them in the wine cellar. They must be awfully uncomfortable by now – I shall have to attend to that.'

He lowered his voice to a discreet drone. 'And your lady was there, too. She, too, objected very strenuously, until I had had a long talk with her and convinced her of the error of her – shall we say, affection, for a gentleman of your instincts. She seemed very frightened at the idea of becoming involved in this case – I'm afraid she will be rather hard to find.'

Druse sighed, lowered his eyes slowly to the rubies, touched the largest of them delicately with one finger. 'And so,' he said, 'to end this vicious and regrettable business – I give you your rubies' – he lifted his hand and made a sweeping gesture towards Mrs. Hanan – 'and your wife – and now I would like your check for twenty-five thousand dollars.'

Hanan moved very swiftly. He tipped the edge of the table upward, lunged up and forward in the same movement; there was a sharp, shattering crash of chinaware and silver. The derringer roared, but the bullet thudded into the table. Hanan bent over suddenly – his eyes were dull, and his upper lip was drawn back over his teeth – then he straightened and whirled and ran out through the door to the living-room.

Mrs. Hanan was standing against the big buffet; her hands were at her mouth, and her eyes were very wide. She made no sound.

Druse went after Hanan, stopped suddenly at the door. Hanan was crouched in the middle of the living room. The Filipino boy stood beyond him, framed against the darkness of the entrance-hall; a curved knife glittering in his hand and his thin yellow face was hard, menacing. Hanan ran out on the terrace, and Druse went swiftly after him. By the dim light from the living room he saw Hanan dart to the left, encounter the wall there, zigzag crazily towards the darkness of the outer terrace, the edge.

Druse yelled: 'Look out!' ran forward. Hanan was silhouetted a moment against the mauve glow of the sky; then with a hoarse, cracked scream he fell outward, down.

Druse stood a moment, staring blindly down. He took out a handkerchief and mopped his forehead, then turned and went into the living room and tossed the derringer down on the big center table. The Filipino boy was still standing in the doorway. Druse nodded at him and he turned and went through the dark entrance-hall into the kitchen. Druse went to the door to the dining-room; Mrs. Hanan was still standing with her back to the buffet, her hands still at her mouth, her eyes wide, unseeing. He turned and went swiftly up the broad steps to the office, took up the telephone and dialed a number. When the connection had been made, he asked for MacCrae.

In a minute or so MacCrae answered; Druse said: 'You'll find a stiff in Mrs. Dale Hanan's apartment on the corner of Sixty-third and Park, Mac. She killed him – self-defense. You might find his partner downstairs at my place – waiting for his boss to come out. . . . Yeah, his boss was Hanan – he just went down – the other way. . . . I'll file charges of attempted murder against Hanan, and straight it all out when you get over here. . . . Yeah – hurry.'

He hung up and went down to the dining room. He tipped the table back on its legs and picked up the rubies, put them back into the case. He said: 'I called up a friend of mine who works for Mahlon and Stiles. As you probably know, Mister Hanan has never made a will.' He smiled. 'He so hated the thought of death that the idea of a will was extremely repugnant to him.'

He picked up her chair and she came slowly across and sank into it.

'As soon as the estate is settled,' he went on, 'I shall expect your check for a hundred and thirty-five thousand dollars, made out to the insurance company.'

She nodded abstractedly.

'I think these' – he indicated the jewel-case – 'will be safer with me, until then.'

She nodded again.

He smiled, 'I shall also look forward with a great deal of pleasure to receiving your check for twenty-five thousand – the balance on the figure I quoted for my services.'

She turned her head slowly, looked up at him. 'A moralist,' she said – 'morbid – and mercenary.'

'Mercenary as hell!' he bobbed his big head up and down violently.

She looked at the tiny watch at her wrist, said: 'It isn't morning yet, strictly speaking – but I'd rather have a drink than anything I can think of.'

Druse laughed. He went to the buffet and took out a squat bottle, glasses, poured two big drinks. He took one to her, raised the other and squinted through it at the light. 'Here's to crime.'

They drank.

THE PERFECT CRIME

C. S. MONTANYE

Carlton Stevens Montanye (1892–1948), an active writer in the early years of pulpwood magazines, appears to have had an exceptional fondness for criminals as protagonists.

Although he wrote for many different periodicals, he achieved the peak of any pulp writer's career by selling numerous stories to *Black Mask*, beginning with the May 1920 issue and continuing through the issue of October 1939. Most were about various crooks, including the Countess d'Yls, who steals a pearl necklace in 'A Shock for the Countess,' Monahan, a yegg, and Rider Lott, inventor of the perfect crime.

His most famous character is the international jewel thief, Captain Valentine, who made his *Black Mask* debut on September 1, 1923, with 'The Suite on the Seventh Floor,' and appeared nine more times in two years, concluding with 'The Dice of Destiny' in the July 1925 issue. The gentleman rogue also was the protagonist of the novel *Moons in Gold*, published in 1936, in which the debonair Valentine, accompanied by his amazingly ingenious Chinese servant Tim, is in Paris, where he has his eye on the world's most magnificent collection of opals.

Montanye also was one of the writers of the Phantom Detective series under the house name Robert Wallace.

'The Perfect Crime' first appeared in the July 1920 issue of *Black Mask*.

THE PERFECT CRIME

C. S. MONTANYE

Two men sat at a table in a waterfront saloon. One was tall, dark and thin. He had the crafty, malevolent face of a gangster or crook. His eyes were beady and set close to a hawk-beak nose. His mouth was loose and weak but his chin was square. The other man was also tall. He was blond and broad shouldered. He was healthy in appearance and youthful looking. He resembled a stevedore or a freight handler from the docks. The two men had never seen each other until ten minutes past.

The dark man absently reached into a pocket and drew out a small, round pasteboard box. He opened it and dipped a thumb and forefinger into it and pinched out some white stuff. This he placed well into a nostril and sniffed it up his nose.

He looked across at the blond, who regarded him curiously.

'Walk in a snow storm, brother?'

'It's dope, isn't it?' the other asked.

The dark man's eyes began to sparkle.

'Happy dust. Have some? No. So much more for me, then. What's your name, brother?'

The blond youth set down his beaker of near-beer.

'My name is Klug – Martin Klug.'

The dark man nodded.

'Martin Klug, you say? I knew a Klug once. He was a gay-cat, which means a blaster or a safe-blower, if you don't happen to know. He was doing a stretch in a band-house in Joplin for a job in Chi. He was old and had big ears. Was he your father?'

'No!' the other replied curtly. 'He wasn't my father. My father was an honest man.'

'Which implies his son isn't, eh? Now, let me see if I can guess what *you* are.'

He cocked his head on one side and looked the youth over.

'You're too big and clumsy for a dip or a leather snatcher. You haven't got enough imagination to be a flash-thief or a con. Your hands are too large for peterman's work and you're too slow to swing on a derrick. What are you? I see your shoes are full of rust and stained with salt water. I'll put you down as a river rat, a rattler grab, which means you're a freight car crook. Am I right?'

The blond youth smiled a little.

'More or less. And you – what are you? *Who* are you?'

The dark man twisted his lips into a grin.

'Me? Brother, I'm Lott – Rider Lott. I'm an inventor. I'm also an author. I'm the inventor of the Perfect Crime. That is to say I've discovered how a job can be turned without any danger of a prison sentence. I'm the author of a little book I hope to publish some day. It's called a Primer of Progressive Crime. I hope you understand me.'

'I don't,' said Klug.

Lott raised a hand.

'Listen. Crime doctors and criminologists say it is impossible to commit a crime without leaving behind a clue. The law of Chance swings an even balance. No matter what is accomplished, so *they* declare, something tangible is always left behind. It might be a finger-print, a drop of blood, a lock of hair, a footprint, a bit of cloth – *something*. Do you get me now?'

Klug nodded.

'And you don't agree with them?'

Lott picked at his right cheek.

'No, I don't agree with them. The Perfect Criminal doesn't have to leave a clue behind. I said the law of Chance swings an even balance. He's not *compelled* to furnish the cops with clues, is he? All he has to do is—'

At this minute a girl came out of the shadows and sat down at the table. She was coarse, voluptuous but possessed of a flashy beauty. She was dressed in tawdry finery and reeked of patchouli. Under a large, dusty picture hat, Klug observed quantities of red-bronze hair. She had cow-like brown eyes, a milk white skin, a vermil mouth. She carried a black satin handbag and a pair of dirty white kid gloves.

'Well, well,' Lott said, as the girl sat down, 'we now have with us Beatrice the Beautiful Brakeman's Daughter. Where have you been keeping yourself, Beatrice? I haven't seen you in six weeks.'

Klug watched the girl curve her painted lips in a smile.

'My name isn't Beatrice,' she said, 'and I never saw you before.'

Lott chuckled.

'Your fault – not mine, then. Beatrice, meet my friend Mr. Martin Klug. He seems to be a nice boy in spite of his name. But he is wasting his youth and ambition robbing freight cars. Stupid occupation, isn't it? Now, if some day he should walk into a bank at twelve o'clock – when the bank cops go and get something to eat – and stick a gun through the wicket of the paying-teller's cage and dip a hand in after it and pick up a package of bills—'

The girl looked at Klug.

'I've got ten cents,' she said. 'Will they back me up a wash of phoney suds for that much?'

'Not while I'm around with a quarter!' Lott said quickly.

He lifted a finger for a lantern-jawed waiter's attention, gave the order and looked at the girl.

'Ten cents is your capital, you say? Beatrice, you surprise me. A swell looker like you and only a thin dime! What's the matter with you? Did you ever happen to fall out of a chair when you were a child? You should be riding around in your limousine. Ten cents! Are you laughing, Martin Klug?'

'I don't see anything funny in that,' Klug growled.

'I was the upstairs maid in a private house,' the girl said moodily. 'Mrs. Cabbler was the madame. She's an old woman with warts on her face. She's about seventy years old, I guess.'

Lott chuckled.

'Seventy, eh? Their necks crack easy when they're that age!'

'I worked there three weeks up to yesterday,' the girl went on. 'I only wanted to get some money together to buy a pair of long white gloves – the kind that come up to your elbows. I'll never be happy until I get long white gloves that come up to my elbows. Look at these dirty things I own. They've been cleaned twelve times—'

'Never mind about the gloves,' Lott said. 'Tell my young friend and myself what happened. You haven't the gloves you yearn for and therefore it stands to reason you weren't paid. You worked three weeks and weren't paid. Why not? What was the trouble? There was trouble of some kind, wasn't there?'

'Yes. Mrs. Cabbler left a ten dollar bill on the bureau in her bedroom. Someone hooked it. She called me in. She said I took it. She discharged me. She wouldn't give me my wages.'

Rider Lott looked hard at the blond youth.

'You hear that, Martin Klug? Mrs. Cabbler said Beatrice took ten dollars from the bureau in her bedroom and discharged her without paying her wages. Clearly an unlawful act.'

'A dirty trick!' The youth said thickly.

'No,' Lott disagreed pleasantly, 'a perfectly proper course to take. Beatrice took the money. But she was forced to give it back. Then her madame took her revenge by discharging her without pay. Only natural, isn't it?'

'She's a devil, that Mrs. Cabbler!' the girl said viciously. 'She looked me in the eyes and seemed to know everything. I gave her back the ten dollars. I didn't know what I was doing, hardly. Now I'll never get those long white gloves that come up to the elbows.'

'I'll buy them for you,' Martin Klug said, 'when I get some money.'

Lott picked at his left cheek.

'You'll never get any if you stick to robbing freight cars. No money in that, my friend.'

The girl pushed aside her glass.

'I wish I hadn't given Mrs. Cabbler back that ten spot. She's got more now than she knows what to do with. Once I was passing along the hall and her bedroom door was ajar. She was counting her money. The whole top of the bed was covered with bills. She keeps it in a trunk under the bed. It is a small black trunk.'

Rider Lott looked across the table again.

'You hear that, Martin Klug? Mrs. Cabbler is seventy years old. She has a trunk full of money. Money isn't much use to a person seventy years old, is it? Young people should have money. You're young – so am I, for that matter.'

He turned his beady eyes on the girl.

'I don't suppose you have the front door key, the back door key, the side door key or any other key, have you Beatrice? I mean to Mrs. Cabbler's house.'

The girl moved restlessly.

'My name isn't Beatrice. But I have the key to the basement door. Just for spite I wouldn't give it back to her. She doesn't know I have it.'

Rider Lott stretched out a thin, pale hand.

'Give me the key you have.'

The girl opened her satin handbag, fumbled in the depths and drew out a key. She gave it to Lott. He dropped it in a pocket and looked at Martin Klug.

'If a person who is an enemy to society works alone,' he stated, 'it is excellent. If two people work together it is less excellent and yet it is not altogether foolhardy. But if three people go out on a job it is flirting with disaster. We are Three. Do you understand what I mean?'

Klug shook his blond head.

'No, I don't.'

'Neither do I,' said the girl.

Lott made an impatient gesture.

'I see why you, Martin Klug, are a river rat. And I see why you, Beatrice, Jewel of my Turban, have never risen above the level of a maid servant. You are both handicapped by the lack of intelligence and imagination. Both of you together don't own the intellect of a common, garden-variety spider. You disgust me.'

Klug scowled.

'Well, what the hell do you mean?'

'Do you mean we should rob Mrs. Cabbler?' the girl asked, breathlessly.

'Ah, a gleam of intelligence!' Lott said mockingly. 'Certainly we shall rob Mrs. Cabbler. Seventy years of age and a trunk full of money! She is made to rob. We have our own particular desires. Beatrice wants a pair of those long white gloves that come to the elbow, to replace the dirty ones she carries—'

'And I,' put in Martin Klug, brightening up, 'need a new pair of shoes. These are all in.'

Lott smiled.

'While I am desirous of placing my books on the newsstands of the underworld. A thousand dollars will float my Primer. It will be of wonderful assistance to young, ambitious crust-floppers, grifters and heavymen. It will make me famous.'

The girl grew animated.

'I should love to rob that skinny witch. And, oh, those gloves—'

Lott picked at his chin with his nervous fingers.

'We shall rob Mrs. Cabbler, the skinny witch. But two of us only must go. Beatrice must be one. She must guide one of us to the bedroom and the trunk with the money. She knows the house. Who will go with her? Martin Klug or myself? We shall draw straws and see.'

He picked up a discarded newspaper, lying beside his chair, and tore two strips of unequal length from it. These he placed in his pale, thin hand and extended the hand toward the blond youth.

'Take one, Martin Klug. If you draw the long strip of paper you go with Beautiful Beatrice and rob Mrs. Cabbler. If you draw the short one I go.'

Klug hesitated a minute and then drew one of the strips of paper from the hand before him. It proved to be the longest piece.

'So be it,' Lott said. 'Go with Beatrice and rob the skinny witch. And remember these things: Use no violence of any kind. Take no chances, leave no clues. Take great pains to cover every step and don't be in a hurry. After you have the money, if you will go back and check over every move you have made, in quest of suspicious or incriminating clues left behind, and then remove them, you will have accomplished the Perfect Crime. I hope you know and understand my meaning.'

Klug inclined his head.

'I do.'

Lott looked at a battered nickel watch.

'Twelve after one.' He considered the two with a roving glance. 'We'll spring this job on a share and share alike basis. We'll divide Mrs. Cabbler's money into three equal portions. But we must decide now on a place where we can cut the swag. It's bad business dividing in a public place. Where can we go?'

The girl stood up.

'I know the very place. I live with my sister. She has a flat up on Tenth Avenue. She's away now. You can both go there. You can stay there as long as you want.'

Lott attained his feet.

'Fine. Let's start for Mrs. Cabbler's now. A woman of seventy sleeps as heavily at twelve o'clock as at three.'

Martin Klug stood up.

'Are you coming, too?' he inquired, as if surprised.

Lott turned up his coat collar.

'Certainly. I shall wait outside for you both.'

II

Two men and a girl sat at a table in the living-room of a cheap Tenth Avenue flat. It was the night following. A gas jet flickered garishly. An empty whisky bottle was on the table. The odor of booze mingled with that of cigarettes.

'Are you sure,' Lott said, 'you left no tell-tale marks behind you, incriminating evidence? Did you follow my instructions to the letter? Did you make it a Perfect Crime?'

Martin Klug shifted about in his rickety chair.

'I'm sure. I remembered what you told me. I went over the ground carefully. I even picked up the burnt matches.'

'Robbery,' said Lott, 'means anywhere from five to twenty years. But murder means the chair. You made a mistake, Martin Klug. You shouldn't have killed the old woman.'

The girl laughed.

'What else could he do? Just when we pulled out the trunk the old witch opened her eyes. She began to squawk.'

Lott shook his head soberly.

'You could have tied her up. You could have gagged her. You didn't *have* to kill her!'

Martin Klug drew a breath.

'I was excited,' he confessed. 'I'm used to freight cars, not bedrooms. I pulled out the trunk. Then I looked up and saw the old woman's eyes looking at me. They were eyes like a fish's, cold and dead looking. Then she began to squawk. So I took her skinny throat between my hands.'

'Bad business,' said Lott. 'Well, there's no use of shedding tears about it. It's over and done with. Get the coin, Beatrice. We'll split it up.'

The girl went to the corner of the room. She pulled aside a couch and drew out a package wrapped in newspaper. She brought this to the table and laid it before Lott. He opened it and drew out three packages of money.

'Nine thousand dollars,' he said. 'Divide it by three and it equals three thousand dollars apiece.'

'I don't see where you come off to get any of it,' Martin Klug grumbled. 'What did *you* do?'

Lott twisted his lips into a grim smile.

'I suppose you want my share because you croaked the old lady? What did *I* do? Nothing, not a thing, except plan the robbery. This three thousand is my royalty on the idea. Get me? What do *you* say, Beatrice?'

'My name isn't Beatrice,' the girl replied. 'And I don't say anything at all. Take the dough – it's yours!'

'You're a droll humorist, my young murderer, if you know what that is,' Lott said to the blond young man.

'Here, take your share of the stuff and keep your mouth shut. Beatrice, Pearl of Price, put your mitts on your three thousand. Take it, my dear. Heaven is witness you earned it!'

The girl grabbed up her package of money and hugged it to her full breast.

'Mine! All mine!' she exulted. 'And that's not all either! No, that's not all! Wait – look! I want to show you something!'

She jumped up, went to her wrap and dug something out of a pocket – something long and supple as a white snake. She held the objects up before Lott's eyes.

'Do you see 'em? *Gloves* – long white gloves that come up to my elbows!'

Martin Klug chuckled.

'She saw them on the dresser in the old woman's room. She made a dive for them. She seemed to want them more than the coin. Women are funny.'

The girl pressed the gloves to her face.

'They're just the kind I dreamed about! It's a joke. I worked there three weeks to get the money to buy them and all the time the old hag had just the gloves I wanted. Well, they're no use to her now. Won't they look swell with that big hat of mine? I'm terribly lucky. When Martin Klug lit the match they were the first things I saw!'

Lott picked at his chin.

'You should have heard the old dame squawk,' Martin Klug said suddenly, with a laugh. 'Then you should have heard her gurgle when I got hold of her windpipe. It sounded like water running out of a sink!'

He sighed.

'We've divided up the stuff, Lott. Let's get down to brass tacks. Let's divide up the girl. You want her. I want her. Who gets her? That's what I want to know.'

The dark man took a deliberate sniff of snow and stretched his long arms.

'I'm in a drift. But don't dig me out! Who gets the girl? Who gets Beatrice the Beaut? Ask her? Who does get you, sweetheart?'

The girl ceased admiring the long, new white kid gloves in her hands.

'They are just my size. It was good to shake the old ones. Now these—'

'Answer the question!' Lott said briskly. 'Who gets you?'

She looked slowly from one to the other.

'Well,' she murmured, 'you're both nice. I like you both.'

'Make a choice,' Lott said brusquely. 'Don't beat around the bush. We both can't have you. That's polygamy; against the law. It wouldn't do to run afoul of the law – that way. So – which?'

The girl let a scowl creep across her beautiful face.

'I think,' she said, after an interval, 'if you would stop calling me Beatrice, I'd like *you* the best!'

Lott picked at his lips.

'Good. Then *I* get you, eh? Is that it?'

Martin Klug lurched heavily to his feet.

'*Like hell you get her!*'

He made a swift lunge at Lott. But the dark man was too quick for him.

Lott jumped to his feet and threw back his head with a quick, feline motion. The blow glided harmlessly over his shoulder. He seized the whisky bottle by the neck as the blond youth sprang at him like a tiger. He side-stepped and brought the bottle down with all his force on the skull of the other.

Klug stopped short, moaned faintly, groaned, and sank in an odd, limp heap on the table.

Then he rolled off it and sprawled, stirless, on the dirty uncarpeted floor.

Lott laughed a little.

'Poor fool! Now we have three thousand more than we had two minutes ago. I guess I've killed him. A tap on the façade is always like that if you use force. Maybe it's just as well. He was only a river rat. Get on your hat and coat, Beatrice. Put the cash in a bag. We've got to get out of here now in a hurry.'

While the girl hastened to obey his orders, Lott took another sniff of dope and prodded Klug's body with his foot.

'No imagination,' he said under his breath. 'It's just as well—'

The girl loomed up before him. She had a satchel in her hand and wore the large, dusty picture hat.

'Wait until I put on these new gloves. They're soft. I love them. I always wanted them.'

She began to flex her hands into them while Lott pushed Klug's body under the table.

'What did you do with the other gloves – the dirty ones?' he asked.

The girl held out a rounded arm and inspected the new glove.

'What did I do with 'em? What do you think? I just naturally chucked them away. What do I want with rotten old gloves like those, that have been cleaned twelve times?'

Lott drew his brows together and glanced at his nickel watch.

'Where did you throw them?'

She began donning the second glove.

'Oh, in the trash basket in the old witch's room. What difference does it make?'

Lott grasped her arm. His face had changed. Color had crept into it. His eyes burned queerly.

'*In the trash basket!* You threw your old gloves in the trash basket in *that room!*'

The girl sought to wrench her arm from the tight grip he put upon it.

'What's eating you!' she said sibilantly. 'You've got too much snow on board—'

Lott drew his lips over his teeth.

'*You fool!*' he cried. '*You little fool!* You've—'

He stopped and dropped her arm. The lids fell over his gleaming eyes. He moved his head to one side as if listening. Something in his attitude caused the girl to listen, too. For a long, tense minute she heard nothing. Then, on her strained ears sounded a footfall on the stairs outside . . . another.

She heard Lott draw a quick breath.

At the same instant the door burst open and two men stepped in, drawn revolvers glinting in the gaslight. Both wore derby hats and an air of authority. One motioned her to fall back against the wall; the other man jammed his gun in Lott's face.

'I'm Davis of Headquarters!' this second man snapped. 'You and the moll are wanted. Case of murder – croaking old Mrs. Cabbler the rich widow! Out with your dukes and let me jewel you!'

Lott, against the table, hands trembling over his head, looked at the cowering figure of the girl.

'*In the trash basket*,' he whispered. 'Oh, God—'

The detective, adjusting steel handcuffs, grunted.

'In the trash basket is right! It was a careful job and neatly turned. Not even a burnt match or a fingerprint. But no crime is perfect. We fished the dirty gloves out of the trash basket. They were full of numbers and those ink marks the cleaners put in them. We spent the day getting a line on the numbers in them. An hour ago we found the establishment that had cleaned them—'

THE MONKEY MURDER

ERLE STANLEY GARDNER

There is a rich tradition in mystery fiction of the Robin Hood thief, the sympathetic figure who steals from the rich to give to the deserving poor. Lester Leith, the hero of more than seventy novelettes, all written for the pulps, approached his thievery from a slightly different angle. He did steal from the rich, but only those who were themselves crooks, and he gave the money to charities – after taking a twenty per cent 'recovery' fee.

Debonair, quick-witted and wealthy, he enjoyed the perks of his fortune, checking the newspapers in the comfort of his penthouse apartment for new burglaries and robberies to solve, and from which he could reclaim the stolen treasures.

He has a valet, Beaver, nicknamed 'Scuttle' by Leith, who is a secret plant of Sergeant Arthur Ackley. Leith, of course, is aware that his manservant is an undercover operative, using that knowledge to plant misinformation to frustrate the policeman again and again.

Leith is only one of a huge number of characters created by the indefatigable Erle Stanley Gardner (1889–1970), many of whom were criminals, including Ed Jenkins (the Phantom Crook), the sinister Patent Leather Kid, and Senor Arnaz de Lobo, a professional soldier of fortune and revolutionary.

'The Monkey Murder' was first published in the January 1939 issue of *Detective Story*.

THE MONKEY MURDER

ERLE STANLEY GARDNER

Lester Leith, his slender, well-knit form attired in a cool suit of Shantung pongee, sprawled indolently in the reclining wicker chair. The cool afternoon breezes filtered through the screened windows of the penthouse apartment. Leith's valet, Beaver, nicknamed 'Scuttle' by Lester Leith, ponderous in his obsequious servility, siphoned soda into a Tom Collins and deferentially placed the glass on the table beside his master's chair.

If Leith had any knowledge that this man who served him, ostensibly interested only in his creature comforts, was in reality a police undercover man, planted on the job by Sergeant Arthur Ackley, he gave no indication. His slate-gray eyes, the color of darkly tarnished silver, remained utterly inscrutable as he stared thoughtfully at the bubbles which formed on the glass only to detach themselves and race upward through the cool beverage.

The valet coughed.

Leith's eyes remained fixed, staring into the distance.

The police spy squirmed uneasily, then said: 'Begging your pardon, sir, was there something you wanted?'

Leith, without turning his head, said, 'I think not, Scuttle.'

The big undercover man shifted his weight from one foot to the other, fidgeted uneasily, then said: 'Begging your pardon, sir, please don't think I'm presumptuous, but I was about to venture to suggest – Well, sir—'

'Come, come, Scuttle,' Lester Leith said. 'Out with it. What is it?'

'About the crime news, sir,' the undercover man blurted. 'It's been some time since you've taken an interest in the crime news, sir.'

Leith sipped his Tom Collins. 'Quite right, Scuttle,' he said. 'And it will probably be a much longer time before I do so.'

'May I ask why, sir?'

'On account of Sergeant Ackley,' Leith said. 'Damn the man, Scuttle. He's like a woman convinced against her will, and of the same opinion still. Somewhere, somehow, he got it through that fat head of his that I was the mysterious hijacker who has been ferreting out the criminals who have made rich hauls, and relieving them of their ill-gotten spoils.'

'Yes, sir,' the spy said. 'He certainly *has* been most annoying, sir.'

'As a matter of fact,' Leith went on, 'whoever that mysterious hijacker is –

and I understand the police are firmly convinced there is such an individual – he has my sincere respect and admiration. After all, Scuttle, crime *should* be punished. Crime which isn't detected isn't punished. As I understand it, the criminals who have been victimized by this hijacker are men who have flaunted their crimes in the faces of the police and got away with it. The police have been unable to spot them, let alone get enough evidence to convict them. Then along comes this mysterious hijacker, solves the crime where the police have failed, locates the criminal, and levies a hundred-percent fine by relieving him of his ill-gotten gains. That, Scuttle, I claim is a distinct service to society.'

'Yes, sir,' the spy said. 'Of course, you will admit that your charities for the widows and orphans of police and firemen killed in the line of duty, your donations to the associated charities and the home for the aged have been steadily mounting.'

'Well, what of it, Scuttle? What the devil has that to do with the subject under discussion?'

'Begging your pardon, sir, I think the sergeant wonders where you're getting the money, sir.'

Lester Leith placed the half-empty glass back on the table, and reached for his cigarette case. 'Confound the man's impudence, Scuttle. What business is it of his where I get my money?'

'Yes, sir, I understand, sir. Oh, quite, sir. But even so, sir, if you'll pardon my making the suggestion, sir, it seems that you shouldn't let such a trivial matter interfere with your enjoyment of life.'

'My enjoyment of life, Scuttle?'

'Well, sir, I know that you always derived a great deal of pleasure from looking over the crime clippings. As you've so frequently remarked, you used to feel that a man could study the newspaper accounts of crime and in many cases spot the guilty party, just from the facts given in the newspapers.'

'I still maintain that can be done, Scuttle.'

'Yes, sir,' the spy said, lowering his voice. 'And has it ever occurred to you, sir, that what Sergeant Ackley doesn't know won't hurt him?'

'Won't hurt him,' Lester Leith exclaimed. 'It's what Sergeant Ackley doesn't know that's ruining him! If knowledge is power, Sergeant Ackley has leaky valves, loose pistons, scored cylinders, and burnt-out bearings. He's narrow-minded, egotistical, suspicious, mercenary, selfish, and pig-headed. In addition to all of which, Scuttle, I find that I don't like the man.'

'Yes, sir,' the spy said, 'but if you'd only interest yourself in the crime clippings just once more, sir, I have several very interesting items saved up for you. And Sergeant Ackley would never know, sir.'

Leith said reprovingly, 'Scuttle, you're trying to tempt me.'

'I'm sorry, sir. I didn't mean to . . . that is, really, sir. Well, of course, you may depend upon my discretion, sir.'

Leith half turned in his chair. 'I can trust you, Scuttle?' he asked, looking at the spy with his inscrutable silver-gray eyes.

'Absolutely, sir, with your very life, sir.'

Lester Leith sighed, settled back, and tapped a cigarette on a polished thumbnail. 'Scuttle,' he said, 'perhaps it's my mood, perhaps it's the weather, perhaps it's the drink; but I've decided to indulge in my hobby *just* once more, only mind you, Scuttle, this time it will be merely an academic pursuit. We'll merely speculate on who the criminal *might* be and keep that speculation entirely to ourselves, a sacred confidence within the four walls of this room.'

'Yes, sir,' the spy said, quivering with eagerness as he pulled a sheaf of newspaper clippings from his pocket.

'Sit down, Scuttle,' Leith invited. 'Sit down and make yourself comfortable.'

'Very good, sir. Thank you, sir.'

Lester Leith snapped a match into flame, held it to the tip of the cigarette, and inhaled deeply, extinguishing the match with a single smoky exhalation. 'Proceed, Scuttle,' he said.

'Yes, sir. The affair of the Brentwood diamond seems to have been made to order for you, sir.'

'Made to order for *me*, Scuttle?'

'Yes, sir,' the undercover man said, forgetting himself for the moment as he perused the newspaper clipping. 'The police have never found the culprit. There's a chance for you to make a good haul and—'

'Scuttle!' Lester Leith interrupted.

The valet jumped. 'Oh, I *beg* your pardon, sir. I didn't mean it in that way, sir. What I meant—'

'Never mind, Scuttle. We'll pass the Brentwood diamond. What else do you have?'

'That was the main one, sir.'

'Well, forget it, Scuttle.'

The spy thumbed through the clippings. 'There's the man who was choked and robbed of some two thousand dollars he'd won at gambling.'

'Skip it, Scuttle,' Lester Leith interrupted. 'A man who wins two thousand dollars at gambling, and hasn't sense enough to go to a downtown hotel and stay there until daylight, deserves to lose his winnings. That's an old gambling-house trick. What else do you have?'

'There was the woman who shot her husband and claimed—'

'Tut, tut, Scuttle,' Lester Leith said. 'You've been reading the tabloids again. That is completely stereotyped. She shot him because he had forfeited her respect. She shot him because she couldn't demean herself to accept the status in life which he thought a wife should have. She had been married ten years, but she made the revolting discovery of his baser instincts at a time when a revolver happened to be handy. She snatched it from her purse, thinking only to bring him to his senses, and then she can't remember exactly what happened. She thinks he started for her, and everything went blank. She felt the recoil of the revolver as it roared in her hand. Then she couldn't remember anything until she found herself at the telephone notifying the police. That was right after she'd slipped out of her house dress and put on her best outfit.'

'I see you've read it, sir,' the undercover man said. 'I didn't realize you were familiar with the case. May I ask, if you don't mind, sir, how you happened to know about it? Were they friends of yours?'

'I'm not familiar with *that* case,' Leith said wearily, 'but with dozens of others of the same type. Come on, Scuttle; let's have something fresh.'

'Well, sir, I don't think there's— Oh, yes, sir, here's something rather unusual. The murder of a monkey, sir.'

'The murder of a monkey?' Leith said, turning half around, so that he could study the spy's face. 'Why the devil should anyone want to murder a monkey?'

'Well, of course, strictly speaking, sir, it isn't murder, but I've referred to it as murder because if what the police suspect is true, that's virtually what it amounted to . . . that is, sir, I trust you understand me . . . I mean—'

'I don't understand you,' Lester Leith interrupted, 'and I have no means of knowing what you mean except from what you say. Kindly elucidate, Scuttle.'

'Yes, sir, it was a monkey belonging to Peter B. Mainwaring. Mr. Mainwaring was returning from a year spent abroad, principally in India and Africa.'

'Come, come, Scuttle,' Lester Leith said. 'Get to the point. Why was the monkey murdered?'

'It was Mr. Mainwaring's monkey, sir.'

'And who killed it, Scuttle?'

'The police don't know. It was a holdup man.'

'A holdup man, Scuttle?'

'Yes, sir. According to Mr. Mainwaring's story, the bandit held up the automobile, shot the monkey through the head, and slit its body open. Mr. Mainwaring thinks the killer came from India. It's some sort of a ceremony having to do with thuggee and the monkey priests who worship the monkeys and exact a death penalty from any monkey that deserts the clan.'

'I've never heard of anything like that before,' Leith said.

'Yes, sir. That's the story that Mr. Mainwaring has given to the police.'

'Bosh and nonsense,' Lester Leith said. 'Thuggee is one thing; the monkey worship of India is entirely different . . . that is, there's no possible connection which could result in a man following another from India to America just to kill a monkey and slit him open.'

'Yes, sir,' the spy said dubiously. 'The police don't know much about it. I don't mind telling you, sir, however, that . . . well, perhaps I shouldn't mention it.'

'Go ahead,' Leith said. 'What is it?'

'I think I mentioned at one time that one of my lady friends was quite friendly with a member of the force, not that she's encouraged him, but he persists in—'

'Yes, yes, I remember,' Leith said. 'A policeman, isn't it, Scuttle?'

'No, sir. He's been promoted to a detective.'

'Oh, yes, Scuttle. I remember now. Where's he stationed?'

The spy said: 'Begging your pardon, sir, I'd rather not talk about that. But I don't mind repeating a bit of information occasionally.'

'Am I to understand,' Lester Leith asked, 'that this detective habitually tells this young woman police secrets, and the young woman in turn makes a practice of passing them on to you?'

The big spy smirked. 'That's rather a bald statement, sir.'

'Bald, nothing,' Leith observed; 'you are doubtless referring to its whiskers.'

'Beg your pardon, sir?'

Leith said: 'Nothing, Scuttle. I was merely making a comment to myself. Go on. Tell me what you were going to say about Mainwaring.'

'Well, sir, the police had an idea that Mainwaring may have been in league with a gang of smugglers and that he *may* have killed the monkey himself in order to cover up the real reason of the holdup. Or, then again, the man may have been an accomplice who had been tricked, and shot at Mainwaring and hit the monkey instead.

'You may be interested in knowing that the police have reason to believe Mainwaring left India in fear of his life.'

'What has all this to do with smuggling, Scuttle?'

'Well, sir, *if* the native rumors are true, sir, Mainwaring *may* have slipped two very valuable gems to some native accomplice with instructions to smuggle them into this country. The gems weren't in the car with Mainwaring, but he *may* have had them in India and intrusted this native to—'

'What gems, Scuttle?'

'The jewels of the monkey god, sir.'

'The jewels of the monkey god? Come, come, Scuttle; this is beginning to sound like one of Sergeant Ackley's wild accusations.'

'Yes, sir. Over in India there's the special god for monkeys, a god that's named . . . Hanne . . . Hanney—'

'Hanuman?' Lester Leith suggested.

'Yes, sir. That's it, sir. Hanuman. I remember the name now that you've helped me, sir. Thank you, sir.'

'What about Hanuman, the monkey god?' Lester Leith asked.

'It seems that back in the jungles, sir, there's a huge statue of the monkey god. He's covered with gold leaf. His eyes were emeralds, and his breast nipples consist of two huge emeralds. It seems that some adventurer managed to gain access to this temple and substituted bits of green glass for the emeralds. The substitution wasn't discovered for some time.'

'And what has this to do with Mainwaring's smuggling?' Lester Leith asked.

'The police, sir, have reason to believe that it was Mainwaring who made the substitution.'

'Peter B. Mainwaring?' Lester Leith asked.

The valet nodded.

Leith said thoughtfully: 'Now, Scuttle, you interest me. You interest me very much indeed. I think you'll agree with me, Scuttle, that if that were the truth, Mainwaring shouldn't be allowed to retain the fruits of his nefarious action.'

'Yes, sir,' the spy agreed, his eyes eager. 'Only Mainwaring apparently doesn't have them.'

'And, by the same sign,' Leith said, 'You will also admit that there is nothing to be gained by sending these stones back to the jungle to become part of the anatomy of a heathen idol.'

'Yes, sir, I agree with you upon *that* absolutely, sir,' the spy said with alacrity.

'Under the circumstances,' Leith announced, 'we'll consider the murder of this monkey, Scuttle. Tell me about it.'

'Yes, sir. Well, you see, sir, the police had been notified. They thought that perhaps Mr. Mainwaring was bringing the emeralds in with him although Mainwaring had denied having them in his possession or knowing anything about them. He admitted that he had been in that section of the country at about the time the stones disappeared. In fact, he said it was due to this fact and only to this fact that the natives thought he was responsible for the theft.'

'Yes,' Leith said. 'I can understand how it would happen that a white man, under such circumstances, would be considered responsible for the loss by ignorant or superstitious natives. Perhaps Mainwaring was telling the truth after all, Scuttle.'

'Well, sir. You see, it was this way, sir. The police and the customs officials were watching Mainwaring closely. Mainwaring made no declaration of the gems, nor did a most thorough search of his baggage reveal them. But he must have been mixed up with Indian gangsters, the disciples of thuggee. At any rate, this stickup looks like it.'

'Mainwaring was traveling alone?' Lester Leith asked.

'His nurse was with him, sir.'

'His nurse, Scuttle?'

'Yes, sir. Mr. Mainwaring is suffering from an indisposition, an organic heart trouble. At times when he's seized with an attack, it is necessary that a nurse administer a hypodermic at once.'

'A male nurse, Scuttle?'

'No, sir. A female nurse, and rather a good-looking nurse at that.'

'*Heart* trouble, did you say, Scuttle?'

'Yes, sir.'

'I can well understand it,' Leith said. 'And the nurse was in India with him?'

'Yes, sir. Airdree Clayton is her name. There's a photograph of both of them here if you'd like to see it, sir.'

Lester Leith nodded. The big spy passed across the newspaper photograph. Leith looked at it and then read the caption.

Peter B. Mainwaring and his nurse, Airdree Clayton, who have just returned from extensive travels in India and Africa. While customs officials were going through the baggage of himself and nurse with what Mainwaring indignantly insisted was unusual thoroughness, Miss Clayton sat on a table in the inspector's office, chewed gum, and entertained Mr. Mainwaring's pet monkey. This monkey was subsequently killed in a most mysterious holdup. Mainwaring threatened to report the customs officials for rudeness, unnecessary search, and unfounded accusations. Miss Clayton, on the other hand, said the customs inspector was 'delightful,' and returned to his office after having been searched by a matron, to thank the inspector for his consideration.

Lester Leith said, 'She chews gum, Scuttle?'

'So the newspaper article says. Apparently she chews gum vigorously.'

Leith digested that information for several thoughtful seconds.

'Scuttle,' he said, 'I can imagine nothing more soothing to the nerves than a nurse who chews gum. There's a quieting monotony in the repetition of chewing, as sedative in its effect as rain on a roof. *I* want a nurse who chews gum. Make a note of that, Scuttle.'

'A nurse who chews gum, sir!'

'Yes,' Leith said, 'and she should be rather good-looking. I noticed that Miss Clayton's . . . er . . . pedal extremities and the anatomical connecties are rather peculiarly adapted to photography.'

'Yes, sir,' the spy said. 'Do I gather that you want a nurse with shapely legs, sir?'

'Not exactly that,' Lester Leith replied. 'I want a nurse who chews gum. If her means of locomotion are attractive to the eye, Scuttle, that'd be an added inducement.'

'But there's no reason why *you* should have a nurse, is there? That is, I mean, sir, you aren't sick?'

'No,' Leith said. 'I feel quite all right, Scuttle. Thank you.'

'Therefore,' the spy said, 'begging your pardon, sir, employing a nurse would seem rather . . . er . . . conspicuous, would it not?'

'Perhaps so,' Lester said. 'And yet, on the other hand, Scuttle, I can imagine nothing which would more readily reconcile me to Sergeant Ackley's continued existence than association with a young woman with shapely pedal extremities, who makes a habit of placidly chewing gum.'

The spy blinked his small, black eyes rapidly as he strove to comprehend the significance of Leith's remark.

'Therefore,' Leith went on, 'since a nurse seems conspicuous, as you have termed it, I shall insist upon a gum-chewing secretary, Scuttle. Make a note to call the employment agencies asking for an adroit, expert, inveterate gum chewer, a secretary with pulchritude and bovine masticational habits, a careless parker— Here, Scuttle, take a pencil, and take this down as I dictate it.'

'Yes, sir,' the dazed spy said.

'A position at good salary is open,' Lester Leith dictated, 'for a pulchritudinous young woman with shapely means of locomotion, amiable, easygoing, good-natured, acquiescent young woman preferred, one who never becomes nervous under any circumstances, a proficient, adroit, expert, and inveterate gum chewer, preferably a careless parker, must be able to pop her gum loudly. Salary, three hundred dollars per month with all traveling expenses. . . . Have you got that, Scuttle?'

'Yes, sir,' the spy said, his voice showing dazed incredulity.

'Very good,' Leith observed. 'Telephone the employment agencies, and now let's get back to Mainwaring.'

'Mainwaring got through customs on the evening of the thirteenth, sir. The customs officials found nothing which hadn't been declared. It was then about seven o'clock and getting dark. Mainwaring's chauffeur was waiting for him. He—'

'Just a minute, Scuttle. Mainwaring didn't take his chauffeur on this tour with him, did he?'

'No, sir. The chauffeur stayed and acted as a caretaker at the house.'

'I see. Go on, Scuttle.'

'Well, the chauffeur loaded the hand baggage into the car, and they started for Mainwaring's house. When they were somewhere around Eighty-sixth Street, the right rear tire blew out; and when the chauffeur went to fix it, he found the jack was broken. He knew of a garage some half dozen blocks away, and Mainwaring said he and Miss Clayton would wait in the car while the chauffeur went to the garage. The chauffeur had some difficulty as the garage was closed. He thinks he was gone perhaps some thirty minutes in all. The robber held up Mainwaring only a few minutes after the chauffeur started out. In fact the chauffeur saw the bandit drive past him, noticed him particularly because of his build. He was big, fat, massive, and with a swarthy complexion. The chauffeur actually saw his features, sir. He was the only one who did. The stickup man had put on a mask by the time he had driven abreast of the Mainwaring car.'

'Why did the chauffeur notice him so particularly, Scuttle?'

'Because he thought the man might stop, pick him up, and drive him to a garage, sir. The chauffeur had his livery on, and he stepped out from the curb and motioned to this man. The chauffeur's quite thin himself, sir, and he naturally noticed the other's corpulence.'

'The man didn't stop, Scuttle?'

'No, sir. He seemed, according to the chauffeur, to be driving fast and with a purpose. When the chauffeur saw his swarthy complexion, he wondered if the man might not be following Mainwaring's car; but he dismissed the thought as being a bit farfetched. Yet there can be no doubt of it that it was this man who held up Mainwaring and killed the monkey.'

'Killed the monkey!' Lester Leith exclaimed. 'Do you mean that this was *all* the man accomplished?'

'Yes, sir. He killed the monkey. That seemed to be what he wanted to overtake the car for.'

'And didn't take anything?'

'No, sir.'

'That's odd,' Leith said. 'And the man was masked?'

'Yes, sir, he was, but the nurse feels quite certain that he was a native of Southern India. Both she and Mainwaring agree that he was very fat although he moved with catlike quickness. He was driving a car which had been stolen.'

'How do they know the car was stolen?' Leith asked.

'Because the chauffeur, returning with the jack, saw this same car again. This time it was speeding away from the scene of the holdup. He noticed that the driver was wearing a mask which concealed his features, so he took occasion to notice the license number. He gave it to the police, of course, as soon as he learned of the holdup. The police found that the car had been stolen. Later on, they found the car itself parked on Ninety-third Street. It had been abandoned there.'

'On Ninety-third Street,' Lester Leith said, frowning. 'Wait a minute, Scuttle. Isn't there a suburban railroad station there?'

'Yes, sir. I believe there is, sir. That's the station where nearly all of the incoming and outgoing trains stop to pick up passengers who prefer to avoid the congestion of the central depot.'

'And the monkey was slit open, Scuttle?'

'Yes, sir.'

'What was the chauffeur's name, Scuttle?'

'Deekin. Parsley B. Deekin, sir.'

'Any photographs of him?'

'Yes, sir. Here's one, sir.'

Leith studied the photograph of the thin hatchet face, prominent cheekbones, and large eyes. 'Rather young to be a chauffeur, isn't it, Scuttle?'

'I don't think he's so young, sir. It's because he's thin that he looks young; the effect of a slender figure, you know.'

'I see,' Leith said, frowning thoughtfully. 'And after the monkey was killed, he was slit open?'

'That's right, cut almost in two, and then tossed back into the car. Mainwaring said he's been afraid all along that an attempt would be made on the monkey's life by some religious fanatic. He said that the monkey was a temple monkey, that his life was supposed to have been consecrated to the priests of Hanuman. He says that in India when a monkey has been so consecrated and then leaves the temple, the priests consider it a desertion just as they do when a priest has consecrated his life to the monkey god and then tries to leave the temple and take up life somewhere else.'

'Sounds like a barbarous custom, Scuttle.' Lester Leith said.

'Yes, sir, it is, sir. Oh, quite.'

'Any other witnesses, Scuttle?'

'None who saw the man's face, sir. A young woman glimpsed a very fat, paunchy man with a mask which concealed his entire face driving a car. She couldn't even tell the make of the car, however. She thought it was a sedan. The car the man used was, in reality, a coupé. It had been stolen about six o'clock in the evening. Because the man took such pains to conceal all of his skin, the police deduce he must have been swarthy.'

Leith grinned.

'Aided in that deduction, of course, Scuttle, by the chauffeur's statement.'

'Yes, sir, I suppose so, sir. But Mainwaring and the nurse both thought he was a native of Southern India, you'll remember, sir.'

Lester Leith held up his hand for silence. 'Wait a minute, Scuttle; I want to think.'

For several seconds he sat rigid in the chair, his face an expressionless mask, his eyes slitted in thought. The valet-spy, his big form perched on the edge of the chair, regarded Lester Leith thoughtfully.

Suddenly Lester Leith said: 'Scuttle, let me have the telephone book, and find out what trains pull out of the Ninety-third Street Station between seven and nine thirty in the evening. Get me the information at once.'

'Very good, sir,' the spy said, vanishing in the direction of the soundproof closet in which the telephone was housed.

Five minutes later, he was back with the information. 'A train leaving the central depot at seven twenty, sir, stops at Ninety-third Street at seven fifty, at Belting Junction at eight ten, at Robbinsdale at eight thirty, and at Beacon City at nine thirty. After that, it becomes a limited train and makes no stops until after midnight. Those other stops are merely for the purpose of taking on suburban passengers.'

Leith said: 'Very well, Scuttle. Plug in the telephone extension, and put the desk phones over here.'

When the spy had done so, Lester Leith called the baggageman at Belting Junction, and said: 'Hello, I'm trying to trace a suitcase which was checked through on the train which leaves Central Depot at seven twenty in the evening. This suitcase went forward on the evening of the thirteenth, and has not been claimed. I have reason to believe it was checked to your depot.'

'Who is this talking?' the baggageman asked.

'This is the claim adjuster's office,' Leith said. 'Shake a leg.'

'Just a minute,' the baggageman said. And then after a few moments, he reported, 'No, there's no such suitcase here.'

'Thank you,' Leith said, and hung up.

He called the station agent at Robbinsdale, made the same statement, and secured the same answer. But at Beacon City, the situation was different. The baggageman said:

'Yeah, we've got a suitcase here. It came on that train, and has never been called for. I've been charging storage on it at the rate of ten cents for every twenty-four hours, after it was uncalled for forty-eight hours. What do you want me to do with it?'

'Describe the suitcase,' Leith said.

'Well, it's a cheap, split-leather suitcase, tan, with straps. It's rather large.'

'Any initials on it?' Leith said.

'Yes, there are the initials A.B.C. in black on both ends of the suitcase.'

'Well,' Leith said, 'a man will probably call for it tomorrow. He won't have his claim check. Make him deposit a bond of fifty dollars and describe the contents, then give him the suitcase.'

'It'll be all right to give it to him if he doesn't have the check?' the baggage agent asked.

'Yes, *if* he describes the contents, and *if* he puts up a fifty-dollar bond. The check's been lost, and this party claims the baggageman here put a wrong check on it. I don't think he did, but anyhow we've located the suitcase, and that's all that's necessary. He'll be out tomorrow. In the meantime you open the suitcase, familiarize yourself with the contents, and don't let anyone who can't describe those contents have the suitcase. That's important.'

Lester Leith hung up the telephone, and nodded to the spy.

'I think, Scuttle,' he said, 'that the situation is now greatly clarified.'

'What do you mean, sir?' the spy asked.

Leith said: 'Has it ever occurred to you, Scuttle, that Mainwaring resorted to rather a clever trick? Before he landed, he opened the mouth of the monkey and forced those emeralds into the monkey's stomach, probably intending to kill the monkey himself and remove the stones when he had reached his home. However some clever holdup man, who deduced what must have happened, swooped down on him, killed the monkey, cut the animal open, and took out the stones. Mainwaring naturally isn't in a position to make a complete explanation to the police because then he'd be guilty of smuggling and subject to a fine. So he had to put the best face he could on the matter and make up this cock-and-bull story about the priests of Hanuman following the monkey and exacting his life as a sacrifice.'

'Good heavens, sir! You're right!' the spy exclaimed.

'Of course I'm right,' Leith said, frowning slightly. 'Don't seem so surprised, Scuttle. I have shown what is, after all, only very ordinary intelligence.'

'But what happened to the gems, sir?'

Lester Leith stared thoughtfully into space for several seconds. At length he said: 'In order to answer that question, Scuttle, I would require two specially constructed canes, four imitation emeralds, a package of cotton, and a gum-chewing secretary.'

'You've already asked me to get the secretary,' the spy suggested.

'So I have,' Leith said, 'so I have.'

'If you don't mind my asking, sir, what type of cane did you have in mind?'

'I would need two canes, identical in appearance,' Lester Leith said, 'two very large canes with hollow handles; that is, there must be a receptacle hollowed out in the handle of each cane. This receptacle must be capable of concealing two of the imitation emeralds; and one cane must have a telescopic metal ferrule so it can be extended and locked into position, or telescoped back and locked into position. Aside from that, both canes must be exactly alike.'

The spy blinked his eyes. 'I don't see what that has to do with it, sir,' he said.

Leith smiled. 'After all, Scuttle, the gum-chewing secretary is of prime importance. However, Scuttle, I think I've exercised my wits enough for this afternoon. I believe I have a dinner engagement?'

'Yes, sir. That's right, sir. But when do you want these canes, sir?'

'I'd require them by tomorrow morning at the very latest. I – What's that, Scuttle?'

'You were talking about the canes, sir, when you wanted them.'

'Good heavens,' Leith said. '*I* don't want the canes. I was merely working out an academic solution for a crime. Under no circumstances, Scuttle, are you to take me seriously.'

'Yes, sir,' the spy said.

'And I don't want the canes.'

'No, sir.'

'Nor the cotton.'

'No, sir.'

'But,' Leith said, 'you *might* get me the secretary, Scuttle. Have each agency send its most proficient gum chewer.'

CHAPTER II

Beaver Reports

Sergeant Ackley sat at a battered desk in police headquarters and scowled across at the undercover man who had finished making his report.

'Damn it, Beaver,' he said. 'The thing doesn't make sense.'

The undercover man sighed resignedly. 'None of his stuff ever makes sense,' he said, 'and yet somehow he always fits everything together into a perfect pattern and whisks the swag right out from under our noses. I'm getting tired of it.'

'Of course,' Sergeant Ackley went on, 'this suitcase is important. You can see what happened, Beaver. The robber, whoever he was, stopped in at the depot and checked this suitcase.'

'That, of course, gives us a clue to work on,' the spy observed. 'But Heaven knows what's in that suitcase. Leith told the baggageman to open it, familiarize himself with the contents, and not to let anyone have it who couldn't describe those contents. Now, of course, we *could* go down there with a warrant and—'

'Absolutely not,' Sergeant Ackley interrupted. 'That's foolish, Beaver. We've been working for months to catch this man, and now that we have a perfect trap all prepared, we'd be foolish to go down and steal the bait ourselves.'

'Then you don't think the gems are in the suitcase?'

'Why the devil should they be?' Sergeant Ackley asked.

The undercover man shrugged his shoulders, and said, 'Stranger things have happened.'

'Well, not *that* strange,' Sergeant Ackley snapped. 'After all, the robber took considerable chances in order to get those gems. He undoubtedly must have followed Mainwaring from India. That much of Mainwaring's story is true; and the robber, once having secured possession of those stones, certainly made tracks for parts unknown. He's probably thousands of miles away from here by this time, traveling by airplane, but there must be something in that suitcase – something which fits into the scheme of the thing. But I don't see how it's going to do Leith any good, because he can't describe the contents of that suitcase any better than we can.'

'Well,' Beaver said, 'I've made *my* report.' And his voice indicated that he considered himself relieved from further responsibility.

Sergeant Ackley said: 'We'll plant a couple of men around the depot. The minute that suitcase leaves the place, we'll get busy and follow it to its destination. If Leith picks it up, so much the better. If he sends some messenger, we'll follow the messenger until he leads us to Leith. If it's an accomplice of the crook, we'll follow him. Of course, we've known all along that Mainwaring's account of the crime was fishy. We felt certain the stickup was over those gems. That was why I wanted you to get Leith interested in working it out. Of course that suitcase may . . . well, we'll just keep that as bait.'

Beaver got to his feet.

'Well,' he said, 'I've told you everything I know. Now, I've got to get busy and give those girls a once-over as they come in. I suppose they'll have chewing gum stuck all over the place.'

Sergeant Ackley assayed a ponderous attempt at humor. 'Be careful they don't gum the works, Beaver.'

The undercover man started to say something, then changed his mind, and marched to the door.

'Be sure to keep me posted, Beaver,' Sergeant Ackley warned. 'This case is the most important one you've handled yet. We'll catch Lester Leith red-handed. We'll get enough proof to convict Mainwaring of smuggling, and if those two gems are equal to descriptions, we'll pick up a nice reward.'

The undercover man said: 'You thought you had him before. If you'll take my advice, you'll figure out what he wants those two canes for and where those four counterfeit stones fit into the picture. Otherwise you'll come another cropper.'

'That will do, Beaver,' Sergeant Ackley roared. '*I'm* running this case. *You* get back on the job and stay there!'

'Very well, sergeant,' the undercover man said with that synthetic humility which he had learned to assume until it had become almost second nature to him.

He opened the door a few inches, oozed his huge bulk out into the corridor, then quietly closed the door behind him.

Sergeant Ackley reached for the telephone.

CHAPTER III

Gum Chewers

The undercover man surveyed the dozen young women who had gathered in response to Lester Leith's summons. They sat grouped about the room in postures which were well calculated to show what Lester Leith's memorandum had referred as to 'shapely means of locomotion.' Each seemed vying with the other to attract attention to the fact that she was possessed of the necessary qualifications.

As might have been expected, however, from the nature of the request which had been sent to the employment agency, only those young women who had seen enough of life to become slightly calloused to the treatment afforded a working girl had applied. The qualification of being a blatant and inveterate gum chewer had also tended to accomplish the same purpose. Had Lester Leith deliberately sought to acquire a young woman who knew her way around, who was willing to take chance, and was unusually self-reliant, he could not have thought of any means better designed to give him exactly what he wanted.

Beaver, the undercover man, entered the room and surveyed the twelve waiting applicants, noted the rhythmic swing of the rapidly chewing jaws, heard unmistakable evidences of a proficiency in gum popping; and his black greedy eyes swept in eager appraisal the exposed lengths of sheer silk terminating in shapely, well-shod feet.

The undercover man took from his pocket twelve twenty-dollar bills, and cleared his throat.

Twelve pairs of eyes fastened on those twenty-dollar bills. The girls, with one accord and as though at some preconcerted signal, quit chewing, some of them holding their jaws poised, the wad of gum balanced precariously between upper and lower molars.

The valet said: 'You young ladies are all applicants for this position. Mr. Leith has instructed me to give to each applicant a twenty-dollar bill. This will be in addition to the three hundred dollars a month salary which is to be paid to the one who gets the job. Mr. Leith has asked me to state that he appreciates your courtesy in coming here, and he wanted me to tell you that he felt quite certain that each of you had . . . "the external qualifications" were the words he used,' the spy said, letting his eyes once more slither along the row of shapely limbs. 'In just a moment Mr. Leith will—'

Lester Leith interrupted him by flinging open the door of his sitting room.

'Good afternoon,' he said.

Twelve pairs of eyes changed from cynical appraisal to interest.

'Good afternoon,' the applicants chorused.

Leith looked them over and said: 'Obviously since there is only one position, eleven of you must necessarily be disappointed. I have tried to make some small contribution which will alleviate your disappointment somewhat, and, as you are all working girls, I believe that it is only fair to all concerned to pick a person to fill the position in the quickest manner possible. I will, therefore, look you over, and interview the person I consider the most talented first. I believe you understand that I am looking for young women with symmetrical limbs, and women who are inveterate gum chewers.'

'Say,' one of them said, 'what's the idea about the gams?'

'Just what do you mean?' Leith asked.

'Is this a *job* or ain't it?' the girl asked.

'This,' Leith assured her gravely, 'is a job.'

'Well,' the girl said, 'I didn't want to have any misunderstandings, that's all.'

Lester Leith surveyed the girl with interest. 'What,' he asked, 'is your name?'

'Evelyn Rae,' she said, 'and I think I'm speaking for most of the others as well as myself when I say that I came up here to look the proposition over. I'm not so certain I'm making an application for the job. I don't like that crack about what you call shapely means of locomotion. I do *my* shorthand and *my* typewriting with my hands.'

One or two of the others nodded.

A blond at the far end of the line shifted her gum, and said: 'Speak for yourself, dearie. *I'll* do my own talking.'

Lester Leith smiled at Evelyn Rae. 'I think,' he said, 'you're the young woman I want to interview first. Come in, please.'

She followed him into his private sitting room, surveying him with frankly dubious eyes.

'You may think I'm the one you want to work for you,' she said, 'but *I'm* not so sure you're the person *I* want to be *my* boss.'

'I understand,' Leith said. 'I understood you the first time.'

'All right,' she said. 'What are the duties?'

'Well,' Leith told her, 'you will take a train out of the city which leaves the depot at seven twenty tonight. You will arrive in Beacon City at nine thirty. From there on, the train is a limited train, making no stops until after midnight. I'll travel with you as far as Beacon City. We will have a drawing room.'

'Oh, yeah?' she said. 'That's what *you* think.'

'At Beacon City,' Leith went on heedless of the interruption, 'a suitcase will be placed aboard the train. You will not open that suitcase. Under no circumstances are you even to look in it. At approximately ten p.m. you will be arrested.'

'Arrested for what?' she asked.

'For being an accessory after the fact in the theft of two emeralds,' Leith said.

'What'll I be guilty of?'

'Nothing.'

'Then how can they arrest me?'

'It's a habit some of the more impulsive officers have,' Leith pointed out.

'Well, I don't like it.'

'Neither do I,' Leith told her.

'What else do I do?'

'You will continue aboard the train in the custody of the officers until they make arrangements to stop and take you off and return you to the city. At that time, you will be released. The officers will apologize. You will retain counsel and threaten a suit for false arrest. The officers will be glad to compromise. I don't think you'll receive a very large sum by the way of a cash settlement, but you doubtless will wind up with sufficient pull to square any parking or speeding tickets you or your friends may get within the city limits for some time to come. There will be no other duties.'

'Is this,' she asked, 'a line of hooey?'

Leith took three one-hundred-dollar bills from his pocket.

'I am,' he said, 'willing to show my good faith by paying you a month's salary in advance. You look honest to me.'

'Honest but direct,' she said. 'What'll *you* be doing in that drawing room between Central Depot and Beacon City?'

'Reading.'

'What'll you be doing *after* the train leaves Beacon City?'

Lester Leith smiled, and said, 'The less you know about that the better.'

Evelyn Rae looked at the three hundred-dollar bills speculatively. 'That,' she said, 'is a lot of money.'

Leith nodded.

'And not much work,' she added.

Again Leith nodded.

'What else am I supposed to do?' she asked.

'Chew gum,' Leith said. 'Chew large quantities of gum. The gum, incidentally, will be furnished as a part of the traveling expenses. You will not have to pay for it.'

She studied him for several seconds with thoughtful worldly-wise eyes, then she slowly nodded her head, and said: 'I don't believe you're on the level, but what's the odds? It's a go.'

Leith handed her the three one-hundred-dollar bills.

'And the first duty which you have,' he said, 'will be to explain to the other applicants that the position is filled.'

She said: 'Well, I've got to talk fast to put *that* idea across, particularly with that blonde.' She moistened her fingers, slipped a wad of chewing gum from her mouth absent-mindedly, and mechanically stuck it under the arm of the chair.

Lester Leith nodded to himself, smiling his approval.

As she reached for the doorknob, Leith said:

'And you will start your duties at once. Please explain to Scuttle, my valet, that I do not wish to be disturbed for the next hour, and, in the meantime, arrange to pack your suitcase and get ready to travel. You will meet me at the Central Depot tonight, ready to board the seven-twenty train.'

When the door had closed behind her, Leith opened a drawer in his desk, and took from it a piece of clear green glass which had been ground into facets, giving it the general appearance of a huge gem. Tiptoeing across to the chair where the young woman had been sitting, he took the piece of glass and pushed it up into the wad of chewing gum, held it there by a firm steady pressure of thumb and forefinger for several seconds, then gradually released it.

CHAPTER IV

Planted Clue

The valet quietly opened the door of Leith's private sitting room, thrust in a cautious hand, and then eased himself through the narrow opening.

Lester Leith, watching him with eyes that were lazy-lidded in amusement, said: 'Scuttle, it doesn't cost any more to open the door wide enough to walk through, instead of opening it a few inches and squeezing through sideways.'

'Yes, sir. I know, sir,' the spy said. 'You mentioned it to me before. It's just a habit I have, sir.'

Leith stared at him with wide startled eyes. 'Scuttle, what the devil are you carrying under your arm?'

'The canes, sir.'

'The canes, Scuttle?'

'Yes, sir.'

'Good heavens, *what* canes?'

'Don't you remember, sir, those that you ordered, the ones that have hollow handles, and one of them has an adjustable ferrule so it can be telescoped and locked in position?'

'Scuttle,' Lester Leith said, '*I* didn't want those canes.'

'You *didn't*, sir? I thought you told me to get them.'

'Why no,' Leith said, 'I merely mentioned that I thought a person who had two canes such as that and an attractive secretary who was addicted to promiscuous gum chewing could solve the mystery of the murdered monkey. But I told you not to get the canes.'

'I'm sorry, sir. I must have misunderstood you. I thought *you* wanted to solve it.'

'No, no!' Lester Leith exclaimed. 'I was merely outlining an academic solution.'

'But you've hired the secretary.'

'I know I have,' Leith said. 'That's an entirely different matter. I hired her on general principles.'

'I'm sorry, sir. I'm frightfully sorry, but I thought you wanted me to get the canes. Now that I have them, sir . . . well—'

Leith said: 'Oh, well, now that you have them, I may as well take a look at them. Pass them over, Scuttle.'

The spy handed over the canes. Leith regarded them with pursed lips and narrowed eyes.

'It's rather a neat job,' the spy said. 'You see, they're canes with just a knob for a handle, and that knob unscrews. The joint is rather cleverly concealed, don't you think so?'

Leith nodded, twisted the head of one of the canes. It promptly unscrewed. Leith looked inside and gave a sudden start of surprise.

'Why, Scuttle,' he said, 'there are emeralds in here!'

'No, sir, not emeralds, sir. Just the imitations which you ordered.'

'Ordered, Scuttle?'

'Well, you mentioned them as being things which would enable you to solve the mystery of the murdered monkey.'

Leith said reprovingly: 'Scuttle, I don't like this. I was outlining merely an academic solution. Why the devil would I want to solve the mystery of the murdered monkey?'

'I'm sure I don't know, sir, except that it would be a source of great gratification for you to know that your reasoning had proved correct.'

Leith said irritably: 'I don't need to go to all that trouble to demonstrate the correctness of my reasoning, Scuttle. It's self-evident when you consider the basic facts of the case.'

The spy wet his thick lips with the tip of an anxious tongue.

'Yes, sir,' he said eagerly. And then after a moment, 'You were about to mention what you consider the basic facts, sir?'

Lester Leith eyed him coldly. 'I was not, Scuttle.'

'Oh,' the spy said.

'By the way,' Leith observed, 'I've given Evelyn Rae a month's wages in advance.'

'Yes, sir. So Miss Rae told me, sir. She said that you didn't wish to be disturbed for an hour so I waited to give you the canes. You were, perhaps, busy?'

Leith said, 'Perhaps, Scuttle.'

'I've just had the devil of a time, sir, if you don't mind my saying so,' the spy complained.

'How come?' Leith inquired.

'Cleaning up after those young women.'

'Were they untidy?' Leith asked.

'Chewing gum, sir. I don't think I ever had quite so disagreeable a job in my life. It was stuck to the underside of the chair arms, the chair buttons, under the table. It was in the most unlikely places and the most annoying places, sir. You'd drop your hand to the arm of the chair, and a wad of moist chewing gum would stick to your fingers.'

Leith yawned, and stifled the yawn with four polite fingers. 'Doubtless, Scuttle,' he said, 'you'll remember in the call which I sent out for secretaries, I asked for gum chewers who were careless with their parking, inclined to be promiscuous with their leftovers. Doubtless, Scuttle, the young ladies were merely attempting to show that they were properly qualified for the position. After all, Scuttle, you know jobs aren't easily obtained these days, so one can hardly blame the young ladies for being anxious to secure one which pays a good salary.'

The spy said: 'That's one of the things I couldn't understand . . . if you don't think I'm presumptuous, sir.'

'What is that, Scuttle?'

'*Why* you wanted a young woman who was such an inveterate gum chewer and what you were pleased to describe as such a promiscuous parker.'

Leith nodded. 'I dare say, Scuttle.'

'Dare say what, sir?'

'That you couldn't understand it,' Leith said.

The spy's face flushed an angry brick-red.

'And now,' Leith said, 'I have some preparations to make. By the way, Scuttle, did you notice in the newspaper that Mr. Mainwaring was to address the Explorers' Club tonight on "Changes in the Psychology of Native Religions"?'

'Yes, sir,' the spy said.

'Probably it will be a most interesting lecture,' Leith observed.

'Did you intend to be present?' Beaver asked.

'I?' Leith inquired. 'Good heavens, no, Scuttle! I'd be bored to death, but I merely commented that the lecture would probably be interesting . . . to those who have a taste for that sort of thing. By the way, Scuttle, you'd better pack my bag, and get me a drawing room on the seven-twenty train tonight.'

'A drawing room, sir?'

'Yes, Scuttle.'

'Very good, sir. Where to?'

'Oh, clean through,' Leith said airily. 'As far as the train goes. I don't believe in halfway measures, Scuttle.'

The valet said, 'I thought perhaps you wanted it only as far as Beacon City, sir.'

'Beacon City?' Leith inquired. 'Why the devil should I want to go to Beacon City?'

'I'm sure I don't know, sir,' the spy said.

'And *I'm* quite sure you don't,' Leith observed in a tone of finality as he terminated the interview.

After Leith had left the room, the big spy, his face twisted with rage, shook clenched fists at the door.

'Damn you,' he said. 'Damn your sneering, supercilious hide! One of these days I'll have the pleasure of watching you in a cell, and when I do, I'll give you something to think of! You're quite sure I don't, eh? You and your chewing gum. Bah!'

The spy sat down in the big chair, mopped his perspiring forehead, then pocketing his handkerchief, wrapped his thick fingers around the arm of the chair. With an exclamation of annoyance, he jumped up and scrubbed at his fingers with the handkerchief.

'Another wad of gum!' he exclaimed irritably. Wearily, he opened the blade of a huge pocketknife, dropped down to his knees, and prepared to scrape off the moist wad of chewing gum.

Something green caught his eye. He tapped it experimentally with the blade of his knife. Then, with sudden interest showing in his eyes, he cut off the wad of gum, and stared at the piece of green glass which had been embedded in it.

For several seconds, the spy stared with wide, startled eyes. Then, with the wad of chewing gum and the glass gem still smeared on the blade of his knife, he stretched his long legs to the limit as he dashed for the telephone to call Sergeant Ackley.

'Hello, hello, hello, sergeant,' Beaver called as soon as he heard the sergeant's voice on the line. 'This is Beaver talking. I've got the whole thing doped out.'

'What thing?' Sergeant Ackley asked.

'That monkey murder.'

'Go ahead,' Sergeant Ackley ordered. 'Spill it.'

'The murder of the monkey was just a blind,' Beaver said. 'The chewing gum is the significant thing about the whole business. Remember that the nurse sat on a table and chewed gum all the time the customs officials were searching Mainwaring, and then, of course, the customs officials searched *her*.'

'Well, what about it?' Sergeant Ackley asked in his most discouraging tone. 'What the devil does gum chewing have to do with it?'

'Don't you see, sergeant?' Beaver said. 'While she was chewing gum with a certain amount of nervousness natural to a young woman under those circumstances, she was able to feed large quantities of gum into her mouth without exciting suspicion.'

'Well?' Sergeant Ackley asked in a voice well calculated to chill even the most loyal supporter.

'Well,' Beaver went on, speaking slightly slower and with less assurance, 'you can see what happened. While she was chewing gum, she sat there on the table, swinging her legs. She'd chew for a while, and then she'd take a wad of gum out of her mouth and stick it on the under side of the table. Then she'd start chewing more gum. Now, *she* had those emeralds with *her*. While they were searching the baggage and asking questions of Mainwaring, she stuck those emeralds in the gum on the under side of the table in the customs inspector's office right under his very nose. Then, after they'd finished searching her and her baggage and Mainwaring and his baggage, she made an excuse to run back to the office of the customs inspector. You'll remember that the newspaper said she thanked him for his courtesy. Well, while she was thanking him, she reached her hand under the table, and slipped out the emeralds and walked out with them. It was cleverly done.'

There was a long pause while the undercover man waited, listening; and Sergeant Ackley remained thoughtfully silent.

'Well,' Beaver asked at length, 'are you there, sergeant?'

'Yes, of course I'm here,' Sergeant Ackley said. 'What else, Beaver?'

'What else? Isn't that enough? I've got it all doped out. That's the manner in which—'

'I think you're getting unduly excited over a very obvious matter, Beaver,' Sergeant Ackley said. '*I* had figured all that out just as soon as you told me Leith insisted upon a secretary who was an inveterate gum chewer and a promiscuous parker.'

'Oh,' the undercover man said, and then after a moment added: 'I see. You thought of it first.'

'That's right,' Sergeant Ackley said. 'By the way, Beaver, how did *you* happen to think of it?'

'I just thought it out,' the spy said wearily.

'No, no, Beaver. Now don't hang up. There must have been something which brought the idea to your mind.'

'I reasoned it out,' the spy said.

'But something must have given you a clue.'

'What was it gave *you* your clue?' the undercover man asked.

'*I*,' Sergeant Ackley said with dignity, 'have risen to greater heights in my profession than you have, Beaver. It stands to reason that my mind is trained to arrive at conclusions more rapidly than yours. Also, I have more time for concentration. You were busy with your duties as valet. I feel certain that something must have given you the tipoff. Now what was it? Don't be insubordinate, Beaver.'

'Oh, all right,' the undercover man said wearily. 'I happened to find where Leith had been rehearsing the secretary. He'd given her a wad of gum and a piece of green glass about the size of a good big emerald. She'd practiced sticking the gum on the under side of a chair arm, and then slipping the emerald up into the chewing gum. Evidently, they're rehearsing an act they're going to put on later.'

'You should have told me *that*,' Sergeant Ackley said reproachfully, 'as soon as you had me on the line, and not tried to make a grandstand with a lot of deductive reasoning. Don't let it happen again, Beaver. Do you understand?'

'I understand,' the spy said, as he dropped the receiver into its cradle.

CHAPTER V

The Rubber Suit

Evelyn Rae was standing by the train gate when Lester Leith arrived. Her jaws were swinging with the rhythmic ease of a habitual gum chewer. Despite the fact that it was only two minutes before train time, she showed no nervousness whatever, but raised her eyes to Lester Leith and said casually:

'Hello, there. I was wondering if you were going to leave me at the altar.'

'Hardly,' Leith said, 'but I've been rather busy. Here, give your bags to this redcap. Let's go.'

The conductor was yelling, 'All aboard,' as Leith grabbed Evelyn Rae's arm and rushed her through the gates. And as soon as the porter had juggled the baggage through behind them, the gateman snapped the brass chain into position, and swung the big doors shut – the seven-twenty limited had officially departed. Actually it waited for Leith and his newly-employed secretary to get aboard before lurching into creaking motion.

Leith settled down in the drawing room, opened his bag, and took out a case of chewing gum in assorted flavors. 'I want you,' he said, 'to try these and see which you prefer.'

Back in the depot, a plain-clothes man telephoned ahead to Sergeant Ackley, who was waiting at Ninety-third Street. 'O.K., sergeant,' he said, 'You've got thirty minutes to get things fixed up and get aboard. Your drawing room is all reserved.'

'He took the train?' Sergeant Ackley asked.

'He's aboard all right. He played it pretty slick. He had his watch set right to the second, and waited to be certain he and the girl were the last people through the gates. He did that so you couldn't follow him aboard the train, but he overlooked the fact that it stopped at Ninety-third Street.'

'Well, *I* haven't overlooked it,' Sergeant Ackley said gloatingly. 'The time will come when that crook will realize that he's fighting a master mind. It's only luck that's enabled him to slip through my fingers so many times before. When it comes to brains, I'll match mine with his any day in the week.'

'Atta boy, sergeant!' the detective exclaimed approvingly, dropped the receiver into place, and then, running out his tongue, showered the transmitter with a very moist but heartfelt razzberry.

Lester Leith took off his shoes, put on bedroom slippers, hung up his coat and vest, slipped into a lounging robe, and took a book from his suitcase.

Evelyn Rae watched him with cautious, appraising eyes. As Lester Leith became engaged in his book, she slowly settled back against the cushions.

Leith rang for the porter, ordered a table, and when it was placed in position in between the seats, put the case of chewing gum on it.

Evelyn Rae moistened her thumb and forefinger, slipped out the wad of gum she had been chewing, and absent-mindedly pushed it against the under side of the table. She tore open a package of Juicy Fruit and fed two sticks into her mouth, one after the other.

'Pretty good stuff,' she said, between chews. 'This must be pretty fresh.'

Leith said: 'It's direct from the wholesalers, and they say it left the factory less than a week ago.'

After she had chewed for several minutes, Leith said: 'I'd like to have you try some of that Doublemint and then contrast that flavor with the pepsin.'

'O.K.,' she said. 'Give me a few more minutes with this. I haven't got the good out of it yet.'

The train rumbled along through the darkness. Evelyn Rae began to make herself at home.

'Gotta magazine or anything?' she asked.

Leith nodded, and took several magazines from his suitcase. She settled down with a motion-picture magazine to casual reading. Soon she became interested.

'Don't forget that Doublemint,' Leith said.

'I won't,' she told him, and pressed the chewed Juicy Fruit against the under side of the table.

At Ninety-third Street, Sergeant Ackley gave last-minute instructions to the undercover man and two detectives who were pacing the platform.

'Now listen,' Ackley said. 'Remember he *may* be looking out of the window, or he may get out and walk up and down the platform. We've got to get aboard without him seeing us. You two birds stand out on the platform when you hear the train coming. He doesn't know you. His reservation is Drawing Room A in Car D57. You two get aboard, go on back to that car and make sure he's in his drawing room. Then signal with your flashlight, and Beaver and I will come aboard and go directly to *our* drawing room which is in D56, the car ahead. Do you get me?'

O.K., sergeant,' the older of the two detectives said.

'Get ready,' Sergeant Ackley warned. 'Here she comes.'

A station bell clanged a strident warning. The big yellow headlight of the thundering locomotive loomed up out of the darkness. Passengers for the limited swirled into little excited groups, exchanging last farewells as travelers picked up their baggage.

The big limited train rumbled into the station. While Sergeant Ackley and Beaver hid in the waiting room, the two detectives spotted Lester Leith's stateroom, flashed a go-ahead signal, and the officers dashed aboard. The brass-throated bells clanged their warning, and the long line of Pullmans creaked into motion.

In Drawing Room A in Car D57, Lester Leith merely glanced at his wrist watch, then took a cigarette from the hammered silver case in his pocket, tapped it on his thumbnail, and snapped a match into flame.

On the opposite seat, Evelyn Rae, her back bolstered up with pillows, her mind absorbed in the picture magazine, slid around to draw up her knees to furnish a prop for the magazine. Absent-mindedly, she slipped the gum from her mouth, pressed it against the under side of the table, and groped with her fingers until she found a fresh package. Without taking her eyes off the article she was reading, she tore off the wrappers and fed sticks of gum into her mouth.

The train, having cleared the more congested district of the city, rumbled into constantly increasing speed.

Belting Junction at eight ten and Robbinsdale at eight thirty were passed without incident At five minutes past nine, Lester Leith said:

'I think I'll take a stroll on the platform when we get to Beacon City.'

Evelyn Rae might not have heard him. She was reading an absorbing article on one of her favorite motion-picture stars. The article told of the gameness, courage, the moral stamina of the star, and Evelyn Rae occasionally blinked back tears of sympathy as she traced the star's unfortunate search for love and understanding through the tangled skein of Hollywood's romance.

Lester Leith picked up his shoes, dropped one of them, and bent over to retrieve it.

Looking up at the under side of the table, he saw wad after wad of moist gum pressed against the wood.

Slipping two of the imitation emeralds from his pocket, he pushed them up into the soft gum. Wetting the tips of his fingers, he kneaded the sticky substance over the imitation gems.

The train slowed for Beacon City, and Evelyn Rae was not even conscious that it was slowing. Busily absorbed in reading the adventures of an extra girl who came to Hollywood and attracted the romantic interest of one of the more popular stars, she barely looked up as Lester Leith slipped out of the door and into the corridor.

As the junction point, Beacon City represented an important stop in the journey of the limited. Here two passenger coaches were transferred from one line and two Pullmans added from another. The station rated a fifteen-minute stop.

Lester Leith picked up a porter and hurried to the baggage room.

'I'm on the limited,' he told the man in charge of the baggage counter. 'I have a suitcase I want to pick up. I haven't the check for it, but I can describe the contents. It came down on the night of the thirteenth on the limited, and was put off here to wait for me. The whole thing was a mistake. I got in touch with the claim office, and they located—'

'Yes, I know all about it,' the baggageman said. 'You've got to put up a bond.'

'A what?'

'A cash bond.'

'That's an outrage,' Leith said. 'I can describe the contents. There's absolutely no possibility that you can get into any trouble by delivering that suitcase to me, and what's more—'

'No bond, no suitcase,' the man said. 'I'm sorry, but that's orders from headquarters. They came from the claim department.'

'How much bond?' Lester Leith asked.

'Fifty dollars.'

The two detectives who had followed Leith into the baggage room were busy checking articles of hand baggage. Apparently, they paid no attention to the conversation which was going on.

Leith opened his wallet, took out ten five-dollar bills, and said:

'This is an outrage.'

'O.K.,' the baggageman said. 'You can get this money back later on. You'll have to take it up with the claim department. This is just the nature of a bond to indemnify the railroad company. Now, what's in the suitcase?'

At this point the detectives seemed suddenly to become absent-minded. They lost interest in their baggage and moved surreptitiously closer.

Leith said, without hesitating. 'It's part of a masquerade costume joke that was played on some friends. There's a costume in there by which a thin man can make it appear he's enormously fat.'

'You win,' the baggageman said. 'I'd been wondering what the devil those pneumatic gadgets were for. Regular rubber clothes. I couldn't figure it. I guess you pump them up with a bicycle pump, and that's all there is to it, eh?'

'Not a bicycle pump,' Leith said, smiling. 'It's quicker to stand at the nozzle of a pressure hose at a service station. All right, make me out a receipt for the fifty dollars, and I'll be on my way. I have to catch this train.'

He turned to the porter, handed him a dollar, and said:

'All right, redcap, rush this aboard the train, put it in Drawing Room A in Car D57. There's a young woman in there. So knock on the door and explain to her that I had the suitcase put aboard. She's my secretary.'

'Yassah, yassah,' the grinning boy said. 'Right away, suh.'

The detectives took no chances. One of them followed the suitcase aboard the train. The other waited for Leith to get his receipt.

'All aboard. All aboard for the limited,' the brakeman cried.

The station bell clanged into sharp summons.

The baggageman looked up from the receipt he was writing. 'You've got a minute and a half after that,' he said.

'All aboard. All aboard,' cried the conductor.

The baggageman scribbled a hasty receipt. The bell of the locomotive clanged into action. The baggageman thrust the receipt into Leith's hand.

'O.K.,' he said, 'you'd better hustle.'

Leith sprinted across the platform. Porters were banging vestibule doors. The long train creaked into motion.

A porter saw Leith coming, opened the vestibule door, and hustled Leith aboard. The detective caught the next car down.

The minute the detective had vanished into the vestibule, Leith suddenly exclaimed, 'Oh, I forgot my wallet!'

'You can't get off now, boss,' the porter said.

'The hell I can't!' Leith told him, jerked open the vestibule door, and stepped down to the stairs. He swung out to the platform with the easy grace of a man who has reduced the hopping of trains to a fine art.

The engineer, knowing he had a straight, uninterrupted run during which he must smoothly clip off the miles, slid the throttle open, and the powerful engine, snaking the long string of Pullmans behind it, roared into rocking speed as Lester Leith, left behind on the station, saw the red lights on the rear of the train draw closer together and then vanish into the darkness.

In the stateroom of Car D56, Sergeant Ackley sat hunched over a table, his elbows spread far apart, his chin resting in his hands, chewing nervously at a soggy cigar. His eyes, glittering with excitement, stared across at Beaver, the undercover man. The two detectives made their report.

'Hell, sergeant,' the man who had followed the suitcase aboard said, 'the thing's all cut and dried. Leith pulled that stickup himself. He's got a bunch of rubber clothes he can put on and inflate with air, and they made him look like a big fat guy. He stuck on a cap and mask, and—'

'Wait a minute, wait a minute,' Sergeant Ackley interrupted. 'Leith didn't pull that stickup himself. Leith is pulling a hijack.'

'Well, that's what's in the suitcase, all right,' the detective said, 'and Leith knew all about it.'

'That's right,' the second officer chimed in. 'He spoke right up and described the stuff in the suitcase – a masquerade costume to make a thin guy look fat.'

Sergeant Ackley twisted the cigar between trembling lips. Suddenly he jumped to his feet.

'O.K., boys,' he said. 'We make the pinch!'

He jerked open the door of his drawing room.

'Do I stay here?' Beaver asked.

'No,' Sergeant Ackley said, 'you can come with us. You can throw off your disguise, and face him in your true colors. You can get even with him for some of these taunts and insults.'

The burly undercover man's fist clenched. 'The big thing I want to get even with him for,' he said, 'is his calling me Scuttle. He Scuttles me this, and Scuttles me that. He says that I look like a pirate, and keeps asking me if perhaps some of my ancestors weren't pirates.'

'As far as I'm concerned,' Sergeant Ackley said, 'the sky's the limit. My eyes aren't very good, and if you say he was resisting arrest and took a swing at you, I'll be inclined to help you defend yourself.'

'I don't want any help,' Beaver said. 'All I want is three good punches.'

Sergeant Ackley turned to the other two officers. 'Remember,' he said, 'if Beaver swears this guy made a swing at him, we're all backing Beaver's play.'

Two heads nodded in unison.

'Come on,' Sergeant Ackley said, putting his star on the outside of his coat, and led the procession which marched grimly down the swaying aisle of the Pullman car where the porter, struggling with mattresses and green curtains as he made up the berths, looked up to stare with wide eyes.

'Do we knock?' Beaver asked, as they swayed down the aisle of Car D57.

'Don't be silly,' Ackley commented. He twisted he knob of the stateroom door, slammed it open. The car porter watched them with wide-eyed wonder. A moment later he was joined by the porter from the car ahead.

Evelyn Rae was sprawled comfortably on the seat, her left elbow propped against the table, a pillow behind her head, her right instep fitted against the curved arm of the upholstering. She looked up with casual inquiry then suddenly lowered her knees, pulled down her skirt, and said:

'Say, what's the idea?'

'Where's Leith?' Sergeant Ackley asked.

'Why, I don't know. Who are you? Why, hello, Beaver. What is this?'

Sergeant Ackley said, 'Come on! Where's Leith?'

'I haven't seen him for a while. I was reading and—'

'How did that suitcase get here?'

'A redcap brought it in. He said Leith told him to put it aboard.'

'Where was that?'

'This last stop.'

'What did Leith say after we pulled out of that last stop?'

'Why, I haven't seen him since the suitcase was delivered here.'

Sergeant Ackley's laugh was scornful and sarcastic. 'Try and get me to fall for *that* one. You must think I'm crazy. Beaver, open the door to the lavatory. Jim, dust out and cover the train.'

The undercover man jerked open the lavatory door.

'No one here,' he said.

The other detective dashed out into the car.

The car porter pushed his head in the door. 'What yo'-all want? The gen'man what—'

Sergeant Ackley held up the lapel of his coat to emphasize the significance of his badge. 'Get the hell out of here,' he said.

The porter backed out, his jaw and lips moving, but no words coming.

Sergeant Ackley slammed the door shut.

'Let's take a look in that suitcase,' he said.

The officers unstrapped the suitcase, opened it. Sergeant Ackley pawed through the clothes.

'O.K.,' he said to the girl, 'where are those two gems?'

'What two gems?'

'Don't stall. The two gems that were in there.'

'You're nuts!' she said.

'I'll show you whether I'm nuts or not,' Sergeant Ackley said. 'You're an accomplice in this thing right now. You give me any more of your lip, and I'll arrest you as an accessory after the fact.'

'After what fact?' she asked.

Sergeant Ackley's gesture was one of irritation.

'Mr. Leith thought he'd left *you* in the city,' she said to Beaver.

'What Lester Leith thinks doesn't count right now,' Sergeant Ackley observed. 'I want those two emeralds.'

'Those two emeralds?'

'Yes.'

Before she could answer, the door of the drawing room burst open, and the detective who had been sent to find Leith said:

'Say, sergeant, here's a funny story from the porter of the second car back. That's the one that Leith hopped when the train pulled out. I grabbed the one behind. I went back and asked the porter what happened to the man who got aboard and—'

'Never mind all that palaver,' Sergeant Ackley interrupted irritably. 'Go ahead and tell me the answer. What happened?'

'He said that Lester Leith climbed aboard all right, and then jumped right back off again.'

Sergeant Ackley's face darkened. 'So you let him give you the slip, did you?'

The detective said indignantly: 'Let him give me nothing! He got aboard the train all right, and I saw the vestibule door shut. The train damn near jerked my arms off when I got aboard the next car back. I hurried up to follow Leith to his stateroom here, but before I could get through the car, he'd had plenty of time to reach this stateroom. Remember, he was one car ahead of me. No one else could have done the thing any differently. How was I to know he was going to jump off?'

Sergeant Ackley whirled to Evelyn Rae. 'I'm going to get those two stones,' he said, 'if I have to search every stitch you have on. So you'd better come through with them.'

'I tell you I don't know what you're talking about,' she said.

Beaver said significantly: 'Remember that piece of glass in the chewing gum, sergeant. I'll bet they were just trying to find out whether a wad of chewing gum would hold—'

'Now,' Sergeant Ackley said, 'you're talking sense.' He grabbed the table, swung it up on its hinges, looked at the assortment of gum gobs which studded the under side of the table. Suddenly a flash of green light caught his eye. With a whoop of triumph, he grabbed at the blob of gum. It stuck to his fingers, but pulled away enough to show the surface of a huge green object which was embedded in the sticky depths. 'Hooray,' Sergeant Ackley cried. 'Caught at last. Snap the handcuffs on that woman.'

CHAPTER VI

The Two Trick Canes

There were lights in the building occupied by the Explorers' Club. From time to time could be heard bursts of laughter or spatterings of applause. The curb around the building was crowded with parked automobiles. Here and there chauffeur-driven cars showed a driver huddled over the steering wheel dozing or, perhaps, listening to the radio.

Lester Leith, swinging along the sidewalk, spotted the license number of

Peter B. Mainwaring's automobile without difficulty. The chauffeur of the car was slumped over the wheel.

Leith walked around the car, and tapped him on the shoulder.

The man snapped to quick attention as he felt the touch of Lester Leith's finger. His right hand started toward his left coat lapel.

Lester Leith said easily, 'You're Mainwaring's chauffeur?'

The man's thin, hatchet face was without expression as he said, from one side of his mouth, 'What's it to you?' His right hand was held hovering over the left coat lapel.

'I have the cane that Mainwaring ordered,' Lester Leith said. 'He told me to deliver it to you, and to show you the secret compartment.'

'Secret compartment?' Deekin said. 'Say, I don't know what you're talking about.'

Leith said: 'Well, I don't give a damn whether you do or not. You don't need to be so short about it. I'm a working man, same as you are, and a damn good cane maker. I'm carrying out instructions, that's all. Now, here's the cane for Mainwaring. You tell him when he wants to get at the hidden receptacle, all he has to do is unscrew the top.'

'What does he want a receptacle in a cane for?' Deekin asked, his voice more friendly.

Lester Leith smirked and said: 'Probably to carry liver pills in. How the hell do I know? I have about a dozen clients who give me orders like this, and I'm paid enough to keep my mouth shut. Do you understand?'

Slow comprehension began to dawn on Deekin's face. The right hand which had been hovering near his chest moved away to rest on the steering wheel.

'What's this about unscrewing the head of the cane?' he asked.

Leith said, 'Let me show you.'

With deft fingers, he unscrewed the head of the cane, showed a cotton-lined receptacle on the interior. He pushed two fingers down into the cavity to show its depth. 'There you are,' he said. 'Four and a half inches deep as ordered, and I defy anyone to look at this cane and tell that there's anything phony about it. Here it is.'

'What's that other cane you've got?' Deekin asked.

'One I'm delivering to another customer,' Leith told him.

'Say, what do you want me to do with this?'

'Just give it to Mr. Mainwaring, that's all,' Leith said. 'It's all paid for. Mainwaring will understand. He told me to be at the Explorers' Club, but not to ask for him, that his car would be waiting outside, and I was to leave the cane with his chauffeur. Don't be so damn dumb.'

'I'm *not* so damn dumb,' Deekin said, inspecting the cane with approval. 'Say, buddy,' with increasing friendliness, 'that's a neat job.'

'You're damn right it's a neat job,' Leith said. 'You ain't telling me anything. . . . Say, I wonder if Mainwaring is interested in knowing that they've caught the guy that robbed him.'

'What do ya mean robbed him?' Deekin asked.

Leith laughed scornfully. 'I wasn't born yesterday,' he said. 'That story about the priests of Hanuman who showed up to avenge the monkey deserter from the temple is a lot of hooey that might go with some people, but you can save your breath as far as I'm concerned. They cut that monkey open to get at the smuggled gems. If your boss had had this cane with him, they wouldn't— Oh, well, never mind.'

'What's this about catching the robber?' Deekin demanded.

'Well, they've just as good as caught him,' Leith said. 'They found out he wasn't a fat man at all. That was just a disguise. The guy stole a car just to pull the stickup, then he ran the car down to the Ninety-third Street Station, went in the men's room and took off his clothes. He had a specially constructed rubber-lined suit. All he had to do was put an air hose on it and blow it up so he looked as though he weighed about three hundred pounds. He stuck that suit in the suitcase, bought a railroad ticket to Beacon City, and checked the suitcase on the ticket. He figured no one would pay any attention to it there, and he'd have a chance to pick it up sometime later.'

'Say, how about this?' Deekin interrupted. 'Who did it?'

'I don't know who did it. I heard this other stuff come in over the radio just a little while ago,' Leith said, 'and I thought Mainwaring would probably be interested.'

'How long ago?' the chauffeur asked.

'Oh, I don't know; ten or fifteen minutes ago. The police said they were working on some hot clues and expected an arrest to be made before midnight. You know how it is, the news announcers don't hand out too much information over the radio in a crime like that until the police tell them it's O.K. to release it. Well, buddy, I've got to be going. Be sure Mainwaring gets this cane. So long.'

'So long,' Deekin said.

Lester Leith walked down the street, swinging the other cane behind him.

The chauffeur mopped cold perspiration from his forehead. He looked apprehensively up at the Explorers' Club, then apparently seized with a sudden inspiration, jumped out of the car, pulled up the front seat, and attacked the body of the automobile with a screwdriver. A few moments later, he had lifted up a cleverly concealed plate and removed two blazing green stones from a hidden receptacle. He unscrewed the head of the cane, dropped the two emeralds into the cotton-lined hollow, and screwed the head of the cane back on. He replaced the front seat in the automobile, jumped out, and started walking rapidly toward the corner, swinging the cane casually in his hand.

He heard running steps behind him.

'Hey,' Lester Leith called. 'I've made a mistake in that cane.'

Deekin stopped, bracing himself ominously. His right hand once more sought the vicinity of his necktie.

Leith, drawing closer, said, 'Gosh, I entirely forgot about the difference in length. The colonel is a longlegged guy, and the long cane is for him. I think I gave you the long cane, instead of the short one.'

Deekin said ominously, 'Well, what *you* think, don't count. *I* think this is the cane that Mainwaring wanted.'

'By gosh,' Leith said, with relief in his voice, 'I guess you're right. That *is* the short cane after all.'

Deekin clutched the cane firmly in his left hand, but appeared somewhat mollified as Leith made the announcement.

'Just a minute,' Leith said; 'let's measure them, just to be sure.'

Still holding his cane firmly in his left hand, his right hand ready to dive under the lapel of his coat, Deekin stood perfectly still while Leith compared the canes. The one which Leith was holding was a full inch longer than the other.

Leith heaved a sigh.

'By gosh,' he said, 'I didn't realize that I was as long-legged as I am. You know, after I left you and started out to deliver this cane to the colonel, I swung it around a couple of times and damned if it didn't almost fit me. So then I got scared and—'

'Well, it's all right now,' Deekin said.

'I'll say it is,' Leith told him, twisting the ferrule of the cane in his gloves hands as though to polish it. 'What were you doing, taking a walk?'

'Yes,' Deekin said shortly.

'Well,' Leith told him, 'I'll go with you as far as the corner.'

Deekin hesitated a moment, then said shortly, 'All right, as far as the corner.'

The two men walked side by side. Lester Leith took out his handkerchief and polished the glass surface of the cane which he held in his hand.

Deekin, after a hundred feet, surreptitiously turned to cast an apprehensive glance over his shoulder.

At that moment, Lester Leith shoved his cane down and to the left. It caught in between Deekin's legs just as the chauffeur was taking a long step forward.

The cane was wrenched free from Leith's grasp. Deekin fell heavily forward, losing the grip on his own cane. At the same time, an ugly blue-steel automatic shot from its holster under his left armpit and slid for a foot or two along the sidewalk.

Leith said: 'Good heavens, man, are you hurt? I'm so sorry. I was polishing that cane and—'

Deekin grabbed for the gun. 'Say,' he said, 'I've seen enough of you. Beat it!'

'But, my heavens!' Leith said. 'It was an accident, purely and simply.

Great heavens, man, what are you doing with that gun? I suppose Mainwaring makes you carry it, but—'

Deekin said: 'Never mind all that talk. Just pass over that cane of mine.'

'Oh, yes,' Leith said, 'a thousand pardons. I'm so sorry. Here, let me help you to your feet.'

'You keep your distance,' Deekin said, menacing him with the gun. 'Give me that cane. Hold 'em out so I can see both of them. Don't try any funny stuff now. Give me that shorter one. O.K., that's it. Pass it over, and don't come close.'

'But I don't understand,' Leith said. 'After all, this was just an accident. Perhaps the blunder was on my part, but still—'

'Go on,' Deekin said. 'Beat it. I've seen all of you I want to see. I crave to be alone. I don't want to have anyone tagging around. Turn around and walk back the other way, and keep walking for ten minutes.'

'But I simply can't understand,' Leith said, 'why you should adopt this attitude. Man, you're pointing that gun at me! You're—'

'Beat it,' the chauffeur ordered.

Leith, apparently realizing all at once the menace of that gun, turned and took to his heels, the cane held under his arm.

Deekin took four or five quick steps, then paused to dust off his clothes, walked another fifteen or twenty feet, and then apprehensively twisted the head off the cane, and peered into the interior. The street light reflected in reassuring green scintillations from the interior, and Deekin, breathing easier, swung into a rapid walk.

CHAPTER VII

Beaver's Deductions

Beaver, the undercover man, coughed significantly until he caught Sergeant Ackley's eye, then motioned toward the door.

They held a conference in the car vestibule.

'There's something fishy about this, sergeant,' the undercover man said.

'I'll say there's plenty fishy about it,' Sergeant Ackley said suspiciously. 'I'm going to put that guy who let Leith give him the slip back to pounding pavements.'

'He couldn't have helped it,' Beaver said, 'but that isn't what I wanted to talk to you about, sergeant.'

'Well, what is it?'

'Those two emeralds *couldn't* have been in that suitcase.'

'What do you mean they couldn't have been?' Sergeant Ackley shouted. 'Where else could they have been?'

'Right in Lester Leith's pockets,' Beaver said.

'Bosh and nonsense,' Sergeant Ackley snapped. 'If that's all you have to offer in the way of suggestions, I'm—'

'Just a moment, sergeant,' Beaver said. 'You forget that Leith told the baggageman to look through the suitcase in order to familiarize himself with the contents. Now, if those emeralds had been in there, the baggageman certainly would have seen them, and then he wouldn't have let the suitcase go for any fifty-dollar deposit. He'd have got in touch with the claim department and—'

Sergeant Ackley's expression of dismay showed that he appreciated only too keenly the logic of the undercover man's words.

'So you see what that means,' Beaver said. 'If those gems weren't in the suitcase, then Leith must have brought them; and if Leith brought them, he'd never have stuck them to the under side of that table and then got off the train.'

'Well, then the girl stuck them there,' Ackley said.

'No, she didn't, sergeant. That girl is just a plant.'

'What do you mean?'

'Just a red herring to keep us occupied while Leith is actually getting the stones.'

'You're crazy!' Sergeant Ackley said. 'We have the stones.'

'No, we haven't, sergeant. You left the chewing gum on them so they'd be evidence, but if you'll pull that chewing gum off and wash those stones in gasoline, I'll bet you'll find they're two of the imitation stones that I got for Leith. He fixed this whole thing so that we'd be carried away on the train 'way past Beacon City while he was doubling back by an airplane to shake down the guy who has those stones.'

'Who?' Sergeant Ackley asked.

'The chauffeur,' Beaver said. 'Can't you see? The chauffeur was a thin guy. He had a board with some nails in it planted so he could puncture a tire on the car right where he wanted to. No one knows that the jack was broken. They only have his word for it. He said he was going out to get another jack. What he really did was climb in this stolen car which he'd planted before he went down to the dock to meet the boat. He slipped this rubberized suit of clothes over his others, drove into a service station, blew himself up, put on a mask, went over to the stalled automobile, stuck them up, killed the monkey, took the stones, drove back, parked the car, deflated the suit, put it in the suitcase, checked it up, salted the emeralds somewhere, and then came back to the car. To keep suspicion from centering on him, he said that he'd seen this fat man and gave the license number of the car. He—'

Sergeant Ackley groaned. 'You're right! But, by gosh, we'll get a plane, we'll telephone, we'll—' His hand shot up to the emergency air cord.

A moment later, the long string of Pullmans, rocketing through the night, suddenly started screaming to an abrupt stop, with passengers thrown about in their berths like popcorn in a corn popper. Sergeant Ackley started forward. His right shoe went stickety-stick – stickety-stick. He looked down at the wad of chewing gum stuck to the sole of his shoe. Curses poured from his quivering lips. He pawed at the wad of moist chewing gum. The motion of the stopping train pitched him forward, threw him off balance. His hat was jerked from his head. With gum-covered fingers, he retrieved the hat, clamped it back on his head, and then, feeling a lump between his hair and the hatband, realized too late that he had pressed the wad of moist gum into his hair.

CHAPTER VIII

Beaver's Big Moment

Sergeant Ackley, Beaver, and the two detectives burst into Leith's apartment to find Lester Leith sprawled in a lounging robe, reading. He looked up with a frown as the men came charging through the door.

'Scuttle,' he said, 'what the devil's the meaning of this, and where have you been, Scuttle? I didn't tell you you could have the evening off— Good evening, sergeant and . . . *gentlemen.*'

'Never mind all that stuff,' Sergeant Ackley yelled. 'What the hell did you do with those emeralds?'

'Emeralds, sergeant?' Lester Leith asked. 'Come, come, sergeant; let's get at this logically and calmly. You're all excited, sergeant. Sit down and tell me what you're talking about. And is that gum in your hair, sergeant? Tut, tut, I'm afraid you're getting careless.'

'Search him,' Sergeant Ackley yelled to the two detectives.

'Now, just a minute, sergeant,' Lester Leith said. 'This is indeed an utterly useless procedure. I certainly don't know what you're looking for, but—'

'Search him!' Sergeant Ackley repeated, his voice rising with his rage. The detectives searched the unresisting Leith.

'Come, come, sergeant,' Leith said, when they had finished with their search. 'I suppose you've made another one of your perfectly asinine blunders, but, after all, there's no use getting so incensed about it. Do you know, sergeant, I'm commencing to get so I'm rather attached to you, and you're going to burst a blood vessel if you don't control your temper. Tut, tut, man, your face is all purple.'

Sergeant Ackley tried to talk, but his first few words were incoherent. After a moment, he managed to control himself enough to say: 'We caught Mainwaring's chauffeur. He had a cane with two imitation emeralds in it.'

'Did he, indeed?' Lester Leith said. 'Do you know, sergeant, *I* gave him that cane.'

'So I gather.'

'Yes,' Lester Leith said, 'I gave it to him. I thought that perhaps Mr. Mainwaring might be interested in it.'

'And why did you think Mainwaring might be interested in it?'

'Oh, just as a curiosity,' Leith said. 'I had two of them, and I really had use only for one, you know. And Mainwaring's a traveler, an explorer who—'

'Where's the other one?' Ackley interrupted.

'Over there in the corner, I believe,' Leith said unconcernedly. 'Would you like it, sergeant? I'll give it to you as a souvenir of your visit. I had some idea for a while that a person *might* be able to work out a solution – and, mind you, sergeant, I mean a purely academic solution – of a crime by using these canes. But I find that I was in error, sergeant. So many times one makes mistakes, or do you find that to be true in your case, sergeant?

'Tut, tut, sergeant, don't answer, because I can see it's going to embarrass you. I can realize that the professional officer doesn't make the errors that a rank amateur would, yet I see that I've embarrassed you by asking the question.

'Anyway, sergeant, I decided there was a flaw in my reasoning so I decided to get rid of the canes. I gave one to Mr. Mainwaring, thinking he might like it – that is, I left it with his chauffeur – and I'm giving you this other one.'

Sergeant Ackley said: 'Like hell you made a mistake. You solved that Mainwaring robbery.'

'Robbery!' Lester Leith asked. 'Surely sergeant, you must be mistaken. It was the killing of a monkey, wasn't it? The malicious, premeditated killing of a harmless pet. I felt very much incensed about it myself, sergeant.'

'You felt incensed enough so you went out and grabbed the emeralds,' Sergeant Ackley charged.

'What emeralds?'

'You know very well what emeralds – the two that were in the monkey's stomach, the two that the chauffeur stole.'

'Did the chauffeur *tell* you that he stole any emeralds?' Lester Leith asked.

'Yes, he did. He made a complete confession,' Sergeant Ackley snorted. 'He and Mainwaring's nurse had been corresponding. She wrote him a letter mentioning the emeralds and their plan for smuggling them in by making a monkey swallow them. Of course, she denies all that, but we know Deekin's right about it. You trapped Deekin into taking two emeralds out of their place of concealment in the car he was driving, and putting them into that cane.'

'Indeed, I did nothing of the sort,' Lester Leith said. 'I had no idea there were any emeralds in the cane.'

'Don't hand me a line like that,' Sergeant Ackley told him. 'You figured it all out.'

'And what did the chauffeur do with the emeralds?' Leith asked.

'Put them into the hollowed-out place in the cane he was carrying.'

'Then you must have *found* them in the cane, sergeant! Congratulations on an excellent piece of detective work! The newspapers will give you a big hand over this.'

'Those emeralds in the cane were imitations, and you know it,' Sergeant Ackley said.

'Tut, tut,' Lester Leith said sympathetically. 'I'm *so* sorry, sergeant. I was hoping you'd been able to solve a case which would result in a great deal of newspaper credit, perhaps a promotion. But you can't go to the newspapers with a lot of hullabaloo about getting two *imitation* emeralds. It's too much like killing a caged canary with a ten-gauge shotgun, sergeant. They'd laugh at you. It's anticlimactic. Now tell me, sergeant, in his confession, did the chauffeur state that the same two emeralds he had taken from the monkey's stomach were in that cane?'

'Yes, he did, because he *thought* those were the two, but by some sleight-of-hand hocus-pocus you must have switched canes and got the cane which had the genuine emeralds.'

Lester Leith smiled. 'Really, sergeant, at times you're exceedingly credulous, and opinionated, and careless with your accusations. If the chauffeur swears that the emeralds *he* took from the monkey's stomach were the ones which were concealed in that cane, then they must be the ones; and if there's anything wrong with those emeralds, any question as to their genuineness or authenticity, it must have been the monkey who made the substitution. Monkeys are quite apt to do that, sergeant. They're very mischievous.

'And, incidentally, sergeant, I'd be very, very careful, if I were you, about making an accusation against a reputable citizen based entirely upon the word of a self-confessed crook, on the one hand, and an assumption of yours, on the other. There's really nothing to connect them up. As I see it, sergeant, you simply cannot make a case against me unless you could find those genuine emeralds in my possession. Of course, I have only a layman's knowledge of the law, but that would seem to me to be the rule. As I gather it, Mainwaring will swear he never had any emeralds. And certainly Mainwaring's word will be more acceptable than that of his chauffeur, a self-confessed crook, according to your statement, sergeant. Of course, if there never were any emeralds stolen from Mainwaring, I could hardly be convicted of taking what had never been taken. At any rate, that's the way I look at it. Larceny involves the taking of property. If you can't show that there ever was any property, you can't support a charge of larceny. That's the way it appears to me, sergeant, although I'm just an amateur.

'What do you think about it, Beaver? You know something of police matters; that is, you're friendly with a young woman who is friendly with— But perhaps I shouldn't mention that in front of the sergeant. He's so zealous, he might resent any possible leak from headquarters.'

Sergeant Ackley stood in front of Leith, clenching and unclenching his hands.

'Leith,' he said, 'you got by this time by the skin of your eyeteeth. I *almost* had you. If it weren't for making myself appear so damned ridiculous if the facts ever became public, I'd throw you in right now and take a chance on convicting you.'

Lester Leith said: 'Well, sergeant, don't let your personal feelings stand between you and your duty. Personally, I think it would be an awful mistake for you to do anything like that. In the first place, you couldn't convict me; and in the second place, it *would* put you yourself in a very ridiculous light. To think that with all the facilities which the police had at their command, they couldn't solve a case so simple that a rank amateur by merely reading a newspaper clipping— No, no, sergeant, it would *never* do. They'd laugh you out of office.'

Sergeant Ackley nodded to the two men. 'Come on,' he said; 'let's go. Beaver, step this way. I want a word with you.

Sergeant Ackley led the undercover man into the soundproof closet where the telephone was kept.

'Beaver,' he said, 'you've got to fix up a story to square yourself.'

'Great Scott, sergeant!' the undercover man exclaimed. 'I can't. He's seen me working with you. He knows—'

'Now listen,' Sergeant Ackley interrupted. 'We've spent a lot of money getting you planted on this job. With you here, we can keep track of what he's doing. The very next time he tries anything, we'll be *certain* to get him. But without you to keep us posted, he'll laugh at us, flaunt his damned hijacking right in our faces, and get away with it. The man's too diabolically clever to be caught by any ordinary methods.'

'I can't help that,' the spy said doggedly. 'I've shown myself in my true colors now, thanks to you.'

'What do you mean, thanks to me?' Sergeant Ackley demanded.

'You insisted that I accompany you.'

Sergeant Ackley's face flushed with rage. 'If you want to come right down to facts, Beaver,' he said, '*you're* the one who's responsible for this whole mess.'

'How do you mean I'm responsible for it?'

'I had the idea all along that those emeralds were in the monkey's stomach. Then you got that brainstorm of yours that the nurse had stuck 'em in the chewing gum, and damned if I didn't let you sell me on the idea. I should have known better. You—'

'I thought that was *your* idea,' Beaver charged.

'Mine?' Sergeant Ackley's eyes were round with surprise. 'Why, don't you remember telephoning me, Beaver, that—'

'Yes, and you said it was your idea.'

Sergeant Ackley said patronizingly: 'You misunderstood me, Beaver. I told you that I'd already considered that possibility. That was all.'

The undercover man sighed.

'Now then,' Ackley went on, 'you'll have to make up for that mistake by devising some way of getting yourself back in Leith's good graces.'

The big undercover man, his black eyes suddenly glittering, said. 'O.K., I have an idea!'

'What is it?' Sergeant Ackley wanted to know.

'I could claim that *I* was under arrest; that you came here and pinched me first and then kept me with you all the time you were laying for him on the train and—'

'That's fine,' Ackley said. 'We'll put that across.'

'But,' Beaver went on, 'it won't explain our conversation in the closet. *You've* spilled the beans now.'

'You'll have to think up some explanation,' Sergeant Ackley said. 'You thought up that other, now you can think up—'

'Of course,' Beaver said, 'I *could* say that you'd called me in here and made me a proposition to spy on him and that I resented it.'

'Swell,' Sergeant Ackley said. 'That's exactly what we want. I knew we could think up something if we put our minds to it, Beaver.'

'Oh, *we* thought of this, did we?' Beaver asked.

'Certainly,' Sergeant Ackley said. 'That is, I outlined to you what was required, and directed your thoughts in the proper channels. It shows you the value of supervision.'

'I see,' the spy said, his eyes still glittering, craftily. 'But Lester Leith won't believe that story unless I tell him that I bitterly resented your attempt to bribe me.'

'Well, go ahead and resent it,' Sergeant Ackley said.

'But how can I resent it?'

'You can shout at me, abuse me in a loud tone of voice.'

'No,' Beaver said, 'this closet is virtually soundproof.'

'Well, think of something,' Sergeant Ackley said impatiently.

'I could push you up against the wall,' Beaver said, 'and he could hear that. Then I'd have to hit you.'

Sergeant Ackley seemed dubious. 'I don't think we need to carry things that far, Beaver. We can scuffle around a bit and—'

'No. That will never do,' Beaver said. 'We have to put this thing on right, or not at all. I won't stay here unless we can do it convincingly.'

'Oh, all right,' Sergeant Ackley said. 'Just to make it seem convincing, I'll hit you first. You hit me easy, Beaver. You're a big man. You don't know your own strength. Come on; let's get started. Now remember, Beaver, after things quiet down, I want you to get him started on the affair of the drugged guard.'

'What's that?' Beaver asked. 'I hadn't heard of it.'

'Well, you will hear of it. We'll give you all the dope. It happened last night. Karl Bonneguard was collecting funds for a political cult movement in this country. We don't know how far it had gone. But he'd collected quite a bit of money. There was a grand jury investigation in the offing, so Bonneguard drew all the money out of the bank and—'

'I get you,' Beaver said. 'What happened?'

'Somebody drugged the guard, and burgled the safe. We can't find out how the guard got doped. It's a mix-up that simply doesn't make sense.'

'You don't think the guard framed it and copped the dough?'

'No. The guard's O.K. He warned Bonneguard soon as he felt drowsy. I'll have to tell you about it later, Beaver. We haven't time to discuss it now. We'll go ahead with the act. We'll open the door. You'll be indignant.'

'O.K.,' Beaver said, 'let's go.'

They raised their voices in loud and angry altercation. Beaver flung open the closet door and said:

'I think it's the most contemptible thing I ever heard of.'

'Go ahead and be a dumb cluck, then,' Sergeant Ackley roared. 'You keep playing around with this crook and you'll wind up behind the bars. You're a crook yourself!'

'Liar!' Beaver shouted.

Sergeant Ackley lunged a terrific swing at Beaver's jaw.

The undercover man, moving with the swift dexterity of a trained boxer, stepped inside of the blow. For a fraction of a second, he set himself. A look of supreme enjoyment became apparent on his face. He moved his right in a short, pivoting jab which caught Sergeant Ackley on the point of the jaw.

Ackley's head snapped back. The force of the punch lifted him from the floor, slammed him back into the arms of the two detectives.

One of the detectives reached for his blackjack. The other dragged out a gun. Beaver whirled to face them, so that his back was to Lester Leith. He gave a series of warning winks and said:

'I call on you to witness that he struck me first, after accusing me of being a crook. Do you know what he wanted? He wanted to bribe me to stay on in this job and act as spy. I told him what I thought of him. I told him Mr. Leith was the best man I ever worked for.'

He took a deep breath and turned to Lester Leith. 'I'm very sorry, sir,' he said, 'for losing my temper. But Sergeant Ackley took me into custody, very much against my will, earlier in the evening. Disregarding my demands that I be taken before a magistrate, he dragged me aboard that train and forced me to accompany him. I didn't dare disobey him. However, when he made this infamous proposal to me, I felt that I was well within my rights as a citizen in couching my refusal in no uncertain language and in defending myself against attack. I trust I haven't done wrong, sir.'

The police officers stared in amazement at the spy. Lester Leith regarded the limp form of Sergeant Ackley with eyes that were half closed in thoughtful concentration. At length he said:

'No, Beaver, you've done exactly what I should have done under similar circumstances. I distinctly saw Sergeant Ackley make an unprovoked assault upon you.'

Turning to the two officers, Beaver said: 'And I call on you two gentlemen to be witness to what has happened. I demand that you take Sergeant Ackley out of here. I think, when he recovers consciousness, he will be the first to tell you that I have done exactly what the situation called for.'

One of the detectives returned the spy's wink. 'O.K., Beaver,' he said, 'you win. Come on, Al. Give me a hand and we'll drag the sarge out of here before there's any more trouble.'

When the door had closed behind them, Beaver said to Lester Leith: 'Disloyalty, sir, is one of my pet abominations. I detest one who is disloyal. I couldn't restrain myself.'

'I don't blame you in the least,' Lester Leith said. 'I'm surprised that Sergeant Ackley had the temerity to arrest you and drag you aboard that train.'

'So am I, sir,' the spy said. And then, with a look of cunning in his eyes, added: 'Incidentally, sir, while I was with them in the drawing room, I heard them discussing a crime which was committed no later than last night; a crime involving a drugged guard—'

Lester Leith held up his hand, palm outward. 'Not now, Scuttle,' he said. 'I don't want to hear it.'

The spy said, 'Perhaps tomorrow, when you're feeling rested—'

'No, not tomorrow, Scuttle.'

The spy did not press the point. 'Very well, sir,' he said.

'By the way, Scuttle,' Leith commented, 'I think I'd like a brandy, and you'd better join me. I derived a great deal of satisfaction from the way you hung that punch on Sergeant Ackley's jaw.'

THE CRIMES OF RICHMOND CITY

FREDERICK NEBEL

Writing in the midst of the Great Depression, Frederick Nebel (1903–1967) wrote prolifically for *Black Mask* and *Dime Detective* and other pulps, producing scores of relatively realistic hard-boiled stories about such fixtures of their era as Cardigan, the hard-as-nails Irish operative working for the Cosmos Agency in St Louis; tough dick Donny Donahue of the Interstate Agency; and, most importantly, the long-running stories about Captain Steve MacBride and the ever-present local reporter, Kennedy, who frequently takes over a story and does as much crime solving as the official member of the police department.

Nebel had two mystery novels published during his lifetime, *Sleepers East* (1934) and *Fifty Roads to Town* (1936). *The Crimes of Richmond City*, a powerful depiction of violence and corruption, has never before appeared in book form. It was published as five separate episodes in *Black Mask* in the issues of September, 1928, through May, 1929.

Publishing novels in serial form was common for *Black Mask* in this era, as it was responsible for such important works as Dashiell Hammett's first four novels, *Red Harvest*, *The Dain Curse*, *The Maltese Falcon* and *The Glass Key*, as well as Paul Cain's *Fast One* and many of Carroll John Daly's books.

RAW LAW

FREDERICK L. NEBEL

Captain Steve MacBride was a tall square-shouldered man of forty more or less hard-bitten years. He had a long, rough-chiseled face, steady eyes, a beak of a nose, and a wide, firm mouth that years of fighting his own and others' wills had hardened. His face shone ruddily, cleanly, as if it were used to frequent and vigorous contact with soap and water. For eighteen years he had been connected, in one capacity or another, with Richmond City's police department, and Richmond City today is a somewhat hectic community of almost a hundred-thousand population.

MacBride sat in his office at Police Headquarters. He sat at his shining oak desk, in a swivel chair, smoking a blackened briar pipe, with the latest copy of the Richmond City *Free Press* spread before him. In one corner a steam radiator clanked and hissed intermittently. There were a half dozen chairs lined against the wall behind him. The floor was of cement, the ceiling was high and, like the walls, a light, impersonal tan. About the room there was something hollow and clean and efficient. About the borders of the two windows at MacBride's left there were irregular frames of snow left by a recent blizzard. But the room was warm and, except for the clanking of the radiator, quite silent.

Reading on, MacBride sometimes moved in his chair or took his pipe from his mouth to purse his lips, it seemed a little grimly and ironically. Once he muttered something behind clenched teeth, way down in the cavern of his throat. Presently he let the paper drop and sat back, drawing silently on his pipe and letting his eyes wander back and forth over the collection of photographs tacked on the bulletin board on the wall before him – photographs of men wanted for robbery, murder, and homicide. One of the telephones on his desk rang. He took off the receiver, listened, said, 'Send him in.' Then he leaned back again and swung his chair to face the door.

It opened presently, and a man neatly dressed in a blue overcoat and a gray fedora strolled in. A cigarette was drooping from one corner of his mouth. He had a young-old face, a vague smile, and the whimsical eyes of the wicked and wise.

'Hello, cap.' He kicked the door shut with his heel and leaned against it, indolently, as if he were a little weary – not in his bones, but with life.

'Hello, Kennedy,' nodded MacBride. 'Sit down.'

'Thanks.'

Kennedy dropped into a chair, unbuttoned his overcoat, but did not remove it.

MacBride creaked in his chair, looked at the newspaper on his desk and said, with a brittle chuckle, 'Thanks for the editorial.'

'Don't thank me, Mac.'

'Your sheet's trying to ride us, eh?'

'Our business is to ride everybody we can.'

'M-m-m. I know.'

Kennedy knocked the ash from his cigarette. 'Of course, it's tough on you.' He smiled, shrugged. 'I know your hands are tied.'

'Eh?' MacBride's eyes steadied.

'You heard me, Mac. This little boy knows a lot. Y' know, *you* don't run the Department.'

MacBride's lips tightened over his pipe.

'*You*,' went on Kennedy, 'would like to put the clamps on this dirty greaseball, Cavallo. Now wouldn't you?'

MacBride's eyes narrowed, and he took his pipe from his mouth. 'Would I?' His hand knotted over the hot bowl of the pipe.

'Sure you would. But—' Kennedy shrugged – 'you can't.'

'Listen, Kennedy. What did you come here for, to razz me?'

'I don't know why I came here. It was cold out, and I know you keep it warm here. And – well, I just thought I'd drop in for a chat.'

'You thought you'd get some inside dope. Go ahead, come out with it. Well, Kennedy, I've got nothing to say. News is as tight here as a drum-head. What a bunch of wise-cracking eggs you've got down in your dump. Gink Cavallo'll laugh himself into a bellyache when he reads it. The lousy bum!'

'Something's got to break, Mac. When a bootlegging greaseball starts to run a town, starts to run the Department, something's got to break.'

'He's not running *me!*' barked MacBride.

'The hell he isn't! Don't tell me. I'm no greenhorn, Mac. Maybe not you personally. But your hands are tied. He's running somebody else, and somebody else is running somebody else, and the last somebody else is running you.'

'You're talking through your hat, Kennedy.'

'Oh, am I? No, I can't lay my hands on it all, but I can use my head. I know a few things. I know that Gink Cavallo is one of the wisest wops that ever packed a rod. He's a brother-in-law to Tony Diorio, and Diorio is president of the Hard Club, and the Hard Club swings two thousand sure votes and a thousand possible votes. And, you know, Mac, that these wops stick together. Most of the bohunks in the mills are wops, and they've sworn by the Hard Club, and – get this, Mac – it was the Hard Club that put Pozzo in for alderman and Mulroy for state's attorney. And it's the state's attorney's office that's running the Department – the rottenest administration in the history of Richmond City. It's just putting two and two together.

'You can't move, Mac. You've got your orders – hands off. What can you do? You're a captain. You've been with the Department for eighteen years. You've got a wife and a kid, and if you were kicked out of the Department you'd be on the rocks. I know you hate Cavallo like poison, and I know you're just aching to take a crack at him. It sure is a tough break for you, Mac.'

MacBride had not batted an eye-lash, had not shone by the slightest flicker of eyes or expression, how he took Kennedy's speech. He drew on his pipe meditatively, looking down along his beak of a nose. It was in the heart of MacBride that seas of anger were crashing and tumbling. Because Kennedy was right; he had hit the nail on the head with every charge. But MacBride was not the man to whimper or to go back on the Department. Loyalty had been ground into him long years ago – loyalty to his badge.

His voice was casual, 'Finished, Kennedy? Then run along. I'm busy.'

'I know, Mac. Kind of touched you on the quick, eh? It's all right, old-timer. Your jaw's sealed, too. You'd be one hell of a fool to tell Steve Kennedy how right he is. Well.' Kennedy got up and lit a fresh butt. 'It's all right by me, Cap. But when the big noise breaks, don't forget yours truly. It can't go on, Mac. Somebody'll slip. Some guy'll yap for more than his share. I've seen these rotten conditions before – 'Frisco, Chicago, New Orleans. I'm hard-boiled as hell, Mac, and there's no one pulling any wool over my eyes. I'm just standing by and laughing up my sleeve.' He took a pull on his cigarette. 'There's one wild Mick in your outfit who's very liable to spill the beans, get himself shoved out to the sticks and maybe poked in the ribs with a bullet, besides.'

'You mean—?'

'Sure. Jack Cardigan. S' long, Mac.'

'Good bye, Kennedy.'

When the door closed, MacBride let go of himself. He heaved to his feet, spread-legged, his fists clenched, his eyes narrowed and burning intensely.

'God, Kennedy, if you only *knew* how right you are!' he muttered. 'If I was only single – if I hadn't Anna and Judith. I'm tied all around, dammit! Home – and *here!*' He sank back into his chair, his head drooping, age creeping upon him visibly.

II

He was sitting there, in precisely the same position, fifteen minutes later. And fifteen minutes later the door swung open swiftly, silently, and Jack Cardigan came in. A tall, lean, dark-eyed man, this Cardigan, rounding thirty years. Men said he was reckless, case-hardened, and a flash with the gun. He was.

'You look down at the mouth, Steve,' he said, offhand.

'I am, Jack. Kennedy—'

'Oh, that guy!'

'Kennedy dropped in to pay me a call. Sharp, that bird. Pulls ideas out of the air, and every idea hits you like a sock on the jaw.'

'Been razzing you?'

'Has he! Jack, he's got the whole thing worked out to a T. He'd just need my O.K. to spill the whole beans to the public, and likely Police Headquarters 'd be mobbed. He's right. He's got the right slant on the whole dirty business. Jack, if I was ten years younger, I'd tell the Big Boss to go to hell and take my chances. That lousy wop is sitting on top of the world, and his gang's got Richmond City tied by the heels.'

Cardigan sat down on the edge of a chair. There was something on his mind. You could see that much. He tapped with his fingers on the desk, his lips were a little set, the muscle lumps at either side of his jaw quivered, his dark eyes were close-lidded, active, flashing back and forth across MacBride's face.

'Brace up, Steve,' he clipped. 'I've got some news that might knock you for a row of pins.'

'Eh?' MacBride straightened in his chair.

Cardigan's lips curled. 'I came up alone. The sergeant said Kennedy'd gone up to see you. Didn't notice if he'd left. So I came up beforehand – to see.'

'Kennedy left fifteen minutes ago. What's up?'

'Enough!' Cardigan took a vicious crack at the desk with his doubled fist. 'The dirty pups got Hanley!'

'What!' MacBride's chair creaked violently. He leaned forward, laid his hand on Cardigan's knee, his breath sucked in and held.

'Two shots – through the lung and the heart! Somebody's going to pay for this, Steve! Joe Hanley was my partner – my sister's husband! There's nobody'll stop me – nobody! I'll—'

'Just a minute, Jack,' cut in MacBride gently. 'How 'd it happen?'

Cardigan got a grip on his temper, bit his lip. 'I was out at Joe's place for dinner tonight, on Webster Road. Marion was a little upset. Kid had a bad cold, and she had a streak of worrying on, just like her. I mind five years ago, how she used to say she'd never marry a cop. She used to worry about me all the time. Not that a cop wasn't good enough – hell no. But she used to say if she married a cop she'd be laying awake all night worrying. So, like a woman, she married Joe, and Joe's been a buddy of mine since we were kids. Well, you know that. Then she had two to worry over – Joe and me.

'And she was worrying tonight. Joe laughed. So did I. She got me alone in the hall and told me to watch out for Joe. She'd always been doing this. I kidded her. She said she meant it, and that she felt something was going to happen. I remember how she hung on to him when we breezed. 'God!'

'Steady, Jack!'

'I know. Well, Joe and I hoofed it to the park, to get a bus into the city. There was none in sight, so we began hiking down Webster Road till one 'd come. Pretty lonesome there. A car came weaving down behind us, and we heard a girl scream. We turned around and held up our hands for it to stop. The driver swerved to one side, intending to duck us. He slid into a ditch, roared his motor trying to get out. The girl was yelling hysterically. We saw her pitch out of the car. Then it heaved out of the ditch and was getting under way when Joe hopped it, pulling his rod. Two shots slammed out, and Joe keeled. I had my hands full with the girl. The car skidded and crashed into the bushes.

'I had my rod out then and ran up. Two guys in the back had jumped out and ducked into the bushes. I nailed the chauffeur. He wasn't heeled, but he was trying to get away, too. He started giving me a line and I socked him on the head so he'd stay put till I looked after Joe. Well, there wasn't much to look after. Joe was dead. The girl – she was only a flapper – was bawling and shaking in the knees. She'd been pretty well mauled. A machine came along and I stopped it.'

'Wait. You say you got the chauffeur?'

'Sure. He says his name's Clark, and he's downstairs, barking for a lawyer.'

'Who's the girl?'

'Pearl Carr's her name. Just a wise little flapper who thought she was smart by taking a ride. She was waiting for a bus – she told me this – when this big touring car stopped and one of the guys offered her a lift. Sure, she got in, the little fool, and these guys started playing around.'

'Know the guys?'

Cardigan growled. 'Two of Cavallo's guns or I don't know anything. Her description of one tallies with Bert Geer, that walking fashion-plate. You remember two years ago they nabbed Geer on suspicion for that girl out in St Louis they found strangled near Grand Gardens. But he got out of it. The other guy sounds like that rat "Monkey" Burns. I took the number of the touring car. I looked up the records downstairs and found the plates had been stolen from a sedan two weeks ago. If they're Geer and Burns, it means that Cavallo's in the pot, too, because they're the wop's right-hand guns. If we make them take the rap, they'll draw in Cavallo, and just as sure as you're born Diorio and Pozzo and our estimable State's Attorney Mulroy'll get in the tangle, and there'll be hell to pay all around. But I'm going through with this, Steve, and the state's attorney's office be damned! Joe was my buddy, closer to me than a brother – my sister's husband! God – can you picture Marion!'

MacBride was tight-lipped, a little pale, terribly grim. The ultimate had come. Would they tie the Department's hands now?

'Did you let Clark get a lawyer?' he asked.

'No – cripes, no!'

'Then get him up here. Where's the girl?'

'Downstairs, still bawling. I sent a cop out to get her a dress or something. I phoned her old man and he's driving in to get her.'

'All right. Leave her there. But get Clark.'

Cardigan went out and MacBride settled back, heaved a vast sigh, crammed fresh tobacco into his pipe. When, a few moments later, the door opened, he was puffing serenely, though deep in his heart there was a great numbness.

Clark came in, aided by a shove in the rear from Cardigan. The detective closed the door, grabbed Clark by the shoulder and slammed him not too gently into a chair.

'Say, go easy there, guy!' whined Clark, a charred clinker of a runt, with a face of seeming innocence, like a mongrel dog.

'Close your jaw!' snapped Cardigan.

Clark spread his hands toward MacBride. 'Tell this guy to leave me alone, Captain. He's been treatin' me hard. First off he beans me with his gat and since then he's been chuckin' me around like I was a rag. I got my rights. I'm a citizen. You can't go cloutin' citizens. I got my—'

'Soft pedal,' said MacBride heavily. 'So your name's Clark, eh? How'd you come to be driving that car?'

'I was drivin' it, that's all. I'm all right. I don't know nothin'. I was just drivin' it. You can't make a slop-rag outta me.'

'Shut up,' cut in MacBride.

'All right, I'll shut up. That's what I'm gonna do. You gotta let me get a lawyer. I got rights. Them's a citizen's rights.'

'Listen to the bum!' chuckled Cardigan.

'There, see!' chirped Clark. 'He's still insultin' me. He's just a big wise guy, he is. I got my rights. I'll see you get yours, fella. I was drivin' a car. All right, I was drivin' it. I know you guys. I ain't gotta talk.'

'You're going to talk, Clark,' said MacBride ominously. 'And none of this cheap chatter, either. Talk that counts – see?'

'I ain't. No, I ain't. I want a lawyer. Gimme that phone.'

He scrambled out of the chair, clawed for the telephone. Cardigan grabbed him by the nape of the neck, hurled him back so hard that Clark hit the chair aslant and, knocking it over, sprawled with it to the floor. He crouched, cringing, blubbering.

'You leave me alone, you! What the hell you think you're doin'? You leave me—'

'Get up – get up,' gritted Cardigan. 'That's only a smell compared with what's coming if you don't come clean. Get up, you dirty little rat!' He reached down, caught Clark, heaved him up and banged him down into another chair.

Clark's teeth chattered. His hands fidgeted, one with the other. His mouth worked, gasping for breath. His eyes almost popped from his head.

'Now,' came MacBride's low voice, 'who were the two guys that got away?'

'You can't make me talk now. You can't!' Clark gripped the sides of his chair, the stringy cords on his neck bulged. 'I ain't talkin' – not me. I want a lawyer – that's what. Them's my rights, gettin' a lawyer. There!' He stuck out his chin defiantly.

MacBride turned in his chair and looked at Cardigan. Cardigan nodded, his fingers opening and closing.

'Take him into the sweat room, Jack,' said MacBride. 'Sweat him.'

Clark stiffened in his chair, and sucked in his nether lip with a sharp intake of breath. He writhed.

'You can't do that, you can't!' he screamed. 'I got my rights. You can't beat up a citizen.'

'Citizen are you?' chuckled Cardigan. 'You're a bum, Clark. You were driving a car with somebody else's plates. You tried to get away with the other two birds but you weren't fast enough. My buddy was killed, see? Now you'll talk. I'll sweat it out of you, Clark, so help me!'

'You won't! I ain't gonna talk. Gawd almighty, I want a lawyer! You can't stop me from gettin' one!'

'You're stopped, Clark,' bit off Cardigan. 'Get up and come on along with me.'

Cardigan reached for him. Clark squirmed in his chair, lashed out with his feet. One foot caught Cardigan in the stomach and he doubled momentarily, grimacing but silent. MacBride was out of his seat in a flash, and Clark was jerked to his feet so fast that he lost his breath. He was wild-eyed, straining at the arms that held him, his lips quivering, groans and grunts issuing from his throat.

'You ain't gonna beat me – you ain't! You'll see! I won't talk! I got my rights. I – I—'

'I'll take him, Steve,' said Cardigan.

MacBride stepped back and Clark struggled frantically in Cardigan's grasp as the latter worked him toward the door.

The telephone bell jangled.

'Wait,' said MacBride.

Cardigan paused at the door.

MacBride picked up the phone, muttered something, listened. Then, 'What's that?' His hands knotted around the instrument, his eyes narrowed, his mouth hardened. 'Are you sure of that?' He groaned deep in his throat, rocked on his feet. Then, bitterly, 'All right!'

He slammed the receiver into the hook and banged the instrument down upon the desk violently. He turned to face Cardigan.

'It's no use, Jack. A runner for that lousy firm of Cohen, Fraser and Cohen, is downstairs, which means this bum slides out of our hands.'

Cardigan's face darkened. 'How'd they know we had this bird so soon?'

'That's their business. They work on a big retainer from the head of the gang Clark belongs to.'

There was a knock at the door, and a sergeant and a patrolman came in. The sergeant showed MacBride a writ, and the patrolman marched Clark out of the office. Then the sergeant left, and MacBride and Cardigan were alone.

'Wires being pulled again,' muttered Cardigan. 'This guy will never come to trial.'

'Of course not,' nodded MacBride grimly.

'What a fine state of affairs! We nab a guy, and have every chance to make him come across, and then he's taken out of our hands. What's the use of a Police Department, anyhow?'

'Clark is one of Cavallo's boys. No doubt about it. And we can't do a thing – just sit and curse the whole thing. It's tough to be on the Force eighteen years – and have to stand for it.'

'I know, Steve, you can't move. Your wife and kid to think of. But there's one way to get back at these wops, and the only way. They killed Joe, and they've got to pay for it! I'm going to make 'em pay – pound for pound! By God, I am, and the Department and the State's Attorney and everybody else be damned!'

'Jack, you can't – alone. You're a dick and—'

'I'm no longer a dick. I'm single and free and my resignation goes in now! I'm going to fight Cavallo, Steve, at his own game!'

'What do you mean?'

'Just what I said. I'm resigning from the Department. I'm going on my own and wipe out Cavallo and every one of his dirty gunmen! Richmond City is going to see one of the biggest gang wars in its history! When they killed Joe Hanley, they killed the wrong man, for my part! I'm going to fall on 'em like a ton of brick!'

'Jack, you can't do it!'

'Watch me!' chuckled Cardigan, his eyes glittering.

III

Men said Jack Cardigan was reckless and case-hardened – men meaning cops and reporters and Richmond City's generous sprinkling of gunmen. Something might be added; he was ruthless. As a detective, he'd been hated and feared by more crooks than perhaps any other man in the Department – inspectors, captain, lieutenants and all the rest included. Because he was hard

– tough – rough on rats; rats being one of his favorite nicknames applied to a species of human being that shoots in the dark and aims for the back.

For three years Joe Hanley had been his partner, in the Department. In life, they'd been partners for years – and the bond of friendship had been welded firmly and topped off with the marriage of Cardigan's sister Marion to Joe. It was a far, long cry from that happy, flowered day to the day when Marion and Cardigan rode home from the cemetery, after the burial of Joe. Cardigan held his sister in his arms on the slow journey. There was nothing he could say to comfort her. Pity, condolence, make empty, meaningless words on such a tragic day. So he held her in his arms and let her sob.

His own face was a mask, grim and carven, the eyes dark and close-lidded. Home, he put her into the hands of their mother. No one spoke. Glances, gestures, conveyed far more. For a long while he sat alone, motionless and thoughtful. The funeral was over, but the dread pall of it still lingered. Even the house seemed to take on a personality of mourning – quiet and hollow and reverent.

A week later Cardigan sat in a speakeasy on the outer circle of Richmond City's theatrical district. He was sipping a dry Martini when Kennedy of the *Free Press* drifted in and joined him.

'What's the idea of shaking your job, Cardigan?'

'What's that to you?'

'Or were you *told* to resign?'

'Maybe.'

Kennedy chuckled. 'Sounds more like it. What you get for bringing in Clark. Lord that was a joke! His lawyer was a sharp egg. Clark played the dope all through. Bet his lawyer spent nights drilling him how to act. Clark was just a hired chauffeur. How did he know the plates were stolen? He was hired a week before the mess out on Webster Road to drive a car. They gave him a car to drive. The whole thing was a joke, and the presenting attorney gave the defense every possible opening. What are you doing now?'

'Nothing. Taking life easy.'

'Don't make me laugh!'

'Well, have it your way.'

'Listen, Cardigan,' said Kennedy. 'You know a lot. The *Free Press* would sell its shirt to get some straight dope from you. That's no boloney. I mean it. I've got the whole thing figured out, but what we need is a story where we can omit the "alleged" crap. Man, you can clean up!'

'Yeah?' Cardigan laughed softly. 'Be yourself, Kennedy. Run along. You're wasting time on me.'

'I don't know about that.'

'Then learn.'

Kennedy had a highball and went on his way. Alone, Cardigan took another drink, and looked at his watch. It was half-past eight at night. He looked across at the telephone on the wall. He drained his glass and lit a cigarette.

The telephone rang. He got up and beat the owner to it. 'This is for me,' he said, and took off the receiver. 'You, Pete? . . . O.K. Be right over.'

He hung up, paid for his drinks and shrugged into his dark overcoat. Outside, it was damp and cold, and automobiles hissed by over slushy pavements.

Cardigan did not walk toward the bright glow that marked the beginning of the theatrical district. He bored deeper into the heart of Jockey Street. Where it was dirtiest and darkest, he swung in toward a short flight of broken stone steps, reached a large, ancient door, groped for a bell-button and pressed it. It was opened a moment later by a huge, beetle-browed negro.

'Pete Fink,' said Cardigan. 'He expects me.'

'Who yuh are?' asked the negro.

'None of your damned business.'

'I'll get Fink,' said the negro and slammed the door in Cardigan's face.

'Takes no chances,' muttered Cardigan. 'Well, that's good.'

Fink opened the door this time, while the negro hovered behind him, his face like shining ebony under the single gas-jet.

'Take a good look, big boy,' Cardigan said, as he passed in.

And the negro said, 'Got yuh, boss.'

Fink led the way up a flight of crooked stairs that creaked under their footfalls. They reached the upper landing. Cardigan placed six doors in a row. One of these Fink opened, and they entered a large, square room, furnished cheaply with odd bits of furniture, no two pieces the same in make or design.

Cardigan stood with his hands in his coat pockets, idly running his eyes about the room.

Fink was leaning against the door he had closed. He was a big, rangy man, with one of his shoulders higher than the other. His nose was a twisted knot; a tawny mustache sagged over his mouth. He had a jaw like a snowplow, and eyes like ice – cold and steady and enigmatic. His hands were big and red and bony. He wore brown corduroy trousers, a blue flannel shirt, a wide belt with an enormous brass buckle. He looked like a tough egg. He wasn't a soft one.

Cardigan sighed and poured himself a drink. He downed it neat, rasped his throat, and looked at the empty glass.

'Good stuff, Pete.'

'Cavallo sells the same.'

They faced each other. Their eyes met and held and bored one into the other. At last Fink grinned and rocked away from the door, sat down at the table and lit a cigarette. Cardigan sat down opposite him, opened his overcoat and helped himself to one of Fink's cigarettes.

'Well, Pete? . . .'

Fink leaned forward, elbows resting on the table, his butt jutting from one corner of his mouth and an eye squinted against the smoke that curled upward.

'Six,' he said. 'I got six.'

'Who are they?'

'Chip Slade, Gats Gilman, Luke Kern, Bennie Levy, Chuck Ward and Bat Johnson. All good guns.'

'Yeah, I know. How do they feel about it?'

'Cripes, they're ripe!'

'They want to know who's behind you?'

'I said a big guy – somebody big, who's in the know.'

Cardigan chuckled. 'Remember, Pete, it stays that way. I'm – it sounds like a joke – the mystery man in this. The master mind!' He chuckled again, amusedly, then grew serious. 'To come out in the open would be to shoot the whole works. I'm too well known as a gumshoe. But I'll manage this, Pete, and supply the first funds. I've got a measly two thousand saved up, but it's a starter. And I'm out to flop on the bums that got Hanley, my buddy. If everybody holds up his end, you'll all make money and Cavallo and his crowd will get washed out.'

'You say the word, Jack. I'm takin' orders from you. The rest take orders from me and no questions asked.'

'Good. I'll give you five hundred bucks to buy a second-hand car. Get a big touring. To hell with the looks of it; buy it for the motor – for speed. Buy half-a-dozen high-powered rifles and plenty of ammunition. Pick up some grenades if you can. How about a storehouse?'

'Got one picked – an old farmhouse out on Farmingville Turnpike.'

'Sounds good. Rent it for a month.'

'It's way out in the sticks,' added Fink. 'Off the main pike, way in on a lane, and no other house inside of a quarter mile. I can get it for fifty bucks a month.'

'Get it. We've got to watch out for tapped wires, though. Here, I'm staying at the Adler House. You know that number. If things get hot and you've got to talk a lot, just call me up and say, 'I've got something to tell you.' I'll hang up and run down to the drug-store on the corner. There's a booth there and I'll get you the number. We'll choose booths all over the city where we can make calls, and we'll get the numbers.'

'O.K.'

'How about the dinge downstairs?'

'He owns a dump. Sees a lot and says nothin'.'

Cardigan ground out his cigarette. 'Then it's all set. Get me straight, Fink. Leave the cops alone. Tell your boys that. We're after Cavallo and his rats – not the cops. If the cops show up, run. I've got a grudge against that wop and the crowd he runs with. I'm playing my grudge to a showdown. If I make some jack out of it, all right. But I'm after rats first – not jack. You and your guns can clean up sweet in this racket, if you use your head and move how I tell you.'

'I got you, Jack,' nodded Fink.

'All right. Let me know when you're all set and I'll map out our first move. Get the rifles, ammunition, grenades. Get a fast car and see that the tires are good.' He drew a wad of bills from his pocket. 'There's a thousand as a starter.'

Fink shoved the money into his pocket and poured another brace of drinks.

'You got guts, Jack,' he said, 'to chuck the Department – for this.'

'Guts, my eye!' clipped Cardigan. 'I've got a grudge, Pete, a whale of a grudge – against the dirty, rotten bums that killed the best friend I ever had.' He raised his glass. 'Down the hatch.'

On that they drank.

IV

Two days later Cardigan was sitting in his room at the Adler House, when the telephone rang. It was the desk, and he said, 'Send him up.' Then he settled back again in his over-stuffed easy-chair. It was ten in the morning and he was still in pajamas and bathrobe. On a settee beside him was a detailed map of Richmond City and its suburbs. Here and there he had marked x's, or made penciled notations.

There was a knock on the door and he called, 'Come in, Steve.'

MacBride came in, closed the door and stood there stroking his chin and regarding Cardigan seriously.

'Sit down,' said Cardigan. 'Take the load off your feet, Steve. You'll find cigars in the box on the table. How's tricks?'

MacBride took a cigar and eased himself down on a divan. 'My day off and I thought I'd drop in and see you.'

'Is that all you came for, Steve?'

MacBride lit up and took a couple of puffs before replying. 'Not exactly, Jack.'

'Spill it.'

'Oh, it's not much. Only I was worrying. You still thinking of butting in on Cavallo's racket?'

'What a question! Why'd you suppose I left the Department?'

'M-m-m,' droned MacBride. 'I wish you hadn't, Jack. You were the best man I had, and, Jack, old boy, you can't buck that crowd. It's madness. You'll get in trouble, and if you make a bad step, you'll get the Department on your neck. You haven't got politics behind you. You'd be out of luck. That's straight. How do you think I'd feel if it came to the point where you faced me as prisoner?'

'I've been thinking about that, Steve,' admitted Cardigan. 'It's the one thing I'd hate.'

'No more than I would.' MacBride licked a loose wrapper back into place on his cigar. 'Kennedy's been in to see me again. That guy's so nosey and so clever it hurts. Look out for him. *He's* got an idea you're up to something.'

'I know. That bird's so sharp he's going to cut himself some day.'

'Made any moves yet – I mean, you?'

'Some – getting things ready.'

'What's up your sleeve anyway?'

'Steve—' Cardigan paused the flex his lips. 'Steve, we've been mighty good friends. We are yet. But I can't tell you. I'm playing a game that can't have any air-holes. You understand?'

MacBride nodded. 'I guess so. But I'm worrying, Jack. I've got a hunch you're going to get in wrong and somebody's going to nail you.'

'Don't worry. Forget it. If I pull a bone I'll take the consequence. But I'm not counting on pulling a bone. This town is going to shake. Somebody's going to get hurt, and, Steve, before long some pretty high departmental offices are liable to be vacated so damned fast—'

'I'd go easy, Jack.'

'I am – feeling my way.'

MacBride shrugged and got up. They shook, and the captain went out, a little mournfully and reluctantly.

Ten minutes later the phone rang and Fink asked, 'How soon can you come out?'

'Five minutes.'

'I'll pick you up at Main and Anderson in the car.'

Cardigan hung up and snapped into his clothes. Five minutes later he shot down in the elevator, strode through the lobby and out on to Main Street. Two blocks south was Anderson. He saw the big touring car idling along – the one that Fink had bought for five-fifty; five years old, but it could do seventy-five an hour. The curtains were on, all of them.

The door opened and he hopped in, settled down beside Fink. They pounded down Main Street, swung into a side street to avoid a traffic stop, and cut north until they struck Farmingville Turnpike.

Then Cardigan said, 'Well?'

'I got the rifles and ammunition and some grenades,' said Fink. 'I want to show you the farmhouse. The boys are ripe to go, soon as you say the word.'

It took them half an hour to reach the ramshackle farmhouse. It was quite some distance from the hub of the city. It stood well off the main highway, hidden behind an arm of woods and reached by a narrow lane where the snow still lay. Fink pulled up into the yard and they got out. He had keys and opened the kitchen door. They entered and Cardigan looked it over. Two big rooms and a kitchen downstairs. Three bed-rooms upstairs. Dust, the dust of long neglect, covered the floor. The windows were small and set with many little squares of glass. The place was old, years old. The walls were lined with brick, a relic of days when houses were built to last for more than one generation.

'Just the thing,' nodded Cardigan. 'Maybe we'll use it tonight.'

'Huh?'

'Tonight. Cavallo keeps a lot of his booze on North Street. Know the old milk stables?'

'Yeah.'

'That's the place. There are three in a row, all joined together. The one in the middle is our meat. It has sliding doors, and there's always a reserve truck inside.'

'How do you know all this, Jack?'

'What do you suppose the Department does, sleep all the time?'

'Oh. . . . I gotcha. Yeah, sure.'

'Get your map out.'

Fink dived into his pocket, came out with a folder that opened to large dimensions. Cardigan also had his out.

'I've figured out the route you're to take,' he said. 'Mark these down now, so there'll be no slip up. The truck is a type governed to do thirty-five per and no more. Four speeds ahead. All right.' And he proceeded to give Fink precise directions to follow, street by street to Black Hill Road which leads into Farmingville Turnpike. 'Got the route all marked?' he asked, as he finished.

'Yeah, all marked.'

'Who'll drive the truck?'

'Bat Johnson and—'

'No – Bat's enough. The rest of you drift along ahead in the touring car and lead the way. One man on a truck 'll cause no suspicion. More might. And get this. Maple Road runs parallel with North street – behind the stables. You park on Maple Road and watch across the lots till you see three blinks from a flashlight. That will mean to come on and take things over. When Bat takes the truck out you boys beat it back across the lots, into the car and fall in ahead of the truck on Avenue C.'

'Who's goin' to blink the lights?'

'I am.'

'Huh?' Fink seemed incredulous.

'That's what I said. I'm going ahead to see if the road's clear. I'll take care of the watchman. If there's more there – the gang, I mean – we'll give up for the night. And mind this, if you don't see any flashes by ten o'clock, breeze. Be on Maple Road at exactly nine fifty, no sooner or later. If everything turns out all right, if you get the booze out to the farmhouse and away safe, call me up and just say, 'Jake'; that's all. And about the truck. Drive it back and abandon it on Black Hill Road.'

'But, hell, Jack, why can't me and the boys bust in the stables and crash the place proper?'

'You would say that, Pete. That's just the way to ball up the whole works. We're not out to butcher our way if we can help it. That's the trouble with you guys. You don't use your head. That's the main reason why Cavallo and his rats are going to blow up. They're too damned free with their gats.'

'Um – I guess you're right there, Jack.'

'All right, then. Come on, let's breeze. Drive me to the bus line and drop me off.'

An hour later Cardigan was eating lunch at his favorite haunt in Jockey Street, with a bottle of Sauterne on the side. It was one of fifteen restaurants circulated throughout the city and owned by a syndicate of brokers that paid a fat sum monthly to the authorities for the privilege. Four were in the financial district, six in the theatrical district, the rest scattered. More would open for business in time. You didn't need a card. The places were wide, wide open. Where the syndicate got the liquor, was nobody's business.

The Jockey Street place was managed by an ex-saloon keeper named Maloney. Cardigan had been a frequent visitor there since his resignation from the force, and they got on well. This day he called Maloney over and asked him to sit down.

He asked, 'Between you and me, what does your outfit pay for good Scotch?'

'That's our business, buddy, if you know what I mean.'

'I know what you mean. Come on, I'm *talking* business.'

'You in the game?'

'I know somebody who is.'

Maloney thought hard. 'Sixty-five bucks a case.'

Cardigan nodded. 'You can get it for fifty-five. Work the deal with your boss and you'll get a rake-off of five bucks on the case.'

'Your friend must be hard up.'

'He's just starting in business.'

'Oh. We'll have to sample it first.'

'Sure. But are you on?'

'It sounds good. How – how many cases?'

'Maybe two hundred.'

'Cripes!'

'Think it over. Speak to your boss. I'll see you again in a day or so.'

He left ten minutes later, pretty certain that he had paved the way nicely. To kill the afternoon, he dropped in at a vaudeville theatre, and ate dinner at the hotel. Later he sat in his room smoking a cigar and going over his plan step by step, searching for a loop-hole. He couldn't see any. Tonight would start the ball rolling. His vengeance would be under way. They'd murdered Joe Hanley. Now they'd pay – pound for pound. It was law of his own making, a hard, raw law – fighting rats on their own ground with their own tactics. Yet he had one advantage; a reasoning, calculating mind, thanks to his service in the Department; strategy first, guns – if it should come to that means – later.

He had a hard crew under him. Pete Fink, a product of the bootleg age – one time in the prize ring, once a sailor. Cardigan knew that he was a tough customer, and he also knew that he could rely on him. The other guns; he relied on Fink to take care of them. He'd arrested Bat Johnson only a year ago for petty larceny. Chip Slade had once felt the rap of his blackjack.

'Hell,' he mused, 'if they only knew who was behind Fink!'

V

Eight-thirty came around. Cardigan put on his overcoat and shoved an automatic into his pocket. He took his time. He wandered leisurely out of the hotel, walked a couple of blocks down Main Street and boarded a bus bound for the suburbs. Half an hour later he got off, lit a cigarette and strolled north. He was a little ahead of time, so he went on at ease.

He reached Maple Road, and continued south. Houses were scattered, and fields intervened. Then, squatting dimly in the murk beyond a field of tall grass, the old milk stables, Cardigan paused behind an ancient oak tree and looked at the illuminated dial of his watch. It was nine-thirty-five. His hand slid into his pocket and gripped the butt of his automatic.

He slipped away from the tree, hunched over and weaved his way through tall weeds. His feet slushed through snow. At intervals he paused briefly, to listen. Then he went on, bit by bit, until he reached the old picket fence behind the stables. In this he found a gap and muscled through, and squatted still for a long moment. From his coat he drew a dark handkerchief and fastened it about his face, just below his eyes. His hat brim he pulled lower.

There was a faint yellow glow shining from a window, and toward this Cardigan crept. A shade had been drawn down to within an inch or two of the bottom of the window. Smoke was drifting from a tin stove chimney. In a moment Cardigan was crouched by the window.

He saw two men sitting in chairs by a little stove. On the stove a kettle was spouting steam. A lantern stood on an empty box nearby. One of the men was asleep. The other was half-heartedly reading a newspaper; Cardigan recognized him, a huge brute of a man called 'Dutch' Weber, with a record. The other he placed as Jakie Hart, sometimes called the Creole Kid, a one-time New Orleans wharf rat. A dirty pair, he mused.

Minutes were flying, and so much depended on chance. Cardigan bent down and felt around on the snow. He found a two-foot length of board, and hefted it in his left hand. His right hand still gripped the automatic. Again looking in, he raised the board, set his jaw and crashed the window. The shade snapped up. The man with the paper spun in his chair, clawed at his gun.

But Cardigan had him covered, his head and shoulders thrust through the window.

'Drop that gat, Dutch!' he barked. 'You too, Jakie – drop it! Fast, you guys, or you'll get lead in your pants!'

The Creole Kid blinked bleary eyes. Dutch Weber cursed under his breath, his huge face flushing, murder in his gimlet eyes, his big hands writhing. But he dropped his gun, and the Creole Kid imitated him a moment later.

'Stand up – both of you,' went on Cardigan. 'Face the wall! Move out of turn and God help you!'

'You lousy bum!' snarled Weber.

'Can that crap, buddy! About face!' bit off Cardigan.

Sullenly they faced the wall, hands raised.

A moment later Cardigan was in the room. He yanked down the shade, picked up the men's discarded guns, thrust them into his pocket. And from his pocket he drew two pairs of manacles.

'Back up six paces, Dutch! Stay where you are, Jakie! Never mind looking, Dutch – just back up. Now put your hands behind your back. Don't get funny, either.' In a flash he had the manacles on Weber. 'Get over against the wall again. Move!' He jabbed the muzzle of his gun in Weber's back. 'Now you, Jakie – back up!'

In a moment he had the other pair of bracelets on the Creole Kid, and forced him back against the wall. Then he took a small bottle of chloroform from his pocket and saturated a handkerchief.

'Back up again, Jakie! As you are, Dutch!'

He clamped his arm around the Creole Kid's neck, forced the handkerchief against his nostrils and into his mouth, held it there, while he still warned Weber to stay where he was. Presently the Creole Kid went limp, relaxed, and Cardigan let him fall to the floor, unconscious.

Then he soaked another handkerchief, approached Weber and planted his gun in the big man's ribs.

'Not a stir, big boy!'

His left hand shot out, smacked the saturated handkerchief against Weber's mouth. The big man struggled, but Cardigan reminded him of the gun.

'Damn your soul!' snarled Weber in muffled tones.

'Shut your trap!'

In a short time Weber joined the Creole Kid on the floor, muttering vaguely, his hands twitching slower and slower. Cardigan pocketed his gun, produced a coil of thin, strong wire and bound their ankles. Then he ripped away strips of their shirts and bound the handkerchiefs securely in their mouths. From Weber's pockets he took a ring of keys.

With his flashlight he started a quick, systematic search of the stables. The large, covered truck was in the main stable. Its tank registered seven gallons of gasoline. Under tarpaulins he saw case upon case of liquor – between two and three hundred. He also saw ten barrels of wine. These he tipped over and sprung the spigots, and the wine gurgled and flowed on the dirt floor.

Chuckling, he hurried into the back room, blew out the lantern and pulled up the shade on the window. He raised his flashlight and blinked it three times. Then he opened the back door, sped into the main stable and unlocked the big sliding doors, but did not open them.

He turned, jumped to a ladder and climbed up to a small loft, drew the ladder up after him. Then he lay flat on his stomach in the pitch gloom, waited and listened. After a few moments he heard a door creak, and then footsteps – saw the reflection of a flashlight in the back room.

'Huh,' muttered a voice, 'the Chief sure paved the way. Lookit the way them two babies is tied up!'

'Shut up, Bat. Come on, gang.' That was Fink.

The beam of light jumped into the stable. Figures loomed in. The flash settled on the draining barrels. Someone chuckled.

'What he can't take he busts,' said a voice. 'This Chief knows his termaters, what I mean!'

The beam of light swept around the stable and found the stacked cases of liquor.

'*Ba-by!*' exclaimed someone, softly.

'Cut the gab!' hissed Fink. 'Step to it! There's the truck! Come on, guys!'

Cardigan watched them spread out. They hauled off the tarpaulins. Two men jumped into the truck. The others leaped to the cases of liquor. They worked swiftly and for the most part silently, passing the cases to the pair in the truck, who stacked them rapidly.

One muttered. 'Y' know, first off I thought this Chief was just a guy wit' brains an' no guts. I mean, like he wanted us to do his dirty work—'

'Pipe down, Gats!' snapped Fink. 'Y' see he's got guts, don't you now?'

'Sure. I'm all for him.'

'You better be,' muttered Fink. 'Any one o' you guys that thinks he's ain't 's got a lot to learn.'

'Where's he now?'

'None o' your business!' said Fink. 'Prob'ly ridin' home in a bus or somethin'. Nemmine the talk. Step on it.'

Cardigan smiled in the darkness. Yes, he could trust Fink; no doubt of it, now. Not even Fink knew he was up there in the loft, a silent watcher.

The minutes dragged by. Case after case went into the truck. The pile on the floor grew smaller and smaller. The men worked rapidly, and now silently. Cardigan looked at his watch. Half-past ten. He was stiff from holding his tense position.

'Cripes, what a load!' a voice said hoarsely.

'How many more?'

'Ten.'

'That,' said Fink, ''ll make two-hundred-and-forty-two.'
'*Ba-by!*'
Cardigan saw the last case go in. Then Fink and two others spread tarpaulins over the rear and lashed them to the sides.
'All right, Bat,' he said.
Bat Johnson climbed up into the seat, juggled the transmission lever. Another man grabbed the crank, heaved on it. The motor spat, barked, and then pounded regularly. Two men jumped to the doors, slid them back. They looked out, came back in and one said, 'Clear! Let her go!'
Bat shoved into gear and the big truck rumbled out. The doors were pulled shut. The men bunched together and at a word from Fink slipped out through the back door.
Three minutes later Cardigan dropped from the loft. He strode into the back room, snapped on his flash, played its beam on the Creole Kid and Dutch Weber, still unconscious. Then he dropped their keys and guns beside them, snapped off his flash and made for the door.
With a brittle little chuckle he went out, crossed the fields and struck Maple Road. He sought the bus line by a different route than the one by which he had reached the stables. At a quarter to twelve he entered his room, took off his coat and dropped into an easy-chair. He lit a cigar and relaxed, a little weary after the strenuous night.
But deep within him there was a great calm. He thought of Joe, and of his widowed sister. He thought, too, of other cops who had met death in strange back-alleys at the hands of rats who always shot from the rear. What protection was a shield nowadays? Protection! He grimaced. More a target! But mainly it was Joe he thought of – mild-mannered, easy-going Joe. Joe with two bullets in him, out on Webster Road. . . .
At half-past one the telephone rang. He picked it up.
'Jake,' said Fink.
'Jake,' said Cardigan, and hung up.

VI

It did not get into the papers. Things like this don't. But the underworld rumbled ominously, and the echoes seeped into the Department, but got no further. The law-abiding element of Richmond City went about its daily tasks and pleasures as usual, all ignorant of the fact that in the world of shadows, wolves were growing and baring hungry fangs.
The very next afternoon MacBride dropped in to see Cardigan.
'Well Jack,' he said.
And Cardigan said, 'Well?'
'M-m-m, you did it.'
'You mean Cavallo?'
MacBride nodded.

Cardigan chuckled.

'We got a whiff of it this morning,' went on MacBride. 'Cavallo must have gone to his brother-in-law Diorio and I guess Diorio went to his friend Alderman Pozzo and then Pozzo had a chat with State's Attorney Mulroy. Jack, for God's sake, watch your step!'

'I am. Why, do they suspect?'

'No, but—' MacBride clenched his fists and gritted his teeth. 'I shouldn't be telling you this Jack. But – we're – old friends, and I'd like to see that dago wiped out. And I guess – if I was younger and single – and a buddy of mine – like Joe was to you – was bumped off, I'd do the same. Maybe I wouldn't. Maybe I wouldn't have the guts. But, Jack, I've got to tell you, for old times' sake. McGinley and Kline, of the State's Attorney's office, have been detailed to get the guys who flopped on Cavallo's parade!'

'Oh, yes?'

'Yes. For my sake, Jack, shake this racket. You can't beat it. You see what you've got against you?'

Cardigan nodded. 'I know, Steve. But I've started, and I'm not going to let the thing just hang in the air. The more I think of Cavallo and Bert Geer and Monkey Burns and all that crowd, the more I want to blow up their racket. Imagine Pozzo for Alderman – a guy that can hardly speak English and calls himself a one hundred per cent American! Cavallo's bulwark! Mulroy having to take these wops' part because they put him in office, and getting a rake-off from their proceeds.'

'I know, Jack, I know. But—'

'No, sir, Steve. I'm playing this to a showdown, and somebody's going to get hurt in the wind-up.'

'It might be you, Jack.'

'Here's hoping it won't.'

'No one gets anywhere today trying to be a martyr.'

Cardigan laughed shortly. 'Martyr! You think *I'm* taking the godly role of a martyr? Hell, no! I'm just an ordinary guy who's sore as a boil. I'm a guy whose buddy got a dirty break, and I'm starting to go after these lads the only way they can be reached.'

MacBride shrugged and remained silent. Then he got up, shook Cardigan's hand and went out.

A little later the phone rang and Fink said, 'I got somethin' to tell you.'

'All right,' replied Cardigan briskly.

A few minutes later he walked into a drug-store on the corner, stepped into the booth and closed the door. A minute, and the bell rang.

'O.K., Pete,' he said.

Fink explained. 'Meet me in the dump on Jockey Street in half an hour. I've got a sample, and it's sure powerful stuff. I'll be waitin' outside the door there. Everything is jake, and the boys are feelin' good but wonderin' about their divvy.'

'Be over,' said Cardigan.

When, later, he strolled down Jockey Street, he saw Fink cross the street, pause on the steps of their rendezvous, look his way, and then pass inside. Cardigan swung up the steps and the door opened. He went in and Fink led the way up to the latter's room. The big man drew a pink flask from his pocket.

'They're all in pints,' he explained. 'Try it.'

Cardigan took a pull on the bottle and let the liquor burn in. 'Good,' he nodded. 'The best I've tasted.'

Fink grinned. 'If that stuff ain't come across the pond I don't know Scotch. It's the first time I ain't drunk dish water in a long time. D' you figger Cavallo's sore?'

'Sore!' echoed Cardigan, and laughed on it.

'Yeah,' droned Fink, 'I guess he'd lookin' to kill. Um. Now the stuff's out there in the farmhouse, what?'

'I'll know by tonight. Keep your shirt on.'

'I ain't worryin'. The gang. They're achin' to see some jack and have a good time.'

'You tell 'em to watch their step, Pete. It's hard lines for any guy pulls a bone. We're not through yet. It would be just like Chip Slade, for instance, to doll up in new duds, pick up a broad, get tight to the eyes and blabber. We've got to watch out for that, Pete.'

'Yeah, I know, Jack. I been keepin' my eye on Chip.'

'I'll see you here tonight, Pete.'

Cardigan went out with the pint flask on his hip and dropped in to see Maloney in the speakeasy. He talked business to him, and let him take a drink from the bottle.

'Boy!' whistled Maloney. 'That's *Scotch*, what I mean!'

'What's the news?'

'The boss says all right, if he likes the stuff. Fifty-five a case.'

'I can get two-hundred-and-forty cases. He can have the lot or none, and he's got to act fast. This is no young stuff—'

'Hell, I know! Ain't I just tasted it? And me – I get my share, when?'

'When your boss pays, you get twelve-hundred bucks, and then forget about everything. There are no names necessary.'

'Of course not,' nodded Maloney. 'How do you get the money?'

'Your boss 'll send it to John D. Brown, at a post office box. You'll get the box number later. Send it in a plain package, with no return address. Thirteen thousand and two hundred dollars in one hundred dollar bills.'

'Insure it?'

'Lord no! Just first class – that's the safest way to send stuff through the mails. It beats registered mail four ways from the jack. I never lost a first class letter, but I've lost 'em registered and I've lost insured packages. A man will pick up the letter at the post office.' He thought for a moment. 'Get the dope from your boss, and let's know where the booze goes.'

'I ought to get my share first,' demurred Maloney.

'I know. You think I'll skip. You'll get yours through the mail, too. That's the proposition. It's up to you.'

'I'll take the chance.' Maloney got up. 'Come in at six.'

Cardigan nodded and left. He took a box at a suburban post office under the name of John D. Brown. When he met Maloney at six that night the ex-saloon keeper was flushed with elation. Everything was settled, and the liquor was to be delivered as soon as possible.

'That means tonight,' put in Cardigan.

'The boss stores it at the Tumbledown Inn. Say the word and there'll be somebody there tonight to meet the truck.'

'It'll be delivered sometime after midnight.'

With that Cardigan went out and met Fink in the latter's hideout. He explained what had transpired, and Fink rubbed his hands in joyful anticipation.

'I know where I can get a truck, Jack. Leave it to me.'

'I am,' said Cardigan.

He explained in detail how the liquor should be transported, how Bat Johnson should drive the truck alone and the others ride in the touring car ahead. The Tumbledown Inn was on Farmingville Turnpike, four miles beyond the farmhouse where the liquor was stored at present.

'It's a cinch,' said Fink.

'When it's all over, ring me up and say the O.K. word.'

They parted, and Cardigan headed for the Adler House. He had proved a successful general on his first try. He believed he could repeat a second time, and then some more. He turned in at eight and set his alarm to wake him at one. He figured that he should get a report from Fink at about two.

When he got up at one a.m., he dressed, in the event of an emergency. He drank some hot black coffee from a thermos and ate some sandwiches which he had brought up before. Then he lounged on a divan with a cigar and watched the clock. The hands moved around the hour and passed two. They passed two-thirty and wheeled on toward three. At three, Cardigan sat up.

He looked grave, a bit tight-lipped. He stared at the telephone. It was black and silent. The hotel was silent as a tomb. Up from the street floated the sound of a lone trolley car rattling across a switch. He sat down, clasping his hands around one knee, tapping an impatient foot. Half-past three.

'Something's gone wrong,' he muttered. He cracked fist into palm, cursed under his breath, bitterly.

Dawn came, and then the sun. And still no word from Pete Fink.

Cardigan put on his overcoat and went out. He bought a paper, thinking he might find some clue there, but he reasoned that if anything had happened in the early hours, the morning papers wouldn't have it yet. The next edition might. He ate breakfast in a dairy restaurant. Then, reasoning that he ought to be at his room in case Fink might call, he hurried back.

At nine Fink called. He said two words. 'My room.'

'Right,' said Cardigan.

VII

Twenty minutes later he was striding down Jockey Street. The negro let him in and he climbed the rickety staircase. He knocked at Fink's door. There was a slow movement.

Then, 'You, Jack?'

'Yes, Pete.'

The door opened. Cardigan went in.

Fink was dropping back into a chair.

'Lock it,' he muttered.

His face was haggard. His left arm was in a sling, and blotches of dry blood showed on the bandage.

'I thought so,' said Cardigan.

'Yeah,' nodded Fink, and forced a grin. 'They got Bat.'

Cardigan sat down. 'Go on.'

'They got Bat. It was all a accident. We delivered the booze and was on the way back. We took Prairie Boulevard. Bat wanted to bring back the truck. The tourin' car got a flat and we stopped to make a change. Bat went ahead slow all by his merry lonesome. We got the spare on, all right, and whooped it up to catch him. You know where Prairie Boulevard goes through them deep woods. It's pretty lonely there.

'Well, our headlights pick up Bat and he's stalled. But we see another car stopped in front of him, facing him. It looks phony, and we take it easy. We see some guys standin' around on the road, but they duck for the car. We stop our car and wait. We think maybe they're dicks, see. Then their car starts and roars towards us. It looks like they're goin' to crash us, but they cut around and slam by, scrapin' our mudguard. A lot of guns bust loose and I'm socked in the arm. Chip gets his cheek opened. Nobody else is hurt. Gats turns around and empties his rod at the back of it. I don't know who he hit, but the car kept goin'.

'I get out, holdin' my arm and Bennie tears off some of his shirt and sops up the blood. Chip is holdin' his cheek and cursin' a blue streak. Gats runs up to the truck and we go after him. Bat is layin' on the road, pretty still. Him and Gats were buddies, you know. You should hear Gats curse!

'Bat is dyin'. They'd busted his knob with a blackjack. He says he was ridin' along when this car stopped him. See, just by accident. Monkey Burns and Bert Geer and two others. They smell there was booze in the truck, and ask him what's he been doin'. He tells them where they can go. They wanter know who he's been runnin' booze for. He ain't talkin'. They sock him, but he don't chirp. That's Bat all over. More you sock him the worse stubborn he gets. Gawd, they batted hell outta him! Ugh! Then they see us. Bat croaks after he spiels us his story. Poor Bat. He was a good shuffer.'

Cardigan stared at the floor for a long minute, his hands clenched.

Fink was saying, 'I took the plates off the truck and disfiggered the engine number and the serial number with a couple o' shots. Then we drove to the farmhouse. The boys are there now. I got here alone, quick as I could. I could ha' sent one o' the boys to call you up, but I didn't want any o' 'em to know where you was.'

'You're aces up in a pinch, Pete,' said Cardigan, and he meant it.

'I did the best I could.'

'I'll say you did. Did Monkey and his gang see you boys?'

'No. And Bat didn't tell 'em. But they know, like everybody else, that Bat was buddies with Gats, and they'll be huntin' Gats. And Gats has gone wild. He wants to go out gunnin' for them guys. He swears he'll do it. And Gats is the best damn gunman I know about.'

'You've got to keep him under cover.'

'Yeah. I got to get back to the farmhouse. Bandage this arm tight so I can put it in a sleeve. I can't go walkin' around too much with a sling. It'll hurt without it, but what the hell.'

'Good man, Pete. Get out there, see how things are. I'll hang around the corner drug-store between two and three. Call me there from a booth and give me a line.'

When he had bandaged Fink's arm, he patted the big man on the back and left him. Below, in the street, he ran into Kennedy, of the *Free Press*, leaning indolently against a lamp-post. He brought up short, his breath almost taken away.

'Hello, Cardigan,' said the reporter in his tired way. 'What's the attraction?'

'You trying to crack wise, Kennedy?'

'Who, me? No-o, not me, Cardigan. See this yet?' He handed Cardigan the latest edition of the *Free Press*.

Rival Bootleg Gangs Clash

That was the headline. Something about an abandoned truck, empty, with license plates gone and engine number disfigured. Blood on the road. Empty cartridges. Nearby trees showing bullet marks. A farmer beyond the woods had heard the shooting about half-past one a.m. No cops on the job. The farmer himself had come out to investigate and reported the abandoned truck. It looked like the beginning of a gang feud.

Cardigan looked up. 'Well that's news, Kennedy.'

'Is it?' Kennedy had a tantalizing way of smiling.

'I'm in a hurry,' said Cardigan, and started off.

Kennedy fell into step beside him. 'I'm not green, Cardigan. You ought to know that by this time. And I know that one of the gangs was Cavallo's. Now the other gang . . . Cardigan, be a sport.'

'What do you mean?'

'Tell me about it.'

'You're all wet, Kennedy.'

'Oh, no I'm not. Listen, Cardigan. You're not pulling the wool over this baby's eyes. The Department knows who the guy was that was bumped off and then carried away by his buddies. They got the dope from Cavallo's friends – maybe Diorio to Pozzo to Mulroy. Then they tell the Department to get busy – just like that, and they're spreading for somebody. That riot squad's on pins and needles, waiting for another break. Now, it would take guts to head a gang to buck that outfit – you tell me, Cardigan.

Cardigan laughed. 'Kennedy, you're funny. So long.' He crossed the street and left Kennedy in perplexed indecision.

But he realized that Kennedy was one man he'd have to look out for. That news hound, in other words, knew his onions. He was nobody's fool.

After luncheon Cardigan went out to the suburban post office, opened his box and took out a solitary package. He thrust it into his pocket and returned to his hotel. There he opened it, and found thirteen thousand, two hundred dollars. Twelve hundred he put in a plain envelope and addressed it to Maloney. In each of five plain envelopes he placed a thousand dollars, for Pete Fink's boys. For Pete he placed aside two thousand. He lost no time in mailing Maloney's letter.

Later, he was at the booth in the corner drug-store to get Fink's prearranged call. Fink mentioned his room, but Cardigan objected, remembering Kennedy, and told Fink to pick him up at a street corner well out of the city. Then he hung up and took a bus out, got off at the street he had named, and waited for Fink. He did not have to wait long. The touring car came up, and Fink was driving with his one good arm. Cardigan got in and they rolled off.

'Gats,' said Fink. 'He slipped out on the boys. He's out gunnin' for the guys who got Bat Johnson.'

'What!'

'Yup.'

Cardigan saw his nicely made plans toppling to ruin. This was one of those things the best of tacticians cannot foresee. An accident. A bad break. Gats gone gun-mad because his buddy 'd been killed by the wops.

'We've got to get him,' he said.

'Yeah, but where?'

Cardigan cursed the luck. Then he said, 'Well, I've got the money. It's all here. A thousand each for the boys. Two thousand for you. Twelve hundred went to the go-between for the booze.' He passed over the envelopes. 'That'll make the boys feel better.' After a moment he said, 'The riot squad's ready for action.'

'It won't take long, if we don't get Gats. He'll start the fireworks sure as hell.'

'Drop me off when the next bus comes along. Look for Gats. Go to all the places you think he'd be. Ring me at the hotel and say 'Jake' if you get him. Then stay out at the farm – all of you – until this blows over.'

A few minutes later he got out of the car, boarded a bus and went back to his hotel. He was very much on edge, and he mused that no matter how perfectly you lay a plan, something is liable to happen that will bring down the whole framework.

At four o'clock the telephone rang, and Fink said, 'Jake.'

'Jake,' said Cardigan.

A great burden was automatically lifted from his mind. He even whistled as he got into his bath. He hummed while he shaved. Then he dressed, spent half an hour with a cigar and the evening paper, and at five-thirty put on his overcoat and went out. As he swung out of the hotel, he heard the scream of a siren. He looked up the street.

Three police cars were roaring down Main Street. Traffic scattered. People gathered on the curb. The three cars shot by the hotel doing fifty miles an hour. They were packed with policemen, and automatic rifles were clamped on the sides. The sirens snarled madly.

Cardigan's breath stuck in his throat. A chill danced up and down his spine. Then his jaw set and he crossed to a taxicab.

'Hit Farmingville Turnpike,' he clipped, and jumped in.

He started to close the door, but something held it. He turned around. Kennedy was climbing in after him.

'Mind if I go?'

Cardigan sank into his seat, his fists clenched. But he managed to grin. 'Sure. The old gumshoe instinct in me always follows a riot call. I'm anxious to see what this is all about.'

'Yeah?' smiled Kennedy.

'Yeah. I'm in the dark, just like you.'

Kennedy frowned after the manner of a man who wondered if after all he isn't wrong in what he'd been supposing.

VIII

Cardigan had a hard time masking his inner emotions. He said to the chauffeur, 'Follow those police cars. It's all right. We're reporters.'

Kennedy lit a cigarette. 'You've got me guessing, Cardigan.'

'Me? Same here, Kennedy. You've got me guessing, too.'

'Have a butt.'

'Thanks.' It was casual, everything he said, but inside of him there was turmoil. What was going on? What had happened to Fink and the boys? He'd formed a strange liking for Pete Fink. In his own way Pete had proved his fidelity, his worth.

The sirens went on screaming. People were still looking out of windows when the taxi shot past in the wake of the police cars. Pedestrians had gathered on street corners and were speculating. Some were talking to traffic cops, asking questions. The cops only grinned and shrugged and waved them away. Other cars were joining in the impromptu parade, breaking all speed laws. The people had been reading of a fresh outbreak in gangdom, of a bitter gang feud. They were obsessed now, rushing to get a bird's-eye view, for human nature is fundamentally melodramatic and its curiosity very close to the morbid.

It was already dark, in the early winter gloom. The taxi struck Farmingville Turnpike, fell into the stream of vehicles that pounded along. Horns tooted, and big, high-powered cars shot by so fast that the taxi seemed to be standing still. Mob curiosity was at its peak. Anything draws it – a fire, an accident, a soap-box orator, a brawl between school-boys, a man painting a flag-pole.

Then suddenly the cars began parking. In the gleam of the headlights two policemen with drawn nightsticks were shouting hoarsely, waving the people away.

'I guess we get out here,' said Kennedy.

'Looks that way.'

'Come on.'

Cardigan paid the fare and they walked ahead. Kennedy showed his card and Cardigan went through with him. They strode briskly along the edge of the woods.

'Hear it?' asked Kennedy.

Cardigan heard it – the rattle of gun fire. Yes, the farmhouse. Alternate waves of heat and cold passed over him. The shadows in the woods were pitch black. Soon they could see the flash of guns, hear the brittle hammering of a machine-gun, firing in spasmodic bursts.

A figure in plainclothes loomed before them.

'Hello, Mac,' said Kennedy.

'Who's your friend?' muttered the captain.

'Cardigan.'

'Oh-o!'

Kennedy pushed on. Cardigan stopped and MacBride came closer.

'Well, Jack, you see?'

Cardigan bit his lip. 'What are you doing, blowing the place up?'

'Yes. Captain McGurk in charge.'

'How'd it start?'

'Headquarters got a phone call about a lot of shooting going on out here.'

Cardigan growled. 'Can't you get 'em to offer a truce? God, Steve, it's pure slaughter!'

He was thinking of Pete Fink and the other boys, trapped in the house.

'There's no use. We came up in the bushes and let go with a machine-gun as a warning. A lot of rifle fire was our answer. This looks like the end.'

'Cripes, Steve, stop it – stop it!' He lunged ahead.

MacBride grabbed him, held him in a grip of steel.

'Easy, Jack. You can't do a thing. Don't be a fool. You took the chance and this is the result.'

'Let me go, Steve – let go!'

'No, dammit – no! By God, if you make a move I'll crack you over the head!'

'You will, will you?'

'So help me!'

Cardigan swore and heaved in MacBride's grasp. They struggled, weaving about, silent and grim. They crashed deeper into the bushes. Then MacBride struck, and Cardigan groaned and slumped down.

MacBride knelt beside him, white-faced and panting. 'Jack, old boy, you hurt much? I didn't mean to hit so hard . . . Jack, but you can't do a thing. It's the breaks of the racket. God! . . . ' He was rubbing Cardigan's head.

The battle was still on. Daggers of flame slashed through the dark. Lead drummed against the walls of the house, shattered the windows, pumped into the rooms. Spurts of flame darted from the house. A policeman crumpled. Another heaved up, clutching at his chest, and screamed.

'Oh, God!' groaned MacBride.

Captain McGurk, in charge, swore bitterly. He looked around. 'That's three they got. We'll have to give 'em the works. Charlie, you got the grenades?'

'Yes, Cap'n.'

'Go to it.'

A machine-gun, silent for a moment, cut loose with a stuttering fusillade that raked every window in sight. Intermittent flashes came from the windows. Lead slugs rattled through the branches and thickets. The breeze of evening carried acrid powder smoke. The men in the bushes moved about warily.

Cardigan lay in a daze, conscious of the shots and the din, but in a vague, dreamy way. He wanted to yell out, and he imagined he was yelling, at the top of his lungs, but actually his lips moved only in a soundless whisper. His head throbbed with pain. MacBride had clipped him not too gently. And the captain was now bent over him, with one arm beneath him, rocking him.

The man called Charlie had worked his way closer, crawling on hands and knees, from tree to tree. Finally he stood up, and his arm swung. A small object wheeled through the dark, smacked on the roof of the house. There was a terrific explosion, and a sheet of ghastly flame billowed outward.

Stones and bits of timber sang through space, clattered in the woods. The roof caved in, parts of the walls toppled in a smother of smoke and dust.

Out of the chaos groped a man, with hands upraised. He stumbled, sprawled and hit the earth like a log. He never moved once after that. Another crawled out of the ruins, turned over on his back and lay as still as the first. The policemen advanced out of the woods. Nothing stopped them now. They closed in around the house, entered here and there through torn gaps.

MacBride hauled Cardigan to his feet, put on his hat. 'You've got to get out of this, Jack,' he muttered.

Cardigan was able to stumble.

'It's all over,' said MacBride.

He half-dragged him back through the woods to the road, walked him along it.

'Brace up!' he ground out. 'I'll put you in a taxi. Look natural. Keep your hat down, your collar up. Get back to your hotel. Stay there, for God's sake. It's all over, you hear? There is no use making a fool of yourself.'

They found a taxi and Cardigan got in. MacBride gripped his hand.

'Good luck, Jack!'

'Thanks, Steve.'

Cardigan rode to his hotel in a sunken mood. He got out, paid his fare, and sagged up to his room. He locked the door and slumped into a chair. He groped for a cigarette and lit it, and stared gloomily into space. He muttered something old – something about plans of mice and men . . .

'Hell!' he mumbled, and sank lower.

Ten minutes later the telephone rang. He looked at it darkly. He didn't know whether he should answer it. But he got up, laid his hand on it, then took off the receiver.

'Hello,' he muttered.

'Jack – my room,' said Fink, and that was all.

Cardigan snapped out of his mood, sucked in a hot breath. He slammed down the receiver and dived for his overcoat.

IX

He climbed the rickety stairs in the ancient house in Jockey Street. He did not know what to expect. He paused a whole minute before the door until he knocked. Then he rapped. There was the sound of quick steps. Then the door swung open and Fink loomed there, grinning. He pulled Cardigan in, closed the door and locked it.

'Park your hips, Jack,' he rumbled. 'Have a drink.'

Cardigan crossed the room, dropped to a chair and slopped liquor into a glass. He held it up. 'I need this.' He downed it neat. 'Well?'

Fink rubbed his big hand along his thigh vigorously. 'Well, Cavallo and his gang oughta be done for. Cripes, it was a great break for us! Well, I picked up Gats all right, and we drove back to the farmhouse. Then I figured maybe one o' Cavallo's guns was trailin' us. I seen a closed coupé follerin' all the way out, but I didn't let on. I swung in by the farm and I saw this coupé slow down and then shoot ahead.

'I put Gats in with the boys, and then I went out and hid in the bushes by the road. An hour later I see a big tourin' car stop down the road and a guy get out. It was Monkey Burns. I run back to the house and plan a trap. I pull down the shades and leave a light lit. Then me and the boys skin out and hide in the bushes with our rifles.

'Little later the bums sneak up. Monkey and Cavallo and Bert Geer and six others. They creep up on the house, and Monkey tries a door. It's open. He turns to his guns and whispers and they all bunch. Then they crash the door and go in shootin'. Before they know what's what, Gats busts loose with his gun and gets the last mutt goin' in. They see they're trapped and they slam the door.

'We surround the place. Then I explain things to the boys. Then I drive off in the car, get to a booth and call Police Headquarters and tell 'em a gun-fight's goin' on out there. Then I drive back and park up the road a bit. The boys was takin' pot-shots at the winders now and then. I tell 'em what I done and then run back to the road. When I see a mob o' cars whoopin' down, I whistle and the boys beat it through the woods. We sit in the car until we hear guns goin'. Then we know the cops is at it, and Cavallo and his bums still thinkin' it's us. Then we drive off, and the boys scatter in the city. Just like that.'

Cardigan regarded Fink for a long moment. Then he wagged his head. 'Pete, you've got a sight more brains than I ever gave you credit for. Every man in that house was killed.'

'Humph. What ammunition we saved. So the cops got 'em after all. Well, who has more right than the cops?'

Cardigan went back to his hotel with a light heart. He turned in, slept well, and got the whole thing in the morning extras. At ten MacBride came in to see him. The captain looked full of news.

'Well, you know it all by this time, eh, Jack?' he asked.

'Yes.'

'No, you don't.' MacBride sat down and took off his hat. 'There's a big shake-up. Cavallo and all his rats were wiped out last night. But Cavallo's brother-in-law, Diorio, president of the Hard Club, goes wild this morning. He got in an argument with Pozzo, his friend, the alderman, and blamed him for it all. Claimed Cavallo was framed because he knew too much – framed by Pozzo and Mulroy. It wound up by Pozzo getting shot. Pozzo passed the buck and drew in State's Attorney Mulroy. Kennedy, that wiseacre reporter, crashed in on the row and got the whole story. What dirt they raked up! It's something nobody can hush. Diorio was pinched and he sprung the whole rotten story of graft and quashed criminal cases. Pozzo threatened to have him sent up for twenty years, but Pozzo can't do a thing. He's in the net. So is Mulroy. The governor's wires have been buzzing, and in a short time we're going to see a new state's attorney and a new alderman. It's the biggest shake-up in the history of the city. And you, Jack, in your own little way, caused it, thank God!'

Cardigan smiled. 'Not me, Steve – exactly.'

'Who, then?'

Cardigan shrugged. 'Well, let it drop. A lucky break – and a certain friend of mine.' He grew grave. 'Now I'm satisfied. Joe Hanley, my buddy, is vindicated. I swore he would be. I was counting on some good breaks. For a while it looked like I was wrong. But the good ones came in the end.'

MacBride nodded. 'It's funny, there wasn't a trace of the gang that was riding Cavallo and his guns – not a trace.'

Cardigan grinned. 'I hoped there wouldn't be.'

'M-m-m,' mused MacBride. 'Well, what are you going to do now?'

'That's a question,' replied Cardigan. 'I was thinking of starting a detective agency. I know the ropes, and I'm through with the Department, and I know where I can get a good right-hand man.'

'Who's that?'

Cardigan chuckled. 'You may meet him some day, Steve.'

He was thinking of Pete Fink.

DOG EAT DOG

FREDERICK L. NEBEL

When Captain MacBride was suddenly transferred from the Second Precinct to the Fifth, an undercurrent of whispered speculations trickled through the Department, buzzed in newspaper circles, and traveled along the underworld grapevine.

It was a significant move, for MacBride, besides being the youngest captain in the Department – he was barely forty – was known throughout Richmond City as a holy terror against the criminal element. He was a lank, rangy man, with a square jaw and windy blue eyes. He was brusque, talked straight from the shoulder, and was hard-boiled as a five-minute egg. Now the Second Precinct is in the very heart of Richmond City's night-life, hence an important and busy station. The Fifth is out on the frontier, in a suburb called Grove Manor, and carries the somewhat humorous sobriquet of the Old Man's Home. Plenty of reasons, then, why MacBride's transfer should have been made matter for conjecture.

MacBride said nothing. He merely tightened his hard jaw a little harder, packed up and moved. To his successor, Captain O'Leary, he made one rather ironic remark: 'Well, I'll be nearer home, anyhow.' He had a bungalow, a wife and an eighteen-year-old daughter in an elm-shaded street in Grove Manor.

He landed in the Fifth in the latter part of August. It was a quiet, peaceful station, with a desk sergeant who played solitaire to pass the time away and a lieutenant who used his office and the Department's time to tinker around a radio set which he had made and which still called for lots of improvement. MacBride's predecessor, retired, had spent most of his time working out crossword puzzles. All the patrolmen, and three of the four detectives, were local men, and well on in years. The fourth detective had just been shifted from harness to plainclothes. Ted Kerr was his name; twenty-eight, sandy-haired, and a dynamo of energy and good-humor. He was ambitious, too, and cursed the luck that had placed him in the Fifth.

'Gee, Cap, it sure is a shock to see you out here,' he said.

MacBride could remember when Kerr wore short pants. He grinned in his hard, tight way. 'Forget it, Ted. Now that I'm here, though, I'm going to clean out a lot of the cobwebs. They say time hangs heavy on a man here. Too bad I haven't got a hobby.'

'Why did they shift you, Cap?'

'Why?' MacBride creaked his swivel chair and bent over some reports on the desk, tacitly dismissing the subject.

A month dragged by, and the hard captain found ennui enveloping him. He was lounging in his tipped back chair one night, with his heels hooked on the desk, reading the newspaper account of a brutal night-club murder in his old district, when an old acquaintance dropped in – Kennedy, of the city *Free Press.*

'Oh, you,' grumbled MacBride.

Kennedy helped himself to a seat. 'Yeah, me. Gone to seed yet, Mac?'

'Won't be long now.'

'What a tough break you got,' chuckled Kennedy.

'Go ahead, rub it in. Pull a horse laugh, go on.'

'I'll bet Duke Manola's laughing up his sleeve.'

'That pup!'

Kennedy shrugged. 'Serves you right for taking the law in your own hands. You birds can shake down a common sneak thief or a wandering wop that goes off on a gun spree coked to the eyebrows. But, Mac, you can't beat organized crime. You can't beat it when it's financed by silent partners – and those silent partners' – he arched a knowing eyebrow – 'on the inside, too.'

'Man, oh, man, I'm going to get that greaseball yet!' MacBride's lip curled and his windy eyes glittered.

'Still got him on the brain, eh?' Kennedy lit a cigarette and spun the match out through the open window. 'He's fire to fool with, Mac. He'll burn you surer than hell. Anyhow, you're out here in the sticks keeping the frogs and the crickets company, and you're not worrying Duke much. He's planted you where you'll do no harm. Oh, I know, Mac. There's a lot I know that the paper can't afford to print. When you raided the Nick Nack Club you stepped on Duke's toes. Not only his – but his silent partner's.'

'Easy, Kennedy!'

'Easy, hell! This is just a heart-to-heart talk, Mac. Forget your loyalty to the badge when I'm around. You've kept a stiff upper lip, and you'll continue to. But just keep in the mind that here's one bird who knows his tricks. I know – see? – I know that Judge Haggerty is the Duke's silent partner in those three night-clubs he runs. Haggerty's aiming for Supreme Court Justice, and he needs lots of jack for his campaign. And he's not going to let a tough nut of a police captain get in his way.'

MacBride bit the reporter with a keen, hard eye. After a long moment he swung his feet down from the desk and pulled open a drawer.

'Have a drink, Kennedy.'

He drew out a bottle and a glass and set them down. Kennedy poured himself a stiff three fingers and downed it neat, rasped his throat.

'Good stuff, Mac,' he said.

'Have another.'

'Thanks.'

Kennedy measured off another three fingers and swallowed the contents at a gulp, stared meditatively at the empty glass, then set it down quietly.

'Now, Mac,' he said, looking up obliquely, while the ghost of a smile played around his lips. 'I'll tell you what I came here for.'

'Came to razz me, I thought.'

'No. That's just my roundabout way of getting at things. One reason why I got kicked off the city desk.'

MacBride felt that something important was in the wind. Sometimes he liked Kennedy; other times, he felt like wringing the news-hound's neck. Clever, this Kennedy, sharp as a steep trap.

'Well,' he said, leaning back, 'shoot.'

'Just this, Mac. Maybe you're going to run up against Duke again.'

'Go ahead.'

Kennedy's smile was thin, almost mocking. 'Duke's bought that old brewery out off Farmingville Turnpike.'

MacBride's chair creaked once, and then remained silent. His stare bored into the lazy, whimsical eyes of the reporter. A sardonic twist pulled down one corner of his mouth.

'What's that wop up to?' he growled, deep in his throat.

'I've got a hunch, Mac. He's getting crowded in the city. He's going to make beer there – the real stuff, I mean. And gin. And—' he leaned forward – 'he's going to rub it in – on you.'

'He is, eh?' MacBride's voice hardened. 'He'll take one step too many. He's getting cocky now. I never saw a wop yet who didn't overstep himself. Riding on my tail, eh? Well, we'll see, Kennedy. Let him move out of turn and I'll jump him. That wop can't kick me in the slats and get away with it. The booze I don't give a damn about. I wouldn't have cared how many speakeasies he ran in the city. But when he ran stud games in the back rooms and reached out for soused suckers I got sore. That's why I broke the Nick Nack Club. It was three in the morning, and among the bums in the back room were two guns from Chicago.'

Kennedy chuckled. 'That was when Captain Stephen MacBride pulled one of the biggest bones in his career. What a beautiful swan song that was! Hot diggity!'

MacBride rose to his lean, rangy height and cracked fist into palm.

'Boy, but I'm aching to meet that dago! I hope to hell he does make a bum move!'

'He put you out in the sticks; out,' added Kennedy whimsically, 'in the Old Man's Home. And you're sore, Mac. I can foresee some hot stuff on the frontier, and Grove Manor on the map.'

MacBride swung to face him, his feet spread wide. 'Just that, Kennedy –

just that. They shoved me out here to cool off and grow stale. But I'm not the guy to grow stale. Duke's cracking wise. Maybe he thinks that the transfer has shut me up. Maybe he thinks he can ride me and get away with it. Let him – that's all – just let him!'

There was a knock at the door, and then Sergeant Haley looked in, his beefy face flushed with excitement.

'Carlson's on the wire, Cap'n. There's been a smash-up out on Old Stone Road. Carlson was riding along in the patrol flivver when he saw a big touring car tangled up against a tree half in the bushes. There's a dead man in the car but Carlson can't get him out 'count of the wreckage.'

MacBride snorted. 'Is Carlson so hard up for company that he has to call up about a wreck?'

'No, but he says he thinks there's something fluky about it. He says there's a woman's footprints near the car, but he didn't see no woman.'

'Maybe she walked home,' put in Kennedy. 'Lot of that going on these days.'

'I'll speak to him,' clipped MacBride, and sat down at his desk.

Sergeant Haley went out and switched over the call and it took MacBride only a minute to get the details. Then he hung up and, pouring himself a drink, corked the bottle and dropped it back into the drawer.

'The ride will do me good,' he remarked as he slapped on his cap.

'Me, too,' added Kennedy.

MacBride looked at him. 'You're out of your territory, aren't you?'

'What the hell!'

On the way out MacBride told the sergeant, 'When Kelly and Kerr drift in – God knows where they are now – tell 'em to hang around. Call up the nearest garage and tell 'em to send a wreckage crew out to Old Stone Road, about a mile north of Pine Tree Park. Buzz the morgue and tell 'em to send the bus to the same place. Tell 'em tonight, not sometime next week. When Lieutenant Miller gets fed up on monkeying with his radio, ask him to kindly take care of things till I get back. When you work out your present game of solitaire, I'd appreciate your getting those delinquent reports as near up to date as you're able. I won't be long.'

Outside, he stopped on the curb to light a fresh cigar. Then he followed Kennedy into the police car, and said, 'Shoot, Donnegan,' to the man at the wheel.

II

Out of the hub of town, the car struck Old Stone Road and followed it past neat, new bungalows and later, past fields and intermittent groves of piney woods. Once through Pine Tree Park, the road became darker, lined by heavier woods, with not even an occasional house to relieve the gloom.

Donnegan, at the wheel, pointed to a pair of headlights far up the road, and when they drew nearer, MacBride saw a small two-seater flivver parked on the side and a policeman in uniform spreading his arms to stop them. Kennedy hopped out and MacBride followed him.

'There it is,' said Carlson, and pointed to a tangled heap of wreckage against a tree alongside the highway. MacBride strode over, and Carlson followed, snapped on a flashlight and played its white beam over the ruined car.

'Three thousand bucks shot to hell,' observed Kennedy. 'And still insurance companies make money.' He sniffed. 'Who's the stiff?'

'Don't know,' muttered MacBride and made a gesture which indicated that the man was so deeply buried beneath the wreck that they could not get him. He turned to Carlson. 'You said something about footprints.'

'Yeah, Cap. See?' He swung his flash down to the soft earth around the car. 'Sure, a woman's.'

MacBride nodded, then said, 'But she never got out of this car after it struck.'

The wreck offered mute evidence to that statement. Its radiator was caved in half the length of the long, streamline hood, and the cowl and part of the hood were crushed up through the windshield frame. Beneath this, and wedged in by the left side of the car, lay the man who had been at the wheel, face downward, the steering-wheel broken and twisted around his chest.

'I been wonderin' where the woman could have went,' ventured Carlson.

'Whoever she was, she must have walked away,' said MacBride. 'Her footprints wouldn't show on the macadam.' He added, after a moment, 'At any rate, I'll bet my hat she wasn't in the car when it socked that tree.'

Donnegan called out, 'Guess this is the wrecker.'

It was. The wrecking outfit from the garage rolled up, and two men in overalls got out.

'Hello, boys,' greeted MacBride. 'Before you haul this piece of junk away, there's a dead man inside. See if you can chop away some of the wreck.'

The two men pulled axes from their car and set to work and hacked away at the snarled mass of metal. MacBride stood at one side, sucking on his cigar, offering no suggestion to men who knew their business and were doing the best they could. Presently he saw them lay down their axes, and he stepped over to help.

Bit by bit they hauled out the broken, blood-stained body, and laid it down on the ground. MacBride bent down on one knee and taking Carlson's flashlight, snapped on the switch. He grimaced, but gritted his teeth. A swarthy young face, the face of a boy in his early twenties.

'Hot diggity!' exclaimed Kennedy.

MacBride looked up. 'What's eating you?

'Don't you know him?' cried Kennedy, his usually tired eyes alight with interest.

'Frankly, I don't.'

Kennedy slapped his knee. 'Duke Manola's kid brother!'

'Hell!' grunted MacBride, and took a swift look at the discolored face.

'He was always a sheik with the ladies.'

'I've heard of him,' nodded MacBride. 'Now what the cripes kind of a stunt did he try to pull?'

'Simple,' shrugged Kennedy. 'Got fresh with some broad probably.'

'But how did the broad shake the wreck? I still say she wasn't in the car when it hit. Man alive, there'd been no chance of her walking after that!'

'The crack reporter of the *Free Press* agrees with the astute captain's common sense remark. But wait till Duke gets wind of it. You know these wops. Tweak the nose of a forty-eighth cousin and the whole shooting-match sharpens up their stilletos. Boy, don't I know!'

'Well, if he started playing around it's his tough luck. The trouble with a lot of these sheiks is that they're so used to the yes-girls that when they meet another kind they get sore – and nasty.'

Kennedy rasped his throat. 'Picture a decent gal trotting out with a marcelled sheik like Joe Manola! Don't tell me!'

MacBride shrugged as he stood up. He took his flashlight and mounted the wreck, shooting the beam down through the twisted metal. A moment later he stood up and held a short, stubby automatic in his hand.

'One shot fired,' he said. 'Not long ago, either.' He had rubbed his finger across the muzzle, and looked at the black streak it left.

A siren screamed through the night, and two headlights came racing down the road. It was the morgue bus, and it pulled up behind the patrol flivver.

'What kind of a gun?' asked Kennedy.

'Thirty-two,' shot back MacBride, and with a sudden movement crossed to the body and knelt down.

Kennedy trailed after him and bent over his shoulder. Then MacBride stood up, wiping his hands, a glitter in his eyes.

'He was shot, Kennedy. Shot through the right side.'

'And then he hit the tree!'

'Exactly.'

Kennedy whistled. 'When the Duke hears this!'

MacBride turned to one of the man from the morgue bus. 'You can take him. But there's a slug somewhere inside. I want it after the autopsy.'

A few minutes later the bus shot off with its dead cargo, and MacBride turned to watch the wrecking-car tugging at the smashed machine. Its derrick hoisted up the front end, and thus the rear wheels were in a condition to move.

'Keep it in the garage,' said MacBride, 'and I'll take care of your bill.'

When the wreck had gone, with the rear red light winking in the distance, Kennedy made for the police car. 'Well, let's be going, Mac. This'll be in the early editions.'

MacBride started to follow, but turned and retraced his steps to where the wreck had lain. His flash played on the gashed tree and down on to the gouged ground. His eyes narrowed and he bent over, picked up something that shimmered in the white light.

In the palm of his hand lay an emerald pendant, attached to a thin gold chain that had been broken. His lips parted in a sharp intake of breath, and his hand knotted over the pendant.

'Oh, shake it up, Mac,' called Kennedy.

MacBride turned and strode to the police car with hesitant steps. He climbed in and closed the door softly behind him. His hand, still holding the emerald pendant, slid into his pocket and remained there.

'Shoot, Donnegan,' he clipped.

III

On the way back through town, MacBride had the car stop in front of a cigar store.

'Want to get some cigars,' he told Kennedy, and strode into the store.

He bought half-a-dozen cigars, spent no more than a minute in a telephone booth, and then returned to the waiting car.

'Have one,' he offered Kennedy.

'You were always a good-natured Scotchman,' grinned Kennedy.

A couple of minutes later they walked into the station, and Kennedy made for the telephone, and shot the news into his office. Then he said, 'Duty calls, Mac. Something tells me I'll be seeing you often.'

'Don't make it too often,' growled MacBride.

Kennedy waved and strolled out to catch a trolley back to the city.

MacBride tipped back his cap, revealing strands of damp hair plastered to his forehead by perspiration. His chiseled face looked a bit drawn.

He addressed Sergeant Haley huskily – 'Call up the Nick Nack Club. Leave word to be delivered to Duke Manola that his brother was found dead at ten-thirty tonight—'

'Dead!' exclaimed Haley, who hadn't recorded a killing in his precinct in ten years.

'Don't butt in,' recommended MacBride, lazily, as though deep within him he was very, very weary. 'Do that. Found dead in a wrecked car on Old Stone Road, near Pine Tree Park. Tell 'em the body's at the morgue and may be reclaimed after the autopsy. No hint as to who shot him. No' – his teeth ground into his lower lip – 'no clues. Make out your regular report and file it. Joseph Manola. We'll get his age and other incidentals later.'

'Looks like murder, Cap'n!'

'Ye-es, it looks like murder,' droned MacBride, sagging toward his office.

Ted Kerr came in briskly from another room, stopped short in the path of the captain.

'In here,' said MacBride, and led the way into his office.

He sank into his chair, slammed his cap down on the desk and took a stiff drink.

'Hear you went out to investigate a wreck,' ventured Kerr.

'Ye-es. And ran into a murder.' MacBride's hand was in his pocket fingering the emerald pendant.

'Well!'

'Don't get worked up,' dragged out MacBride.

'You look all in,' said Kerr, seriously.

'Never mind me. What's on your mind?'

'Well, nothing much. Kelly and I were out to the Blue River Inn. You know there's been some complaints about raw parties being pulled off there. Pretty quiet tonight. Couple of drunken dames and a few soused college boys. And then – well. . . .' He hesitated, and looked away, his lips compressed.

'Well, what?'

'Oh, nothing much. Just. . . .' He paused again.

'Come on, Ted. Let's have it.'

'Well, I just got a bit of a shock, that's all.' His clean-cut face bore a vaguely hurt expression. 'Well, Judith was there—'

MacBride snapped forward, his eyes keened. 'Yes!'

'Why, what's the matter, Cap?'

'Keep talking. Judith was there. Who with?'

'Oh, hell, I shouldn't have said anything about it. But I've sort of liked Judith—'

'Don't say like when you mean love. And?'

'Well, she was there, that's all. Was another girl with her. Never saw the other girl. Kind of – well, brassy type. Chic looking and all that but – brassy. And two fellows. The one with Judith was young and dark – looked like an Italian sheik. The other fellow was older – so was the girl. I didn't let on I saw them. They had a couple of drinks, then breezed in a big, classy touring car. Don't bawl Judith out, Cap. I shouldn't have told you, but – well, it just came out. Judith's a good girl. I guess I've got a nerve to think I ever had a chance – me just a dick. Promise me you won't say anything to her about it.'

MacBride drew in a deep breath and held it trapped in his lungs for a long moment. Then he let it out, slowly, noiselessly, and followed it with a sigh.

'Ah-r- it's a rough, tough world, Ted, old timer.'

Kerr attempted to change the subject. 'But what about this murder, Cap?'

'It's going to start something – something big – big! Well, I've got my wish – but not in the way I'd expected.' He was thinking of his wish that Duke Manola would face him again for a showdown.

'What wish, Cap?' asked Ted Kerr.

'No matter. Joe Manola was the bird got killed. He's Duke Manola's brother, and the Duke can call two dozen gunmen any time he wants to.'

The telephone on the desk jangled. MacBride leaned forward, picking up the receiver and said, 'Captain MacBride—'

'Yes, MacBride,' came a voice with a hint of a nasal snarl. 'This is your old playmate, Manola.'

'The elder,' supplemented MacBride.

'Be funny,' snapped Duke Manola. 'I just heard my kid brother was bumped off out in the sticks. What's the lay?'

'No lay yet, Duke. When I get the lay I'll send you an engraved copy of the report, autographed.'

'Crack wise, big boy, crack wise.'

'And—'

'You better snap on it, MacBride. I'm just telling you, get the pup or pups that winged the kid before I do. And don't get tough, either. Kind of a sock on your jaw, eh? You having to work for the guy gave you a buggy ride out to God's country!'

'Lay off that, Duke. And don't *you* get tough. You keep your hands out of this. And take a tip: Try to play around in this neck of the woods and I'll flop on you like a ton of brick. I'll handle this case, and I don't want any dirty greaseball getting in my light.'

'I may drop in for tea soon, big boy.'

'If I never saw you, Duke, that 'd be years too soon. There's no Welcome sign hanging out here, and there's no good-luck horseshoe parked over the door. In short, I'm not entertaining.'

'Whistle that, guy, and go to hell!' With that a sharp click indicated that Duke Manola had hung up.

MacBride slammed down the receiver, and Kerr offered, with a half-grin, 'You men don't seem to get along so well.'

'We get along worse every day,' replied MacBride.

Kerr lit a cigarette. 'Any clues on that murder, Cap?'

MacBride's hand was in his pocket, and it clenched the emerald pendant in sweaty fingers.

'No, Ted,' he muttered.

IV

Mrs. MacBride was a woman of thirty-eight who still retained much of her youthful charm. The onyx sheen of her hair was not threaded by the slightest wisp of gray. Ordinarily, at breakfast time, she was a bright-eyed, animated woman, with a song on her lips and pleasant banter for her husband; and occasionally, as she passed back and forth from the kitchen, a kiss for the captain's cheek. Secretly, MacBride cherished this show of affection.

But something in his attitude that morning – or it may have been something in the heart of his wife – tended to eliminate this little by-play. There was a song on her lips, but it was in an unnatural, off-tone key.

When they sat down at the table facing each other, MacBride, without looking up from his morning paper, said, 'Judith up yet?'

'Yes. She'll be right in, Steve.' She went about sprinkling sugar on the grapefruit. 'Grove Manor must have gasped this morning when they read the papers about – about—'

'Yes,' nodded MacBride. 'Haven't had a murder here in ten years.'

'You'll be careful, Steve.'

He glanced up. 'Careful, Ann?'

'Well – you never can tell. I'm always worried.'

'Oh, nonsense, Ann. You shouldn't worry—'

There was a step on the stair, and Judith came in, quietly. Ordinarily she entered at a skip, vivacious, animated. Her hair was jet black, and bobbed short, in the extremely modern manner. Likewise was her mode of dress extremely modern.

'Morning, dad. Morning, ma.' Cheerful the tone, but with a faintly hollow ring.

As she crossed to the table she limped a trifle, but it escaped MacBride's eyes. His gaze was riveted on the newspaper.

'Morning, Judith,' he said.

When she was seated, he folded his paper and laid it aside.

It seemed that Mrs. MacBride was holding her breath.

Hard on the outside, hard with men who were hard, he had always found it difficult to be hard at home. He wanted to eliminate a lot of preliminary talk. Somehow, he did not want to see a woman of his own crumpling bit by bit under a lightning parry and thrust of words.

He drew his hand from his pocket and laid the emerald pendant on the table.

'Yours, Judith?'

But the girl had already blanched. Mrs. MacBride sat stiff and straight, her hands clenched in her lap, the color draining from her tightly compressed lips.

'It was found,' went on MacBride slowly, clumsily gentle, 'beside a wrecked car on Old Stone Road last night.'

'Oh!' breathed Judith, and looked to left and right, as if seeking an avenue of escape.

'Come, now, little girl,' pursued MacBride. 'Tell me about it. What happened?'

Judith jerked up from her chair, started for the stairs leading to her room.

'Judith!'

She dragged to a stop and turned.

'Please, Steve!' choked Mrs. MacBride. She got up and put an arm around her daughter.

'Ann, please stay out of this,' recommended MacBride; and to the girl,

'Judith, tell me about it. I know you were out in the company of the man who was murdered last night! I'll have to have an explanation!'

'I – I can't tell!' came her muffled, panicky voice.

'But you must!' he insisted sternly.

'No – no! I can't! I won't! Oh, please! . . .'

He crossed the room and laid his hand on her shoulder. 'Do you realize the significance of this? I don't say you killed Manola. But you were out with him, and you know what happened on that road. Judith! Out with one of the worst rakes in the city – the brother of Duke Manola, the gang leader and – my enemy! My God, girl, what have you been thinking of? Isn't Ted Kerr good enough for you? Or does a classy car and a marcelled wop win you?'

She was crying now, but through it all she kept reiterating – 'I won't tell! I won't tell!'

'Judith, so help me, you will!'

'No – no! I won't! You can beat me! You – can – beat – me! I won't tell! Oh-o-o-o! . . .'

'Steve,' implored Mrs. MacBride, 'don't – please!'

'Ann, be still! Do you think I enjoy this? How do you think I felt last night when I picked that pendant up by the wreck? God, it's a wonder the hawk-eyed Kennedy didn't see me! Judith, listen to reason. You've got to tell me!'

She spun back, her hands clenched, a storm of terror in her moist eyes – tense, quivering, like a cornered animal, and defiant.

'No – no – never! You can't make me. Dear God, you can't!'

She pivoted and clawed her way up the stairs, fled into her room and locked the door.

Half-way up the staircase, MacBride stopped, turned and came down slowly, his face a frozen mask.

'To think, to think!' he groaned.

His wife touched him with her hands, and he took them in his own and looked down into her swimming eyes.

'Ann, I wish you could make me happy, but just now – you can't. I'm as miserable, as sunk, as you are.'

Years seemed to creep upon him visibly. He picked up the pendant and dropped it into his pocket.

V

At five that evening MacBride was sitting at his desk in the precinct, when Ted Kerr breezed in, closed the door quietly and stood, wiping perspiration from his forehead.

'Well?' asked MacBride.

'I was out there. Kline, the bird that runs the Blue River Inn, acted dumb. He didn't remember the party of four. Had never seen them before. In short, didn't know them.'

'Think he's on the level?'

'No.' Kerr dropped to a chair. 'I could see he was walking on soft ground, watching his step. It's my bet that he knows the two fellows.' He paused. 'How – how's Judith?'

'Still love her?'

'Well, God, Cap, she's in trouble—'

'Sh! Soft pedal, Ted!'

Kerr spoke in a husky whisper. 'I don't believe she's done bad. She wouldn't. Just lost her head. Damn these oily birds with their flashy cars!'

'Listen. If you saw the guy who was with Manola again, would you recognize him?'

'Sure.'

'Then take a trolley to Headquarters and look over the Rogues' Gallery. Call me up if you have any luck.'

Kerr took his departure, and a little later Kelly entered and said, 'Yup Cap, there's men out in that brewery where you sent me. I heard some hammerin' goin' on like, and the windows on the third floor – that's the top, you know – them windows was open, they was. Then I seen two cars parked inside the fence, under the sheds where the beer used to be loaded on trucks. Classy cars – one a big sedan, all black – number A2260. The other was a sport roadster, C4002. Nobody was around them.'

On his desk pad MacBride marked down the type and number of the two cars. He dismissed Kelly and then called up the automobile license bureau. The sport roadster, he found, belonged to a man named John A. Winslow. The sedan was owned by Judge Michael Haggerty.

MacBride sat back with a bitter chuckle. 'That sounds like "Diamond Jack" Winslow, the race-track kid. H'm. And Mike Haggerty. Cheek and jowl with Duke Manola.'

He lit a cigar and looked up to find Detective-Sergeant O'Dowd, from Headquarters.

'Hello, O'Dowd.'

'Hello, Mac. I just dropped in with a little order from the big cheese. Know that brewery out off Farmingville Turnpike?'

MacBride nodded.

O'Dowd said, 'Well, don't let it worry you, Mac. They're making some good beer there, and orders are to leave 'em be.'

'I've been waiting for those orders,' said MacBride. 'So long as they bust the Volstead act and don't make any noise, it's O.K. by me. Anything else, though—'

'Let your conscience be your guide, Mac,' grinned O'Dowd, and left.

The machinery of the underworld and politics, mused MacBride, was getting under way. Kerr called up a little later, and he had information.

'I'm sure it's the same guy, Cap,' he said. 'Chuck Devore. The records show he was arrested two years ago in connection with the shooting of a taxi driver named Max Levy. But he wasn't indicted.'

'We're hot, Ted,' shot back MacBride. 'Devore is a gangster, and a pretty tough egg. He used to run with Duke Manola. In that killing two years ago we had the hunch that Manola tried to frame Devore to take the rap. Then they broke and Devore drifted. If he's back in town, there's a pot of trouble brewing.'

'You mean a gang war?'

'Right. Dog eat dog stuff, and hell's going to pop or I miss my guess. All right, Ted. Hop a trolley home.'

MacBride slammed down the receiver and sat back rubbing his hands. Devore back in town! But what had he been doing in the company of Duke Manola's brother? And who was the woman in the case – besides Judith? A chill shot through MacBride. His own daughter mixed up in an underworld feud!

He snapped up to his feet, changed from his uniform coat and cap into a plain blue jacket and a gray fedora. He strode out of his office, told Donnegan to get the car out, and left brief instructions with Sergeant Haley.

Outside, he climbed into the car and said, 'Know the Blue River Inn?'

Donnegan said, 'Yes.'

'That's where we're going. Don't run right up to it. Park back a distance, out of sight.'

The car shot off through town, hit Old Stone Road and followed it into Farmingville Turnpike. Half an hour later Donnegan pulled up on the side of the road, in the shadow of a deep woods. Up ahead they could see, *Blue River Inn*, picked out in electric light bulbs.

'You wait here, Donnegan,' said MacBride. 'I won't be long.'

The inn was large and rambling, two storied, with many windows. MacBride entered the large, carpeted room that served as a lobby, and the head-waiter, with a menu in his hand, bowed.

'I'm not eating,' clipped MacBride. 'Who runs this dump?'

'Sir?'

'Cut out the flowers, buddy. I'm from the precinct.' He flashed his badge. 'Snap on it!'

A short, rotund man in dinner clothes came strolling in from the main corridor, and the head-waiter, a little troubled, beckoned to him.

'You the owner?' asked MacBride. 'What's your name?'

'Hinkle, owner and manager. What can I do for you?'

'I'm MacBride, from the precinct. There were two couples in here last night— *You!*' he suddenly shot at the head-waiter. 'Stay here! Now,' he went on, 'who were the two men?'

'Of course,' said Hinkle, 'there are so many people come here, we cannot recall them. So many are transients.'

'Look here,' pursued MacBride. 'One of those men was Joe Manola, who was later killed in a wreck last night. Now who was the other guy – the guy with him?'

Hinkle moistened his lips and his eyes shifted nervously. 'I'm sorry. I don't know. Nor does my head-waiter.'

The girl at the desk trilled, 'Mr. Hinkle, telephone.'

Hinkle went over to the desk, and MacBride followed, stood beside him. Hinkle picked up the telephone, and said, 'Yes, Hinkle talking.' And then his face blanched, and his lips began to writhe.

MacBride's gun came out of his pocket, jammed against Hinkle's adipose paunch. He tore the receiver from Hinkle's hand and clasped it to his own ear, heard—

'. . . and get that, Hinkle. Act dumb, all the time, see. And if it gets too hot, call me on the wire. Got that number? Main 1808?'

MacBride's lips moved silently, forming the words, 'Say, yes, Hinkle.'

'Yes, yes,' said Hinkle, his face pasty white.

'O.K. then,' was the reply, and the man at the other end hung up.

MacBride hung up, set down the telephone, a thin, hard smile on his face. 'Who was that, Hinkle?'

Hinkle wilted, blubbered, kept shaking his head.

'Chuck Devore, eh?' grinned MacBride, without humor.

'Oh, G-God!' choked Hinkle, gasping for air and reeling backward.

MacBride picked up the telephone and called the precinct. To Sergeant Haley he said, 'Send a man out around to the telephone exchange. Tell the operators there to allow no calls incoming or outgoing from' – he looked down at the number on the phone – 'Farmingville 664. Also, no calls to be connected, outgoing or incoming, to Main 1808. Until further notice from the station. Also, get me the address of Main 1808, quick, and ring me at Farmingville 664 before the order to shut off. Snap on it, sergeant!'

He hung up, stepped to the door and blew his whistle. When Donnegan came in on the run, MacBride said, 'No hurry. Just stay here and keep your eyes on these two men till you get word from the precinct. Don't let them get out of sight. Go in the dining-room and tell all the guests to clear out.'

There were only a dozen-odd persons in the dining-room, and they made an angry and protesting exodus. When they had gone, MacBride said to Donnegan. 'Let no more in. See that no more cars leave.'

The telephone rang, and he picked it up, listened. 'All right, sergeant,' he said. 'I'll have to pass there on the way through. Tell Kelly and Kerr to be ready and I'll pick them up.'

He turned from the telephone, looked at the group of waiters and at Hinkle and his steward. Then he looked at Donnegan. 'Keep them salted, Donnegan, right in this room. You, Hinkle, have your sign shut off and all the lights in the house except in this room. You're temporarily closed for business.'

'It's an outrage!' choked Hinkle.

'See if I care,' chuckled MacBride; and to Donnegan, 'I'll take the car.'

VI

Kelly and Kerr were waiting outside of the precinct when MacBride drew up.

'Hop in, boys. We're going for maybe a little target practice.'

Kelly shifted his chew and climbed in, and Kerr, eagerness sparking in his eyes, followed. MacBride stepped on the gas and they shot off.

'What's the lay, Cap?' asked Kelly.

'We're going to look up Chuck Devore, at a dump in lower Jockey Street. There may be a fight. You boys well heeled?'

They were. And as they drove on, MacBride explained about his pilgrimage to the Blue River Inn.

They made good time into the city. Traffic on Main Street, the artery of theatres and cabarets, held them up.

Presently MacBride turned into Jockey Street and followed it west. Near Main Street, small restaurants, Chinese or Italian, displayed their signs. Further along, it changed to blank-faced brick houses, old and peeling, with here and there a single globe of light marking out a speakeasy. The municipal lighting system was poor, and the way was dark.

MacBride pulled up in the middle of a block and said, 'It's on the next block, but we'll leave the car here. Come on.'

They got out and continued down Jockey Street with MacBride taking long strides in the lead. There was a noticeable jut to his teak-hard jaw and a windy look in his blue eyes. He was not the man to grow stale from sitting on his spine in a precinct office. The game on the outside still lured him – the somewhat dangerous game of poking into back alleys and underworld hide-outs.

He slowed down, but did not stop. 'This is the house, boys. Number 40. Don't stop. All dark except the third floor. Shades drawn there, but you can see the light through the cracks. I know this neighborhood. They have a lookout in the hall, and a man needs a password to get in. A red light dump without the red lights. We'll see if there's a way to it from the next street.'

At the next block they turned south, and then east into the next street. Between the houses here they could see the backs of the houses on Jockey Street.

'There it is,' pointed out MacBride. 'That three-story place, taller than the others.' He stopped. 'Here's an alley. Come on.'

They swung into a dark, narrow passageway that led between two wooden houses and on into a small yard criss-crossed with clothes-lines. Separating this yard from that of the one belonging to the house in Jockey Street, was a high board fence. Behind this the three paused and looked up. All floors were dark except the third and top-most.

MacBride gripped the top of the fence, heaved up and over, landed in soft earth. Kerr and Kelly followed and they stood hunched closely, whispering. MacBride pointed to the fire-escape.

'Up we go. You boys trail me. Easy!' he warned.

He led the way up the ladders, his gun drawn. Nearing the top story, he went more cautiously, more quietly, and turned once to recommend silence with a finger tapping his lips. At the third floor he stopped, hunched over. The window was open, a half-drawn shade crackling in the draft.

Slowly MacBride raised his head and peered in over the sill. Four men were sitting around a table in shirt-sleeves, their collars open. A bottle and glasses were on the table, and MacBride caught whiffs of cigarette smoke. He saw Chuck Devore in profile. Devore was a tall, smooth-shaven man of thirty, with curly brown hair and a cleft chin. His eyes were deep-set and peculiarly luminous. In repose, his face was not bad to look at – except for the strange, impenetrable eyes. MacBride had never seen the others, but all of them bore the stamp of hard, dangerous living. The most outstanding, besides Devore, was a huge bull of a man with flaming red hair and a heavy jaw.

'It will be a cinch,' Devore was saying. 'We can bust in about three a.m. and stick up the works, and you can take it from me, there'll be no small change. Not with Diamond Jack Winslow in on the show and a lot of big political guns. And they can't yap. That's where we've got them. They're playing a crooked game, and if the public got wind of it, Perrone would have about as much chance of getting in the aldermanic show as I would. And Haggerty'd land on his can, too.'

'And won't Duke Manola get sore!' chuckled the red-head.

'Yes, the lousy bum!' snapped Devore. 'Cripes, his kid brother spilled a lot of beans. Wild sheik, that bird was.'

'Yeah – *was*,' nodded the red-head.

'I feel a draft,' said Devore, and got up, coming toward the window.

He walked into the muzzle of MacBride's thirty-eight.

'Nice, now, Chuck!' bit off MacBride. 'Up high.'

He stepped in through the window, and Kerr was half-way through behind him, his gun covering the startled group at the table.

Then came Kelly, slit-eyed, dangerous.

'What's the meaning of this, Mac?' snarled Devore.

'Be your age, Chuck,' said MacBride.

No one saw a hand sliding in through a door that led to another room. This hand, slim and white, felt for the light-switch, found it, and pressed the button.

The room was thrown into sudden darkness. Chairs scraped. A door banged.

A dagger of flame slashed through the gloom, and a man screamed, his body hit the floor with a thud.

MacBride found Devore on his hands, and the gangster was trying to twist the captain's gun arm behind his back.

'No, you don't, Devore!'

MacBride heaved with him, spun through the darkness, crashed into other struggling figures. He slammed Devore against the wall, and Devore tried to use his knee for a dirty blow. MacBride blocked with his hip and banged Devore's head to the wall, again and again. Then Devore twisted and dragged out of the jam, but MacBride heaved against him and they crashed to the floor.

Struggling feet stumbled over their twisting bodies, and curses ripped through the darkness. Another shot banged out, went wild and shattered a light bulb in the chandelier. The table toppled, and somebody crashed over a chair.

Then the door leading to the hall was flung open and dim figures hurtled through it on the way out, their feet pounding on the floor. Devore planted his knee brutally in MacBride's stomach and the captain buckled, gasping for breath. Then Devore tore free, reeled about the room and dived for the open door.

But MacBride caught his breath, heaved up and lunged after him. Doors opened and banged, but nobody came out to get in the way. Somewhere far below MacBride heard a sharp exchange of shots. He catapulted after Devore who was racing down the staircase. Near the bottom, he leaped through space and landing on Devore's neck, crashed him to the floor.

Devore groaned and relaxed. MacBride straddled him, drew out manacles and settled Devore's status for the time being. He stood up, wiping blood from his face, shoving wet strands of hair back from his forehead. He heard footsteps rushing up from below and swung around with his gun leveled.

It was Ted Kerr, his clothes in tatters and a couple of blue welts on his face.

'They got away, Cap,' he explained. 'Through the back. Went through a door, slammed it and locked it. Kelly and I tried to bust it, but no can do. I came up to see if you were all right. One was wounded. Here's Kelly.'

Kelly puffed up, his collar gone but his tie still draped around his neck.

'Take this guy,' MacBride said, jerking a thumb toward Devore. 'I'll be right down.'

He went upstairs two steps at a time and entered the gang's quarters. He lit a match, found the light switch and snapped it. The room was in ruin, and the shade still clicked in the draft. He crossed to another door, stood to one side, then turned the knob and kicked the door open. A light was burning inside, and a breeze blowing through an open window.

Entering, MacBride set it down as a room used by a woman. There was a littered dressing table, and a bureau with several drawers half out and signs indicatory of somebody having made a quick getaway. A cursory examination revealed no tell-tale clues. MacBride turned out the lights, left the rooms, and descended the staircase.

Devore was standing up now, between Kerr and Kelly, and venom was burning in his strange, enigmatic eyes.

MacBride said, 'Now for a little buggy ride, Devore.'

'You're going to regret this MacBride,' the man snarled. 'By cripes, you are!'

'Cut out the threats, you bum!'

'Cut out hell! Before you know what's what I'm going to have you tied by the heels.'

'Should I sock him, Cap?' inquired Kelly.

'No. He'll get a lot of that later, where it's more convenient.' MacBride's hand clenched, and his lips flattened back against his teeth.

Devore smiled, mockingly. 'We'll see, MacBride – *we'll see!*'

VII

It was about half-past ten when the police car rolled into Grove Manor. Ted Kerr was at the wheel. Devore sat in the rear, between MacBride and Kelly.

'Looks like a crowd in front of the station,' sang out Kerr.

''Swing into the next block,' said MacBride. 'Probably some photographers and – no doubt – that very good friend of mine, Kennedy, with his nose for news, and his wisecracks.'

The car turned into a dark street several blocks this side of the police station and halted.

'What should I do, Cap?' asked Kerr.

MacBride was thinking. 'Let's see. H'm. Drive around the back way, Ted. Park a block away from the station. I'll run this bird in the back way, right into my office. You and Kelly drive up a little later. And don't spill any beans – keep your traps shut. Then you come in my office, Ted, and we'll see.'

Kerr drove off slowly, cut around the back of the town and came up a dark, poorly paved street that ran back of the station. When he pulled up, MacBride hauled Devore out and marched him off. They took a path that led through a vacant lot and on up to the back of the station.

Here MacBride, using a key, opened a door and shoved Devore in, then followed and, locking the door, guided the gangster along a dark hallway that ended against another door. MacBride unlocked this and stepped into his office, relocked it quickly and crossing to the door that led into the central room, shoved shut the bolt. Then he turned with a sigh of relief, took off his cap and sailed it across his desk.

'Take the load off your feet, Devore,' he droned, and pulling open a drawer in his desk, hauled out a bottle and downed a stiff bracer. He turned to Devore. 'Dry?'

'I don't drink slops, thanks.'

'You can go to hell,' chuckled MacBride, slamming shut the drawer.

'Listen,' jerked out Devore. 'Let me use that phone. I gotta talk to my lawyer.'

'Try setting that to music, guy. You're calling no lawyer. You're seeing no one. And the newspapers aren't going to know I've got you. I'm top-dog, you dirty slob, and you're going to come across!'

'About what?'

'Ask me another,' scoffed MacBride. 'About the killing of Joe Manola. Now don't try to hand me a song and dance, Devore. I was listening outside the window on the fire-escape. I heard you and your guns talking.'

'How did you get the lay on me, MacBride?'

'Don't worry about that, Devore. The thing is, I've got you, and you're going to come across.'

Devore leaned forward, his teeth bared, but not in a smile. 'How about your kid daughter, big boy?'

'Yes, you pup, how about her?' exploded MacBride, a bad light in his eyes.

'Sound nice, won't it? Daughter of Captain MacBride linked up with gangsters. Think it over, MacBride.'

'I'm thinking it over, Devore. It's a blow – a sock flush on the button, but I'll weather it. She'll have to talk, sooner or later, even though she is my daughter. But she's been framed somehow. And what I want to know is, who's the woman who was in the quartette last night at the Blue River?'

'Ah, wouldn't you like to know!' Devore snarled; and then snapped, 'Try and find out, you big bum!'

There was a knock on the door. MacBride walked over and asked, 'Who is it?'

'Ted.'

He opened the door and Ted Kerr slipped in. MacBride snapped shut the bolt. Kerr scowled at Devore.

'Right at home, eh, Devore? You won't be,' he threatened.

MacBride said, 'Keep your eye on him, Ted. I'm going out and give the gang the air.'

There was a sizable crowd waiting for news. Four reporters, three photographers. And Kennedy, with his whimsical smile.

'Ah, captain,' he chortled, 'and now you broadcast.'

MacBride bored him with a keen stare. 'You're wasting your time, Kennedy. On your way – all of you boys. No news tonight.'

'But who's the bird you've got?' demanded a reporter from the city news association.

'You heard me,' shot back MacBride. 'No news. There's a trolley goes through here in five minutes. Take a tip. Hop it.'

'Aw, for cripe's sakes,' protested Kennedy. 'Be a sport, cap. Think of all the good breaks I've put in your way.'

'Think of all the good drinks I've handed out,' replied MacBride. 'No use, Kennedy. Beat it, all of you. You're cluttering up the station.'

The outer door opened and a man strolled in nonchalantly smoking a cork-tipped cigarette. He was of medium height, slight in build, dressed in the acme of fashion. He wore a gray suit that could not have been made for less than a hundred dollars, a cream-colored silk shirt, a blue tie, and a rakish Panama hat. He carried a Malacca stick, and now he leaned on it, his hand aglitter with diamonds, a lazy, indolent look in his slitted brown eyes.

'Hello, MacBride,' he droned through lips that scarcely moved.

'Aren't you late for tea, Duke?' asked the captain.

'Kind of. But I heard you've been shooting the town up. Where's the catch?'

'Rehearsing. No public showing just yet, Duke.'

'Forget it. I got a right to a private interview.'

MacBride shook his head. 'That's a lot of noise. You've got no rights at all so far as I'm concerned. The door's behind you, Duke. The air 'll do you good.'

Duke Manola snarled, 'Can that tripe, Mac. I didn't come out here to chin with you. I came out to see who you picked up. Cut the comedy!'

'Soft pedal, Duke. You're in bad company right now.'

'Why, damn your soul, MacBride!—'

'Shut up!' barked the hard captain. 'You might be a big guy in other circles, but just now, as far as I'm concerned, you're only a little dago shooting off a lot of hot air.' He stepped to the outer door and yanked it open. 'Now get the hell out!'

Manola's lips moved in a silent oath, and his eyes flamed behind lids that were almost closed. Then he shrugged. 'All right, MacBride. Have your way. I see you're not tamed yet.'

'Not by a damned sight, Duke!'

'Maybe – I'll try a little more – taming.' With that he sauntered out, a leer on his dark, smooth face.

A moment later the newspapermen followed.

From then on until midnight MacBride sat in his office, behind locked doors, and raked Devore with a merciless third degree. But Devore only taunted him. He made no confession. He gave no details. He weathered the gale with the hardness of his kind, and at midnight MacBride, worn and haggard, torn inwardly by emotions that he never revealed, called it a day.

'All right, Devore. That'll do for tonight. More later, buddy.'

He called in a policeman and directed him to put Devore in a cell.

'Listen here, MacBride,' the gangster protested on the way out of the office. 'I want a lawyer. I want him mighty quick.'

'Dry up. You're not getting out on bail while I'm alive.'

Still protesting, Devore was dragged away to a cell.

Weary, sunk at heart, MacBride slumped back in his chair, his chin dropping to his chest, his tousled hair straggling down over his red-rimmed eyes. He was up against it. He dared not look ahead. There was no telling what the morrow would bring. But one thing was certain. His daughter would be drawn into the net, linked with a gangster's crime, her name and likeness published throughout the country. Judith MacBride, daughter of Captain MacBride, feared by the criminal element of Richmond City. A stickler for the law. A hard man against crooks. Possessed of an enviable record.

He shuddered; the whole, big-boned frame of him shuddered.

And then the telephone rang, and he picked up the receiver.

'Is this you, Steve?' came his wife's anxious voice.

'Yes, Ann.'

'Steve! I don't know where Judith is. She went to a movie tonight – to – forget for a little while. She'd promised to go with Elsie, from the other end of town. You know the show's out at eleven. And she hasn't come home yet. I called up Elsie and she said they parted in front of the theatre at eleven and Judith started walking home.

'And Steve, listen. At about ten some woman called up and asked for Judith. I said she wasn't in, that she'd gone to the movies. Then she hung up. What do you suppose could have happened?'

Under the desk, MacBride's clenched fist pounded against his knee.

'I don't know, Ann. But don't worry. I'll be home right away. Don't worry, dear. I'll – be – home.'

The color had drained from his face by the time he slipped the receiver back on to the hook. He sat back, his arms outstretched, the hands knotted on the edge of the desk, the eyes wide and staring into space. And then the eyes narrowed and the lips curled.

He heaved up, banged on his cap and strode out of the station. When he reached home his wife was sobbing, and she came to his arms. Hard hit as he was, he, nevertheless, put his arms around her and patted her gently.

'Buck up, Ann. That's a brave girl. Maybe it's nothing after all. Maybe—'

The ringing of the telephone bell interrupted him. Slowly, he approached the instrument, unhooked the receiver.

'Who is this?' grated a voice.

'MacBride.'

'Get wise to yourself, MacBride. You see that Devore gets free by tomorrow midnight, or your daughter gets a dirty deal. This is straight. The gang's got her at a hide-out you'll never find. I'm calling from a booth in the railroad station. By tomorrow midnight, MacBride, or your daughter gets the works! Good-bye!'

A click sounded in MacBride's ear. He turned away from the telephone, met his wife's wide-eyed stare.

'Steve! Steve!' she cried.

'Judith's been kidnapped by Devore's gang. Devore's the man I've got in jail. His freedom is their price – for Judith.'

'Oh – dear – God!'

Ann MacBride closed her eyes and swayed. The hard captain caught her, held her gently, carried her to a sofa and laid her down, kneeling beside her.

For the first time in his life MacBride prayed – for his daughter.

VIII

Next day he sat in his office, with the doors bolted, and Ted Kerr facing him.

'Ted, I'm cornered,' he muttered. 'I've got to pay through the nose.'

'The skunks!' exclaimed Kerr. 'God, can't we comb the city? Can't we run the pups down?'

'It would take two or three days. They demand Devore by midnight. I've got to swallow my pride and let him go.'

'But, Cap, you can't let him just walk out.'

'I know I can't. There must be another way. He must escape.'

Kerr bit his lip, perplexed. 'Escape? Can you imagine the razzing you'll get?'

MacBride nodded. 'Yes, more than you can. I've been called a tough nut, Ted. Well, I won't deny it. And my pride's been one of the biggest things in me. Swallowing it will damn near choke me. But my daughter – my flesh and blood – is the price, and, by God, I can't stand the blow!'

'But can't it be fixed so the blame 'll fall on me? Hell, Cap, you've got so much more at stake.'

'No. I'm the guy pays through the nose. Devore must escape.'

'What about those birds at the Blue River?'

'They're not in the know. I hauled Donnegan off last night. Devore was just their bootlegger. Hinkle came across. He said Devore warned him to close his trap and keep it closed, or wind up wrestling with a bullet. No, there's no alternative. Sometime tonight I've got to pull a bonehead move and let Devore blow. Afterwards, Ted, I'll clean him out. But Judith comes first.'

'Suppose they double-cross you?'

'I'll take care of that before Devore goes.'

The day dragged by, and at nine that night MacBride had Devore brought in from the cell. He dismissed the officer with a nod. Devore sat down – he was without manacles – and helped himself to a cigarette from a pack on the desk. He needed a shave, and he looked down at the mouth – and nasty.

'What a crust you've got, MacBride! Dammit, I want a lawyer. I want to see something besides polished buttons. I gotta right to that, MacBride.'

MacBride rocked gently in his swivel chair. 'Pipe down. And listen. You're going to slide out of here tonight.'

Devore looked up, suspecting a trick. 'What d' you mean?'

'The rats you run with kidnaped my daughter last night. Their price is – your freedom. They've got me buffaloed, and I know they'd slit her open if I didn't come across.'

'Told you I'd get you tied by the heels.'

'Shut up. It's a bum break, and I'm not yapping. You slide out tonight.'

Devore looked around. 'Which way?'

'Not yet, buddy. You're going to call up your gang and tell 'em to let my daughter go.'

'Do you see any green on me, Cap?' snarled Devore.

'You can take my word or leave it. I've never framed a guy yet, Devore. You ought to know that. Here's my proposition. You call up your gang and tell 'em it's all fixed. They let my kid go. You breeze. I'll give you twelve hours' grace. But after that I'm going after you. I'll know what number you call up, so don't hang around there after you're out. You're getting a lease on life, a twelve hours' lease. Grab it before I change my mind.'

Devore leaned forward, his luminous eyes roving over the captain's face.

'Call Northside 412,' he breathed.

MacBride reached for the telephone and put through the call. When he heard the operator ringing, he passed the phone over to Devore and watched him intently.

'Hell – hello,' snapped Devore. 'This you, Jake? . . . Yeah, this is Chuck. It's all fixed. Let the dame go – right away. Put her in a taxi and send her home. Then clear out and I'll meet you at Charlie's. . . . Of course, I mean it. For God's sake, don't act dumb! . . . Yeah, right away. S' long.'

He hung up, his eyes narrowed. 'Now, MacBride!'

MacBride pulled open a drawer and laid an automatic on the desk. 'The gun you shot Joe Manola with. It's empty. You grab it and cover me and beat it out the back way, through the lots, and run for three blocks. There's a main drag there, and a bus goes through to the city in five minutes.'

Devore grabbed the gun, his eyes brilliant in their deep sockets, his lips drawn tight.

'Paying through the nose, eh, MacBride?'

'Shut up. When I meet you again, Devore, I won't be taking any prisoners. The morgue bus will gather up the remains. Breeze!'

Devore snapped to his feet, leered, and sped out through the rear door. MacBride sat still, his face granite hard, his fingers opening and closing, his teeth grinding together. For two minutes he sat there. Then he jumped up, ran to the door leading into the rear hall and banged it shut.

He spun around and dived for the door leading into the central room. Sergeant Haley was playing solitaire. Kerr was sitting at a table playing checkers with Kennedy, of the *Free Press*.

'Snap on it!' barked MacBride. 'Devore's escaped! He pulled a fast one. Grabbed a gun lying on the desk. Come on!'

Kerr kicked back his chair. Two patrolmen came running from another room, drew their nightsticks.

MacBride led the way out, and on the street said, 'We'll split.' He directed the patrolmen to head for the trolley line. To Kerr he said, 'We'll watch the bus line.'

A moment later he and Kerr were running for the bus line, and when they reached the highway, MacBride pointed to a red light just disappearing around a bend.

'That's the bus,' he said. 'And Devore.'

'So you did it, Cap.'

'Hell, yes!'

IX

An hour later, MacBride and Kerr stopped in at the captain's house. Judith was weeping in her mother's arms and her mother was shedding tears of happiness.

'Judith just came in,' she said.

MacBride took his daughter and stood her up, placing his hands on her shoulders. 'Poor kid – poor kid. Now tell me, Judith, tell me – all you know.'

Ted Kerr stood a little back, ill at ease.

'Oh, daddy, I've been a fool – a little fool. When I was walking home from the movies last night that girl drove up in a car, called to me – and then two men jumped for me, gagged me, and they drove off.'

'What girl?'

'Arline Kane. I met her a month ago at a hairdressing parlor in the city. She said she was an actress, and marveled at my hair. She said I ought to go on the stage. She took me to lunch, and then promised to introduce me to some theatrical men. She was going with a man named Devore. I met him several times, and then the other night we went to the Blue River and there was another fellow – for me. Mr. Manola. I – I didn't like him. He – he drank too much.

'When we drove away from the Blue River, he wanted to park on a dark road. But I didn't want him to. He was pretty drunk, and he wanted to make love to me. I fought him off, and then he turned to the others and said, "I thought you said I'd find a good time." And Mr. Devore said, "Don't crab, Joe. Drive on." And Mr. Manola said, "Nothing doing. I've got a mind to make you all walk. Go on, get out, all of you." Well, he meant it, and he was pretty angry, too. And Mr. Devore got angry. They began swearing. Then Mr. Manola said, "You *will* get out, all of you!" And he drew his gun. But Mr. Devore, who was sitting in the back, jumped on him, and the gun went off, but it was twisted around so that the bullet struck Mr. Manola.

'He screamed, and then he shouted, "I'll wreck all of you!" He seemed crazy, and threw into gear, and the car started. Then Mr. Devore yelled, "Jump! We'll have to jump!" And we all did. And the car gathered speed, and Mr. Manola must have fainted, because it swerved to right and left and then hit a tree.

'We fled through the woods, after I'd gone to the wreck to see if he was alive. But he wasn't. Then Mr. Devore told me to say nothing about what had happened. He threatened that if I did he'd wipe out my whole family. That's why I wouldn't tell you, dad. I've been terrible – a fool – a fool!'

'Yes, you have,' agreed MacBride. 'But did Devore and Manola talk about – well, business?'

Judith thought; then, 'No. But I remember, at the Blue River, when Arline and I had come back to the table from the ladies' room, Mr. Devore was saying to Mr. Manola, "And they think hooch is being made there! A good blind!" And then he laughed.'

MacBride stepped back, stroking his jaw. Judith threw Kerr an embarrassed look, but he came to her and took her hand. 'It's all right, Judith. I'm awfully glad you're safe.'

'I've been awful, Ted. And yet you're so kind.' Feeling his arm about her, she laid her head on his shoulder. 'I'll never – never do it again, Ted – never.'

MacBride clipped suddenly, 'Ted, I've got a hunch. That brewery. I wonder if something besides beer and hooch is being made there.'

Kerr looked up from Judith. 'What do you mean?'

'I don't know. But I'm going to find out. Come on.'

Leaving Judith, Kerr flicked her cheek with his lips, and she pressed his hand.

But MacBride was calling him, and he hurried out at the captain's heels. They strode back to the station, and MacBride hauled out Donnegan and the police car.

'Drive to that old brewery,' he clipped.

He sat back beside Kerr and lit a fresh cigar.

Kerr said, 'I thought the orders were to lay off that place?'

'I said I'd lay off if they were busting the Volstead act. But I've got a hunch something else is going on there.'

'What, Cap?'

'That's what I'm going to find out. Shoot, Donnegan!'

Donnegan nodded, and as the car moved away from the curb, there were running feet on the sidewalk, and a moment later Kennedy was riding on the running-board.

'Mind if I tag along, Mac?' he grinned.

'You're like a burr in a man's sock, Kennedy. But get in beside Donnegan.'

'What's the lay, Mac?'

'Stick around and see if you can find out. Here's a cigar. See if that 'll keep your jaw shut.'

'Thanks, Mac. Only I'm sore as hell that you didn't tell me beforehand it was Devore you had. Cripes, won't they hand you the razzberry! I shot the story right in. I said you were sitting with Devore alone in your office, with the automatic lying on the desk. You were trying to make him swear it was his gun, and in the heat of the argument Devore grabbed it and covered you. I had to make up a lot of fiction, but that was because you didn't explain. I ended up by saying that you were sure you'd recapture him, and all that sort of boloney.'

'That's as good as anything,' muttered MacBride. 'Now jam that cheroot in your mouth and sign off.'

Twenty minutes later they were driving along Farmingville Turnpike. The night was dark, and within the past ten minutes a chill Autumn drizzle had started, the kind of drizzle that is half rain and half mist – penetrating and clammy. The rubber tires hissed sibilantly on the wet macadam, and the beams of the headlights were reflected back from the gray vapor.

Presently Donnegan slowed down and swung in close to the side of the road, extinguished the lights.

'Can't you drive into the bushes?' asked MacBride. 'We ought to get the car off the road and out of sight.'

Donnegan tried this and succeeded. Then they all got out and stood in a group.

MacBride said, 'We'll walk up. There's a lane a hundred yards on, leading into the brewery, which is a quarter of a mile off the Turnpike. You,' he said to Kennedy, 'better stay out of this.'

'Try and do it, Mac. I didn't come out here to pick wildflowers.'

MacBride growled, turned and plowed through the bushes. The others followed, and in short time they reached the lane. It led through vacant fields, fenced in, where in the old days horses belonging to the brewing company had grazed.

'Here comes a machine!' warned Kerr, and they dived into the tall grass by the fence.

Two beams of light danced through the gloom. The machine was bound in from the Turnpike, and presently it purred by – a big, opulent limousine. When its tail light had disappeared behind a bend, MacBride stood up, motioned to the others, and proceeded. The visor on his cap was beaded with the drizzle.

Gradually the buildings loomed against the blue-black sky – the big main plant, surrounded by stables and storehouses. Not a light could be seen. They reached the first outbuilding, and from where he stood MacBride could see a half-dozen automobiles parked near the main building, by the loading platform. Here and there he saw a faint red glow near the machines.

'Chauffeurs, smoking,' he decided, and his gaze wandered up the dark face of the big three-storied building, which an ancient brewing company had evacuated three years ago.

'Something phony going on there, or I don't know my tricks,' remarked Kennedy.

'Guess this is the time you do,' replied MacBride. 'Let's work around to the rear.'

They retraced their steps a short distance and then began creeping around the outside of the building, weaving through tall grass and dried out weeds. Ten minutes later they were at the off-side of the main building, deep in shadows. MacBride found a window with broken panes, nodded to the others, and crawled through. He dropped a few feet into a chill, damp cellar, black as pitch; stood waiting while Kerr, Kennedy and then Donnegan, followed.

'Your flash, Donnegan,' he whispered, and felt the cylinder pressed into his hand.

He snapped on the light. The beam leaped through the clammy gloom, shone on stacks of dusty kegs, long out of use, and on stacks of bottles musty with cobwebs. The odor of must and mold seeped into the men's nostrils.

MacBride led the way, winding in and out between the rows of barrels. Further on he came to a small, heavy door which, swinging open under his hand, led into another section of the cellar. Here were more barrels, but they were standing upright, and the smell of new wine was prevalent. Barrels of it. Kennedy licked his lips, then pointed ahead.

The beam of light swung back and forth across stacked cases of liquor. The men crept closer.

'Hot diggity!' whispered Kennedy. 'Look at the Dewar's, and the Sandy MacDonald. And – say! . . . Three Star Hennessy!'

'Pipe down!' snapped MacBride under his breath.

'Maybe you got a bum steer after all, Mac. If it's only liquor, and you dragged me all the way out here—'

'Nobody dragged you out here, Kennedy! Quit yapping!'

'I know, but—'

Bang! Bang!

Kerr tensed and his breath shot out with – 'What's that?'

Bang! Bang!

MacBride had his gun out, his lips pursed, his eyes looking up toward the unseen regions above.

'One thing,' he muttered. 'It's not just target practice. Come on!'

X

Four shots, muffled by floors and walls but, nevertheless, somewhere in that building.

MacBride, with his flash sweeping around furiously, finally located a staircase that led up to the ground floor. At his heels came Kerr, trailed closely by Donnegan and Kennedy. MacBride paused to get his bearings.

Another shot rang out, echoes trailing, commingled with the sounds of banging doors and the shouts of men.

'This way!' clipped MacBride, espying another stairway.

He ascended two steps at a time, reached the next landing. He looked up into the gloom above just in time to see a slash of gun-fire rip through the darkness. In the sudden flare he saw a man with hands upthrown. Then there was a thumping sound, as the man fell.

MacBride's flash was out. His lips were set. He whispered to his men, 'Watch it, boys! This place is a death trap! Stick close!'

A sudden exchange of shots burst out on the floor above, and the rebound of bullets could be heard intermingled with screaming oaths and pounding feet. Then, nearby, MacBride heard a body hurtling down the stairs. He jumped in that direction, caught a man in the act of scrambling to his feet. Heaving up, the man struck out and the barrel of a revolver whanged by MacBride's cheek and stopped against his shoulder.

MacBride struck back with his own thirty-eight and landed on the stranger's skull. Then Donnegan was there to help him, gripping the man's arms from behind. They dragged him down the hall, felt their way into a room, and then MacBride snapped on his flash and looked at their catch.

It was the bull-necked red-head whom he had seen in Devore's hide-out in Jockey Street. The man was streaked with blood.

'What the hell are you doing here?' MacBride wanted to know.

'Playin' Santy Claus—'

'Cut out the wisecracks! What's going on upstairs?'

'Go up an' find out. Go on. Slugs are sailin' around up there like flies in the summer time.'

'I'll tend to you later,' bit off MacBride; and to Donnegan, 'Get out your bracelets and clamp him to the water pipe on the wall.'

This done, MacBride again led the way back up the hall. As they reached the foot of the staircase leading to the floor, they partly heard, vaguely saw, a knot of men milling down the steps.

MacBride squared off and pressed on his flash.

'Good cripes almighty!' exploded one of the men.

'As you are!' barked MacBride.

The man in the lead was carrying a canvas bag. The man was Chuck Devore, and behind him were six others. One of these snapped up his gun and fired. The shot smashed MacBride's flashlight, tore through his left hand that held it. He cursed and reeled sidewise, and Kerr's gun boomed close by his ear, and the slug ripped through the gang on the stair.

'Back up!' one of them called to his companions.

MacBride thrust his wounded hand into his pocket and fired at them.

'Come on!' he snapped, and leaped up the staircase.

Kerr passed him on the way up, and let fly with three fast shots. A gangster crumpled near the top, spun around and came crashing down. He reeled off MacBride and pitched over the railing. At the top, a gun spat and a bullet grazed Kerr' cheek, leaving a hot sting. Then they were on the top floor.

In a close exchange of shots Kennedy gasped and clutched at his left arm, and Donnegan stopped short, his legs sagging. His gun dropped from his hand and he crumpled. MacBride stumbled over him and sprayed the gloom with three shots. A man screamed and another flung out a bitter stream of oaths that died in a groan. MacBride plugged ahead, reeling over prone bodies, himself dazed with the pain of his wounded arm.

He saw a square of the night sky framed in a window, saw it blocked suddenly by a figure that stepped out to a fire-escape. The figure twisted and a slash of gun-fire stabbed the darkness. MacBride's cap was carried from his head. His own gun belched and the man in the window doubled over and fell back into the hall.

Then he brought up short, looked out and saw, vaguely, a couple of automobiles tearing away into the night. He spun around, expecting another enemy, but a dread pall had descended after that last shot. Kerr limped up to him, panting. Kennedy was swearing softly. MacBride snapped on his own flash and saw them, bloody and torn; Kerr with a gash on his cheek, Kennedy slowly sopping a wound in his arm. The beam picked out dead bodies on the floor. He swayed back and bent over Donnegan, then stood up, wagging his head.

'I'll never say, "Shoot, Donnegan," again,' he muttered.

His light swung around and settled on the man he had shot by the window. It was Devore, still gripping the canvas bag. MacBride bent down and opened the bag, and saw a mass of bills – fives, tens, twenties. He gave the bag to Kerr, and moved on toward a door. He threw his light in here and saw a large, square room whose expensive furnishings were in ruin. He espied a light switch and pressed the button, and a big chandelier sprang to life.

'Hot diggity!' exclaimed Kennedy.

Dead men were here, too. But what had caused Kennedy's exclamation was the gambling layout. There was a roulette wheel. There was a faro table. There were a half dozen card tables, two of them overturned. There were cards and chips spread over the floor. The windows were covered by heavy curtains, and ventilators were in the ceiling.

'My hunch was right,' nodded MacBride, bitterly.

'And look who's here!' cried Kennedy. 'Duke Manola – dead as a doornail. And – oh, boy! – the late Judge Mike Haggerty – *late* is right. Where,' he yelled, looking around, 'oh, where is a telephone? What a scoop!'

There was a shot below, and MacBride whirled. He dived out into the hall, with Kerr at his heels, and went down the stairway on the fly. His flash leaped forth and spotted two figures running for the lower staircase.

'Stop!' he shouted.

His answer was a shot that went wild. But MacBride fired as he ran, and saw one of the figures topple. He kept going, furiously, and collided with the other.

'All right, Cap. You've got me.'

His flash shone on the face of a woman.

The man lying dead on the floor was the red-head.

XI

'Well,' said MacBride, 'who are you?'

'Arline Kane, and what about it?'

'No lip, sister. What are you doing here?'

She laughed – a hard little laugh. 'Came in to look around. I heard the fireworks from the road. I found Red tied to a pipe and I shot away the nice little bracelet.'

'You come upstairs,' directed MacBride, and shoved her toward the staircase.

Once in the hidden gambling den, Arline stood with her hands on her hips and looked around with lazy eyes.

'Hell,' she said, 'what a fine mess. Real wild West stuff. Jesse James and his boy scouts were pikers alongside these playboys. Well, there's Duke, the bum. Good thing.'

'What do you mean?' asked MacBride.

She sat down and lit a cigarette. 'Don't know, eh? Well, Duke used to be my boy friend, until he got hot over a little flapper not dry behind the ears yet. Gave me my walking papers. That was after he tried to frame Chuck Devore, and Chuck breezed for a while. But when Chuck came back, I looked him up and we consolidated our grudge against the wop.

'We got one good break. Duke and his kid brother were on the outs. The kid wanted more money, but Duke was nobody's fool. He told Joe where he got off. I understand they actually came to blows. Well, it was about that time I met Joe, and like a kid he handed me his sob story about Duke landing on him.

'I got him tight one night and he sprung his tongue for a fare-ye-well. Told me about Duke buying this brewery to make and store booze. But some politicians, and Diamond Jack Winslow – laying there, with the busted neck – were behind him. Diamond Jack installed the games here and Haggerty was to get a thirty per cent split from Jack on the house winnings. Duke had some money in it, but he was mainly for the booze end. Haggerty promised protection, and Duke, in payment, promised three thousand votes for Haggerty's party.

'Well, Duke's kid brother was hard up for money, and Duke would never let him run with the gang. So Chuck and I got the kid one night and put it up to him: He could clean up by raiding this dump, by tipping us off when the games were running high. Then the other night, he got drunk and sore and—'

'Pulled a bone,' put in MacBride, 'on Old Stone Road. I know all about that. And then tonight Devore and his rats thought they'd pull a fast one – do what we'd least expect after their first fumble – jump this joint and clean out before we'd caught our breath. Well, they would have fooled me, sister. I *didn't* expect them. I came here on a hunch to look around, and found fireworks. And you – you're the last one.'

'Out of luck again,' she nodded.

'You could make some money,' put in Kennedy, 'writing a series of articles for the *Evening News* on "How I Went Wrong".'

'You would say that, ink fingers,' she gave him, derisively. 'But I'll do no writing. And because I'm the last straggler, I'll take no rap.' She bit off the end of her cigarette and flung the other part away with a defiant gesture. 'A pill was in the tip. Always carried one for just a tough break like this.' Her eyes were glazed. 'Not lilies, boys . . . something red . . . roses.'

A day later MacBride sat at his desk in the station, his cap tipped back, one eye squinted against the smoke from his cigar while he read the *Free Press*' account of last night's holocaust. Sometimes he wagged his head, amazed at remarks which he was alleged to have made.

The city was shocked to the core. Election possibilities had turned more than one somersault during the past twelve hours. Big officials were making charges and counter charges. And MacBride, with his hunch, was mainly responsible for it.

He looked up to see Kennedy standing in the doorway. He put down the paper and leaned back. Kennedy's arm, like his own, was in a sling.

'Greetings, Mac. No end of greetings.' He wandered in and slid down on a chair. 'How do you like the writeup I gave you?'

'You're a great liar, Kennedy.'

'Well, hell, I had to make up a lot of goofy stuff, sure. What's the biggest lie, Mac?'

'Where the account says, "Captain MacBride, having received a tip from an unidentified person, probably a stoolie, that a certain gang was planning to raid the near-beer plant on Farmingville Turnpike last night, immediately drove out to forestall any such attempt".' He jabbed the paper with a rigid forefinger. 'That's the part, Kennedy.'

Kennedy shrugged. 'Yeah, you're right. When I got back to the office and wrote the thing up, I wondered how you *had* got the tip. Well, I was in a hurry, so I wrote in that – just that. It sounded all right, fitted all right – and look here, Mac. It just about cinches any chance of the big guns bawling you out. You were tipped off by a stoolie – a phone call – no name. You shot out there and the raid was under way. What developed later was not your fault. It's air tight!'

MacBride creaked his chair forward, sighed, and drew a bottle and glasses from his desk. He set them down.

'Have a drink, Kennedy.'

Kennedy edged nearer the desk and, arching a weary eyebrow, poured himself a stiff three fingers. MacBride poured himself a drink, and leaned back with it.

'Kennedy,' he said, 'there have been times when I ached to wring your neck. You're a cynical, cold-blooded, snooping, wisecracking example of modern newspaperdom. But, Kennedy, you've got brains – and you're on the square. Here's to you.'

Kennedy grinned in his world-weary way. 'Boloney, Mac. No matter how you slice it, it's still boloney,' he said.

THE LAW LAUGHS LAST

FREDERICK L. NEBEL

A tough precinct was the Second of Richmond City, lying in the backyard of the theatrical district and on the frontier of the railroad yards.

A hard-boiled precinct, touching the fringes of crookdom's élite on the north – the con men, the night-club barons; and on the south, the dim-lit, crooked alleys traversed by the bum, the lush-worker and poolroom gangster. On the north were the playhouses, the white way, high-toned apartments, opulent hotels, high hats, evening gowns. On the south, tenements, warehouses, cobblestones, squalor, and the railroad yards. The toughest precinct in all Richmond City.

Captain MacBride, back again in the Second, ran it with two fists, a dry sense of humor and a generous quantity of brass-bound nerve. He was a lean, windy-eyed man of forty. He had a wife and an eighteen-year-old daughter in a vine-clad bungalow out in suburban Grove Manor, and having acquired early in life a suspicion that he was going to die young and violently in line o duty, he had forthwith taken out a lot of life insurance. He was not a pessimist, but a hard-headed materialist, and he rated crooks and gunmen with a certain species of rodent that travels by dark and frequents cellars, sewers and garbage dumps.

He was sitting in his office at the station house a mild spring night, going over a sheaf of police bulletins, when Kennedy, of the *Free Press*, strolled in.

'Spring has come, Mac,' Kennedy yawned.

'Why don't you set it to poetry?'

'I got over that years ago.' He drifted over to the desk, helped himself to a cigar from an open box, sniffed it critically. 'Dry,' he muttered.

'I like 'em dry.'

'I always keep mine moist.'

MacBride chuckled. 'That's rich! First time I see you smoking a cigar of your own I'll buy you a box of Monterey's. Well, what's on your mind?'

Kennedy looked toward the open window through which came the blare and beat of a jazz band muffled by distance.

'That,' he said.

MacBride nodded. 'I thought so. I'll bet if something doesn't bust loose over there you'll get down-hearted.'

Kennedy shrugged, sank wearily to a chair and lit up. 'And I'll bet you're happy as hell they're staging that political block-party. You look it, Mac.'

'Don't I!' muttered MacBride, a curl to his lip. 'Yes, Kennedy, I'm happy as a school kid when vacation time comes. Of all the dumb stunts I can think of, this block-party takes the cake. If this night passes without somebody getting bumped off, I'll get pie-eyed drunk and take a calling-down from my wife. A political campaign in Richmond City makes a Central American rebellion look comical.'

'And how!' grinned Kennedy. 'But I only hope Krug and Bedell get kicked out of office so hard they'll never get over it. As State's Attorney, Krug's made a fortune, and Alderman Johnny Bedell's his right-hand man. I'm all for Anderson for State's Attorney and Connaught for alderman of this district. They're square. But I wouldn't be willing to bet on the outcome. The Mayor and his crowd are behind Krug.

'And here's the nigger in the woodpile. Connaught and Anderson are square men. They deserve to get in office. But there's a gang in this city that's taken it into their own hands to make things hot as hell for Krug and Bedell, and by doing this they're going to cramp the Anderson-Connaught square style. Connaught and Anderson don't want their support, but they've got to take it – through the nose, too.'

'Say who you mean, Kennedy,' broke in MacBride. 'Come on and tell me you mean Duveen and his guns.'

'Sure – Duveen. Duveen hasn't got a good break since Krug's been State's Attorney. But who has? Simple, Bonelio, the S.A.'s friend. And Bonelio is sure tooting his horn for the Krug-Bedell ticket. If Anderson gets in for State's Attorney he'll put a wet blanket on Bonelio's racket; and if Anderson sweeps Connaught in with him, it'll mean that Bonelio's warehouses this side of the railroad yards will be swept clean.

'And that's what Duveen wants, because he wants to run the bootleg racket in Richmond City, and so long as Bonelio has the present State's Attorney and the alderman for this district on his side, Duveen's blocked. What a hell of a riot this election is going to be!'

MacBride grunted, opened a drawer and pulled out a bottle of Three Star Hennessy.

'Have a drink, Kennedy,' he said. 'There are times when I'd like to kick you in the slats, but I admire your brains and the way you get the low-down on things.'

Through the window came another burst of dance music. On Jackson Street couples were dancing, political banners were flying, ropes of colored lights were glowing. And policemen were on the walkout, idly swinging nightsticks, watching, waiting, prepared for the worst and hoping for the best.

MacBride lit a cigar and looked up to find Detective Moriarity standing in the doorway.

''Lo, cap. 'Lo, Kennedy.' Moriarity was a slim, compactly built young man, short on speech, quick in action – one-time runner-up for the welterweight title.

'How do things look?' asked MacBride.

'Depends,' said Moriarity. 'Committeeman Shanz is a little tight. Bedell ain't there yet. Shanz expects him, though. Says Bedell's s'posed to speak at eleven.'

'See any bums?'

'No. But pipe this. I just been tipped off that a crowd of Anderson-Connaught sympathizers from the Fourth Ward are making a tour of the town. About ten machines. Band and flags and all that crap. I figure this way. Ten to one all o' them have got some booze along, to make 'em feel better. They're mostly storekeepers and automobile dealers, but if they get tight they'll get gay. Like as not they'll wind up at the block-party and some wiseguy will haul off and talk outta turn.'

MacBride doubled his fist and took a crack at the desk. 'Just about that, Jake! All right. Get back on the job. Cohen with you?'

'Yeah, Ike's over there. Patrolmen Gunther and Holstein at one end the street. McClusky and Swanson the other. Things are running smooth so far. Don't see any o' Duveen's guns, or Bonelio's.'

'That,' said MacBride, 'is what itches me. Bonelio ought to be there. He's Shanz's friend.'

'He's not there. None of his guns, either. Tell you who is there, though, cap.'

'Who?'

'Bonelio's skirt. That little wren he yanked from the burlesque circuit and shoved in his ritzy night-club on Paradise Street. Trixie Meloy. Ask me and I'll crack she still oughter be back in burlesque, and third rate at that.'

'Who's she with?'

'Alone. High-hatting everybody. But she sticks close to Shanz.'

'I got it!' clipped MacBride. 'She's waiting for somebody, for Bonelio. Watch her, Jake. It's ten-thirty now. Bonelio should have been on hand long ago. He shows up at all of the district's balls and dances. Until he comes anything can happen. Tell the cops to keep their eyes open. Tell Cohen to tend to business and quit trying to date up the gals. I know Ike. On the way out tell the sergeant to see the reserves are ready for a break. First time you pipe a Duveen gun on the scene, run him off. If he cracks wise, bring him over here.

'Remember, Jake, this precinct is just about as safe as a volcano. We've heard rumblings for the past month, and God knows when the top'll blow off. It's a tough situation. I'm all for the Anderson-Connaught ticket, as you know, but no rat like Duveen is going to get away with anything. He doesn't give a damn for the Anderson-Connaught combine. He's sore at the present State's Attorney and the greaseball Bonelio. Both of them ought to be in the pen, and before this election is over I've got a hunch one of them will be – if he doesn't get bumped off during the rush. On your way, Jake, and good luck.'

Moriarity went out.

Kennedy said, 'I'm going over and look around, too, Mac.'

'You smell headlines for tomorrow's *Press*, don't you?'

'Yeah – the city of dreadful night. Hell, man, we ain't had a good hot story since that Dutch butcher tapped his frau on the knob with a meat ax. Years ago, Mac, old bean!'

'Two weeks ago last night,' mused MacBride. 'Ah-r-r, when will this crime wave stop? Wives killing husbands; husbands killing wives! College kids going in for suicide and double death pacts! Men braining little kids! Men willing to kill to get power!'

'That,' said Kennedy, pausing in the doorway, 'is what keeps the circulation of the daily tabloids on top. See you later.'

Alone, MacBride stared into space for a long moment, his eyes glazed with thought. Then he sighed bitterly, flung off the mood with a savage little gesture, and continued looking over the collection of police bulletins.

Fifteen minutes dragged by. The dusty-faced clock on the wall ticked them off with hollow monotony.

Then the telephone rang.

MacBride picked up the receiver, said, 'Hel-lo.'

'MacBride?'

'Yup.'

'Bedell's slated to get the works tonight.'

The instrument clicked.

'Hello – hello!' barked MacBride.

There was no use. The man behind the mysterious voice had hung up. MacBride rang the operator, gave his name.

'Trace that call,' he snapped. 'Fast!'

II

He pressed one of a series of buttons on his desk. The door opened. Lieutenant Donnelly tramped in wiping the cobwebs of a recent nap from his eyes.

'On your toes, lieutenant!' cracked MacBride. 'Just got a blind call that Bedell's going to get bumped off. You'll take charge here tonight while I'm on the outside.'

The telephone rang. MacBride reached for it, said, 'Yes?' A moment later he hung up, snorted with disappointment. 'Call was from a booth in the railroad terminal.'

'Who d' you suppose it was, captain?' ventured Donnelly.

'How the hell do I know?' MacBride was on his feet, buttoning his coat.

He reached for his visored cap, but changed his mind and slapped on a flap-brimmed fedora.

'I'll be over on Jackson Street,' he told Donnelly crisply. 'Bedell's supposed to pull a campaign speech at eleven. I'll put the clamps on that. Bedell's no friend of mine, but I'm damned if any bum is going to kill him in my precinct. If Headquarters wants me, give 'em the dope and tell 'em where I am.'

He strode into the central room and shot brief orders to the desk sergeant. Then he drafted four policemen from the reserve room. They came out buttoning their coats, nightsticks drawn. The lieutenant, the sergeant, the four policemen – all were affected by the vigor, the spirit with which MacBride dived into the middle of things. No captain liked more to get out in the raw and the rough of crime than MacBride. The crack of his voice, the snap of his movement, made him a man whom others were eager to follow. Hard he was, but with the hardness of a man supremely capable of command. He had turned down a Headquarters job on the grounds that it was too soft – that he would stagnate and grow old before his time, grow whiskers and a large waistband.

He led the way out of the station house. His step was firm and resolute, and he carried himself with a definite air of determination. One block west, and two south, and they were at Jackson Street.

The band was playing a fox trot. The block was roped off at either end, and a hundred couples were dancing on the street pavement. On the sidewalks and the short stone flights before the tenement were a hundred-odd onlookers. Strung from pole to pole were rows of colored electric lights. Banners were waving; posters showing likenesses of Alderman Bedell and State's Attorney Krug emblazoned the houses and the poles. A temporary bandstand had been erected in the middle of the block, and from this, too, the candidates for re-election were expected to speak.

MacBride looked the place over critically. Detective Ike Cohen left a couple of girls to join the captain.

'Something up, cap?'

'Maybe. See any old familiar faces around?'

'None that'd interest you. Here comes Moriarity.'

At sight of the captain Moriarity frowned quizzically. 'Huh?' he asked.

MacBride explained about the telephone call. Gunther and Holstein, the patrolmen stationed at that end of the block, mingled with the four reserves, all wondering what was in the wind.

'Where's Committeeman Shanz?' MacBride asked.

'I'll get him,' said Moriarity, and faded into the crowd.

He reappeared in company with Shanz, district committeeman and chairman of the night's carnival. Shanz was a German-Jew, though he had more of the beer-garden look about him. A short, rotund man, beefy-cheeked and spectacled, with a jovial grin that was only skin deep.

'Well, well, captain,' he boomed, waddling forward with his hand extended, 'this is a pleasure.'

MacBride shook and said, 'Not so much, Shanz. You've got to bust up this picnic.'

Shanz's grin faded. 'How's this?'

'The ball is over,' explained MacBride. 'There's trouble brewing and it's liable to boil over any minute.'

'But I got to make a speech,' argued Shanz. 'And Alderman Bedell is due here now.' He looked at his watch. 'He's going to make a speech, too.'

'I don't give a damn! You're not going to broadcast and neither is Bedell. I tell you, Shanz, this block-party scheme is the bunk. It's the best way I know of to start a riot.'

'Do you say that, heh, because you favor the opposition? Ha, I know where your sympathy lays, captain!'

'Don't be a fool! I just got a tip that Bedell's set to get bumped off, and it's not going to happen in my precinct.'

Shanz leaned back and threw out his chest. 'What is the police for? What are you for?'

'I've got a hunch I'm supposed to side-track crime. I'm no master mind, Shanz. I don't go in for solving riddles. I'm just a cop who tries to beat crime to the tape. Now don't stick out your belly and hand me an argument. I'm not in the mood.'

Shanz was troubled. 'I can't stop it. If I do that and Bedell can't make his speech he'll land on me. Wait till he comes. Talk to him. But I ain't going to call it off. We staged this so Bedell could make a speech.'

MacBride, impatient, cracked fist into palm. 'Cripes, I want to clear this crowd out before Bedell gets here! I told you he's not going to make a speech. I won't let him.'

The dance number stopped. But from the distance came the sound of another band, with brass and drums in the majority. It drew nearer with the minutes, and then a string of cars appeared, flaunting banners that exalted the virtues of the Anderson-Connaught combine. Colored torches smoked from every machine, and the roving campaigners cheered their candidates lustily.

'What in hell is this?' roared Shanz, reddening.

'Competition,' said MacBride.

The automobiles stopped, and the brass band attained new heights of noise commingled with the singing voices of the men. The carnival orchestra, not to be outdone, burst into action, hammering out a military march. The result was boisterous, maddening, and everybody began yelling.

The first symptoms of mob hysteria were apparent.

MacBride snapped quick orders to the policemen. 'Chase this crowd! The dance is over!'

He pivoted sharply, set his jaw and plowed through the crowd on a bee-line for the leaders of the parade.

'You move on!' he barked. 'Come on, no stalling. Get out of here, and I mean now!'

'Aw, go fly a kite,' came a bibulous retort. 'Everybody havin' helluva good time. Who's all right? Hiram Anderson, the next State's Attorney's all right! Y-e-e-e-e!'

Others took up the cry. Somebody flung a bottle and it crashed against a house front, the glass spattering.

'Dammit,' yelled MacBride, 'you're starting a riot! Get a move on!'

One of the cars started moving. Others honked their horns. Many of the occupants had piled out and several of them, far gone with walloping liquor, hilarious as sailors on a spree, were trying to tear down the banners of the Krug-Bedell faction. The supporters of Alderman Bedell objected strenuously, and fists began flying about promiscuously. It was, now, anybody's and everybody's carnival. Admission fees were waived. The two bands continued to add to the din and clamor. The tempo of their combined efforts went far toward heightening the strain of hysteria that had taken hold of the mob. The streets were jammed with motor cars, and the horns honked and bleated.

Women screeched, and men began striking out without apparent provocation. The crowd surged this way and that, but never got anywhere. Nightsticks rapped more frequently on stubborn heads. Somebody heaved a brick that crashed through an automobile windshield and knocked the man at the wheel unconscious. The machine swerved, bounded and banged head-on into a doorway.

'Good God Almighty!' groaned MacBride.

He plunged through the mob, fought, pounded, hammered his way to the big touring car that carried the musicians. He leaped to the running-board, wrenched a trombone from the player's hand.

'Stop it!' he yelled. 'I'll cave in the next mouth that pulls another toot!'

He silenced them.

He turned and weaved toward the bandstand, and on the way ran into Alderman Bedell.

'Who started this, MacBride? What is it? What's going on?'

'What the hell does it look like, a May party?'

'Don't get sore – don't get sore!'

'Listen to me, Bedell!' MacBride gripped his arm hard. 'You're no friend of mine, but I'm giving you a tip. Get out of here! Jump in your car, go home and lock all the doors. Some pup is out to get you!'

'He is, eh?' snarled Bedell, a big whale of a man with gimlet eyes. 'Let him!'

'Don't be a blockhead all your life! I tell you, man, you're in danger!' A whiff of Bedell's breath told him the man had been drinking. Drink always made Bedell cocky, and he spoke best from a platform when he was moderately soaked.

'I'm going to d'liver a speech here tonight, MacBride—'

MacBride snorted with disgust and went on his way. He reached the bandstand and ripped the baton from the leader's hand. He kicked over the drum and shot out short, sizzling commands. He left a silenced bandstand.

The policemen had managed to club into submission the instigators of the riot. Swollen heads, black eyes and bruised jaws were in abundance. The best argument in a riot is a deftly wielded nightstick. A clout on the head is something a temporarily crazed man will understand.

The hysteria was dwindling. A dozen of the rioters were hastily escorted away from the scene by four policemen and taken to the station house. The crowd quieted, took a long breath generally, and waited.

MacBride climbed back upon the bandstand, rumbled the drum in plea for silence, and then raised his voice.

'Please, now, everybody go home!' he demanded. 'The party is over. It's too bad, but nothing can be done.' He waved his arms. 'Clear out, everybody – now!'

A figure bulked at his elbow. It was that of Alderman Bedell, and before MacBride could get a word in edgewise, Bedell roared, 'La-dies and gentlemen, it grieves me to see this sociable gathering break up because of the undignified actions of the hirelings – yes, hirelings, I say – of the party which is trying to drive me out of office. As alderman of this district, I want to say – I . . . ugh!'

He clapped a hand to his chest, swayed, then crumpled heavily at MacBride's feet.

'Heart attack,' cried someone in the crowd.

MacBride knelt down, turned the alderman over, felt his chest, ran his hand inside the shirt. It came out stained with blood. Bedell twitched, stiffened, and was dead.

Cohen said over MacBride's shoulder, 'Headlines, Mac, in the first edition. Hot diggity damn!'

III

An hour later MacBride stood spread-legged in his office at the station house. His coat was unbuttoned, his hair was tousled, and his lean cheeks looked a little drawn.

Among the others present were Committeeman Shanz, Trixie Meloy, Moriarity and Cohen, and the inevitable Kennedy. No one had been apprehended. No shot had been heard. Obviously a silencer had been used on the gun that sent Bedell to his death. Bedell's body was at the morgue being probed by the deputy medical examiner.

'Now look here, Miss Meloy,' MacBride said. 'You say you were standing on Jackson Street near Holly. You saw a man wearing a light gray suit and a gray cap drift down Holly, get into a car and drive off when Bedell was shot. Why didn't you yell out?'

'Does a lady go shoutin' out like that?' she retorted, tossing her peroxide bob. 'Besides I didn't know what it was all about. I didn't know he was shot. I thought he fainted or something. I didn't connect the two up until I heard you yell he was killed. Then I thought of the other man.'

'In that case, how does it happen you remember what he wore?'

'Well, I got an eye for nice clothes. He was dressed swell, that's why. A woman notices clothes more than a man does.'

'Remember the car?'

'Not so good. It wasn't so near. It looked like a roadster.'

'How about the man – besides his clothes?'

'I didn't see his face – only his back as he was walkin' away.'

'I see. You're a friend of Tony Bonelio's, aren't you?'

'Yes. Antonio's a good friend of mine.'

'My mistake. Antonio.' He smiled drily. 'How come Antonio wasn't at the dance with you?'

'He was at his night-club. I never seen a block party, so I come down to look it over. Mr. Shanz here invited me. He's a friend of Antonio's.'

'Yes, that's right,' put in Shanz.

'And listen,' said Trixie, looking at her strap-watch. 'I got to dance at the Palmetto Club tonight.'

'All right, Miss Meloy. You run along. Keep in mind, though, that I may want to ask you more questions.'

Shanz stood up. 'I'll take Miss Meloy to the club in my car,' he said.

'Suit yourself,' shrugged MacBride. 'Maybe this'll be a lesson to you about block parties.'

'It cooks the Anderson-Connaught goose, too, captain,' replied Shanz. 'Connaught's a guy preaches a lot and then goes and hires gunmen.'

'Careful how you talk,' warned MacBride. 'If it was a gunman of Connaught's I'll nail him. But I've got a hunch it wasn't.'

'Then who was it?'

'If I could answer that right now, d' you think I'd be losing a night's sleep?'

'See you get him, anyhow. There's lots o' captains want this job here.'

'That's my worry, Shanz, not yours.'

'Well, I'm just telling you, see you get him.'

'See you mind your own business, too.'

Shanz and Trixie Meloy went out.

MacBride opened his desk and passed around the Hennessy. He downed a stiff bracer himself and lit a fresh cigar.

'Cripes,' he chuckled grimly, 'this'll mean one awful jolt to Connaught.

It'll be hard to believe that the guy got Bedell wasn't on Connaught's payroll.'

'If,' said Moriarity, 'we only knew who the guy was sent in that tip you got.'

'That's the hitch, Jake,' nodded MacBride. 'The guy who called up is the key to who killed Bedell.'

There was a knock on the door, and Officer Holstein looked in.

'Say, Cap, there's a Polack out here wants to see you. He lives on Jackson Street.'

At a nod from MacBride, an old man came in, fumbling with his hat.

'Hello,' said the captain. 'What's your name?'

'Ma name Tikorsky. I got somet'in' to tell. See, I live number t'ree-twent'-one Jackson, up de top floor. I look out de window, watch de show, see. When de big fellar drop down, I hear' – he looked up at the ceiling – 'I hear noise on de roof, like a man run, see.'

MacBride jerked up. 'You heard a man run across the roof?'

Tikorsky nodded.

'Is there a fire-escape back of where you live?'

'Yeah, sure.'

MacBride reached for the phone, called the morgue. In a moment he was speaking with the deputy medical examiner. When he hung up he pursed his lips, and his eyes glittered.

'All right, Mr. Tikorsky,' he said. 'You can go home. Thanks for telling me. I'll see you again.'

The Pole shuffled out.

MacBride looked at Kennedy. 'Out, Kennedy. Go home and hit the hay.'

'Ah, Mac, give a guy a break,' said Kennedy. 'What's in the wind?'

'A bad smell. Come on, breeze, now. When there's any news getting out, I'll let you know.'

Kennedy got up, shrugged, and sauntered out.

Moriarity and Cohen regarded the captain expectantly.

MacBride said, 'I just got the doctor's report. The bullet was a thirty-eight. It hit Bedell in the chest, knocked off part of his heart and lodged in his spine. But get this. The angle of the bullet was on a slant. It went in and *down*.'

'Then,' said Cohen, 'it couldn't have been fired from the corner where the broad saw this guy she was beefin' about.'

'No,' clipped MacBride. 'The Polack was right. He heard a guy on the roof. The guy who was on the roof bumped off Bedell.'

'What about this guy in the gray suit?'

'I'm wondering. But we know he couldn't have done it. A bullet from him would have gone up and hit Bedell on the left somewhere.' He tapped his foot on the floor. 'Well, the show is on, boys. Bonelio, the late alderman's buddy, has a whale of an excuse to oil his guns and start a war of his own.

And Krug, the State's Attorney, will give him protection. Bonelio will suspect the same guy we do.'

'Duveen,' said Moriarity.

'Exactly. I know just what the greaseball will do.'

'Let him,' suggested Cohen, with a yawn. 'Let the two gangs fight it out, exterminate each other. Who the hell cares?'

MacBride banged the desk. 'You would say that, Ike. But I'm responsible for this precinct. I've got one murder hanging over my head as it is. Personally, I wouldn't care if these two gangs did mop each other up. But in a gang war a lot of neutrals always get hurt.' He put on his hat. 'Let's look over the Polack's roof.'

The three of them went around to 321 Jackson Street, located the rooms where the old Pole lived, and then ascended to the roof. Moriarity had a flashlight. They discovered nothing to which they might attach some relative importance. They took the fire-escape down to a paved alley that paralleled the back of the row of houses and led to Holly Street.

'See here, boys,' MacBride said. 'Wander around and get the low-down on Duveen's gang. If you see Duveen, cross-examine him. Better yet, tell him I want to see him.'

The two detectives moved off. MacBride headed back for the station-house and requisitioned the precinct flivver. A man named Garret was his chauffeur. After brief instructions on MacBride's part, they drove off.

Twenty minutes later they stopped on Paradise Street, uptown. It was a thoroughfare of old brownstone houses that, following the slow encroachment of the white lights, had been turned into tearooms, night-clubs and small apartments, patronized mostly by people of the theatre.

Garret remained with the flivver. MacBride entered the Palmetto Club, to which an interior decorator had tried his best to give a tropical air. The manager did not know him, and said so.

'That's all right,' said MacBride. 'I don't want to see you, anyhow. Where's Bonelio?'

A moment later he met Bonelio in a private room handsomely furnished. Bonelio was a chunky Italian of medium height, dressed in the mode. He had smooth white skin, dark circles under his eyes, and an indolent gaze.

'Sit down, MacBride. Rye or Scotch?' he asked.

MacBride noticed a bottle of Golden Wedding. 'Rye,' he said.

'Ditto.' Bonelio poured the drinks, said, 'Well, poor Bedell.'

'What I came here about.'

They looked at each other as they downed their tots.

'About what?' Bonelio dropped on to a divan and lit a cigarette.

'Just this,' said MacBride. 'I'm banking on the hunch that you suspect who's behind the killing. I'm asking, and at the same time telling you, to keep out of it. We've never been friends, Bonelio, and don't get it into your nut that I'm making any overtures. But I don't want any rough work done in my precinct. I'll handle it according to the law. You just stand aside and keep your hands off. You get me?'

'Sure. But let me tell you, MacBride, that the first pup gets in my way or monkeys around my playground, I'll start trouble and I don't give a damn whose precinct it's in. I'm sitting on top of the world in Richmond City and no guy's going to horn in.'

'I'm telling you, Bonelio, walk lightly in my precinct. I'm giving you fair warning. I'm putting on the lid and I'm locking up any guy that so much as disturbs the peace. That goes for you and your gang as well as anybody else. You can sell all the booze you want. Much as I dislike you, I've never bothered your rum warehouses down by the railroad yards—'

'You were told not to. The big boys are my friends.'

'Don't take advantage of it. I could be nasty if I wanted to. And I will, if you butt in in my precinct.'

'Here's hoping you get Duveen for the murder of Bedell.'

'Make sure *you* don't try to!'

MacBride banged out, hopped into the flivver and Garret drove him back to the station-house.

Moriarity and Cohen were playing penny-ante, half-heartedly.

'What news?' asked MacBride.

'None,' said Cohen. 'Duveen hasn't been seen for the past week.'

'Hasn't, eh? All right, we want him, then. Sergeant,' he called to the man at the desk, 'ring Headquarters. General alarm. Chuck Duveen wanted. Ask Headquarters to spread the news and start the net working. I want Duveen before' – his lips flattened – 'before somebody else gets him.'

IV

Next day the papers carried big headlines. The sheets that were in sympathy with the current administration bellowed loudly and asked the public to consider the drastic measures used by the opposition to gain its own end. The others, among them the *Free Press*, employed a calmer, more detached tone, and pleaded with justice to get at the root of all evil. Both Anderson and Connaught, aspirants for the offices of State's Attorney and alderman of the Sixth Election District respectively, deplored the tragedy and promised all manner of aid in running down the person or persons who had murdered their opponent, the late Alderman Bedell. State's Attorney Krug promised quick action in the event the criminal was apprehended. Charges and counter charges ran rampant.

MacBride, having gone home at three in the morning, did not get back on the job until noon. He felt rested and his clean-clipped face glowed ruddily from recent contact with lather and razor. He had read the papers on the way in from Grove Manor with the attitude of a man who knows the inner workings of politics and newspaperdom. In short, a slight morsel of what he read was worthwhile, and the rest was bunk – salve for an outraged public.

The one item that drew his attention was anent the fact that Adolph Shanz was to run for alderman in place of the late Alderman Bedell. This made him chuckle bitterly. As committeeman Shanz had been, ever since he was elected, clay in the hands of Krug and Bedell. If elected for alderman, he would be one of Krug's most pliable tools.

The police net was spread for Duveen. The city was combed up, down and across. But the man was not caught. The only information available, gleaned as it was from old familiar hangouts of the gang boss, showed that Duveen had not been seen for a week. A day passed, and then two and three, with the man still at large.

Wherefore, on the fourth day, Captain MacBride was convened for a solid hour with the Commissioner of Police, a man who ran the Department and gave quarter nowhere. The meeting took place in the morning, and before noon MacBride was back in the station-house. There he held a brief consultation with his assistants.

In conclusion, he said to the sergeant at the desk, 'When Kennedy, or any other of his breed drifts in, tell him I have a statement for the press.'

Alone in his office, he drank his first bracer and started his first cigar of the day. He chafed his hands vigorously, paced the floor with a little more than his customary energy, trailing banners of excellent cigar smoke behind him. A beam of sunlight streamed through the open window. On the telephone wires that passed behind the old station-house, birds were swaying and chirping. MacBride's eyes were keen and narrow with thought.

An hour later, when he was writing at his desk, a knock sounded on the door.

'Come in,' he yelled.

Kennedy came in. 'What the hell's this I hear about—'

'Sit down. Glad to see something can work you up and make you look as if you weren't dying on your feet.'

'Come on, spill it, Mac!'

'My wife's birthday.'

'Cripes—'

'Should see the new spring outfit I bought her. Kennedy, she gets younger every day. Well' – he cleared his throat with a serio-comic air – 'look who her husband is.'

'For the love o' God, what's the matter, are you batty?'

MacBride grinned – one of his rare, broad grins that few people knew, outside of his wife and daughter.

'All right, Kennedy,' he said. 'I said I'd give you a break when I started broadcasting. I'm broadcasting. Tune in. Early this morning Detective Moriarity picked up a man for violating the state law regarding the possession of concealed weapons. This man was carrying an automatic pistol.

'He was cross-examined by Captain Stephen J. MacBride – don't omit the J. Intense questioning brought out certain interesting facts, in the light of which Captain MacBride hopes to apprehend – and don't insert "it is alleged" – Captain MacBride hopes to apprehend the man who killed the late Alderman Bedell within the next twenty-four hours.

'For certain reasons known to the Department alone, the informant's name will not be divulged for the present. Suffice it to say that during the course of the cross-examination it was learned that this man was the one who phoned anonymously to Captain MacBride about one hour before Alderman Bedell was murdered, warning him that the murder was prearranged.'

He rubbed his hands together. 'How does that sound? Pretty good for a plain, ordinary cop, eh? And I never took a correspondence course, either.'

'But who's this guy you picked up?' demanded Kennedy.

'You heard me, didn't you? He's under lock and key right here in the precinct. Put that in, too, Kennedy. He's locked up at the precinct. But who he is – that's my business for the time being. Headquarters is standing by me to the bitter end on that. Now pipe down and consider yourself lucky I've given you this much. Here, sink a drink under your belt and see that story gets good space.'

Still curious, Kennedy, nevertheless, went out. Within the hour other reporters got the story. It would be on the streets at four that afternoon.

Moriarity dropped in, when MacBride was alone, and asked, 'Think it will work, Cap?'

'Man, oh, man, I'm banking everything on it right now. It's a bluff – sure, a hell of a big bluff. And if it doesn't trap somebody or give me a decent lead I'll take the razz. Just now the underworld is stagnant, Jake. This will be the stone that stirs the water. We're supposed to have somebody here who knows who killed Bedell. Whoever killed him, will make a move. What that move will be, I don't know, but I'm ready to meet it.'

Moriarity was frankly dubious. 'Dunno, Cap. Maybe I'm short on imagination. You're taking a long chance giving out the news we got a mysterious somebody picked up and locked in.'

'I'm willing to take it, Jake. It's a bluff – the biggest bluff I ever pulled in my life. Just play with me, Jake. Appear mysterious. All you've got to keep saying is that you picked a guy up – but no more. I've got all the keys to that cell and nobody, I don't care who he is, is going to see that it's empty.'

'Gawd,' muttered Moriarity, 'I hope you don't get showed up.'

'That's all right, Jake. Cut out worrying. Just play your part, and if the breaks go against us, I'll take the razz personally.'

Moriarity wandered out, far from overjoyed.

At four the news spread. Quick work, mused many – an important prisoner in the hands of the police already, with the account of the murder still vivid in the city's mind. And the mysterious tone of it; that was intriguing, MacBride holding the man's name a secret.

MacBride read three different sheets.

The *Free Press* mentioned his name more than the others. That was Kennedy's work. Good sort, Kennedy, even though he did get on a man's nerves at times. Kennedy's column was well-written, concise, cool, almost laconic.

At four-thirty a big limousine pulled up before the station-house. State's Attorney Krug, a large, faultlessly groomed man, innately arrogant, strode into MacBride's office swinging his stick savagely.

'Look here, Captain,' he rapped out, 'what is the meaning of this? I refer to the late editions, and to this fellow Moriarity picked up.'

'What does what mean?' MacBride wanted to know, unperturbed.

Krug struck the floor with his stick. 'Why, as State's Attorney of this county, I think it is no more than pertinent that I should be informed of such important news before it comes out in the newspapers.'

'Dark secret, Mr. Krug,' said MacBride. 'The Department's prisoner. When we get through with him, we'll turn him over to the State Attorney's office.'

'But I should like to have a preliminary talk with the fellow, so that I may go about preparing briefs. I tell you, Captain, action is what is necessary.'

'I agree with you. But as it is, Mr. Krug, the prisoner is still in the Department's hands.'

'Nonsense! We can have just an informal little chat. I want to see the fellow. What is he called, by the way?'

MacBride shook his head. 'The whole thing is a dark secret. When I spring it, everybody'll know.'

'But dammit, man, I am State's Attorney! I demand to interview the prisoner!'

'I ought to add,' put in MacBride, 'that I have the backing of the Department. There's the phone if you care to call the Commissioner.'

State's Attorney Krug departed in high heat, bewailing the fact that the Department was trying to double-cross the very efficient State's Attorney's office.

'You know why he's in such a hurry, Jake?' MacBride asked Moriarity.

'Sure. Stage a fast trial, get a quick conviction. It'd help him for re-election.'

MacBride chuckled grimly. Moriarity drifted out, leaving the captain alone.

It was about half an hour later that the door swung open, and a tall, broad-shouldered man entered casually. He kicked the door shut with his heel, stood with his hands thrust into his coat pockets, a cigarette drooping from one corner of his mouth. His face was deeply bronzed, his eyes pale and hard as agate.

'My error,' he said, 'if I didn't knock. Thought I'd drop in and see why you've been looking for me.'

'Sit down, Duveen.'

'I'll stand.'

MacBride leaned back in his chair. 'Are you heeled?'

'No. Want to look?'

'I'll take your word. But you've got one hell of a lot of nerve to come in here.'

'Open to the public, ain't it? Duveen gushed smoke through his nostrils. 'I want to know what's all this crack about you looking for me.'

'Where have you been for the last ten days?'

'I don't see where that's any of your business. I was touring. I took a ride to Montreal. Get up on your dates, skipper. I've been gone two weeks. Scouting around for good liquor. Got two truckloads coming down for the election – and afterwards.'

'Counting on Anderson and Connaught getting in?'

'Yup.'

'Won't do you any good. Connaught's going to clean up this district, and you'll never be able to buy off Anderson.'

'All I want is the bum Krug out. Well, you were looking for me. Here I am.'

'About that Bedell killing.'

'What about it?'

'You'll need a strong alibi to prove where you were on that night, Duveen.'

'Talking of – arrest?'

'About that.'

Duveen laughed. 'Not a chance, MacBride. Krug would frame me so tight I'd never have a chance. Guess again.'

'Nevertheless. . . .' MacBride's hand moved toward the row of buttons on the desk.

Duveen snapped, '*Kid!*'

'Up high, Cap!' hissed a voice at the window.

MacBride swivelled. A rat-faced runt was leaning in through the open window, an automatic trained on the captain.

Duveen ran to the window, stepped out. There was an economy of words. With a leer, the rat-faced man disappeared.

MacBride yanked his gun, blew a whistle.

The reserves, Moriarity and Cohen came on the run. They swept out, guns drawn.

But the city swallowed Duveen and his gunman.

MacBride took the blow silently, choking down his chagrin.

'Did he wear a gray suit?' asked Moriarity.

'Yes,' muttered MacBride. 'Block all city exits, place men in the railroad station. Tell Headquarters to inform all outlying precincts and booths, motorcycle and patrol flivvers, Duveen's in town. What I can't understand is, why the hell he came strolling in here?'

'Crust, Cap. Duveen's got more gall, more nerve, than any bum I know of. Probably came looking for information.'

'Yes, and I pulled a bone,' confessed MacBride. 'I should have played him a while, drawn him out. But seeing him here, I wanted to get the clamps on him right away. He had no gun – he's wise. But he had a gunman planted outside the window. If I can get him, get this Trixie Meloy gal to identify him as the man walked down Holly Street toward the roadster, we can crash his alibi. We know he couldn't have fired the shot, but it's likely one of his rats was planted on the roof, and Duveen was on hand to see things went off as per schedule.'

An hour later the telephone rang.

'MacBride?'

The captain thought fast. 'No. You want him?'

'Yes.'

'Wait a minute.'

MacBride dived into the central room, barked, 'Sergeant, call the telephone exchange – quick – see where this guy's calling from.'

The sergeant whipped into action, had the report in less than a minute. 'Booth number three at the railroad waiting room.'

'Good. Call the Information Desk at the railroad. Cohen's there. Tell him to nab the guy comes out of booth three. Fast!'

The sergeant put the call through, snapped a brief order to Detective Cohen.

MacBride was on the way back into his office. He stood before the desk, looked at his watch. He would give Cohen two minutes. The two minutes ticked off. He picked up the instrument, drawled 'MacBride speaking.'

'Just a tip, MacBride. Your station-house is going to be blown up. If you're clever, you'll get the guys. Sometime tonight.'

That was all.

MacBride hung up, sat back, his fists clenched, his eyes glued on the instrument.

V

Who was the man behind the voice? Who was he double-crossing, and why?

MacBride went into the central room, called out four reserves. 'Look here, boys,' he said. 'I've got a tip somebody's going to try to blow up this place. One of you at each end of the block, the other two in the back. Let no machines come through the street. No people, either. Make 'em detour. Anybody around the back, pick him up. Anybody tries to hand you an argument, get rough. All right, go to it.'

He went back into his office, clasped his hands behind his back and paced the floor.

Twenty minutes later the door opened. Cohen came in with a man. The man was a little disarranged. His natty clothes were dusty and his modish neckwear was askew. His derby had a dent in it, and wrath smoldered in his black eyes. Slim and lithe he was, olive skinned, with long, trick sideburns that put him in the category familiarly known as 'Sheik.'

Cohen's explanation was simple. 'He tried to argue, Cap.'

MacBride rubbed his hands together briskly. The mysterious informant was in his hands. His enormous bluff, recently put into print, that he had a valuable suspect in connection with the murder of Bedell, had worked out admirably.

'What's your name?' he asked.

'I'm not telling,' snapped the high-strung stranger, struggling for dignity.

'I want to thank you for those tips,' went on MacBride, 'but I want to know more. Now cut out the nonsense.'

'I'm not telling,' reiterated the stranger. 'It was a dirty trick, getting me this way. If those guys knew I'd been tipping you off, my life wouldn't be worth a cent.'

'You tell me your name,' proceeded MacBride, 'and I'll promise to keep your name mum until the whole show is over.'

'That's out. I don't want your promise. I didn't do anything. I'm not a gangster. I was just trying to help you out and keep my name out of it at the same time. It wouldn't do you any good to hold me. I've got no record. I didn't do anything.'

MacBride told him to sit down, then said, 'I'm sorry we had to grab you, buddy, but I've got a lot to answer for, and I've no intentions of getting tough with you. Just come across.'

The man was losing his dignity rapidly. His black eyes darted about feverishly, his fingers writhed, his breath came in short little gasps. Fear was flickering across his face, not fear of MacBride, but of something or someone else. Mixed with the fear, was a hint of anguish.

'Please,' he pleaded, 'let me go. My God, if I'd thought it would come to this, that I'd be picked up, have my name spread around, I'd never have tipped you off. Give me a chance, Captain. Let me go. I told you this place is going to be blown up tonight.'

'Who's going to blow it up?'

'Don't make me tell that! God, don't. I guess I've been a fool, but I – I— Oh, hell!' He choked on a hoarse sob. 'I told you what's going to happen. Lay for them. Get them when they try to blow you up. You'll learn everything then.'

'Why have you been tipping me off?'

'I – for many reasons. A grudge, but behind the grudge – something else. It's been driving me crazy. Haven't been able to sleep. I was going to kill –

but – I didn't.' He raised his hands and shook them. 'I'm lost, Captain, if you keep me, if you let loose who tipped you off. Dear God, give me a break – won't you?'

He leaned forward, extending his hands, pleading with his dark eyes, his face lined with agony.

MacBride bit him with an unwavering stare. What tragedy was in this fellow's life? He was sincere, that was certain. Something terrible was gnawing at his soul, making of him a shivering, palsied wreck, pleading eloquently for mercy.

'I don't want anybody to know I've been in this,' he hurried on. 'It's not only my life's at stake, it's something else – something bigger and deeper. Don't make me explain. I can't. Isn't it enough I warned you about this – this bombing?'

MacBride looked down at the desk, tapped his fingers meditatively. Then he looked up. 'I'll give you a break,' he said. 'I'm going to lock you up for the night. If I get the men I want, you slide out quietly, and my mysterious informant remains a mystery. That's a promise. If Cohen here can find a Bible, I'll swear on it.'

'Not a Bible in the whole dump,' said Cohen.

The stranger was on his feet. 'You promise, Captain? You will promise me that?'

'I've promised,' nodded MacBride.

'Thanks. God, thanks! I've heard you were a hard-boiled egg. I – I didn't expect—'

'Pipe down. Ike,' he said to Cohen, 'lock him up and keep your jaw tight about what's just happened.'

Cohen took the man out, and MacBride leaned back to sigh and light a fresh cigar, musing, 'Maybe I ought to get kicked in the pants for making that promise. But I think the guy's hard-hit.'

Half an hour later he was visited by State's Attorney Krug. Krug was pompous. 'What are the latest developments, Captain?'

'Got some dope this joint is going to be blown up. You better get on your way.'

Krug's eyes dilated. 'Blown up!'

'Right.'

'Then why don't you clear out?'

'See me clearing out for a lot of bums like that!'

'But this fellow you've got – this mystery man. Hadn't you better get him out of here? Don't you realize that it is possible they intend blowing up the place so that the man will be exterminated? Dead, he can give no evidence. I say, Captain, you ought to turn him over to me. Consider that I am eager to start a trial. We can use him, put the blame on him temporarily, at least make some headway. Come, now.'

MacBride shook his head. 'Nothing doing, Mr. Krug.'

'This,' stormed Krug, indignantly, 'is monstrous!'

'If I were you, I'd get out of the neighborhood. Hell knows when these birds will show up. You don't want to follow in Bedell's footsteps, do you?'

'Damn my stars, you are impossible!' With that Krug banged out.

The echoes of his departure had barely died when Kennedy wandered in.

'How about some more news, Mac?'

'Thanks for mentioning my name so much in your write-up,' replied MacBride. 'When there's more news, you'll get it.'

'Meaning there's none now.'

'How clever you are!'

'Applesauce!'

'On your way, Kennedy.'

'I'm comfortable.'

'You won't be if you hang around here much longer. Now cut out the boloney, old timer. I'm busy, there's no news, and you're in my way.'

Kennedy regarded him whimsically. 'When you talk that way, Mac, I know there's something in the wind. All right, I'll toddle along.' He coughed behind his hand. 'By the way, I intended buying some smokes on the way over, but—'

MacBride hauled out his cigar box, and Kennedy, helping himself to a cigar, sniffed it as he sauntered to the door.

'I wish you'd keep 'em a little moist, Mac,' he ventured.

He was gone before MacBride could throw him a verbal hot-shot.

The captain put on his visored cap, strode into the central room, looked around and then went out into the street. At the corner he paused for a brief chat with the policemen stationed there.

'Everything okay, boys?'

'So far, Cap.'

'Keep a sharp lookout. If it comes, it will come suddenly.'

The men nodded, fingering their nightsticks gingerly. A street light shone on their brass buttons, on their polished shields. Beneath their visors, their faces were tense and alert.

MacBride made a tour of the block, and then through the alley in the rear. Everything was calm, every man was in readiness. They spoke in voices a trifle bated. They exuded an air of tense expectancy, peering keenly into the shadows, moving on restless feet.

As MacBride swung back into the central room he almost banged into the desk sergeant.

'Just about to call you, Cap,' the sergeant puffed. 'Holstein and Gunther just picked up a touring car with three guys, and a machine-gun and half-a-dozen grenades.'

'Where?' MacBride shot back.

'Down near the railroad yards. They were coming north and stopped to fix a flat. Holstein and Gunther are bringing 'em in.'

'Good!' exploded MacBride, and punched a hole in the atmosphere. 'By George, that's good.'

Moriarity and Cohen were grinning. 'Looks like them guys got one bum break,' chuckled Moriarity.

'Sure does, boys!'

MacBride strode up and down the room grinning from ear to ear. He kept banging fist into palm boisterously. He was elated.

A little later there was a big touring car outside, and a deal of swearing and rough-housing. MacBride went out, and found Holstein and Gunther man-handling three roughnecks. Kennedy was there, having popped up from nowhere.

'Knew something was in the wind, Mac,' he chortled.

'You'll get plenty of headlines now, Kennedy,' flung back the captain.

Patrolman Gunther said, 'Nasty mutts, these guys, Cap. One of 'em tried to pull his rod and I opened his cheek.'

'G' on, yuh big louse!' snarled that guy.

'I'll shove your teeth down your throat!' growled Gunther, raising his stick.

'All inside,' clipped MacBride.

The roughs were bustled into the central room. A reserve carried in the grenades and the machine-gun. There was a noticeable lack of politeness on the part of the three gangsters. Also, there was noticeable lack of gentleness on the part of the policemen. One of the gunmen, a big, surly towhead, was loudest of all, despite the gash on his cheek. He started to make a pass at Gunther, but MacBride caught him by the shoulder, spun him around and slammed him down upon a chair.

'That'll be all from you, Hess,' he ripped out warmly. 'I guess we're near the bottom of things now.'

'Who is he?' asked Kennedy.

'"Slugger" Hess, Duveen's strong-arm man.'

'Hot diggity damn!'

'Now where's Duveen?' MacBride flung at Hess. 'I want that guy. Every damn gangster in this burg is going to get treated rough. Now you come clean or you get the beating of your life!'

'And I'd like to do it, Cap,' put in Gunther.

'Yah, yuh big hunk of tripe!' snarled Hess.

'Can that!' barked MacBride. 'Where's Duveen?'

Hess was not soft-boiled. Despite the roomful of policemen, he stuck out his jaw. 'Go find him, Captain. You can't bulldoze me, neither you nor that pup Gunther!'

'Where's Duveen?' MacBride had a dangerous look in his eyes, and his doubled fists were swinging at his sides.

'You heard me the first time.'

Gunther flexed his hands. 'Should I sweat him, cap?'

'Sweat the three of them,' said MacBride. 'In my office. Ike, Jake, you'll help,' he added to Moriarity and Cohen.

Eager hands took hold of the three gangsters and propelled them toward MacBride's office.

But before they reached the door there was a terrific explosion, and the walls billowed and crashed.

VI

Stone, splinters, plaster, beams thundered down. Yells and screams commingled with the tumult of toppling walls and ceilings. Lights were snuffed out. The roof, or what remained of it, boomed down. There were cries for help, groans, oaths. Tongues of flame leaped about, crackling.

MacBride found himself beneath a beam, an upturned table, and an assortment of other debris. Near him somebody was swearing violently.

'That you, Jake?'

'Yeah, Cap . . . if I can get this damn hunk of ceiling off my chest. . . . '

MacBride squirmed, twisted, heaved. He jackknifed his legs and knocked aside the table. He brushed powdered plaster from his eyes, spat it from his mouth. The beam was harder. It was wedged down at both ends by other weighty debris, and MacBride could not shove it off.

But he twisted his body from side to side, backed up bit by bit, finally won free and stood up. His face was bloody, the sleeve of his right arm was torn from shoulder to elbow. He did not know it. He stumbled toward the pinioned Moriarity, freed him from the weighty debris pressing upon him and helped him to the sidewalk.

Going back in, he ran into Cohen. Ike was carrying a semi-conscious desk sergeant.

A crowd had already gathered. People came on the run from all directions. Somebody had pulled the fire-alarm down the block. The flames were growing. From a crackling sound they had been whipped into a dull roar.

Two battered but otherwise able policemen came out and MacBride sent them to chase away the crowd. Blocks away fire-engines were clanging, sirens were screaming. The policemen fought with the crowd, drove it back down the street. MacBride and Cohen were busy carrying out those they were able to pry from beneath the debris.

The first fire-engine came booming around the corner, snorted to a stop, bell clanging. Helmeted fire-fighters with drawn axes ran for the building. A couple of flashlights blinked. The big searchlight on the fire-engine swung around and played its beams on the demolished station-house. The firemen stormed into the mass of wreckage, hacked their way through to the pinioned men.

MacBride plowed back into the cell where the mysterious stranger had been placed a few hours before. He had trouble finding him. The man was deep beneath the wreckage. MacBride ran out, got an axe and came back to chop his way through. He carried out a limp dead weight.

Other engines came roaring upon the scene. There was a din of ringing bells, hooting motors, loud commands. Hose was being strung out. Streams of water began shooting upon the building, roaring and hissing. A grocery store down the street was used to shelter the injured men, all of whom had been taken from the building. An ambulance was on the way.

MacBride and Cohen were bending over the stranger. He was a mass of bruises, scarce able to breathe, let alone talk.

'Guess . . . I'm . . . dying,' he whispered, his eyes closed, his body twitching with pain.

'The hell you are!' said MacBride. 'We'll have an ambulance here in a minute.'

'Don't . . . tell.' He struggled for breath, then choked. 'Two ten . . . Jockey Street. . . . Get 'em!' Then he fainted.

One of the gangsters was dead. The two others had escaped in the wild mêlée.

Kennedy was alive, though pretty much the worse for wear. He was hatless, covered with soot and grime, one eyes closed, a welt on his forehead. He limped, too, but he was not daunted.

'What next, Mac?'

MacBride turned. 'God, Kennedy, you look rotten!'

'Feel rotten. I'd like to find the guy put his heel on my eye. I'm out of smokes. Who's got a butt?'

Moriarity had one.

The battalion chief for the fire department came up. 'Hello, Mac. Bomb, eh? Yeah, I know. I've just been around. It was pitched through a window in the back.' He looked up. 'Good-bye, station-house, Mac!'

Even as he said this the front swayed, caved in with a smother of smoke, cinders and flame. Firemen rushed to escape the deluge. The hose lines pounded the place with water.

Detective Cohen appeared, with a bad wrist – his left hand.

'Where you been, Ike?' asked MacBride.

'Looking around. Guy in a cigar store around the corner said he was looking out the window a few minutes before the fireworks. Saw a big blue sedan roll by slow. He noticed because it's a one-way alley and classy machines don't often go through it. Runs back of the station-house, you know – Delaney Street.'

'See here, boys.' MacBride's voice was tense. 'You all well heeled? Good. We're going to take a ride up to 210 Jockey Street, and I smell trouble. There's something here I don't understand. We were caught napping. I'll say I was – I'm the dumb-bell. There I thought I had the case all ready to bake, and we were blown up.'

He found Lieutenant Connolly and gave him brief orders. He gathered together six reserves and Moriarity and Cohen. They used the big touring car in which Hess and the other two gangsters had been brought to the precinct. Gunther drove, and as he was about to slide into gear, Kennedy came up on the run.

'Room there for me, Mac?'

MacBride groaned. Getting rid of Kennedy was like getting rid of a leech. But taking a look at Kennedy, seeing him all banged up but still ready to carry on, the captain experienced a change of heart.

'Hop in,' he clipped.

The big machine lurched ahead. Once in high gear the eight cylinders purred smoothly.

Two left turns and a right, and they were on a wide street that led north. In the distance the reflection of the white light district glowed in the sky. Ten men were in the car. There was no room for comfort.

The white light district grew nearer.

MacBride and his men ignored traffic lights. They struck Jockey Street. Jockey Street is like a cave. At one end it is lit by the glare of the theatrical district. As one penetrates it, it becomes darker, narrower, and the street lamps are pallid. Two and three-story houses rear into the gloom, lights showing here and there, but not in abundance. Most of the doors are blank-faced, foreboding. It is a thickly populated section, but pedestrians are rare. More than one man has been killed in lower Jockey Street. Patrolmen always travel it in pairs.

The machine stopped.

'Two ten's on the next block,' said MacBride. 'We'll leave the car here. Gunther, you and Barnes go over one block south and come up in the rear. Hang around there in case anybody tries to get out. The rest of us will try the front.'

They all alighted. Gunther and Barnes, their sticks drawn, their pistols loose in their holsters, started off purposefully. MacBride, though he saw no one, had a vague feeling that eyes were watching him from darkened windows. People might have been curious in Jockey Street, like all humanity, but they differed materially in that they rarely came into the open to vent their curiosity.

As the men walked down the street, their footsteps re-echoed hollowly; a nightstick clicked against another. MacBride led the way, a jut to his jaw, his fingers curled up in his palms. Home, in peaceful Grove Manor, his wife was probably mending socks. Maybe his daughter was playing the piano; something about Spring from Mendelssohn or one of those Indian love lyrics. Well, he carried lots of insurance.

How about the men with him? Most of them married, too, with little kids. Moriarity, Cohen, Feltmann, Terchinsky, O'Toole, Pagliano. Gunther and Barnes in the back. Two hundred a month for the privilege of being a target for gunmen. They made far less – and paid double the life insurance premium – than many a man whose most important worry was a cold in the head or the temperature of his morning bath.

'This is it,' said MacBride.

Kennedy said, 'Dump.'

'You stay out of it, Kennedy.'

'If you've got a pen-knife I'll sit out here and play mumble-peg on the pavement.'

In front of the house, which was a two-story affair built of red brick, was a depression reached by four stone steps that led down to the basement windows. At a word from MacBride, the men hid in this depression. A single step led to the front and main entrance, where there was a vestibule with glass in the upper half.

Alone, MacBride approached this, tried the door, and finding it locked, pressed a bell button. Somewhere distant he heard the bell ring. He took off his cap of rank and held it under his left arm, partly to hide his identity. His teeth were set, his lips compressed. He rang again.

Presently he heard a latch click. It was on the inner door. There was a long moment before a face moved dimly in the gloom behind the vestibule window. MacBride made a motion to open the door. The face floated nearer, receded, remained motionless, then came nearer again. Then it disappeared abruptly. The inner door banged. He heard running feet.

'We crash it, boys!' he barked in a low voice.

His revolver came out. One blow shattered the glass in the vestibule. He reached in, snapped back the latch. His men swarmed about him. He leaped into the vestibule, tried the next door. It was locked, built entirely of wood.

'All together, boys,' he clipped.

En masse, they surged against the door. Again they surged. Wood creaked, groaned, then splintered. The door banged up under the impetus, and the law swept in. MacBride had a flashlight. It clicked into life, its beam leaped through the gloom. He turned.

'Holstein and Feltmann! Guard the front!'

'Yup, cap!'

His flashlight swung up and down, back and forth, showed a stairway against one wall, leading to regions above. In the lower hall, he saw two closed doors.

'Bust these!'

He was the first to leap. The first door opened easily. The room was bare, unfurnished. He dived out and tried the next. It was unlocked. Empty. But it was meagerly furnished; a cot, a table, a rocking-chair, a gas stove.

'Lookout's room,' he speculated. 'Guy who came to the door.'

Sentences, words, were clipped.

The flashlight's beam picked out the foot of the stairway.

'Up, boys!'

MacBride was off on the run. He led the way up the stairs.

Came two gun reports, muffled.

'Gunther and Barnes,' he said. 'These guys are trying for a break.'

They were in the hall above. The first door they tried was locked. MacBride hurled his weight against it.

Bang!

A shot splintered the panel, passed the captain's cheek. He sprang back.

Moriarity, leaning against the bannister, shot from the hip. He plastered four shots around the doorknob. Pagliano put three more there. Then they waited, silent, all guns drawn. They listened. Men were moving inside the room. There was an undertone of voices.

MacBride turned to Cohen, 'Ike, go downstairs and get the chair in that room.'

Cohen departed, returned carrying a heavy kitchen chair. MacBride took a chair, hefted it, then swung it over his head and dived with it toward the door. The chair splintered; so did the door. A couple of shots banged from the inside. MacBride felt a sting on his cheek. Blood trickled down his jaw.

Two policemen stood side by side and pumped bullets into the room. There was a hoarse scream, the rush of bodies, the pound of feet. Glass shattered.

Firing, MacBride and Moriarity hurtled into the room. Moriarity saw a dim figure going out through the window. He fired. The figure buckled and was gone.

'They've made the roof!' clipped MacBride.

He jumped to the window, out upon the fire-escape, up to the roof. He could see vague blurs skimming over the roof of the adjoining house. For a block these roofs were linked together, trimmed with chimneys, ventilating shafts, radio aerials.

Cohen went past MacBride in leaps and bounds, stopped suddenly, crouched and fired two shots. One knocked a man over. The other whanged through a skylight. Moriarity cut loose, missed fire.

Then the gunmen, near the end of the row of roofs, stopped and hid behind chimneys and the projections that separated one roof from another. They sprinkled the night generously with gunfire. Officer Terchinsky went down with a groan, came up again.

The policemen advanced warily, darting from chimney to chimney, crouching behind a skylight, wriggling forward. MacBride was mopping the wound on his cheek with a handkerchief. His gun was in the other hand. Moriarity was with him. A slug chipped off the corner of the chimney behind which they crouched.

Moriarity fired.

'Got that bum!' he muttered.

Both sides suddenly opened a furious exchange of shots. Lead ricochetted off the roof, twanged through aerial wires, shattered the glass in skylights.

Shouts rose, sharp commands and questions. The policemen rose as one and galloped forward, firing as they ran.

The gunmen loomed up in the darkness – four, five, six of them. Guns bellowed and belched flame at close quarters. Terchinsky, already wounded, went down again, this time to stay. Guns empty, the men clashed, hand to hand, clubbing rifles. Nightsticks became popular.

Below, crowds were gathering, machines coming from other districts. Police whistles were blowing.

Gunther and Barnes came up from the rear, joined the fight. From then on it was short-lived. Every one of the six gunmen, rough customers to the last man, were beaten down, and most of them were unconscious.

The policemen were not unscathed, either. Terchinsky, of course, was dead. Cohen was on the point of collapse. MacBride was a bit dazed. They handcuffed the gangsters. MacBride looked them over, one by one, with his flashlight, and then went off to examine the ones who had been shot down. Moriarity was with him.

'Recognize anybody, Cap?'

'One or two, but can't place 'em. I'd hoped to find Duveen.'

'Didn't you pot a guy going through the window? Maybe he fell down the fire-escape.'

'That's right, Jake. Let's look.'

MacBride gave brief orders to his men, told them to carry the prisoners down to the ground floor. Then he went off with Moriarity, descended the fire-escape, followed it down to the bottom.

Lying on the ground, face down, was a man dressed in a tuxedo. MacBride turned him over.

'Alive,' he muttered, 'but unconscious.'

'Who is he?' asked Moriarity.

MacBride snapped on his flash, leaned over, his eyes dilating.

'*Bonelio!*' he muttered.

Kennedy was coming down the fire-escape.

VII

A day later MacBride stood in a large room in Police Headquarters. He was a little pale. His cheek was covered with cotton and adhesive tape. Moriarity was there, strips of tape over his right eye. And Cohen's left arm was in a sling.

Against one wall was a bench. On this bench sat Trixie Meloy, Adolph Shanz, and Beroni, manager of the Palmetto Club. All three were manacled, one to the other. Shanz was despair personified. Beroni was haggard. Trixie wore a look of contempt for everybody in the room.

Kennedy came in, sat down at a desk and played with a pencil.

MacBride said, 'I have a letter here that I'm going to read. It will interest you, Miss Meloy.'

He spread a sheet before him, said, 'It was dictated to a stenographer at the hospital by a man named Louis Martinez.'

Trixie bit her lip.

MacBride read, '"To Captain Stephen MacBride: The man you want is Tony Bonelio. I worked in his club. I was Miss Meloy's dancing partner. We'd danced before, all over the country. I loved her. I thought she loved me. Maybe she did until Bonelio won her with money. It drove me crazy. I wanted to kill him. But I didn't. But I learned a lot. He killed Bedell. I heard the plans being made. Bedell was getting hard to handle. State's Attorney Krug and Shanz and Bonelio got together. Shanz was to get Bedell on the speaker's platform, so Bonelio could shoot him from the roof. Shanz and Krug staged the block-party just for that. When Bonelio read that you had a man prisoner who was in the know, I heard him phone Krug. Krug promised to go down and get the man from you. Whoever he was, they were going to pay him a lot of money to take the rap. But when you wouldn't give him up, Bonelio told Krug there was only one way – blow the station up.

'"I tipped you about all this because I wanted to see Bonelio get his. I wanted to win back Trixie's love. But I knew if she knew I'd done all that, she'd never look at me again. I was crazy about her. I was, but that's over. I was lying here, dying, and I called her up to come over. She told me to go to hell and croak. I've been a fool. I see what she is now. But go easy with her, Captain, anyhow. The only thing she did was to go to the block-party and say she saw a man in a gray suit walking away. She didn't see anybody. It was just a stall. That's all she did, except what she did to me. I don't know, maybe I still love her."'

MacBride concluded, and you could have heard a pin drop. Then he said, 'That was Martinez' death-bed confession.'

'The damn sap!' snapped Trixie, her face coloring.

'What a fool he was to waste his time on a hunk of peroxide like you,' observed Kennedy. 'And what a dirty write-up I'm going to give you, sister.'

'Rats for you, buddy,' she gave him.

'Here's hoping you become a guest of the state. Don't forget to primp up and look pretty when the tabloid photographers get around. I don't even see what the hell Bonelio saw in you.'

'Damn you, shut up!' she cried fiercely.

'Now, now,' cut in MacBride, 'that'll be enough. You, Shanz, are under arrest, and your trial won't come up till the new administration's in.'

'Where's Krug?' he grumbled.

'Still looking for him,' said MacBride. 'He slipped out at three this morning. Moriarity was over to his house and saw signs of a hasty departure. Krug got cold feet when he heard we had Bonelio. He knew he couldn't help Bonelio, because the wop staged a gunfight with us. And he knew that if

Bonelio knew Krug couldn't help him, then Bonelio would squeal. As a matter of fact, Bonelio has squealed. You'll go on trial in connection with the killing of Bedell. The net is out for Krug.'

Even as he said this, the telephone rang. He picked it up.

'Hello,' drawled a voice. 'I want MacBride.'

'You've got him.'

'Well, MacBride, this is Duveen. I was sore as hell because you picked up Hess and the other two boys. They were on the way to blow up one of Bonelio's warehouses. Say, I hear you're looking for Krug.'

'Yes, I am. He's wanted – bad.'

'I've got him. I'm calling from up-State. He ran into me a little while ago with his car. I nabbed him. I'm sending him in with a State trooper. That's all, MacBride.'

'Thanks. Drop in for a drink some time.'

'I might, at that.'

That was all.

MacBride rubbed his hands together. 'And now we've got Krug,' he said. 'Krug, Shanz, Bonelio. And thank God, they'll go on trial when Anderson is State's Attorney.'

Shanz groaned. A little man, a tool of others, he had tried to barter honor for power.

The three of them, including Trixie Meloy, were marched out and locked in separate cells.

The commissioner came in, a large, benign man, mellow-voiced, steady-eyed.

'Congratulations, MacBride,' he said, and shook warmly. 'It was great work. You've broken up an insidious crowd in Richmond City, and there's every possibility you'll be made inspector and attached to my personal staff.'

'The breaks helped me,' said MacBride. 'I got a lot of good breaks toward the end.'

'That may be your way of putting it. Personally, I attribute your success to nerve, courage and tenacity.'

With that he left.

MacBride sighed, sat down, and felt his head. It hurt, there was a dull pain throbbing inside. He would carry a three-inch scar on his cheek for life. He felt his pockets.

'Thought I had a smoke. . . .'

Kennedy looked up, grinned, pulled a cigar from his pocket. 'Have one on me, Mac.'

MacBride eyed him for a moment in silent awe. Then he chuckled. 'Thanks, Kennedy. I see where I have to buy you a box of Montereys.'

'See they're good and moist, Mac,' said Kennedy.

LAW WITHOUT LAW

FREDERICK L. NEBEL

Kennedy chuckled. 'So you're back in the Second, Mac.'
'See me here, don't you?'
'Ay, verily!'
The old station-house blown up during the last election had been rebuilt, and the office in which Captain Stephen MacBride sat and Kennedy, the insatiable newshound, stood, smelled of new paint and plaster. Something of the old atmosphere was lost – that atmosphere which it had taken long years to create: dust, age-colored walls decorated with news clippings, 'wanted' bulletins, likenesses of known criminals.
Two days ago MacBride had been suddenly and inexplicably shifted from the suburban Fifth to the hectic Second. He was surprised, more than a little incredulous; and he suspected some ulterior motive behind the new Police Commissioner's leniency.
So did Kennedy. And Kennedy said, 'This is funny, Mac.'
'As a crutch.'
'Now, if you'd asked me a week ago, I'd have said you were stuck in the Fifth for the rest of your term – or shoved farther out in the sticks. What did Commissioner Stroble say?'
'Said we ought to get on well.'
'Was he nice?'
'Gave me a drink and asked about the health of my family.'
'Hot damn!' Kennedy clasped his hands and with a serio-comic expression stared at the ceiling. 'O, Lord what hath come over the powers that be in this vale of iniquity, Richmond City?'
'You jackass!'
'Mac, poor old slob—'
'Don't call me a slob!'
'Mac, my dear, what's up now? Why did the Commissioner suddenly put you in the precinct nearest your heart's desire?'
'Out of the pure and simple goodness of his heart.'
'Amen!'
Kennedy sagged limply and supported himself with one extended arm against the wall.

'Of course, Mac,' he said, 'you know and I know that this is one awful lot of liverwurst.'

'Then why ask?'

'Kidding you.'

'Ho!'

'Getting your goat.'

'Ho! Ho!'

Kennedy left the wall, crept dramatically across the floor and slid silently upon the desk. And in a hushed voice, with mock seriousness, he said, 'Mac, somebody's trying to make a boob out of you!'

'How do you know?'

'I suspect, old tomato – I suspect. It's too sudden, Mac. Stroble has got something up his sleeve. He's brought you back into the town for a purpose.'

'How big do you think he is?'

'Pretty big.'

'Big enough to be the Big Guy?'

'Almost – and yet, not quite.'

'Who is?'

'Beginning to get a faint idea. If I'm right, the Big Guy has been behind it all from the very beginning. The gangs have come and gone, but the Big Guy has succeeded in remaining hidden. If it's the bozo I think it is. . . .'

'Yes?'

'I don't think you'll reach him.'

'Oh, go to hell, Kennedy! Listen, I'll get to him. Man alive, I *couldn't* lay off now! The thing's got in my blood. I've got to see it through. And I'm going to.'

'Well, Mac, so far you've surprised me. Why you aren't occupying a snug grave in somebody's cemetery, is beyond me. But you've still got lots of opportunity of following in Jack Cardigan's footsteps. He was a poor slob.'

'A martyr, Kennedy.'

'Well, dignify it.' Kennedy put on his topcoat. 'I'm going places, Mac. Good-luck.'

He wandered out, trailing cigarette smoke.

MacBride creaked back and forth in his chair, stopped to light a cigar, went on creaking. Damn new chairs, the way they creaked! The whole room was strange, aloof. Not like the old one, not as dusty – as intimate. Those three chairs standing against the wall – mission oak, bright and shiny, like the desk. Everything trim and spic and span – on parade. Even the clock was new, had a fast, staccato tick. He remembered the old one, a leisurely, moon-faced old chronometer, never on time.

A noise in the central room roused him. He raised his eyes and regarded the door. It burst open. Rigallo and Doran and a third man weaved in. The third man looked like a Swede, and was a head taller than either of the detectives. He slouched ape-like, great arms dangling, and his sky-blue eyes were wide and belligerent. He wore corduroy trousers, a blue pea-jacket.

'What's this?' asked MacBride.

Rigallo said, 'Know him?'

'No.'

The two detectives steered the man across the room and pushed him into one of the three chairs. He looked more the ape than ever – an ape at bay – sitting there with shoulders hunched, jaw protruding, huge hands dangling across his knees.

'Who is he?' asked MacBride.

'Says Alf Nelson,' clipped Rigallo. 'Me and Tim here were poking around the docks. We caught this baby trying to set a Tate & Tate barge adrift. He'd slipped the bow line and we caught him as he was on the stern.'

'H'm,' muttered MacBride. 'That right, Nelson?'

'It ain't.'

'He's a lousy liar!' snapped Rigallo.

'We saw him,' supplemented Doran.

MacBride said, 'Come Nelson, why did you do it?'

'I tell you, I didn't do nothin'.' His Scandanavian accent was barely noticeable. 'These guys are tryin' to frame me.'

'Ah-r-r!' growled Rigallo. 'Can that tripe, buddy! D' you think we waste time framin' guys? Come down to earth, you big white hope!'

'Look here, Nelson,' said MacBride, rising. 'This is damned serious. It's a rough night on the water, and that barge would have caused a lot of trouble. Riggy, was anybody on the barge?'

'Yeah, guy sleeping. We woke him up. Scoggins. He was scared stiff, and I'll bet he doesn't sleep a wink the rest of the night.'

MacBride took three steps and stood over Nelson. 'Did you have a grudge against Scoggins?'

'No. I tell you, I ain't done nothin'. I found the lines loose and was tryin' to fix 'em.'

'Cripes!' spat Rigallo.

'Who's he work for, Riggy?'

'Dunno. Frisked him for a gat. Here it is. Thirty-eight.'

MacBride said, 'Who do you work for, Nelson?'

Nelson growled, pressed back in his chair. MacBride reached down toward his pockets. Nelson raised a hand to block him. Doran caught the hand and knocked it aside. MacBride went through the man's pockets.

'H'm. Badge,' he said, 'of the Harbor Towing. This guy's a barge captain. Here's his Union card. Name's right. Thirty-five. Unmarried, citizen. Listen, Nelson, come across now. Why the hell did you try to cut that barge loose?'

'I told you I didn't try to cut no barge loose,' rumbled Nelson.

MacBride turned on Rigallo. 'You're sure he did, Riggy?'

'Ask Tim.'

'Sure he did, Cap,' said Doran.

MacBride put Nelson's belongings in the desk and said, 'Tim, plant him in a cell. I'm going down to the river. You come along, Riggy. There may be something in this, and there may not.'

II

It was cold and windy on the waterfront. The pier sheds loomed huge and sombre, and overhead the sky arched black as a cavern roof. And there was not a solitary star afield, not a vagrant moonbeam, not a patch of color against the black inverted bowl.

The river was a dark mystery moving restlessly toward the sea, and fringed sparsely with pier-head lights which probed its surface with thin, tremulous needles of radiance. And here and there, between the fringes, other lights – red, green, white – marked black shapes that moved through the thick gloom. The sound of bells, rung intermittently, skipped across the water with startling clarity.

MacBride and Rigallo strode down Pier Five and came to a barge moored at the end. Beneath them the water gurgled among the piles, and the barge thumped dully against the wharf. The tide was high, and they leaped to the barge without difficulty.

A man was standing in the doorway of a small, lighted cabin, smoking a pipe.

'Scoggins,' said Rigallo.

'Hello, Scoggins,' said MacBride. 'Let's go inside.'

They entered and Scoggins closed the door and leaned back against it. He was a small man, knotty in the framework, weather-beaten, steady-eyed.

MacBride said, 'You know Nelson?'

'Yeah, years – from seein' him around the docks and in the lunch-wagon sometimes. Works for the Harbor Towin'.'

'Ever have a scrap with him?'

'Nope.'

'Sure?'

'Yup. But I got a scare tonight, though!'

'You figure he tried to cut you loose?'

'Says he didn't. I ain't never had a line slip on me yet, and I been twenty years on the river.'

'Well, look here, can you think of anything that might cause him to do it?'

Scoggins frowned thoughtfully and rubbed his jaw. 'Gosh, I dunno. Of course, Tate & Tate, the comp'ny I work for, had a split with the Union, and they ain't hirin' Union men 'less they can help it. The Harbor Towin' 's all Union. Guys get in scraps over that sometimes. Day before yest'day Bill

Kamp, who's on Number Three Barge, got in a fight with a Harbor Towin' guy. The guy called Bill a scab and Bill poked him.'

'What caused this split with the Union?'

'Dunno. Just know they split. Young Mr. Tate was sore as hell over somethin'.'

'Do you know what barge Nelson is on?'

'Number Three. Up at Pier Twelve now.'

MacBride turned to Rigallo. 'Come on, Riggy, let's snoop around.'

They left Pier Five, reached the cobbled street and walked north. Fifteen minutes later they turned into a covered pier, met a watchman, flashed their shields and passed on down the vast interior.

On the south side of Pier Twelve they found a lighter flying a metal pennant numbered Three. A light shone in the little cabin. They leaped down from the wharf, pushed open the door and walked in.

A girl sat on the bunk. She was a large girl – not fat, but large, broad in the shoulders, wide at the hips. Her skin was fair, her hair light brown; and her cheek-bones were high, prominent; her mouth wide with lips full and frankly sensuous. Her clothes were cheap and not precisely in the mode, and she regarded the two intruders with a dull stare.

Rigallo smiled. 'Hello, girlie.'

'Hal-lo.'

'Where's Alf?' asked MacBride.

'Ay don't know.'

'H'm. We were supposed to meet him here tonight,' lied Rigallo.

'Yes,' nodded MacBride.

She shrugged her broad shoulders. 'So vas I. Dat Alf iss neffer on time.'

'Ah, he's a good guy, though,' said Rigallo.

She regarded him stolidly for a moment, then grinned, showing large white teeth. 'Yah, Alf iss good fal-ler. Ay vait. You fal-lers vaiting for Alf?'

'Sure,' nodded Rigallo. 'We're his friends. Eh, Mac?'

'You said it, Riggy.'

'Alf's some guy,' said Rigallo.

'Yah,' nodded the girl, shedding some of her nerves. 'Alf iss good fal-ler.' She paused, meditated heavily, then laughed and slapped her knee. 'Ay tal you, Alf is vun big guy. Dis Meester Braun he likes Alf much.'

'Sure,' said MacBride. 'Mr. Braun's a good guy, too. But he should treat Alf better.'

Still more of the girl's reserve vanished, and she leaned forward, waxing confidential. 'Yah, like Ay tol' Alf. But Ay t'ank dis Meester Braun iss be sqvare by Alf. Alf he tal me he vill get lots dol-lars.'

'Well, it's no more than right,' put in Rigallo.

'Yah. Alf vill be rich fal-ler some day.'

MacBride and Rigallo grinned at each other. Then they grinned at the girl, and MacBride said, 'Gosh, miss, Alf's been holding back on us. Never told us he had a nice girl like you.'

She dropped her eyes. 'Yah, Ay t'ank Alf luffs me lot. Ay luff Alf lot.'

'He'll invite us to the wedding, though, I hope,' said MacBride.

'Sure,' nodded Rigallo.

'Yah,' said the girl.

MacBride tried. 'When did Alf say he would be back?'

'Vun hour ago. But Ay vill vait.'

'Yeah,' said Rigallo. 'Alf said something about a job down on Pier Five. I wondered what he meant.'

'Vass it Pier Five?' asked the girl.

'Yeah,' said Rigallo.

'Ay vill go.'

'No. You stay here,' put in MacBride. 'We'll look him up and tell him you're waiting. What did he say he was doing?'

'Alf didn't say. Alf ain't tal me much, but he say he be very busy dese nights soon.'

MacBride stood up. 'Well, if we see him, we'll tell him you're waiting. What did you say your name was?'

'Hilda. Hilda Yonson. Ay come from Oslo two year' ago.'

'See you again,' said MacBride.

'Yeah, see you again,' said Rigallo.

'Yah,' said Hilda Yonson.

MacBride and Rigallo climbed back to the wharf and strode through the pier-shed.

'Who is Braun?' asked Rigallo.

'Don't know. Probably one of the bosses. We'll ask the night watchman.'

In a little office at the far end of the pier they found the watchman, and MacBride asked, 'Who is Mr. Braun?'

'Manager. Yeah, he's the manager.'

'Good-night,' said MacBride, and steered Rigallo into the street.

'What now, Cap?'

'Nothing, until I see Braun.'

'It looks as if Nelson is somebody's dope.'

'What I think, Riggy. Flag that taxi.'

MacBride went home that night, pounded his ear for eight hours and was back on the job at eight next morning. In plain clothes, he left the station-house and went down to the general offices of the Harbor Towing Company, which were located over Pier Nine.

Braun had evidently just arrived, for he was going through the morning's mail. He was a fat, swarthy man, nervous and shifty, with a vague chin.

'Oh, Captain MacBride,' he said. 'Ah, yes. Won't you sit down? Won't you have a cigar?'

MacBride sat down but refused the cigar. 'You probably know,' he said, 'that I've got one of your barge captains over at the station-house.'

Braun's eyes squinted, and he licked his lips. 'Why, no! That's too bad. Likely a drunken brawl, eh? Well, I suppose I'll have to bail him out – mark against his salary.'

'Not quite,' said MacBride. 'He was caught trying to cut a barge adrift last night. Pretty serious.'

'Well, I should say so! Can you imagine! Humph! You never know what these drunks will do.'

'But Nelson wasn't drunk.'

'Well, that *is* strange! Now why do you suppose he tried to do a fool thing like that, Captain?'

'Search me. Thought maybe you might know.'

'Me?'

'Uhuh.'

'But, Captain, I'm surprised, how should I know why these fool Swedes—'

'Aboveboard, now, Mr. Braun!'

'Why – um – why, what do you mean?'

'Don't make me go into detail.'

'But I tell you, Captain, I don't understand—'

'Aboveboard, Mr. Braun!'

Braun pursed his lips, his eyes dilated. He looked amazed. 'Really, Captain—'

'Oh, for God's sake, cut out this stalling!'

'I tell you, Captain, I'm in the dark. I don't know what you're driving at.'

MacBride's lips curled. 'There's something crooked somewhere.'

'Well, if there is, I'd certainly like to know about it. If Nelson has been going wrong, I'll certainly fire him. Tell you what, I'll go down to the station-house and give him a talking. Let's see. It's nine now. I'll be there at ten, Captain.'

MacBride stood up. 'I'll be waiting there.'

'Good! Won't you have a cigar?'

'No.'

MacBride's exit was like a blast of wind.

III

Twenty minutes later he walked into the offices of Tate & Tate, and a boy piloted him into the sanctum of Hiram Tate, the younger and executive member of the firm. Tate was a lank, rock-boned man of forty-odd, with flashing dark eyes.

'I came over,' said MacBride, 'about that bit of business on Pier Five last night.'

'Oh, you did? Good! I'll go right over with you and prefer charges against this bird you've got.'

'What is your opinion?' asked MacBride. 'Why do you suppose he tried to cut that barge loose?'

'Captain, my answer will be heavily prejudiced. You want to know what I think? I think that the Harbor Towing is trying to intimidate me. We're non-Union. I'll tell you why. Mike Tate, my old man, was double-crossed. And keep this under your hat. The Harbor Towing and Tate & Tate have always been rivals for the river trade.

'We've had more damned inspectors on our tail than I thought were in existence. What for? For little things. Unsanitary lavatories. Doors that opened in instead of out. Electric wiring. Unsafe barges. Condemned tugs. Ever since we kicked the Union in the slats.

'And what started it? The municipal pier at Seaboard Basin. It was offered for sale, and we wanted it. The Harbor Towing wanted it. We claimed it should come logically to us because we had no uptown terminal and did a lot of uptown business. The Harbor Towing carried it right to the Union. I was out of town. The old man represented us, and he's known for a convivial old souse. They got him tight at the board meeting, and he signed all the dotted lines he could find.

'Well, we couldn't retract. The whole mess was attested by a notary, and when the old man came to he discovered that the Harbor Towing owned the municipal pier. When I came back to town I found him raving mad. I got sore, too, and we told the Union what we thought of it, and dropped. What's the use of catering to an outfit that kowtows to big money? The Harbor Towing is a big outfit, and they get all the court decisions, too. It's damned funny. When we get a square deal, get at least one section of the municipal pier to unload and load freight, we'll go back into the fold. That's my story. Believe it or not.'

'I'll think it over. If you want to press a charge against Nelson, we'll indict him.'

'I'll press charges, all right!' Tate rose and put on his overcoat. 'Have a cigar?'

'Go good. Thanks.'

They drove to the station-house in Tate's private car, and as they entered the central room, they found Rigallo pacing up and down in something akin to rage.

'Hell, Cap, where have you been?' he snapped.

'What about it?'

'Bower came down from Headquarters and took Nelson up for a quiz.'

MacBride tightened his jaw. 'Why'd you let him?'

'How could I stop him. I'm only a dick.'

'What's this?' put in Tate.

MacBride said, 'Nelson's at Headquarters.'

'I want to place that charge.'

'All right,' said MacBride; then to Rigallo, 'You go along with Mr. Tate, Riggy.'

They went out, and MacBride banged into his office. Kennedy was parked in his chair before his desk, immersed in solitaire.

'Out of my throne, Kennedy!'

'Just a minute, Mac. I've almost got this.'

MacBride grabbed the back of the swivel chair, hauled it and Kennedy away from the desk, slid another into its place, and sat down. He studied the cards for a moment, made several swift moves, filled the suits and said, 'Learn from me, Kennedy.'

'That was good, Mac. How about two-handed poker.'

'No. Busy.'

'What doing?'

'Thinking.'

'Bower came down and got Nelson.'

'Don't I know it!'

Kennedy chuckled. 'Bower's the Headquarters "yes" man. Guess the Commissioner wanted to see Nelson, shake his hand, and tell him to go home.'

'H'm.' MacBride stood up, put on his coat and strode out.

Ten minutes later he entered Police Headquarters.

Commissioner Stroble regarded him through a screen of excellent cigar smoke.

'How about Nelson?' asked MacBride.

'We let him go,' said the Commissioner.

'Let him go!' echoed MacBride.

'Why, certainly. No case at all, MacBride. We had a chap named Scoggins here, too. I weighed both testimonies. Scoggins was asleep. Nelson saw that one of the cables had slipped and was trying to fix it. Scoggins was vague. Don't bother with such small change, MacBride.'

'Small change!' MacBride curled his lip. 'If it was so small, why did Bower take Nelson from the precinct, and why did you bother with it?'

Stroble's eyes narrowed. 'Remember, MacBride, I took you out of the Fifth, gave you another chance. Don't be a fool!'

'You're trying to make a fool out of me! I know the situation on the waterfront, and it's not small change. That guy Nelson is guilty as hell. And the outfit he works for is a damned sight guiltier!'

Stroble leaned forward, pursing his lips. 'MacBride, I said it was small change. Now don't hand me an argument. Go back to your roost and forget about it. This interview is over.'

MacBride went out with a low growl. He walked back to the station-house, certain now that trouble was breeding on the river. Small change! He cursed under his breath. He was very near the end of his tether. Time and time again someone in the machinery of the city government had tried to balk him.

In his office that day he had moments of black depression. He wondered if after all he were not beating his head against a stone wall. What was he? Only a common precinct captain, with strong ideas of his own. How could he hope to carry out his own straightforward plans when the Department sidetracked him?

Yet there was the strain of the hard in his blood. To give up now, to fall in line with the long column of grafters, would be a tremendous blow to his conscience – and to his stubborn pride. Rigallo and Doran would razz him. And Kennedy! And a lot of other men who were aware of his single-handed struggle against graft and corruption.

No, there was no backing out now. He had built a structure of two-fisted justice, escaped death, release from the Force, by the skin of his teeth. The game at this stage was far too interesting. He had wiped out some of the most notorious gangs in Richmond City, had made the political racketeers squirm, had driven some right out of office.

But still he had not got to the roots. Had the Commissioner before his appointment, been the drive wheel in the racket? And now, being in a position of vital importance, would he rebuild all that MacBride had knocked down? How big was he? How far could MacBride push him? Why had he permitted Nelson's release on such short notice?

Small change! Hell!

It was strange that a month should pass without an untoward murmur on the river. At times MacBride wondered if after all Nelson had been innocent. But then it wasn't like Rigallo to make such a raw blunder. He was not a detective who usually went in for small game.

An interesting and significant bit of news drifted in one morning. Kennedy, the inevitable, walked in on MacBride and said:

'What do you think, Mac?'

'What?'

'A Tate & Tate barge sank last night. One of their oldest. Just foundered, so the report goes, off the coast. Sprung a leak. Went down with one hundred thousand dollars' worth of copper wire. The barge captain was saved. The tug *Annie Tate* was towing, and saved him. Read what the *News-Examiner* says.'

He scaled a newspaper on the table, and MacBride conned a terse editorial:

> Last night the Tate & Tate barge Number Two sank off the Capes. It is evident that this barge was sadly in need of repair. The sea was only moderately rough and the tug *Annie Tate* had good steerageway.
>
> A cargo valued as $100,000 was lost in fifty fathoms, and the barge captain, Olaf Bostad, is in the City Hospital suffering from exposure. It

seems to us that there is a deplorable lack of efficiency somewhere. Why the Number Two, one of the first barges built for Tate & Tate, was allowed to go to sea, is beyond us.

It seems incredible that a reputable company should place a man in jeopardy by sending him on a coastwise voyage in a barge of such ancient vintage. The company, of course, does not lose. The underwriters do. We no longer wonder why marine insurance is at such a premium, and why many underwriters refuse to insure coastwise barges.

'H'm,' muttered MacBride.

'I wonder who paid for that,' said Kennedy. 'Tate & Tate are in hot water now, for sure. Watch the insurance company go into action!'

'And the waterfront bust wide open,' said MacBride.

Indeed, the first rumble came on the following day, when not a single tug or barge of Tate & Tate moved. Captain Bower, of Headquarters, boomed into the station-house with orders from the Commissioner.

'MacBride, you've got to patrol the river,' he said. 'Use all your available men. Two cops on each pier where there's Tate & Tate shipping. The insurance company has refused to allow Tate & Tate to move until every barge and tug has been inspected. The city is also sending its own inspectors, and there's a complete tie-up.'

'All right,' nodded MacBride.

He called on his reserves, dispatched them to six different piers, and himself went down to the Tate & Tate general offices.

Young Hiram Tate was in high heat. 'What do you think of this, MacBride? By God, can you beat it? That barge was overhauled only two months ago and the underwriters O.K.'d it. Now we're tied up. Not a thing allowed to move. We've got thousands of dollars' worth of freight that has to move – has to make trains, ships – and some of it's perishable. Hell, we'll go bankrupt!

'What happens now? Consignees and consignors are bellowing. But we can't move. We lose our contracts, and the movement of freight is taken over by other companies. And what company mainly? The Harbor Towing. God, what a blow below the belt this is!'

'We're putting men on the piers to prevent trouble,' said MacBride.

But trouble broke. When a Harbor Towing tug and three lighters warped into Pier Eight to move perishable freight from a Tate & Tate shed, a fight started. Fists flew, and then stones and canthooks. The police joined, and shots rang out, and one man was wounded before the outbreak was quelled.

But the feud had taken root and spread the length of the waterfront, and MacBride was here and there and everywhere, struggling for law and order.

The Commissioner called him and said, 'Clamp the lid, MacBride. It looks as if Tate & Tate employ a lot of hoodlums. This can't go on. Pitch 'em all in jail if you have to.'

MacBride had been up most of that night, and he was weary. 'If you'd get the inspectors on the job and make that insurance company snap on it, this would stop. I'm doing the best I can.'

'Keep up the good work, MacBride!' was Stroble's parting shot.

MacBride slammed down the receiver, whirled and stared at Rigallo. 'Now I know why I've been shifted here! I'm getting a beautiful kick in the slats! I'm told to ride Tate & Tate, and, Kennedy, way down in my heart I believe Tate & Tate is the goat!'

'Mac, I'm with you, you know. So is Doran.'

'Thanks, Riggy. It's good to know.'

Reports came in continually from the river. All the reserves were out. Fights occurred every few hours – uptown – downtown.

MacBride slept at the station-house that afternoon, awoke at six, had hot coffee and a couple of hamburgers sent up, and prepared for another night. Tate & Tate were at the breaking point. The inspectors were taking their time, and the first barge that was looked over was held up for some minor detail that was not yet settled among the inspectors.

On the other hand, the Harbor Towing Company was reaping a harvest, taking over all the freight that Tate & Tate could not handle. And the Union men of the Harbor Towing, old enemies of the non-Union crowd of Tate & Tate, took every opportunity to bawl insults at the men whom circumstances had forced to a stand-still.

Hiram Tate called MacBride on the telephone and yelled, 'Look here, MacBride! You've got a good name in this lousy burg. What am I going to do? These pups from the Harbor Towing are getting away with murder. You can't blame my men for fighting. I've bailed twenty out already. If this keeps up, if my floating equipment isn't allowed to move, we'll go bankrupt. It's dirty, MacBride. There's some underhand work somewhere. I tell you, if it keeps up, I'm going out on the river myself and bust the first Harbor Towing bum that opens his jaw!'

'Sit tight, Tate,' said MacBride. 'I've got to maintain law and order.'

'Law and order, hell!' exclaimed Tate, and hung up.

Rigallo asked, 'What's the matter, Cap?'

'Tate's sore. Can you blame him?'

'No.'

'Riggy, this is getting worse. There's big money in it, and between you and me it looks as if the Harbor Towing is trying to wipe out Tate & Tate, their biggest competitors. And how they're doing it! That sunken barge was just what they needed. Graft all around. Ten to one the underwriters were bribed. The *News-Examiner* was bribed. The city is being bribed.'

'D' you ever stop to think, Cap, that the barge might have been monkeyed with?'

'You know, I wonder!'

The hours dragged by, with more reports coming in, and at midnight came a staggering report from one of the patrolmen stationed at Pier Fifteen.

'We just found a stiff, Captain.'

'Who?'

'Guy named Nelson. We heard a shot and ran down the dock and found him dead in his barge. Right through the heart.'

'Hold everything, Grosskopf. I'll be over.'

MacBride hung up and looked at Rigallo. 'Riggy, somebody plugged Alf Nelson of the Harbor Towing.'

'God help Tate & Tate!'

'Let's go!'

IV

Officer Tonovitz met MacBride and Rigallo at the entrance of Pier Fifteen.

'Grosskopf's on the barge,' he said.

They strode down the covered pier, came out in the open, and saw Grosskopf standing outside the cabin door. MacBride and Rigallo jumped down to the barge.

Nelson was lying on the floor, flat back, one arm flung across his chest, the other extended straight from his shoulder. A chair was overturned.

'Fight,' ventured Rigallo.

'Maybe not,' said MacBride. 'He might have been sitting on the chair, and jerked up when he was hit.'

'Door and windows were closed,' put in Grosskopf.

'Didn't find anything?'

'No.'

MacBride went out and up to the dock, and found a knot of men hovering nearby, expectantly.

'You guys knew Nelson, didn't you?'

Most of them did.

'See anybody around here tonight?'

One replied, 'I seen Gus Scoggins.'

'Going or coming?'

'He must ha' been goin' to the barge. I seen him on this dock. Was about nine o'clock. He said, "Hello, Joe." And I said, "Hello, Gus."'

'You didn't see him go back?'

'Well, no. I didn't hang around. I was on the way to my own barge when I saw Gus.'

'Who do you work for?'

'Harbor Towin'.'

'Sure you're not tryin' to frame Scoggins?'

'Who? Me? No. I'm a' old timer. I know Gus for years. I don't figger he did anything.'

'He might have,' said another voice. 'Him and Nelson ain't been good friends since Scoggins claimed Alf tried to cut him loose.'

MacBride left the group and called Grosskopf. 'Ring the morgue and have them get Nelson. Tonovitz, you stay on this barge. Riggy, come with me.'

MacBride and Rigallo went to the float dispatcher for Tate & Tate and got from him the position of Scoggins' barge. It was at Pier four, and ten minutes later they found it. No lights shone. MacBride boarded, tried the door, found it padlocked from the outside.

'He should be on board,' remarked Rigallo.

'He should,' agreed MacBride. 'Cripes, if Scoggins did this, Tate & Tate will be swamped!'

They climbed back to the pier and accosted the patrolman on duty, O'Toole.

'You know Scoggins? Have you seen him?'

'Saw him about eight-thirty, Cap, leaving.'

'When he comes back, hold him and ring the station-house. If he doesn't show up by the time you leave, call me and tell your relief to watch for him, too.'

'O.K.'

MacBride and Rigallo shot back to the station-house. Rigallo went home, and MacBride hauled out a blanket and curled up on a cot in one of the spare rooms.

By morning he had the medical examiner's report. The bullet had gone through Nelson's heart aslant and lodged in his spine. A thirty-two.

O'Toole had rung in with no word of Scoggins. MacBride called the patrolman at Pier Four, and found that Scoggins was still absent. He hung up, went down to the pier, picked up the harbor master for Tate & Tate, and had him open the door to the little cabin. Everything was in order. Scoggins' suitcase, clothes, and other odds and ends, were still there.

MacBride went back to the pier, and found Hiram Tate, just arrived.

'What do you think about this killing, MacBride?'

'Looking for Scoggins. Somebody saw him around Nelson's barge last night.'

'This is a rotten break, MacBride! Do you think it was Scoggins?'

'It looks as if it might be. He hasn't showed up all night.'

They walked back to the street, and then MacBride made for the barge that had been Nelson's home. Officer Pallanzo was on duty, and he was having his hands full.

'I can't get rid of her, Cap,' he complained.

MacBride stood with arms akimbo and stared at Hilda Yonson, who sat on the dock beside the barge. Her hands were clasped about her knees, and she was rocking back and forth and moaning. Her yellow hair blew in coarse wisps across her hueless face. Her hat was askew.

'Alf. . . . Alf. . . .'

She was dazed. When MacBride spoke, it seemed she did not hear him. She rocked on – and on, staring with red-rimmed eyes.

'Look here, Hilda,' MacBride said, bending down. 'Come on. Don't sit around here. I'll take you home.'

He shook her. She looked up, and her lips quivered. 'You – you said you vass Alf's friend. All de time you had Alf in de station-house.'

'Forget that. I was doing my duty. Come on, Hilda, I want to get the man who killed Alf. I want you to help me get him.'

'Ay vill keel him!' She doubled a fist and squared her jaw.

'No, you leave that to me. Let's go.' He took her arm, urged her.

She rose and permitted MacBride to lead her from the barge. She walked with a steady, purposeful tread, her face grim.

MacBride found a room at one corner of the warehouse, and they entered it, Rigallo close behind.

'When did you last see Alf, Hilda?' asked MacBride.

'Ay see Alf last night.'

'What did he say?'

'Ay didn't talk. Ay go down by de dock und Ay see Alf iss playin' cards vit two fal-lers. So Ay don't go in. Ay go home.'

'You know the men?'

'No. Vun vass dressed like vat you call sheik. Ay looked in by de vindow. De odder vun vas dat fal-ler Scoggins.'

'About what time?'

'Vas maybe half-past nine.'

MacBride turned to Rigallo. 'This looks queer, Riggy – Nelson and Scoggins playing cards.'

'With another guy – yeah.'

'Ay vill keel him, whoever it vass dat keeled Alf. O-o-o-o, my poor Alf!' she moaned, rocking on the chair.

'Listen, Hilda,' put in Rigallo, 'buck up. And don't do any killing. Leave that to us. We'll get this bum and he'll burn for it.'

'Ay vill bet it vass dat Scoggins.'

They took her home, where she lived with an elder sister, and then went over to the station-house.

'The Commissioner's been calling you, Cap,' said Sergeant Flannery. 'Wants to talk to you.'

MacBride took the phone and called Headquarters, and the Commissioner said, 'That Scoggins is a good lead, MacBride. Tail him and get him. He's the guy we want, all right.'

'I'm not so sure,' said MacBride.

'Get him, MacBride. Grill young Tate. Maybe Tate knows a lot about it. Maybe he knows where Scoggins is.'

Hanging up, MacBride swore softly. 'Riggy, they're sure out to crush Tate & Tate, and making no bones about it.'

Sergeant Flannery knocked and came in. A little boy accompanied him. Flannery said, 'Kid, just came in with a note.'

MacBride took a rumpled piece of brown wrapping paper, and read:

For Cap. MacBride, Second Police Precinct. I been took here and held. Looks like these guys are going to kill me or something. Get me out of it. I can't write more now. Gus Scoggins.

MacBride looked at the boy, who was standing on one foot, twisting a cap which he held in his hand.

'Where'd you get this, son?'

'I picked it up in the gutter on North Street.'

'You know just where?'

'Yes.'

MacBride stood up and put on his overcoat. 'Come on, Riggy. Where's Doran?'

Flannery said, 'Playing poker with the reserves.'

'Call him.'

MacBride and Rigallo pushed out into the central room and a moment later Doran appeared and joined them.

'We're going places, Tim. You heeled?'

'Yup.'

'Then let's go. Come on, sonny.'

V

MacBride flagged a taxi, and they all piled in. Ten minutes later they alighted and walked down North Street.

'It's on the next block,' said the boy, 'on the other side of the street. See that red brick house? I found it right in front of that, in the gutter.'

'All right,' said MacBride. 'Here's a half-dollar. Run home.'

The boy ran off and MacBride stopped. 'Riggy, Tim, we've got to get Scoggins. The Commissioner wants him.'

'I wonder if he really does,' said Rigallo.

MacBride grinned. 'I'll be doing my duty. He told me to get him.'

They walked on, crossed the street and drew near the red brick house. An empty store was on the street level , windows soaped and pasted with *To Let* signs. Above this ranged two stories. North Street is a mongrel street. There are warehouses, garages, poolrooms, a few tenements.

'There's an alley,' said Doran, pointing a few doors further on.

'Good idea,' said MacBride. 'We'll go around to the back.'

They entered the alley, followed it to the rear, vaulted a couple of board fences and eventually found themselves in the yard back of the red brick house. A door that apparently led into the back of the store barred the way. There were two windows.

'We don't want to make any noise,' said MacBride. 'Cut the putty away from that top pane and we'll pry it out.'

They used jack-knives, succeeded in removing the pane with a minimum of noise. MacBride reached in, unlocked the window, pushed it up. Then he crawled in. Doran and Rigallo followed, and they stood in an empty room littered with paper and old boxes.

'Upstairs, I guess,' said MacBride, and opening a door, stepped into a musty hallway.

Each man carried one hand in his pocket, on his gun.

MacBride led the way up a flight of stairs. He stood on the first landing, looking around. Doran and Rigallo joined him. There were four doors along the side, and one at either end of the corridor.

MacBride whispered, 'You guys park on the next stairway and watch. Quiet, now.'

They nodded and cat-footed off.

MacBride stood alone, deliberating. Now that he was here, what should he do? The situation presented some difficulties. Where was Scoggins? What room? How much of a gang was here? Where was the gang? Why hadn't Scoggins been more explicit?

Questions? The answers would be arrived at only through action. He shrugged. Couldn't stand here all day. Supposed he picked a door at random and knocked?

Well, try it. He did. Squared his shoulders, assumed an innocent expression and rapped on the nearest door. Whom should he ask for? . . .

The door opened and a man in an undershirt and trousers looked out.

'Hello,' said MacBride.

'Hello,' grunted the man.

'I'm a tenement-house inspector,' said MacBride. 'I'd like to look through the rooms. Won't take long.'

'What do you want to look for?'

'Just see about lights, fire exits. Won't take long. Few minutes. Hate like hell to bother you, but the boss has been riding me.'

'Well, come in, then,' grunted the man.

MacBride entered, wondering what tenement-house inspectors were supposed to do. He took out a pencil, however, and a batch of old envelopes from his pocket. He made a few lines, looked very thoughtful, went to each of the two windows in the room, opened and closed them. The man in the undershirt watched him closely.

'Well, this room's all right,' said MacBride. 'Now the next.'

'Wait a minute,' grumbled the man, and entered the next room, closing the door behind him. MacBride heard subdued voices during the brief moment the door was open.

He stepped to the hall door, swung it open, caught Rigallo's eye, and put a finger to his lip. Rigallo, hiding with Doran on the staircase, nodded and grinned. MacBride closed the door softly.

A second later the other door opened, and the man in the undershirt came back. With him was another man, a tall, slim, saturnine man smoking a cigarette through an ivory holder. He eyed MacBride with a cold stare.

'Who sent you here?' he clipped.

'My boss.'

'Well, come around some other time.'

'Can't. I'm taking this block today.'

'Well, take this dump some other day.'

'What's the idea?' shot back MacBride. 'What do you suppose the boss will say if I take all the houses on this street except this one?'

'That's your lookout. Here's twenty-five bucks. Mark this place as okey.'

'Sorry,' said MacBride.

'Then clear out.'

MacBride didn't know how tenement-house inspectors acted in such a case, but he knew how a cop acted. 'Now look here, mister,' he said. 'My job is to look these places over, and I'm going to look it over. Don't get snotty, either, or I'll condemn the damned joint right off the bat.'

'You will, eh?'

'You said it.'

'Who cares?'

'I don't,' shrugged MacBride.

'And neither do I. Can that crap and on your way, buddy.'

'Well, all right, then, if you want to get mean about it,' said MacBride. 'I'll hand in a bum report.'

'Sure. Go ahead. I don't care.'

MacBride put away his pencil and paper and pulled open the door, shoved his hand into his pocket, and stood there.

'Now I'll get mean,' he ripped out. 'Just like this!'

His gun jumped into view, and the two men gasped.

'Raise 'em high!' snapped MacBride; and over his shoulder, 'Come on, boys.'

But Doran and Rigallo were already beside him. 'Frisk 'em,' said MacBride.

Rigallo entered the room and approached the man in the undershirt, relieving him of an automatic. The other man snarled:

'What the hell kind of a stunt is this?'

'Shut up!' said MacBride. 'Get your hands up.'

He snatched a gun from the man's pocket and put it into his own.

'It's a frame-up!' yelled the man.

'Damn you, close your trap!' barked MacBride.

The door to the next room swung open. He caught a momentary glimpse of a group of startled faces. Then the door banged, as Doran leaped toward it and tried to keep it open.

'Hold everything, gang!' yelled the saturnine man.

A shot crashed, splintered the door.

Doran stepped back, leveled his gun and put three shots through the lock.

Rigallo handcuffed the two men together. MacBride took another pair of manacles and secured them to a waterpipe.

'You guys are dicks!' cried the saturnine man.

'God, but you're bright!' chuckled MacBride.

Somewhere below, glass crashed. Doran reloaded his gun. Rigallo fired a couple of shots through the door.

Footsteps were pounding up the stairway. MacBride jumped into the hall, his gun leveled. Two policemen appeared, guns drawn.

'Take it easy, boys,' called MacBride. 'Stay here in the hall. We've got some bums bottled up.'

Even as he said this a door further down the hallway burst open and men rushed out. Revolvers blazed, and one of the policemen went down. MacBride fired and Doran joined him. Eight men swept down upon them like an avalanche. Rigallo came hurtling out of the room.

Doran sank under a blackjack. MacBride put two shots through the head of the man who had wielded it. A clubbed revolver skimmed along his skull and thudded on his shoulder. He twisted and clubbed his own gun, and broke a man's nose. Blood splashed over him.

Somebody reeled, balanced on the balustrade, and then pitched down into the hallway below. Somebody else kicked MacBride in the stomach while he was trying to reload. He doubled and fell to the floor, and another foot cut open his left ear.

Rigallo, holding the doorway of the room wherein the two men were manacled, put a slug in the back of the man who was kicking MacBride's head. The man fell over the captain and never moved once, until MacBride shoved him over and staggered to his feet.

Two men rushed Rigallo, and one swore in Italian. Rigallo snarled, 'As one wop to another, back up!' The man struck with his blackjack. Rigallo dodged and blew out the man's stomach.

'Cripes!' choked the other.

'Stay back,' warned Rigallo, 'or I'll spill your guts, too.'

Two more policemen rushed up the stairs, met two gangsters at the head, forced them back. Suddenly the shots ceased, and the hallway was strangely quiet. Six men, one of them a policeman, lay on the floor, dead. Three gangsters stood with their backs against the wall, disarmed, breathing thickly, one with a broken and bloody nose.

Rigallo still stood in the doorway. MacBride lifted up Doran, shook him.

'You all right, Tim?'

'Yeah – sure,' mumbled Doran.

'Hold him,' MacBride said to one of the policemen.

Then he turned toward the door, laid his hand on Rigallo's shoulder. 'Riggy, this was a hell of a blow-out!'

'Sloppy,' nodded Rigallo.

MacBride entered the room and looked at the two men manacled to the water-pipe.

'Well, you satisfied?'

The man in the undershirt said nothing. The other said, 'No, are you?'

'Not yet.'

MacBride entered the other room. A table was littered with bottles and glasses. He looked around, rubbing his jaw. He crossed and opened another door, looked into a bedroom. It was empty. He backed up, called Rigallo.

'You and Doran hunt for Scoggins. He must be hidden somewhere. Go right to the roof, if you have to.'

They went out, and MacBride sampled a bottle of Three Star Hennessy. It was good stuff, warmed him up. He noticed a closet door, and with the bottle still in his hand, walked over and grasped the knob. He pulled, but the door resisted, yet it was not locked. He dropped the bottle and drew his gun. Someone was in that closet, holding the door shut.

'Come out!' MacBride called.

There was not a murmur.

'Out, or I'll riddle the door!' said MacBride.

Still no answer.

'I'll count three,' said MacBride. 'Ready. *One!*' He marked time. '*Two!*' His gun steadied. '*Three!*'

His finger tightened on the trigger. He aimed low.

Bang! Bang!

Rigallo and Doran came in, with Scoggins between them.

'Found him, Cap,' said Rigallo.

'Just a minute, Riggy,' said MacBride. 'I've found something else.'

He waited. He saw the knob move.

'Atta boy!' he called. 'Open it or I'll shoot higher. Ready!'

The door burst open and a wild-eyed man tottered out.

'Well!' exclaimed MacBride. 'Greetings, Mr. Braun!'

'G-God!' stuttered Braun.

A new voice penetrated the room – 'Is that Braun of the Harbor Towing, Mac?'

MacBride pivoted.

Kennedy of the *Free Press* was leaning in the doorway, tapping his chin with a pencil.

VI

Braun, that short, round, dark, nervous man, seemed to be swallowing hard lumps.

MacBride spoke to a policeman, 'Ed, you shove those three bums in the hall into the next room with the other two.'

'Right-o, Cap.'

'Riggy and Tim, you stay in here with me,' went on MacBride. 'Kennedy, you can stay here on the condition that you don't publish anything unless you have my consent.'

'Suits me, Mac.'

MacBride rubbed his hands gingerly. 'This will be interesting. Make yourselves at home, men – you, too, Braun, and you there, Scoggins. There's a bottle and glasses. Let's get clubby.'

Braun was not in a clubby mood. He was emphatically nervous, and kept biting his thin red lips.

MacBride said, 'Now, Scoggins, what happened?'

Scoggins had taken a drink. He wiped his mouth. 'Gosh, I was scared. T' other afternoon me and Alf Nelson met in the lunchroom across from Pier Ten. I said, "Hello, Alf." And he said, "Hello, Gus." Then I said, "Look here, Alf, we know each other for years. We worked together. What's the sense o' bein' mean? I know you tried to cut me loose t'other night, but I'm willin' to forget it." And Alf said, "I been a big bum, Gus." And I said, "You been a fool, Alf. You never had much brains. You're lettin' some big guys talk you into doin' things. You'll get in trouble, Alf, if you don't look out." So Alf looked kinda guilty, and he said, "Yeah, I been a big bum, Gus. I been wantin' to get some money ahead, so me and Hilda could get hitched. You and me been friends for years, Gus." And I said, "We sure have, Alf. And like one friend to another, I'd warn you to look out for them big buys. If you get in Dutch, they ain't goin' to help you." So he said, "I guess you're right, Gus. I been a dumb-bell." I said, "You sure have, Alf." And he nodded and then said, "Gus, come over my barge tomorrer night and have a game of pinochle like old times." So I said I would, and I did.

'So I went over. We played for an hour, and then some guy came in, and Alf said, "This is a friend, Gus. Call him Pete." So I called him Pete and he called me Gus, but I didn't like him. He wasn't a waterfront man. Along about 'leven o'clock I figgered I better go, and Pete said, "Me, too. I got a motorboat out here. I'll take you upriver." I said, "Thanks," and we went.

'There was another guy waitin' in the boat, and when we got out in the river they jumped me. I was knocked out. When I come to I was in a room upstairs. I was sore. I wonder if Alf double-crossed me.'

'Alf is dead,' said MacBride.

Scoggins squinted. 'What!'

'Was killed about an hour after you left.'

'Dead!'

'Uhuh.'

'But who did it?'

'I don't know – yet.' MacBride turned to Braun. 'Maybe you know.'

Braun started. His eyes blinked. He moistened his lips. 'Captain, I seem in a peculiar position. Unfortunately, circumstances are against me. I believe I'll not say anything until I've thought things out more.'

'Until you've seen a lawyer?' sneered MacBride.

'Until he's seen the Commissioner,' sliced in Kennedy.

It was like dropping a bomb. MacBride swung on him. Braun shuddered, clenched his hands, pursed his lips. Rigallo tapped the floor with his toe. A long moment of silence enveloped the room. Kennedy smiled whimsically, one eyebrow slightly arched.

MacBride said to Rigallo, 'Bring in those guys we hitched to the pipes inside.'

Rigallo grinned, entered the adjoining room, returned a minute later with the saturnine man and the man in the undershirt. The saturnine man had tightened his dark face, and his eyes were two black slots of malevolence, his lips were flattened against his teeth.

Scoggins said, 'That's the guy we played cards with. He's the guy took me for a motorboat ride.'

'The guy that killed Nelson, eh?' put in Kennedy. 'Know him, Mac?'

'Not yet.'

'He's from Chicago, if I've got my mugs right. Pete Redmond.'

'Well, what about it?' snarled the man.

'Soft pedal,' said MacBride. 'I'm going to plant you for a long while, buddy.'

'Like hell you are!' snapped Redmond.

'Sh!' put in Braun.

Redmond turned to him. 'What's the matter with you? You look yellow around the gills. Come on, tell this guy who we are. I can't hang around here all day. I got a date. Call the Commissioner on the telephone.'

Braun turned a shade whiter. 'Sh! Don't be a fool, Redmond!' he gulped.

'Well, then, let's go. He can't hold us. Telephone the Commissioner. I tell you, I got a date.'

MacBride said, 'Braun, do you want to make a telephone call?'

Braun shifted nervously, wore a pained look.

'Go ahead,' urged Redmond. 'Call him up.'

Braun went over to the telephone, called a number. 'Hello, George,' he said. 'Listen, George. . . . Huh? You know. . . . Well, what are you going to do? . . . Yeah, Pete is here. . . . Well, how could I help it? . . . Well, don't bawl *me* out, George. . . . All right.'

He hung up, said, 'He'll be right over.'

Kennedy licked his lips. 'Hot diggity!'

Braun was pale. Redmond scowled under MacBride's steady gaze and said, 'Think you're wise, eh? I get a great kick out of you, big boy. I didn't think they came that dumb.'

'You'll find how dumb I am,' said MacBride.

'Wait till the Commissioner comes,' smirked Redmond.

'Ah, just wait,' said Kennedy.

So everybody waited. Thirty minutes passed, and then an hour.

Braun said, 'I wonder what's keeping him.'

'He'd better hurry,' said Redmond. 'I got a date.'

'Oh, damn your date!' cried Braun.

'Yeah?' snarled Redmond.

MacBride took a drink and said, 'Pipe down.'

The telephone rang. Rigallo was nearest and took the call. When he hung up, he said, 'We should all go over to Headquarters.'

'Now why the hell should we go to Headquarters?' snapped Redmond. 'I'm not going.'

'Let's go,' said MacBride.

'I don't savvy this at all,' complained Redmond.

'It will be all right,' soothed Braun.

'It better be,' said Redmond.

MacBride called the morgue, said, 'There are a lot of stiffs at 46 North Street. Better come up and collect 'em.'

He went into the next room, and told one of the policemen to remain with the dead until the men from the morgue arrived. To the others he said, 'We're taking the rest over to Headquarters.'

MacBride, Rigallo and Doran and the three policemen gathered the six gangsters together and marched them down the stairs. All were handcuffed, including Braun, who stumbled as he walked. MacBride hauled him along roughly. Scoggins walked beside Kennedy.

Below, a crowd of people swarmed on the sidewalk outside the door. MacBride chased them as he led the way. Rigallo and Redmond were behind him. They marched down the street, two by two.

'I don't like this,' complained Redmond. 'I don't see why the hell we have to go to Headquarters.'

'Be quiet,' called back Braun.

'I tell you, guy, if—'

Bang!

VII

Redmond sagged, belched blood.

Bang!

Braun stopped in his tracks, buckled, groaned.

'Duck!' yelled MacBride, and dragged Braun into the nearest hallway.

Rigallo lugged Redmond into a fruit store.

Four shots rang out, and the four gangsters behind crumpled.

Kennedy and Scoggins dodged into a hardware store as a shot smashed the window beside them.

MacBride had disengaged himself from Braun. Braun was dead.

Rigallo joined the captain and said, 'Redmond's cooked, too. What the hell do you suppose happened anyway?'

'God knows, Riggy! Those shots came from that store across the way. Come on!'

He rushed into the street, blew his whistle. Doran came on the run, followed by the policemen. Doran said, 'Every guy was picked off, Cap, and there was some straight shooting! That store—'

'Yeah. Let's go,' clipped MacBride, and crossed the street on the run.

The store was empty, but they broke through the door and cascaded into the interior. The men bunched around MacBride.

'They've cleared out – through the back! Come on!' he said.

He led the way into the rear, and they found a back door open and thundered out into a yard. A fence barred the way, but they vaulted over it, crashed through the back door of another house and milled in a dark hallway.

MacBride rushed headlong, came to another door, yanked it open and looked out upon Jackson Street. He started to step out, when a machine-gun stuttered and the door frame splintered. Rigallo yanked him back, slammed the door.

'Don't be a fool, Mac!'

They heard the roar of a motor. It diminished in a few seconds. MacBride again opened the door, stepped out, looked up and down the street, said over his shoulder, 'Come on.'

His men came out warily. The street was empty – not a car, not a person in sight.

'Dammit!' muttered MacBride.

'Well, why worry?' asked a policeman. 'One gang against another. That's a good way of getting rid of rats.'

'It sure is,' said another cop.

MacBride grumbled.

Kennedy said, 'Come on, Mac. I've got several ideas.'

'I'm going to Headquarters,' growled MacBride. 'Riggy, you and Doran go back to North Street and see the morgue bus gets those bums.'

He turned on his heel and strode down the street. Kennedy fell in step beside him.

'Mac, we're near the end. It won't be long now. I figure you're just outside the Big Guy's doorstep.'

MacBride made no comment. His jaw was hard, and his eyes glittered.

They entered Police Headquarters. Kennedy lingered at the desk while MacBride went on to the Commissioner's office. But the Commissioner was not in. MacBride rejoined Kennedy at the desk, prodded him and marched out.

'What's the matter?' asked Kennedy.

'He's not in.'

'Where'd he go?'

'Left no word.'

They stopped on the wide steps outside, and MacBride lit a cigar.

A big black limousine drew up, and Commissioner Stroble alighted. He stood speaking with someone who remained in the tonneau behind drawn curtains. Then he suddenly spun around and saw MacBride and Kennedy standing on the steps. He spoke hastily in an undertone and stepped back to the sidewalk.

The car started off. Kennedy ran down the steps, called, 'Hey, how about a lift?'

The Commissioner looked startled. Kennedy jumped to the running-board, but the car jerked ahead, and he slipped, fell, rolled into the gutter.

Stroble mounted the steps, eyes narrowed. 'What do you want, MacBride?'

'Just wanted to see you.'

'Come up to my office.'

As MacBride followed Stroble in, he turned and saw Kennedy standing on the sidewalk, grinning.

In the Commissioner's office, a tenseness became apparent. Stroble took off his overcoat and sat down.

'Well, MacBride.'

'I thought you were coming over to North Street.'

'I was. But when I reached the street there was a gun-fight going on. I'm too old for gun-fights, MacBride.'

'Braun was killed. He was a friend of yours.'

Stroble sighed. 'Poor Charlie. Yes, he was a friend of mine, from school days. What kind of a mess did he get into?'

'I'm sure I don't know,' said MacBride. 'I caught him with a bad gang. A bird named Pete Redmond, from Chicago, and some other guns.'

'My!' exclaimed Stroble. 'That was strange. Charlie shouldn't have done that.'

'He was sure you could help him,' gritted MacBride.

'Yes, for old times' sake. Months ago he came to me and said Tate & Tate were riding him. Trade was falling off. He wanted more police protection. Well, I tried to make it easy for him. You'd do the same, MacBride, for an old friend. I didn't know he'd gone bad.'

MacBride restrained himself with an effort. Deep in his heart he knew that Braun had been double-crossed, yet what could he do? There was no evidence.

Stroble was saying, 'It was strange, too, how that other gang popped up. Why do you suppose they committed such wholesale slaughter?'

MacBride blurted out, 'It looks to me like a double-cross.'

Stroble blinked. 'I say, now, do you really think so?'

'Yes.'

'H'm. That is possible. Poor Charlie! He was a good chap, MacBride, but a bit of a fool. No clue to who did it?'

'No. All the cops ran to North Street when the shooting started. The gang, after they killed Braun, and the others, beat it through to Jackson Street and made a clean getaway. We tried to follow, but I damned near got plastered by a machine-gun. We had to hide.'

'Sensible, MacBride – very sensible. Personally, I believe that in such a situation, you should be careful. Gangs often destroy each other, and take that task off a policeman's hands. Of course, we must spread an alarm. But poor Charlie! I didn't think he'd take advantage of me – of a good thing, MacBride.'

'Scoggins, you know, was kidnapped and held by Braun's gang.'

'Goodness; Now why do you suppose they did that?'

MacBride leaned forward, barbed every word – 'So that we'd think Scoggins killed Nelson. So that red tape would tie up Tate & Tate a little longer, drive them nearer to bankruptcy, give the Harbor Towing a big lead.'

'Could that be possible!' exclaimed the Commissioner. 'And there I was trying to do Charlie a good turn, for old times' sake! It wasn't fair of Charlie. Do you think so, MacBride?'

'I don't know.'

'H'm. Well, run along. I've some work to do. File the report on this when you find time. Good luck.'

MacBride almost lost control of himself. His fingernails dug into his palms. A grunt escaped his lips.

The Commissioner looked up. 'Eh?'

MacBride snapped, 'Good day,' and banged out.

In the street he found Kennedy, and the reporter said, 'You look fit to be tied, Mac.'

'I am! I'm stumped!'

'Mac' – Kennedy took his arm and steered him down the street – 'Mac, buck up. Before very long you're either going to get the Big Guy – or he'll get you.'

'What do you mean, Kennedy?'

'I know things. Come on over to the station-house.'

They tramped into MacBride's office. Kennedy closed the door and locked it. He rubbed his hands together, smiled his tired, whimsical smile. He slid upon the desk, and tapped the blotter in front of MacBride.

'Get this, Mac, and think it over,' he said. 'I've been keeping a few things under my hat. Yesterday I made a discovery. Why do you think Stroble was giving the Harbor Towing all the breaks?'

'Braun was a friend of his.'

'Nonsense! Stroble is a big stockholder – silent one, you know – in the Harbor Towing.'

'How do you know?'

'I found out. I went to that lousy brokerage firm of Weber & Baum. They used to handle Stroble's business, but he broke with them, and they got sore. In confidence Baum told me that Stroble practically owns the Harbor Towing. And look here. The Mayor owns the Atlas Trucking Corporation – under cover – and the one is practically linked with the other.

'I've got the whole thing doped out, Mac. Pete Redmond was head of Stroble's private gang, and Braun had to move as he was told. When they balled things up that way, and when you flopped on their big parade – and I turned up at the right moment – the Commissioner knew that he was cooked.

'You had Braun and Redmond cold. Even Stroble, with all his power, couldn't get them clear. So what did he do? Wiped them out! Double-crossed them! Got another gang to kill everyone of them as you marched down the street.'

'Good God!' groaned MacBride. 'I believe you, Kennedy. I'm sure you're right. But the Mayor – man – the Mayor! You're sure he's mixed up in it?'

'I'll say this, Mac. I'll bet my shirt that the gang that wiped out Redmond was the Mayor's own. Stroble went to him, told him the fix he was in. The Mayor knew that if Braun and Redmond were caught, they'd squeal on the Commissioner and that Stroble would yap on the Mayor. So he lent Stroble his gang.'

'But who is the Mayor's gang?'

'That's for you to find out.'

'And you think the Mayor is the Big Guy?'

'If he isn't, I'm all wrong.'

MacBride snorted. 'Hell, Kennedy, it's incredible. I never thought much of him, but—'

'Look here, Mac,' cut in Kennedy. 'The Atlas Trucking Corporation has been having hard sledding, too. The Harbor Towing will have to shut up. Tate & Tate will get that concession at Seaboard Basin. But the Colonial Trucking Corporation is a subsidiary of Tate & Tate, and I'll bet that before long this trade war will be carried toward that end.'

'If it is, Kennedy—'

'You'll find a hard nut to crack.'

'I'll crack it or croak.'

Kennedy lowered his voice. 'I didn't tell you, Mac, who was in that limousine I tried to hop.'

Their eyes met, MacBride's wide and blunt, Kennedy's narrowed and smiling.

'Who, Kennedy?'

'Don't you know?'

'You mean, the. . . .'

'Sure,' nodded Kennedy. 'The Mayor!'

GRAFT

FREDERICK L. NEBEL

Police Captain Steve MacBride, elbow on desk, chin on knuckles, looked down along his nose at the open dictionary, and concentrated his gaze on the word 'graft.' Now graft is a word of various meanings, and the definitions, as MacBride discovered, were manifold. But the definition that attracted and held his eyes longest, was clean-cut, crisp and acutely to the point:

> Acquisition of money, position, etc., by dishonest, unjust, or parasitic means.

His lips moved. 'Parasitic. Humph! That's what they are, parasites!'

He sighed, creaked back in his swivel chair, and stared absently at the night-dark window. Cold out. The panes rattled. The wind hooted through the alley. More distant, it keened shrilly over housetops, whinnied through the complicated network of radio aerials. Even the poor had radios – bought tubes and what-not and went without shoes.

But graft. Parasitic. Parasites in the Town Hall. Hell, why hadn't he taken up plumbing, after his father? You could straighten out a bent pipe, plug a leak. But, as a police captain, with a wife and a daughter to support, and three thousand still due on that new bungalow in Grove Manor. . . .

He banged shut Webster's masterpiece with a low growl, got up and took a turn up and down the room. Straight was MacBride – morally and physically. Square-shouldered, neat, built of whip-cord, hard bone, tough hide. His face was long, rough-chiselled, packed well around cheek and jaw. His mouth was wide and firm, and his eyes were keen, windy – they could lacerate a man to the core.

He ran the Second Police Precinct of Richmond City. His frontiers touched the railroad yards and warehouses, plunged through a squalid tenement district and then suddenly burst into the bright lights of theatres, hotels, nightclubs. It was the largest precinct territorially in Richmond City. It was also the toughest.

Beyond the rooftops, a bell tolled the hour. Midnight. MacBride looked at his watch. Home. He could catch the last street car out to Grove Manor.

Stifling a yawn, he walked to a clothes tree and took down his conservative gray coat and his conservative gray hat. He had one arm in his coat when the door opened and Sergeant Flannery, bald as a billiard ball, poked in.

'Just a minute, Cap. Girl outside pestering me—'

'Why pass the buck?' MacBride had his coat on. 'I'm going home, Sergeant.'

'But I can't get rid of her. She wants to see you.'

'Me? Nonsense. You'll do for a sob case, Flannery. I mind the last sob sister you pawned off on me. Was hard up for a drink, the little tramp. Widowed mother and all that crap. Bah!'

'This one's different, Cap. Married a little over a year. Left her kid, three months old, home with her old lady. Name of Saunders. Lives over on Haggerty Alley. Damn near bawling. Wants to see you.'

'Well' – MacBride started to put on his hat, but changed his mind and flung it on the desk – 'send her in.'

Overcoat partly buttoned, he dropped into the swivel chair and sighed after the manner of a man who has to listen, day in and day out, to tales of woe, of stolen cats, strayed dogs, blackened eyes, and broken promises. Well, another wouldn't kill him. . . .

The girl came in timidly. She wore no hat, and her coat was a cheap thing, and she looked cold and forlorn and afraid. Pity – MacBride claimed there was not an ounce of it in his make-up – prompted him to say:

'Take that chair by the radiator. Warmer.'

'Thank you.'

Pretty kid. Young, pale, brown-eyed, hatless, and hair like spun copper. A mother. Haggerty Alley. God, what a draughty, drab hole!

'Well?'

'I came to you, Captain, because Jimmy – he's my husband – because Jimmy always says, "MacBride, the gent runs the Second, is one reason why there ain't more killings in this neighborhood." '

MacBride was on guard. He hated compliments. But, no, this wasn't salve. Her lower lip was quivering.

'Go on, madam.'

'Well, I feel funny, Mr. MacBride. I feel scared. Jimmy ain't come home yet. I've been reading things in the newspaper about some trouble in the trucking business. Jimmy drives a big truck between Richmond City and Avondale – that's thirty miles. He leaves at one and gets back to the depot at nine and he's always home at ten. He's been carting milk from Avondale, you know – for the Colonial Trucking Company.'

MacBride's eyes steadied with interest. He leaned forward. 'What makes you afraid, Mrs. Saunders?'

'Well, I was reading the paper only the other night, about this trouble in the trucking business, and Jimmy said, he said, "Wouldn't surprise me if I got bumped off some night." You know, Mr. MacBride, only last month one of the drivers was shot at.'

'H'm.' MacBride's fingers tapped on his knee. 'Don't worry, Mrs. Saunders. Everything's all right. Truck might have broken down.'

'I phoned the depot, and they said that, too. But the drivers always phone in if they're broke down. Jimmy ain't phoned in. The night operator was fresh. He said, "How do I know where he is?" So I hung up.'

'Listen, you go right home,' recommended MacBride. 'Don't worry. They don't always break down near a telephone. Run home. Want to catch cold chasing around the street? Go on, now. I'll locate Jimmy for you, and send a man over. Got a baby, eh?'

Her eyes shone. 'Yes. A boy. Eyes just like Jimmy's.'

MacBride felt a lump in his throat, downed it. 'Well, chase along. I'll take care of things.'

'Thank you, Mr. MacBride.'

She passed out quietly; closed the door quietly. Altogether a quiet, reticent girl. He stood looking at the closed door, pictured her in the street, rounding the windy corner, with shoulders hunched in her cheap coat – on into Haggerty Alley, dark, gloomy hole.

Jerking himself out of the reverie, he grabbed up the telephone, asked Information for the number of the night operator at the Colonial Trucking Company's River Street depot. He tapped his foot, waiting for the connection.

'Hel-lo-o,' yawned a voice.

'Colonial?'

'Yup.'

'That driver Saunders. Heard from him yet?'

'Cuh-ripes!' rasped the voice. 'Who else is gonna call about that guy? No, he ain't showed up, and he ain't called, and if you wanna know any more, write the president.'

'I'll come down there and poke you in the jaw!' snapped MacBride.

'Aw, lay off that boloney—'

'Shut up!' cut in MacBride. 'Give me the route Saunders takes in from Avondale.'

'Say, who the hell are you?'

'MacBride, Second Precinct.'

'Oh-o!'

'Now that route, wise guy.'

He picked up a pencil, listened, scribbled said, 'Thanks,' and hung up.

Then he took the slip of paper and strode out into the central room. Sergeant Flannery was dozing behind the desk, with a half-eaten apple in his pudgy hand.

'Sergeant!'

Flannery popped awake, took a quick bite at the apple, and almost choked.

'Chew your food,' advised MacBride, 'and you'll live longer. Here, call the booth at Adams Crossing. We're looking for a Colonial truck, number C-4682, between Avondale and here. Call the booths at Maple Street and Bingham Center. Those guys have bicycles. Tell 'em to start pedaling and ring in if they find any trace. Brunner – you can locate him at the Ragtag Inn. He hangs out there between twelve and one, bumming highballs. Tell him to fork his motorcycle and start hunting.'

He paused, thought. Then, 'Where's Doran and Rigallo?'

'Stepped out about eleven. Down at Jerry's, shooting pool. Should I flag 'em?'

'No.'

MacBride turned on his heel, entered his office and kicked shut the door. He sat down, bit off the end of a cigar, and lit up. He hoped everything was all right. Poor kid – baby three months old – Haggerty Alley – eyes like Jimmy's. Bah! He was getting sentimental. Did a man get sentimental at forty?

The door opened. Kennedy, of the *Free Press*, drifted in. A small, slim man, with a young-old face, and the whimsical, provocative eyes of the wicked and wise.

'Cold, Mac. Got a drink?'

MacBride pulled open a drawer. 'Help yourself.'

Kennedy hauled out a bottle of Dewar's and poured himself a stiff bracer – downed it neat. He slid on to a chair, coat collar up around his neck, and lit a cigarette. The cigarette bobbed in one corner of his mouth as he said:

'Anything new about this trucking feud?'

'Not a thing.'

Kennedy smiled satirically. 'The Colonial Trucking Company versus the Atlas Forwarding Corporation. Hot dog!'

'Take another drink and breeze, Kennedy.'

'Cold out. Warm here. Say, Mac, look here. What chance has the Colonial against the Atlas when the Atlas is owned – oh, privately, sure! – by the Mayor? Funny, how those inspectors swooped down on the Colonial's garage last week and condemned five trucks as unfit for service and unsafe to be on the public highways. Ho – protecting the dear, sweet public! D'you know the Atlas is worth five million dollars?'

'Shut up, Kennedy!'

'Funny, how that driver was shot at last week. He was going to tell something. Then he turned tail. Who threatened him? Or was he paid? The new State's Attorney, good chap, could get only negative replies out of him. Hell, the guy got cold feet! Then he disappeared. This State's Attorney is ambitious – too clean for this administration. He'll get the dirty end, if he doesn't watch his tricks. So will a certain police captain.'

MacBride bit him with a hard stare. Kennedy was innocently regarding the ceiling.

'Some day,' he went on, 'or some night, one of these drivers isn't going to get cold feet. I pity the poor slob!'

Sergeant Flannery blundered in, full of news.

'Brunner just rang in. Found the truck. Turned upside down in a gully 'longside Farmingville Turnpike. Milk cans all over the place. Driver pinned underneath. Brunner can't get him out, but he says the guy's dead. He's sent for a wrecking crew, nearest garage. Farmingville Turnpike, two miles west of Bingham Center.'

MacBride was on his feet, a glitter in his windy blue eyes. Haggerty Alley – eyes like Jimmy's. Hell!

'Haul out Hogan,' he clipped, 'and the flivver.' He buttoned his coat, banged out into the central room, fists clenched.

Kennedy was at his elbow. 'Let's go, Mac.'

'It's cold out, Kennedy,' said MacBride, granite-faced.

'Drink warmed me up.'

No use. You couldn't shake this news-hound. Prying devil, but he knew his tricks.

Outside, they bundled their coats against the ice-fanged wind, and waited.

The police flivver came sputtering out of the garage, and the two men hopped in.

MacBride said, 'Shoot, Hogan!'

II

Have you ever noticed how people flock to the scene of an accident, a man painting a flag-pole, or a safe being lowered from a ten-story window?

MacBride cursed under his breath as, the flivver rounding a bend on Farmingville Turnpike, he saw up ahead dozens of headlights and scores of people. A bicycle patrolman was directing traffic, and the flivver's lights shone on his bright buttons and shield. Automobiles lined either side of the road. People moved this way or that. One pompous old fellow, with a squeaky voice, remarked that truck drivers were reckless anyhow, and served him right for the spill.

MacBride stopped on the way by, glared at the man. 'Did you see this spill?'

'No – oh, no, no!'

'Then shut your trap!'

The captain was thinking of Haggerty Alley, and his tone was bitter. He moved on, and Motorcycle Patrolman Brunner materialized out of the gloom and saluted.

'Right down there, Cap. Guy's dead, and the truck's a mess. Can hardly see it from here.'

'How'd you spot it?'

'I went up and down this pike twice, and the second time I noticed how the macadam is scraped. The guy skid bad, and you can see the marks. Closed cab on the truck, and he couldn't jump.'

'Wrecker here yet?'

'No – any minute, though. Hoffman's handling traffic.'

'Give me your flashlight. Go out with Hoffman and get these cars moving.'

'Right.'

MacBride took the flash and started down the embankment. Kennedy, huddled in his overcoat, followed. The way was steep, cluttered with boulders, blanched bushes; and as they descended, they saw turned earth and split rocks, where the truck had taken its headlong tumble.

Then they saw the truck, a twisted heap of wood and metal. A ten-ton affair, boxed like a moving van. But the truck had crashed head-on into a huge boulder, and the radiator, the hood, the cab and the cargo were all jumbled together. And somewhere beneath this tangled mass lay the driver.

Kennedy sat down on a convenient stump and lit a cigarette. MacBride walked around the wreck, probing with his flashlight. The beam settled on an arm protruding from beneath the snarled metal. Bloody – the blood caked by the cold.

He snapped out the flash, stood alone in the chill darkness, quivering with suppressed rage. The wind, whistling across the open fields, flapped his coat about his legs. Probably that girl was still sitting up, with her slippered feet in the oven of the kitchen stove, and her wide, sad eyes fixed on the clock. Brutal thing, death. It not only took one, but stung others. He wondered if there were any insurance, and thought not. Good thing, insurance. He carried twenty thousand, double indemnity, in case of accident. Could a guy in the Second Precinct die any other way but through an accident? Or was getting a slug in your back by a coked wop, death from natural causes?

A broad beam of light leaped down into the rocky gully.

'Wrecker,' said Kennedy.

MacBride nodded, watched while several men came weaving down the slope.

'Cripes!' muttered one, upon seeing the wreck.

Another said, 'Hell, Joe, we can never haul this out. Need a derrick.'

'Well,' said MacBride, 'you've got axes. Hack away enough junk so you can get the man out.'

MacBride stood back, hands in pockets, chin on chest. Axes flashed, rang. Crow-bars heaved, grated.

Brunner came down and said, 'Morgue bus just came, Cap.'

They got the body out, and one of the men became sick at his stomach. Another – case-hardened – chuckled, said, 'Hell, buddy, you should ha' been in the war!' War! This was war – guerrilla warfare! War of intimidation!

They put a blanket over the dead man, laid him on a stretcher, carried him up over the hill and slid him into the morgue bus.

'I want the report as soon as possible,' MacBride said to the man from the morgue.

The bus roared off into the night.

MacBride and Kennedy climbed into the police flivver. It was a bleak, cold ride back to the precinct.

The captain, without a word, went straightway into his office, uncorked the bottle of Dewar's and downed a stiff shot. He rasped his throat, stood staring into space.

Kennedy drifted in, espied the bottle, rubbed his hands together gingerly. 'B-r-r! Cold out.'

MacBride turned, eyed him, then waved toward the bottle. 'Go ahead.'

'Thanks, Mac.'

Alone, MacBride went out into the black, windy street, turned a corner, crossed the street and entered Haggerty Alley. He stopped before a drab, three-story dwelling. Aloft, one lighted window stared into the darkness. He drummed his feet on the cold pavement, then suddenly pushed into the black hallway, snapped on his flash, and ascended the worn staircase.

Third floor. One lighted transom. He knocked. The door opened. That pale young face, wide, questioning eyes. Shoulders wrapped in a plaid shawl.

'Come . . . in.'

MacBride went in. Yes, the kitchen, and an old woman sitting before the open oven of the stove, and clothes drying on a line above the stove. Faded wallpaper, hand-me-down furniture, warped ceiling. Cracked oilcloth on the floor. Neat, clean – poverty with its face washed.

The girl knew. Oh, she knew! Her breath, bated for a long moment, rushed out.

'Is he . . . ?'

MacBride stood like an image of stone. 'Yes. Bad wreck.'

She wilted, like a spring flower suddenly overcome by an unexpected frost. The old woman moved, extended a scrawny arm.

'Betty!'

The girl reeled, spun, and buried her face in her mother's lap. The mother cradled her in ancient arms.

MacBride wanted to dash out. But he held his ground, and something welling from the depths of him melted the granite of his chiseled face. The old woman looked up, and though her eyes were moist, there was a certain grimness in her expression. Age is strong, mused MacBride. It meets fate with an iron jaw.

The old woman, looking at him, shook her head slowly, as if to imply that this was life, and we either died and left others to mourn, or mourned while others died.

MacBride put on his hat, backed toward the door, opened it softly. He bowed slightly, and without a word, departed.

He was a little pale when he reached the station-house. Doran and Rigallo, his prize detectives, and four or five reserves were hanging about the central room, and Kennedy, his coat collar still up to his ears, was leaning indolently against the wall and blowing smoke circles.

MacBride nodded to Doran and Rigallo and strode into his office. Kennedy tried to edge in but MacBride closed the door in his face. Doran hooked one leg over a corner of the desk and Rigallo stood jingling loose change in his pocket.

He said, 'Trouble, eh, Cap?'

'Plenty!' MacBride bit off.

'Was the guy shot?'

'No telling yet. Too messed up to see. That's the morgue's job. We'll get news soon. But I'm willing to bet my shirt the guy's been done in. If he has, I'm going to bust loose and drive the Atlas Corporation to the wall.'

Doran grunted. 'Fine chance, with that bum of a mayor back of it. How the hell did he ever get in?'

'Don't be dumb,' said Rigallo 'That last election was a farce. All the polls in the Fourth and Fifth wards were fixed. Guys voted twice, and the polls committee scrapped a lot of votes for the opposition because of some lousy technicality – illegibility, unreadable signatures and all that crap. Who votes in this city? The better element yap at conditions and turn up their noses and don't even go near the polls. The bums, the bootleggers, the blockheads and gunmen vote! And the New Party sends loud-mouthed guys to ballyhoo the mill and river bohunks during lunch-hour, and under-cover guys go around near the employment agencies, the bread-lines, and the parks. They find guys out of work and up against it, and they slip 'em a ten-dollar bill to vote. The Atlas Corporation employs eight hundred men, and they vote right or lose their jobs, and their wives, mothers and the whole damned family are dragged to the polls. Now d'you wonder why we have this bum of a mayor?'

MacBride said, 'Sounds like Kennedy.'

'It is,' replied Rigallo. 'Kennedy and I have the whole thing thrashed out.'

The telephone rang. MacBride picked it up, muttered his name, and listened. When he put the instrument down, he sucked in his breath and curled his lip.

'Poisoned,' he said. 'Saunders, the driver, was poisoned. A stuff that he could drink and it wouldn't have any effect for an hour. Then it hits a man like a stroke of paralysis. That's how it hit Saunders.'

Doran said, 'Must have stopped at a roadhouse for a snifter and got poisoned liquor.'

'Just that,' nodded MacBride. 'I'll find that roadhouse. Some pup is going to hang for this, just as sure as God made little green apples!'

'Remember, Cap, the mayor,' put in Doran.

MacBride doubled his fist. 'I'll bring it right to his doorstep if I have to, and I'd like to see the bum try to can me. I'm sick and tired of these conditions! I'm going to put a dent in the Atlas Corporation, and wipe out this graft, this dirty, rotten corruption.'

'They'll bump you off, Mac.'

'I'll take the chance! I'm insured for twenty thousand, and my plot in the cemetery is paid for!'

It took a tough man to run the Second.

III

Next day the noon edition of the *Free Press* gave the wreck and the death of Saunders a front-page column. It recited the details in its customary offhand manner, giving the place, the approximate time, name of the deceased, and financial loss. It wound up with the non-committal statement that the police were investigating the matter, but did not say why.

MacBride, reading it over his coffee, at his home in Grove Manor, was a little disgruntled at its apparently disinterested attitude. But, turning the pages, his eye rested on the editorial columns, and particularly on an item labeled,

CRIME – CORRUPTION

Crime. We've always had it. It is a disease, recurring every so often, like smallpox, diphtheria, and scarlet fever. It lays waste, like any and all of these diseases, and causes suffering, misery and despair.

And on the other hand, wealth, affluence, power. To whom? Why, to those, quite often in high place, who like parasites, feast avidly upon the meaty morsels gathered by vultures who swoop in the dark, kill from behind, and crow at the dawn.

What we need is a crusader. Not a preaching, scripture-quoting, holier-than-thou sort of fellow. Not an altruist, nor a gavel-thumper. But a Man, and we capitalize that symbolically. A man somewhere in the rusty machinery of this municipality, who cares not a whoop for authority and is willing to stack the possibility of losing his job against the possibility of sweeping out the unclean corridors of intrigue and corruption, and satisfying the ego of his own morals and ethics.

A two-fisted, slam-bang, tougher-than-thou sort of man! The streets of Richmond City are more sordid than its sewers. They smell to high heaven. We need a chunk of brimstone to sterilize them. Amen.

'Whew!' whistled MacBride. 'This will cause apoplexy in the Town Hall. The *Free Press* is out to ride 'em.'

He was back in his office at the precinct at one, and Kennedy was sound asleep in the swivel chair. He kicked it, and Kennedy awoke.

'Hello, Mac.'

'Hello. Pretty ripe, that editorial.'

'Thanks.'

MacBride looked at him. 'You didn't write it.'

'Yup. My name'll go down in posterity.'

'If the Big Gang knew you did it, it would go down in the Deceased Column. Get out o' that chair.'

Kennedy got out and sat on the desk, swinging his legs.

MacBride said, 'I see, now, that you were shooting in my direction. Humph. Crusader!'

Kennedy smiled. 'Would you, Mac.'

'I am,' snapped MacBride, 'but there's nothing of the crusader about me. I'm sore, and I'll bust up this racket if it's the last thing I do. That poor kid, Kennedy – her name's Betty. . . . God Almighty! Government of the people, by the people and for the people! What a bromide!'

He pulled an empty cigar box from his desk, took a pen and a piece of paper, and on the paper printed, in large letters:

SPARE CHANGE, BOYS,
FOR A HARD-HIT NEIGHBOR

This he pasted on the cover of the box, and said, 'Dig down, Kennedy.'

He himself dropped in a couple of dollars, and Kennedy added another and some odd change. Then MacBride carried the box into the central room and placed it on the desk, where none might pass without seeing it.

Still in plain-clothes, he shook Kennedy, and walked down to River Street. He found the Colonial depot, and from a number of drivers learned that, on cold nights, they usually stopped at the *Owl's Nest*, out beyond Bingham Center, on the pike, for a shot of rum. Reasoning that Saunders had lived, driven and drunk similarly, he took a trolley car to the outskirts of the city, alighted where Main crossed Farmingville Turnpike, and boarded an outbound bus.

It was a long ride, and they passed the shattered truck on the way. It still lay in the gully, but a derrick was at work, and one of the Colonial's trucks was gathering up the remains. At four-thirty he left the bus, and stood regarding the *Owl's Nest*. It stood well back off the highway, a low, rambling casino with many windows. The main entrance was decorated with colored light bulbs, but on one side was a sign, *Delivery Entrance*, and MacBride judged that this also was the logical entrance for truck-men in quest of a drink.

He pushed this door open and found himself in a hallway that turned sharply to the left. But directly in front of him was an open door leading into a small, shabby room containing two tables and a half dozen chairs, and a fly-specked electric light hanging from the ceiling.

MacBride sat down, and presently a man in shirt-sleeves entered.

'Rye highball,' said MacBride.

The man, large, beetle-browed, hairy-armed, looked him over, then shook his head. 'No drinks here, buddy.'

'Tripe! I know.'

'Not here, buddy.'

'You the boss?'

'No.'

'Flag the boss.'

The man disappeared, and a few minutes later a short, fat, prosperous-looking man entered with a frown of annoyance. But the frown disappeared like a cloud and sunlight beamed.

'Oh, hello, Mac.'

'Didn't know you ran this dump, Hen. Sit down.'

Hen sat down, cheerful, twinkle-eyed, and said to the hovering waiter, 'Make it two, Mike.' And a moment later, to MacBride, 'What *you* doing out this way, Mac?'

'Poking around.'

'I mean – really, Mac.'

'Trailing a clue. Hear about that truck smash-up?'

'Sure. Tough, wasn't it?'

'You don't know the half of it. And that's why I'm up here, Hen.'

Hen's eyes widened perplexedly. He started to say something, but the drinks arrived, and he licked his lips instead. The waiter went out, and the two men regarded each other.

MacBride jerked his head toward the door. 'How long has that guy been working here? What's his name?'

'A month. Mike Bannon.'

'He serves all the drinks?'

'Ye-es.'

'All the truck drivers stop in this room, I guess?'

'Sure.'

MacBride took a drink and let it sink in. 'Good stuff,' he nodded, and then leaned across the table. 'You're a white guy, Hen, and you're sensible. Fire that man.'

'What's the matter?'

'Fire him tomorrow. If he gets sore, tell him the cops are tightening down on you, and you're cutting out the hooch for a month or more. I'm doing you a turn, Hen. You want to keep your hands clean, don't you?'

'Cripes, yes, Mac!'

'Then bounce him – tomorrow at noon.'

'Okey, Mac.'

MacBride was back in the precinct at seven. He picked up Rigallo and Doran and they all went over the Headquarters and sought out the Bureau of Criminal Identification. This was a vast place, lined with rows of card-indexes, and on the wall were several huge metal books, attached by their backs, so that a man could swing the metal pages back and forth and scan the photographs of those men who, having stepped outside the law, were recorded therein, with further details of their crimes recorded in the surrounding files. MacBride, turning page after page, suddenly grunted and pointed.

'There's the guy, boys,' he said.

He noted the number, gave it to the attendant, and while waiting, said to his prizes, 'Working at the *Owl's Nest*.'

The attendant reappeared with a card and handed it to MacBride. MacBride scrutinized it. 'H'm. Michael Shane, arrested for criminal assault against Rosie Horovitz, June 12, 1924. Indicted, June 13th. Acquitted July 2nd. Lack of evidence. And again: Arrested October 5, 1925. Charge, felonious assault with attempt to rob. Charge preferred by Sven Runstrom. Indicted October 6th. Sentenced October 15th, sixty days, hard labor.'

'Let's go out and nab him,' said Rigallo.

'No,' said MacBride. 'He's working as Mike Bannon. Come on.'

They returned to the precinct, and in the privacy of his office, MacBride said, 'This guy poisoned Saunders' liquor, but I'm after bigger game. He's a tough nut, and he'll hold his tongue until some shyster, retained by the gang, gets him out of our hands on a writ. What we want to know is, who's the boss of the gang, the mayor's right-hand man. *That* is the guy we want. We've got more to do than apprehend the actual murderer of Saunders. We've got to grab the mob and their boss, and prevent further killings, and when we do this we'll have the mayor against the wall. Shane is a stoical bum, and a rubber hose wouldn't work him. We've got to get the big guy – the one with the most brains and the least guts.'

'What's your idea?' asked Rigallo.

'Just this. At tomorrow noon Shane gets his walking papers from Hen Meloy. You go out there tomorrow morning in a hired flivver, and when this guy gets a bus headed for town, tail him. He'll head for his boss, to report. Tail him that far and then give me a ring.'

MacBride went home early that night, slept well, and was back on the job at nine next morning. He took the cigar box from the desk in the central room, went into his office, and counted out forty-two dollars and fifty cents. This he shoved into an envelope, with the brief message, 'From the bunch at the Second Police Precinct.' He called in a reserve, gave him the envelope and the Haggerty Alley address, and then, sitting back with a sigh, started his first cigar of the day.

Kennedy dropped in on his way to Headquarters, and said, 'The municipal inspectors condemned two more Colonial trucks. Said Saunders death was caused by a faulty steering gear. Nobody knows the details? What did the morgue say, Mac?'

'Run along, Kennedy.'

'Keeping it under your hat, eh? It's all right, Mac. I can wait. Here's another tip. The Colonial people aren't dumb, and there's a guard riding on all their night trucks now. They're die-hards, Mac. These guys liked Saunders, and they're primed to start shooting first chance they get.'

Kennedy went out, and MacBride cursed him in one breath and complimented him in the next.

At two o'clock the telephone rang and MacBride grabbed it.

'Cap? Rigallo.'

'Shoot, Riggy.'

'Tailed him okey. Two-ten Jockey Street. I'm waiting in the cigar store on the corner. Come heeled.'

MacBride hung up, slapped on his visored cap, and strode into the central room. 'Six reserves, Sergeant! Ready, Doran!'

A windy look was in his eyes, and his jaw squared.

IV

Jockey Street is hell's own playground. You enter it from the theatrical center, and all is glittering, blatant and intensely alive. But as you bore deeper, riverward, the street lights become further apart, the chop suey joints disappear, and the houses, losing height, likewise lose color.

It was cold that afternoon, and fog smoked in from the river, damp and chill. The din of upper Jockey Street died to a murmur, and on its lower reaches few men were afield. Here or there you heard footsteps, and soon, dimly at first, then clearer, a pedestrian materialized out of the fog, swished by and gradually disappeared again, trailing his footsteps. Up the man-made causeway came the muffled rhythmic tolling of a pier-head fog bell.

Down it rolled a black, inconspicuous touring car, with drawn side-curtains. Nearing a side street, the door to the tonneau opened, and MacBride leaped out. The car rolled on, was swallowed up by the wet gray clouds.

MacBride strode toward a cigar-store. Rigallo came out, smoking a cigarette, looking unconcerned. They fell in step and strolled down the side street, leisurely.

'He hasn't come out, Riggy?'

'No. Came on the bus to Main and Farmingville. Took a taxi from there. Got off at Main and Jockey. Walked. I left the car there and walked, too. Saw him go in 210. There's a gray touring car parked outside – powerful boat.'

'I'll crash the joint.'

'They'll never open the door. Bet you need signals.'

'Try my way.'

They circumnavigated the block, and came out upon Jockey Street a block nearer the river. Here the police car was parked, the men still hidden inside. MacBride stood on the edge of the curb, spoke to the curtains.

'I'm aiming to get in 210. Two minutes after I leave here you boys get out and surround this block. It may be messy.'

'Okey,' came Doran's low voice.

MacBride said, 'Come on, Rigallo,' and they walked up the street. He explained. 'We'll both climb the steps to the door. I'll knock. Somebody will come, but if he doesn't get the proper signals, he won't open. But he'll listen. Then you walk down the steps, hard as you can, and walk away. He may open then and peek out. I'll crash it.'

'What then?'

'Hell knows!' MacBride's fists clenched. 'Just let me get in that dump!'

They reached the four stone steps that led to the door of 210. They mounted them, and MacBride, one hand on the gun in his pocket, knocked with the other.

They waited, looking at each other. Presently they heard the padding of footsteps, then silence. MacBride knocked again, insistently. No, that wasn't the signal. He nodded to Rigallo. Rigallo nodded back, stamped heavily down the steps and walked off.

MacBride flattened against the doorframe, breath bated, gun half-drawn. The latch clicked. A hinge creaked. The door moved an inch, another inch. A nose appeared. Then two beady eyes, and a pasty, pinched face.

MacBride cannoned against the door, and knocked the look-out sprawling. The door, working on a spring, slammed shut. The captain was bent over the prostrate, speechless form, with the muzzle of his gun screwed into a sunken chest.

'Chirp and I'll bust you!'

The man writhed under the firm pressure of the gun. His mouth worked, gasping. His eyes popped.

'Cripes!' he moaned.

'Pipe down! Quick, now. What's the lay? Where's the gang?'

'Cripes!'

'Spill it!

'Cripes!'

Desperate, MacBride rapped his jaw with the gun barrel.

'Ouch!'

'Then talk!'

'Second floor, door t' back o' the hall. Cripes!'

'Open?'

'Uh – yup.'

'How many?'

'Tuh – ten.'

'Get up!'

MacBride hauled the runt to his feet, dragged him to the front door, opened it. Rigallo was on the curb. MacBride motioned to him, and Rigallo skipped up.

'Take this, Riggy!'

Rigallo grabbed the look-out, clapped on manacles. 'Should I get the boys?'

'No. I'll start the ball. There are ten guys upstairs, and I feel ambitious. Besides, if we all crash it, it will be a mix-up and the boys might get hurt. One man can crash a room better than six. I'll blow when I need you. You hang here, and then blow for the boys.'

'It's a long chance, Cap!'

'I carry heavy insurance. Don't let this door close.'

MacBride turned and re-entered the hall. Gun drawn, he went up the stairway, paused at the first landing, listened, and then ascended the next flight. He was wary, alert, dangerous. There were captains on the Force who directed operations from the outside, smoking cigars on street corners, at a safe distance. MacBride was a man who never sent his men into a trap before first examining the trap himself. One reason why his wife lay awake nights, thinking.

Door in the rear. He stood at the stair-head, muscles tense, gun pointing toward the door. He advanced straight, light-footed, primed to go off. He stood before the door, the muzzle of his gun an inch from the panel.

His left hand started out, closed gently, carefully, over the knob. Some said you should turn a knob slow, bit by bit, until you could not turn it any more; then heave and rush. But sometimes you never got that far. A knob might creak. A wandering gaze on the other side might see it turning.

Turn, heave and rush all at once – that was it. MacBride did it. The door whanged open and he crouched on the threshold, poised and deadly.

A woman, alone, looked up from the depths of an overstuffed chair. She had been trimming her fingernails with a steel file, and she sat there, apparently unperturbed, the file, in her right hand, poised over the thumb of her left. She wore a negligée, pink and sheer. Her hair was peroxide treated, bobbed and fuzzy.

MacBride reached back and closed the door. The woman, with a shrug, went on trimming her nails, and said, in an offhand manner,

'Got your nerve, Cap, busting in on a lady.'

'What's wrong with that sentence, Gertie?'

'Well, rub it in.'

'Get dressed.'

'I'm not going out.'

'No?' He leaned back. 'I'm waiting.'

She rose, running her hands down her sides and lodging them on her hips, thumbs forward.

'Suppose I yell?'

'You'll be the first woman I ever killed.'

'You would?'

'I sure would.'

They stood staring at each other, the lynx and the lion.

'Think I can get dressed with you in the room?'

'I'm not particular. If you're too modest, put on that fur coat.'

'I'm not modest. *Particular*, guy.'

'Put on the coat.'

She tilted her chin, cut MacBride with a brassy, withering look. Then she sauntered over to the coat, picked it up and slipped into it. She thrust her hand into a pocket.

'Careful!' warned MacBride.

She laughed, drew out a handkerchief, touched her nose and then shoved the handkerchief back into her pocket. A split second later flame and smoke burst through the fur, and hot lead ran up MacBride's gun arm. His gun clattered to the floor.

The woman leaped for the switch, threw off the lights. With his left hand MacBride, gritting his teeth with pain, recovered the gun. Another burst of flame slashed through the darkness, and a shot whanged by his ear. He dived, headlong, collided with the woman and knocked her over. Again her gun went off, wildly, and the shot banged through the ceiling.

With his wounded hand MacBride groped for hers – found it, wrenched away her gun, groaned with the pain of it. He heaved up, rushed to the door, shot home the bolt. Then he dived for the light switch, snapped it, and a dazzling radiance flooded the room.

The woman, on her feet, flung a Chinese vase. MacBride ducked and the vase crashed through a mirror. She crouched, quivering in every muscle, her breath pumping fiercely from her lungs, eyes wide and storming with anger.

'You – lousy – bum!' she cried.

'Pipe down!'

Fists hammered on the door, feet kicked it. Voices snarled.

The woman laughed hysterically. 'The Gang! The Gang! They'll riddle you! They'll cut your dirty heart out!'

'Will they?'

MacBride drew his whistle, blew it.

V

Abruptly, the scuffling and pounding stopped. A moment of silence, then retreating footsteps.

MacBride stood with his cap tilted over one ear and a slab of hair down over one eyebrow. His right arm hung down, blood weaving a red tracery on his hand, then dropping to the floor. His hand felt heavy as lead, dragging at wounded muscles. A thought struck him, and he shoved the hand into his coat pocket.

Footfalls sounded again, hammering up the stairs. Cops' shoes – heavy-soled, thick-heeled. Now they were out in the hall, moving about, whispering hoarsely. MacBride backed against the door, unbolted it, pulled it open.

Rigallo came in. 'Hell, Gertie!' he chuckled, sarcastically.

Gertie thumbed her nose and wiggled her fingers.

'You trollop!' snapped Rigallo.

'Pst, Riggy,' said MacBride. 'Where's the look-out?'

'Doran's got him in the machine.'

'Jake!' He looked into the hall. Six cops out there and two closed doors. They had the doors covered. 'Take her downstairs, Riggy.'

'Who's her boy friend?'

'That's what we'll find out. She's not talkative just now. Grab a dress, sister, and take it along.'

'If you think I'll spill the boy friend's name, MacBride, you're all wet,' she snapped.

'Take her, Riggy.'

Rigallo grabbed a dress from a hanger and flung it at her. It draped across her shoulder. She left it there.

'Get out,' he jerked.

She put one hand on her hip and sauntered leisurely. Rigallo took a quick step, gripped her by the arm and propelled her out not too gently. She cursed and added something relative to his maternity. He trotted her down the stairs.

MacBride joined his cops. 'Let's bust this door.'

Seven guns boomed, and seven shots shattered the doorknob and crashed through the lock. Patrolman Grosskopf, one-time leader of a German mud-gutter band, hurled his two hundred and twenty pounds of beef against the door and almost ripped it from its hinges.

MacBride waved his men back and stepped in. The room was empty. His right hand was still in his pocket. His men did not know he was wounded. He came out in the hall and nodded at the other door.

Bang! Seven shots sounded as one.

'Now, Grosskopf.'

Grosskopf catapulted, and the door capitulated.

The room yawned empty. It showed signs of some having made a hasty departure. Bureau drawers were pulled out, a chair was overturned. Glasses, some of them still containing liquor, stood on the table. A chair, also, stood on the table.

'Up there,' said MacBride, pointing to a skylight. 'To table, to chair, to roof.'

He led the way up to the roof, and they prowled around, from one roof to another. Wind, fog, and emptiness. They came to a fire-escape in the rear.

'They skipped,' he said. 'Come on back.'

Below, in the hall, they found Rigallo and the woman, Doran and the look-out. MacBride looked at the woman but addressed his men. 'We've got an ace-in-the-hole now. Let's go.'

They went out into the foggy street, and MacBride said to the look-out, 'Thought you tricked me, eh? Ten men in the back room!'

The woman laughed. 'Ten! That's headquarters, Cap, not the barracks. What a joke! There was only three – in the front.'

Rigallo said to the look-out, 'Boy Scout, we will entertain you a while at the precinct. I have a nice new piece of rubber hose.'

They piled into the police car. Its motor roared. It turned about and purred up Jockey Street, and at Main Rigallo got out and picked up his flivver, and the two cars proceeded toward the Second.

The prisoners were locked up in separate cells. Then MacBride, alone, went out and walked several blocks and entered a door above which was a small sign bearing the legend, Dr O. F. Blumm, M.D.

'Oh, hello, Mac.'

'Hello, Doc. Fix this.' He drew his blood-soaked hand from his pocket, and the doctor frowned, murmured, 'H'm,' and added, 'Take off the coat, shirt.'

The bullet had struck just above the wrist, sliced open three inches of the forearm and lodged in the hard flesh just short of the elbow. MacBride, teeth clamped, his eyes closed, shed streams of sweat while the doctor probed for the bullet and finally removed it. Then MacBride sank back, a little pale, very grim.

'It might have been worse,' remarked the doctor.

'Sure,' said MacBride, and breathed quietly while the wound was cauterized, stitched and bandaged.

'Most men take a little dope for this, Mac.'

'Uh!' grunted MacBride through tight lips.

Through the fog, he returned to the station-house, his hand concealed in his pocket, his wound throbbing.

Kennedy was lounging in the office. 'You look yellow around the gills, Mac.'

'Liver,' clipped MacBride, and took a drink.

'Hear you got Gertie Case and Midge Sutter.'

'Um.'

'How long do you suppose you can hold 'em?'

'Watch me.'

'There'll be a writ of release here before you know it,' said Kennedy. 'How come you didn't get the gang?'

'Breeze, Kennedy! Dammit, I'm not in the mood!'

Kennedy shrugged and went out.

Alone, MacBride drew out his hand, laid it on the desk. God, how the arm throbbed! He heard a voice outside the door and slipped the hand back into his pocket. The door opened and a big, bloated man, with a moon-face, large fishy eyes, and an air of pompous importance, sailed in.

'Hello, Mac.'

'Hello.'

Captain Bower, plainclothes, a Headquarters 'yes man,' and the mayor's bodyguard. MacBride drew into himself, wary, on guard.

Bower deposited his indecent bulk in an arm-chair and sent a tobacco shot into the cuspidor. 'This latest business, Mac. The Jockey Street fizzle.'

'Fizzle?'

'Well, whatever you like. Anyhow it's out of your district, and Headquarters is going to handle it. Another thing. We're also handling the case of Saunders. Of course, there's nothing to it, and we'll dispose of it right off.'

MacBride's jaw hardened. Graft again! Nothing to it! Bah! They knew he was out to riddle their racket. They were cornered, and playing a subtle game. They could not fire him immediately, could not shove him out in the sticks while this thing was hanging fire. But they *could* take a case out of his hands. Could they?

'It's my case, Bower,' he snapped. 'My men got the clues, did the tailing, and we've got Midge Sutter and that Case broad salted.'

'On what charge?'

'Suspicion. That's enough for any cop.'

'We'll work it out at Headquarters,' said Bower, very matter-of-fact. 'I'll take the pair along with me, now.'

Color crept into MacBride's face. 'Not before I indict 'em – tomorrow.'

Bower frowned. 'Don't be a goof. What can you indict 'em on?'

MacBride was in his last ditch, his back to the wall. He had hoped to conceal this, but—'

He drew out his wounded arm, placed it on the table. 'This, Bower. The woman potted me.'

Bower's face dropped, and his mouth hung open. He stared at the bandaged hand. Then he drew his face back into place and got up.

'Good-bye,' he sniffed, and pounded out.

MacBride waited a few minutes, then called in Rigallo. 'Riggy, take Sutter in the sweat room. Sweat him.'

'Right,' nodded Rigallo, and went out.

MacBride sat back in his chair and lit a cigar. The pain pounded furiously, shot up and down his arm, reached his neck. Sweat stood out on his forehead, and muscles knotted on either side of his wide, firm mouth. An hour dragged by.

Then Rigallo came in, brushing his hands together. His hair, ordinarily neatly combed, was a bit disheveled.

'Well?' asked MacBride.

Rigallo shook his head. 'No go. The guy is little but tough. He's been through it before. Knows if he squeals the gang will crucify him.'

MacBride held up his wounded arm. Rigallo clicked his teeth.

'Hell, Mac. I didn't know.'

'The broad got me. Look here, Riggy. You're the whitest wop I've ever known. My back is to the wall, and I need a guy who's willing to kick authority in the slats and play this game to a fare-three-well.'

'Shoot, Mac.'

'Take the broad and bounce her around from one station to another. They'll have a writ out for her, or some trick. The idea is, the writ mustn't find her. When they come here, I'll say she's over at the Third. Then I'll ring you and you take her to the Fourth and so on, and the guys at the Fourth will tell the runner you've taken her to the Fifth. Keep ahead of the runner. The precincts will play with us. They're good guys. Keep moving until tomorrow morning. Judge Ross will be on the job then, and he's the only judge we can depend on. He'll indict her. We'll get hell, Riggy, but we'll crash this racket.'

'Right!'

Five minutes later Rigallo was headed for the Third with Gertie Case.

Ten minutes later a runner appeared with writs for Gertrude Case and Midge Sutter.

'Sutter's here,' said MacBride, 'and you can take him. But the Case woman's over at the Third.'

And he telephoned the Third.

A little later a doctor from the Medical Examiner's Office, accompanied by Captain Bower, entered, and the doctor said:

'I'll look at your wound, Captain.'

Grim, stony-faced, MacBride allowed his wound to be looked at.

The doctor said, 'Bad, Captain. You can't carry on.'

'The hell I can't!'

'Nevertheless—' The doctor sat down and affixed his signature to a document, scaled it across to MacBride. 'You're released from active duty until I sign a health certificate of reinstatement. Signed by the Commissioner and attested by me. Go home and rest.'

MacBride saw through a red haze. Vaguely, he heard Bower's words. 'Your lieutenant will take charge until a captain can be sent over.'

MacBride's heart sledge-hammered his ribs. The men went out, and he sat alone, like a man in a daze. Alone against graft, corruption and the very Department to which he had given eighteen years of his life! The blow should have crushed him, sent him storming out of the station in rage and righteous indignation. It should have driven him to ripping off his uniform, throwing his badge through the window, and cursing the Department to the nethermost depths.

But tough was MacBride, and a die-hard. He heaved up, swiveled and glared at the closed door. His lip curled, and challenge shone in his eyes.

'Home – *hell!*' he snarled.

VI

But he went out, his slouch hat yanked over his eyes. Night had closed in, half-brother to the fog. And both shrouded the city. Street lights glowed wanly, diffusing needle-like shafts of shimmering radiance. Headlights glared like hungry eyes. Autos hissed sibilantly on wet pavements. Faces appeared, palely afloat, and then disappeared.

Cold and wet and miserable, and MacBride tramping the streets, collar up, hands in pockets, pain pumping through his arm. In minutes he aged years. Why not let things slide? Why go to all the bother? What reward, what price honour? Let Headquarters take 'em. Let Bower frame their getaway. Cripes, but Bower would get a nice slice of graft out of this! How could a single precinct captain hope to carry his white plume in this city of graft?

He dragged to a stop at an intersection. Well, Rigallo was standing by him. And the State's Attorney was a square-shooter.

'H'm.'

He suddenly flagged a taxi, climbed in and gave an address. Out of the dark of the street another figure appeared, got into a second taxi.

Ten minutes later MacBride alighted in a quiet, residential street, told the driver to wait, and ascending a flight of brown-stone steps, pushed a bell-button. A servant appeared and MacBride gave his name. A moment later he was ushered from the foyer into a spacious library.

State's Attorney Rolland, thirty-eight, lean, blond, clean-cut in evening clothes, extended a hand. MacBride shook with his left, and though Rolland's eyes flickered, he said nothing.

'You look worn, Captain. Sit down. Cigar?'

'Thanks – no. Am I keeping you?'

'No. Dinner at eight.' He leaned against the side of a broad mahogany table, arms folded loosely, eyes quizzical.

MacBride detailed, briefly, the fight in Jockey Street, the apprehension of Gertie Case and Midge Sutter; the release of Sutter on a writ, the game of hide and seek even now being played by Rigallo.

'I'll pick up Rigallo and the woman around dawn,' he went on. 'I'll get her indicted. I thought if you could be around there, to take her in hand before her lawyer gets to her— Hell, we've got to get the jump on these pups!'

'Don't know her man, eh?'

'No. That's why we've got to hold her. If she's faced with twenty years for shooting an officer, she'll think. She's thirty now, and no guy is worth enough in her eyes to take a twenty-year rap for him. She'll come across. Ten to one her boy friend realizes this.'

'And you believe that Saunders chap was poisoned?'

'Yes. Bannon did it. He's been lying low for a couple years. Always lone-wolfed. That's why we can't connect him with the gang he must have hooked with. If the Case woman squeals, we'll get the gang, and getting the gang means—'

'Ah, yes,' nodded Rolland.

It was politic, in the State's Attorney's rooms, not to mention the name both men had in mind.

Then Rolland said, 'Good you have the woman. These gangsters laugh at a prison sentence. But a woman – and especially one of her type – looks upon prison as death. I'll be there in the morning. Take care of your wound.'

They shook, and MacBride departed. The Regime thought they had picked soft clay in Rolland. What a shock when they had discovered cement instead, unpliable!

Entering the taxi, MacBride drove off, and further back, another taxi began moving.

He left his taxi at the Fourth, and discovered that Rigallo and the woman had gone on to the Fifth ten minutes before. He hung around, saw the runner with the writ rush in and start broadcasting to the desk. The sergeant told him where the woman had gone, and cursing, the runner went off and out like a streak.

MacBride followed from station to station, and at the Seventh, just after the runner had gone on, he met Bower.

'Look here, MacBride. What's your game?'

'What's yours, Bower?'

'Cut that boloney.'

'Then cut yours.'

Bower scowled. 'You'll get broke for this. Stop that guy that's got the dame.'

'I don't know where he is. What's more, Bower, I'm off duty. Got nothing to say. You find him – and try stopping him. Your job depends on that, Bower.'

Bower worked his hands. He started to say something but bit his lip instead and stormed out.

A game was being played on the checkerboard of Richmond City's police stations. Rigallo moved from one to another, doubled back, moved across town, uptown, downtown. Midnight passed, and dawn approached, and still Rigallo kept the lead; and Bower blundered in his wake, fuming and cursing; and the man with the writ, worn to a frazzle by the chase, now tottered at Bower's heels.

MacBride, weary, haggard, sapped by the pain in his arm, sometimes dizzy, met Rigallo in the Eighth at four a.m. Gertie cursed and protested at such inhuman treatment, but no one paid her any attention.

MacBride and Rigallo formulated plans, and then MacBride took the woman and carried on the game. When Bower caught up with Rigallo, the latter wasted half an hour of the other's time by stalling, kidding and then finally telling Bower that the woman was probably uptown. Bower saw the trick and bowled off in high heat.

When he caught up with MacBride, he discovered that the woman had again changed hands and was now probably downtown. Bower cursed a sizzling blue streak and was indiscreet enough to call MacBride an untoward name.

With his one good hand, MacBride hung a left hook on Bower's jaw and draped him over a table. Then he went out into the wet gray dawn, and felt a little better.

At half-past eight he met Rigallo in the Third, joined him and the woman in Rigallo's flivver.

'Cripes, I'll never get over this!' rasped Gertie.

'You said something, sister,' nodded MacBride.

'You're a big bum, MacBride,' she stabbed. 'And you're another, Rigallo.'

Rigallo spat. 'Three of a kind, eh?'

'And your mother's another,' she added.

Rigallo took one hand from the wheel and with the palm of it slapped her face.

She laughed, baring her teeth, brazenly.

A block behind, a taxi was following.

Ahead yawned the entrance to Law Street, and half way down it loomed the Court.

'Here's where you get indicted, sister,' said MacBride.

'I'm laughing.'

'You don't look that way.'

On one side of the entrance to Law Street was a cigar store. On the other corner was a drug-store. As the flivver crossed the square, a man sauntered from the drug-store, and at the same time another sauntered from the cigar-store. They looked across at each other, and both nodded and shoved hands into pockets.

Bang! – bang! Bang – bang!

VII

Rigallo stiffened at the wheel. Gertie screamed, clutched her breast. MacBride ducked, and the flivver leaped across the square, slewed over the curb and crashed into the drug-store window.

Pedestrians stopped, horrified, frozen in their tracks. The two well-dressed men who had stood on either corner joined and walked briskly up the street toward a big, gray touring car.

The taxi that had been trailing the flivver stopped, and Kennedy, leaping out, ran across to the demolished flivver. He reached it as MacBride, streaked with blood, burst from the wreckage.

'There's the car, Mac!' He pointed.

'Where's another?' clipped MacBride.

Kennedy nodded to the taxi, and they ran over.

'Nossir,' barked the driver, 'I ain't chasin' them guys.' He climbed out. 'You guys go ahead.'

'I'll drive,' said Kennedy casually.

'Kennedy,' said MacBride, 'you stay out of this.'

'What! After tailing you all night! Coming?'

He was beside the wheel, shoving into gear. MacBride clipped an oath and hopped in, and the taxi went howling up the street.

He muttered, 'Pups – got – Riggy! Step on it, Kennedy!'

'The broad?'

'Dead.'

'They made sure you wouldn't indict her.'

'Pups! *Watch that turn!*'

'Yu-up!'

Kennedy took the turn on two wheels, knocked over a push-cart full of fruit, and jammed his foot hard down on the gas.

'Applesauce!'

'And crushed pineapple!'

Bang!

A cowl-light disappeared from the taxi.

Bang – bang – bang! went MacBride's gun.

People scattered into doorways. Moving cars stopped. Heads appeared at windows.

The gray car swung into a wide street set with trolley tracks. It weaved recklessly through traffic, heading for Farmingville Turnpike, where speed would count. It roared past red traffic lights, honking its horn, grazing other cars, swerving and swaying in its mad, reckless flight.

The taxi hurtled after it no less recklessly. MacBride was leaning well out of the seat, twisting his left arm to shoot past the windshield. Kennedy swung the machine through startled traffic with a chilling nonchalance.

MacBride fired, smashed the rear window in the tonneau.

'Lower, Mac. Get a tire,' suggested Kennedy.

'Can't aim well around this windshield.'

'Bust the windshield.'

MacBride broke it with his gun barrel. He dared not fire again, however. People were in the way, darting across the street in panicky haste. A traffic cop was ahead, having almost been knocked over by the gray touring car. MacBride recognized him – O'Day. He leaned out, and as they whanged by, yelled:

'O'Day – riot squad!'

The gray car reached Farmingville Turnpike, a wide, macadam speedway, and its exhaust, hammered powerfully. The taxi was doing sixty miles an hour and Kennedy had the throttle right down against the floor boards.

'Faster!' barked MacBride.

'Can't, Mac. This ain't no Stutz!'

Bang! No shot that time. The rear left had blown, and the taxi skidded, bounced, and dived along like a horse with the blind staggers. Kennedy jammed on his brakes as a big powerful car slewed around him and slid to a stop ten yards ahead. It was a roadster, and out of it jumped Bower.

'Well, MacBride, see what you've done!'

'Pipe down, Bower!' clipped MacBride, starting for the roadster. 'Come on, Kennedy. This boat looks powerful.'

Bower got in his way. 'MacBride, for cripes' sake, lay off! You'll get broke, man!' His voice cracked, and he was desperate.

'Out of my way!' snapped MacBride.

Bower tried to grasp him. MacBride uncorked his left and sent Bower sprawling in the bushes. Then he ran toward the roadster and Kennedy hopped in behind the wheel.

'Step on it, Kennedy!'

Kennedy stepped on, and whistled. 'Boy, this is *my* idea of a boat!'

Inside of three minutes he was doing seventy miles an hour. MacBride's hand dropped to the seat, touched a metal object. He picked it up. It was a pistol fitted with a silencer. Kennedy saw it out of the corner of his eye.

MacBride opened the gun. A shell had been fired.

'Now,' said Kennedy, 'you know how we got a flat.'

MacBride swore under his breath.

Soon they saw the gray touring car, and Kennedy hit the gun for seventy-five miles an hour. They were out in the sticks now. Fields, gullies, occasional groves of sparse timber flashed by. Curves were few and far between. The road, for the most part, ran in long, smooth stretches.

The roadster gained. MacBride screwed open the windshield, fired, aiming low. He fired again. The touring car suddenly swerved, its rear end bounced. Then it left the road, hurtled down an embankment, whirled over and over, its metal ripping and screeching over stones and stumps.

Kennedy applied his brakes, but the roadster did not stop until it was a hundred yards beyond the still tumbling touring car. MacBride reloaded his gun, shoved the one with the silencer into his pocket, and started back. Kennedy was beside him. As they left the road and ran through the bushes, they saw two figures staggering into the timber beyond.

MacBride shouted and fired his gun, but the figures disappeared in the woods. Kennedy brought up beside the shattered touring car. Four broken, twisted men were linked with the mangled wreckage.

'They're done for, Mac,' he said.

'You stay here, Kennedy. I'm going after the others.'

'So am I.'

'Kennedy—'

'Let's go, Mac.' He was off on the run.

MacBride galloped past him, dived into the timber. Somewhere ahead, two men were thrashing fiercely through the thickets. Five minutes later MacBride caught the fleeting glimpse of one. He yelled for the man to stop. The man turned and pumped three shots. Two clattered through the branches. A third banged into a tree behind which MacBride had ducked.

Kennedy, coming up at a trot, raised his automatic and blazed away. MacBride saw the man stop, throw up his arms, and buckle.

'Come on,' said Kennedy.

They plunged ahead, reached the fallen man.

'Bannon!' muttered MacBride. 'You finished him, Kennedy.'

'Good.'

Bang!

Kennedy and MacBride flung themselves into a convenient clump of bushes. They lay still, back to back, until they heard the sounds of continued flight up ahead.

'Let's,' said MacBride, heaving up.

'Sure – let's.'

MacBride started, hunched way over, darting from tree to tree, bush to bush. He stopped, to listen. Kennedy puffed up behind him.

'Come on,' said MacBride.

'Sorry, Mac. . . .'

MacBride pivoted. Kennedy was sitting on the ground, holding his right leg.

'Hell, Kennedy!'

'Hell, Mac!'

MacBride bent down.

'Go on,' grunted Kennedy. 'Get the slob!'

'I'll get him,' said MacBride, and started off.

Dodging from tree to tree, he finally came to the edge of the timber. Before him lay a wide, marshy field, and the wind rustled in blanched weeds and bushes.

Bang!

MacBride's hat was shifted an inch, and the bullet struck a tree behind his head. His teeth clicked and he fired three shots into the weeds, then ducked. He crouched, breath bated, and listened.

The weeds crackled, and he heard a groan. Warily he crawled out into the weeds, worming his way over frozen puddles. A groan, and a rasped oath reached his ears. Sounded a bit to the right. He wriggled in that direction. He stopped, waiting. Five, ten minutes passed. Half an hour.

Then, ten yards from him a head appeared above the weeds, then a pair of shoulders. MacBride stood up.

'Drop it, guy!' He leaped as he said it.

With a snarl the man spun, but not completely. MacBride jabbed his gun in the man's side, and the latter regarded him furiously over one shoulder.

'Hello, Sciarvi.'

Black and blue welts were on Sciarvi's face. He was hatless, and his overcoat was ripped in several places.

'Where'd I pot you?' asked MacBride, snatching his gun.

'In the guts,' grated Sciarvi.

'Didn't know you had any.'

'Get me to a doctor. Snap on it, and can the wisecracks. You don't worry me, MacBride.'

'Get going.' MacBride prodded him. 'And lay off the lip, you lousy Dago! You're the guy I've been looking for, Sciarvi, and I'll see you to the chair!'

'Yeah? Laugh that off, MacBride. I got friends.'

'I'll get your friends, too.'

'That's a joke!'

'On you, Wop.'

They passed into the timber, and came upon Kennedy leaning against a tree and smoking a cigarette.

'Sciarvi, eh?' he drawled. 'Spats Sciarvi, the kid himself, the Beau Brummell of crookdom, the greasy, damn dago.'

'Yeah?' sneered Sciarvi. 'When I get out of the doctor's care I'll come around and pay you a visit.'

'Tell me another bed-time story, Sciarvi!'

They moved along, Kennedy limping in the rear. They came upon Bannon, alias Shane, lying face down, quite dead. They walked past, rustled through the bushes, and came out near the wrecked car.

Half a dozen policemen and a sergeant looked up, and then Bower appeared, red-faced and bellicose.

'Oh,' grumbled MacBride, 'the riot squad. What did you do, come around to pick souvenirs?'

'We'll take the prisoner,' rumbled Bower.

'You'll take hell!' said MacBride.

'Damn you, MacBride!' roared Bower.

MacBride pulled the gun with the silencer from his pocket, held it in his palm, looked at Bower. 'Don't you think you'd better pipe down?'

Bower closed his mouth abruptly, stood swaying on his feet, his bloodshot face suffused with chagrin.

'Come on, Bower,' snarled Sciarvi, 'do your stuff.'

Bower caught his breath, glared at Sciarvi with mixed hatred and fear. Then he stamped his foot and pointed a shaking finger at MacBride.

'You'll see – you'll see!' he threatened, but his tone was choked and unconvincing.

MacBride chuckled derisively, turned to the sergeant and said, 'There's a stiff back in the woods. Better get him.'

Then he pushed Sciarvi up the slope toward the road, and Kennedy limped after him. They reached the roadster and Kennedy eased in behind the wheel.

'Your leg,' said MacBride.

'It's the right one, Mac. I'll use the hand-brake.'

Sciarvi was shoved in and MacBride followed, and the roadster hummed back toward Richmond City.

'Now the big guy,' said Kennedy

'Now the big guy,' said MacBride.

'Jokes!' cackled Sciarvi.

VIII

The Mayor paced the library of his opulent, fifteen-room mansion. He wore a beaver-brown suit, a starched, striped collar, a maroon tie and diamond stick-pin. He was small, chunky, with a cleft chin, a bulbous nose, and shiny red lips. He wore *pince-nez*, attached to a black-ribbon, and this, combined with the gray at his temples, gave him a certain *distingué* air. He was known for a clubable fellow, and a charming after-dinner speaker; and he went in for boosting home trade, sponsoring beauty contests, and having his picture taken while presenting lolly-pops to the half-starved kids of the South Side, bivouack of the bohunks.

He was not his best this morning. There was a hunted look in his usually brilliant eyes, and corrugated lines on his forehead, and he'd lost count of how many times he'd paced the room. He stopped short, to listen. There was a commotion outside the door, a low, angry voice, and the high-pitched, protesting voice of Simmonds, his man.

Perplexed, he started toward the door, and was about to reach for the knob when the door burst open. He froze in his tracks, then elevated chest and chin and clasped his hands behind his back.

MacBride strode in, kicked shut the door with his heel. He was grimy, blood-streaked, and dangerous. A pallor shone beneath his ruddy tan, and dark circles were under his eyes. He was weary and worn and the hand of his wounded arm was resting in his pocket. His coat collar was half up, half down, and his battered fedora, with Sciarvi's bullet hole in the crown, was jammed down to his eyebrows.

'Well?' said the Mayor.

'Well!' said MacBride.

And they stood and regarded each other and said not a word for a whole minute.

'Who are you?' asked the Mayor.

'MacBride. A common precinct captain you never saw before. But you know the name, eh?'

'Humph,' grunted the Mayor. 'I shall refer you to my secretary. I'm not in the habit of receiving visitors except by appointment.'

MacBride lashed him with windy blue eyes, and a crooked smile tugged at his lips. 'Mister Mayor, Spats Sciarvi's dying. He wants to see you.'

The Mayor blinked and a tremor ran over his short, chunky frame.

'Sciarvi? Who is Sciarvi?'

'Better come along and see.'

'I don't know him.'

He turned on his heel and strode away.

MacBride put his hand on the knob. 'Remember, Mister Mayor, I carried a dying man's wish. He's at 109 Ship Street.'

The Mayor stopped, stood still, but did not turn.

MacBride left the room, and as he went out through the front door he ran into Bower. They stopped and stared at each other.

Bower snarled, 'Where's Sciarvi? What did you do with him? He ain't at Headquarters. He ain't in none o' the precincts. He ain't in the hospitals.'

'Ask the mayor,' said MacBride, and passed on.

He got into a taxi, sank wearily into the cushions, and closed his eyes. Twenty minutes later the taxi jerked to a stop. The driver reached back, opened the door and waited. After a moment he looked around.

'Hey,' he called.

'Um.' MacBride awoke, paid his fare and entered a hallway.

The room he walked into was electrically lighted. Sciarvi lay on a bed, his face drained of color. Kennedy sat on a chair while a doctor was bandaging his leg. Another doctor hovered over Sciarvi.

'MacBride. . . ?' a question was in Sciarvi's tone.

MacBride shook his head. 'Your friend wouldn't come. Never heard of you.'

Sciarvi stared. 'You're lyin', MacBride!'

'God's truth, Sciarvi!'

Their eyes held, and in the captain's gaze Sciarvi must have read the awful truth.

He closed his eyes and gritted his teeth. Then he glared. 'Damn your soul, MacBride, why are you hidin' me here? Why didn't you take me to a hospital?'

MacBride said, 'You started yelling for a doctor. This was the first M.D. plate I saw.'

'Why the hell didn't you turn me over to Bower?'

'You're in my hands, Sciarvi, not Bower's. I've got two doctors here. You wanted your friend, and I went for him. He said he didn't know you. You've gotten a damned sight more than you deserve already. Quit yapping.'

'Cripes, what a break!' groaned Sciarvi, relaxing, closing his eyes.

MacBride sat down, stared at Kennedy's bandaged leg. Kennedy looked sapped and drawn. But his cynical smile drew a twisted line across his jaw.

'I needed a vacation, Mac,' he drawled.

'Hurt?'

'Hell, yes!' And still he smiled, eyes lazy-lidded, features composed.

The one doctor left Kennedy, and joined the other doctor and the two doctors put their heads together and conversed in undertones. Then they looked at Sciarvi, examined his wound, took his temperature. After which they went back to the window, put their heads together again, and mumbled some more.

The upshot of this was quite natural. One doctor said, 'Captain MacBride, we have come to the conclusion that, for the sake of everyone concerned, this man should be removed to the City Hospital.'

'Gawd!' groaned Sciarvi.

'Huh?' said MacBride.

'Gawd!' groaned Sciarvi.

All eyes looked toward him. He glared at the doctors. 'City Hospital, eh? Why the hell don't you come right out and say I'm done for? I know the City Hospital. You saw-bones always send a dyin' guy there. It's just a clearin' house for stiffs. Come on, mister, am I done for?'

The doctor who had spoken before spoke again. 'I will tell you frankly – you have one chance in a hundred of living.'

'What odds!' cackled Sciarvi, sinking again. Then a shocked look came into his eyes, and he stared with the fierce concentration of those who are outward bound.

'MacBride!' he choked.

Kennedy drew a pencil and a couple of blank envelopes from his pocket.

MacBride stood at the bedside. 'Yes, Sciarvi?'

'The Mayor – the pup! He hired me, at a thousand a month to wage a war of – whaddeya call it? – intimidation? – against the Colonial Trucking. He promised absolute protection in case I got in a jam. For the killing of Saunders – Bannon did it – I got a bonus of fifteen hundred. The Mayor supplied that special kind o' poison. He got it from the City Chemist. When you got Gertie, I wised him and he started working to nip an indictment in the bud. His right-hand man is Bower. Bower flopped, and two this mornin' I told the Mayor that if Gertie was planted in the State's Attorney's hands, we were done for. He turned white. He was in a hole, and he asked me what idea I had. I told him we could block off Law Street and get rid of Gertie. He said go ahead. We went ahead. Huh – and now the pup says he don't know me! Ugh. . . . Get a – ugh. . . .'

'Get an ambulance,' said one doctor.

'He wants a priest,' said MacBride, understanding.

'He won't die for half an hour,' said the doctor. 'And if we get him to the hospital—'

'He'll burn in the chair eventually,' said MacBride.

'That's not the point,' said the doctor, and took up a telephone.

When he put it down, Kennedy said, 'I wrote it down, Mac. I've signed as a witness. You sign and then the doctors.'

All signed, and then MacBride stood over Sciarvi. 'Want to sign this, Sciarvi?'

'Read it.'

MacBride read it. Sciarvi nodded, took the pen and scrawled his signature. 'Get a . . . ugh. . . .'

Five minutes later an ambulance clanged to a stop outside. Two men came in with a stretcher, a hospital doctor looked Sciarvi over briefly, and then they carried him out, and the ambulance roared off.

Kennedy hobbled out on MacBride's arm, and they entered a taxi. Twenty minutes later they drew up before an imposing mansion. Kennedy hobbled out and with MacBride's assistance climbed the ornate steps.

MacBride rang the bell and a servant opened the door. MacBride brushed him aside and helped Kennedy into the foyer.

The mayor was standing in the open door of his library, and his face was ghastly white. Toward him MacBride walked and Kennedy hobbled, and the mayor backed slowly into the room. MacBride closed the door. Kennedy sat down in a comfortable chair and lit a cigarette. The mayor stood with his hands clasped behind his back – very white, very still, very breathless. MacBride looked around the room, and then walked toward a table. He pointed to the phone.

'May I use it?'

The mayor said nothing. MacBride picked up the instrument and gave a number. A moment later he asked, 'That Sciarvi fellow. What about him?' He listened, said, 'H'm. Thanks,' and hung up.

Then he drew an envelope from his pocket and handed it to the mayor. The mayor read, and moved his neck in his stiff collar, as though something were gagging him. His hand shook. Then he laughed, peculiarly, and scaled the letter on the desk.

'His dying confession,' said MacBride, picking up the envelope.

'Confessions made at such times are often worthless. This Sciarvi was a little off. A dead man makes a poor witness.'

MacBride nodded. 'Yes. But, you see, Mister Mayor, he is not dead. He had one chance in a hundred, and he got it. They just told me he'll live. Of course, it will mean the chair.'

The mayor drew a deep breath. MacBride bit him with keen, burning eyes, and nodded toward Kennedy.

'This,' he said, 'is Kennedy, of the *Free Press*. Of course, this confession will appear in the first edition.'

He said no more. He shoved the envelope into his pocket and turned to Kennedy. 'Come on.'

They went out, arm in arm, and left the mayor standing transfixed in his ornate library.

MacBride went home that night, and his wife cried over his wounded arm, and he patted her head and chuckled and said, 'Don't worry, sweetheart. It's all over now.'

He had his wound dressed and went to bed and slept ten hours without so much as stirring once. And he was awakened in the morning by his wife, who stood over his bed with a wide look in her eyes and a newspaper trembling in her hands.

'Steve,' she breathed, 'look!'

She held the paper in front of him, and he saw, in big, black headlines, three significant words:

'*Mayor Commits Suicide.*'